SUZANNAH ROWNTREE

A Conspiracy of Prophets

Watchers of Outremer, Book Four

First published by Bocfodder Press 2022

Copyright © 2022 by Suzannah Rowntree

All rights reserved. No part of this publication may be reproduced, stored or transmitted in any form or by any means, electronic, mechanical, photocopying, recording, scanning, or otherwise without written permission from the publisher. It is illegal to copy this book, post it to a website, or distribute it by any other means without permission.

This novel is entirely a work of fiction. The names, characters and incidents portrayed in it are the work of the author's imagination. Any resemblance to actual persons, living or dead, events or localities is entirely coincidental.

First edition

Editing by S J Editing
Cover art by Seedlings Design Studio

This book was professionally typeset on Reedsy.
Find out more at reedsy.com

Author's Note

This book depicts religiously motivated and justified violence in the context of the medieval crusades, as well as war, violence, blood, death, anxiety, disordered eating, and loss of a loved one, among other things. I have done my best to communicate the truth of history in a way that is both accurate and sensitive, but if this kind of content may be triggering for you, please be aware and stay safe.

Map of Antioch

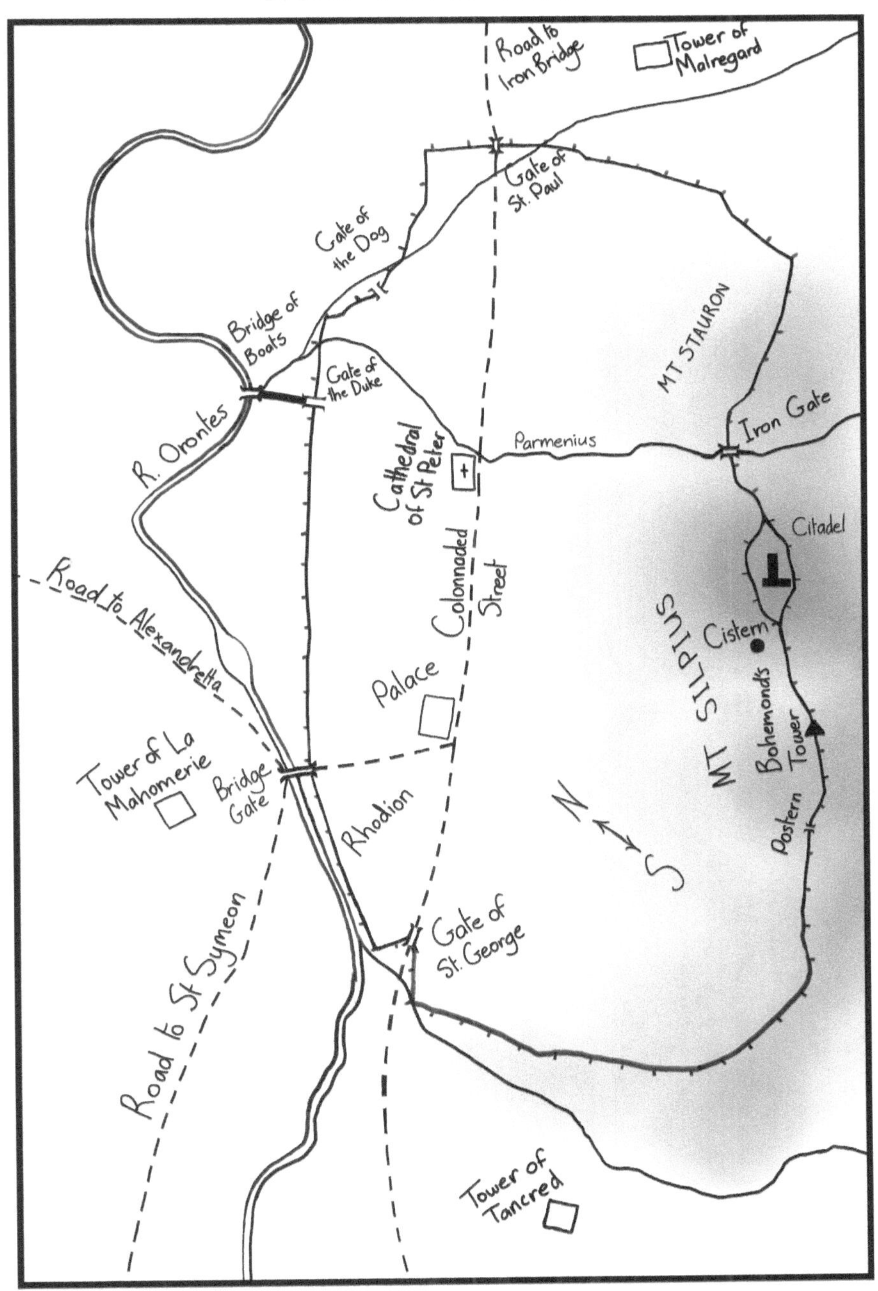

Prologue.

Syria, AD 1098

Winter in the Syrian highlands was brutally cold, the high red plateau scoured by chilling winds and freezing rain. Summer was worse; the land fired like clay in a furnace until the living flesh of the half-stone sorcerer baked and blistered in heat that would kill any man not sustained by the cursed existence of the demon to which he was bound.

Four hundred and sixty-one years the sorcerer had endured the turning seasons, sometimes in silence, sometimes in raving madness, before anything like hope had come to him. Hope which came in the shape of one who might, if he wished, release him from torment and return his limbs from stone to flesh.

The one who had come, had seen, had understood—and had turned his back.

Lukas Bessarion, the son of his enemy.

What else did he expect? Surely not the mercy for which he had begged? After the boy's departure, his laughter at his own self-delusion rose into a cackling shriek of madness and died away into racking sobs.

He had heard it said that justice must be equal. Tooth for tooth. Eye for eye. Life for life. All things in due proportion. Thus, for four hundred and sixty-one years he had kept his grip on sanity by dreaming of shackling the Bessarions on this mountain, prolonging their lives until they had endured a torment matching his own.

Now, in the four hundred and sixty-second year of his suffering, Khalil ibn Hassan decided that this was not enough. It would never be enough. There could be no limitation upon their sentence.

Khalil no longer wished for justice. Now, he desired only vengeance.

Chapter I.

Lukas Bessarion took care to stay out of sight on his journey, worming part of the way on his belly, among the pale tumbled rocks and scrubby pines of the mountainside, until he reached his meeting-place: a ruined shrine high above Antioch, on the eastern slope of Mount Stauron. The shrine was little more than a face chiselled from the living rock at the entrance to a small grassy bay running into a cleft of the mountain. Though its features were blunted by centuries of wind and rain, Lukas doubted anyone had forgotten the warning it signified. In these mountains, noxious vapours sometimes rose from clefts and chimneys in the rock. One treated such places with respect.

To reach this destination, he'd had to bypass the Norman camp on the north side of Antioch, then venture past the tower of Malregard, a squat structure of scavenged limestone and rough-hewn wood. From Malregard, Count Bohemond's men kept watch on the secret paths leading across and around the mountain.

If Bohemond's men caught him, he would be in all kinds of trouble, and not just from the Norman count. Lukas heaved an inward sigh, imagining how his master, Count Raymond, would react if he was careless enough to let Bohemond discover what he was doing here. If he was lucky, the count would flay him with incisive, devastating contempt. If he was unlucky…

Lukas shuddered, imagining what it would be like to be driven off like a stray dog. Once, he thought he knew what it was to be hungry and lonely, at the mercy of cold and heat, not knowing whether to expect death at the point of an enemy's blade or amidst the pangs of hunger and dysentery. He'd been a fool. They'd all been fools, the whole pilgrimage. For the last seven and a half months the Franks had camped outside Antioch subject to fear, battle, sickness, desertion, cold, disease and, worst of all, starvation. The shiver that ran through him at the memory took uncontrollable possession of his body in spite of the late May heat, and it was some time before he was able to quell it.

Working for the count was the only thing keeping him alive, but Lukas had no reason to love the Franks. Because of them, he was trapped in this living nightmare. Because of them, he could not get inside Antioch to retrieve the weapon his father had hidden there four and a half centuries before.

Because of them, Ayla had died two hundred and twenty-four black days ago.

For two hundred and twenty-four days she had mouldered beneath a cairn of stones in the northern hills, her soft wry lips and impudent brown eyes becoming worm-eaten and foul. For two hundred and twenty-four nights she had haunted his dreams, always in the distance, always agonisingly out of reach.

Calm down, he imagined her telling him now. *Don't get your knickers in a twist. You have a job to do, remember?*

Lukas closed his eyes, breathing deeply. He wore Ayla's old sling around his waist, and now threaded the faded blue-and-orange cords slowly through his bony fingers, concentrating on the rasp of old sheepswool until his bones ceased their rattling and the looming shadow of the past retreated.

He could hear the wind on the mountain again. He could feel the sun on his skin now, and this hunger was only a momentary thing. Winter's cold—winter's starvation—was behind them. Antioch could not stand much longer; the Bessarion Lance was within reach, and soon he would have his fill of vengeance.

Footsteps and crackling twigs roused him from his reverie and brought him up against the rocks with a racing heart. It was the man he'd been sent to meet, a young Turkish renegade in beggar's rags—one of Count

Raymond's regular informants.

"Mergen," Lukas said, relaxing. "God have mercy, man, you walk like a whole herd of cattle."

It was Lukas' job to meet the man every week or so, gleaning what information he could. Somehow over the past seven months, Lukas had become the count's envoy of choice in his dealings with the locals, whether Greek, Syriac, Armenian, or Turkish.

He still wasn't sure whether that meant the count trusted him, or merely found him useful.

"What news? Tell me about conditions inside the city."

"Nothing new. It is known that Lord Yaghi Siyan and his garrison cannot hold the city much longer. The Iron Gate through the mountains is still open, but your raiders keep a watch on the road for supply caravans. Food and morale are still low."

"And the Franks? Is there any movement to treat with them?"

A shrug. "Of course, but Lord Yaghi Siyan refuses to entertain such ideas."

Does anyone in that damned town have an agreement with Bohemond? Count Raymond's instructions had been puzzlingly specific, but Lukas hesitated to put the question so bluntly. If the Turks were unaware of the rivalries and resentments that divided the Frankish war council, it wasn't Lukas' place to enlighten them. "Yaghi Siyan may refuse to deal with these people, but I'm sure the Franks would be eager to meet them. Could an envoy get inside the city? Not a whole party, like the last one. Just one man."

Only last week, a party sent by the North Franks had come to grief within the city, their heads appearing on spikes along with those of other captured Frankish knights, grimacing down at the Frankish camp. In turn, the bones of captive Turks littered the muddy fields dividing the camp from the city, left to rot where they had fallen after bloody torture prised soul from body. After months of brutal attrition, Lukas knew only the very brave or the very stupid would dare to enter the city...but what if he volunteered for the mission? Inside Antioch, he could go straight to the basilica and retrieve his father's lance. Then he could slip back out again, and the world would be at his feet. He'd no longer be dependent on the stipend of a servant. He'd be a warrior, a worthy successor to the great John Bessarion. He could name his own price and win the Franks' respect.

Or, better yet, he could lead the Syrians against their Turkish overlords, and take possession of Antioch right under the noses of seven Frankish princes and the greatest army the world had ever seen. Prince Thatoul had done it at Marash, shrewdly exploiting the pilgrimage's reluctance to take up arms against fellow Christians. If Lukas did it at Antioch, what could the city not become? A sanctuary where his people might be ruled by one of their own, delivered from the exactions of foreigners.

The Franks would be violently opposed to such a plan, it was true, but they hadn't managed to overcome Antioch's defences for seven months, and they were now reduced to hoping the city would be delivered to them by treachery.

It was a dream as lucent and glorious as coloured glass, but the Turk shattered it with a shrug. "Impossible. I left the city with a supply train bound to Aleppo. We were counted, and our names taken at the Iron Gate. No one else will be allowed back in, unless they're Turkish reinforcements for the garrison. Since catching the last Franks, Yaghi Siyan is taking no chances."

That was disappointing, but he ought to be used to it by now. A whirr in the thornbushes uphill caught Lukas' attention, but it was only a small bird, probably a quail, launching from the covert. "Very well. Meet again here in a week."

If the city's so close to falling... Ayla seemed to prompt him, and he interrupted the other man's farewells. "One last question. Does the name Ilkay of Antioch mean anything to you? I'm looking for his family."

The Turk's eyes widened, and he muttered something under his breath—it sounded like one of the incantations Ayla used to recite against demons. He backed away, towards the path that would lead him back to the city. "How do you know *that* name?"

For a few short, foolish days I was married to his daughter. The words would have laid bare a wound Lukas never wanted anyone else to see. "I knew one of the daughters. She's dead now. I'd like to tell her family."

Ayla had always worried what would happen to her mother and siblings once the Franks reached Antioch, and Lukas knew he had to find them before anyone else did. The Franks were looking for vengeance, and it would be a bloody day when the city fell.

The Turk shook his head, backing another step. "Ilkay is dead. I don't know his family, but I'd stay away from them if I were you."

Mergen wasn't the only Turk who didn't want to speak or think about Ilkay and, as always, Lukas wondered whether it was because the man had been in league with demons, or because of the manner of his death. He had no time to say more for, at that moment, three men rounded a spur of the white rock that concealed the shrine from the path, nearly colliding with Mergen. At the sight of the Turk, they all stopped dead in their tracks. The tallest of them caught his breath and swore in unmistakeable Frankish.

Like the other two men, he was wrapped up in a homespun cloak, despite the warmth of the day. Then, Lukas saw his face and for a moment could not move, could scarcely even breathe.

This man. Ayla's killer.

Evrard of le Puiset.

The next moment there was a flash of armour as another of the men threw off his cloak. A knife appeared in the knight's hand.

Mergen turned, startled. He carried no significant weapons; his thin, half-starved frame was no match for the Franks. Lukas started forwards with a yell, grasping the iron-shod staff he'd carried all the way from Constantinople—his best weapon, now that the sword he'd plundered from the battlefield near Dorylaeum was half eaten with rust.

Too late. Mergen didn't even have the time to react before the knife was planted in his chest. He gave an odd, painful-sounding cough and fell to his knees. All three of the newcomers had swords out now and Le Puiset swept his, sending Mergen's head rolling down the mountain with one powerful stroke.

Lukas froze. The metallic scent of blood mingled in his nostrils with the astringent scent of pine; he heard the *thump, thump* of the rolling head for what seemed an excruciating length of time. At last it was gone and a strangled sound escaped him. Mergen had been harmless—as Ayla had been harmless. An ally. A *friend*.

And Evrard of le Puiset had killed both of them.

For so many months he'd moved through a numb haze, barely able to feel any emotion at all. Now, wrath flooded through him.

He knew, even as he raised his staff, that it was a stupid thing to do. Le Puiset was a count. Not even Count Raymond would protect him if he got his man—and the odds were three to one.

He didn't care. He'd been fighting with the staff now for more than a year—knew what a formidable weapon it could be in the hands of a man who knew what he was doing. He took his fear and turned it to a cold shard of ice, used it to steady his hands and fuel his silent charge.

"Ware, Barisan! Get the other one!"

The third man—a native, going by his neatly-trimmed beard and smooth brown skin—hung back uncertainly, as though reluctant to fight, but the second Frank—Barisan—bore down on Lukas, sword raised. There was no time to think, to bargain, even if he had meant to. Lukas gripped his oaken staff one-handed at the end, raising it behind him, then snapped it forward. The momentum was relentless. The staff struck the Frank's uplifted sword, caving in his guard and striking his skull. Barisan staggered and fell. Catching the staff in his open left hand, Lukas pivoted to face the native, sending the man staggering backward with a thrusting feint. Then Count Evrard pressed in on his left.

Lukas brought his staff around in a strike, but le Puiset was more agile and cunning than either of the others. He raised his sword one-handed—an easy target, Lukas thought, beating through his parry; but it was a deflecting blow and the Frank slid under the oaken shaft. The next instant, le Puiset smashed his great heavy hilt upon Lukas' unprotected neck and shoulder. It was meant to be the blade; but even misaimed it was a crushing blow, and Lukas staggered to his knees with firebursts of pain dancing before his eyes.

Dimly he heard the whistle of the count's blade and Lukas realised his own head was about to follow Mergen's down the hillside. Instead, there was the whine of steel as another sword met le Puiset's, deflecting it.

"Wait!" the third man said in breathless Armenian.

Lukas scarcely heard the interruption. He sucked in a breath, eyes locked on le Puiset's sword-hand. He was about to surge to his feet again, putting all his strength behind a thrust to the count's jaw, when the Armenian pulled up Lukas' left sleeve, exposing the Watcher's Mark inked into his forearm beneath the elbow: an *I* and *X* superimposed on each other.

"You're a *Watcher.*"

Count Evrard seemed not to understand the Armenian's words. "What's this?" he snarled in Frankish, stepping backward. The point of his sword wove in the air, from Lukas to the Armenian and back again. "How do you know this—"

His eyes fastened on Lukas, and not until that moment did a flash of recognition show in the count's eyes. Le Puiset drew a hissing breath. The point of his sword lowered.

With a snarl, Lukas surged to his feet. But the Armenian still had a grip on his arm, his staff. His attack slowed. The next instant Count Evrard's blade was up again, settling cold and prickling at the hollow of his throat.

Checkmate. For a moment it was all Lukas could do to draw breath. Then the edge wore off his anger: he understood, suddenly, the position in which he'd put himself. A mere servant didn't strike a count, not even in self-defence. It was le Puiset who had taught him that lesson in the first place, and now—

Now, not even grovelling would save him. Instead, he straightened, raising his staff from guard.

"The question is, do you know *me?*" he rasped between heaving breaths.

"Lukas Bessarion." Count Evrard of le Puiset pressed his lips together until they nearly disappeared. "You just can't stay away from the damned Turks, can you?" He moved and, for an instant, Lukas thought he was about to strike. Instead, the count shuddered and collapsed onto a rock, breathing much too quickly, as though the brief combat had utterly exhausted him.

In the silence, the Armenian repeated, "Bessarion? You're descended from *the* Bessarion—John Bessarion?" He shook back his sleeve to display his own Watcher's Mark. Not any Watcher's Mark: not the chi-rho of Constantinople or the triple-pointed cross of Alexandria, but the rimless *IX* of Lukas' own.

Lukas stared. Ayla had sworn her father's friends had eradicated all the Watchers from Antioch—yet this man was a Syrian Watcher. One of his own people.

Someone who knew his name, yet did not recoil in loathing.

Lukas found himself letting out an overwrought laugh. "Descended from him? You might say that."

"This upstart is *my* prisoner, Syrian," le Puiset began, pushing his way off the rock. He seemed unsteady on his feet, but the Armenian retreated a step, speaking in conciliatory Frankish this time.

"He's one of ours, my lord. Don't you see that Mark? My master will wish to speak with him."

For a moment le Puiset swayed on his feet, his grip white and trembling on the hilt of his sword. The count looked more like death than usual, Lukas realised: there was no visible wound on him, but the skin was thin and drawn over his bony frame; he appeared gaunt, almost skeletal. It struck Lukas that the Frank had come down the path from the east—from the direction of the city, not the camp. Captive knights were sometimes rescued by Antiochene Christians, returning via forgotten posterns and secret paths to the Frankish camp. The count had stumbled upon him in the moment of escape.

Be that as it may, Lukas still didn't mean to stand still while le Puiset sent his head down the mountainside after Mergen's. His grip tightened on his staff, but before the count could move, the Frank whose head Lukas had struck came to, lifting his bleeding head from the grass with a groan. With a grunt of irritation, le Puiset sheathed his sword and went to help him up.

With the immediate threat gone, Lukas turned to the Armenian, breathing a little more easily. "Are you from inside the city? Are there more of you? They told me all the Watchers of Antioch were dead."

The Armenian nodded eagerly. "I'm Tigranants. There are two dozen of us now. More will come when they know a Bessarion is with us."

He was a young man, though evidently prosperous: although he was dressed in serviceable travelling-clothes—a light tunic of fawn-coloured chequered linen worn over white trousers, the whole surmounted by a blue turban—they were new and well-fitted, lacking the rents or stains or straining seams of hand-me-downs.

Lukas stole a glance at le Puiset, who glared at him from the other Frank's side. "What are you doing in this Frank's company, my friend?"

"Sending him on his way. He entered the city a week ago, with an embassy. The Turks had an ambush waiting, but our people managed to save these two."

Several days ago the Constable of France's head had appeared on the battlements above the Gate of St Paul, facing the encampment of the North French who had sent him. Le Puiset and his knight must be the only survivors of that mission.

"You might have done me a favour and left him to the Turks," Lukas grumbled under his breath. He didn't mean the words, of course. If the Turks got le Puiset, he'd never have the chance to deal with Ayla's murderer himself.

"Are you quite finished?" The count interrupted Tigranants' laughter, eyes narrowed as though he realised they spoke of himself. "I know my way home from here, Armenian. Leave the Syrian to me and go."

Tigranants stopped laughing—he must be somewhat cowed by le Puiset, despite the Frank's evident weakness. "Will I meet you again?" he asked Lukas.

"I'll meet you here at the kalends of June. Wait," he added, as le Puiset made towards them. "If the city falls, the Franks will kill indiscriminately. Tell your people to pin crosses to their clothing. Assemble them in Saint Peter's basilica and bar the door. I'll find you there. Understand?"

"Yes."

"Then go now. Don't be caught."

Tigranants nodded, bowed to Count Evrard, circled Mergen's body, and disappeared beyond the great rugged wall of rock. Lukas let out a sigh and turned to face the count, whom he now realised had been speaking to him.

"Now, if you will, explain yourself." Le Puiset gestured towards the dead Turk. "Watcher or no, if you have no good explanation for this, I will strike off your head as I did his."

There was a time when Lukas would have responded to such a demand with equal hauteur. Now, he measured his words carefully before speaking. He was here on Count Raymond's orders, but those orders included definite instructions to keep his meetings with Mergen a secret, especially from Count Bohemond. On the other hand, if he concealed his legitimate excuse, le Puiset would be all too happy to kill him.

"You were the man who squandered the opportunity to take Nicaea, my lord. Will you waste the opportunity to take Antioch, too?"

He stalked towards the downward path, the iron-shod foot of his staff grinding against the stones. It almost worked, but not quite.

"Stop," the count ordered. Le Puiset stood for a moment breathing heavily, as though trying to command his own anger. Then he sheathed his sword and strode forward, grabbing Lukas by the scruff of his neck.

"Come," he growled. "I'll take no chances. You'll explain yourself before Count Bohemond."

Ah, devil take it, Lukas thought. Count Raymond was going to be *furious.*

Chapter II.

"What the hell are you playing at?" Raymond of Saint-Gilles burst into angry speech the moment the door of Malregard tower opened to admit him, Count Galdemar Carpenel, and their small retinue to Bohemond's presence. "Where's my interpreter? What right have you to harass—"

As his one remaining eye adjusted to the darkness within, Saint-Gilles bit off what he was going to say. Within the rough stone room, a single lamp burned on a rough board table, where Bohemond of Taranto sat with his legs stretched out savouring a beaker of wine. Lukas Bessarion was on hands and knees on the rush-strewn floor, his sides heaving with great labouring breaths as though in some terrible agony.

"Ah, Saint-Gilles." Bohemond straightened a little in his chair and his teeth flashed, impossibly white and predatory in the lamplight. "What can I offer you? Wine? Figs?"

Saint-Gilles paid him no heed. A Norman knight bent over Bessarion and Saint-Gilles moved without thinking, grabbing the other man by the shoulder and hurling him away from the young Syrian. The next instant his sword was halfway out of its scabbard; Galdemar caught his arm in warning.

"No one," Saint-Gilles growled, *"no one* touches my people and lives to boast of it."

"That's not what I heard," someone said in an undertone.

The blood roared in Saint-Gilles' ears, but when he glared around the room, none of Bohemond's men met his eyes. He knew what they meant. William. His infant son had been killed, and he'd sacrificed his just vengeance for a promise of safety from the duplicitous Greeks. Saint-Gilles ground his teeth and added, just as softly: "What have you done to my man?"

Bohemond's eyes were round with exaggerated innocence. "My dear Saint-Gilles, no one has touched your man. We all know better than that."

Saint-Gilles glanced down at the gasping Syrian. "What, you mean to tell me you were in the midst of a civilised discussion, and he began having fits for no reason at all?"

"Marvellous that you should put it like that." There was mockery in the younger count's eyes. "In a word, yes. That's precisely what occurred."

"Bessarion?" Saint-Gilles bent over the interpreter, touching his shoulder. "Did they hurt you?"

There was no answer from the boy. The Syrian's eyes had rolled back in his head, leaving only the whites. His teeth were clenched; his breath coming and going like a bellows. There was no blood, no bruising to be seen.

"Bessarion," Saint-Gilles repeated, feeling curiously powerless beneath Bohemond's smirking gaze. Was the boy fainting? Was he having a fit? Or…a darker premonition teased at the corners of his mind. He made the sign of the cross. "Pull yourself together, man!"

A faint groan escaped the boy. His eyes closed. The next moment he blinked and was himself again, though still breathing hard, sweat standing out on his forehead. "My lord." He grasped Saint-Gilles' arm with feverish strength. "You've come. I have to—" and then he caught himself with a glance at the stiff figure standing at Bohemond's right hand. It was a young count that Saint-Gilles knew slightly, to his regret; by this stage of the pilgrimage, he had a peculiarly gaunt and bony look to him, his once fine armour now rusted and rent, its links badly mended.

Evrard, the count of le Puiset. There had been some sort of grudge between his interpreter and the thin-skinned young count ever since the unfortunate business at Nicaea.

"No one is going to hurt you," Saint-Gilles told Bessarion, straightening. Bessarion must have been having an attack of nerves. In the endless nightmare that this siege of Antioch had become, such things had begun to happen with increasing frequency: strong men, good warriors, breaking beneath the weight of invisible wounds. He didn't know exactly why the sight of le Puiset would provoke such an attack, but he'd heard rumours. Bessarion had had a friend—a Turkish beggar. Saint-Gilles gathered there had been a tragedy, and that le Puiset was responsible.

"Was this your doing, le Puiset?"

"Your interpreter's a filthy spy, meeting with Turks behind your back." Le Puiset scowled. "I could have told you he'd turn against you."

Bessarion used his staff to lever himself off the floor, brushing the dust from his garments with shaking hands. The boy remained as fastidious as a cat, for all that cleanliness was a losing battle in this muddy wasteland.

"I appeal to my master, the count of Toulouse," he muttered with a defeated air. But Saint-Gilles was near enough to see the quick, imploring glance Bessarion sent him.

So that was it. Rather than betray Saint-Gilles' confidence, the boy meant to pretend he was guilty of fraternising with the enemy. It was a rare sort of loyalty, and for a moment Saint-Gilles could scarcely trust himself to speak.

Le Puiset, like a fool, took the opportunity to dig himself deeper. "It was on the slopes of Stauron. As I was fleeing the city, I caught him thick as thieves with a Turkish beggar. Who knows how he got past Malregard without being seen."

"Whatever mission he was on, it certainly wasn't yours, my lord." Bohemond spoke with a sincerity that was flawless and yet somehow unconvincing. "Naturally I sent for you at once. I'm sure you'll be happy to know the Turk in question is dead. That was his head you passed on the way in."

"I'll thank you to let me deal with my own servants, count." Saint-Gilles bit the words off sharply. He could feel his anger mounting, and he drew a long slow breath. While both of them were locked in an unspoken rivalry for control of the pilgrimage, he couldn't afford to provoke the slippery young South Norman to open hostility. Bohemond was not merely in possession of uncommon looks, charm, and panache: he was also a brilliant commander who had saved all of their lives in battle after battle.

Was this a warning, then? Both of them knew Antioch would never fall to storm; only treachery would win them the city now. Meaning the siege was less a matter of forcing a breach than seducing a traitor, and Bohemond had cut off Saint-Gilles' best chance of that along with Mergen's head.

Saint-Gilles turned to le Puiset, judging it wise to expend some of his anger on a safer target. "As for you, le Puiset, you're a lord—a count, for heaven's sake. Don't you have better things to do with your time than bother an obscure servant?"

Of course, the young Syrian claimed to be some sort of highborn exile, but le Puiset was apparently unaware of this. "This upstart villein has continually insulted me! I don't know why he has singled me out for harassment, but so it is. He needs to be taught a lesson, and if his own lord won't do it, then I will."

A villein was the lowest of the low, a slave. Bessarion was at least a free man, but le Puiset chose to exaggerate. Saint-Gilles permitted himself a small hard smile, already feeling more in control. "I'm old enough to be your father, le Puiset, so allow me to give you some advice. I know what you're thinking. A common servant put your nose out of joint. Your pride is injured, and you can't let it alone. Honour demands vengeance, eh?"

A dull flush crept along the young man's cheekbones. "I'm not a child, my lord."

"Then stop acting like one," Saint-Gilles said. "Persecuting my servant doesn't make you look bigger, you fool. Pick a fight with someone your own size and leave my people alone, or I'll take it up with your liege. Is that clear?"

Le Puiset's face glowed with embarrassment and helpless wrath, but he swallowed whatever objection he might have been about to make. "As noonday," he said bitterly. "I'm grateful for your counsel, count…and you're right. That *is* how my father would have spoken." He turned to

Count Bohemond. "You'll excuse me? I haven't slept in nearly a week. Come, Barisan."

Not until the young count and his man had left did Saint-Gilles recall that le Puiset was, in a way, back from the dead. Hadn't he gone with the French constable into the city? For some days already, Galon of Chaumont's corpse had decorated the battlements of Antioch. By what miracle had le Puiset escaped? And why did he surface *here,* in Bohemond's tower?

Bohemond, he thought sourly, had a finger in every pie.

Still lolling at the table, Bohemond shoved forwards an untouched wine beaker. "You might as well drink le Puiset's wine, now that you've read him his lesson."

"Thanks, but no," Saint-Gilles said. "I'm a busy man. If you don't mind, I'll take my interpreter and go."

"One moment." Bohemond got up, flicking a hand to dismiss all his men. "Leave us a while." They filed out, blocking the light that flowed in through the door.

In the silence that followed, Saint-Gilles ironed his lips shut, refusing to send his own supporters—Galdemar, Bessarion, a brace of squires—out after them.

Bohemond smiled patiently and said, "I meant to ask if you had the chance to consider my recent proposal."

The proposal. Saint-Gilles clenched his teeth a moment before replying.

"There's no need to consider it. It's out of the question. Thousands of men have perished in this siege, and to hand the city to one man would be to spit on their graves. If you have a way to get into the city, it's your duty to share it freely with all of us." Saint-Gilles narrowed his eyes, sending Bohemond the kind of look that made strong men quake, back home in Toulouse. "And you *do* have a way into Antioch, don't you?"

"What makes you say that?" It was outrageous, how bland and innocent Bohemond looked.

"You came to the council and proposed that the prince who brings about the fall of Antioch should be given the city to rule," Saint-Gilles said in his softest, most perilous voice. "Why would you propose such a thing unless you already had hope of grabbing the prize for yourself?"

"Out of desperation; what else?"

He spoke so calmly, Saint-Gilles could only shoot a long-suffering glance at Galdemar, who took that as a cue to say mildly, "Desperation, count?"

"We pinned all our hopes on Galon of Chaumont's embassy, and now his head is decorating the Gate of St Paul," Bohemond pointed out. "Meanwhile, my scouts have confirmed that a great Turkish army is mustering in the east. What happens when they come here? What if they catch us out in the open, camped before Antioch's walls? We cannot allow this siege to drag on any longer. If we want a great victory, we must hold out a great prize."

It sounded plausible—devil take him.

"Duke Godfrey informs me the *great Turkish army,* as you call it, is besieging Edessa," Saint-Gilles said curtly. Godfrey, one of the seven great princes leading the pilgrimage, was a weak-willed man; but his brother Baldwin of Boulogne was a man of great ambition, who had struck east into Syria and seized the ancient city of Edessa, beyond the river Euphrates. "Godfrey should know; his brother sent to warn him. The army is not large, and Boulogne is confident he can hold the city against them. It's ten to one against their coming here, and so what if they do? We have already taken the field against two relieving armies and routed them."

Bohemond gave a hum of assent. "You participated in neither of those fights, as I recall."

Saint-Gilles felt his face getting hot. "What's that supposed to mean?"

"Only that you were not there in person to fully grasp the difficulties of the situation."

"God fought for us," Saint-Gilles said stubbornly. He wasn't about to admit that their miraculous victories so far had depended in large part upon Bohemond's genius, his cunning. "He will again. Come, Galdemar."

He turned and stalked to the door, but Bohemond's voice stopped him before he made it outside.

"We have never faced anything like this," Bohemond said. "Godfrey's information is old. My scouts tell me the Turkish army has doubled and tripled in size since the siege of Edessa began. Their leader is Kerbogha, commander-in-chief of the sultan of Persia. Edessa is only the mustering-point, Saint-Gilles. Their true goal is Antioch."

* * *

Outside the tower, a squire held Saint-Gilles' horse and Galdemar's, poor dispirited beasts whose every rib was visible beneath their dull coats. Neither were western horses: two years' hard travel, fighting, and exposure to the elements had taken its toll on the beasts as well as the people. These were local horses, remounts sent from Edessa; yet a few months of life in the camp had left them, too, ailing. Saint-Gilles had done what he could—he was able to afford feed and even some cramped stable facilities—but it was no life for man or beast here.

And now Bohemond claimed a fresh danger was coming.

Despite the sticky warmth of the day, Saint-Gilles felt chilled. He pulled himself into the saddle, moving stiffly so as not to disrupt the pain in his gut. He'd been sick most of the winter. He'd been sick most of the *pilgrimage.* Yet somehow, it never occurred to him except in a vague, unbelievable way that he might actually die. Not before reaching Jerusalem, at any rate.

He glanced down at Bessarion, who had followed him from Malregard and now leaned upon his staff, eyes a little too wide, staring into an unfathomable distance. "Can you walk, Bessarion?" he demanded, and the boy jumped as though he had been a thousand miles away.

"Yes, my lord." Bessarion seemed to be about to say something, and then stopped.

"You can report when we get home," Saint-Gilles turned his horse's heads towards the west. Only once they had left the tower behind them did Saint-Gilles send a sidelong glance at his friend. "You're unusually silent today, Galdemar."

The winter had left even Galdemar looking less sleek and jovial. He'd plucked a stem of grass from somewhere on their way out of the tower, and now chewed it thoughtfully before replying. "Bohemond is pushing you. I don't like it."

"Don't worry. Two can play at this game. It's only a matter of pushing back hard enough."

"That's what I don't like about it. It's one thing to intimidate people who can't hit back. Something tells me Bohemond is a tougher nut to crack. Remember what you yourself said to le Puiset."

"That child? Picking on a servant to make himself feel like a better man. You would compare me to *him?*"

Galdemar raised a sardonic eyebrow. "You're right. I would hate to know anyone who would behave like that."

"One of these days I'll blacken your eye," Saint-Gilles muttered. Ridiculous. Bohemond was nothing if not a worthy opponent. "This is different, and you know it."

He took the ride slowly, allowing the squires and Bessarion to keep up on foot. Positioned on high ground north of the city, Malregard commanded an excellent view of the city, as well as the camp where seven princes and seven armies waited to break in.

Antioch stood between mountains and river. All along its eastern spine, its houses washed up against the lower slopes of the twin mountains Silpius and Stauron. These imposing, craggy peaks soared overhead, casting a stark shadow across the city each morning. The city's founders had made the most of these natural defences by half enclosing them within massive walls, crowning both mountains with distant towers that appeared deceptively tiny and toy-like with distance.

To the west, Antioch's boundary was marked by the winding Orontes river, which kissed the wall only at the Bridge Gate to the southwest, where a massive stone bridge led from the city to the western bank and the road to the sea. The easiest approach to the city lay where the pilgrimage had encamped on the city's northwest, in the narrow, swampy meadows of the river's east bank; but only three of Antioch's six gates were located here. The Bridge Gate was accessible only if you crossed the river, and to reach the city's southernmost gate you must cross the river a second time, or take the punishing hidden paths through the wilderness of Silpius and Stauron to the Iron Gate on the east.

No wonder it had taken the army of God so many months to tighten the blockade and shut five of those gates. Occasionally some of the pilgrims—mostly ignorant peasants or foolish hotheads—complained at the delay. The goal of their pilgrimage was not Antioch, after all. Why should they linger'in Syria when the holy places of Jerusalem beckoned? Few paid any attention to such madness, and for good reason. For one thing, Antioch was a holy city in its own way: the first see of Peter the Apostle, the place where the followers of Christ had first been named Christians, its mountains riddled with the cells of hermits and holy men.

For another thing—and far more important to Saint-Gilles' mind—taking the city was a tactical necessity. Here they were, unimaginably far from home, terribly far even from the Greek emperor upon whom they relied for supplies and relief. Jerusalem might be their ultimate goal, but they could not risk leaving Antioch in the hands of the enemy. Do that, and the Turks would easily cut their supply lines. They would be surrounded in enemy territory, easy pickings.

Descending from the slopes of Mount Stauron, Saint-Gilles bypassed the city's north gate and entered the pilgrim's camp, an unsightly, endless suburb of diseased tents, makeshift huts and shanties, all wedged between the wall and the river. The camp stretched from Bohemond's Normans at the northernmost St Paul gate, past the barricaded Dog Gate where Saint-Gilles had settled with his own Provençals, to the Gate of the Duke towards the south where Godfrey of Lorraine guarded a rickety pontoon bridge across the Orontes. Thankfully the winter's mud had dried, but now a thick layer of dust coated everything, working its unwelcome way into mouth, eyes, nose, and lungs. Throughout the rank-smelling camp, laundry fluttered from lines strung between dying trees, while beneath them, emaciated beggars picked through rubbish-heaps alongside the rats and mangy dogs the pilgrimage had somehow collected.

Saint-Gilles heaved a sigh. When the pilgrimage had arrived before the gates of Antioch last winter, the Orontes river-meadows had been lush and green, their orchards and vineyards full of returning life after the scouring heat of summer. Now the army of God had scarred and blighted the land, fouling the river with their refuse. All the same, the true reason the sight broke his heart was that there were not more of them. The winter had been especially harsh to his Provençals. A particularly large number of common people had followed Saint-Gilles on his pilgrimage. Disease and starvation, desertion and cold had thinned their ranks ruthlessly.

Perhaps it was that Antioch was such a large city, making the pilgrimage appear smaller by comparison. But Saint-Gilles doubted he was mistaken: the pilgrimage had dwindled terribly. Easily half of the pilgrims who had followed him and the six other princes from the West had died, been captured, or simply wandered away, too exhausted—or terrified, or sick—to keep fighting.

Even the survivors would likely never see their homes again.

What if Bohemond was telling the truth? What if this was more than an effort to gain power by spreading panic—what if another Turkish army really was on its way to relieve Antioch?

Saint-Gilles shivered, feeling once again so far from home, so vulnerable, so *weak*.

"Saint-Gilles?" Galdemar jolted him out of his thoughts before he could ride blindly past the gate of the adobe farmhouse he'd commandeered by the river. Saint-Gilles blinked away the fog of worry and let his horse take them into the courtyard—a sleepy place at this point in the afternoon, full of knights and sergeants, squires and servants who diced or dozed or polished armour in the afternoon's heat.

Before he entered the house, Saint-Gilles snapped his fingers at a sergeant of his household. "Send for Bishop Adhemar." The papal legate was not just a vassal, but one of his closest friends as well, with the kind of influence over the unruly counts that Saint-Gilles could only dream of.

"He's waiting for you upstairs, my lord."

"Good." Saint-Gilles swivelled until he could pin Bessarion with his one good eye. "Stay here, Bessarion. I'll receive your report as soon as I'm done speaking with the bishop."

Despite the hot wind—May was never so warm in Provence—the house was blessedly cool, its thick mud walls retaining the previous night's chill. In the private quarters on the second floor he found Adhemar sitting thoughtfully over a cup of abstemiously mixed water-and-wine, his fingers moving anxiously over a set of well-worn rosary beads.

"Saint-Gilles," he greeted, getting to his feet. "They told me you'd gone to Malregard. I thought—"

"Calm yourself, my friend." Saint-Gilles reached for the wine-jug, hesitated a moment, and then poured himself an undiluted beakerful. "I saved my breath. Bohemond remains unchastised—for now."

Adhemar drew a deep breath, letting it out again in a slow, cautious stream. "Bohemond is a reasonable man. If he has done wrong he will be quick to set it right."

"I'd sent Lukas Bessarion to meet with my usual informant," Saint-Gilles said briefly. "That busybody le Puiset collected him and took him to Bohemond, and Bohemond took it upon himself to question the boy. Yes, he's in one piece," he added, as concern shone in the bishop's eyes. He took a swallow of the wine—it wasn't bad, this local stuff, although difficult to come by in lands so recently ruled by Turks. "As for Bohemond's reason," he said bitterly, "it's his conscience that's defective, not his wits. It may interest you to know that last week I received a letter from the Duke of Apulia."

"Isn't that Bohemond's younger brother?" said Adhemar, frowning slightly.

"Roger Borsa. The one to whom old Guiscard left his whole Sicilian empire, because Roger's mother was a princess and Bohemond's was not."

"I suppose old Guiscard thought he'd left Bohemond more than enough in the way of wits and looks and sheer bloody-minded audacity." Galdemar snickered.

Saint-Gilles glared at his friend, wondering why even Galdemar must rub salt in that particular wound. His friend and vassal swallowed the laughter instantly, and Saint-Gilles went on.

"When the lord Pope declared an armed pilgrimage to liberate the holy places and the eastern church, Bohemond was with Roger and their uncle laying siege to Amalfi. The news arrived when Bohemond just *happened* to be wearing his most costly mantle. He pulled it from his shoulders and cut it into strips of cloth for crosses. Maybe he was filled with devotion and wanted to atone for his sins. Roger thinks differently. Nearly the whole army followed suit. Roger had to call off his siege and wave his vassals goodbye as they followed Bohemond across the sea to Constantinople." Saint-Gilles paused, letting this sink in. "It's Roger's opinion that he was swindled. He suspects Bohemond came to Amalfi for one purpose only: to poach his brother's best warriors for a war of conquest in the east."

Adhemar looked troubled. "Borsa cannot know that for certain. Bohemond took the same oath as the rest of us, to worship in Jerusalem. Who knows what was in his heart?"

"Oh, don't be such a gull, Adhemar! I *told* you Bohemond had an understanding with the Greek emperor. At Marash he boasted to Thatoul that he would make himself supreme commander of the whole pilgrimage, and then to me that he meant to defy Alexius. It's all part of the same picture. Bohemond used pious pretences to equip himself with his brother's crack troops, purely for the purpose of conquering himself a lordship in the East. Never forget that Bohemond's father disinherited him for the sake of Borsa. *He* surely hasn't."

Saint-Gilles let his words ring in the air, irrefutable. In the last seven months he'd spent at least as much time watching Bohemond as he had watching the Turkish garrison behind Antioch's walls. Each new piece of evidence fitted into a larger, more sinister picture. It astonished him that no one else saw it as clearly as he did.

Galdemar lifted a half-mocking eyebrow. "Now I wonder what urged Borsa to write to you, Saint-Gilles?"

"I wrote first," Saint-Gilles admitted curtly. "A man should know his enemy."

"Count Bohemond is no enemy!" Adhemar protested. "Do I need to remind you how he saved all our necks at the battle near Dorylaeum?

What about the kalends of January? What about the Lake? And—"

"Please," Saint-Gilles said in a very quiet voice, "believe that I remember."

There was a silence in the airy upper room. *Seven hundred knights,* Saint-Gilles thought for the hundredth time since the Lake battle three months before. *No infantry at all. Who wins a battle against a force of twelve thousand using just seven hundred starveling knights, some of them riding cows?*

"He may be one of us," Saint-Gilles added. "But Bohemond is a danger to the whole pilgrimage. All he cares for is his own ambition—not the lives of these people, not performing his pilgrim vow—and he will ride roughshod over everyone that stands in his way. *That* is what stands behind his proposal to the council—and I suspect that is also what stands behind his tales of a Turkish army. We can't afford to let him seize control. We all swore the same sort of oath in Constantinople. All the territory we recovered, as far as Antioch, must be ceded to the emperor. If we fail in that, then Alexius stops sending us food, money, reinforcements." He sighed, dragging a hand through his hair. "I shouldn't have to explain this to you. *No* army can survive this far from home without help. Without support from Alexius, we'll be cut off, surrounded, slaughtered. Us, our knights, all these helpless commoners. And *now* Bohemond proposes that whoever can take the city should be allowed to rule it?"

The bishop tried to say something, but Saint-Gilles was too angry to be halted. "Wake up, Adhemar! The only possible reason he might have to propose such a thing would be if *he was already in communication with a traitor inside the city.* He already has Antioch in the palm of his hand! How many weeks has he been keeping this traitor of his up his sleeve? How many people have died for the sake of his ambition? How many more will it take?"

Again, Adhemar tried to speak, but Galdemar held up a hand. "Let me try," he said to the bishop, but there was a twinkle in Galdemar's eye that told Saint-Gilles he was hardly taking the affair seriously enough. "Look, Saint-Gilles, I'd agree with you, except that the Greek emperor *hasn't* been much help lately. The winter storms prevented his supply fleets from Cyprus reaching us, remember? Then, in February, right before the

Lake battle, Tatikius up and announced he was leaving, with all of his two thousand men. He promised he was going back to his master to fetch supplies, but we've seen neither hide nor hair of him since, and no news from Alexius."

Saint-Gilles' mouth set stubbornly. "That's what the other princes said."

"And why shouldn't they? How long has it been since Alexius was any use to us? Christmas? If he won't send help or come himself, the next best thing would be to install Bohemond here in Antioch! *And why not?* Once he's made himself master of the city, he'll be far too busy to play the gadfly. The rest of us can take the pilgrimage south to Jerusalem, as we vowed, and Bohemond can support us from Syria."

Saint-Gilles gritted his teeth. When Galdemar put it that way, the thought was only reasonable. Except that Bohemond had only gotten to this point by lies and deceit, trickery and subterfuge, and meant to keep lying until he made himself overlord of them all. Give an inch, and Bohemond would take all the miles he could get.

"It's the principle of the thing," he growled. "Devil take it! It was Bohemond who hounded us all into swearing the oath in the first place!"

"I *agree.*" Adhemar finally managed to squeeze a word in. He levelled an exasperated look first at Saint-Gilles, then at Galdemar. "Most of us at this rank have done homage and vowed fealty to Alexius. To award Antioch to any one of us would void that oath entirely. An oath each of us swore on the Crown of Thorns and the True Cross."

Saint-Gilles tried to cut in, but it was Adhemar's turn to raise his voice—once an unusual occurrence, though it seemed to be getting more common as the pilgrimage dragged on.

"Breaking an oath doesn't just have consequences in the temporal world, you know. It won't merely strike at the foundation of our society, the trust we all have in our vassals and our vassals in us. It doesn't just risk bringing the emperor down on our heads to take his revenge, if God puts it in his mind to do so. It has grave spiritual consequences as well. When you swore those oaths to Alexius, you called God himself to bear witness. Here you are on the most perilous adventure of your lives, assailed daily by the enemy and with nowhere to turn but Heaven when things go wrong. Here you have no walls to hide behind, precious few allies to avenge your deaths, and no monasteries endowed to pray for your souls. Will you *really* provoke the Lord to abandon you?"

Galdemar had paled, but Saint-Gilles burst into laughter. "God help us, Adhemar! Couldn't you have said that yesterday in council, when everyone was discussing the question so calmly?"

Adhemar looked abashed. "I only just thought to say it now."

Saint-Gilles snorted. "I know you, Adhemar. You *hate* confrontation. When Bohemond proposed awarding the city to one man, their only objection was that since all had borne the labour, all should share equally in the lordship. God help us when Alexius *does* come to claim his own. After the winter we've had, he'll eat us alive."

"*If* Alexius comes," Galdemar said, cheerfully.

"I've sent to him," Saint-Gilles snapped. "He's campaigning in Anatolia, remember? I've told him we destroyed the armies of Aleppo and Damascus in pitched battle, the Turks are in disarray, and the city is at the point of falling. It's a golden opportunity to secure the empire's great border outpost in the east. He'll come. He'd be a fool not to." He tossed back the rest of his beaker of wine and went to the door, throwing it open and shouting for Bessarion.

Galdemar cleared his throat. "And in the meantime, what about Kerbogha?"

"Kerbogha?" Adhemar echoed anxiously.

"Bohemond says the sky is falling," Saint-Gilles snapped. "It's likely nothing. *My* scouts—"

"My lord." Lukas Bessarion interrupted him from the doorway. "I beg your pardon, but please, Count Bohemond is right. The Turks are coming here."

Chapter III.

Lukas' visions came upon him these days with swift inevitability. All the warning he ever had was the tell-tale dizziness dancing through his head before his eyes stopped seeing his surroundings in favour of vivid, unreal colour and light. This was what happened to him in the tower of Malregard: one moment he was sweating beneath Bohemond's rapid-fire questioning, the next he had fallen to his knees, clinging to reality for a few futile moments before the vision took him.

He stood at a crossroads in a broad river valley between two arms of the mountains somewhere between Marash and Antioch. In a cloud of dust, an army passed before him: rank after rank of heavily armed cataphracts, lightly mounted horse archers, and infantry bearing spears. Banner after banner, many of them bearing the crescent symbol of the Mahometan faith. Troop after troop; an immense host as great as the Frankish army had been at Nicaea.

They streamed down the road from the east; overwhelmed the narrow, overgrown stones of the ancient Roman way. At the crossroads, they turned south towards Antioch and kept marching.

Rank after rank. Troop after troop. Banner after banner. They were still marching when the vision faded: he knew in his bones that it would take two or three days before they had finished passing the crossroads.

Count Bohemond thought he'd had a fit. Count Raymond seemed to think it was an attack of panic, common in the pilgrimage after so much hardship and anguish. God knew he was no stranger to those, either. The visions were intense, not so different to the times at which he helplessly relived the moment when the life faded from Ayla's eyes, and all light went out of the world…No, he mustn't think of that. Think of the army coming for them. The Turkish sultan at Baghdad must have finally called together the splintered lordships of Mesopotamia and Syria, determined to secure his western frontier. How could the weakened pilgrimage possibly resist an army twice their own size?

At first, Lukas had kept silent. Count Raymond would not thank him for blurting out confirmation of Count Bohemond's words, certainly not in front of his rival. Back at the count's headquarters, he'd been told to wait, and so he had, gnawing at his ragged fingernails. Count Raymond's patronage had begun to give him an illusion of safety: he might not have enough to eat, but he had more than most; he had regular pay, even if it couldn't buy what he needed, and a place to sleep, and a measure of protection. Now that illusion had been broken. The whole pilgrimage was in danger. He had no way into Antioch. Le Puiset still nursed a grudge against him—he knew well that only Count Raymond's name protected him.

Perhaps, once he had warned these people, he should go. What sort of life was it here, anyway? Lukas glanced around the farmhouse's lower room—a dark, bare, crowded room full of bedrolls, spare armour and weapons and other belongings, the coughing and retching of sick men, the stench of unwashed clothes and bodies, the smell of mildew that speckled all their clothes and belongings after spending so long cramped on a river marsh during the winter's relentless downpours. He was living like a beast. When was the last time he'd had a real bath?

Others had already deserted the pilgrimage. Yet who else did he know in this strange and inhospitable future? Service with the Franks was still preferable to starvation in the wilderness, and the only thing that gave him purpose was the hope of getting into besieged Antioch and retrieving his father's lance from its hiding-place. The sorcerer in the mountains said it was a powerful weapon—that the bearer of that lance would never be defeated in battle—and it did not occur to Lukas to doubt him. Khalil ibn Hassan had called on demons and slaughtered hundreds in a blood sacrifice to get his hands on that lance.

The Bessarion Lance would give him everything he still wanted in this life. The respect and status the Franks denied him. The certainty that he could protect his people from anyone who wanted to subdue them.

And vengeance. Ayla's death must not go unpunished.

No, if he left the pilgrimage he might as well cut his own throat, for there would be no other purpose left to him. And since he meant to stay with the pilgrimage, he must do more than warn them. He must make sure they believed him.

He must try to save them.

So, when he ascended the stairs and found Count Raymond protesting that Bohemond was in a panic, he blurted out his news, despite the knowledge that the count would not thank him.

** * **

Count Raymond might have only one eye, but he used it to pin Lukas with a look that could curdle milk. "What do *you* know about it, Bessarion?"

He'd have to tell them *something*. Anything, other than the truth. Lukas knew what would happen if he started giving prophecies. He'd become a demagogue, a holy fool. He had no aspirations to sainthood; he was born to be a warrior.

He swallowed and cut the truth as fine as he could. "I managed to speak to Mergen today, before Count Evrard killed him. I imagine it's common knowledge among the Turks."

"What else did Mergen say?" the count demanded. "Did he say how many? Or when they will arrive?"

"No, my lord. He had little to report, and now he is dead."

The count turned to meet Bishop Adhemar's worried look. "All *right*," he said. "I'll send scouts. Well done, Bessarion. I'm pleased with you."

His voice had warmed unexpectedly, and Lukas felt his face warm in turn. Count Raymond was an exacting, often harsh master; but if he could be resentful or blunt, he was also loyal and straightforward. And somehow, over the last terrible year, Lukas had earned the count's trust.

It still hurt to be treated like a servant, with unthinking contempt, when he had been born nobly and trained to rule. But if he had never known to want more from his life, he might have been satisfied in this humble position. He must be careful. He might yet learn to be satisfied with being base and despised. *No.* He wouldn't let himself slip into obscurity. He would make a place for himself, for his people, in this future.

"There's more," he blurted. "Count Evrard was with an Armenian from inside the city. Tigranants, he calls himself. I've arranged to meet him again at the kalends. They could be of use to us."

"Can they get us into the city?" Lord Galdemar put in dryly.

"I don't know."

"It hardly matters." Count Raymond ran a thoughtful finger along the drooping lid of his lost eye. "If it was so easy to betray the city, they would already have done it. Bohemond must have found someone manning the walls. A Turk, or at least a convert. If Bohemond succeeds, we'll need these people as our allies."

Lukas hesitated. He shouldn't get involved in Frankish politics; surely it made no difference to him who ended up ruling Antioch, so long as they treated his people with kindness. But no, there was a difference. That difference was that Count Raymond was the nearest thing he still had in this pilgrimage to a friend; or at least, a patron.

"It turns out Tigranants and I had something in common, my lord." Lukas pushed up his sleeve and extended his arm, showing his Watcher's Mark. His voice could not help shaking with emotion. "He is one of the Syrian Watchers we were told had perished. He's not the only one."

"A Syrian Watcher?" Bishop Adhemar straightened, his eyes widening in awe. "God be thanked! But they told us in Constantinople there were none left…"

"Watchers?" Count Raymond looked from Lukas to the bishop, confused. "A lay society of do-gooders? How will they help us?"

"Watchers aren't just a charitable organisation," Adhemar said in a voice of repressed excitement. "They promote holiness in laymen, and are blessed with extraordinary gifts. Interpretation. Perception. Prophecy."

"You're joking," said the count with a snort of laughter. "All this time you've had prophets up your sleeve, Adhemar?"

"Messengers and other giftings are rare," the bishop added, touching his own Mark almost unconsciously where it lay beneath his sleeve. "But they tend to reach a higher concentration in times or places of particular trouble. If most of the Syrian Watchers have disappeared and the rest are living in hiding, then it's quite possible there are powerful giftings among them."

Lukas shifted uncomfortably, thinking of his visions. His prophetic gifting hadn't been enough to save Ayla, and it wasn't something he was ready to tell anyone.

"Then we want them on our side." Count Raymond slapped his shoulder. "Don't miss that meeting at the kalends, Bessarion. And in the meanwhile, go downstairs and feed yourself. I'd better get to La Mahomerie before nightfall; the Turks have been amusing themselves each night trying to burn us out."

So dismissed, Lukas descended into the courtyard, where he paused, the vision once again flickering before his eyes.

Troop after troop. Rank upon rank.

The pilgrimage was sick, tired, desperately low on horses, and stranded outside the walls of Antioch. They would be crushed like a nut.

He'd been sent down to get some food, but his stomach seemed full of snakes.

"Lukas?" Bishop Adhemar had followed him, and now put a hand on his shoulder, stooping to look into his face. "What is it? Are you ill? Did le Puiset injure you?"

"It's nothing." Lukas wished the bishop would be less perceptive. Certainly the shock of this morning's confrontation had done his peace of mind no favours. "I'm hungry, that's all."

Adhemar watched him with shrewd eyes that, perhaps, suspected him of lying. "Some food for the count's interpreter," he called to one of the sergeants dicing on the doorstep leading to the farmhouse kitchen. "Bread *and* meat, as much as you can find." He turned back to Lukas. "Let me know if le Puiset ever troubles you again. Saint-Gilles and I will both speak to his liege lord. That's a promise."

"It won't work," Lukas said. If he wouldn't confess to having visions, perhaps he should confess to this: "Even if Count Evrard leaves me alone, I'm still vulnerable to any bully with a sword and a title. You speak of liberating the Christians of the east, my lord, but to the rest of these people I'm just another peasant to be ordered around. I won't be safe—none of us will be safe until they respect us."

The bishop frowned slightly. Lukas watched in him speechless hope. Adhemar was the only Frankish noble he knew who made a point of treating him like an equal, not a servant. He knew it wasn't just himself, either. Adhemar had also forged a friendship with the exiled Patriarch of Jerusalem over the winter, travelling to meet him in Cyprus and deferring to his claims of authority even where they conflicted with those of the Latin pope.

It struck him that alone among the Franks, Adhemar of Le Puy cared about other people more than he cared about his own honour. Adhemar might possibly sympathise with his hopes, even if he couldn't grant them.

"If Count Raymond would make me one of his knights," Lukas blurted out, "*then* I would be safe. And I'd be able to keep my people safe. I'd have power."

Adhemar looked disappointed. "Power again, Lukas?"

"I know," he said bitterly. "You've told me time and again that I should learn to pull my head in, to serve. I suppose it's easy to give such advice when you have all the power in the world."

"It isn't that," the bishop said quickly. "It's only that I've spent all my life in the company of men who think that all their troubles would be over if they were only given more power, that wrongs are righted in taking vengeance against their foes. But it doesn't work that way."

"Then how does it work?" Lukas sucked in a ragged breath. "I'm not asking for myself. Only I have to protect my people *somehow*."

The bishop looked about them—towards the mountains, the city, the sprawling, filthy camp. "I wish I knew," he said in a curiously bleak voice. "I ought to have faith. *The meek shall inherit the earth.* But…"

His voice trailed away. In the silence, a sergeant emerged from the kitchen carrying a bundle of food, wrapped in a tolerably clean cloth. The evening meal was over, but evidently some food had been kept back; some of it was even warm. Lukas took it gratefully.

Adhemar touched his shoulder again. "Neither Saint-Gilles nor I have forgotten the purpose of this pilgrimage, Lukas: to liberate the eastern church. We can't do that without interpreters and liaisons—without you. Perhaps you have more power than you think. You've served Saint-Gilles faithfully. He wouldn't rely on just anyone to deal with such people as the Syrian Watchers. He trusts you, and that in itself gives you power to protect them."

Not anywhere near enough…but the bishop was only trying to comfort him. With a grunt of assent, Lukas tucked the bundle under his arm and stalked away. At the courtyard gate he glanced back. The bishop of le Puy stood alone in the courtyard staring at the cracked pavement beneath his feet. It struck Lukas how thin and frail the old man looked, how the once ropy sinew had withered from his forearms, how hollows formed in his cheeks. His hair was almost completely grey now.

It wasn't just Lukas. Everyone in the pilgrimage had been through hell, and now this Kerbogha was on his way, and they were exposed and helpless. But what could he do? He'd given his warning and helped persuade the count to act on it. If only Tigranants had been able to get him inside Antioch. Then he might have retrieved the Bessarion Lance. Saint George…he might have even been able to *bathe.*

As it was, all he had was a little food and a little time of peace in which to eat it. Lukas made his way towards the marshy land bordering the river, trying not to breathe in the clouds of midges he disturbed as he walked. A few late spring flowers still bloomed among the lush untrampled grass, for the ground was too damp here to pitch camp. Lukas found a fallen tree too rotten for building and too wet for burning, and sank onto it to inspect his meal. The bread was hard, but the meat was warm, and there was also a canteen of watered wine. Lukas yanked the cork with his teeth and poured a few drops of it onto the ground. "Here's to you, Ayla." The thought reminded him of someone else, and he splashed a little more after it. "And to you, Bertrand." The bishop's squire had died in one of the many skirmishes outside the Bridge Gate, sometime between Christmas and Epiphany. Lukas didn't remember the precise day. Sickness, hunger, cold, violence…what was the point of remembering a death? Far better to recall a life.

The sound of tramping feet echoed hollowly along the great sweep of the Orontes as Count Raymond and a band of his men crossed the Bridge of Boats, a rickety pontoon bridge the Franks had constructed from shallow-hulled vessels seized on the river. The bridge groaned, bobbed, and swayed until the count and his men gained the western shore and moved south—doubtless to relieve the garrison of the small fortress the Franks had recently constructed to blockade the Bridge Gate. Before the fortress had been constructed, the Turks used the Bridge Gate to make raids, galloping up the river's western shore to shoot clouds of arrows into the Frankish camp.

Although the river-marsh was green with grass, it was still littered with arrows and bones. Lukas sighed. The spectre of death haunted him even here.

Why did he bother trying to survive this? It would be easier to succumb, to let the Turks kill him, since hunger and disease had not. Ayla was dead, Bertrand was dead, and he would never find his way home across the gulf of time to his own time, his own family. He was so very weary of fighting.

God be merciful, Greek, Ayla would say, if she were here. *Lie there and whine some more, why don't you? You've done nothing else since you got here!*

What else was there to do? His reason to live had died with Ayla.

Then you ought to avenge me.

Ayla's words had given him purpose once, and they still gave him purpose now—but he sometimes wondered how long they would keep him going. Vengeance was a grim, cold sort of motivation, compared to the flicker-fire of home and family. Even the desire to protect his people felt distant and bloodless when he had no real friends among them. Lukas thought his will might give out one day soon, and he would sink into this soft wet earth and become food for the flowers.

He took a swig of the watered wine and thought about le Puiset. Would Count Evrard never tire of tormenting him? Was the Frank not content to have killed the only woman he would ever love? Lukas wished the mixture was strong enough to make him forget the thick, acrid emotions that drifted through him like the smoke of a burning city. He felt a measure of loyalty towards Count Raymond and Bishop Adhemar, but he found with a jolt of surprise that it was Count Evrard he really cared about. He hoped viciously that the count would live through whatever was coming, that he would stay hale and able-bodied until Lukas could call Ayla's name and put the Bessarion Lance through his ribcage.

He couldn't do that as a peasant, without the formalities and protections of knightly combat.

Lukas swallowed as much food as he could stomach before hiding the remainder down the front of his tunic. The bedroll waiting for him in the lower room of the count's house contained a sack that held a great many pieces of old dry meat and mouldy bread, and he'd add these remainders to the collection as well. Lukas knew very well he shouldn't be saving food until long after it went bad, and there was still a part of him that recoiled in disgust from the thought of ever eating it, but he couldn't bring himself to throw it out. He might be glad of it yet.

Not that he meant to return just yet to that suffocating, crowded room. He pulled his cloak around himself and lay back, breathing deeply of the warm, humid air as the spring stars appeared in the darkening sky. It was hard to believe it had already been a year since the pilgrimage was camped outside Nicaea, and he and Ayla had been playing foolish riddle games. *I have a bagful of walnuts I can never finish counting.* His breath hitched as memory stabbed him, sharp as a blade.

Stars. The answer was stars.

* * *

He must have slipped into sleep, for he began to have troubled dreams.

Ayla was there, as always. Tonight, she walked on the opposite bank of the river, her forehead still marked by the red mess where Count Evrard's crossbow bolt had struck her. It should have been too dark to see her, but there was a glimmer like moonlight where she trod.

"Ayla," he called. His voice was surely too soft to carry, but she turned, saw him, and waited.

Ignoring the cramps in his stomach, he got to his feet and staggered closer to the water before falling to his knees in the shallows. "I miss you," he whispered.

"I miss you too." Her distant voice carried faintly across the water, and Lukas shivered with happiness. She had never spoken to him in his dreams before.

"Have you come to take me home?"

"Not yet. There is work for you here."

"I only want you." For the first time since he'd known her, she was wearing women's clothing—during her life he had only ever seen her in men's tunics. He swallowed and whispered, "You look beautiful. Are you in Paradise? Tell me if you are in Paradise."

"Cucumber," she said with a soft snort, and Lukas felt the tears springing to his eyes.

"Then *please* take me with you."

"I will, one day. But first you have work to do."

"I'm not a prophet, Ayla."

"Don't you remember the Message Kari gave you on the day of the great battle? It's your duty to protect Antioch and Jerusalem. Your own people."

He closed his eyes. Kari, the emperor's Varangian, who had turned out to be a Messenger. Just another of the allies he had lost to this war. "I would need power, and becoming a Messenger won't give me that kind of power."

"Why not?" She let him think about that a moment before adding: "The Franks are trapped out here in the open, aren't they? And you have the opportunity to save them."

"They *killed* you," he growled through his teeth. "That's why not."

Either she didn't hear him, or she pretended not to. "Deliver your Message, save them from the hands of their enemy, and they'll obey you in everything. Just think: all that power, in the hands of one who *cares* for the Syrians."

It wasn't the first time he'd considered it, but Lukas ground his teeth. "That isn't the kind of power I want. I'm a cataphract—a *knight.* Prophets are outsiders, madmen, curiosities. I want respect. I want friends."

"Put yourself at the head of this army, and you needn't be an outsider for long."

Lukas looked up at her. The red wound in her head was gone and she was watching him with Ayla's familiar smirk. But there was something wrong. *Save them from the hands of their enemy*—when had the real Ayla ever spoken with such poetic words? When had the real Ayla ever encouraged him to take power and make himself the leader of a Frankish army?

It may have been seven months since her death, but his memory was not quite so bad as *that.*

"You aren't my wife. Ayla never cared about power."

"I care about *you.*" She sounded injured now.

He dragged himself to his feet. "Stop this. Who are you really? Who gave you leave to come here wearing that face?"

She blinked at him, her borrowed features uncannily still. "Wouldn't you rather I lied to you?"

"I've had enough of lies."

"Yet still you listen to me."

"Who are you?" he shouted. "In God's name, answer me!"

Her features blurred: for a moment, Lukas found his eyes would not fix on her. Then he blinked and a woman stood near him, close enough to reach. Her smile was as red as a slash of blood; her arms and body dripped with black, iridescent vulture-feathers.

"Who am I?" said Lilith. "I am your reckoning. I am the one who shields you when the arrows fly. I am the one who sets boundaries on your diseases. I am the one who owns you, Lukas Bessarion, until you keep the oath you made on the mountain of Oliveta. Does that answer your question?"

Lukas' throat dried. When he lifted the arm with the Watcher's mark, it was shaking. "You don't own me."

She smiled. "This isn't a struggle you can win, Bessarion. The harder you fight me, the more you'll slip into my grasp."

He backed away, his gut a pit of snakes. Lilith followed, Fate on taloned feet.

"You might as well get something out of it," she prompted. "Why be my slave when you might be my champion?"

Lukas tried to recall the words of his mother's exorcism prayer. "May the Lord rebuke thee," he began, but despite the movement of his lips, no sound came from them at all.

And Lilith only laughed at him. "That might have worked for you once, my gilded boy, but not anymore."

In another blink, she was Ayla again, leaning forwards as though she meant to press a kiss on his lips.

Lukas awoke screaming.

* * *

A day passed, and then another. Ayla haunted his dreams as she always had, a voiceless ghost he could never catch no matter how far or fast he ran. Still, Lukas was not fool enough to believe Lilith had forgotten him. Waking or sleeping, the back of his neck always prickled with the feeling that he was watched.

In Oliveta after Ayla's death he had sworn to free Khalil ibn Hassan from the enchantment that kept him prisoner, half stone from the waist down. That vow he had broken, and given Lilith power over him.

Power that would only increase the longer he failed to keep that vow.

What could he do about it? He could not free Khalil to become Lilith's slave, to wreak fresh evil upon the world. Perhaps he might confess the vow and be absolved of it, but he was doubtful that would work. He had sworn of his own free will, to his own hurt, and had changed. What power would protect him from his own word?

Three days passed, and Lukas was running a message from the fort at the Bridge Gate to Count Raymond's headquarters. He had crossed the Bridge of Boats and was hurrying through the Lorrainers' camp when a voice called his name and he turned to see a tall young Frankish woman with ash-blonde hair, alone save for a young squire who tugged on the girl's arm with a sound of protest.

"Stop it, Reynald; I *know*," the Frankish lady said in a thin wisp of a voice. She turned back to Lukas, her brows knitting anxiously. "I thought it was you. I wanted to say that I'm sorry about what happened the other day."

Lukas stared, uncomprehending.

"Oh," she said. "You don't remember. Silly me! I'm Evrard of le Puiset's sister."

Memory flooded back to him. The faded blue of her dress, the reliquary around her neck, the wide blue eyes and ashen hair—it was the Frankish girl he'd had the misfortune to liberate from Turkish captivity after the great battle at Dorylaeum.

A decision he had regretted ever since, for it had tripped the series of events that led to Ayla's death. Lukas recoiled. "Excuse me, mademoiselle. You shouldn't speak to me."

He turned abruptly and made towards the Provençal camp. To his chagrin, Emelota of le Puiset darted after him, catching his arm.

"No! Wait! It's all right. I won't tell my brother we've spoken."

"We haven't spoken." He tried to move past, but she caught his shoulders, stopping him in his tracks. Lukas found himself unable look away from her wide blue gaze: for a moment he had the eerie feeling that she looked into his heart and sifted through his thoughts.

"I love my brother," Emelota said. "But he's made an enemy of you, and I know it was a terrible mistake."

"Yeh, well, perhaps you should tell him that."

"I did." She still wouldn't release him. "There's *good* in my brother, Lukas Bessarion."

"A man is only as good as the way he treats those he despises." He pulled from her grasp and set out again, trying not to let her see the rage in his eyes—nor the grief trembling beneath it. Trailed by her anxious companion, Emelota fell into step beside him. Lukas growled, "Why are you following me?"

She glanced down at the basket she carried. "I visited Duke Godfrey's apothecary for some mandrake root. My sister lost her husband a week ago. They say that putting an immersed mandrake root by her bed will chase away her melancholy."

"Melancholy, hm?" Lukas stifled his mocking laughter. "What can you recommend for a persistent panic?"

"For courage? Bear's hair, to lay on your chest." She frowned. "I'm not sure the apothecary would have any of *that* left. Are there any bears in Syria? Quite likely lion's hair would do as well."

"Saint George," Lukas swore, unable to stand the conversation any longer. If word of this meeting ever got back to Evrard, not even his liege lord's displeasure would keep the count from hunting Lukas down and peeling the flesh from his bones. "Be well, mademoiselle."

He turned abruptly, but once again she caught his arm. She was taller than he was, and he could not risk trying to push her away.

"I haven't forgotten that you saved my life at Dorylaeum and, despite how it may seem, neither has Evrard."

"Nor have I forgotten that he murdered my *wife*," Lukas snarled.

Emelota's mouth dropped open. She lost her grip on his arm, and he stalked on, blinking the angry tears from his eyes.

He had only the barest moment to pull himself together, and then she was beside him again, clutching her basket with wide eyes. "I didn't know that," she said solemnly. "But I knew there had to be something terrible… I am so sorry."

That took him aback. "You believe me?"

Her voice dipped "I can tell when people are lying to me. It's like shadow spewing from their mouths." She paused. "Yours spews blood."

Every hair on his neck stood up. Lukas turned to look at her. "I beg your pardon?"

"You're dangerous," she said. That was the urgency in her wide blue eyes: fear. "You hold all our lives in your hand, Lukas Bessarion. And I don't want my brother to die unconfessed."

Fear. She was afraid of him. Lukas took half a step towards her and said huskily, "Good. You ought to be afraid."

Her eyes widened. The squire caught up with them, a little out of breath. "Please, my lady, come away."

This time, speechlessly, she obeyed. As Lukas watched them go, Emelota glanced over her shoulder at him as she went. Pleading.

She saw...*blood,* spewing from his mouth? For a moment, Lukas felt an ice-cold chill that had nothing to do with the unseen watcher who lay in wait for him. Then he recalled her mandrake's root and bear's hair, and told himself not to fall prey to a foolish girl's fancies.

He returned to the Provençal camp to find an uproar sweeping from tent to tent. A pale-lipped messenger waited at the farmhouse with a message for Count Raymond, and within minutes Lukas was on his way back across the Bridge of Boats, the pontoons swaying dizzily beneath his hurrying feet.

The Provençal scouts had returned bringing the news that confirmed his vision. All the lords of Syria and Mesopotamia were on the march. The sultan had gathered an army great enough to wipe the Franks from the face of the earth, and now it was marching to Antioch.

Chapter IV.

It was three months ago that the Greeks had deserted them, silently, suddenly, at first light on a miserable, wet February morning.

Saint-Gilles remembered well how the icy rain blew directly into his face, making it impossible to see far ahead as he rode after them. He didn't see the Greek cataphracts until he'd blundered directly into their ambush.

That it was an ambush, he was left in no doubt. Tatikius' heavily-armed knights emerged from the trees with levelled spears and drawn swords, to surround him and his small entourage. Immediately upon the road before him, the gold-nosed Greek general waited, huddled beneath an oiled cloak.

Saint-Gilles raised both his hands, palm open. "It's me!" he shouted through the pelting rain. "Saint-Gilles!"

"I can see who you are," the Greek said coldly. His men did not move, still surrounding the Provençals in a ring of steel. "Why are you following me?"

"Why," Saint-Gilles countered hoarsely, "are you leaving the pilgrimage in such a hurry? Is it something I've done? This isn't about our little disagreement, is it? Because I don't think Emperor Alexius will be happy to see you throw away this alliance for something so trivial."

Only a week previously, Tatikius had once again recommended retiring from the walls of Antioch to conduct a looser siege from a distance, starving Antioch out from the warmth and safety of the surrounding fortresses.

"Trivial?" Tatikius kneed his horse forward, breaking through the ring of steel to confront Saint-Gilles eye to eye. "It's no trivial matter, to see the emperor's gold and food squandered on such a costly siege, when a distant campaign would serve just as well."

"So, what? You're abandoning us?"

"Of course not. I go in search of the emperor. In person, I'll be able to explain how affairs stand here and make sure he sends the supplies we need." Tatikius' voice was as bland as ever, but he was frowning behind the shiny gold nose he wore to replace the original, lost in some battle or other. Saint-Gilles realised with a jolt of surprise that even the sleek, well-groomed Greek had suffered from the winter's siege. He was thinner, his hair sprinkled with more grey, his once immaculate linens now drab and mildewed. He looked tired, puffy around the eyes. Perhaps it was the rain, the fact that both of them were soaked to the bone and had no hope of getting dry before summer arrived. Or perhaps this siege had broken even Tatikius, trusted general and own foster brother to the emperor, Alexius Comnenus himself.

"This is madness," Saint-Gilles said more calmly, wiping a palmful of water from his forehead and flinging it into the road. "I wanted a close siege because it took power from Bohemond and gave it to me. Now you'll leave altogether? How will I hold this alliance together then? The counts have been complaining all winter that Alexius sends less help than they'd like. Should you leave, it will be all too easy for Bohemond to repudiate the emperor."

The Greek's face was like clay, cold and motionless. "Perhaps not so easy as you think," he said in a voice no more expressive. "Bohemond has sworn oaths that even he will find it difficult to break. Keep your oaths, Saint-Gilles. I *will* return to claim this city."

* * *

Bohemond had waited three months to make his next move, and now Saint-Gilles could only wish he had warned Tatikius—and through him, the emperor—more strongly. (He ground his teeth at the memory of how for a while on the march through Anatolia Bohemond had won his trust—almost his friendship. That had been embarrassing, but Saint-Gilles was not in the habit of making the same mistake twice.)

Even since discovering the true depths of Bohemond's duplicity—that he had beguiled the emperor into promising him the lordship of the east—the two of them had managed to ignore their differences and work together in the siege of Antioch, secret rivals for the leadership of the pilgrimage and the emperor's favour. Now that Bohemond had claimed the city for himself and begun harassing Saint-Gilles' servants, the situation had changed.

Retaliation was now necessary—and Saint-Gilles knew exactly which step to take.

As he and Galdemar arrived in the courtyard of Bishop Adhemar's house where the princes' council had gathered to debate their next steps—and plan their survival in the face of Kerbogha's approach—Saint-Gilles paused to strip off his gloves. "I know *exactly* what is going to happen next," he said gloomily. "Bohemond will charm them into giving him what he wants, and nothing I say will make any difference. I wish Adhemar hadn't gone off on that mission to the coast."

"Keep your chin up," Galdemar put in. "With any luck, the Turks will slaughter the lot of us before Bohemond ever gets his hands on Antioch."

Saint-Gilles was in no joking mood. "What's that supposed to mean?"

Galdemar raised his hands. "Nothing, nothing. Look, there's Tancred."

While the seven great lords of the pilgrimage assembled upstairs on the bishop's rooftop, many of their greatest vassals would sit here in the courtyard, drinking wine and trading gossip. Bohemond's nephew Tancred sat at the head of the great rough trestle table that had been set up in the courtyard, laden with wine and walnuts and fresh peppered bread. Saint-Gilles stopped beside him, leaning on the spear he used as a staff. "May I have a word in private?"

The young Norman sent him a calculating look. As Bohemond's right hand, Tancred had to know about the unspoken rivalry between the two counts. But rumour had it that the nephew's ambition was no less rapacious than the uncle's—a fact that could not sit well with Bohemond. Sure enough, Tancred hesitated barely a moment before getting to his feet and following Saint-Gilles and Galdemar to a quieter corner of the courtyard, where an olive-tree in a tub half concealed them from onlookers.

Saint-Gilles swivelled, pinned Tancred with his one remaining eye, and said, "Tell me, young man, do you mean to play second fiddle all your life?"

Tancred's eyes opened in shock—no doubt after a lifetime dancing attendance on Bohemond, he was unaccustomed to such directness. After a moment, however, he let out a laugh and said "To my uncle? Of course not."

"Look," Saint-Gilles said. "You've proven yourself these last two months overseeing the blockade of the south gate. You deserve to be up there with the great men, not down here among the second rank." He nodded to the rooftop where the seven great princes gathered. "What's holding you back?"

Any other man, from any other family, might have responded with *my sworn fealty.* Tancred, however, let a smile play over his lips. "Money. I can't afford my own knights, and I haven't the land to support them."

Saint-Gilles had never corrupted other people's wives, but he was practised in the seduction of other people's vassals. Women were skittish and wanted all sorts of peculiar things, but there was usually only one thing a count ever wanted, and that was power. So he said offhandedly, "If money's all that's lacking, I have enough to set you up as your own man. Pay your own knights, seize your own lordship, and make your own name."

"And the terms?" Tancred's mouth quirked in a mocking smile. "Or is this pure charity?"

"Pure charity, out of the goodness of my heart," Saint-Gilles told him, meeting the other man's raillery with a little of his own. "You'll pay it back, of course, but only once you've set yourself up in a few of these Syrian fortresses, which you'll have no trouble manning once you've poached your uncle's men."

"You're a saint," Tancred said, but the smile on his face was real now. "I'll consider it."

Galdemar whistled long and low as the young Norman swaggered back to his seat at the table. "That went easier than I expected. Think he'll take it?"

"There's no use beating around the bush on such things," Saint-Gilles said. He might have begun by seizing Toulouse from his niece, but from there he'd made himself into one of the most powerful men in Europe by having precisely this sort of conversation with neighbouring counts. "And it hardly matters whether he takes it or not. Bohemond stands to lose his right hand and half his men if Tancred defects. At best, he'll be paying through the nose to make Tancred stay. Either way, he'll think twice before interfering with me again."

Galdemar made a non-committal sound and caught a walnut in his mouth. "And what if he doesn't? You'll hit back harder next time?"

"Until he breaks, if I must."

Another grunt. "Did you ever hear the story of Bohemond's name?"

"No."

"Well, I was dicing with some of the Normans last night, and they say Bohemond isn't his baptismal name. His real name is Mark. Soon after his birth, at dinner one evening, a bard was telling the tale of a giant named Bohemond, a doughty warrior. Old Guiscard declared his son was made for just such a destiny, and called the boy by the giant's name from then on."

Yet another tale of Bohemond's precocious brilliance, bravery, and good looks. Wonderful. "Why are you telling me this?"

"Because that boy grew up to become the victor of Dorylaeum and the Lake Battle and half a hundred other skirmishes over the last few months. How often does early promise bear such fruit?" Galdemar paused, then continued quietly. "We're caught in a trap. I know it, you know it, all these people know it." He nodded towards the pilgrims who had assembled in dead, expectant silence at the bishop's gate. "In a crisis like this, Bohemond might still be the best man to save us all."

Saint-Gilles snorted in derision. "I hardly need *you* to tell me that, Galdemar. Don't worry; I won't put the pilgrimage in danger for Bohemond's sake."

All the same, as he left his friend sipping wine with other lords in the courtyard, he allowed himself to imagine a different possibility. He'd had a strange dream last night, imagining that a beautiful, black-haired woman had come to offer him the lordship of the whole crusade. *Bohemond has a secret,* she'd said. *He never wants anyone to know the true nature of his relationship with Alexius.* Then, because it was a dream, there'd been some disturbing nonsense about swearing fealty to her in return for information and supreme command. *You shall have a gift, a weapon that will make you invincible in battle.* Dreams! It was one thing when a holy man had visions, but the day Raymond of Saint-Gilles started making prophecies would be the day they shipped him off to a monastery to die.

He laughed, but it was not a bad idea. He should find out exactly where Bohemond stood with the Greek emperor.

Owing to the day's heat—moist and sticky, with a faint cool breeze running through it—the council met on the flat roof of the bishop's house, a vantage-point from which the princes could see almost the entire city and its surroundings. Chairs had been provided, as well as more wine, nuts, and bread—but no one seated himself during the discussion that followed, let alone took anything to eat or drink.

The situation was too dire for that.

"Ah… I believe we're all here," Count Stephen of Blois remarked, as Saint-Gilles emerged onto the roof and glanced around the small assembly. Even the princes' council had shrunk since the previous year at Nicaea. The duke of Normandy, famously indolent and fonder of comfort than glory, had retired to the coastal port of Laodicea some months before to enjoy a life of peace and quiet—whence Adhemar of le Puy had now gone, partly in order to retrieve him.

Other than that, they were all present: Blois, Flanders, Vermandois, Godfrey, Saint-Gilles…and Bohemond, who was leaning against the parapet in an overlooked corner, playing with a bejewelled gold toothpick.

At Blois' words, he straightened and saw Saint-Gilles, and if Saint-Gilles hadn't known better he would have sworn that his rival was genuinely delighted to see him.

"Saint-Gilles! Now that Father Wisdom is here we can get started."

The words might have held an undercurrent of raillery. Or they might not. With Bohemond, one never knew. Saint-Gilles harrumphed. "Didn't you know, count? Too much honey turns the stomach."

Blois gestured to the tall blond duke of Lorraine. "I'll let Godfrey explain the situation."

Saint-Gilles scowled. "We all know the puzzle we're facing. The question is how we solve it."

"Go on, Godfrey," Bohemond said generously. "We can stand to hear it again."

Some months ago, Stephen of Blois had been appointed to chair the princes' council in hopes of avoiding the wrangling that normally characterised the meetings of seven men accustomed to supreme power within their own realms. Naturally, the only candidate everyone had been able to agree on was also one of the least strong-willed. Only Godfrey, Saint-Gilles thought, could possibly have been a less effective leader.

Duke Godfrey cleared his throat elaborately. "My lords, as you know, Edessa is presently ruled by my brother Baldwin."

Saint-Gilles dragged a hand down his face, but omitted to point out that since everyone knew this, there was no point in repeating it. After more than a year on pilgrimage together, he knew better than to try to hurry along the ponderous young duke. Sure enough, Godfrey laboriously recounted the entire story:

"Some weeks since, the sultan's commander-in-chief Kerbogha arrived outside my brother's gates and laid siege to the city. It was at this time that Baldwin sent messengers to let us know of his predicament. Rumours reached us, however, that Kerbogha's true target was Antioch herself. Thanks to the scouts we sent, who have now returned, we know this was true. Kerbogha used Edessa as the gathering-point for an immense force of pagans: Turks, Arabs, Saracens, Paulicians, Azymites, Kurds, Persians,

Agulani, and many others who cannot be counted. This army is greater than any we have yet faced. It has now abandoned the siege of Edessa and begun its journey towards us."

"How long?" Saint-Gilles could no longer keep silent.

Godfrey blinked at him. "My lord?"

"How long do we have before they arrive?"

"It's hard to say precisely."

"Then don't say precisely. A month? A week? A day?"

Godfrey's eyes went vacant as he thought. His men had spent more time coming and going between Antioch and Edessa than anyone else's. "A week," Godfrey said at last. "If they tarry. But if they send a vanguard, four days, maybe five."

Absolute silence settled upon the small council. Saint-Gilles glanced over the parapet at the people waiting below, gazing upon them in a hushed mixture of desperation and hope.

"Days," he said softly. "Saint James…"

Blois had a hand over his mouth, looking pale and sick. "Saint Maurice, pray for us. What are we going to do?"

No one spoke. They all turned to look at Bohemond, who leaned against the parapet with his toothpick jutting from his lips, eyes fixed on his steel-gaitered feet. Saint-Gilles allowed himself a grim smile. "Baffled, count?"

Bohemond blinked up at him mildly; then his white teeth flashed in his sunburnt face. "Thinking it over, Saint-Gilles."

"There's nothing you'd like to share with us?" If Bohemond had a traitor in Antioch, four days might possibly be enough time to take the city and be waiting behind its massive walls by the time Kerbogha arrived.

The alternative was unthinkable.

But Bohemond made no answer, and Count Robert of Flanders spoke suddenly. "I don't see what the problem is. We've dealt with this sort of thing before. Damascus sent an army, and we fought them to a standstill. Aleppo sent an army, and we tore them to shreds. So now Persia sends an army. What of it? We may be fewer than we were, but our men are seasoned—tempered like steel."

"March out and confront them, you mean?" Blois looked alarmed.

Saint-Gilles scowled. "Battle is a terrible risk, but Flanders is right. We had this conversation four months ago, before the Lake. Unless *someone* has a way into the city, we cannot afford to fight defensively. Our only hope is to strike hard, strike fast, and smash this threat before it reaches Antioch."

"The lord of Aleppo is with them," Godfrey said softly. "He'll warn his commander. They won't fall into the same ambush twice."

"Well, of course not," Saint-Gilles snapped. "We'll come up with a different ambush. That's all."

"Bohemond?" Blois turned to the Norman count, as though he was the only one of them with any real combat experience. "What are your thoughts?"

Bohemond straightened, taking the toothpick from his lips. "It would be suicide."

He spoke lightly and with a smile, as though the words meant very little.

"It's a simple matter of the available resources," he went on. "As Duke Godfrey has already pointed out, we have already used our best ambush. Moreover, I understand Kerbogha's army is far greater than the one we fought at the Lake—by three or four times. And finally, the reason I had to fight that particular battle with only seven hundred knights, was that we could barely find seven hundred beasts to put them on, counting oxen and mules. How many horses do we have now? Fifty? If you really wish to send fifty knights into battle against an army of fifty thousand, you may, but I certainly don't mean to join you. It would be suicide."

"Sitting here outside Antioch waiting for them to catch us would be suicide," Saint-Gilles said, "and I don't hear you proposing anything different."

Bohemond looked injured. "Three days ago I *did* propose something different."

Saint-Gilles felt as though a pot of Greek fire had smashed against his forehead.

"That is out of the question," he growled. "We made a solemn vow to restore Antioch to Alexius. We swore to that vow before Christ and all his saints, on the Crown of Thorns and the True Cross." He glared around him, wishing any of them would back him up. But, despite the experiences of the previous months, there was an inner circle he had never managed to break into: he was too old, too sick, not closely related to the others by ties of marriage or kinship. All the influence he'd tried to win during the winter, spending Greek gold like water on horses, armour, and food for the needy, and he still had no more command of them than he had at Nicaea. "Devil take it, how can you call yourselves the army of God and break your own vows like this?"

"Saint-Gilles is right," Godfrey said unexpectedly. "We cannot save ourselves by breaking our oaths. If that means we must march out and risk battle, so be it."

"I'm inclined to agree," said Flanders.

Bohemond spread his hands. "Fair enough! Fair enough! But you need a better plan than fifty knights."

"We'll march the whole army out together on foot, then." Flanders slumped against the parapet with his broad shoulders bowed, but his jaw was set stubbornly.

"And lose the element of surprise?" Bohemond objected.

"We don't necessarily need to win a battle," Saint-Gilles put in. "We only need to stay alive long enough for Alexius to come from the west. The last I heard, he's already in Pisidia—halfway from Constantinople. I've already alerted him to the situation here." He did not add that his alert had had more to do with Bohemond's machinations than Turkish attack; but he would be sending his last brace of pigeons with the news before nightfall. "With any luck, Alexius will be here within the month. In Antioch, we can hold out until our relief comes."

"But we have no way into Antioch," Godfrey said, frowning slightly.

"Don't we?" Saint-Gilles swung to confront Bohemond. "Count?"

"Devil take it, he's right," Flanders burst out, as though he was only just seeing it. "Why else should Bohemond suggest the city should be given away on such terms? *Does* he have a way in?"

"Gentlemen, gentlemen," Bohemond protested, laughing. "If I had a way into Antioch, I would already have taken it, surely!"

"Not if you wanted our blessing with it," Godfrey put in. He frowned faintly. "Our oaths to Alexius would stand in the way, unless you convinced us to abandon them."

"I thought we trusted one another," Bohemond said after a moment. Perhaps there was real hurt in his voice, or perhaps it was all play-acting. "How many times have I saved you and your people from disaster, my lords? Did I fail you at Dorylaeum? Did I betray you at the Lake? Did I flee when we fell into ambush on the kalends of January?"

Saint-Gilles kept his lips ironed shut; he could tell from Godfrey's and Flanders' faces that they were unconvinced.

Bohemond sighed and grabbed his gloves from his belt, pushing away from the parapet as if to leave. "I see how it is. But you cannot expect me to make you battle plans when I am under such a cloud of suspicion."

"We do trust you," Blois said hurriedly, standing up. "Perhaps it would be best to adjourn until Count Bohemond can prepare a battle plan, or Count Raymond can find a way into Antioch."

Adjourn—with this threat hanging over them, and Bohemond determined to continue playing games with them! All the same, Saint-Gilles chose not to object: he had said his part, and he was fairly certain that Flanders and Godfrey were on his side.

He followed Bohemond downstairs using the butt of his lance to measure each step—since he had lost his eye, he always had trouble with heights. In the courtyard, Tancred got up from his seat and approached Bohemond; the two of them spoke together a few moments. Saint-Gilles let a small hard smile escape him, before turning his attention to the assembled crowd beyond the gates. They murmured, rattling the gates as though they expected an announcement.

Saint-Gilles turned and shouted, "Blois!"

Blois descended the stair behind him. "I'm not feeling very well," he protested. Indeed, he looked pale and sea-sick. "You speak to them."

"I'm not sure the poor beggars deserve me," Saint-Gilles said under his breath. Then he raised a hand and his voice. "Good people! The rumours are true. The sultan's army is coming down on us from the north, and we intend to give battle. No doubt God, who has kept us safe thus far, will continue to do so." There was an awkward silence. What more did they expect? "You are dismissed," Saint-Gilles snapped, and with a shuffling of feet, they began to disperse.

"Truly, a stirring speech," Bohemond said at his elbow.

Saint-Gilles restrained his desire to strike the smirk off the Norman's face. He was fairly sure he'd given worse speeches. "What did you expect me to do? Lie to them?"

"Pay them some compliments. Tell them why you think they can win."

Saint-Gilles shot him an incredulous look. "I *don't* think they can win. We're going to need a miracle."

"Ye-es," Bohemond said thoughtfully. "That explains a great deal. You should have a little more trust in people, my friend. Let them know you expect to be pleasantly surprised."

"If I expect it, it isn't a surprise," Saint-Gilles snapped. "And when people surprise me, it's invariably unpleasant. Don't leave; I want to speak with you."

"As do I with you. I didn't want to tell just anyone, my lord, but I think I may have the raw materials for the miracle we need. Are you interested?"

Saint-Gilles was assailed by powerfully conflicting emotions. There was no doubt they needed a miracle…but did Bohemond really have the cheek to reveal a way into the city *now,* after denying it to the council? Was Bohemond trying to manipulate him again? No, that was a foolish question. Bohemond was *always* trying to manipulate people. The question in this instance was: how?

In any case he had no time to refuse. "Walk with me," the South Norman count offered, leading Saint-Gilles towards a narrow passage piercing through the house, and leading to a small garden behind that ran down towards the river. "You too, Duke Godfrey, Flanders."

Half a minute later the four princes stood beneath the apple-trees beside the river.

"Let me guess," Saint-Gilles said between gritted teeth. "You have a way into the city."

Bohemond gestured expressively. "It's more a *potential* than an *actual* way into the city."

He and the slippery South Norman had come close to blows once, on a spring morning much like this one, in Constantinople. Saint-Gilles' fist itched to complete the transaction, but the same consideration that had stopped him then, stopped him now. The knowledge was as bitter as death: Bohemond once again had the upper hand. He was their best battle leader. It wasn't merely his experience; it was something more—that brilliant, alert, calculating mind that combined cunning and temerity in equal measure. Saint-Gilles was steadily coming to hate his rival, but even he could admit that the qualities that made Bohemond a treacherous friend also made him their best general.

He couldn't afford to antagonise this man. It helped, a little, that Flanders gave vent to the anger that he could not.

"Devil take it, man! You have a way into Antioch, and you've been keeping it from us? How long? How soon can you get us in?"

Saint-Gilles smiled tightly. "Keeping it from us, *and* lying about it to the council—yes. Wasn't it obvious from the beginning? Out with it."

Indulging his flair for the dramatic, Bohemond turned and pointed towards the broad crest of Silpius. "Do you see those towers near the citadel? They are commanded by a man named Firuz, who desires vengeance for a slight done him by the lord of Antioch. He has offered to admit our men by ladder to the wall. From there, we do the rest."

Beside Saint-Gilles, Godfrey made a worried sound. "Can he be trusted? After what happened to Galon of Chaumont..."

"That can't be helped," Saint-Gilles put in harshly. "We can afford the men for the task. What we can't afford is to be caught outside the wall when Kerbogha arrives."

"Our aged friend is correct," Bohemond said.

Saint-Gilles turned on him. "The other thing we can't afford is to break our oaths to the emperor. Or have you seen sense? Are you repudiating any claim to rule the city?"

"Now wait a moment," Bohemond said, as though Saint-Gilles had just suggested something particularly foolish. "*I* went to all the trouble of cultivating this Firuz. *I* mean to risk my men on the entry. Am I to have no reward for my labours?"

Saint-Gilles stared at the South Norman speechlessly. Then he turned. "I've heard enough. I don't wish to hear more."

"Wait, wait, wait a moment." Bohemond was laughing. "I heard what you said about the oath. I agree with you. We can't risk offending heaven." He crossed himself. "So I propose that you cede me the city until such time as Alexius shall come to claim it, and then I will either deliver it up to him or receive it from him in fief. Although I sorely doubt he still cares for us."

Saint-Gilles stared at the Norman count, speechless. So that was it. He, Godfrey, and Flanders had all objected to handing the city to Bohemond for fear of violating their oaths—so Bohemond was giving them an alternative.

A patch. A shred of respectability. Like the little bloody scrap of cloth flying from the chin of a man who has cut himself shaving—it rather called attention to the breaking of the oath than excused it.

And there was nothing he could do to prevent it, because Bohemond was right. The only alternative was a suicidal battle.

Godfrey, ever pliable, said: "I suppose that *would* be acceptable."

"It deals with the problem of the oath, perhaps," Flanders growled. "But there's also the question of what is due to us. All of us have lost men and money on this venture."

"That's why I'm telling you about it now," Bohemond said winningly. "My men will handle the most dangerous part—climbing the wall—but I want to co-ordinate the infiltration of Firuz's towers with an attack on the citadel to distract the Turks from what's happening on the wall. Meanwhile, I'll need someone poised down here on the plain to seize the advantage when the north gates open. You three are the most energetic men in the army. You and your men will be the first inside the city, the first to the spoils."

First to the spoils. Saint-Gilles turned, glancing towards the city. Say Godfrey and Flanders managed to seize the Citadel. Say he, poised at the Bridge Gate, managed to seize the wall and the palace.

Bohemond had taught him that trick in the Cilician business. You didn't have to defeat a foe in order to render him powerless. All you had to do was counterbalance him.

"All right," Saint-Gilles said. "On two conditions. First, I'd like to see the chrysobull Alexius gave you when you swore your oaths to him."

Bohemond raised an eyebrow. "The chrysobull! Why ever do you want to see *that?*"

Because I was warned in a dream... "Because if you're to be playing fast and loose with the Greek alliance, the least you can do is show us exactly where you stand with him, so that we don't offend him through helping you."

"Well, that seems fair. I don't know just where to find it, but I'll ask my chaplain to hunt it up. What was the second condition?"

"That you'll swear on the True Cross that you'll cede the city to Alexius if he comes." And of *course* Alexius would come, he'd be a fool not to, when Antioch had been the empire's richest and strongest border outpost within the last fifteen years. "We'll take the oath now, using the relic Adhemar has up there in the house. I take it you have no objections, count?" he added, as Bohemond seemed to hesitate. Saint-Gilles smiled inwardly. As self-interested as Bohemond was, not even he was quite ready to defy heaven.

"No objection," Bohemond said blandly. But as he accompanied Saint-Gilles and the others towards the bishop's house, he added in an undertone: "Tancred asked me to give you a message. He thanks you, but believes his chances of advancement are greater with me."

Using, no doubt, the bait of a captured Antioch. Well, that didn't matter now; Tancred had always been a long shot.

It was Cilicia all over again, Saint-Gilles thought. Only this time, he meant to be the victor.

Chapter V.

The moment Emelota of Le Puiset saw Humberga's face, she knew what her half-sister had come to say.

"Humberga is here," she announced, retreating into the cramped, musty tent she had for the past month shared with her brother, his men, and her own attendant. Her own tent had rotted, and Evrard had spent all his money trying to keep his men fed and armed; an extra tent for his half-sister was the least of his worries.

Evrard, discussing something with one of his few remaining knights over the remains of a scanty dinner, glanced up at her with a look of relief. "Thank God for *that*. Barisan, I'll pay you tomorrow if you can stick it out that long." Shaking hands with the knight, he ushered Barisan to the tent-flap and waited to welcome their sister.

Emelota bit her lip with misgiving at the sound of her brother's overly hearty voice. She could guess what Evrard wanted from their eldest sister, and she didn't think he was going to get it. Emelota could hardly say as much—people found it disconcerting to hear their innermost feelings and intentions bandied about—but Humberga had the look of one driven by fear, willing to run far and fast to get away from it.

Not so that anyone else would sense it, of course. For Emelota, it wasn't just that she found people easy to read. It was something more than that.

When Humberga entered the tent, Emelota bowed. "My lady, I trust the mandrake helped your melancholy a little?"

Humberga looked her up and down with distaste. The hardships of the past year had roughened her pale complexion and sprinkled grey hairs amidst the flax-coloured locks. Her eyes were bloodshot with grief, but she remained irritable, haughty. "Oh, did *you* send the mandrake? I couldn't imagine what it was meant to be for. I suppose it must have gone into the rubbish. Next time, you ought to bring your gifts in person."

Behind Humberga, Evrard's jaw clenched; he knew Emelota had gone to Humberga's tent in person, only to be turned away at the door. But he offered her a stool and kept his voice civil.

"What brings you, sister? I meant to visit you myself; only I did not wish to intrude."

It was little more than a week since the mission to Antioch in which Galon, Humberga's husband, had been killed. Evrard had been saved as though by a miracle, but Emelota knew the disaster had given her brother bad dreams: some nights, he disturbed the tent with his shouts. She missed Galon herself: he had been kinder to her than most. It would have been comforting to be allowed to mourn with Humberga, but her half-sister would not have it.

Even now, she evaded Evrard's question and took the offensive. "I suppose you want more money?"

Evrard cleared his throat, looking uncomfortable. "Only until I can find some plunder worth anything. There's usually an enemy caravan going in at the Iron Gate at the kalends. If I seize it, I can return your loan and still have something left to pay my knights." An awkward pause. "I've asked Blois, but I take it he's running low on funds as well."

Like most of the other counts on the pilgrimage, Evrard had sold and mortgaged huge amounts of property in order to finance his journey. The le Puiset money had lasted a respectable time, bolstered by pay from his liege Count Stephen of Blois and plunder seized in war. But now, at last, the coffers had run low, the land around Antioch had been scoured bare of anything valuable, and what small amounts their feudal master could pay was not enough to keep them solvent.

"You're trying to feed too many mouths," Humberga told him. "Turn some of them away to serve new masters. The bastard, for instance."

Emelota felt that her blood had frozen. For a moment she was unable to breathe. *The bastard.* Herself. Until now, Humberga's insults had been veiled behind a poisonous sweetness. In some ways, it was a relief to hear the ugly truth spoken so plainly.

"Humberga," Evrard said warningly. "We aren't discussing this again."

Perhaps Humberga was right. She *was* an extra mouth to feed. Emelota heard herself saying in a shaky voice, "Do you think anyone would have a use for me? I'm no good at servants' work, and I always thought..."

A sheltered upbringing as the old count's bastard daughter had left Emelota with little education: she had not been made to do servants' work, but neither—since she did not have the lineage to make her of any value as a wife—had she been taught to administer an estate or defend a fief, as Humberga and the other sisters had. Her only gift was the ability she kept a secret: that uncanny capacity to read intentions, emotions, and purposes. If Humberga thought she might be of value to someone else, then she wanted to hear of it.

"That's not going to happen," Evrard said, the same warning in his voice.

"It will if you die," Humberga told him. "No, don't speak over me! You may be the head of this family now, but I was Galon's lady when you were scarcely out of swaddling-clothes. It's bad enough that Father treated that muck-born bastard better than his own children, without you following suit. Stop coddling the creature, for the rest of the family certainly will not!" She turned hostile eyes on Emelota. "With good fortune, someone might make you his mistress. There's nothing else you're good for, and if Evrard had an ounce of sense, he'd have arranged it long ago."

There was a prickling feeling at the back of her throat but, perhaps, as Humberga had said, it was a false kindness to ignore the truth. So Emelota ducked her chin and said, "Or a convent might take me in. I'll consider it, my lady. Thank you."

Evrard's lips were pressed together, fury bleeding from him in thick black clouds, but he kept his voice level and soft as he said: "Is that your price? To receive your gold, am I to make a whore of my sister?"

"Not my price, but my advice." Humberga stood up, so that her eyes were on a level with Evrard's—gathering courage, Emelota realised. Everything she had said since entering the tent, hostile as it has been, was like another piece of armour strapped on for this very moment.

"I can lend you no more money." Humberga's shame was acrid as an unwashed body, but her voice was iron. "I came to say farewell. I'm leaving the pilgrimage for Alexandretta tomorrow."

A silence. Evrard's face went tight and stiff until his gaunt face looked almost skeletal. "Leaving? At a time like this? With Kerbogha marching down on us from the north with God knows how many thousands?" Humberga made no reply. "We're recalling all our garrisons from the outlying towns to take our stand here, at Antioch. If you go to Alexandretta, God knows what will happen. We surely won't be able to protect you."

"I will be perfectly safe," Humberga snapped. "Haven't you heard? Count Stephen finds his health has been suffering, and is going to Alexandretta to recover it. Drogo and I will travel with his party."

"Drogo?" Evrard looked dazed. "Party? Surely *all* these people can't be in poor health?"

Couldn't her brother read the truth in Humberga's set jaw and narrowed eyes? Emelota sighed, suppressing the urge to say anything.

"I came to ask if you would accompany us," Humberga said after a chilly moment.

A shiver ran through Evrard. Very quietly, he said: "You're deserting the pilgrimage."

"This isn't desertion. It's common sense."

"It's dishonourable," Evrard said harshly. "I'm a count, Humberga. I don't have the right—"

"Then I'm fortunate to be a woman." Humberga's voice cracked with sudden emotion: she pressed a trembling hand over her mouth. "I have endured this long, but I tell you: I am at the end of my strength. This hopeless war—it's no way for decent people to live. I'm done, Evrard. Perhaps if Galon was still alive..."

She took a slow, shaking breath. Ever since Galon's death, Emelota had sensed that Humberga's pilgrimage was over. Poor lady, she must have been fighting the decision all week, hating herself for her own cowardice.

Evrard seemed oblivious to her struggle. "I can make allowances for *your* weakness, sister. But you ought to know better than to ask me to share in it."

"It's no weakness," Humberga said. "As I said, Count Stephen is leaving too."

Evrard paled a little. "Then Count Stephen is a coward! What, swear to fight for Christ in the east, and then run away at the first sign of trouble? As for Drogo, I thought the boy had been raised better than that. Galon would be ashamed of him."

Humberga paled with fury. "It is a coward's trick, Evrard, to say such a thing to a grieving widow." A pause, loaded with anger. "You're exactly like Father."

Humberga had always known exactly how to slip the knife in. Evrard fell back a step, speechless. Humberga watched him with a small, thin smile on her lips, savouring the impact of her words.

"Farewell, brother. To God and his saints I commend you, if they truly are watching over this foolish expedition."

She turned to leave, but Evrard stopped her.

"Wait," he said hoarsely. "Take Emelota with you."

Humberga turned with a look of incredulity.

"I don't ask you to support her. Only see her to a convent somewhere she will be safe—in Cilicia or further afield."

Go to a convent—take vows. Emelota had always supposed such would be her destiny; but not now—not in her youth—not while she might yet have children. The religious life was a boon for those called to it—for the pious, the scholar, the herbalist or artisan scribe wedded to her calling...

The people of Emelota's world were, all of them, going somewhere. They might go willingly or unwillingly, but at least they were going. She was the only person for whom she had never been able to read a purpose, but she felt very sure that this was not it.

"Let me stay with you, Evrard. I'm not afraid."

Evrard turned to her, jaw set. "Father entrusted me with your protection. And Humberga is right. It's too dangerous. Don't be afraid to go with her.

She shall swear to deal honestly with you."

Emelota spared their sister a glance. Humberga's lips were shut in a thin straight line, but Emelota knew she would do as she promised, albeit with ill grace.

"I trust Humberga," she said softly. "But it's all right. You'll be glad of me in the end, I swear it."

It wasn't only that she would rather face an army of Turks with a brother who cared for her than flee to safety with a sister who did not. She might not be able to divine her own purpose, but she felt certain of Evrard's. She felt nothing clearer than a sense that she *must* remain at his side; that she had a part to play in whatever was about to happen.

Evrard frowned, evidently puzzled by her insistence.

"I made promises of my own," she added, in case it helped. "I told Alice I'd take care of you."

"I'm not the one who needs taking care of," he growled, but Emelota knew she had carried her point—for now.

After Humberga had made her farewells and departed, he let out a long, slow breath, seeming to shrink in on himself.

"I'm sorry our other siblings are all so hateful. They feel that you got all Father's attention."

"But *you* got all the lands," Emelota said, quite honestly. "They're more resentful of you than they are of me, in truth. Only they can afford to show it to me."

For a moment, the hard shell Evrard had built around himself since Alice's death seemed to crack open. The look on his face was soft, almost wistful.

"What was it like, having a father who cared about you?"

"I wouldn't know." She drew in a deep breath. "It sounds horrible, I know. But all those gifts, all the attention—I always felt he was trying to buy my love."

He was unsure what to make of that. "Well. I'll find some other deserter to take you to Alexandretta."

Emelota smiled at him, knowing that if he truly wanted her gone to

Alexandretta, he would be ordering her to go. "But then Alice would be disappointed in me."

"Of course," he said in the voice he used when trying to humour her.

Already, the hard shell was back in place: the mask he wore, trying to be more like Father, trying to care less about his loss. Things had been different when Alice was alive. *Evrard* had been different: less touchy, more at peace.

And now she had lost both of them.

He murdered my wife. Emelota frowned at the memory of Lukas Bessarion's impassioned words. She knew better than to doubt him; she well remembered the evening that Evrard had come back to camp with his hands stained a spectral red. For months now, the shadow of blood had followed him, unconfessed, unabsolved. She might have asked about it before, but it seemed as though it would be ungrateful, somehow. As kind as Evrard was to her, it was impossible to forget that, if not for him, she would be alone in the world and uncared-for.

And now he seemed sure he was going to die—with a mortal sin on his conscience. So she said, "Did you really kill Lukas Bessarion's wife?"

Evrard choked on his own breath. "Who told you that?"

"Someone who was there."

"Was it Sir Barisan?"

"That would be telling."

His jaw clenched. "Well, it's not true. I killed a Turk, that's all."

"So you did kill someone," Emelota said sadly. "I thought so."

Evrard had gone as white as paper. "Perhaps I'm not proud of some of the things I've done, but I'm a knight, Emelota. I kill people all the time. And this one was a *Turk.* I gain indulgence for all my sins on this pilgrimage…"

His voice trailed away.

"But is the indulgence for killing Turks, or for liberating the holy places?"

"Can't do one without the other."

"Which holy place was the one you killed oppressing at the time?"

"She had a sling," Evrard said. "I feared for my life."

"I see," Emelota said thoughtfully. Evrard shot her an unguarded look. Furtive, anxious, guilty. He was so afraid, and so much of that fear was bound up in Lukas Bessarion and the girl he had killed at Marash.

"It was Lukas Bessarion's fault," he growled. "The boy is nothing but trouble. Tell me you weren't speaking to *him*."

"All right, then," she said agreeably. Evrard frowned, but before he could piece together what she had just said, Emelota's maid ventured out from behind the tent partition. She held her meagre belongings under one arm, all bundled up in her travelling cloak. With a shock, Emelota realised what she meant to say even before she said it.

"My lord," the girl stammered with a stiff, frightened bow. "If you please, I…I would go to Alexandretta with my lady of Chaumont."

The girl had followed them all the way from France, the closest thing Emelota still had to a friend, the only other woman remaining in Evrard's household. "Of course," Emelota said, although her face had gone stiff and her voice seemed to come from a long way away. She fumbled in her purse for a coin. "Take this, with my love."

Evrard caught her wrist. "Keep it," he told her. Emelota looked down at the coin and saw that it was a gold bezant, the last from a gift Evrard had made to her after the emperor's largesse at Nicaea. Already he had dipped into his pouch and put five silver coins in the girl's cupped hands. "Tell Humberga I beg her to take you into her service. Now go."

The girl ran from the tent, leaving behind an echoing silence. Evrard dragged gaunt hands down a haggard face.

"Galon and Humberga are gone," he muttered, as though the truth had only now struck him. "Even Count Stephen is abandoning us. What will I do? I can't pay my knights like this. What sort of count am I, Emelota?"

She considered that. "One who is loyal to his friends, and worries a great deal about things he cannot change."

Evrard sent her a distracted smile, as though he'd scarcely heard what she said. "I *can* change this. I need plunder and pay. And for that, I need to take service with another of the princes. Bohemond, most likely."

The purpose settled over him; and something more—a sense of purpose that went beyond Evrard's own. "Do that," she told him. "I think Bohemond is planning something."

Evrard gave her one of his half-mocking, half-mystified looks. "Now how could you know that?"

Emelota leaned over to kiss his cheek. "If I told you, you wouldn't believe me. Just trust me." But still she stayed close to him, searching his face, before she let out a sigh. "It won't kill you, at any rate. At least not in the next few days."

Chapter VI.

Lukas jolted awake with a sound of alarm and found himself staring into the blazing light of an oil-lamp held in the fist of a Frankish sergeant.

"You're awake," the man said tersely. "It's time."

He stomped away and Lukas sat up, working the cricks out of his neck. Vespers was being sung somewhere nearby, signalling sunset. He was expected at Duke Godfrey's camp within half an hour. The kitchen would be holding some food for him, but Lukas was still half asleep. He closed his eyes, drawing in a deep breath through his nose and letting it out again slowly, through his lips.

It wasn't the light that had awoken him. It was the dream.

He'd dreamed himself in the streets of Antioch by night, running through the narrow alleyways trying to escape roaming bands of Franks.

They'd killed everyone they met. Without mercy. Without hesitation. Without even knowing if they were killing enemies—or friends, like Tigranants the Watcher and the thousands of other Syrians, Greeks, and Armenians within the city.

It had been so vivid. So real. Lukas shivered, recalling the wet *thwack* of blades meeting flesh, the hoarse screams of deathly agony. It was a vision, no doubt, but what could he *do* about it? He had already warned Tigranants to gather the Watchers and anyone else he wanted to save in the church of Saint Peter. According to Kari's Message, he was intended to save Antioch; but he was powerless… until he retrieved his father's lance.

The basilica. The Bessarion Lance. That was the entire plan he had to save his people.

It had better be enough.

Rubbing the grit out of his eyes, Lukas got up and stumbled towards the kitchen in search of food. There was a long night's work ahead of him.

* * *

Lukas glanced into the sky where the ramparts of Antioch loomed black against the racing clouds. Lonely watchfires shone from the towers, but they shed no light on the landscape of tumbled white rock across which the Franks had picked their way in the total darkness of storm and new moon. The momentary lapse in concentration was a mistake: a stone caught his foot, and he only saved himself from falling with a quick motion of his staff. To his relief, the hot wind was strong enough to muffle the sound of his scuffle.

If the Turks patrolling the wall above heard or saw them as they passed, the Franks were as good as dead—and Lukas with them.

Under the cover of darkness, the small band of Frankish foot soldiers had crossed the Orontes before looping south of the city and making the punishing ascent to the crest of Mount Silpius and the foot of the wall that ran atop it. Hours had passed and Lukas was already exhausted, but the night's work was still ahead of them.

The Franks were cutting things terribly fine. It was four days since the scouts had brought news of Kerbogha's approach, and his vanguard would arrive any day now. Lukas shook his head, wondering just how much luck had been involved in the Franks finding this way into Antioch at the eleventh hour. It was fairly evident, even to those not in Count Raymond's confidence, that the one-eyed count suspected slippery dealing on Bohemond's part.

Now they had reached the crest, a whispered signal was passed to sit down and take a moment's rest. All the same, Lukas had only stooped to find a place to sit when Duke Godfrey passed by, hissing his name. "Bessarion? Has anyone seen that interpreter of Saint-Gilles'?"

Lukas straightened with an inward groan. "Here, my lord."

"Follow us."

Lukas fell into step behind the duke, the count of Flanders, and their handful of attendants as they picked their way towards the black rampart of the wall.

Count Raymond had not explained the plan beyond telling Lukas to sleep through the afternoon and then accompany Duke Godfrey on an unspecified mission. He had, however, given Lukas an outline of his task: once the Franks were inside the city, should they get so far, Lukas must raise the Christian populace to join the fighting. At first, the prospect of retrieving the Bessarion Lance had filled Lukas with exhilaration. Now he was haunted by the afternoon's vision. What bloodshed lay ahead of them?

Bishop Adhemar had also given some instructions. "I'm anxious to have you inside the city as soon as possible for my own reasons, Bessarion," he had said. "We came to liberate the eastern Church, and it will do us no good to do them an injury."

Now, following the counts towards the wall, Lukas felt his heart almost hammering against the back of his teeth in excitement. Despite his worry, he could almost *feel* the Bessarion Lance in his grip. He had crossed hundreds of years in the blink of an eye, escaped slavery and enemy Watchers, and traversed Anatolia on foot. He'd survived Nicaea, Dorylaeum, and dozens of skirmishes outside Antioch. He'd suffered agonies of cold, hunger, and sickness, but he had survived them all—and he did not believe he had been brought this far, only to fail at the last.

His right hand clenched on the iron-shod staff he had carried since Constantinople, and he imagined that it was already his father's lance.

When he heard the murmur of sign and countersign ahead of him, Lukas came to a blind halt in the shadow of the wall. No one wanted to risk a light, and it was the night of the new moon, dark as pitch, save for a faint glimmer of starlight. Thankfully, the paths up the mountain were of white stone, and the Franks had a Turkish renegade to guide them.

Duke Godfrey's voice drifted impersonally out of the night: "Ah,

Bohemond? I trust all is well, my lord?"

"Everything went off without a hitch." The Norman count sounded pleased with himself. "It can't be long till dawn now. We've spoken with Firuz and the ladder's been sent up."

"Thanks be to God," said the duke, with the hushed voice of one in a church.

"And a little credit to Bohemond, I hope?"

"As you say," Godfrey said with a faint sigh. "I have that interpreter of Saint-Gilles here with me."

"Oh, the Bessarion?"

Evidently, Count Bohemond remembered his name—a bad omen, although he had done Lukas no harm at Malregard. "Here, my lord."

"You can go by the postern. Go and make yourself known to the count in command. It's along the wall south of here." Any further instructions were interrupted by the sound of footsteps hurrying towards them, and Lukas heard a voice hissing that Count Bohemond was wanted at the tower. Bohemond said something in return, and the princes set off northwards, their voices and the chime of their armour quickly lost in the wind.

Lukas turned to his left and clambered over rocky, uneven ground towards the looming bulk of another nearby tower. On any other night he would have felt vulnerable without the protection of a high-ranking Frank, but tonight all he could think of was the basilica and what was kept there.

As he neared the tower, a hushed voice commanded him to halt, and he thought he saw a dark knot of men huddled in the shadow beneath the wall. "Give the watchword."

"*Non nobis, Domine, non nobis,*" Lukas said.

"*Sed nomini tuo da gloriam;* all right. Do you have a message?"

"I do. From the princes." Lukas stumbled over his words: for an instant he had thought the man meant something different by asking for a Message. Once again, the nightmarish imagery of his dreams flashed through his mind. The army of the east, blackening the earth like a plague of locusts. The Franks moving through the city at night, slaughtering as they went.

Clearing his throat, he added: "I'm Count Raymond's interpreter. Count Bohemond told me to make myself known to the count in command of the postern sortie."

"Devil take it, *what?*" a new voice demanded, flat and incredulous. The dark figures before him shifted as one pushed forward.

Lukas almost recoiled. The voice was Count Evrard's and for a bare moment the sound dragged him back to the dark road outside Marash, to Ayla's cold weight in his arms on the longest night of his life. Lukas shuddered, pushing the memory away.

He shuffled back, out of arm's reach of the lanky, skeletal Frank; but he could sense le Puiset's bulk and height as though his hands had already knotted into the front of Lukas' tunic. "Count Raymond and Bishop Adhemar have sent me to approach the local Christians and assure them of our friendship."

For what seemed like an age, he stood waiting for le Puiset's banked-down violence to erupt in rage. Instead, the dark shadow looming over him turned its head at last and spat on the ground.

"Take excellent care of this man, my friends. There are lessons he has yet to learn at my hands. Let no Turk cheat me of that pleasure."

With that the huddle of knights re-formed, leaving Lukas on the margin and in no doubt of his exclusion. He glanced over his shoulder, but the night was much too dark to show him the tower where Bohemond's men were attempting to scale the wall.

Count Bohemond must know le Puiset hated him, must have sent him here on purpose as part of his unspoken rivalry with Count Raymond. Like two dogs with a bone, and Lukas was the bone. He shivered, then jumped as he realised that Count Evrard stood beside him, motionless and watchful.

"What are your orders?" le Puiset growled.

"I'm to guide you to the basilica of Saint Peter, where some of the Syrians and Armenians will be waiting. We're to enlist their help to raise their men to join the fighting, and mount guard over their weak and infirm."

"We spend the sack of Antioch on *guard duty?*" another Frank said incredulously. "Will they guarantee us a share of the plunder?"

Lukas didn't wait for permission to speak. "I don't know, but the papal legate bids you remember why you came east."

"To take vengeance upon Our Lord's enemies, these damnable Turks," the Frank said, with offhand laughter.

"I think you mean, to liberate his people and patrimony."

The words came out more passionately than Lukas intended and, despite the truth in his words, Count Evrard was swift to stamp out what he saw as insolence.

"Watch your tone, Greek. As for the rest of you, you have Bishop Adhemar's orders. I need not remind you he represents the Pope himself."

"But these locals are *heretics,*" someone grumbled. "To think of risking our lives and those of our men..."

"If it wasn't for these heretic locals, I'd have died with Galon. Plunder or not, we'll stand by them. I won't have it said that I don't pay my debts; do you hear me?" There was a taut silence before le Puiset turned to Lukas again. "You need to understand two things, Greek. One: stay with us. It's going to be hard fighting in there and I won't be slowing down for stragglers. You get separated from us, you can die on your own. Two: give me the slightest reason to doubt your loyalty, and I'll spit you like a rat, bishop's messenger or not. Understood?"

"Understood," Lukas muttered, banking his rage down where it would smoulder, hotter than ever, in his heart. He must be patient only a little longer. Within hours he would be inside Saint Peter's basilica, his father's lance within reach. And then Count Evrard would answer for every insult, every threat, every act of violence.

But first, he'd take a bath. He was sick of smelling like a barbarian.

Shouts drifted to his ears from further along the wall, a faint clamour of "God's will! God's will!"

"They are on the wall," one of the faceless shadows announced. "To the postern!"

"To the postern!" le Puiset echoed, and the threat of his presence retreated as he beckoned the others nearer the wall. As he followed them, Lukas loosened his slim, straight Turkish sword in its scabbard; the winter's damp had corroded the steel, but he had spent the afternoon sharpening what remained of it.

The wall above erupted into shouts and the crash of steel as Bohemond's scaling-party encountered the Turks in the neighbouring towers. The song of striking steel and dying shrieks was like a fever in Lukas' blood; the Franks found the postern and hurled themselves against it like wolves scenting blood, all pretence of secrecy abandoned as they shouted for help. "Over here! Let us in!"

But in the end, there was no need to wait for the gate to be unbarred. One of the Franks called for rocks to use as makeshift battering-rams. His call was taken up. Someone dropped a small pale boulder into Lukas' arms and he passed it on. A rhythmic pounding shook the gate—then, with the crack of splintering wood, le Puiset's pack staggered forwards. A faint light, door-shaped, broke through the shadow of the wall as the gate burst open and Lukas followed the Frankish sortie into Antioch.

Antioch. At long last.

They stood upon the high crest of Silpius, buffeted by the wind. Although the ground was rough and uneven, here at the foot of the wall a path of white gravel glowed faintly in the darkness. Below their vantage-point—so dizzyingly far below that one of the knights drew back with a frightened curse—the tower watch-fires of Antioch's great encircling wall blazed, specks of distant light that circled the city and zig-zagged up the jagged mountainside towards them.

Not far away, a trumpet sounded, its brazen shriek nearly swallowed by the wind. From the great citadel fortress along the wall to the north came the sound of shouts and the clashing of weapons: Godfrey and Flanders must be assaulting its gate from outside the city. On the wall above them, armour glinted and torchlight flared as Bohemond's men secured tower after tower.

"Leave them," Count Evrard said sharply, as some of his men turned towards the citadel. "Our business is below in the city."

"It's too dark," someone said. "We'll break our necks."

"Then it's a good thing we have a guide." A hand fastened on the scruff of Lukas' neck, dragging him to face the tall dark shadow of le Puiset. "You, Greek. You'll lead us."

"I don't know the way any better than you do!"

"You cost us our plunder. It's the least you can do." Count Evrard shoved him along the white path to the left, his sword a pale gleam in the dark. "Keep well ahead of us unless you want to taste the goads. No need for all of us to break our necks on this mountain. The rest of you, keep your heads. Getting into this city is the easy part, as I know to my cost."

Lukas swore under his breath, but there was no point arguing. Taking his iron-shod staff in both hands, he set out tapping the stick ahead of him like a blind man, watching the white path in his peripheral vision and listening for the crunch of the gravel.

The going was slow at first, but dawn was near and his staff led them true until the darkness fled. By the time they were halfway down the mountain, it was light enough to see the path without the help of his staff, and Count Evrard pushed past him with the other knights—twenty or thirty of them formed this advance guard, although when Lukas glanced behind them he saw other, larger bands darkening the mountainside on their trail. Soon, they descended low enough to enter the populated area of the city. The road beneath their feet turned to stone pavement and they made their way between the fine adobe villas rising from the mountain's lower slopes.

Lukas had walked these streets hundreds of years before, and the sight horrified him now. Even in this, the city's wealthiest quarter, the houses appeared shabby: their windows barred, their courtyards filled with rubbish, and the stucco flaking from adobe walls weakened by earthquake and rain. Even in his own time, men had considered Antioch shabby and down-at-heel compared to her former splendours, but this was a step further into decay.

The first citizens they met were a pair of men dragging a nightsoil cart from the courtyard of one of the houses. Thin and attenuated from the long siege, they looked up in numb disbelief as the Frankish band descended upon them.

"Wait!" Lukas yelped, as Count Evrard and his men broke into a run, but there was nothing he could do as his nightmares came to life. Heavy Frankish swords flashed in the dawn gloom. One of the men crumpled, but the other reacted more swiftly, turning with a shriek of fear to run before a thrown battle-axe took him between the shoulders.

At once, some of the Franks disappeared within the courtyard from which the nightsoil-men had appeared, no doubt scenting more valuable plunder than would be found in the city below.

"No looting, damn you!" Count Evrard bellowed, dragging another knight back from the open gate, even as crashes and shouts of alarm echoed within. "Either we stick together or we die apart!" He turned and seized Lukas by the front of his rusted mail shirt. "You. Which way to the basilica?"

"Those men were probably Christians," Lukas hissed. It felt good to stand up to le Puiset, even if he could only do so under the protection of Count Raymond's name. "They might have helped us."

The count's eyes narrowed, his voice lowering. "Don't try my patience, peasant—"

"I'm not a peasant," Lukas interrupted. It might be insane to bait him like this, but he was past caring. "Today, I'm the personal envoy of Bishop Adhemar and Count Raymond themselves. Show some respect."

Le Puiset's jaw bulged. "Respect? I've had to fight all my life to win a measure of respect, and I won't squander it on an upstart like you. Where's the basilica?"

"North." Lukas pointed.

Le Puiset shook him before releasing him. "Lead us."

Lukas turned away with rage and disgust boiling in his gut. Count Evrard, a barbarian raised in the lap of luxury, to claim *he* had struggled to earn respect? How dare he? He should put himself in Lukas' shoes—penniless, powerless, far from home, assailed by enemies, desperate to protect what few people remained to him.

Keeping his thoughts to himself, Lukas led them up the street in the direction of the palace—or where the palace had been, four hundred years ago. From there, unless things had changed, the city's main thoroughfare would lead them directly to the basilica.

Although his feet ached from first climbing and then descending a mountain in the dark, Lukas forced the quickest pace he dared, anxious to leave the Franks no time for slaughter and plunder. Behind them, shouts and screams warned him that subsequent looters had made their way down from the city and were immersing themselves in the pleasure of the sack; and he felt the mailed footsteps behind him falter as some of le Puiset's men looked back with hungry, half-starved eyes.

It wasn't simply greed that drove them. Lukas, with the bits of mouldy bread and dry meat hidden in his bedroll, had to acknowledge that. It was the mindless will to survive at any cost.

Without warning, a flash of colour seared his vision. Lukas stumbled, but the vision was a fleeting thing. A moment later he caught himself on his staff and turned to confront Count Evrard.

"This way," he gasped. Before the scowling Frankish count could stop him, Lukas turned into a covered street to his right.

The count lunged after him. "What are you up to, Greek?"

"There are Turks coming from the palace. A hundred, maybe two hundred of them, headed up Silpius to the citadel."

Count Evrard's eyes flicked towards the shadows of the covered street, jittery with fear. "I saw nothing. Are you in their confidence? Are you leading us into a trap?"

Le Puiset raised a sword wet with Antiochene blood. Lukas sucked in a breath. "No! Please, my lord, you have to believe me!"

"Turks! 'Ware Turks!" The shout echoed from the street, along with the distant echo of tramping feet. Le Puiset didn't lower his weapon, but at least that seemed to convince him.

"Take cover," he called. "Let them pass!"

The men crowded into the shadows around them, filling the silent darkness with their breaths. For what seemed an endless length of time, Lukas remained where he was, shoved against the wall with le Puiset's blade at his throat. The tramping feet came closer; then all of a sudden shadows crept in at the mouth of the alley.

Lukas looked up.

A gigantic figure stood in the street's archway, bleeding shadows. Half woman, half bird, all nightmare. Her war-mask was a great hooked beak that concealed her face, and her wings swept up behind her; it was Lilith as he had seen her at Dorylaeum, dressed for war.

She raised her arms, her shadows creeping through the alley to enfold them. In the street, tramping feet passed them: a detachment of Turks from the palace, sent to investigate the disturbance on Silpius. In the unnaturally darkened alley, silence reigned. Lukas felt his heart racing, heard the jerky breathing of the fearful men around him, and saw le Puiset's face, ghastly and terrified, as he stared through Lilith into the street.

The garrison's footsteps died away towards Silpius before being swallowed up in the sound of shouts and clashing weapons as they ran into the larger Frankish forces behind them. Lukas blinked. Lilith was gone; the knights in the covered street drew breath, seeming to wake from bad dreams. But Count Evrard bared his teeth and yanked Lukas back against the wall as he tried to slide away.

"How did you know they were coming?" Flecks of spittle hit Lukas' face. "Answer me!"

"Saints! I saw them, all right?"

"You saw them? In this murk?" Le Puiset shook him, knocking his head against the mud-brick wall.

"I *saw* them." Lukas wished he could say anything else to allay his enemy's suspicions, but all he could see, even with his eyes open, was Ayla's dead face, the bloody crater between her brows where le Puiset had panicked and shot her.

Somewhere in the city, alarm bells began to ring, and the blare of trumpets sounded thin and strangled on the gusting air.

"You're in league with them." There was something like a sob in Count Evrard's voice. His sword bit into the angle beneath Lukas' jaw and a hot trickle ran down his neck.

All his being was terror and grief and the count's face was like a death's head in the shadows. He couldn't die here; not without making it to the basilica. "I *saw* them," Lukas repeated in desperation. "I have visions. I saw them in a vision. I knew where they were going."

"You lie!"

"Count," one of the other knights said, putting a hand on Evrard's shoulder. "They're sounding the alarm. We must go."

Le Puiset swallowed, hard, before pulling himself together with a deep breath. "Onwards, then."

The next instant Lukas was dragged out into the street again. A bony hand planted between his shoulder-blades and shoved. Lukas caught himself on his staff and set off at a run, leading le Puiset and his men deeper into a waking, wailing, terrified city.

Dawn came slowly to Antioch, the shadow of the city's twin mountains clinging stubbornly to her narrow streets. All around, the sound of battle spread as more of the Franks entered the city from above. Ahead, the road leading from the mountains grew wider. They passed the great forum where the Senate stood, and the basilica built on the ruins of Jove's temple, flattened in an earthquake long ago. The old structures were still there, looking shabby in the dim morning light with the folded-up remnants of a market slumped at their feet. The great Omphalos stone was still there, but the statue of Emperor Theodosius upon it was long gone.

Beyond, the broad Colonnaded Street running the length of the city had changed since Lukas' time, most of the great marble columns that had once shaded the thoroughfare having vanished—carted away to be used in other buildings. The remainder stood white and stark, denuded of their gilding and of the statues that once stood atop them. The palace, however, was still much as it had been in Lukas' time: an imposing, graceful edifice of plastered white adobe. In its forecourt, a small band of Turkish knights waited.

Lukas halted, but it was too late: the tramp of Frankish feet and the chime of Frankish armour had already warned the enemy. At once, a small party of the Turks broke off from the main band and spurred their horses towards Lukas and the Franks behind him.

"Swords out! Hold!" Count Evrard called to the others.

Lukas transferred his staff to his left hand, drawing his rusted Turkish blade with his right. At once, le Puiset towered over him. "Hand that to me."

"What?" Lukas hissed.

"It's about to be busy. I don't want to worry about a blade in the back. Hand it over."

There was nothing he could do. Lukas looked daggers—they lost their way in the dark—and slammed the hilt into the count's left palm.

"Turkish rubbish," Count Evrard said contemptuously, hefting the slim, rust-eaten blade. *"Le Puiset!* God's will!"

He brought up the sword in his left hand and struck it at one of the columns still bracketing the street where they stood. There was a sharp *snap* as the weakened blade broke and fell into the shadows with a metallic rattle.

"You *bastard!*" Lukas howled, goaded beyond bearing. The count paid no notice. Flinging the broken hilt into the face of the foremost Turk, le Puiset surged forward, hefting his own shorter, stouter blade. The other Franks followed in a berserk frenzy, and all Lukas could do was sink back into the shadows beneath the abbreviated colonnade, grasping his staff and hoping he would escape the enemy's attention.

Not that the Turks had a hope of reaching him. Covered in blood, both their own and others', the Franks appeared gaunt and skeletal, living corpses. For all that, they fought like demons. They swarmed the approaching horses, dragged the Turkish knights from the saddle and hacked them to pieces; their eyes were alight with madness. When a man fell, mortally wounded, the Franks finished him off with brutal blows of their feet.

Ayla would want him to do something. *What will the Franks do when they take Antioch, teach us all to play polo?* But fear was like a chain weighing down his limbs. How could one unarmed man halt this bloodshed?

Lukas was unsurprised when he turned his head away and saw Lilith stalking amidst the carnage with her beak tilted to the sky and her arms spread wide, shivering in some unholy ecstasy. He remembered how Khalil had slaughtered the town of Oliveta as a sacrifice to her. Now the slaughter of Antioch was a new sacrifice, and he was as helpless as he had been before.

Within a short and hectic time most of the Turks were dead, five of their precious horses were in Frankish hands and the two or three remaining enemy had fled. But their diversion had served its purpose: the palace gate was now closed and barred.

"Now we are men again!" Count Evrard cried, swinging up into the saddle of one of the horses. He threw a reluctant glance at the palace, then snapped his fingers at Lukas. "Onwards!" he commanded for the tenth time that morning, and Lukas set off up the Colonnaded Street at a stumbling run.

Saints, what would happen when he led them to the basilica? Behind him, any of the townspeople who stumbled into their path were brutally cut down. A tall girl ran swiftly towards him, seizing his arms. Her eyes were milky and blind; her loose dark hair was matted with the blood that spilled down her front from a gash in her throat. *"Do* something, Watcher," she whispered in a husky, bubbling voice. Lukas recoiled with a cry, but in the space between one breath and the next she had vanished.

Was he mad? Were the visions walking into his waking life now?

"Onwards," le Puiset repeated with a snarl.

What other choice did he have? These Franks were barely in control, and from the many-throated scream even now spreading throughout the city behind them, the rest were still more unrestrained and savage. The only thing that could save them was the Bessarion Lance.

Lukas was not as familiar with Antioch as with Jerusalem, and to him it was nearly a year since he had been in the ancient Syrian capital. But if the basilica was still there, it ought to be unmistakeable, and he doubted whether another year, or twenty would ever serve to blot the memory from his mind. Soon enough, he glimpsed the great dome where it towered above the surrounding buildings, now denuded of the gold that had once covered it.

"That's the basilica."

He was still pointing when a rush of feet interrupted his thoughts. Lukas turned as a band of civilian Turks wielding makeshift weapons erupted from a narrow alleyway. As they plunged towards him, Lukas instinctively grabbed at his hip, but empty air met him in the place where his sword-hilt should have been.

Count Evrard spurred his horse between him and them, his blade singing in the air. The Turks broke ranks with panicked shouts, dispersing into the morning shadows.

"What's the matter, Greek? Have you run out of visions?" the count taunted.

Lukas gritted his teeth. "You might have left me my sword."

"Be glad I left you breath to complain with," le Puiset said. Lukas muttered a curse and kept moving.

The basilica stood in the midst of a great walled courtyard on the street named Singon, running parallel to the Colonnaded Street. Even in Lukas' time, the basilica had been the most ancient building in the city, miraculously preserved amidst the destruction of the Persian wars and the great earthquakes of the century before he was born. Today it looked shabby and in disrepair, cracks webbing between its stones.

That didn't matter, so long as his father's lance remained hidden in the crypt. Lukas tried the small wicket-gate in the great double door and found it barred.

Count Evrard stepped beside him and smashed the heavy iron pommel of his sword against the timbers. "Open, in God's name!"

"Right," Lukas muttered, "yell at them in Frankish, why don't you? That'll make them trust you."

The count sent him an angry frown and Lukas couldn't help flinching. Would he be forced to explain to his wife's murderer that, in fact, not every person in the world viewed the Franks as saviours?

Instead, le Puiset stood back with an imperious gesture. "So you call them."

Lukas rapped on the wicket and shouted in Greek. "Tigranants! It's me, Bessarion! Open up—we've come to protect you!"

At first there was no sound from within. The Franks fidgeted behind him, shooting fearful looks towards the silent, watchful buildings that overlooked the courtyard. Should anyone at those windows have a bow...

Something rattled on the other side of the door and the wicket-gate opened a crack. "It's me, Lukas Bessarion," he said in Greek as Tigranants appeared in the gap. "May we come in?"

The man looked frightened at the sight of the bloodstained Franks, but then le Puiset pushed Lukas aside. "It's me, le Puiset," he said in loud, overbearing Frankish. "You hid me—after the ambush—remember?"

Whether Tigranants understood the count's words or not, he evidently remembered, for he bobbed his head and stood aside. Lukas preceded the Franks into a great, dark, empty space. The contrast with the basilica he had visited on his last visit to Antioch was stark. Then, the great octagonal chapel had blazed with light and colour reflected from gold, precious stones, polished marble and glittering mosaics. In the galleries above, uplifted on columns, magistrates gave judgement and students gathered to the feet of logicians and grammarians. Now, the windows were shuttered and the precious things had been stripped away, the mosaics covered with crude, flaking whitewash, the high altar torn from its place on the western wall. The space was empty and echoing save for covered stalls and folded furniture, which blocked his view of the steps leading down to the crypt. In place of incense was the stench of livestock; underfoot, the once-shining flagstones had been scuffed to a dull patina.

Somehow, this shocked him more than the bloodshed outside. This was a house of God, and they had turned it into a marketplace.

Standing in the centre of all this was a lone man with a lantern in one hand and a naked sword in the other.

Lukas glanced from the lantern-bearer to Tigranants, near the door. "What is this? Where are the Watchers?"

"They're surrounding you." The man with the lantern spoke in a voice ringing with authority. "Tell your Franks to put their weapons away and keep their hands where they can be seen. And you, Lukas Bessarion… come over to us."

Lukas followed the Watcher's glance. From the shadows around them rose a small ring of grim-looking young men. They were not Turks—their skin was not pale enough—but like Tigranants they were all young, well-dressed and, most troubling of all, well-armed. Some held swords, others short horn bows with arrows ready on the string.

These were the Syrian Watchers? He'd expected…more. Women and children, the old or infirm.

"What's the meaning of this?" Le Puiset's voice was a roll of thunder in the empty basilica. "These men harboured me."

"I don't know!"

The Watcher, ignoring le Puiset's demands, addressed Lukas again. "He's a Frank and a foreigner. You're a Syrian and a Watcher. You're one of us now."

One of us now.

Lukas drew a deep, unsteady breath. It felt as though he had been waiting a year or more to hear words like that. He had little time to savour them, before one of other Watchers repeated the words in accented Frankish.

For a moment Lukas could have heard a fly draw breath. Then Count Evrard turned on him, red with anger.

"You led us into a trap. You're a dead man, Bessarion."

His sword flickered in the lamplight as it drew back to strike.

The man with the lantern snapped his fingers. Somewhere in the basilica a bowstring twanged, sending an arrow flying past the count's head. Le Puiset froze, and the man with the lantern smiled at him, shaking his head.

"You don't want to touch one of my Watchers." He spoke in Greek, but his meaning was clear from the tone of his voice. Le Puiset lowered his sword, flushing red in the dim light.

His men shuffled. "Hold still," the count hissed. "There are fewer of them than us. Wait for my signal to rush them."

"No, no—it's all right." Lukas found his voice. He didn't want to see what these blood-crazed Franks would do to the only remaining Syrian Watchers. Changing to Greek, he said: "For God's sake, these men were sent to protect you. Let them do it." Turning back to le Puiset, he added in Frankish, "These are the Syrians we were sent to protect. Put your weapons away."

"The hell we will! You said they would be weak and infirm!"

"Because I thought they would be!" Lukas turned back to the Watchers. "Stand your men down if you don't want bloodshed. And where are the rest of the Watchers? The women and children, the old and sick?"

"There are none. We are all the true Watchers left in Antioch."

Impossible. Whoever heard of a Watcher's Council that consisted only of rich and able-bodied men? Outside, the screams of a dying city rang louder and louder in the air, and the sounds went through Lukas like a knife. Were these men fools?

"Have you no families? Have you no friends that you love? I *told* you that blood would flow like water in this city! I told you to gather *all* your people to the basilica!"

The lantern-bearer's aristocratic face darkened. "You don't know what it's like here. You don't know how we are hated and distrusted. The people of this city are weaklings, willing to collaborate with the Turks for their own safety."

Lukas looked the man up and down—his fine clothes, his sturdy frame, despite the seven month siege that had left so many others gaunt and desperate even within the city. He heard Ayla in his head, and couldn't resist giving voice to her. "Yeh, you look like you've been through some real disasters." He turned to Count Evrard. "I told them to bring all their people to the basilica, but it seems only these twenty qualified."

"What?" The count's voice was flat with disbelief. "They didn't even bring their own wives and parents? Saints, you Greeks."

Another of the knights snorted in derision. "What do you expect from heretics?"

"We aren't heretics." Lukas' throat was suddenly dry with terror, but they didn't hear him.

"Come on. Let's go and join the sack while there's still something left."

It was exactly what he had feared, but to his surprise le Puiset's voice cut through the sounds of agreement. "Do that and I'll tell everyone in the camp you abandoned your duty like the worthless idler you are. The bishop gave us a mission, and I'm not leaving it unfinished. Have you forgotten that our survival depends on securing the city? We can't do that if we loot until the Turks rally and slaughter us." Le Puiset turned back to the lantern-bearer, squaring up to the other man. "You helped me once. Now I am asking your help again. I am Count Evrard of le Puiset, and I bring greetings from Bishop Adhemar of le Puy, the appointed legate of Pope Urban. He sends his assurances that he will do all he can to protect the lives of the Christians in Antioch, but he asks for your help. The army of God is within the city, and we need your help to secure it. The gates are still closed. Do as you promised. Help us defeat the garrison and open the gates."

He snapped his fingers to Lukas, who quickly translated. The lantern-bearer shot Lukas a dubious glance. "There would have been terms for our help. Antioch belongs to the Greeks, not the Franks."

"Then die where you stand; it's your choice."

The two men watched each other; it was the Watcher who gave in. "The Turks are on the defensive. Let's take back what is ours. We can debate terms after."

Lukas felt a thrum of eagerness as he translated the words, unable to avoid emphasis on some of the phrases. *Antioch belongs to the Greeks. Let's take back what is ours.* Perhaps the Watcher was right; perhaps he didn't understand just how difficult it was to be a Watcher in Antioch these days. Ayla's people had tried to hunt them to extinction, after all. And now these Franks thought they would walk in and dictate. The lantern-bearer was making it clear from the beginning that he meant to hold an equal partnership with the Franks.

Perhaps these Watchers were men Lukas could work with, after all.

"We'll split up," said le Puiset, apparently still believing himself in command. He glanced around the great empty space. "Half of us to rouse the Christians of Antioch and open the gates. Half to round up those who cannot fight and escort them here for safety."

"I'll stay here," Lukas offered. "There needs to be someone who can speak both languages to those who come." And in the meantime he could explore the crypt. His hands tightened longingly on his staff.

Count Evrard threw him a disdainful look, clearly presuming that Lukas was showing cowardice. "We can easily spare you," he said. "Have one of these Watchers remain as well."

A little more wrangling in two different languages—Lukas thought it would never end—and then, at last, the Franks and Watchers divided into two roughly equal bands and left the basilica to Lukas and Tigranants.

"You weren't at our rendezvous yesterday," the Armenian said.

That was right—he'd had an appointment for the kalends. "Something came up. To be precise, this." Lukas glanced around them. It was difficult to get his bearings with the basilica so altered from what he had known. "Look at what they've done to this place..."

"When the Turks took Antioch thirteen years ago they seized all our churches except St Mary. Barbarians. It's about time civilisation returned to this city."

Lukas paid little heed to the Armenian's words. Instead, he took the lantern the Watchers' leader had left behind—a simple horn and bronze affair—and lifted it high, picking his way towards the northern wall. Columns ringed the octagonal church, creating an aisle that circled the space. Here, a clear path had been left for shoppers to circumnavigate the market. Small semicircular apses opened from the aisle, the shrines they once held now empty and desecrated.

Trembling a little with eagerness, Lukas flashed his lantern to and fro, looking for the small dark stairs leading down into the crypt.

"What are you doing?" the Armenian's voice demanded from the basilica's centre.

"Just looking around," Lukas assured him, anxious now that no one else should get between him and the treasure he sought.

His father's lance. Excitement quickened his pulse. He'd grown up seeing the awe in other boys' eyes when he told them he was the son of John Bessarion, hero of the Persian wars. When a new war started with the Arabian heretics, Lukas had been eager for his chance to prove himself a true son of the great Bessarion line. But his father had refused to let him march to war. Instead, he'd told Lukas that not all problems could be solved with a sword, before attempting to pack him off to Constantinople with the women.

Hadn't he had enough of such a life? Lukas was too young to recall much more than the very end of the Persian wars, when he'd lived with his mother and Marta in the imperial stronghold of Trebizond. For a barracks town it had been an idyllic life, sheltered from the war; swimming in the surf of the Black Sea and play-fighting with the other generals' sons. But then he had grown. And still it was *War is no life for a dog, much less my son.*

Lukas shivered. He knew, now, exactly what horrors his father had spoken of, and maybe if he'd had a son himself... But no: war was the crucible of heroes as well as beasts. He had lived like the latter; it was past time he ascended to the former.

The pavement was smooth, uninterrupted. Perhaps he was misremembering the location of the crypt steps. He circled towards the missing altar, then back to the doors. There ought to be an opening, fenced by a low baluster with a chain fixed across to warn idle wanderers away. No, there was certainly no sign of the stairs in the north aisle. This basilica was a little strange, after all, oriented towards the west rather than the east. Nearly suffocated between eagerness and fear, Lukas passed before the double doors and circled the south aisle.

Tigranants strolled after him with both his thumbs stuck in his belt. "Has it been long since you were last in Antioch?"

"It's been a while." Four hundred and sixty years, give or take. Lukas flashed the lantern to and fro, cold knots forming in his gut as he turned the final angle and found himself once again upon the scarred dais from which the altar had been roughly torn. He stopped dead, then crossed into the north aisle again. It couldn't be. Where was the crypt? It had to be here somewhere!

"Something wrong?" Tigranants sounded mystified.

"The crypt," Lukas said, unslinging his staff and drumming it against the flagstones, listening in vain for a hollow boom. Perhaps the stairs were here, only paved over. "There ought to be an entrance to the crypt."

"A crypt?" Tigranants' voice lilted up, amazed. "But there's no crypt. There's never been a crypt."

"There *was* a crypt." His heart was racing again, a dreadful rhythm in his chest. He pounded on the flagstones, and then dropped to his knees where he was sure the steps had been, wedging his eating-dagger between the stones. After a struggle, he got his fingers around the edge of a flagstone and levered it up. Beneath, flat pale earth stared back at him. Solid, packed as hard as stone. Lukas leaped to his feet, seizing his iron-shod staff and pounding it into the pale earth. The dirt flaked away, but revealed no hidden door, no secret way. Lukas stopped, panting.

"There *was* a crypt, I know it," he repeated, as though if he said the words with enough certainty the ground would split open, letting him pass. "Centuries ago. The Patriarch Anastasius was buried there."

"It's just a story, if you ask me. Or if there was a crypt once, an earthquake must have caved it in."

Lukas stared at the solid ground, clenching and unclenching his grasp on the staff.

"How long?" he whispered.

"How should I know?"

His father's lance was buried deep, God only knew where, beneath a solid weight of earth and stone. Hidden. Safe.

Completely out of his reach.

Chapter VII.

"Bohemond lied," Saint-Gilles growled.

The slippery mountebank *said* he would have the gates opened for us by now, Saint-Gilles thought. Devil take it! When would he learn? He slammed his fist into his gloved left palm, wincing as it hit home with more force than he had intended. It might have been more satisfying to break something, but Saint-Gilles didn't believe in wasting perfectly good resources, no matter how easily he could replace them. Besides, the only breakable within reach was the enamelled glass beaker from which Galdemar was drinking wine. His friend had taken advantage of the prolonged wait to finish his breakfast, miserable as the fare was—the bread was full of barley husks and there was definitely something doubtful about the roast lamb. Galdemar chewed his last mouthful in silence, washed it down with the last of his wine, heaved a dissatisfied sigh and leaned down from his saddle to hand the empty glass to a servant, who ran back towards La Mahomerie with it. The servant's path took him down the long fidgety column of Provençals—counts, knights, and rabble—waiting between the fortress and the Bridge Gate to enter the city.

If only the Bridge Gate would open—and it remained resolutely shut, the massive timbers of its double doors barred fast in the shadow of the colossal square towers to either side.

Only once his mouth was empty did Galdemar bother answering Saint-Gilles. "Bohemond might have run into trouble on his way down the mountain. Must be a long road."

"It's been two hours," Saint-Gilles said, jabbing a finger towards the mountain peak. Even two hours since dawn, the sun had not yet risen above the crest of Silpius, and Antioch lay in shadow. All the same, the distant line of ramparts atop the mountains were gilded by sunlight, and even his single eye could see, small and far-off but bright in the morning light, the blood-red banner of Bohemond snapping above one of the towers. "He's in control of the ridge and you can hear perfectly well the sack is underway. By Saint Giles, I wouldn't put it past him to keep the gate closed until he's scoured the town clean, walked into the palace, and sat down on whatever Yaghi Siyan uses as a throne."

"Then I suppose we'll just have to walk into the palace after him, pull him off the throne, and shake him till he disgorges the loot," Galdemar said placidly. Then, suddenly, came a grinding sound, and a flurry of activity atop the Bridge Gate's barbican, between the towers. "Or," Galdemar added, nodding towards this disturbance, "perhaps that won't be necessary."

A small postern was set within the larger gate; this burst open suddenly, and a small figure emerged, gesticulating and shouting wildly in one of the native languages—Greek, Syriac, or Arabic, Saint-Gilles wasn't sure. He did, however, wear a cross of white fabric stitched hastily to his dark mantle. Instantly, all Saint-Gilles' resentments were swallowed up by feverish anticipation.

"Now!" he bellowed. "Infantry! Secure the gate! Go, go, go!"

Not so long ago, the pilgrimage's foot soldiers were little more than a rabble of indigents strengthened by the presence of lightly-armed but well-trained sergeants. Now, with so many heavily-armed knights having lost their horses, they had become a force to be reckoned with.

Lord Raymond Pilet, whose last horse had died two months ago, brandished his sword and shouted a war cry before dashing towards the gate. A column of horseless knights followed at his heels, holding the tight-packed formation they had learned to use when facing the Turkish arrow-storm. Saint-Gilles held his breath as they entered the kill zone, already littered with arrows and rotting corpses from previous skirmishes. Two, maybe three arrows spat from the north tower, then—nothing. The garrison must have its hands full: Saint-Gilles thought he could hear the sounds of battle echoing faintly behind the barbican, and found that his hands were gripping the reins of his horse painfully tight.

It was happening. It was really happening. Turkish resistance had crumbled. The advance guard made it across the bridge without losing a single man. At the postern there was a little hesitation: the first two or three men through such a narrow passage faced the risk of being isolated and cut down if the garrison should have regained the upper hand. Saint-Gilles found himself praying under his breath as Pilet, obliged by his station to take the lead, vanished within that low black maw.

But the men followed after him, one by one vanishing into the city beyond. Just as the last man turned to follow, a dark shape dropped from the barbican above, landing square on the Provençal's neck and knocking him to the ground. A knife flashed, the knight stilled, and one of the Turkish defenders limped to his feet before dashing back within the postern.

"Holy Virgin!" Galdemar swore under his breath. "Did you see—"

"I saw," Saint-Gilles said tightly. "Our turn; quickly, before we lose momentum."

Seven months was a long time to bully and terrorise each other, and the garrison must know they could not expect the slightest mercy. Franks and Turks alike had captured, tortured, and slaughtered each other's envoys or prisoners all winter, and now it was no surprise if these cornered Turks fought like demons. Saint-Gilles didn't blame them. It was only honourable to fight one's way to a red death, rather than fall into the hands of such enemies.

Galdemar looked dubious, but he didn't object as Saint-Gilles signalled to his standard-bearer. "Onwards, by Saint Giles!"

He set spurs to his horse, thundering into the kill zone, across the great stone bridge. This time there were more arrows, one of which nicked his hauberk. Behind him, someone less fortunate yelped with pain as another sank home. The garrison must have secured at least one of the towers. An ominous sign. In any other city, on any other day, he would already have plans for a retreat should the assault go sour. Today, it never even occurred to him: he would never be able to dispute Bohemond's mastery of Antioch if he didn't get inside the city *now*. Retreat was out of the question.

Beneath the shadow of the gate-towers, Saint-Gilles didn't hesitate, slipping from his horse and plunging through the postern-gate. Beyond, the barbican and towers were a battleground. The Turks seemed to have barricaded themselves within the south tower, the townspeople and a handful of Pilet's Provençals had seized the north tower, and the barbican over the gate itself was a furious mêlée, as was the gate itself. The Turks had it barred and barricaded from within, and stood atop the barricade of timbers and rubble aiming missiles and sword-blows upon the Franks and the Syrian rabble below.

From the Bridge Gate a wide road led east, towards the glimmering whitewashed battlements of Yaghi Siyan's palace. Saint-Gilles had only a glimpse of the palace beyond the lower buildings surrounding it, but that was enough to drive all else from his head, even the battle at the gate. From the palace wall yet fluttered Yaghi Siyan's banner. Bohemond had not yet taken the palace. Likely, the lord of Antioch was still there, a trump card nearly the value of the citadel itself.

Ducking behind his shield, Saint-Gilles turned to the lords who had followed him through the postern.

"Get that gate open!" Outside the city, a great crowd of the poor still waited across the bridge, gripping makeshift weapons but unwilling to come nearer while the fighting was underway. The sooner they swarmed in, the better Saint-Gilles would like it. Capturing a city was a numbers game. "Change of plans. I have business in the city. Vigeois, Polignac, and the rest of my own household—with me!"

His lords stared at him, uncomprehending. Galdemar said, "You're leaving the gate?"

Saint-Gilles flinched as a Turkish javelin spitted a squire standing beside him. The missile must have been aimed at him, but between the sheer jadedness of war and the white-hot focus that possessed him, he felt almost numb to the danger.

"You take the gate. I want the towers secured and a Provençal garrison installed—Provençal, you hear me? Montmerle, Lastours, take your people down the wall and capture as many of the towers as you can. Then hold them. Galdemar—"

"I have the gate," Galdemar assured him. "But, Saint-Gilles—"

A volley of Turkish arrows rained down on them, cutting off Galdemar's protests. Luckily—unlike some of Provençals crowding through the postern—Saint-Gilles had his shield up. "No time," he snapped. "Polignac, with me."

It was the standard-bearer's job to make sure the fifty knights of his own household followed him, so Saint-Gilles barely bothered to make sure he had his men before starting up the road towards the palace. Warnings teased at the corners of his mind. If Galdemar had trouble securing the gate…if he and his household were cut off from their reinforcements…if all the horrible stories he'd heard came true, tales of small bands getting cut off and massacred because they plunged willy-nilly into the narrow streets of an enemy city…Saint-Gilles ignored them all.

The city had descended into chaos. Armed men of every faction roamed the streets: it seemed there was a battle on every street corner and arrows flying without warning from upper windows. Saint-Gilles avoided the fights as best he could, and led his men in a tightly-packed phalanx through the ones he couldn't, scattering the combatants with little regard for whom he was fighting or why. The street emerged into a broad forum within half a mile of the Bridge Gate, surrounded by beautiful white-stuccoed buildings. The palace was nearest; Yaghi Siyan's banner still floated above it. Here at last they found determined resistance: the thick timber gates were barred and, as his Provençals entered the forum, a volley of arrows flew over the parapet of the wall to greet them.

Saint-Gilles didn't have to give orders: his men drew tightly together and formed a shield-wall before he pulled them back within the shelter of a side street.

He felt a flicker of pride. The other princes mocked him for having built his considerable dominions in Provence more through inheritance and hard bargaining than the noble art of war. Perhaps it was true; a year ago he hadn't had a fraction of Bohemond's experience on the battlefield, and neither had his men. But things were different now. Anyone who had survived the winter had been tempered like steel.

There was a second, more important message in that volley of arrows: Yaghi Siyan's hand-picked guard must still be holding the palace. The lord of Antioch was within his grasp.

Saint-Gilles could scarcely assault the citadel—the true key to the city's power—for that was located on the crest of Silpius, still flying the green flag, and Bohemond was no doubt already doing his best to take it. But the palace was the seat of government, and Yaghi Siyan might yet prove a powerful player in the handover of the city, to say nothing of negotiations with Kerbogha. If Bohemond failed to take the citadel this morning—and Bohemond was an able man but no miracle-worker—then Yaghi Siyan might be employed as a hostage to crack open those stubborn gates.

Saint-Gilles' hostage.

"The Turkish lord is hiding behind those gates," he barked to his men, jabbing his finger at the gates. "Bring up the battering-ram. Antioch is ours!"

He'd arranged for his men to bring a ram, a short timber beam with its nose sheathed in iron. It only took four men to carry, and the gates looked formidable. Still, it was better than nothing. At his signal, the four knights and two replacements raised their shields and dashed into the forum. Saint-Gilles found himself praying under his breath as they swung and released the ram, as missiles from above tested every inch of their shields.

"My lord." Someone plucked at his elbow. "My lord, Count Galdemar sends from the gate. He begs you to return. He cannot—"

"Not now." Saint-Gilles barely heard the man's words, so absorbed was he in what was happening in the forum. God was with them: at the third blow of the ram there came a great crack and the gates shivered. Even as they drew back for another blow, Saint-Gilles called the charge. His men surged from their hiding-place full into the empty forum, easy pickings for the archers on the palace wall.

If the gate held, the Turks would pick them off like fish in a weir.

The gate did hold.

Arrows drummed against their uplifted shields as they advanced. Some sank between the jostling plates. Saint-Gilles heard cries and yelps as the barbs sank home, as some of his men fell. Then they made it across the forum and the gate groaned as his men threw themselves bodily against the great barrier. It sagged beneath their onslaught and held—once, twice, three times they battered beneath the hissing of arrows. Then, with a final blow of the ram, the gates burst open and Saint-Gilles staggered into the broad forecourt at the head of his men.

He came face to face with Yaghi Siyan. The Turkish lord faced them astride his horse, wearing armour beneath his embroidered silk tunic, and a round steel cap from which a chainmail coif descended. A phalanx of his men waited at his back. As Saint-Gilles and his men burst into the courtyard, the Turkish lord levelled his lance with a yell, spurring his horse.

Evidently, they had been preparing to leave the palace—perhaps to retreat to the citadel or a gatehouse, perhaps to flee entirely—when Saint-Gilles and his men attacked. Now a fresh volley of arrows tore into Saint-Gilles' men from the wall flanking the gate. Saint-Gilles staggered a little as an arrow struck his own hauberk. It pierced through rings and gambeson to lodge between his shoulders, just deep enough to annoy and hamper his movements but not enough to disable him.

While his men were still recoiling behind the cover of their shields, the Turkish charge tore into them.

The world became a nightmare of shrieks and trampling hoofs and flailing swords. Half his men were underfoot, being trampled by the horses. Those who managed to keep their feet plucked at the riders without attacking the steeds, endangering their own lives to preserve the precious horseflesh.

"Don't spare the horses!" he yelled. The distraction cost him. A Turkish knight struck at him with a hand-axe, the blow glancing off his helmet but filling his vision with bright bursts of light. He staggered backwards and got his sword up, managing to spit his attacker through the midsection even as another blow—from where, he could not tell—caught him on the shoulder, sending him to his knees. In the same moment, the Turk he'd just killed folded around the hilt of his sword and slid off the horse onto him.

Saint-Gilles fought off the stifling weight and rose to his feet. With a start he realised he'd lost his shield. Then he looked around him and saw that the battle was already over. The courtyard was littered with dead and injured men, riderless horses, and the pale, gasping faces of his surviving followers. Yaghi Siyan, surrounded by a scant handful of men, was already disappearing at a desperate gallop down the Colonnaded Street to the southwest, and the archers on the wall had sheathed their bows and retreated along the ramparts towards the palace.

Saint-Gilles snatched the reins of the nearest horse from the knight who had commandeered it, but his efforts to get into the saddle failed as a wave of dizziness passed through him—whether from loss of blood, or shock of pain, or just the ever-present sickness roiling in his gut, who could tell?

He dragged in a breath—his first, it seemed, since he had called the charge on the gate. Every inch of his body ached and the arrow had been torn from his back leaving a bloody, stinging mess. He felt sick as a dog.

"Devil take it!" he bellowed when he was able to speak again. "What are you waiting for? Yaghi Siyan's headed for the south gate! Get on these horses and follow him! Bring him back alive and the horses are yours!"

With that there was a rush at the animals and moments later a small band of knights had dashed down the Colonnaded Street in pursuit. Saint-Gilles took another deep breath and pounded his fist into his left hand again. *Hell.* Had things gone differently, Yaghi Siyan might have delivered the citadel and by extension all of Antioch into his hand. He'd been so close, and now all he could do was rely on his men to catch the Turkish lord.

Something told him not to get his hopes up.

In the meantime, he had yet to secure the palace. Saint-Gilles turned on his heel, surveying the silent building, its doors barred and windows tightly shuttered. After the cost of storming the forecourt and pursuing Yaghi Siyan, he needed reinforcements if he was to clean out the palace.

"Bessarion," he called, before recalling that the Syrian had gone via Silpius on Adhemar's orders. "Polignac. Return to the Bridge Gate. If it's secure, have Galdemar send me as many as he can spare." He faltered then, vaguely recalling a hand on his arm and a pleading voice, just before he'd called the charge. Galdemar had sent for help. The messenger was nowhere in sight. A thin trickle of smoke rose over the Bridge Gate in the west. What if Galdemar had failed at the gate? Better to risk it all on the palace than retreat outside the city: "If not, have Galdemar draw as many as he can back to the palace. The rest of you, come with me." *And pray we don't get cut up piecemeal, scattered as we are.*

Polignac paled and looked nervous at the prospect of picking his way back through the havoc of the city to a gate that might or might not be in the hands of the enemy, but he didn't question Saint-Gilles' orders. There were no horses left in the courtyard, or Saint-Gilles might have given him one. He sent a quick prayer up for the standard-bearer's safety, then put the matter out of his mind. He still had half his men and the palace would never be riper for the taking. Calling them to follow, he stalked his away across the forecourt towards the entrance hall.

The work that awaited him within was long, tedious, and bloody, for the Turks were bold men and hard fighters, and nothing fights more desperately than a man who knows he has been caught in a trap. No news came from the gate, nor reinforcements. Saint-Gilles was in the courtyard asking if his hunting-party had returned with Yaghi Siyan when a slow beat of hoofs interrupted him, and Saint-Gilles looked up to see Polignac leading a horse upon which Galdemar Carpenel slumped with one arm done up in a makeshift sling. He had lost his conical helmet and must have received some kind of head wound, for his face was masked in dried blood.

Saint-Gilles' heart stopped. It had never occurred to him to think Galdemar might be *hurt.*

"Galdemar!" He rushed to the other man's side, gripping the hands that clung limply to the saddle horn. "What happened? Are you much hurt?"

Galdemar grunted and slid from the saddle. Saint-Gilles put his arms around him to help him stand. "I'm all right. I lost a lot of men in the towers and nearly got encircled, that's all."

A chill went through him. "Encircled."

"The Turks rallied. At least forty of them came up from the wall to the south. If the poor hadn't ventured across the bridge to help us we would have been dead meat." Galdemar shrugged him off, nearly tripping over one of the bodies still littering the courtyard. "Seems you had your hands full here as well. Did you secure Yaghi Siyan?"

"He, ah, slipped through our ranks and fled. I've sent men after him."

What had he done? It was a decision made in the blink of an eye, in the snap of a finger—to leave the battle at the gate, and come to the palace instead. Consumed by thoughts of his rivalry with Bohemond, he'd chosen to forget that the Turks were still the most immediate danger.

He'd abandoned a friend—no, it was worse; he'd abandoned a *vassal,* and Galdemar had lost some of his own men, and it was Saint-Gilles' fault. He'd sinned against friendship and perhaps injured the fealty Galdemar had sworn him. Without his vassals' trust, what right did he have to call himself count? Guilt rushed through him in a hot, sickening wave.

He remembered that last black morning at Nicaea, when Galdemar had nearly died and he'd come near to blows with the Greeks because of it. "Galdemar, I'm sorry. In the heat of the moment—I didn't think. I'll make it up to you, I promise."

Galdemar turned, and if there had been something standoffish in his bearing a moment ago, it was gone now. "It's all right, Saint-Gilles. It's war. The outcome is never certain."

Saint-Gilles nodded and helped Galdemar limp into the palace to get his wounds seen to. But the guilt remained like the wound between his shoulder blades, lurking at the edge of consciousness, catching him unawares. It was as though, for a moment, he'd glimpsed himself in a mirror of clear silver. Galdemar might shrug it off, but he alone knew exactly how coldly and selfishly the decision had been made. When the choice was put before him, Saint-Gilles had sacrificed his own people's safety for the sake of his feud with Bohemond.

Chapter VIII.

Fists pounded against the basilica's door and Lukas opened the small wicket to appraise those who sought entrance. There were three veiled women, with smooth olive skin; he guessed they were Armenians. Two of the women had their arms around the third, who held a young child in her arms, her head bent beneath her thick black veil. A man brought up the rear, hunched over with a fold of his turban draped across his face.

Fugitives had been fleeing to the cathedral all day as word spread that the Franks had designated it a sanctuary for their fellow Christians. The space was crowded now, packed with Syrians, Greeks, Armenians, and even a handful of Amalfitan merchants from across the sea. In their rush to secure the city, slaughter the Turks, and strip all the loot they could find, few of the Franks would have the patience to identify and spare Christians, even if they were inclined to do so. Many of the townspeople would seek refuge in their own cellars and storerooms, of course, but doubtless the basilica was presently the safest place in the city for them.

"Thank God, it's true," one of the women murmured when she saw him, lowering the icon of the Virgin and Child which she held before her like a buckler. "We seek sanctuary!"

Lukas was about to welcome them in when Tigranants, behind him, said sharply: "Wait. Who's that with you?"

"It's only one of our neighbours—" the Armenian began. Ignoring her words, Tigranants brushed past Lukas and yanked the cloth from the man's face. He was a young man, very little older than Lukas himself, with skin nearly as fair as that of the Franks. He blinked at the Watcher in something close to terror, and Tigranants growled. "No Turks. *Or* their concubines," he added, turning to the Armenian women. "Go home."

"Wait," Lukas said.

Tigranants turned to him with a scowl. "You can't seriously think to let these women in here, after they've tried to smuggle Turks—"

"We aren't smuggling anyone," one of the Armenians said indignantly. "We would have *told* you if you'd—"

"Are you crazy, bringing one of the enemy into a place of sanctuary?" Tigranants put a hand on the hilt of his sword. Thinking it was time he acted, Lukas lifted the iron-shod staff and rapped the other man on the knuckles. Tigranants yelped with pain.

"They have a child," Lukas said firmly. "They are here as supplicants, not enemies. They may come in."

Tigranants flushed a dark, dull red. "You dare give orders to me?"

Lukas swallowed the hot retort that sprung to his lips. "I'm not giving you orders. I'm simply telling them they may enter."

"And if I tell them they may not?"

"Then you'll need to ask yourself if you wish to bring a sword to a staff fight."

Tigranants dropped his hand to his sword-hilt again, but after a moment he spat on the floor and stepped aside. "You call yourself a Bessarion? John Bessarion would be ashamed of you."

Lukas almost laughed. He would have done this for Ayla's sake regardless, but he was also confident that this was one action of which his father would wholeheartedly approve. He beckoned the Armenian women and their Turkish neighbours through the low door into the basilica.

As they vanished into the gloom within, Tigranants glowered at Lukas. "This land doesn't belong to the Turks and the Saracens. We remember that. Do you?"

"Every day," Lukas said quietly. The land didn't belong to the Armenians either; it belonged to his own people, but he didn't mean to pick a fight with Tigranants. He turned his back on the Watcher, seeking out the young Turkish couple where they cowered in the shadows, little more at their ease than they had been in the courtyard outside. Lukas knelt to put himself on a level with them. "Do you speak Greek?" he ventured, in that language.

The man's eyes flickered with understanding and he reached out to grasp Lukas' hand with both his own. "Thank you," he said. "I do not want trouble. I only want my wife and daughter to be safe."

Lukas glanced down into the little girl's face, still round and childish despite the hardships of the siege. She seemed exactly the age of his youngest sister Elisa, with Elisa's curling dark hair and big brown eyes; for a moment he felt almost suffocated by the memories. Had his mother and Elisa survived that dreadful night at Oliveta? Had anyone given them sanctuary?

And yet the Turks were invaders just as bad as the Saracens, and if he could only get his hands on his father's lance he would dethrone their lords and sweep them out of the land. They'd visited untold horrors upon his people as part of the siege; they'd even dragged the venerable Patriarch of Antioch onto the walls and flogged him in full view of the Frankish camp—a display the Franks had returned in kind with their own Turkish captives.

He might not view these people as enemies, but he surely couldn't accept them as friends. Feeling awkward, Lukas pried his hand from the other man's grasp.

"I'm looking for the family of a man named Ilkay," he said. "He left wives and children. Do you know them? I don't mean to hurt them," he added as the man and his wife looked at each other warily, "but I promised I'd take care of them, and Antioch isn't safe for your people today."

The man shook his head. "No, sir. I'm afraid we don't. We're newcomers to the city…I was part of the garrison in Marash before the Franks came."

I'm sorry, Ayla. I'm trying. Lukas retreated to his post by the door, breathing in the soft sounds of talk from the crowd of fugitives hidden with him. If only he could control his visions… But it seemed the flashes of foresight came completely at their own will. Finding that his teeth were clenched together and his shoulders were stiff with tension, he forced himself to release them.

He couldn't find Ayla's family to save them. His father's lance was buried beneath the basilica pavement and short of excavating the entire floor, he couldn't imagine how he was going to retrieve it from its long rest.

If he was going to protect his people and Ayla's family, he needed more power than this.

A loud boom shook the doors, jolting him from the anxious treadmill of his thoughts. Muffled shouts could be heard from without. Lukas leapt to his feet, imagining fugitives pounding on the doors for help as Frankish or Turkish pursuers swept into the courtyard on their trail. Hastily he lifted the latch and threw the wicket open.

He faced a band of Franks—poor, half-starved, more than half-crazed peasants that had formed themselves into hungry bands and taken to roaming the countryside, scouring it for food. At their head was a boy his own age sporting a patchy beard. There was something wrong with the young Frank's eyes, a little too hot and glassy for comfort.

Lukas tightened his grip on his staff, all too aware that he was at a disadvantage before their numbers, their brandished knives and clubs. "What do you want?" he asked in the Provençal dialect. "This is a house of God and there's nothing here to loot, anyway."

The boy facing him raised his fist—a severed Syrian head dangled from his hand: a horrible sight, for it was beaten and bruised and had been hacked none too gently from the parent body. "You're right, this is a house of God, and it's time it was cleansed of all the Saracen rats and heretics you've got hiding here."

Lukas wanted to retch, but if he lost his self-command, all these people might lose their lives. "There are no heretics here."

"I hear their brats crying." The boy shoved forward, throwing the head past Lukas. There came a dull *thunk* as it hit the flagstones behind him. Inside, a woman shrieked. Abruptly the boy's followers began to chant.

"Send them out! Send them out!"

Oh, God. Plenty of the Franks saw everyone in the east—Turks or Greeks, Saracens or Syrians—as heretics, deserving of death. There was no reasoning with such people. Lukas jabbed the end of his staff into the boy's guts and doubled him onto the courtyard pavement. That bought him a precious moment, and he got the wicket shut and latched a moment before the great doors began shaking.

He turned to find Tigranants facing him. "They'll break down the door," the Armenian hissed as the assault intensified. "Just give them what they asked for. Give them the damned Turks."

"They don't just want the Turks. They want all of us."

With a muffled curse, Tigranants tried to get past him to the door. Quarters were too close to use his staff, so instead Lukas drew his dagger, making the Armenian go very still.

"If you won't hear my word as a brother Watcher, then hear this," Lukas hissed. "I'm here on behalf of the count of Toulouse and the personal representative of Pope Urban, and if you are even faintly interested in remaining on good terms with them, you'll do as I say."

Once again, Tigranants had not the courage to challenge Lukas to a fight, despite Lukas' far inferior weapons. Seeing the impotent fear in the other man's eyes, Lukas felt momentarily at a loss. He, too, had once been an untried boy, cosseted and deferred to, more entitled than truly capable. All that had been beaten out of him in the last terrible year, but it had left something behind, something hard and implacable; a core of cold ice that left him able to intimidate others. First Emelota of le Puiset, and now this youth.

Women and boys. What did that make him, but a bully?

Outside, the mob rattled the doors and the little wicket began booming hollowly to the rhythm of their clubs. This was the relative weak point in the structure, and Lukas could not stifle a sound of alarm as the timbers groaned and the iron strapwork began to bend.

"They're getting in!" someone gasped in Greek. The fugitives put their arms around each other. A woman cried, "Don't let them take me alive! I saw what they did to the women in the palaces on the hill!"

Lukas backed away as the wicket shook and rattled in time with the chant outside. *Send them out! Cleanse the church!* Ayla's old sling was knotted around his wrist for a keepsake—he raised it to his lips and kissed it in farewell. Thanks to the count of le Puiset, he didn't even have a sword to use, only his staff, a formidable weapon but no match for a bloodthirsty mob. Tigranants had a blade, but the Armenian was no trained warrior—especially not compared to the hardened killers outside. As for the Syrians, even those with knives and daggers were women, old men, boys. Lambs to the slaughter.

There was no fighting this. The door shook. The timber around the latch was splintering, tearing away. Lukas threw a desperate glance over his shoulder towards the high altar.

Send me a vision, he pled. *Show me the Bessarion Lance. Show me how to get at it. Oh, God...*

Nothing.

Any vision, then. Nothing. He glanced to the galleries above. Already some of the people had fled upstairs and now leaned over the balusters, as though they could delay the inevitable. *Show me a way out. Show me a hiding place. Show me a miracle. Please!*

Nothing.

A rivet popped from the splintered wicket and the latch gave an inch or so, letting the door open a crack. He saw grey morning sky, distorted faces, weapons lashing against the door. Lukas took another step backwards. No matter what the Franks believed, Bessarions were warriors, leaders, noblemen. He knew what that was supposed to look like: his father had done it again and again, without hesitation. It meant he was supposed to stand between his people and their enemies until he hadn't two limbs left to stand with.

Dismemberment seemed an imminent possibility.

The people behind him wailed on the brink of panic. The woman who had begged not to be taken alive pointed to Tigranants' sword. "Kill us," she shrieked. "Better to die a clean death with honour than be taken by those beasts."

Shouts of agreement echoed through the church. Shuddering, Tigranants turned towards the Turks cowering in the corner. "This is happening because of *them!* We must give them up!"

The atmosphere thickened within the basilica, hot and sharp as though the blood had already started to flow. Lukas felt himself sweating beneath the oppressive cloud—and then suddenly he knew what it was.

This was Lilith's maddening influence. This was Lilith's mind-numbing fear. This was Lilith's will, not God's: blood, terror, slaughter.

He took a long, deep breath and reached out with both hands, raising his staff above his head. In the midst of the maelstrom, he reached for peace—and found it.

Show us, then. Show us your salvation.

The vision came bright and searing. The doors were no barrier to his sight. He watched as a band of Frankish knights and Watchers swept into the courtyard and drove towards the basilica.

"Don't be afraid!" Lukas shouted. His voice rolled around the basilica, echoing in the great dome. "Wait and watch for your deliverance!"

For a heartbeat, a breath, the people stilled. If not for that, they might not have heard the rattle of many mailed feet against the stones outside, nor the assault on the door faltering as the frenzied peasants realised they were no longer alone. The stifling terror that moments before had reigned in the dim church dissipated, like mist on a sunny morning. Those who held blades to their own throats blinked like sleepers waking, and lowered their weapons with trembling hands. Lukas gulped a deep, cleansing breath.

"Take yourselves off, villeins." Count Evrard's voice, cold and arrogant, sounded faintly through the splintered door. "I am in command here."

"Who are you calling villeins?" a voice shouted. Their leader, the evil-eyed boy. "In God's holy army, every peasant has the dignity of a knight."

Lukas didn't hear exactly what le Puiset said in reply; only that there was an undercurrent of laughter in his voice. The next moment came an indistinct sound of shouts and screams and running feet. Moments later, a fist pounded against the shattered door.

"Bessarion! Are you still in there? Open up and let these people take sanctuary."

Lukas fumbled with the deformed latch and swung back the door. Outside, le Puiset and his band of knights and Watchers guarded a column of pale, trembling townspeople clutching makeshift crosses or hastily seized icons. There was no sign of the peasants or their rabid leader. Lukas held the door open to let the townspeople pass; but when Count Evrard tried to follow them into the church with his Franks, he stepped in front of him.

"They don't want to see Franks today, my lord. Trust me on this."

"Stand aside," le Puiset growled.

Perhaps not all the devils were gone. Perhaps some of them still remained, whispering in his ear. "You don't need to put on a display for these people. They're already terrified of you."

Count Evrard didn't answer, but he caught Lukas by the tunic, jerked him forward an inch, and then cracked his head against the door. Pain exploded behind his eyes and he crumpled helplessly to the stones as the count stepped over him and stalked into the church.

His knights remained outside, looking down on Lukas with scornful eyes. The Watchers seemed too overawed to do anything: one took a step towards him, but then glanced at the Frankish knights and decided against it.

So he was the only one who would stand up to the Franks? All right then. Lukas pushed himself to his feet and staggered after the count, whom he found facing the silent, wary Syrians within the church.

"By order of the good Bishop Adhemar of le Puy, this place is under the protection of le Puiset," Count Evrard announced. "Don't be afraid. I am indebted to your people…" He turned to Lukas. "They don't understand me. Translate. Tell them I'm taking them under my protection, that my men and I will stay here and make sure no one harms them."

His teeth were aching from where they'd crashed together when Evrard shoved him, but Lukas ground them together a little harder.

Why? Le Puiset didn't care for Lukas' people, not really. All the foul names he'd called Lukas came back to mind. *Greek. Heretic. Traitor.* If he was protecting them now it could only be out of self-interest, even if only the kind of self-interest that wouldn't be able to think highly of itself if it didn't spare them.

And there was nothing he could do about it. Without the Bessarion Lance, he was powerless to protect them himself, and Count Evrard was the only Frank willing to forego the sack in order to guard them. Lukas stepped forward.

"This is Count Evrard of le Puiset. He has agreed to remain here and put you under his protection. He pledges that no one will trouble you."

Even without a vision, he could have predicted what happened next. Relief swept into their faces as the crowd flocked to the count, kissing his hand, thanking him, calling down blessings on his head. "Don't leave us," one woman sobbed in the broken Frankish of the Italian merchant states.

Evrard of Le Puiset bowed his head and lifted his bloodstained sword up to kiss the hilt. "On this sword, so long as this danger lasts I will not abandon you."

Lukas turned his head away in disgust as they fawned on him. Le Puiset was one of the very Franks who had put them in danger, slaughtering their people in the streets. They were *his* people to protect, but even his visions painted Count Evrard as their saviour. Why? Weary bitterness swept over him. Why did every vision he had revolve around the Franks? Why was he obliged to warn them, to save them?

Was *this* what it meant to be a Messenger?

Chapter IX.

The day and its horrors were alike interminable. Antioch might not be what she once had been, the capital of an empire, but she was still populous and wealthy, the greatest city between Constantinople and Alexandria, and a rich nexus of trade. From the rumours flying as fugitives continued to stream into the basilica, Lukas gathered that resistance had been determined. There had been fighting in the streets between the Christians and Mahometans of every people. In parts of the city, the fractured Turkish garrison lay in wait to ambush isolated bands of Franks; in others, the Syrians joined the Franks, looting the homes of their Saracen neighbours. Despite the ferocity of the struggle, resistance could not last much longer. The Franks had seized the wall and all its gates, and the whole pilgrimage was now inside the city. By nightfall, when silence began to descend, Lukas wondered how many of the Turks in the city were dead or flown, and whether those that remained would simply throw away their weapons and sue for peace.

Bishop Adhemar did not come, but he had not forgotten them. Around sunset, one of the papal legate's senior clergymen, Peter of Narbonne, arrived with an escort of Provençal footmen. He took over from Count Evrard and ordered Lukas back to the palace.

Antioch at night had once blazed with the light of a thousand street-lamps, but tonight the city was dark and still, lying exhausted and spent like the bodies littering its streets. Thankfully there was still enough light in the western sky to guide Lukas down the Colonnaded Street. He moved cautiously, hoping the cross stitched to his tunic was visible enough to save him from any sudden ambush, for a few late bands of Franks still roamed the city, seeking enemies and plunder. The day had been warm and already the city stank of blood and entrails: he kept stepping into pools of cooled and congealed blood.

His heart sank. Hundreds of people had found refuge in the basilica, but if the rest of the city looked anything like the Colonnaded Street, thousands must be dead.

Were Ayla's family among them? He'd *promised* to find them, to protect them. *What a fool,* he told her. *I don't have the power. I couldn't protect you. I couldn't protect anyone.*

Well, yeh, she would say if she was here. She'd send him an impish smile. *It's all right. I don't recall asking you to protect me, or anyone else. Never mistook you for a djinn or demigod.*

Still, he and she were supposed to be bound by fate. He had wanted to do something for Ayla's family, and now perhaps he would never know if they had lived or died.

In bitter self-reproach, Lukas came to the palace and found carpenters already hard at work mending its broken gates in blazing lamplight. Perhaps Count Raymond expected trouble within the city... In the courtyard, a bonfire had been kindled, and some women were playing music and dancing while the Franks either rolled dice for plunder or lumbered up to join the dance themselves. There was not much food, and very little wine; if the men were drunk it was on blood. Lukas watched the women as he made his way around the bonfire. They weren't Frankish; they hadn't the fair hair or the ragged clothing of the women in the camp. Defeat was stamped on their faces, even as they held their bodies poised and erect, going through the motions of dance for their captors. He wondered if any of them were Ayla's sisters, but he didn't stop to ask. Even if they had been, he was unable to protect any of them. He would succeed only in drawing the Franks' wrath on his own head.

He'd thought Count Evrard an indiscriminate killer, and that was true, but he wasn't the only one. The Franks were ready to unleash unrestrained violence on anyone who resisted them, no matter which direction they prayed in. Kari, the Varangian who had died at Dorylaeum, had told Lukas it was his mission to save Antioch and Jerusalem, to be the Watcher they needed. Today he had failed the first part of this mission. What happened when the pilgrimage got to Jerusalem? How many more of his people would die?

And the damned visions kept prompting him to *help* the Franks?

He couldn't help anyone like this. He needed real power, not the intangible abilities of a Messenger, and not even the slight authority he had working for Count Raymond and Bishop Adhemar. Now, more than ever, he needed the Bessarion Lance.

Receiving directions from the guard on the door, Lukas made his way into the palace's entrance hall, noting all the changes the centuries had made in it. The wall frescoes he remembered, depicting emperors and saints, had been plastered over and replaced with new bright patterns, partly floral and partly geometric. But the hall itself was the same shape, the mosaics underfoot were sharply familiar, and the same faint smell of rosewater hung in the air. This, at last, was a place he really knew. It ought to have felt like a homecoming, but Lukas felt only a dreamlike sense of unreality.

Hushed voices caught his attention. Count Raymond stood in the doorway to another hall, speaking in a hurried undertone to someone inside.

"I know, Adhemar, but they're only human."

The bishop emerged, looking uncharacteristically agitated. "There's no excuse for such murder and rapine. The pilgrimage was a chance to fight in Christ's name, to liberate his people in the East. Not to satisfy base passions."

"Why are you telling me? With all respect, Adhemar, we knew this was going to happen the moment all these peasants and indigents decided to come. Why, I have a couple of them in custody right now for attempting to steal relics from the Church of the Virgin! The count of Die caught them making off with milord Saint Joshua's staff and the keys to the Ark of the Covenant."

"That's all very well, Saint-Gilles, but it wasn't only the indigents who have done such things." The bishop lowered his voice as though nervous of how that would be taken. "And it wasn't only the enemy that suffered. It was the very people we came to help! If we don't protect the local Christians—if we treat them no better than Yaghi Siyan did, what right have we to be here at all?"

Count Raymond's lips pressed together. "I'll have a word with the men. And I'll hang those relic thieves as an example. But there's only so much I can do, Adhemar; you know that. I can only command my own household and hector *my* vassals. If you want to hand down moral edicts, talk to your own clergy."

"Of course." Adhemar sighed and rubbed his eyes. His face was hollow and gaunt from the long winter; Lukas wondered if he still subsisted on quarter-rations, giving everything else he had to the poor.

"Ah, Bessarion. There you are." Count Raymond beckoned Lukas to join them, then swivelled back to face the bishop. "Speaking of the local Christians, I hear the Patriarch is still languishing in a prison around here somewhere."

"Oh, heavens! I'd better go in person." Adhemar hastened towards the forecourt, hardly even seeing Lukas. He was only halfway to the door when he wheeled around and rushed back to Count Raymond. "At least one of the Syrians ought to be put in a position of authority to safeguard his people. I mean to have the Patriarch reinstated with full honour."

The one-eyed count gave a huff of laughter. "Saints! You should be telling this to Bohemond, since he is the one determined to rule this city. *I* still mean to hand it back to Alexius, and no doubt he will install whatever Patriarch he likes."

"But I can depend on you to support me in this?"

"Against Bohemond?" A grim look settled on the count's scarred face. "Never doubt it."

A worried smile from Adhemar, and the bishop turned once again to go. Lukas cleared his throat. "Should I come and interpret, my lord?"

"Lukas!" Relief drifted over the bishop's face. "I hear you did well at the basilica today."

"I need him here," Count Raymond called harshly, and Adhemar put a hand on his shoulder with a smile.

"I'll find someone else to interpret. But thank you."

The bishop left, leaving Lukas feeling conflicted. He was already sick of watching his fellow Syrians fawning over the so-called liberators who had half destroyed them. Still, Adhemar seemed really to have their best interests at heart, and until Lukas could recover his father's lance, who else had the power and desire to protect them?

Count Raymond beckoned Lukas towards the audience-hall he seemed already to have taken over, like a man stepping into another's cast-off mantle. "You have done well, Bessarion. If not for your Syrian friends, I've no doubt I'd still be waiting outside the Bridge Gate. You won't find me ungrateful… What the devil is it?" he added as a guard called out to him.

"I don't know what this man wants, my lord, but he keeps repeating the name of Yaghi Siyan."

Count Raymond swivelled on his heel, suddenly eager. "It's about time. Send him in!"

The man who entered was dressed like a local peasant, his hands speckled with a crust of blood. Bowing to Count Raymond, he lifted a lapis signet ring.

"Yaghi Siyan," he announced.

"What's this?" Count Raymond snatched the ring, holding it up to the light to inspect the emblem carved upon the flat face of the stone. "Bessarion! Ask him where he got this."

Lukas put the question to him in Armenian, since that seemed to be the man's native tongue. The man spoke volubly, and when he fell silent at last, Lukas turned to Saint-Gilles. "It seems the Turkish lord was escaping south from the St George Gate and stopped in this man's village to rest. Since he had taken the heads of many Armenians, and they wished for vengeance, the men of the place banded together and cut off his head."

"Beheaded him? Devil take it!" the count erupted. "I wanted that man alive!"

Lukas flinched, afraid of the oncoming storm; but after a moment Count Raymond swallowed his wrath and waved a hand. "I want to see the body. Where is it?"

Lukas was not privy to all the details of the count's feuds, but even he knew that the answer was not likely to be well received. "They…they took it up Silpius, my lord, and gave it to Count Bohemond in exchange for a guarantee of freedom for their village." Count Raymond's face reddened, but he didn't say a word. Lukas added, "Count Bohemond, knowing that you were anxious for news of Yaghi Siyan, sent this man down to deliver the signet ring."

After a long, awful silence the count said, "Of course he did." He tossed the signet ring contemptuously to the Armenian. "Tell him he may keep it as his reward. Yaghi Siyan is useless to me now."

Lukas obeyed before rejoining Count Raymond in the audience hall. The one-eyed count had sunk into a chair, a hand clasped over his mouth, his mind clearly still half focused on Bohemond's act of provocation. When Lukas cleared his throat, Count Raymond glared up at him. "What is it now?"

"You were just saying how grateful you were, my lord," Lukas said hopefully. Since he did not have the lance, he must still rely on Count Raymond's favour, at least until he could unearth the weapon. Beyond that, something in him craved the count's respect. God knew he'd had little enough of it in the past year, and the count was one of the few Franks he genuinely respected himself.

"Ah, yes," Count Raymond said, a little of the growl leaving his voice. "I'll have Vigeois take you into the treasury tomorrow; choose something for yourself, anything you fancy."

If the count really wanted to give him his heart's desire, he might ask for permission to dig in the basilica—but how would he explain a request like that, without betraying the reason? And if he tried to conceal the reason, what was to prevent the count hanging him as a relic thief? Perhaps he ought to ask to be knighted and receive arms. Lukas opened his mouth to ask, but his courage failed him. Count Raymond knew him as an interpreter, not a warrior. Perhaps he should retrieve the lance first and prove himself as a knight.

He hesitated, and his chance was lost. Count Raymond said, "The real reward is that you're about to become a valuable player in this city, Bessarion. Bohemond is planning to build his own dominion here in Antioch, in defiance of our vows to Alexius. I mean to stop him, but in order to do that I will need a base of support here in the city, among the natives. Adhemar will deal with the Patriarch, but you said you were in communication with other local leaders—Watchers and such. Whoever you know in this city, I want to meet them. Can you arrange it?"

Lukas hesitated again. Only yesterday he might have been glad to obey, but tonight he could not bear the thought of acting as the Franks' go-between with the locals.

While the words might have been phrased as a question, the count's tone left Lukas in no doubt that it was a command and not to be denied, no matter how he felt about it. "Yes, my lord."

"See to it first thing in the morning," Count Raymond added. "Once Kerbogha arrives at our gates, we shall have other things to occupy our time."

Lukas found that he had already been assigned quarters in the palace. He had been looking forward all day to the prospect of sleeping beneath a real roof again: luxury of luxuries, he even had a room to himself. His bedroll had been tossed into a small cell not far from the audience hall, in the administrative section where Yaghi Siyan's messengers and secretaries had worked. Bare and comfortless except for a tiny window and a low wooden bed, it felt like an entire palace of his very own.

His whole body ached and he felt desperately short on both sleep and food. Too tired to go to the trouble of locating the kitchens or wheedling food out of them, Lukas dug into his unappetising hoard for some of the fresher bits of bread and meat. As he swallowed the morsels, he considered the next morning's mission. Willing or not, he could scarcely refuse to bring the local Watchers to Count Raymond for a meeting. But despite his confrontations with Tigranants today, these Watchers were his own people, not the count's. He meant to restore them to greatness, not help subordinate them to the Franks, even the few he respected.

Since discovering that there was no way home from this strange future, Lukas had often told himself a time would come when he must cut loose of Count Raymond and seize control of his own fate. He'd make himself a warlord like Thatoul of Marash, thumbing his nose at Franks and Turks alike. But, in his mind, that only happened *after* he found himself the lance. Now the decision would be forced upon him. Either he must hand over his allies to the Franks, or he must strike out without the lance.

If only he could find a pretext to dig beneath the basilica! Lukas waited, but no vision came to enlighten him. It seemed the visions were not remotely interested in his success. Swallowing a dry mouthful of bread, Lukas pushed the remainder of his scraps back into his bedroll. The count had sent him to the Watchers, but regardless, he would need to speak to them before he came to a decision. He remembered the alert, clean-cut face of the lantern-bearer in the basilica. There had been something very attractive in the man's commanding manner, in his easy assumption of power. Tigranants, rather grudgingly, had given him the name of a street in the northwest corner of the city. It was a few minutes' walk from the palace, and if he went tonight under cover of darkness, Count Raymond need never know.

With a sigh, Lukas splashed cold water over his aching eyes and ventured into the night.

Chapter X.

Tigranants' instructions led him into a small quarter of the city near the St George Gate, where the houses had once been very fine but were now shabby and run-down. Centuries ago, before the great earthquakes of Justinian's time, this road had led south into the mountains where the rich took their ease amidst the pleasure-gardens and temples of Daphne. Even in his own time, a memory of wealth and excess still clung to this part of the city, named Rhodion in memory of the rose-gardens that had once clustered in the villa gardens. Even in the darkness of gathering night, Lukas could see that this wealth, like the roses, was now a distant memory. Underlying the day's stench of fresh slaughter were the mingled smells of old refuse. Gardens had been torn up and overbuilt with slums. The great houses were divided into tenements, single rooms let out to poor families who now sat up by lamplight bewailing their dead.

The house of which Tigranants had told him was an old empty mansion, such a bare shell that the sack seemed to have passed it by. A grey cat yowled at him and scampered away as he entered the courtyard, where a lamp shone from the window of one of the lower rooms, shedding a beam of light into the peristyle. The shadow of a seated woman stretched out from an ancient bronze statue set near that same window. She had been torn from her plinth and her eyes had been pierced with nails; the gold leaf had long ago been scoured from her diadem and the sheaf of wheat she carried in her right hand, but Lukas recognised her all the same. This was the city's Fortuna, worshipped in pagan times for the luck it was thought she would bring to Antioch. Later, after the temple of Jupiter in which she had originally stood had been converted to Christian worship, her statue had been removed to the forum outside the senate—though not banished altogether, to appease the conservative-leaning pagan faction that retained some power in the city. There must have been a significant value of bronze in her, and Lukas was astonished to find the statue still in this unguarded courtyard.

Venturing further, Lukas noticed a very fine mosaic decorating the pavement. Though some of its tesserae were broken and lost, it still depicted a tree bearing round golden fruit, bordered with an undulating snake catching its tail in its mouth. When his feet touched the image, blinding light drowned his senses.

Not now. This couldn't have happened in the basilica?

Lukas resigned himself to the vision.

He stood in this same courtyard on a day of strong sunlight. At first, the smell of blood and ordure thick on the air made him presume he was seeing something that had happened earlier today, or would happen tomorrow. Then he glanced around the courtyard and realised that it had a comfortable, lived-in feel. Signs of industrious domestic work were everywhere. Beside the statue of Fortuna was a tub carrying a small lemon-tree. Other plants grew in old troughs: herbs for the most part, though there were some vegetables as well. Near them lay some gardening tools and a small heap of weeds. Dry laundry flapped from a line at one corner of the courtyard above an abandoned washtub. A lap-desk laden with bottled ink and weighted papers stood to one side.

A ring of men surrounded the mosaic with their sleeves rolled up to display the Watchers' Marks on their forearms. Beyond them, a smaller number of women paced the perimeter, spinning industriously from the distaffs tucked beneath their elbows. In the centre of the circle, kneeling between two of the Watchers upon the faded tree of golden fruit, was a Turkish man with terror in his eyes.

The eldest of the Watchers addressed the kneeling man. "You are accused of consorting with demons and dabbling in magic. For this, you face the penalty of death. Have you anything to say, Ilkay of Antioch?"

Ilkay of Antioch. It ought to have surprised him, but it didn't. He knew where he was, now: Ayla had described to him the terrible day when the Watchers of Antioch murdered her father.

Lukas turned and startled as he saw that the statue of Fortuna had changed. It was a living woman, a girl about his sister Marta's age, with blinded eyes and dark hair escaping from beneath her diadem. There was something familiar about her… Lukas caught his breath. It was the girl he had seen in the streets today, with the gashed throat.

She ought not to be able to see him or anything else, but she tilted her head and looked over her shoulder, pointing at the window tucked into the peristyle behind her. Lukas' heart wrung as he saw a small pale hand pressed against the ancient, cloudy glass. *Ayla.* She had been only nine years old when she watched her father die. Involuntarily, he took two steps towards her.

"Help me, Aemathe!" In the courtyard, Ilkay reached a desperate hand towards the Fortuna, tears of desperation streaking his face.

"Your familiar cannot help you now," one of the younger Watchers sneered. Lukas was surprised to recognise the voice.

"Destroy them, Aemathe! I command it!" Ilkay cried again. A small line etched between the Fortuna's brows, and she tilted her head as though listening for a sound far away, but she made no sound or movement.

"This is all the proof we need," said the eldest Watcher. "Kill him, Leo."

The young Watcher's sword flashed in the sun as it was drawn. Nearly in the same movement it scythed down. Ilkay crumpled to the stones, but the job was not done. Again and again the young Watcher struck, until the head finally rolled free of its torso and he straightened, arms and face speckled with blood. "There," he panted. "It's done, Presbyter."

Lukas recognised him, too. The man from the basilica, the lantern-bearer. Again, he felt dimly aware that he ought not to find this surprising.

"Good. Now we must go," the old Presbyter announced. The circle broke, moving quickly and furtively, as though afraid of something. The women stopped spinning, and in a moment all of them had collected their tools and gone out of the gate. Lukas was left standing in the sunlit courtyard, looking down at the shattered bone and dark blood oozing across the mosaic at his feet.

He drew in a breath and the smell assailed him again: blood and ordure.

A door slammed, making him jump. The vision blew to bright shreds, leaving him standing in the same courtyard on the night of the sack. Lukas turned to see a man approaching him in the faint light that shone from the window. The man from the basilica, Ilkay's killer. Lukas gulped, managing not to flinch.

"Tigranants told me I would find you here."

The other man's voice was warm. "Welcome home, Watcher. I knew you would come to me."

He stepped past Lukas and began to close the gate. Alarm swept through him. "Wait," Lukas said in a half strangled voice.

The Watcher lifted an inquiring eyebrow. Lukas swallowed. He didn't particularly relish the thought of the gates being closed; that felt too much like being trapped. Then again… Ayla's father had traded his own daughter's soul to a demon in exchange for power. If anything merited a death sentence, surely that did—and it wasn't as though the Syrian Watchers had carried out their sentence without severe consequences, anyway. Ilkay's family and allies had hunted them down and exterminated every Watcher they could find—which might explain why there had been no elderly or female Watchers in the basilica this morning.

The thoughts went through his head in a flash, but the Watcher was still waiting for him. "Don't bother closing the gate," Lukas managed to say. "I don't mean to stay long. I have been awake a very long time."

The Watcher shrugged. "There's plenty of room here if you need a place to sleep."

"There's no need for that." Who knew what kind of visions he would have if he tried to sleep here? The atmosphere was almost tangible—full of blood and darkness and terrible bargains. Lukas shivered. "Is this your headquarters, then?"

"Yes." The Watcher moved again, pacing like the lion he was named for until he stood near the Fortuna, backlit by the lamplight from the window.

Like everyone else in Antioch, the lantern-bearer spoke Greek with an Arabic accent. At least he was able to speak it at all; some had forgotten it altogether. "This was the site of a glorious victory for the Antiochene Watchers. Seven years ago, we killed a sorcerer, Ilkay the Vowed, on these very stones."

Lukas dared not say anything in response to that. Instead he gestured to the Fortuna. "And the old pagan statue? Why do you keep that around?"

"We keep it to remind us of the greatness of our forefathers," the Watcher said gravely. "It is said the statue commemorates a noble maiden, the offspring of demigods, who gave up her life in ancient times for the sake of the city and now watches over it. Ilkay used it for some barbaric purpose or other." A pause. "Tigranants said this man was known to you."

Lukas resisted the urge to run a nervous tongue across his lips. "By repute only. Seven months ago in Marash, I confronted the last of his confederates."

"Tigranants said you asked for news of Ilkay's family." The face of the man opposite him was in shadow.

"Ilkay's daughter helped me destroy the last of the Vowed. Thanks to her they will trouble us no longer." He cleared his throat. "She died helping me. The least I can do is protect the rest of her family."

He sensed the Watcher's amusement. "And you'd harbour the offspring of a sorcerer?"

"I would repay a debt of blood," Lukas growled. "This is a matter of honour."

"What kind of Watcher acknowledges debts of honour to a *Turk?*"

For a moment, Lukas forgot himself in his anger. "I'll answer that if you tell me what kind of Watcher tries to save his own neck and leaves the rest of his people to die in a sack!" He took a calculated step backwards, towards the gate. "Perhaps we don't have as much in common as I hoped."

The other man capitulated: "Ilkay's family left Antioch a year ago. That's when we came to this house."

"Where did they go?"

"I don't know. We tracked them as far as Laodicea, but there the track went cold. Perhaps they took ship to Smyrna or one of the other emirates in Asia Minor. Perhaps they went south to Tripoli." His eyes narrowed. "Look, Tigranants had reservations about you. Antioch may be in Christian hands again, but the entire Watchers' Council was obliterated after Ilkay's death and I only saved myself by three years' exile. If I make a mistake, everything I've built since my return will be destroyed. I need to know you're on my side."

Lukas wondered again whether he could really trust this man. Only the reflection that he was desperately short on allies made him pull back his sleeve to show his Watcher's Mark.

The other Watcher pursed his lips in a soundless whistle. "So Tigranants was right. A Syrian Watcher. But not from around here, or I'd recognise you. Where are you from? Is your name really Bessarion?"

Bessarion... When he'd confessed his name and identity to the Watchers in Constantinople, they'd called their guards and tried to have him killed, since they blamed his father for destroying the Watchers' Council at Oliveta. In Antioch, barely two days' journey from the site of the massacre, memories would be even sharper. Still, the gate behind him was open, and this might be the quickest way to find out whether he could trust this man.

"I'm a long way from home," he said cautiously. "Nearly four hundred years from home, to be exact."

For a moment the Watcher looked puzzled. Then his eyes widened in an expression that made him seem suddenly much younger. "Oliveta," he breathed. "My God, you're one of *those* Bessarions?"

Lukas inched back a step, tightening his grip on his staff. If the Watchers had men hiding in the courtyard shadows, he'd be dead. *Now would be a wonderful time for a vision,* he thought, but none came. Instead, he lifted his chin.

"And what if I am?"

"It was John Bessarion who slaughtered the corrupt Watchers at Oliveta. It was John Bessarion who gained enough power to bind the half-stone sorcerer, then vanished along with two of his children... Legend always had it you would return—I thought it was only a story." The look that burst onto the Watcher's face was ecstatic. He seized Lukas' hands. "God be thanked, you're one of the sons! You've come back! Is he here?"

Lukas blinked, fastening on to the only part of this that he felt he understood. "Is who here?"

"John Bessarion, the hero of Oliveta! Please tell me he's returned! He'll know me, I'm sure. I'm Leo Zarides. My family has ruled in Antioch since ancient times. My forefather was Thomas Zarides—they fought side by side at Nineveh—"

Lukas was overwhelmed. "My father...a hero?"

"Of course! Thanks to him, the half-stone sorcerer was trapped in Oliveta, limited to using the Vowed as his puppets."

The Vowed weren't Khalil's puppets; they were Lilith's. All the same... "You know of Khalil?"

"Of course I know of him—and of what your father did to stop him. Saints, it must have taken some guts to slaughter an entire Watcher's Council. They don't make men like *that* anymore! You can't imagine how much trouble we had convincing the old Watchers to execute *one* of the Acolytes of the Mountain. Now that he has returned, we will take such a vengeance upon our enemies, to make them fear the Watchers forever!"

"He hasn't returned," Lukas said, retreating another step; Zarides' enthusiasm was overpowering. "And..." He caught himself. *He* knew his father hadn't killed those people—that John Bessarion, the real one, would never have committed such an atrocity. It was a slander invented by his enemies. It was Khalil who massacred the town, and he got trapped in his own black magic when Paulus ruined his sigil. But if he admitted this to Zarides, would these Watchers accept him? Would they respect him? Would they do what he needed them to do?

"One day, I'll tell you what really happened at Oliveta," he said after a moment's hesitation.

Oh, you cucumber! Ayla's voice echoed in his memory, but he cleared his throat and rushed on. "Listen well: I'm Lukas Bessarion, son and heir to John Bessarion. I know your family. I used to play with Constantine

Zarides in Trebizond while our fathers were away fighting the Persians. So trust me when I tell you that my father meant to do more than turn Khalil half to stone: he meant to destroy him altogether."

"So why didn't he?"

Lukas shut his eyes for a moment, the answer lying heavy and bitter on the tip of his tongue. "Sometimes, no amount of foresight can stop fate. Oliveta was like that. The Saracen heretics caught us unaware. My father and siblings are gone, God knows where, but if it's vengeance you want, then we have something in common. This is my homeland, Zarides. I'm taking it back from Khalil; from the heretics; from the *Franks*. Are you with me?"

"God be praised! I've been waiting all my life for this. But how?"

Could he trust Zarides with the secret of the Bessarion Lance? Perhaps the Watcher would be just as happy to wield it himself as cede it to Lukas. To buy time, he said, "Tigranants told me you were seeking an alliance with the Franks, and Count Raymond sent me to offer you a meeting."

"Yes, but..."

"There's to be no more of that. We want an Antioch ruled by Syrians, for Syrians."

"Yes, but the Franks hold all the power, Bessarion. Wise men put themselves where the power is."

Power. There it was again: he had no power at present.

The only way he could get the power he so desperately needed was through this alliance. And the only way to get this alliance was to part with a scrap of information.

"My father had a weapon," he confessed. "Something that could end Khalil for good. Something that would allow us to dictate our own terms to the Franks and build a dominion where our people will be safe. And it's hidden here in Antioch. When I retrieve it, all the power will be with me. So which of us will you ally with then?"

Zarides didn't hesitate. "With Lukas Bessarion," he said softly, seizing Lukas' hand in a crushing grip. "How could I choose differently?"

* * *

Lukas kept to the shadows on his way back to the palace. Once again he tripped and slipped his way over corpses and through fluids he didn't want to think about, but this time his thoughts thrummed with nervous excitement. Zarides had made an undertaking not to ally with the Franks without consulting him first, but time was now short and ready to run out. If he didn't move fast…if the Watchers got tired of waiting for him to act, and went over to the Franks, or if Lukas couldn't unearth the lance, all tonight's bargaining would be for naught. At worst, Zarides might even betray Lukas' double-dealing to Count Raymond.

He'd gone through all the agony of trying to prove himself to the count once before. A second betrayal would not be forgiven; even Lukas could tell that.

No, he must recover the lance quickly—if, of course, it was still here. He wiped a sleeve across his sweating forehead and focused on what he could control. He couldn't afford to ask for permission to excavate the basilica: if anything of value was found, Count Raymond would certainly make him hand it over for his own use, or hang him for stealing if he refused.

He'd simply have to break into the basilica one night and dig until he found what he sought. For that he needed help, a team of workers. Which meant trusting Zarides further.

It would help if I had a vision telling me where to dig, he thought pointedly, but was unsurprised when no answering vision came.

Lamps were still burning in the palace when he returned, although the bonfire in the courtyard had sunk to a smouldering glow. This time, when he returned to his cabinet he fell asleep almost instantly and dreamed of Ayla.

"You might ask for permission to dig in the basilica," she suggested from where she lay beside him, warm and clinging. "Nothing easier. You've been having visions, haven't you?"

"Yes, but they don't come at my command. It isn't as though I can say, oh, the lance is beneath *this* stone."

"Of course not, but there's another way. You've been keeping your visions secret. Why not deliver one? Give the Franks a prophecy and let it come true. After that, they'll believe anything you say. You could order them to dig up the basilica to look for any sort of relic, and they'll ask how deep."

For a moment, no more than a heartbeat, Lukas was tempted. Then he shook his head. "That would make me a prophet, and anybody can be a prophet. I have birth and training. I'm a knight."

"If you don't do as I say, you *cucumber*, the only thing you'll be is a corpse."

It was Ayla's favourite insult, but the venomous way she hissed it now was worlds away from the irascible, half-joking way she'd always used it before. And if she were a figment of his own memory, surely she would know he had already decided against asking permission.

Suddenly, Lukas felt cold all over.

"You aren't my wife." He tried to pull away from her clinging arms, suddenly too tight and constricting. "Ayla would *never* advise me to use my gifts for deceit. Who are you?"

"I'm trying to help you," she hissed, following him as he tried to roll away.

"Who are you?" Lukas whispered. His voice was failing as his horror built. "Show your true face, you harpy!"

She straddled his body to hold him down, and his limbs turned into ice as she bent down to whisper in his ear. "Show you my true face? Perhaps I will. The last man who saw me died of terror. Can *you* survive it?"

Her face blurred, eyes and mouth dissolving into a blank, glassy surface as smooth and black as obsidian. Shadows moved deep within. Lukas felt certain that *something* would come out of that glassy darkness and look him in the eyes and send him mad. He tried to scream, but no sound came out. He tried to repeat his mother's exorcism prayer, but instead his lips moved as of their own accord and he said:

"Hail Lilith, Poison Mother."

He stopped, an agony of fear tearing through him. A shape deep within the black glass resolved from the murk and began to approach him. Fixing the words of his mother's prayer in his mind, he tried to speak again. "Hail Lilith." He stopped again, tried to scream to the heavens, but again the words twisted on his lips. *"Hail Lilith!"*

His heart was racing and he couldn't wake. The figure came nearer the obsidian surface, peered into his eyes. Thank God!—she was veiled, although he could see writhing shapes in the periphery of his vision, as though she was partly made of worms, or snakes.

A dreadful voice whispered to him: *Pretty creature of flesh, ripe and waiting to fall into my hand. No longer may you command me. I command you now.*

Lukas woke drenched in sweat, his throat hoarse from his own screams. What did it mean? This was the second dream in which Lilith had visited him in Ayla's shape. It was an unspeakable violation. After the years Ayla had spent fearing Lilith. After the agony with which she'd battled free of the terrible demon at last… He dug his fingernails into his thighs in a futile rage, partly at Lilith and partly at himself. He'd failed to protect Ayla when she was alive, and now Lilith was violating Ayla's memory in death.

As he himself was violating his father's memory by letting Zarides continue believing that pack of lies about Oliveta. The thought struck him like a javelin. No, he must tell these Watchers the truth. After he'd found the Bessarion Lance. After he'd shown them his mettle. They would follow him for himself, then, not just for the sake of their idea of his father.

Too unnerved to sleep again, Lukas spent the long hours inventing a story to tell Count Raymond about his visit to Leo Zarides. But, in the end, he had no need to say anything, for the next morning a vanguard of thirty Turkish scouts appeared and slaughtered fifteen knights who rode out to face them.

Kerbogha had come.

Chapter XI.

At night, in the great limestone massif above Antioch, no lamps burned to dazzle the eyes. The stars blazed like a great welt of light splashed across the sky. Only the flat sands of the desert would have been a better place for stargazing.

Khalil ibn Hassan watched the stars dance in their slow circles across the night, familiar by position and brightness, if not always by name. Among those he knew was a small cluster burning bright above the Bull's horns: the Pleiades.

He listed them by their Greek names, checking the position of each. *Maia, Electra, Taygete, Alcyone, Celaeno, Sterope.*

Perhaps it meant that his lance had not yet been discovered or broken, and the spirit trapped within had not been freed, and his vengeance was still there for the taking. Or perhaps it meant nothing at all.

There was nothing else to do, so Khalil began counting again, reciting the names under his breath: *Maia, Electra, Taygete, Alcyone, Celaeno, Sterope.*

This time he was only halfway through when the skin on the back of his neck prickled, and he knew he was being watched. He looked down from the starry dome above and saw *her.* Lilith. She was dressed like a queen tonight, her tall womanly body draped in a long cloak of flowing, iridescent black feathers and her face concealed by the great hooked beak of a vulture. Khalil could not tell whether this was a mask or simply the form she had chosen to take. He swallowed in a hopeless attempt to irrigate his dry throat, and hoped this was her chosen face for tonight. The other possibility was that she was hiding something worse under a mask, and he did not want to see anything worse.

"Are you forgetting something?" she demanded.

In unwilling obedience, Khalil bowed from the waist. "Hail Lilith, Poison Mother. I am your humble slave. Command me."

"Better," Lilith declared, stalking in a circle around him, her cloak flying out on the wind like a memory of beating wings. "As useless as you are to me, your attitude has certainly improved of late."

Khalil ground his teeth, conscious that his obedience was not entirely show. He had meant to use the rite at Oliveta to force *her* into *his* service. Instead, she had made him immortal and left him to rot, and only when his spirit was finally broken did she return to force him into her service.

He had only wanted to tip the divine balance in his favour, do enough good deeds to outweigh his sins. He had never planned to fall into the power of a demon, much less to become the tool of her dark appetites.

He didn't want to be Lilith's slave, but he was weakened beyond bearing. If she commanded him, he would obey, no matter how much he hated doing it.

And perhaps she knew that. Perhaps she counted on it. Perhaps she liked it better this way.

"You said you would free me," he reminded her in an empty show of defiance.

"And I will," she soothed. "Lukas Bessarion is rotting on the tree. Soon he will fall into my mouth."

She made a snapping motion with her beak, and Khalil shivered.

"Soon," she murmured, bending down to caress his cheek, "you will be free, and you will be mine."

He flinched as her fingernails scored through the exposed, sunburnt flesh on his face. "To do what?" he demanded with a flash of hope. "To destroy the Franks and their coreligionists?"

A soundless laugh. "By the bridge of swords, no!"

"You said you meant to slaughter them." She had also meant to slaughter his own people, but Khalil was beginning to wonder if it was a price he could pay, after all. He swallowed hard. "I have given my help. All I ask is justice against the Bessarions."

"Justice? Why, you think that they have done you some great wrong! Do you forget that it was *I* who bound you here? Do you forget it was *you* who instigated the slaughter of Oliveta? This is justice, Half-Stone."

"They stole what was mine," he said, doggedly. "Promise me that they, at least, shall pay…and do as you like with the Franks."

"As you like it. I care nothing for the Bessarions. But you should not give me the Franks so readily, Half-Stone."

There was a mocking note in her voice. Khalil's mouth had gone dry. "What do you mean?"

She knelt before him, her black eyes glinting in the starlight above her beak. The light was so soft and tricky; he still did not know whether she was wearing a mask. "There's more to these Franks than I thought. You should have seen the creatures in Antioch today, killing without restraint, maddened by vengeance." The eyes closed and she shivered, ecstatically. "I haven't fed like that in years. Do you know what they did in the west, before they came here? Some of them were hag-ridden with nasty curses. It seems that in Germania or whatever they're calling it these days, some of them began their pilgrimage by dispatching the local Jews."

The Jews? Khalil thought of the merchantmen that had formed trading enclaves, schools, and synagogues across the Levant. Arrogant swine, who'd rejected the prophet and persecuted the house of faith. "What do the Franks care about the Jews?"

"They don't. They care about honour. Vengeance." Lilith laughed. "Their code says that if someone strikes you on the cheek, you must strike them back, and harder. The Jews killed the Galileean they pretend to worship, so they took their vengeance. Isn't it too perfect? Their Galileean taught them to turn the other cheek to the smiters. But he has *failed.* I ought to have seen it sooner. These Franks may fight in his name, but they've been serving me all along."

She laughed, a dreadful sound. Understanding her meaning, Khalil felt sick. Of course these infidel invaders were little better than mindless beasts, but it was *his people* at their mercy. And Lilith was more than happy to feed on their slaughter.

"You want me to help the Franks," he whispered.

Lilith smiled. "Oh, no. This is so much greater than the Franks. Listen, Half-Stone, and I will tell you how we made the djinn and demigods—how we spat in God's eye, and lived."

Chapter XII.

The only saving grace to this hellish week, Saint-Gilles reflected, was that Bohemond had not succeeded in taking the Antiochene citadel.

If it *was* a saving grace, and not the instrument of their own destruction.

He tightened his fingers around the hilt of his sword and threw a glance over his shoulder to the several hundred men waiting in expectant silence with him. Huddled in the shadow of the great limestone wall, they reminded Saint-Gilles of the line of debris washed up against a sea wall at high tide. The crest of Silpius, a wind-scoured landscape of stunted pine, tangled thornbush, and tumbled stones, was supposed to be cooled by mountain breezes but, in the morning's still heat, Saint-Gilles already felt sweat trickling down his back. A postern gate stood open behind them—the very same by which the city had been taken—but it was too narrow to permit his men to retreat; the infantry had taken half an hour to file through the narrow passage in the first place. Here, outside the wall, there was no shelter, either from the glaring sunlight or from the Turks.

From where the Franks massed silently for their attack, the wall angled slightly towards the north, climbing towards the highest point of the mountain and the enemy-held citadel beyond it. The postern itself was just out of sight of the citadel, making it a reasonable enough sally-point, but Saint-Gilles scowled as he watched the young count of le Puiset lead his mounted troop through.

A hundred precious horses they were committing to this sally, to say nothing of the men. If anything went wrong in the next half-hour, the postern was too narrow to save them.

Seven days ago, the pilgrims had taken Antioch. Six days ago, Kerbogha's vanguard had arrived outside the city. At first, the fighting was concentrated upon the outlying fortresses, Malregard and La Mahomerie, until hard fighting had forced the Franks back within the city, setting fire to the outposts as they retreated. Now, with splinters of the mighty Turkish host camped outside each gate, the Frankish besiegers had become the besieged. The roads to the sea and to the Armenian-held hinterland were blocked, along with any hope of reinforcements or supplies. Meanwhile, Kerbogha's main army was camped across the Orontes two or three miles north of the city. Saint-Gilles had glimpsed the vast host from afar on his way up the mountain, like nothing he'd ever seen, save for the pilgrimage itself.

Even at that distance the sight put a slowly churning knot of fear in his gut. It would take a formidable relief army to save them now—which meant their only hope was Emperor Alexius. But would he arrive on time? Once again, Saint-Gilles tried a mental calculation of the limited manpower and even more limited food stores in the city. Once again, he caught himself in a treadmill of worry. Best not to dwell on it. Best only to be grateful so many men had been recalled to the city from surrounding outposts, together with at least a measure of food.

Meanwhile, the camp north of the city wasn't even the totality of Kerbogha's great army. After the fall of La Mahomerie two days ago, a good half of Kerbogha's men marched through mountain paths to the rear flank of Silpius and pitched camp on the gentler eastern slope of the mountain. A two-day lull had followed, but Saint-Gilles and the other princes knew it was merely the breath of calm before the storm. The citadel was built on the city wall itself, its courtyard forming a small enclave of Turkish-occupied land at the crest of Silpius. Equipped with small, easily defended gates, the citadel had become a vestibule through which the entire Turkish host, if left unattended, might stroll into Antioch herself.

And that was evidently what Kerbogha meant to do: force his way through the citadel's gates, past Bohemond's blockade, and down the narrow road leading to the city. Saint-Gilles recognised the irony. It had taken the Franks seven bitter months to find even such a small crevice by which to sneak into Antioch and take the city, but Kerbogha arrived to find his entrance ready and waiting.

That was why he shouldn't worry about food, Saint-Gilles thought grimly. Even if Alexius tried to reach them in time, it was ten to one the siege had only days—perhaps hours—left to run. And the climax would be both brief and bloody beyond imagining.

Saint-Gilles sighed, pushing his conflicting thoughts aside as the count of le Puiset finished assembling his men. Turning to Saint-Gilles, the gaunt young count nodded and touched the hilt of his sword. Saint-Gilles nodded back. That was all the discussion needed: they had laid their plans an hour ago in the tower that served as Bohemond's headquarters. Le Puiset swung up into his saddle. Harnesses creaked and hoofs scraped against the stones as the hundred knights followed le Puiset single file up a narrow path that dipped into a gulley before rising again towards the citadel—and to the Turkish camp beyond. Beside Saint-Gilles, his interpreter let out a breath that sounded as though he'd been holding it a while. Bessarion was always on edge around le Puiset, more so now that the younger count had entered Bohemond's service.

With all Bohemond's attention on the citadel and everyone else occupied in guarding the wall or manning the outposts, Saint-Gilles had taken the opportunity to consolidate power with a few alliances of his own. Bessarion's negotiations with the Watchers had not yet borne fruit—some nonsense about the Antiochenes wanting greater autonomy than they were likely to get under either Turks or Franks—but others were not so troublesome. There were the Italian merchant lords: he had already promised trading privileges to the Genoese on the pilgrimage, and was leaning on the existing Amalfitan mercantile community to support him as well. The Syrian Patriarch, now out of prison and being nursed back to health under Adhemar's care, had sworn on the bones of Saint Ignatius to support Saint-Gilles and the emperor against Bohemond. And, perhaps best of all, during the sack Saint-Gilles had managed to secure the city's major granary. Now, not only the indigents on pilgrimage, but all the common Antiochenes depended upon him for their daily bread. By the time Bohemond took the citadel—*if* Bohemond took the citadel—Saint-Gilles aimed to be unshakeably entrenched in the city.

The blast of le Puiset's horn cut into his thoughts, a reminder that all this work was for nothing so long as the Turkish threat continued. Instantly, the thunder of charging horses rumbled through the still morning air. From the citadel, a gong clanged wildly to raise the alarm. Too late: within moments, the distant screams started as le Puiset's knights ploughed into the Turkish camp.

Behind Saint-Gilles, the infantry stirred restively. "Wait on my signal," he growled. "Stick to the plan."

It was Bohemond's plan, of course. Not that Saint-Gilles meant to stick by it if the opportunity arose.

It had been dawn when he and his men made the arduous climb up Silpius to the small canvas city that had sprung up opposite the citadel, where Bohemond and his South Norman veterans waited like a cat by a mouse-hole. Bohemond had met Saint-Gilles outside his own tent. Unlike everyone else in this doomed city, the Norman count seemed refreshed, well fed, and indecently on his mettle: even his armour was scoured bright, and his chin freshly shaved. Only a limp betrayed how he'd been pierced in the leg by an arrow on the day the city fell, leading a determined storming-party along the wall to the citadel. Beside him, the count of Flanders and the duke of Normandy seemed bleary, unkempt, and down in the mouth.

"Saint-Gilles! Well met!" Bohemond clasped Saint-Gilles exuberantly to his bosom. "Welcome to our summer palace. It might not look like much, but the breezes keep us cool even on the hottest day, and the hunting is *sublime*."

From the direction of the citadel, panicked shouts had rung out and Saint-Gilles heard the crash of steel, the screams of the dying.

"Charming," he said dryly.

"It's only the dawn attack. Nothing to worry about, we're just making sure they're awake. Come up into the tower, and you shall see the lay of the land and hear our plan for the sortie."

Energetic despite his limp, Bohemond led them towards the wall. Saint-Gilles followed, leaning on his own spear to prevent himself stumbling upon the tumbled rock that littered the hilltop. His one remaining eye was keen enough, but it gave little clue as to depths and distances.

The camp atop the mountain was small, inhabited almost exclusively by fighting men: there were few laundresses, cooks, or servants to be seen, and if Bohemond was concealing any ulterior schemes, there was no sign of it in the camp. They came to the foot of the wall and went single file up one of the infrequent narrow stairs leading onto the broad ramparts. The towers fortifying the wall were built of baked brick atop massive piers of solid stone, accessible only from the ramparts. At the first tower facing the citadel on the south, Bohemond led them in at an entrance that smelled faintly of rotting blood. Then, despite his injured leg, Bohemond managed to pull himself up the narrow wooden ladder leading to the second level, which differed from the first only in the walls being pierced by loopholes. Some knights with bows and crossbows were stationed here, and gave quick respectful bows as the four princes and their retinue trailed Bohemond up a second ladder onto the tower's flat roof.

"Here we are," Bohemond said with a flourish. Saint-Gilles followed the Norman count to the parapet overlooking the citadel. The highest point of the mountain was a little behind them now, and ahead the wall sloped away before them, partly descending into a narrow, thorny gulley that contained a large open cistern. Beyond that, the wall rose again to meet the citadel, a massive square keep encircled by a broad enclosure, before falling away again steeply towards the Iron Gate. From the citadel there were onto two narrow paths towards the city: the white gravel road to the left (littered with bodies and broken machines) that threaded the ridge between the gulley and the western cliffs, and a small footpath running beneath the line of the wall.

"Look at it," Bohemond said admiringly, waving a hand towards the citadel. "It's practically impregnable. I should know; I've tried."

"Not hard enough," Saint-Gilles said disagreeably. His own ambitions aside, it seemed that Bohemond, who had been trying for a full seven days to seize the citadel, ought to be abashed by his failure. Particularly since it put the entire pilgrimage in very immediate danger. From the tower, Saint-Gilles saw the slope beyond the wall where the fringes of Kerbogha's new camp could be seen just beyond the gulley, the smoke of its fires making a haze in the blue air. They had arrived late the day before yesterday, and no doubt would make their move shortly.

Unless the Franks struck first.

Bohemond laughed, and Saint-Gilles said irritably, "I'm not sure why you're enjoying yourself so much."

"You're not a gambling man, count?"

"No."

"No, I didn't think so. But this game comes with the highest stakes I've ever diced for." Bohemond had shed a warm smile on Flanders and Normandy, reminding Saint-Gilles how pleasant it had been, for a few short months, to let himself like this man. "No matter what happens in the next few hours, we will always be remembered, my friends."

Not that deathless glory was the reason Saint-Gilles and his men were now broiling in the Syrian sun against the limestone wall of Antioch, awaiting le Puiset's next signal. Sheer survival was more like it. Bohemond's plan had been simple, but effective. Even a large army could be smashed by a small, determined surprise attack, and given the desperation of their position, any other tactics were beyond them at present. Either they must strike with audacity or face the slow, grinding defeat of attrition and starvation, hoping that Alexius arrived before the last of them perished.

So le Puiset had volunteered to lead a small cavalry charge into the Turkish encampment. Saint-Gilles and his infantry were to provide support, whether as a second wave should le Puiset's charge succeed, or as a rear-guard should the mounted knights fall back. Routing Kerbogha's men from the mountain might be a small victory within the drama of the larger siege, but it would undermine morale in the all-important citadel and might thus prove decisive.

Time lengthened, marked by distant screams, the blood-quickening sound of metal striking metal. Still le Puiset did not wind his horn. Either he was dead, or things were going well in the Turkish camp. As a new note entered the sound of the fighting, Saint-Gilles ventured out of his hiding-place in the angle of the wall to peer towards the citadel. It took him a moment to realise what he was seeing. The roof of Bohemond's tower was empty, and there was a sound of battle within the wall.

Bohemond was attacking the citadel again.

That decided him. It was high time Saint-Gilles took a hand in whatever was going on. "Come on!" he ordered, taking to the path. He hesitated when he came in view of the citadel. He could hear Bohemond's attack more clearly now, the pound-pound of a battering ram against a distant door. East of the citadel, but still hidden behind the swell of the mountain, the grey smoke of the Turkish campfires had turned to a black, angry column. Le Puiset's attack must be prospering.

Saint-Gilles sucked in a breath and made his choice. "Advance on the citadel," he commanded. With the garrison's attention pinned by Bohemond at their front door, there might be a chance for him, Saint-Gilles, to break in by the rear—and then the citadel, as well as the city, would be in his hands.

"But, my lord—" Polignac began to protest. Saint-Gilles fixed him with a glare, and the young standard-bearer subsided.

"Le Puiset doesn't need us," Saint-Gilles said. "And if he does sound his horn, we'll hear it. Onwards!"

He set a quick pace down the slope, through the gulley, and up the other side again. The Turkish camp came in view, full of raging flames and running and struggling figures. Many of Saint-Gilles' men looked longingly in that direction, scenting plunder. Saint-Gilles called, "Steady! There'll be loot enough in the citadel!"

The outer entrance of the citadel was a small postern protected by an outer wall, preventing anyone from coming at it head-on. Many loopholes overlooked the long, narrow passage leading towards it, but no arrows flew as Saint-Gilles ventured within. Just as he thought: the garrison had its hands full with the Norman attack.

He turned to his men. "Volunteers to break the door open! A hundred gold bezants to the first ten who answer!"

Within moments ten sturdy peasants had disappeared down the narrow passage. Rhythmic thuds echoed as they attacked the door with stones and axes. The garrison was bound to hear—bound to send men to answer the knock on their back door—and then which would take the citadel first, Bohemond or Saint-Gilles?

"My lord!" Bessarion said.

"Not now, Greek," Saint-Gilles said testily, for a ringing *crack* had already sounded, as though something in the battered door had given way.

"My lord, it's the Turks!" That was Polignac, a note of panic in his voice. In the same moment came the blast of a horn—le Puiset's horn—three short blasts. The retreat.

Despite the summer heat, Saint-Gilles felt as though he had fallen into icy water. "Devil take it," he breathed, turning away from the citadel to scan the hillside. What was le Puiset playing at? Three blasts meant the charge had run into trouble and must retreat. It was Saint-Gilles' signal to organise his men in a shield-wall around the postern, holding the Turks at bay until the knights with their precious mounts could retreat within the city again.

Except that now, as le Puiset's knights fled from the camp in a seething, panicked mess and ran pell-mell for the postern—as the Turkish counterattack emerged through smoke and flame on their trail and hounded them across the rocky, uneven hillside—Saint-Gilles and his infantry were nowhere near the postern.

Le Puiset didn't know that. He thought he was headed for safety.

(It was too late. He was a *fool*, a besotted fool, and he was about to get them all killed.)

"Fall back! Fall back!" Saint-Gilles yelled. "Get back to the postern and form a shield-wall! Go! Go!"

Polignac caught his arm. "Give me leave and I'll run to Count Evrard, tell him to make a stand. If he protects our retreat, we can protect his."

There came a scream from the battered citadel door as arrows flew from the loopholes above, felling the men he had sent to break it open. Overhead on the citadel ramparts came the tramp of feet as Turkish archers took their places, bent their bows.

"No," Saint-Gilles barked. "It's suicide." Polignac, his standard-bearer, was from a noble family.

"Bessarion," he said. "You go."

Chapter XIII.

Count Raymond had asked a great many things of Lukas over the last few months, but he had never sent him running into a rout with a message for his worst enemy. *It's suicide.* The implication of the count's words hit him like a fist to the gut and, for a moment, all he could do was stare.

"Run," the count ordered in a voice like the scrape of a sword on a whetstone. "Tell them we can protect them. But we need time."

There was no arguing with a drawn sword. Lukas unslung his staff and began running, zig-zagging perilously amidst tumbled rocks and stunted scrub, aiming to intercept the retreat at the narrow path crossing the gulley. Le Puiset's retreat was almost level now with the citadel. Not all the knights were a-horse: he saw one of the men on foot in the rear raise a horn to his lips and blow the triple blast of alarm again. There was Count Evrard.

It's suicide.

Lukas crossed himself without slowing. War fodder. Was that all he'd ever been to Count Raymond?

He reached the gulley path before the Franks did. The Turks poured after the Franks and caught them; swords and spears flickered like flame as they shouted their ululating war cries. Le Puiset signalled a stand as the rout devolved into a string of desperate, lonely combats. Some of the more panicked Franks kept fleeing, forcing Lukas off the path as they and their terrified steeds stormed by. Others followed on foot, tripping among the stones and the fallen bodies of their fellows.

Lukas stopped in his tracks, realising the running battle was about to overwhelm him. *Strife!* He didn't want to die here, so close to recovering his father's lance. And he had only a rusted mail shirt and a wooden staff with which to defend himself.

He'd never get a message to le Puiset now.

Lukas turned to flee for the postern, but he didn't get far. Someone shoved him in the back and he fell heavily among the rocks at the wayside. Only the unevenness of the ground saved him as the rout passed him by. Lukas gasped for breath until the dizziness of pain passed, and then he scrambled to his feet again. He leaped for smoother ground, but then a Frankish knight came staggering backward towards him, fending off the attentions of three heavily armed Turks.

It was too late to scrounge himself a better weapon, for battle had found him. Lukas swept up the weighted iron foot of his staff and jabbed it past the retreating knight, straight into the jaw of one of the attackers. The Turk's head snapped back with a crack and he fell like a sack of rocks. In the same moment, another of them landed a blow with his long-handled axe on the Frankish knight's left thigh: a direct hit that crumpled the man into the stones with a high, terrible cry of anguish.

Before the axe-wielder could recover from his blow, Lukas lashed his staff against the man's temple, striking off his helmet and laying him beside his fellow. The third Turk levelled a wild swing at Lukas' head on his way past. Lukas threw himself forwards and the blow fell on his shoulders, a stunning buffet that laid him flat on the path. The Turk's charge carried him past, and then it was much too late to think of fighting.

Lukas lay still, feigning death as the onslaught of Turks swept past. Someone trod heavily on his leg, grinding it into the stones until Lukas thought it would break; but then the counterattack was past and Lukas rose up on his elbows to see what was happening at the wall.

Count Raymond and his infantry hastened back to the postern along the narrow path at the foot of the wall, but they must be barely halfway; the one-eyed count's decision to assault the citadel could not have been made at a worse moment, and now Lukas and heaven knew how many others would die because of it. The crest of Silpius blocked his view of the postern, but the slope towards the mountain's highest point was now speckled with desperate combats. The Franks were not quite routed; some of them were still fighting in desperation, having realised by now that their retreat through the postern was impossible.

Lukas heard screams, the crash of arms, the awful shriek of horses in pain. He imagined the scrum by the gate as the panicked Franks trampled and crushed each other in their haste to find safety. Then from the Turkish camp, a drum began to beat, and Lukas turned on his elbow to see more Turks advancing towards them.

"Saint George, pray for us," he sobbed.

The knight on the stones beside him groaned. Frantic for weapons, Lukas turned, hoping to find the man dying and vulnerable to plunder. Instead he found the knight half sitting, half reclining against the rocks. Both hands were clamped over the oozing wound on his thigh and his face, blank and ghastly pale, was yet recognisable.

Count Evrard.

Of course.

Lukas knelt looking at him for a long, speechless moment. Le Puiset hardly noticed him: his eyes were unfocused with shock. Lukas glanced towards Count Bohemond's tower beyond the steep gulley walls where the pale faces of onlookers still watched the disastrous battle. If he robbed or abandoned le Puiset, they would stand witness.

Le Puiset stirred, making a strangled sound as he recognised Lukas. To Lukas' surprise, the Frank sighed a little and turned his head away, still grasping his wound.

"Either kill me or leave." Le Puiset's voice was scratchy with agony and something Lukas didn't expect: resignation. "But for God's sake don't stand there gloating."

Lukas reached for his anger, trying to summon up the raw, harrowing memory of the night he'd spent holding Ayla's corpse in his arms outside Marash. The glassy dead eyes, the sickly crater in her forehead…but all he found was the memory of le Puiset saving the lives of everyone locked inside the basilica a week ago, when the rabble were beating on the door.

Le Puiset attempted to rise, but his wounded leg jarred against Lukas' knee and he sank back onto the ground wincing, sweat beading his lip.

Rocks and scrub obscured them from the Turks coming down from the camp, but in another moment the enemy would be close enough to see them. Lukas swore under his breath and then bent to get his arms under the count's shoulders. "Here. Let's get you to—"

"I said *leave*," the count growled, and suddenly there was a dagger in his hand and it was rasping against the underside of Lukas' chin.

"You don't want my help?" Lukas raised his hands. "You want to die? Perfect! I'll come back in a day or two and dance on your grave, by your leave."

"I don't—need your help," le Puiset panted, lurching to his knees. Blood sobbed from his wound, and his face went grey.

Lukas shouldn't care whether this murderer lived or died. He had bigger things to concern himself with. Zarides had promised to help him retrieve the lance. He should find a hiding place, focus on staying alive…but he couldn't leave le Puiset to die at the hands of the Turks. Apart from anything else, Lukas had promised himself the pleasure of killing the count himself, in single combat, with the Bessarion Lance in his hands and Ayla's name on his lips.

"You know what, I think I'll go," he snarled. "With you out of the way, I'll be able to continue my acquaintance with your sister. I don't remember her name, but she's a fine bit of damask and she thinks I'm *preux*."

Le Puiset roared, surged up, swung. Lukas was waiting for him. He caught the count's arm, heaved him to his feet and braced his shoulders under his weight. After hauling the unsteady Frank down the steep path into the gulley, Lukas started along it, forcing a way past the thorns that slashed his undefended legs, scanning the rocks for shelter.

"You villein," le Puiset panted, when he had gained enough breath for it. "I'll kill you if you so much as look at my sister."

"My lord, I wouldn't look at your sister if I were the Emperor of Rome and she the only daughter of Khosrau the Victorious."

"What are you saying, Greek?"

Of course, le Puiset knew nothing of the wars between Rome and Persia. Ignorant barbarian. "Make up your mind, Frank! Do you or do you not want me to admire your sister?"

"I want you to stop talking about her," le Puiset said faintly.

"Try to stop me," Lukas said, with a hard laugh.

"When I'm whole again, I'll kill you with my own hands."

There was something exhilarating in baiting the count like this. "You can try," Lukas promised, thinking of the Bessarion Lance. "I'm counting on it."

Behind them, the battle cries of the Turkish reinforcements became louder as they reached the gulley and swept across it, heading for the cacophony at the postern. Two of the enemy peeled off and made towards them, swords hefted.

"Give me your sword," he demanded, turning to le Puiset.

"Go to hell."

"All right." Shifting his staff to his left hand, Lukas threw off the count's arm and dodged away. Le Puiset flung out his arms, wind-milling as he lost balance. Lukas plucked the sword from its sheath as le Puiset collapsed onto the rocks, then he turned to face the Turks. The odds were poor, two to one, but Lukas' exhaustion left him at the feeling of a finely balanced sword in his hand.

Count Evrard, sprawled on the rocks behind him, left him little room to manoeuvre. Instead, Lukas rushed to meet the enemy. The foremost Turk swiped at him. Using his staff to deflect the blow, Lukas put his whole body behind a retaliatory thrust. Too late—the other man raised his buckler and caught the blow, staggering back a pace or two.

The other closed in on him from the side. Lukas turned to parry the thrust, but suddenly a flash of certainty blazed across his mind: the Turk was only feinting. Instead of meeting the blow, he raised his staff to guard and thrust the other man through; he felt the resistance of chainmail, heard the shriek of parting links as the armour gave way.

Another flash: in his mind's eye he saw the first Turk recovering and closing in on him. Lukas lashed out with his staff, not even looking. He heard the other man's grunt as the iron-shod end sank into his gut. Lukas pivoted, bringing the sword down with his right on the man's unguarded neck as he folded to the ground.

Lukas fell back, breathing hard and watching the bodies for any sign of life. For the moment, the gulley was clear again, the wave of Turks having rushed on without waiting to see the outcome of the struggle. As he stood gasping for air, a third splinter of vision came to his mind's eye. Between himself and le Puiset, a thorn-bush grew against a steep rock. Lukas pushed the bush away with the end of his staff and saw a shallow cleft between two rocks: open to the sky, but well hidden on all other sides.

"Quickly," he told le Puiset, grabbing him by the arms. The count staggered to his feet, and the two of them shoved past the thorn and into their sanctuary.

Chapter XIV.

For a while they lay side by side, only breathing, only listening to the nightmarish sounds of the battle. "They must be getting slaughtered out there," Lukas said under his breath. There was no response from Count Evrard. He turned to find the count slumped against the rock beside him, face blank and slack, eyes glassy. Suddenly fearing that le Puiset had died, Lukas gripped his shoulder and shook him. "Count?"

For a moment le Puiset did not respond. At length, however, he focused on Lukas and took a heaving breath. "You can fight."

It wasn't a question, but there was a note of disbelief in it. "That's what I told you at Nicaea," Lukas said. "I have a knight's training."

He sat up, feeling light-headed. Count Raymond had his whole household on starvation rations, or something close to it, and breakfast had been a long time ago. Lukas glanced up at the sky—it was still no later than mid-morning. "Do you have any water?"

"No."

"Then it'll be a long, thirsty day. There's no point trying to get back into the city until it's dark." He got to his feet, risking a peek over the rocks, outside the gulley. There was still fighting going on at the hilltop and beyond. Meanwhile, the Turks had brought ladders and were attempting to mount the wall. Uphill, towards the citadel, reinforcements entered the citadel in a long stream.

He slid down again and caught his breath, running his hands through his hair. Saints, he wanted a bath! He wanted a bath, and a square meal, and a good night's sleep uninterrupted by visions or portents. Instead…

"The Turks are entering the citadel," he said. "And assaulting the wall. And fighting to take the postern."

Le Puiset didn't answer, but there was a haunted look on his face. Both of them knew what that meant. The Turks meant to force their way past Bohemond and down into the city, where there would be a repeat of last week's sack.

"So there's a battle to fight," le Puiset whispered at length. "What the hell are *you* doing here?"

"Saving your worthless life." Lukas squatted down beside him. "Here, I'm going to look at your leg."

"Don't *touch* me. And give my sword back."

Lukas jostled the wound spitefully. "I'm not asking your permission. And I'm keeping the sword. I might need it. To save your worthless life, again."

With a groan of pain, le Puiset let his head drop back among the stones. "This doesn't wipe out what's between us, Greek."

For a moment Lukas could scarcely breathe. The *audacity* of the Frank, to presume Lukas wanted to curry favour with him—as though all the debt was on his side—as though Lukas was the one who had done wrong. "Far from it," he muttered at length, inspecting the gash across the count's leg. There may have been a fervid tremble in his voice, for le Puiset shot him a narrowed glare.

Lukas kept a kerchief in his pouch—his father had always recommended a clean kerchief—along with a small pot of cleansing salve that looked almost useless beside the count's welling wound. He dabbed his cloth against the wound, noting that though deep, it had missed any major veins or arteries. The blood was still welling. Taking out his canteen, Lukas drank a swig of the watered wine inside before trickling some of the rest over the wound. It would need sewing up, but he didn't have the materials for that now. Lukas took out his dagger to cut a strip from the embroidered tunic the count wore beneath his mail.

"What are you doing?" le Puiset snapped. Until now, he'd been silent, lying with his head turned towards the sounds of battle from within the wall. Now, he half-sat, snatching for Lukas' wrist.

"I need cloth to wrap your wound."

"Tear your own clothes, then."

Lukas gave a wordless growl of frustration. "Saints! What have I done to be saddled with *you*? Don't you have servants of your own?"

"My squire died of fever two weeks ago," le Puiset said baldly. "Half the men who followed me from France are dead now and, because I could not afford to feed them, most of the rest have gone to follow other counts." He left the silence hanging a moment before adding—half gruff, half pleading—"My wife made this tunic."

Lukas looked down again at the tunic. It was worn and stained—like everyone's clothes after so long in the mud and dust of campaign—but had been carefully washed and mended, time and again. The fine linen had faded and the embroidery was worn, but it had been made with care, the stitches painstaking and perfect.

He hadn't known le Puiset was married. Was the countess with him on pilgrimage? Unlikely, since the tunic meant so much to him. Lukas' fingers found Ayla's sling where it was knotted around his wrist, stroking the faded orange-and-blue woollen threads.

"Yeh, well," he said at last, "it's not my leg, and if I ruin my own tunic, I've no one to make me another."

He tore into the garment with his dagger and cut a strip from the hem; it came away with a long whine. Le Puiset didn't protest; only gazed up at the sky with his lips compressed.

Using his own kerchief as a pad, he wrapped the wound tightly before wiping his bloody hands on a dry tuft of grass and sitting back, bone-weary. His shoulders hurt where the Turk had struck him. When he reached between his shoulder-blades, something twinged in his back and his fingertips came away wet with blood. His hauberk must have saved him from the worst of the blow, but the chain links had broken and now sagged open across his shoulders. The wound, from what he could tell, was shallow. It was the bruising that would give him trouble.

Awful sounds still poured from the postern, but Lukas felt curiously detached from what was happening. Count Raymond's words still rang in his ears. *It's suicide...You go, Bessarion.* The one-eyed count had never really valued him—or his people, he thought bitterly.

"Did you meet with those Watchers of yours?" Count Raymond had asked a few days ago. At first Lukas had been kept busy running to and fro across Antioch with messages to the other princes as they rapidly co-ordinated their defence, bringing in what supplies and reinforcements they could from the Frankish-held fortresses around Antioch. Once Kerbogha had established his blockade, however, Count Raymond returned to his politicking. "Will they swear fealty to me?"

Lukas had his speech prepared. "Do you know who built this city, my lord? It was a Greek emperor, Seleucis, a successor to Alexander the Great. He named the city after his father Antiochus. For hundreds of years, she ruled an empire stretching from Anatolia to Persia. Even under the Romans, Antioch remained a queen. The capital of Oriens, responsible for all Syria, Palestine, and Egypt."

"And?"

"The people of this city are not accustomed to serve foreigners, my lord. They like their independence."

At that, Count Raymond snorted explosively. "Then they're fools. This isn't a little town like Marash, it's a great city claimed by the emperor, the Turks, and Count Bohemond. If they want autonomy, they should leave and found their own city. Unless they can raise a third army, greater than either ours or Kerbogha's. Can they?"

Put like that, it *did* sound ridiculous. "No, my lord."

"Then they should be grateful for what they can get. Adhemar plans to reinstate their Patriarch. I mean to see the city ceded to Alexius as we all promised. Tell your precious Watchers that Bohemond certainly doesn't mean to give them any sort of independence, and their best hope is to stick by me—and Emperor Alexius."

"Yes, my lord. I'll tell them that." Not that it would make any difference. He might not have an army, but he meant to have the Bessarion Lance. That same evening, he'd gone to Zarides and revealed the secret of the lance's hiding-place. The Watchers had been eager to help him. Everything was arranged: the sacristan bribed to hand over the key, the picks and shovels to break the ground, even an official-looking seal affixed to a paper licensing a team of workmen to excavate the ancient crypt. With the basilica back in Christian hands, a great deal of work was being planned to restore the church. No one would be surprised to come across workmen by night.

Above the gulley, the sun moved across the sky towards its zenith, beating down on Lukas and Count Evrard with a foretaste of summer's heat. The scar that Ayla had left on his face the night of their marriage itched with sweat. Beyond their hiding-place, the sound of battle ebbed and flowed.

"It's a good sign," le Puiset said at length in a strained whisper. "If we can still hear the battle, the Turks haven't broken through to the city. Our men are holding."

"No thanks to you and your friends." Lukas had spent so much of the last year biting his tongue and hiding his thoughts. Now he spoke with a freedom that was as terrifying as it was intoxicating. "What went wrong, out there at the camp?"

Sweat glistened on le Puiset's forehead, and his face twisted in agony. "The plan was to fall back to a shield-wall like the one we used at Dorylaeum. Count Raymond ought to have been there. Instead he chased off to the citadel."

"Only because he thought you had everything in hand. Didn't you?" No answer from the count. "The Turks didn't see you coming, or you'd never have made it so far into their camp. They should have been caught unawares. Instead they rallied and counterattacked. You must have lost the initiative somehow. Saints! You scattered to plunder, didn't you?"

Le Puiset scowled. "There was nothing I could do. If the men won't listen to their commander…"

"Then the whole debacle is still your fault," Lukas said with a derisive laugh. "He who excuses, only accuses."

Le Puiset's hand tightened on the hilt of his dagger, and for a terrifying moment Lukas thought the count would lunge at him. Instead, his throat worked and he turned his face away, as though consumed by shame and in too much pain to hide it.

Presently, the count growled, "Why are you here, Greek?"

"Count Raymond sent me with a message. For what it's worth, he wanted you to rally your men and buy him time to defend the postern."

"I didn't mean that." Le Puiset fell silent. For a moment Lukas thought he would let the matter drop. Then he said, "First you fraternise with the Turks, then you hide me from them. I would have thought you'd be happy to let them kill me."

Lukas waited until the count looked up at him before replying: he wanted to savour the look on le Puiset's face when he leaned close, trembling a little before the enormity of what he was about to say.

"I don't mean for you to die at their hands. I mean for you to die at mine."

Something like fear flickered over the count's face.

"You wouldn't dare."

"You think I am some frightened little peasant. You constantly underestimate what I would or would not dare."

"Then do it. I dare you. Cut my throat. No one will see. Have your revenge like the coward you are."

Again, Lukas felt the heady consciousness of power: the count was in his mercy, and knew it. And to think he had nearly left him behind, to a quick clean death at the hands of his enemies!

"Kill you now?" he said, with a laugh. "No. Ayla deserves a better vengeance than that."

Le Puiset's eyebrows arched in outrage.

"You're weak," Lukas went on, sensing the words that would cut deepest. "It would be like killing a child. That's what you expect, isn't it? That I'll cut your throat when you're helpless? Oh, no. When I kill you, you'll be whole. You'll be armed. You'll have every advantage due to you by birth and station, and *then* I'll destroy you. And you'll know *exactly* how far from being your equal I am."

For an instant le Puiset was speechless—perhaps out of incredulity or anger, but Lukas thought it was at least partly out of fear. Then he gave a forced laugh. "You're deluded. You've been listening to minstrels and it's turned your head."

"Tell yourself that, if it makes you feel better." Lukas glanced towards the sky. It was now noon, and his stomach had been aching with hunger for three hours at least. It wasn't the worst hunger he'd ever felt, but the day's exertions had left him feeling almost dizzy. "I don't suppose you managed to come back from that little jaunt with any food."

"*I* wasn't trying to loot."

"Maybe you should have, since you couldn't achieve anything else."

Le Puiset sucked in a laboured breath. "If we get out of this alive, I'm going to whip you like a mule."

Lukas ground his teeth. If they got out of this alive, he would have his father's lance. Let Count Evrard try to whip him *then*.

Beside him, le Puiset gave a hiss of breath. "That bird—!"

Lukas followed his gaze to where a raven had alighted on an outcrop of stone above them. He blinked, disbelieving. In its beak it carried a fragment of bread as big as Lukas' fist. Soft, fresh, smelling faintly of yeast.

For a moment he and le Puiset were both still and speechless. Then the raven's mouth opened, dropping the morsel straight into Lukas' lap. This done, it spread its wings and soared away, only to be followed by a second carrying a strip of dried meat that landed beside the first.

Lukas felt numb. This couldn't be happening. Not to *him*. He was dreaming, or sun-struck. He looked into the sky to see a cloud of ravens circling above them, winging from the plundered Turkish camp and back again. A third bird began its descent, another small object in its beak.

"Lord, have mercy," Count Evrard muttered, raising a hand to cross himself.

With that, Lukas found his wits again. He hurled a pebble at the next bird, driving it back into the air with a startled caw. "Get away from us!" he hissed.

"What are you doing?" le Puiset sputtered as Lukas flung stone after stone at the birds. "Stop it! Are you mad? They're bringing us food!"

One bird swooped low, releasing a small glass bottle that hit Lukas on the head before falling into the rocks with a clatter. Lukas could have shouted in frustration. Instead, he got to his feet and hurled one last stone with such force and accuracy that the raven folded its wings and plummeted from the air, dead.

The spell broke.

With loud, angry caws, the drifting flock broke up and scattered in every direction. Lukas dropped to his seat among the stones, his hands shaking as though he'd run a mile. When he lifted his face from his hands, the count was staring at the tiny bottle in his hand.

"This is medicine," he whispered. "Honey salve. They brought us food and medicine. Just...just like milord Saint Elijah, when he was hiding in the desert..."

He hated the way the Frank looked at him, anger lost in awe and a kind of fear that brought Lukas no pleasure at all. *Food and now medicine. Whoever's responsible for this is overdoing it.*

"What does this mean?" Le Puiset licked his dry lips. "You said you had visions...you were telling the *truth?*"

Devil take it. This was exactly what he'd been afraid of. "You Franks shouldn't be so credulous," Lukas snarled, picking up the meat and bread, and tossing it into the gulley.

"What—! Our *food!*"

"Who knows where it's been." As though he hadn't been happy to eat boiled grass and three-days-old carrion, during the winter. As though he hadn't been eating mouldy bread from his hoard just within the last week. He put out his hand for the salve. "Give me that."

"No! What kind of heathen *are* you?" Le Puiset clutched the medicine to his chest. "My God, I wish you *would* kill me."

"Those birds would have given us away to the Turks." Giving up on the salve, Lukas settled back against the rocks, trying to find a spot that was shaded from the hot sun but did not chafe his aching shoulders. Little as he liked to admit it, even to himself, le Puiset's objection worried him. What kind of heathen turned down a genuine miracle? Well, at least some of his dreams and visions lately had come from Lilith. Perhaps she had sent the ravens, too.

Of course Lilith didn't send ravens to feed you, you walnut, his memory of Ayla commented. *That was someone who* cares *about you.*

The ravens were feeding him. His dead wife was calling him a walnut. Le Puiset was staring at him again with a mixture of awe and loathing. Lukas wished he were anywhere but here: perhaps rescuing the count had been a mistake after all.

"We can't move till after dark," he growled, deciding to change the subject. "I'm going to get some rest." If he was to get safely back into the city, descend the mountain, and unearth the Bessarion Lance, he'd want all the sleep he could get. Settling le Puiset's sword across his knees, he lay back, ignoring the pebbles that ground into his shoulders. Le Puiset began fidgeting with his bandages, doubtless meaning to treat the wound with the salve.

Lukas had learned to sleep anywhere. He woke once or twice as the afternoon progressed. Each time the battle continued without losing intensity, so that the day itself took on the quality of a nightmare. Around sunset he slept again, and this time he saw a vision.

He stood on Bohemond's tower atop Silpius where the princes had gathered to plan the sortie. The sun was going down in the west in a welter of red and gold. Beneath Lukas, the mountain and the city were alike dead and decaying. The river was dry, its water mills broken and lifeless. Smoke rose from the city's bones. All about him, on the wall, and on the road that led to the citadel, and heaped around the cistern in the gulley between, lay the bodies of men. Swollen and stinking within their shredded tunics and bloodied armour, their purple fingers still clutched swords and lances.

The world was silent, silent as the tomb: no wind blew, the sounds of battle had faded away, and the stench of corruption was suffocating. Lukas looked for some sign of life, but there was not even a bird in the brazen sky.

He knew at once this was no common dream: it had none of the unreality. On the contrary, it was sharp and hard-edged. He could feel his tunic itching under his sticky arms in the heat.

He stiffened as he realised that Someone stood behind him, hot as fire. It was like standing in front of a furnace: the sweat dried from the skin on the back of his neck.

Speak. It was less a word than a thought imposed upon his soul: a single compelling instinct. Lukas opened his mouth as the word welled up inside him, too great for him to carry, as a woman falls into labour when her child is grown.

And as a woman does not know the face of her child until it is born, the shape of the word that burst from his lips was unknown to him until he spoke it.

"LIVE," he said.

It was no language he knew. It burst into the air like a living, burning thing. Something went out from it and passed through him like a tide of fire. The corpses rattled in their armour and stood on their feet again, Franks and Turks together, and all of them looked up at the tower and at Lukas.

He heard a sound at his elbow and turned to find the count of le Puiset watching him with reverent awe. Count Evrard had always seemed deathly gaunt, as long as Lukas had known him, but that look was gone from him now. There was flesh on his bones, and his cheeks were no longer hollow; the wolfish light was gone from his eyes.

The light changed, losing its bloody aspect. Lukas turned to the western horizon. Above Antioch, the sun rolled up towards noon. The haze cleared. Destruction reversed; Antioch returned to life. Even the grass growing among the rocks became green as spring, and the thorns put out blossoms.

"No," he choked in his own language and, with that, the vision vanished and he was awake.

Night had fallen and the wind had turned cold. Lukas's skin, where he had been unable to protect it from the sun, was hot and tight. The rest of him was shivering with cold and he felt sick, almost feverish. Count Evrard lay at his feet breathing steadily. There was something different about the night, and after a moment he realised it was the silence: the fighting was over. But how had the battle ended? If he approached the wall, would he find Turks holding the ramparts, or Franks?

Lukas climbed to his feet and regretted it at once, for he was light-headed with hunger. When the dizziness passed off, he crawled up the rocks and lay watching the wall, listening for the clink of sentries on patrol. The light had completely faded from the western sky, and watchfires flickered serenely from the towers and the citadel. *Strife...*it must be approaching midnight, and here he was sleeping away his first real chance at getting his father's lance.

Except for the cool breeze, the night was perfectly still, unsullied by the sounds of battle or plunder, near or far. The Franks must have held their position, though at what terrible cost Lukas could not tell.

The pilgrimage had survived another day.

He thought of his vision and the hairs prickled on the back of his neck. He'd seen Antioch filled with the dead... Obviously it was a message, and he was intended to tell someone. Somehow he must reverse the impending destruction, call them back from the brink of the grave.

This time, he did not dare even imagine this to be a lie of Lilith's. Had not the northern Messenger, Kari, begged him to do as much at Dorylaeum? Was he not a Messenger of the Watchers?

Still, devil take it, he *did not mean to be a prophet.* Frustration escaped his clenched teeth in a groan. His mother was the Messenger of the family. Though he had respected her gift, he had never coveted it. It was his father he longed to emulate. And what about Count Evrard? Le Puiset didn't deserve to be pulled back from the brink of the grave, and the longer Lukas thought about it, the less he believed the rest of the Franks deserved it either. That was a dreadful thought, and one that gave him pause. Here they stood on the edge of a sword, and Lukas could save them if he spoke.

He shook himself. Time was short, and he had much to do. The first task was to get le Puiset and himself inside the wall again while the night was quiet and still. Lukas slid down the stones and prodded the mail-clad shape on the stones. "Wake up, count."

There was no response. Lukas took the opportunity to unbuckle the count's sword-belt and put it around his own waist, sliding the blade into the scabbard. After that, he struck le Puiset lightly across the face with his open hand. At this, the count surfaced with a startled yelp. "I'll obey!" he cried, cringing away from Lukas. Then, as he properly awoke: "…Greek?"

For once, Lukas didn't feel like mocking the Frank's frightened outburst. It sounded too much like the frightened vulnerability he felt himself, and he didn't want to let himself feel any sympathy for Ayla's killer. All he said was, "It's time to go. Can you walk?"

Le Puiset snarled that of course he could walk, but Lukas ended up having to lever him to his feet and sling his arm across his shoulders before the two of them were able to venture out into the gulley again. The worst part was getting out of the gulley without making too much noise, but once they reached the level ground sloping towards the postern, the going was easier. The moon had waxed since the night Antioch fell, so there was a little light to show them the way.

They had reached the shadow of the wall and were fumbling for the postern when the sound of scuffling and hard breathing stopped them. Lukas stiffened, tightening his grip on his staff.

"Who goes there?" Count Evrard hissed as muffled feet dropped to the ground beneath the shadow of the wall. In the dark, someone swore in an explosive whisper and then came at them out of the dark with a drawn sword. Just in time, Lukas deflected the wild cut with his staff. For a moment their attacker was face-to-face with them in the faint moonlight, just near enough to discern features. Le Puiset stiffened. Then someone came up behind their attacker, hissing, "Come on!" and a rush of footsteps went down the mountain to the south—fifteen or perhaps twenty men.

"What was *that?*" Lukas panted: the sudden terror of the sword in the dark had left him dizzy with fear.

"That was Guy Trousseau," the count said numbly, staring towards the retreating footsteps. "My cousin…perhaps he's on a mission for the princes."

"Didn't seem that way to me," Lukas said. There'd been a steady stream of deserters from the pilgrimage whenever things became bad enough. "Looked more like your cousin was running away with his tail between his legs."

This time, le Puiset didn't bother answering. Lukas found the postern at last, and beat his staff against the solid timber door as loudly as he dared. "Anyone there? Let us in!"

There was no reply, and he had to abandon all caution and hammer on the door as loudly as he could before a sleepy answer came. "Who's that? I mean, give the watchword."

"*Non nobis, Domine, non nobis, sed nomini tuo da gloriam*—let us in, for heaven's sake; we've been lying low on the mountainside all day. I have the count of le Puiset, and he's injured."

"All right, but we'll have to clear the door." The guard on the other side sounded half asleep, and no wonder, if he'd been fighting all day without a break. There were grumbles and yawns and the sound of grating stone for an agonisingly long time before the postern opened and Lukas dragged the count inside.

"Is there a surgeon on this mountain?" Lukas demanded.

"No. We sent the wounded down at sunset. There's a hospital in the city; we might find a mule to take him down there..."

"No," le Puiset said faintly. "Report first, then hospital."

Lukas rolled his eyes, but the sentry said blankly, "My lord, you can hardly stand."

"I'm not *dead*," le Puiset said testily. "Take me to Count Bohemond."

Count Bohemond was in his headquarters, the tower facing the citadel. As for Count Raymond, the sentry explained, he had survived the battle and retreated into the city to quell some disquiet there. Lukas could not help feeling abandoned. It made no sense to have hard feelings: so many knights and counts had been left for dead in the same way, even le Puiset. And yet...

It was a difficult journey in the faint moonlight, le Puiset dragging on him like a dead weight but angrily denying any need to stop, to rest. There wasn't a single sound on the hilltop apart from the sighing of the wind. Once, Lukas tripped over a body and had the dreadful feeling that he had wandered back into his vision. Instead there was a dim mutter from the man underfoot and a moment later he rolled away.

Lukas began to realise just how ferocious the battle must have been, for the men to have fallen asleep where they stood.

The climb up the narrow stairs to the tower was punishing but, at last, sweating and shaking with hunger, Lukas manhandled the fainting le Puiset through the narrow archway leading from the wall to the tower's interior. Within, a light was burning as Count Bohemond spoke in an undertone with five other knights as bleary and exhausted-looking as himself, their armour hacked and bloody. All of them turned and stared as Lukas staggered within and deposited le Puiset unceremoniously on the floor.

He straightened slowly, realising that he was once again facing Bohemond in a tower, far from his own master. The South Norman count's eyebrows climbed as he recognised le Puiset, then Bessarion. This was going to be awkward; worse, in a way, than explaining his reasons for meeting clandestinely with the enemy. And with le Puiset back among his own people, he *must* get down to the city; Zarides was waiting for him. So he simply said, "I believe this is one of yours. Good evening."

"Don't leave."

"My lord, I have errands to run in the city."

"They'll wait." Bohemond squatted beside le Puiset. "Count. Are you with us?"

Le Puiset rallied a little. "I'm with you," he said in a voice of drunken clarity. The torn strip of cloth around his thigh showed fresh blood where it had soaked through the bandage, and his face was pale and covered in perspiration. "I beg your pardon, my lord. The fault was mine. A better leader would have kept them from dispersing to plunder, and then, like a fool, I went and got myself wounded..." A shuddering breath. "This whole disaster is—"

"Don't blame yourself," Bohemond said quickly. "No man can do more than his best."

Le Puiset made no reply; he seemed to drift away into some waking dream. Bohemond glanced up at Lukas.

"You've tended his wound? Was it serious?"

Lukas shook his head. "Deep, my lord, but not mortal, and we had ointment for it. But we hid all day in the gulley in the hot sun with no food and water. And then he insisted on coming directly to you." That triggered a memory. Lukas hesitated for a moment, then decided to buy goodwill, if he could. "My lord, did you send Guy of Trousseau on a mission outside the wall?"

"Did I—no! I've sent no missions outside the wall. What have you seen?"

Briefly, Lukas described their encounter with le Puiset's cousin. By the end of it, Count Bohemond was exchanging tight-lipped glances with his council.

"Deserters," one of them spat before Lukas was even halfway through his tale.

Another of the Norman knights shook his head. "There's only so much we can take. We've had seven months of nightmare and now *this*? We're surrounded and the Turks have an open door into the city. It's useless. I'm telling you! We should negotiate a surrender and leave."

"No, by the Virgin! I won't have it," Bohemond spat. "We can *do* this, I tell you. We fought back and forth across this scrap of wilderness for ten hours straight, and against all the odds we kept the Turks out of the city. The terrain works in our favour. There is Kerbogha with the greatest army in the history of the world, and what can he do with it—nothing!"

"He has an open door into the city," someone repeated.

"Yes, but what can he *do* with it? It's like pouring a bottle of wine: there may be any amount of liquid in the bottle, but only so much of it can flow through the opening at once. We held them off, gentlemen! All day, with a fraction of their men—and it will never be forgotten as long as the world lasts."

Such was Bohemond's magic that the atmosphere in the tower lightened at once, even when the pessimistic knight muttered, "It's not like we have any other choice."

Still lost in his waking dream, Le Puiset seemed not to have heard any of the conversation. Desperate to escape, Lukas cleared his throat. "Should I find someone with a mule to carry Count Evrard down the mountain?"

Bohemond shook his head. "We used all our beasts of burden getting the wounded down at sunset. Le Puiset might as well stay here in the tower; it's the safest place on this mountaintop, which isn't saying much. You had better go down into the city and find his people. Make sure they come up to fetch him by dawn, for Kerbogha hasn't finished with us yet. There will be hard fighting tomorrow, too."

At last. Lukas found himself nearly trembling with nervous energy. The additional errand was a small price to pay for his escape, and perhaps there was still time to make his rendezvous. Squatting beside le Puiset, he waved a hand before the count's unresponsive face. "Tell me where to find your people."

Count Evrard turned slowly to look at him, eyes unfocused. "What?"

It wasn't physical shock this time; it must be a reaction to the fighting. Lukas had seen this often in the past seven months. Mortal flesh could take only so much danger and fear.

"I believe his sister has a house in the city, east of the basilica on the bank of the Parmenius stream," Count Bohemond volunteered.

That woke le Puiset. "No!" he slurred. "Don't you dare—!"

"Don't worry," Lukas told him with a sigh. "Believe me, I won't spend any more time in your sister's company than I can help." Bowing, he let himself out of the tower and unslung his staff. He had a long walk ahead of him, but already his heart beat like a winging bird at the thought of the basilica and the treasure within.

One step at a time, Greek. Ayla's voice echoed in his mind. *One step at a time.*

Lukas took a deep breath…and then that first step.

Chapter XV.

His first hint of something amiss was the fire.

The white mountain path glimmered with reflected red light. In the city below, bonfires crackled like torches in the forums and intersections. In places, whole buildings were on fire. Once or twice, as the steep path brought Lukas nearer the city, he heard the faint sound of battle-cries and crashing weapons. The sounds came and went swiftly, nightmarishly.

Near the foot of the mountain where the road entered the city, Lukas found a barricade manned by some of Count Raymond's Provençals. "Don't shoot! It's me, Lukas Bessarion," he told them. "What's going on?"

"Some Turks got down the mountain and made trouble with their coreligionists in the city," said the knight in command. "Turns out we didn't clean house as well as we might have, last week." He turned, scanning the sergeants and peasants manning the barricade. "I'll send you an escort to the palace if you want."

That would be a comfort—if he were going to the palace, which he wasn't. Lukas readjusted le Puiset's sword-belt, a comforting weight on his bony hips. "Don't worry, I can take care of myself," he said with more bravado than he felt. He ventured into the fitfully lighted streets, thinking that if it came to the worst, at least Lilith was trying to keep him alive, and so, for that matter, were his visions. Neither of which was a particularly comforting thought.

The going was easy enough at first, the broad street leading from the mountain to the palace lighted with blazing lamps and patrolled by huddled, nervous parties of Frankish knights. Thanks to the brown skin and dark hair marking him as something other than Frankish, Lukas was stopped again and again, but each time he was recognised and allowed to proceed. In the forum outside the palace—lit with a bonfire and surrounded by skittish-looking Provençals—Lukas hesitated, keeping to the shadows and trying to decide where to go first. Zarides would be waiting for him with the other Watchers at Ilkay's house in Rhodion, but he could hear the sounds of intermittent fighting within the narrow, barricaded streets.

Better to go directly north on his most urgent errands. The eastern half of the city, like the west, was filled with disturbance—barricades, skirmishes, fires. In order to avoid both the insurgent Turks and the Frankish patrols, Lukas was forced to take a roundabout journey to the great church of the Virgin. This stood not too far from the basilica, one of the few churches in the city that had not been desecrated by the Turks. A small complex of buildings stood beside it to house the canons. As Lukas felt his way to the low door Zarides had described, he wondered whether he was wasting his time entirely. Zarides had told him to be here hours ago. Most likely, he had missed the rendezvous.

All the same, when he rapped against the heavy wooden gate, a small hatch in the door opened at once, letting through a ray of lamplight. A pair of eyes appeared behind the wrought-iron grate. "What is it? Who's there?"

"A son of Heraclius," he said, using the password Zarides had given him. Himself, Lukas didn't think much of the emperor who'd abandoned Antioch to the heretics so many centuries before, but Zarides seemed to venerate the past as an imaginary golden age in which no one had ever disputed the right of a Roman lord to rule. The truth, Lukas knew, was a good deal messier. When they recovered their birthright, Zarides would learn.

"And about time!" the man on the other side of the door hissed. "Here." He shoved a small item through the grate, wrapped in a scrap of papyrus. Lukas seized it, unrolling the paper until a key lay on the palm of his hand—the key to the great basilica.

"Thank you," he whispered. "You've done your people a great service tonight. You'll boast of this in coming years."

"Dear God, I hope not. Don't go telling anyone I helped you," the sacristan said, alarmed. A moment later, the grate slammed, plunging Lukas once more into darkness.

By touch alone, Lukas got Ayla's sling unlooped from his wrist and used it to hang the key around his neck inside his mail and tunic where it would be safe. As he did so, he considered his next steps. It had taken him far longer to cross the city than he expected, and much of the night must already be past. Beyond that, with so much of the city in uproar and the Franks out for blood, it wouldn't be safe to march a band of Watchers across the city to dig in the basilica, even now that he had the key. The delay made him grind his teeth, but at least they *had* the key now. It was only a matter of waiting for the right time to use it.

Meanwhile, he had another errand to run.

Lukas found Emelota of le Puiset in the upper storey of a dingy house built beside the Parmenius torrent not far from the basilica. The lowest floor of the building was home to some sort of shop, which stood dark and silent in the equally dark and silent street; but a flight of external stairs led to an upper room where lamplight flickered at the windows. Lukas didn't know what he expected to find as he knocked on the door, but certainly it was a surprise when Emelota herself opened it. Her face was white and strained, as though she expected bad news—or perhaps that was only her reaction to finding him on the doorstep.

"Lukas Bessarion?" she whispered.

He gave her the news without ceremony. "Your brother's wounded."

She stared at him with enormous, stricken eyes. "How?"

"I didn't do it, if that's what you're asking. The count was assigned to command a sortie, and he took a gash in the thigh. Now he's up in a tower on Silpius, and they want him out of the way. They're expecting an attack at dawn."

At that she nodded, regaining a little composure. "I'll come at once."

For a moment Lukas wasn't sure if he'd heard correctly, but he reminded himself that the Frankish hubris knew no bounds. "Mademoiselle, there's rioting in the streets and the mountain road is treacherous in the dark. Send someone else."

She gave him a rather expressionless look, then stood aside so that he could see past her into the room. "This is all I have."

As he stepped over the threshold, the smell hit him—the sickly scent of fever and bloody flux. The bare, comfortless room was stuffy, its small windows providing little ventilation. Soiled cloths were piled haphazardly into a tub. On a bed in a dark corner, a man lay moving restlessly. A woman sat near him, trying to spoon a tisane down his throat. When she looked up, Lukas recognised one of the Armenian women from the basilica.

"My brother took every spare man up Silpius for the fighting," Emelota added, retreating into the room to take a saddlebag, and beginning to fill it with clean cloths and medicine-jars. "I have no attendants but this good neighbour and Father Adso, our chaplain, and he is as you see him." To Lukas' astonishment, she addressed the other woman in what sounded like broken Arabic. The Armenian nodded, then caught Emelota's hand and murmured something that sounded like a prayer.

She couldn't actually mean to disregard his warning. Lukas cleared his throat, bemused. "You'll never make it—a woman on your own. It's suicide."

She turned to look at him. "I won't be alone. You'll be with me, surely?"

Ah. Well, that was absolutely typical. "Certainly not. I'm due at the palace—"

"At midnight?"

All right, so perhaps Saint-Gilles wouldn't thank him for barging in to report in the middle of the greater sleep: most people woke for a short time around Vigils to pray, relax, or conduct business, but that was still two hours away at least. Lukas tried again. "Your brother won't be pleased if I spend any time with you."

"He can scold me later, when he's safe and mending."

Lukas ran a hand through his hair. He should be in the basilica digging up the Bessarion Lance, not bandying words with an arrogant Frank. "Mademoiselle, you he may scold, but me he will whip like a mule if he gets the chance. I'm not your servant, and I've already gone far beyond the extra mile for your brother today. Now, if you'll excuse me, I'll return to my own master."

"Wait," she said, grasping his hand even as he went to slam the door behind him. Her voice dipped. "I know what you are, Lukas Bessarion."

All the hairs on the back of his neck stood up as he turned to look into her eyes. She could mean anything at all, he reminded himself. "Are you threatening me?"

"What? No!" She sucked in a deep breath, scrutinising his face with great dark eyes as though he was a book to be read. "You see things others don't. You have a gift. So do I… You're meant to help me."

He hadn't even told the Watchers about his gift. Lukas yanked away from her almost violently. "The devil I am!" He was halfway down the stairs when she followed him at a run, tossing a thin mantle over her shoulder as she came, and settling the bag of supplies at her hip.

"I'll prove it to you," she told him breathlessly when she'd caught up to him in the street.

"Go home, mademoiselle."

"You know I can't do that."

A cacophony broke out nearby, the sound of shouts and the clash of steel forming a chaotic counterpoint to Emelota's pattering feet and startled gasp. Lukas lifted his eyes to the waxing moon and sighed, coming to a halt. She couldn't trail through the streets like this at his heels. Perhaps if he humoured her, he might persuade her to go home.

"All right, prove it to me."

Her face was a pale blur in the darkness beside him. "You need to ask for guidance."

"It won't work. My visions don't come at command."

"That's only because you don't know how to ask."

"All right," he snapped, turning his face to the sky. "Go on, give me a vision."

And the vision came.

The air took on the familiar crystalline clarity, everything within eyesight springing into sharp focus so that it was like looking at a tapestry or an icon. Even the colours and shadows intensified, the darkness of the night no longer a barrier to sight. His spirit rose from his body and flew through the twisting streets of Antioch at a dizzying speed. Every turn impressed itself upon his mind, along with the dangers that awaited them. Here, they must turn aside to avoid a barricade some of the Turks were erecting in one of the narrower streets. There, they must stop and wait until a handful of soldiers who had stolen from the citadel and made their way down by secret mountain paths into the city could pass by and vanish within one of the houses. There, again, he must call out the watchword so that a gang of Franks with crossbows and uneasy trigger-fingers did not shoot him down.

All of this unspooled in his mind's eye within a few heartbeats. Then he was back in his own body, breathing hard and more than a little terrified.

He reeled. Emelota of le Puiset caught him by the shoulders—she was taller than him and nearly as strong as a man—but he threw off her steadying hands and backed away.

"What are you?" he asked raggedly.

"I don't know. I can usually tell what people intend to do, and sometimes I can tell the purpose they are meant to fulfil. I knew you were supposed to ask for guidance about me. What happened? What did you see?"

God have mercy, she's genuine! Ayla's remembered voice was excited. *Lukas, don't you see what this means? She could help you with your visions!*

He let out his breath in a rush. "You're a Revealer."

"I like the sound of that," she said in an absurdly pleased tone. "I've never had a name for it! Are there others like me? And will you take me to my brother now?"

"Saints." There was no point denying he'd seen something; his reactions would have told her that. *Yeh, reactions or not, you won't shrug this one off so easily.* Lukas blinked, pushing Ayla to the back of his mind. "Look, I've better things to do with my time than to run up and down mountains for your brother. I'm going back to Count Raymond, and he'll send someone up the mountain to fetch the count."

"But it's supposed to be us. Isn't it?"

He had the feeling she would be difficult to lie to. The silence stretched out. The practical side of him that sounded so much like Ayla pointed out helpfully that he had not received instructions for how to return to the palace. With the unrest in the city, he could be killed half a dozen times between this house and the palace.

"This is madness." He rubbed his eyes, conscious of a headache building after spending a whole day in the hot sun. "The city's up in arms, and I won't be able to protect you."

"After the year I've passed, I don't frighten so easily. You had a vision, didn't you?"

He didn't have time for this! Lukas wanted only to dig in the basilica, to unearth the lance. The night was fleeting: dawn must only be two or three hours away. *A fat lot of digging you'll manage in that amount of time,* put in the part of Ayla he still carried with him, and he had to admit she was right. Even if he survived the trek across the city, even if he was able to lead his Watchers back to the basilica in safety, it would be nearing dawn by the time they arrived.

Beyond that, he felt quite certain that if he walked away from the Frankish girl, she would either trail behind him, or worse, try to climb the mountain alone. She would never survive: she had neither Ayla's survival instincts nor even his sister Marta's impulsive physical courage. If he left her, he left her to die. Rescuing her at Dorylaeum, being cheered for it even by the Franks, was one of the few memories he was truly proud of, and he couldn't tarnish that moment by abandoning her now.

"All right, have it your way!" The sooner he washed his hands of the whole fool family, the sooner he could see to his own affairs. "I'll take you up Silpius on one condition. I may be a Messenger, but I don't want anyone to know about it; understood? Keep it to yourself."

"Oh, a *Messenger?* Is that what I call you?"

"Not if you want my help."

She must have smiled, because he could hear it in her voice. "As you like. Lead on."

Resigned to his fate, Lukas hurried Emelota along the path he had been shown, keeping to the shadowed streets where the lamps had not been lit. He had no difficulty finding his way, for the moon shed a faint light and the vision remained crisp in his memories.

Despite his hurried pace, Emelota kept up with him as easily as ever, her long legs swallowing up the distance. "You know the city well," she observed.

"I came here several times with my family," he admitted. "I still have… unfinished business here."

"Oh?"

Ask her about it, you walnut! Ayla prompted. She had a point. Just as he had given up hoping his visions might be of any real use, along came Emelota. With a Revealer's guidance, he might be able to do more with his visions; might know better when to seek them out.

If only Emelota had been anything but a Frank, and the sister of his enemy.

Look, why are you calling me a walnut all of a sudden? It used to be cucumber. *Cucumbers are just green and silly, but walnuts are dense and hard to crack. Well, if I am dense, at least I'm not green and silly any more.*

He sighed.

"I don't suppose you've any idea how I'm supposed to go about it," he said. *Or whether you're intended to succeed at all,* Ayla put in, but he didn't say that aloud. Failure was the one eventuality he refused to contemplate.

"Go about what?—Oh, your business." There was a silence. "I don't know. Perhaps if you told me more, I could help you better."

But he couldn't risk that. "Never mind," he growled. It wasn't as though he hadn't asked for visions concerning the lance, and received only more silence. What was it all supposed to mean? That he wasn't meant to know? Or that he wasn't meant to know *yet*?

Ahead, just as his vision had shown him, three Turkish townsmen pelted around a corner into the street. They wavered when they saw Lukas and Emelota, but then made up their minds and charged directly for him.

Lukas grabbed Emelota by the shoulders and shoved her towards a door set in a nearby alcove. "Get back."

"I'm not leaving you," she protested, eyes wide.

The doorway offered protection on three sides and a step to give him the advantage of height. Even without the guidance of his vision Lukas knew he'd have to be a madman to make a stand anywhere else. "You aren't," he snapped.

He put his back to the door and turned, raising his staff. But, as he'd foreseen, the Turks never came near him. They only sidled past watchfully, not close enough to engage. A moment later they vanished into the shadows, and the sound of their footsteps faded into the night.

"You let them go?" Emelota sounded horrified.

Lukas stepped into the street again, his hands shaking around his staff, weak defence as it would have been against three desperate foes. "They were too many and glad to let me be. We aren't looking for trouble."

With a beckoning gesture he set off down the street again. What did she expect of him? Was he inhuman? Could he go a year without the proper food or medicine, carry her brother from a battlefield, climb down a mountain, and then take on three enemies alone? They would have gone through him like a winter wind.

The thought distracted him at the moment he should have been finding a hiding-place for them both. The narrow street they were following spat them out into the very path of a company of well-armed Turks that marched down the street in a phalanx. By the time his ears heard the scuff of feet it was too late. His heart leaped into his throat and he swept Emelota back into the alley.

"Get into one of the houses, if you can," he told her, pointing towards a small door with a solitary lamp burning over it.

"These ones want blood," she whispered, with a terrified look at the coming soldiers, who had turned aside to follow them.

He didn't need a Revealer to tell him that. There was no time to reply, no time to plan. In a bright shard of vision Lukas glimpsed the foremost of his attackers closing in. Reversing the iron-shot foot of his staff, he shot it viciously into the unsuspecting Turk's gut. The man went down, winded. Beyond him, the next Turk crouched behind a light buckler. Lukas backed away to buy time. The Turk charged.

Another flash of vision: a warning, the exact path of the enemy's sword-point. Lukas flung himself to the left, dodging the blow and putting every ounce of strength into a backhanded riposte from his staff, dealing the enemy a ringing blow to the man's cheekbone beneath his steel cap. With a crunch of broken bone the enemy crumpled onto his face, his hands clutching the stones at Emelota's feet.

She looked up at him with a milk-pale face. "They're running," she murmured.

Lukas turned to find the alley empty but for themselves and the two groaning men on the stones. The Turks on the street shouted a warning as they fled. Moments later, shadows clad in the silvery glint of Frankish mail raced after them.

He was still watching when there was a scuffle behind him, and Emelota screamed a warning. One of the Turks had climbed dizzily to his feet, the one Lukas had only winded. He supported himself against the wall, breathing hard and fumbling for his sword. Lukas moved without thinking, snatching le Puiset's sword from the scabbard and spitting the Turk through the midsection. The man stared at him with shocked eyes and a dim gasp. Blood spilled from his mouth, but his left arm came up with a dagger, arcing for Lukas' unprotected neck. Releasing the sword, Lukas thrust his staff up, striking the Turk's wrist and flinging the dagger into the gutter.

The man fell to his hands and knees, but he was still fumbling for his sword. Emelota had been silent for a moment; Lukas turned to find her watching him with enormous eyes. He motioned her to turn away, then retrieved le Puiset's sword from between the defiant Turk's ribs. He wished he'd also told her to put her hands over her ears: the Turk found his voice as he died.

He took a deep, shaken breath as whatever had stampeded through his veins like fire half a minute ago began to recede, leaving him with feeble hands and a hammering heart. The knot of pain that was never entirely absent from his stomach tightened. It had been an ugly fight, culminating in inglorious butchery, but it wasn't revulsion he felt: it was sheer numbness. Surely he ought to feel something more than this...

"Can I look now?"

"Yes, come on." He took Emelota's hand. The street beyond the alley was clear again now, and he guided her swiftly across the intersection into the welcome darkness of the alley beyond, following the path laid down in his vision.

Were they becoming stronger, more regular, these visions of his? Lukas wished they would confine themselves to saving his life in battle; that, he could manage. He wished he didn't have to wonder whether they were only trying to keep him alive for some unfathomable purpose.

"You fight differently to anyone else I've met," Emelota observed, as the streets they followed began to slope upwards at the foot of Silpius.

"Oh?" Lukas felt exhausted: from the danger, from the battle, from the constant keyed-up tension. He didn't particularly want to have this conversation now, especially when she went on:

"You fight like a peasant. You don't mind running away."

He let go of her and came to a halt in the street, still breathing hard from the battle. "You must be joking."

"Why would I be joking? It's true."

"Saints, you Franks," he growled. "You think nothing of throwing yourselves half-prepared into impossible situations, and then it amazes you when you're mown down by your hundreds. *Oh, God's will, hooray for the martyrs.* I'll tell you why I run away. The last time my belly was full was October. I have nothing to protect me, save for a mail shirt and a quarterstaff. I have no particular wish to die, and I take it neither do you. Or your brother, for that matter."

"Oh, I didn't mean to insult you. It's good sense. I wish my brother saw it the same way."

Her words cut his anger off at the knees. "I beg your pardon?"

"That's the problem with Evrard. All the things they say about honour and courage and shame…he takes them all quite seriously, you know. Most knights know they aren't demigods; they know how much of it is just talk. But Evrard doesn't. He believes it, and since he knows he'll never measure up…" She took a deep breath. "It's why he hates you, even though everyone is laughing up their sleeve at him for being so obsessed. He's so careful of his reputation that he doesn't know how to respect himself, simply for doing the right thing."

"Then he's a fool," Lukas snapped, but he felt a hot delight in his heart. If that was true, then when the time came, le Puiset would fight him just to save face. Good.

"Oh, I think peasants have very good sense sometimes."

"I'm not a peasant," he said. Then his stomach cramped, reminding him that he had not eaten since very early the previous morning. "Did you bring any food?"

She glanced down at her saddle-bag, embarrassed. "No. Evrard ate our last bread the night before last, when he went up the mountain. And in the morning Father Adso had fallen ill… Lusine brought what she could, but it's all gone."

Lukas swore in Greek, under his breath, and glanced at the eastward sky. It was difficult to say how long they had been twisting through the streets of Antioch, and they yet had to find their way up Silpius—carefully, in the dark—by dawn. After only a week's siege, food was already becoming scarce in the city, and they couldn't spare the time to look for some now. "It doesn't matter. Let's go."

The rest of the journey went smoothly; they were able to keep clear of both Turks and Franks a little while, until they reached the barricade across the narrow white road leading up Silpius. His vision had warned him of this: the guard had been changed since he descended the mountain, and Lukas approached with his heart in his mouth, wishing he was enough of a peasant to feel comfortable hiding behind Emelota.

"Ho there!" He called out in Frankish, stepping into the light of the last street-lamp. At once a bright shard of vision struck him: he recoiled even as Emelota made a sound of alarm, seized him by the loose mail between his shoulders, and yanked him backwards.

A crossbow-bolt hissed through the darkness where he had just stood.

"Hold it, Saracen! What's your business?" a Frankish voice challenged them.

"I'm Syrian! I work for Count Raymond, and I know the watchword," he protested in Frankish—his knowledge of the language, as always, his best passport.

"You do, do you? Let's hear it." But when he recited the *Non nobis,* there was a grim silence. "Wrong watchword. The count changed it at midnight, but it's not being given out to just everyone. Don't you know they need all able-bodied men on the wall? Have you reported to the palace?"

With a high-pitched and wholly feminine sound of disgust, Emelota stepped into the lamplight and drew herself up to her full—considerable—height. "Kindly stop shooting at us. I am Emelota of le Puiset, and I'm going up Silpius to fetch my brother, the count. He's been wounded, and Count Raymond's interpreter is here as my guide."

"Holy Virgin!" The involuntary oath was followed by the scrape as a lantern-shutter opened. A group of men hurried from the darkness, holding a lantern of their own. The Franks were pale and grim, bloodstained and exhausted. The wounds they had sustained would ordinarily have put them in the infirmary, yet here they were on watch duty at the foot of the mountain. The princes must be desperate, if they had begun to press injured men into service.

"Forgive us, mademoiselle, we didn't realise it was a lady. Your brother's on Silpius, you say?"

"In Count Bohemond's tower," Lukas put in.

"That's where your brother is?" The Franks looked at Emelota with new respect. "Mademoiselle, it's dangerous up there. They're expecting an attack at dawn."

"I know." Her lips pulled thin. "Sir, the sooner I see him the sooner I'll be able to get him to safety."

The Frank shrugged, glancing to the sky above the mountain, as though he expected to see the dawn-light already crowning the embattled slopes. But the sky was dark, and he gave a resigned sigh. "Do as you will, but I won't be responsible for it."

Chapter XVI.

"Ah, there you are," Galdemar called out as Saint-Gilles and Adhemar led their small retinue through the palace gates. "I've been looking for you all morning!"

"Then you can't have been waiting long." Saint-Gilles glanced towards the east. The twin mountains—the black bulk of Silpius and the narrower peak of Stauron to its left—were only black outlines against the faintly lightening dawn sky. It was still too dark to see the small dark blot of Bohemond's flag flying from the tower he had made his headquarters. Was the Norman count still the master of Silpius? Saint-Gilles paused, raising a hand for silence, but if the morning's battle had already begun, he could not hear it.

Bohemond must hold the mountaintop. Otherwise all of them were lost; and thanks to the previous day's debacle it would be at least partly his fault. All night Saint-Gilles had felt the eyes of his men on him like rasping sand on a sunburn. No one was fooled as to why yesterday's sortie had ended so badly; he'd even heard two of his vassals, Raymond Pilet and Isoard of Die, muttering about rivalries growing out of all bounds.

They were right. That was the part that irked him most. He ought to have been focused on the job at hand, defending the pilgrimage from Kerbogha. Instead, he was caught up in his feud with Bohemond. He'd lost sight of the real threat, and now he was going to pay for it with the loyalty of his own followers.

"I've been patrolling the city, seeing that the gates are locked and the wall secure," Saint-Gilles explained, laying his spear in the crook of his arm so that he could ease off his gloves. After spending most of the previous day caught in the battle on Silpius, his whole body ached and one hand was swollen from a crushing blow: the flat of a Turkish battleaxe had beaten it against the wall. He had slept a bare couple of hours before rising at Nones to patrol the city, and this morning he felt strangely vulnerable, as though he was made of glass and all men could see through him. To distract Galdemar from the fact that all this vigilance was at least partly in atonement for yesterday's mistakes, he added: "It seems some of the men let down ropes and fled in the night."

Galdemar blanched. "How many?"

"We don't know. Some of them were quite highly placed, though. Grandmesnil and his brother, and Guy of Trousseau."

Galdemar drew in a hissing breath. "They've made cowards of themselves?"

"There's only so much mortal flesh can endure before it breaks," Adhemar put in. "After the last seven months we should all know that." The bishop looked pale and attenuated this morning, as though the wind might blow him away, and his words struck Saint-Gilles with an ominous ring.

"Have you eaten this morning, Adhemar?"

"Yes, mother." The gleam of humour in the bishop's eyes reassured him, but only a little. "I'm only tired, old friend. I've been on the wall all night, like you."

While Saint-Gilles had busied himself in the city, Adhemar had taken command of the wall itself. Saint-Gilles didn't trust him to take proper care of himself; not when food and sleep were at such a premium, and the papal legate felt responsible for the whole pilgrimage. The bishop seemed loath to admit that he, too, had a breaking point. Saint-Gilles sighed and turned towards the palace itself, determined that Adhemar should have a square meal and a good sleep before he went out on the wall again.

"The desertions are only part of the problem," he told Galdemar as they crossed the entrance-hall and went towards an inner courtyard, where immense marble pillars bordered a small garden of roses and aromatic herbs, and a little pool of water to cool the air. "I met Flanders trying to assemble a new battalion to replace the wounded and exhausted up on Silpius. There were not many volunteers. It's as though our fighting force is melting away—and they can't have all fled over the walls. They must be lying low, hiding in the houses."

He couldn't entirely blame them for it, not after disgracing himself yesterday. His own head did not feel particularly secure on his shoulders. Kerbogha's threat lay on the city like a cloud, and he read fear and desperation in the eyes of every man in his following.

There was only one man in the city that seemed to be having the time of his life. Up on Silpius, Bohemond was swaggering about, accentuating his limp. Did the South Norman mean to turn the situation to his own advantage somehow? Stupid question: of course he did. But how? How many magnificently audacious plans could one man have hiding up his sleeve?

"All we can do is pray for help," Saint-Gilles added in a growl. If his messenger had got through to Alexius—if they dug in their feet atop Silpius and refused to budge, if their food held out, if no one's nerve broke, if, if, *if...*

Galdemar snapped his fingers. "As it happens, that's why I was looking for you."

Saint-Gilles pulled to a stop so abrupt that Adhemar almost sleepwalked into him. "What's this? You have help?"

His friend shook his head. "Look, I don't know. You should speak to the boy yourself." A glance at Adhemar. "Bishop, you'll want to see him, too."

"What boy?" Saint-Gilles demanded. For an instant he hoped Galdemar meant Lukas Bessarion—but Bessarion was dead, trapped in the rout outside the walls yesterday.

Here in the palace's central courtyard, some comfortable, low-backed chairs and a table bearing a scanty breakfast had been set out in the peristyle. Nearby, a young man was waiting for them, flanked by two sergeants of Saint-Gilles' household. It was not Lukas Bessarion for, despite his dark hair and browned skin, this young man was certainly

Provençal. Dressed in ragged clothes with a patchy beard, he was dirty and unkempt: spattered with blood, some of which appeared to be his own, and terribly thin, like many of the peasants in the army of God. His eyes, however, were hot like molten glass.

He did not wait for an invitation to speak. "My lords," he rasped, taking a painful limp towards them, and then falling upon his knees. "I come bearing good news. My lord Saint Andrew has appeared to me four times in a vision, and he bade me say this: *Arise, go and tell the people of God to have no fear. For they shall be victorious everywhere, and within five days God will send them such a sign as shall fill them with joy and confidence, so that if they will fight, their enemies shall all be overcome, and no one shall stand against them.*"

The hoarse voice filled the courtyard, echoing from the polished stone of the floor. Saint-Gilles' eyebrows rose, and he shot a reproachful look at Galdemar. The bishop had been up on the ramparts all night, and Galdemar dragged this madman in to be questioned and doubtless debunked?

At Saint-Gilles' incredulous look, Galdemar shrugged. "I think you should hear what he has to say."

"Of course we will," Adhemar put in, as gracious as ever.

Very well, Saint-Gilles thought, if the man chose to turn demagogue he might be trouble, and it made sense to investigate his claims quickly, before sending him on his way.

Sinking into one of the seats provided, Adhemar blinked at the young man. "Saint Andrew, you say?"

"Yes, my lord. Again and again he has commanded me to bring you this message, but I was too fearful to put myself before such great lords."

"You had better explain it all from the beginning."

"My name is Peter Bartholomew." Despite his claim to be fearful of thrusting himself upon their attention, the boy spoke with conscious dignity. "The apostle first visited me during the earthquake shortly after Christmas. He was clad in brilliant, shining garments like an angel of light; his hair and beard were red speckled with white, his eyes were black, and his countenance agreeable. The one with him was younger, taller, and…"

His voice trailed off for a moment.

"And?" Adhemar prompted.

"Fairer than the sons of men," the boy said.

Adhemar glanced towards Saint-Gilles, alarm deep in his eyes. It was only with that look that Saint-Gilles realised exactly what Bartholomew was claiming.

"Did *He* speak to you?" asked the bishop.

"No, only the apostle. Saint Andrew and his companion came to me three times more: at Edessa, at Saint Simeon, and at Mamistra, as I was travelling in search of food. Each time he gave me the same message: *Arrange a meeting with the bishop of le Puy and the count of Saint-Gilles. Ask them: Why doesn't Adhemar spend more time preaching and exhorting the people, blessing them with the Cross he carries? They are weak and fearful; this would give them strength."*

The bishop gave no sign of resenting this; Saint-Gilles wondered at Adhemar's humility and self-command. "It is a reasonable question. Was there more?"

"Yes." Bartholomew rose to his feet and turned to face Saint-Gilles directly. "The apostle commanded me to follow him, and he would show me a relic of unmatched holiness which has been set aside for the count of Saint-Gilles since birth. Although the Turks still held the city, the apostle led me into Antioch by the north gate and brought me to the church of the blessed apostle Peter. Two lamps shone, filling the church with light. The apostle and his companion brought me to the column adjacent to the south steps leading up to the altar. There Saint Andrew reached beneath the ground and drew out an ancient lance."

Saint-Gilles' throat was dry; he didn't know why, unless he was fearful before the intensity of the boy's hot eyes—which was ridiculous. He swallowed, levelling a haughty stare at the boy. "A lance?"

"The apostle placed it in my hands," Bartholomew said hoarsely. "And he said, *Look upon the lance which pierced Christ's side, from which the world's deliverance arose.* He made me swear most solemnly that, once the city was captured, I would return to the basilica with twelve men to search for the lance in the place where it had been revealed—and to deliver it to you, for whom it has been set aside as a mark of favour and as a sign that you will never be defeated."

Bartholomew was promising a relic of unimaginable power and sanctity. For *him.* Saint-Gilles' mind whirled. Could it be true? Come to think of it, had he not been given dreams of his own? *I have a gift for you, a weapon that shall never be defeated in battle.* The words came back to him in a husky whisper. He could remember little else, including the identity of the one who had spoken to him. Had he, too, been visited by a saint in his sleep?

"Thank you, Bartholomew." Adhemar's voice broke into his thoughts, shattering the spell in which the young peasant had gripped him. "You did well in coming to us."

Saint-Gilles waved to the sergeants to show the young Provençal out. Of course, one could not take such visionaries at face value. Adhemar, as the papal legate, must now consult with other clergymen and debate the veracity of the vision. As a layman, he must not leap to any conclusions.

And yet…God knew they needed help. God knew *he* needed help. Especially after yesterday's disaster. He'd nearly doomed the whole pilgrimage, and everyone knew it. If this Bartholomew was genuine, he might be exactly what Saint-Gilles needed to keep these people safe, to prevent Bohemond diverting the pilgrimage to serve his own selfish ambitions.

To consolidate power.

He turned to Adhemar with an uncertain smile. "What do you make of *that?*"

With a laugh, Galdemar threw himself down in one of the empty seats and caught an almond in his mouth. "I knew you'd wish to hear him."

The bishop stared at the bread and meat on the table without reaching out to take any of it. "I don't know, Saint-Gilles. How can this be the Holy Lance?"

"Surely all we need do to prove or disprove him is dig in the basilica." Saint-Gilles shoved a plate of food towards his friend. "Eat, Adhemar. No,

I don't care if you've already eaten this morning. All year you've been keeping yourself on starvation rations and giving the rest to the poor. What have we got to lose, anyway? If he finds nothing, then his vision was false. If he finds something, then evidently it was true, and we disregard it at our peril."

Adhemar reached out with a sigh to pick up a piece of the coarse bread, but didn't raise it to his lips. "My friend, I've *seen* the Holy Lance, under lock and key in the basilica of Saint Sophia in Constantinople."

Saint-Gilles wasn't ready to give up so easily. "Oh, hogwash! You know as well as I do that not everything displayed as a relic, really is!"

Adhemar stared at him, puzzled. "This isn't like you, my friend. You've always been happy to leave dreams and visions to me. Why is *this* one so terribly important?"

Saint-Gilles let out a gusty breath. "Because we *need* it," he muttered, throwing himself backward into his seat. After his sleepless night, his head ached nearly as badly as his injured hand. "Because God knows how desperately we need a way to keep morale up until Alexius comes. A relic like this is *exactly* what we need."

Adhemar looked startled, and even Galdemar was looking at him strangely. "Even if not genuine?" the bishop asked. "There have been other prophets, Saint-Gilles. Other demagogues who've claimed to have unearthed powerful relics, who've led hosts of enthusiastic followers into the jaws of death, because of a mistaken belief that God was on their side."

Saint-Gilles felt his cheeks redden. "Of course. But I would let Bartholomew dig, and if he finds something, I would put my faith in it. What other choice do I have, now that I've lost the trust of my own people?"

There. He'd said it. Galdemar might gape at him, but it was true. He'd spent so much of the pilgrimage fighting sickness or distracted by politics, he'd never had the chance to prove himself to the people as their leader. Meanwhile, Bohemond sailed in to win the victories and snatch the glory. People loved Bohemond. They didn't love him. Unless he could find a way to change that, he would always be fighting at a disadvantage.

"That's nonsense," Galdemar reassured him. "Don't be maudlin, my friend."

Still, Adhemar's face had settled into drooping, leaden lines. "What has happened to you, Saint-Gilles? There was a time when you hated the thought of manipulating your followers, even for the sake of morale."

"Nothing's happened to me!"

Saint-Gilles' voice echoed in the courtyard, far too loud. Adhemar got to his feet, sighing heavily. "Please believe me, Saint-Gilles; I'm only trying to do what's best—"

"Where do you think you're going? Sit down and eat!"

"I'm not hungry. I need to rest. And pray."

That restored him to a little hope. "You'll think of it, then? You won't object if I send the boy to dig in the basilica?"

Adhemar looked at him sadly, and Saint-Gilles had the feeling he might be about to hide himself away, not to pray, but to weep. "I can't give my blessing to this vision, Saint-Gilles. I believe it's a fraud."

When the door closed behind the bishop, Saint-Gilles threw up his hands with a wordless exclamation.

Galdemar sat at his left with arms folded, studiously staring at his feet.

"What's wrong?" Saint-Gilles growled at him.

Galdemar blinked up at him. "With me? What makes you think there's something wrong?"

"You're not even eating."

"Ah." Galdemar shook himself, then reached forward for a piece of bread and some spiced, skewered meat. "That better?"

Saint-Gilles looked away, letting out a deep slow breath. "A little; thanks."

Galdemar spoke through a full mouth. "Do you want *my* opinion on all this?"

Saint-Gilles waved a permissive hand. "Why not?"

"Honestly, I think you're right," Galdemar announced. "I think the least you could do is let this madman have a dig in the basilica, and see if there's something there. If there is, it could make all the difference between life and death for the whole pilgrimage. Even if Adhemar's correct…even if there's a risk of Bartholomew leading the people to their own deaths…it's still worth the risk."

"I'm glad you understand, at least," Saint-Gilles muttered.

"Don't say that yet; I'm not finished." Galdemar swallowed a bite and leaned forward. "I said all that because I need you to realise that I understand the practicalities of this situation. Bartholomew could be a boon to us. But is he worth burning down your friendship with Adhemar?"

Saint-Gilles felt cold. The image of the bishop's leaden face rose up before his eyes. "I'm not—" he began.

"I know the bishop, Saint-Gilles. I've never seen him speak to you like that before. I saw what it cost him."

"Saint Giles!" He had to admit it was the truth: Adhemar was serious about this. Moreover, not only was the bishop a friend; he was also the most powerful ally he'd ever have in the East.

"Besides, the bishop has a point." Galdemar watched Saint-Gilles with shadowed eyes. "You've changed, Raymond. All the way across Anatolia, you would have sacrificed anything to spare people's lives. After Marash, things changed. *You* changed. Tatikius and Bohemond wanted to blockade Antioch from a distance, sit the siege out in comfort in the neighbouring fortresses. You insisted on a field siege. Everyone told you it would cost lives, but you said you would pay the price."

"And I *did* pay the price." With the money he'd received in secret from Tatikius.

"You did, but people still starved, and sickened, and died. Then there were the rumours, that you'd created a situation where the whole pilgrimage, from the lowest to the highest, must depend on you and serve you in order to survive."

Saint-Gilles hoped he didn't look as guilty as he felt. So his plans hadn't been as secret as he'd hoped. Well, it wasn't as though anyone could *prove* anything. He lifted his chin defiantly. "I did what I believed best for the whole pilgrimage."

Galdemar's eyes dropped. This had cost him something, too. "I know," he said, putting his food back on the table as though he'd lost his stomach for eating. "If I'd thought you were mistaken, I would have said something. I'm not making accusations; I'm telling you what must have been galling that tender heart of Adhemar's all winter. The bishop is a good man, my friend, but he's no fool."

Saint-Gilles rubbed a thoughtful hand against his mouth. By the Virgin, perhaps Galdemar was right. He recalled little things—the soft-spoken objections Adhemar had made, which he'd barely even noticed. Perhaps Adhemar had been trying to take a stand for months already.

"I don't believe it," he said after a moment. "Adhemar and I are *friends.* Pope Urban gave both of us command of this pilgrimage. A little thing like this…"

He glanced up to find that Galdemar shaking his head. Slowly, but very certainly.

Saint-Gilles didn't feel hungry anymore, but he made himself reach forward to help himself to some bread and meat, and splashed himself a generous cup full of the clear, crystalline rainwater that flowed from the mountains by a cunning system of pipes to every house in the city. How long did they have until this promised deliverance? Five days? That left him until Monday. He would give Adhemar a few days to think it over, before asking him again.

He felt exhausted, but he had no time to rest. His thoughts—as they so often did now—drifted back to Bohemond, to the unparalleled opportunity he had to consolidate his grasp on the city while the wily South Norman was still occupied on Silpius. It was a shame that his interpreter had been lost. Where in this immense city would he find the Watchers, now that Bessarion was gone?

Chapter XVII.

When the drums began pounding outside the wall, it was barely light enough for Emelota to see the road beneath her feet. An answering horn blew from the distant tower where Count Bohemond's red banner smouldered like a dying flame. Ahead of Emelota, Lukas Bessarion stopped short with a grunt of annoyance. She nearly blundered into him, then paused, trying to catch her breath.

After the past year's campaign, even Emelota knew what those drums meant. The morning attack had begun, and they were not yet three-quarters of the way up the mountain.

Lukas lifted both hands, shoving his dark hair away from his eyes, muttering under his breath. He turned to Emelota. "It's no use. I'll have to take you down again."

The climb up Silpius had been agony, especially on an empty stomach. By unspoken consent, they'd settled into a punishing pace, Lukas extending his staff for her to hold onto, a precaution lest either of them blunder off the path in the dark. Gradually, Emelota had become aware that she could see Lukas' bowed shoulders before her, moving doggedly in time with his breath. At about the same time, the birdsong began. Dawn was coming. Neither of them spoke—they were both too exhausted for that—but both silently increased their pace. The light grew stronger, a haze of blue mist washing the world around them through which the lights of Antioch glimmered like haloed stars, until Emelota could see Lukas' feet plodding against the white path before her. With her gift, she saw them swathed in shadow, heavy and dragging. At that she let go of his staff. They were both climbing as quickly as they could, but from that moment she had known they would never reach Evrard before the dawn attack. Minutes later, the drums began.

She was therefore ready with her reply. "I won't go back without my brother."

Lukas sagged against his staff, his free hand fastened around something at his breast, hidden beneath his mail shirt. "Is your gift telling you that?"

Emelota shook her head. "It doesn't show me my own purpose, only that of others." Her entire life had revolved around others: her father, then Evrard, and then, for a small time, Alice... She'd found her only identity in them, her gift little more than a useless curiosity. She had never dared to tell anyone else about it, except Alice, who had never scoffed at anyone in her life. She hadn't even known there was a word for an ability like hers, let alone a real use. *I'm a Revealer,* she thought, trying the name on, as she might a new gown or a pair of gloves. A smile tugged at the corners of her mouth. *I'm somebody.*

The smile was a mistake: Lukas Bessarion was looking at her as though he thought she might be tormenting him on purpose. "Then I'm not taking you to a battlefield," he said flatly. "Your brother would murder me and I've enough to do keeping myself alive as it is."

Emelota drew a deep breath. "I can see *your* purpose, though," she told him, before stepping around him and continuing up the narrowed path. All right, perhaps *see* was too strong a word. Her gift did not usually manifest in visible ways: more often it was an inchoate certainty pooled in her gut. She knew Lukas Bessarion was *meant* to go up the mountain, and from that she had deduced that she was *meant* to go with him. In the same way, she felt obscurely certain he would be unwilling to abandon her if she went on. For the first few steps, she wondered if her gift had failed her, but then he let out a huff of breath and a bit of muttered Greek that did not sound complimentary, and hurried after her.

A quarter of an hour later, with the morning sunlight gilding the ramparts of the wall and towers, Emelota and her guide stood atop the highest point of Silpius. Behind them, tents dotted the sloping backbone of the mountain where Bohemond's camp was pitched. One of them, faded and ragged, was Evrard's, but they'd already checked it: it lay empty and deserted. Her brother's last squire lay dead across the threshold, and the belongings had been ransacked, although there was no sign as to whether the looters had been Turkish or Frankish.

Now, atop the knoll of Silpius, Emelota caught her breath, trying not to gag. It wasn't just the slaughter-yard smell of a hot day's battle that oppressed her; it was the stink of rage and vengeance, acrid and stinging in her nostrils.

The battle was concentrated on two narrow fronts. A moatlike gulley, full of thorns and a deep cistern, protected the citadel from any attack except by the road that approached it on the left, or by the city wall on the right. On the road, the Frankish shield-wall was locked in line, desperately withstanding the onslaughts of Turkish infantry along a path already heaped with bodies. But it was along the line of the wall to their right that the real battle raged. A whole Turkish battalion must be assaulting the wall from outside, their siege-ladders jutting over the ramparts. Frankish knights manned the wall or clustered atop the great square towers, wielding their bows as the Turks attempted to swarm up and gain a foothold on the wall.

Emelota swallowed hard and kept her voice steady. "Where is he? Where is Evrard?"

Lukas pointed towards the wall. "Somewhere in that tower."

The tower that flew Bohemond's blood-red banner was the eye of the storm. Atop the wall ran a narrow stone pathway along which it was possible to circle the entire city unless one of the towers barred its doors, and that was exactly what was happening here. A strong contingent of Turks had issued from the citadel and driven along the wall to Bohemond's tower; they now battered against the north door, attempting to break through. Another contingent had gained a foothold on the wall and attacked the tower from the south. As she watched, one of them hurled a spear from the ramparts to the tower's roof; it struck a knight leaning from the battlements, about to draw his bow.

Emelota's throat went dry. Was Evrard in there, wounded and surrounded? "You have to help them," she whispered, catching Lukas' arm.

"*I* have to help them?"

"What will happen if that tower falls?" *What will happen if my brother dies unconfessed?*

His mouth set stubbornly. "Everyone inside will be killed or captured, including Count Bohemond. And with a tower in their pocket, our whole defence collapses. Kerbogha will slaughter your people, and punish mine for rising against him. But if you think one man more or less will make a difference…"

"Not even one Messenger?"

He looked up at the heavens in despair. "I should never have told you that. Mademoiselle, with all respect, I'm not your servant. I have business of my own to see to. I have a master of my own to serve, and I've already wasted far too much time playing nursemaid to someone who wants to kill me. Now, if you'll excuse me, I'm going back to the city. You can take your chances here in the camp, or you can come back down the mountain with me, but I'm washing my hands of your brother." He turned away, but he muttered the next words in Frankish so that she could understand them. "If you had any sense you'd do the same."

"You're right, you know." Emelota hurried after him as he began walking briskly towards the camp, away from the battle. She certainly was spending a great deal of time running after Lukas Bessarion, but she felt it was not a hopeless cause. His intentions were not so clear today as they had been a fortnight since, before the city fell. "You've gone to great lengths for my brother, and he doesn't deserve it at all; not from you. But are you going to let all that effort go to waste? You saved his life for a reason, didn't you?"

He turned on her with a scowl. "You wouldn't thank me if I had."

"Then if you won't do it for my brother, do it for your own sake. Do it to save Antioch. That's…" The certainty struck her. "That's what you're meant to do, isn't it?"

He went as still as stone, the only part of him that moved a lock of dark hair whipping across his face. After a moment, he ran his tongue across his lips and said, "This is madness. There's nothing I can do."

He was going to do as she asked. "You can ask for a vision."

"It's like I told you. I can't just *ask*."

"Of course you can ask. The only reason you don't get what you ask is because…" Sensing danger, she stopped.

"Because what?" His voice was dangerously quiet.

"Because you don't ask for the right thing," she said with a sigh, substituting the words for what she had been going to say: *because your mind is consumed with blood and glory.*

Something made him swallow whatever he had been going to say. His jaw worked stubbornly for a moment, but then he said: "All right. It worked well enough this morning. Tell me."

And here, at last, was her purpose: something no one else in the world could do. This time, Emelota didn't bother to hide her smile. From where they stood on the mountain's backbone, the whole city was spread out at their feet, still veiled in the morning's haze. "Look at Antioch," she whispered. "Ask how to save her."

"What's left of her," Lukas muttered, but he focused on the view, his brows knitting together.

"Don't try too hard," she murmured. "Just be patient."

Even as she spoke, he staggered and sat down abruptly on the ground. His stare was fixed and far away, but she had the feeling he was not looking at the city at all. Moments later, he blinked and looked at her. "A frontal assault on the citadel? That's madness. I'll never convince the princes to do that."

"Which prince?" she prompted him.

"Flanders." Lukas nodded towards the count's banner floating above the shield-wall on the road to the citadel's gate.

Emelota nodded. "You need to persuade him. Ask for another vision."

"I…" Lukas let out a puff of breath. "All right." He slid back into his trance instantaneously, and stayed there longer. Emelota waited patiently, wondering why she felt disappointed. The visions were not *hers*; she had a different gift. But it was one that only seemed useful in tandem with Lukas Bessarion, and she was not sure how she felt about that, or about him.

She was still thinking so when he came back to her and muttered, "That will never work."

"Then perhaps you'd better ask for a vision of what happens if you don't," she said, more tartly than she intended. Lukas looked unsettled.

"I don't need to," he muttered. "I've already seen that vision. Antioch, full of corpses. And I didn't like what came after, either." He rubbed weary, red-rimmed eyes, as though steeling himself for what he needed to do next. "Find somewhere to hide, mademoiselle. Among the rocks, preferably; not in the camp. Try the steep ground beneath the road; look for shade and water, and if I don't return by nightfall, find your way down to the city in the dark."

It was going to work. She didn't know how—he hadn't shared his visions with her—but she knew it would work. "Thank you."

"I'm not doing this for you."

For some reason, his irritation pleased her. Emelota sent him a smile. "Not all of it, but some of it for certain—and for that I thank you."

* * *

Lying against the tumbled rocks of the hillside, Lukas closed his eyes and wished for water. His head pounded, and his arms lay uselessly by his side, aching from the strain. How long had he been standing behind Flanders' shield-wall, bracing himself against the men in front of him, sweating and swearing in the intolerable heat? Each time he thought he had come to the end of his strength, he'd found more to draw upon. In the small hours of the morning, fighting their way through the streets of Antioch, he had fumed at Emelota for thinking him a demigod. But after hours in the thick of battle beneath this blazing sun, perhaps he was beginning to forge himself into one.

He let his head sag to his left. He was not alone: a row of exhausted men sat or lay beside him, their sunken eyes feverish in their bloodstained faces.

One of them dabbed at his split lip, searched his mouth with his tongue, and spat a tooth. "We can't do this much longer," he said bleakly.

No one replied.

Thanks to his visions—and to Emelota's guidance—Lukas had a vague idea of what he was meant to do. He dragged a hand down his face, still a little overwhelmed by the discovery that his visions *would* answer to him—if properly requested. Still, the moment had not yet come for him to act. That was why he'd spent the morning in the Frankish shield wall, a bit of human reinforcement in the endless surge and flow of the battle.

Now, a lull in the Turkish attack had enabled them to withdraw from holding the road just long enough for Flanders to bring up a fresh company. Lukas turned his head to the right, where Bohemond's banner still floated above his tower, but that was the best that could be said. The tower was surrounded on all sides: the Turks had driven Normandy back along his stretch of the wall to his own tower and had also forced their way across the thorny gulley beneath the wall, occupying the ground beneath the redoubt. Bohemond's was no longer the only tower under siege. Evidently, the only thing keeping the Turks from sweeping through the camp and down into the city beyond was the worry that if they relieved the pressure on Bohemond for even a moment, he might issue from the tower and surprise them from the rear, cutting them off from their retreat.

"Where the devil is everyone else?" someone grumbled. "We had thousands of men when we took this city a week ago. Now, suddenly, we only have hundreds to hold this damned knoll. They can't *all* have gone rope-dancing!"

"They've sent for reinforcements," Toothless pointed out. "Duke Godfrey and Count Hugh."

"Well, I wish they'd hurry. The Giant can't hold out much longer. Sooner or later the Turks will break down the doors; and then what happens to the rest of us?"

Someone passed a canteen of warm, stale water down the line. Lukas took a mouthful—not enough, but better than nothing—and passed it on, pressing a hand once more to his chest to feel the shape of the key beneath the hauberk. If he didn't help the pilgrimage survive then his own people would suffer as well as the Franks, but that didn't stop the restlessness crawling up and down his limbs like ants. He was *so close* to his father's lance. Tonight…

A rolling tramp of footsteps came from the distance, disrupting his thoughts. Lukas tried to push himself up again. It took several efforts of will before his limbs responded; he must be more exhausted than he knew. But he remembered what he had seen in this morning's vision: a stream of reinforcements crowding into the citadel from the Turkish camp, four men carrying a small battering ram.

The *coup-de-grace*. With reinforcements arriving, the Turks could no longer afford to hold back. They must crack open the tower, slaughter Bohemond and his best knights, and force their way through all resistance, down into the city.

Around him, men staggered to their feet as Duke Godfrey's banners bloomed above the crest of the hill. The duke had brought only a small band of reinforcements: so far he had spent the siege stationed on Stauron watching the city's northeastern walls. Yet a ragged cheer arose from the browbeaten Normans and Flemings at his arrival.

The duke halted atop the crest of the hill, speaking to Count Hugh—another of the great princes, brother to the French king—and a battered, desperate-looking Count Robert of Flanders. Lukas watched them pointing and debating, as though they thought they had all the time in the world. He limped across the hard rocks of the mountainside and approached the great lords where they stood flanked by their high-ranking vassals.

"They're about to counterattack," Lukas called out when one of the knights stepped in front of him to bar his way. "They're gathered in the citadel to counterattack—no, listen to me!"

"Let him approach," someone said, and the knight stood back reluctantly to let him pass. Lukas looked up into the face of Duke Godfrey: his imposing height had become hollow and bowed, and his fair hair had greyed over the past few months. All the same, he looked kindly on Lukas.

"Go on, youngster. What have you seen?"

Lukas repeated his message. "Kerbogha is packing the citadel with his men. I saw four of them with a battering-ram preparing to take the tower."

Flanders scowled, throwing a glance towards the citadel's massive wall. "And how exactly did you see *that*? Did you sprout wings and fly, maybe?"

"I…" Lukas' throat was dry. For a moment he thought of giving in, doing what the visions prompted, admitting to being a Messenger. The le Puiset siblings already knew. And perhaps, if the visions were going to continue saving his life in combat, it was worth humouring them.

But no: they helped him only because if he died, he couldn't become a prophet to the pilgrimage.

And that he would never do. If he meant to use the visions, he'd use them on *his* terms.

"I crept through the gulley and peered through a chink in the citadel gate," Lukas lied. He could feel the guilt twisting across his face, the tell-tale stiffness his parents or siblings would have recognised at once. But none of these men knew him so well.

"That was *preux*," the duke said warmly. Flanders turned away, shouting for every spare man to prepare to reinforce the shield-wall behind Godfrey's newcomers. As the men of Lotharingia filed down to create the shield-wall, Godfrey beckoned a sergeant and put a hand on Lukas' shoulder.

"I presume they'll bring the ram along the wall and attack the door facing the citadel," he said. "Once outside that door, our archers won't be able to reach them from this slope. If I give you five archers, can you lead them to a place in the gulley where they can cover the door?"

Lukas' mouth went dry. In the gulley, six men would be terribly vulnerable. The Turks could pick them off with their own archers.

The duke must have seen the hesitation in his eyes. "I know it's dangerous, but that's why I want to send them with you. You found a way through once without being seen. Can you do it with five?"

Could have told you that was a bad idea, Ayla remarked.

Then why didn't you?

I'm your wife, not your mother.

There was nothing he could say. He'd brought it on himself with his own lie, and now he would have to go through with the mission. Lukas gulped and nodded. "I think so."

Chapter XVIII.

When Lukas Bessarion came to find her, Emelota nearly brained him with a rock.

She'd spent the morning curled into the scanty shade of a rocky overhang beneath the road, listening to the horrible sounds of battle and staring at the city, which was spread like a carpet far below. Heat and exhaustion weighed down her head and eyes, but she dared not sleep. After a while, she'd built herself a little pile of rocks small enough to lift in one hand but large enough to do some damage when hurled with force. When Lukas slid from the road and landed on the small shelf where she lurked, she'd thought him an enemy and acted accordingly.

"Easy." He caught her outstretched arm. "I thought you were the le Puiset who *didn't* mean to kill me."

She pulled away from him, brushing dust from her linen tunic, hoping it would conceal the trembling in her hands. "Forgive me. Some of *them* got in over the wall a while ago. They made it into the camp before…before they were stopped."

"And you thought I was one of them?" Lukas sniffed. "I thought you could sense intentions."

In that moment she regretted revealing her gift as much as he seemed to regret revealing his to her. "I can," she said. "Remember? I see you covered in blood. So I thought…"

He flinched as though she'd slapped him in the face. "I *am* covered in blood. Don't ask," he added as she assessed the rents in his tunic, the welling scratches that marked his arms and legs. "The princes sent me on a mission into the gulley, leading some archers to cover the tower. But it's all done now. We forced the Turks into the citadel and relieved Bohemond."

At that, her heart leaped painfully within her. "Evrard?"

His face turned wooden. "Alive. We've carried him to his tent. But…it isn't good. Prepare yourself."

Emelota swallowed, trying to remind herself that Evrard was not the only one suffering wounds and sickness. Her brother's chaplain, Father Adso, was lying in a delirium in the city below, whom she had abandoned for Evrard's sake. And there were all the men wounded in the fighting this afternoon. "What of the rest of the battle?"

Lukas explained as they crossed the dusty road to the camp. The plan to relieve Bohemond's tower by increasing pressure on the citadel gates had been on the point of failing, even with Godfrey's reinforcements, had it not been for Count Tancred's leadership. Borrowing one of his uncle's tactics, Tancred had charged the scrum at the gulley with a large body of reserves, managing to break the Turkish resistance and hurl them back into the citadel. Meanwhile, archers had successfully harassed the attackers on the wall from the hiding-place Lukas had found them in the gulley. The ram had fallen with two of its wielders into the thorns below, irretrievable. That was Bohemond's chance to issue from his tower at the head of his knights, to ecstatic cheers from the men.

It wasn't enough to turn the tide, either to seize the citadel or to secure the wall; only enough to restore Frankish morale and give them a breathing space. Now the hillside was dotted with exhausted men as well as corpses. Emelota was glad to shut out the sights of battle, if not the sounds or the smells, behind the flaps of her brother's tent.

The tent was horribly hot and stuffy, empty but for her brother on his low camp bed to one side—someone, thank God, had moved the squire's corpse. Evrard lay pallid and restless, still wearing his bloodstained armour—he must be half suffocated in this heat. Emelota fell on her knees, seizing his hand. "Evrard! I'm so sorry I didn't come sooner. I tried."

He was too weak to lift his head, but his muttering quieted a little, as though her voice comforted him. She dropped a swift, fierce kiss on his slack hand, and then looked up at Lukas. "He can't be moved. I'll have to tend him here until..." she waited, but no certainty came to her, one way or another. So, she pretended she knew. "Until the fever breaks and he can be moved down the mountain."

At this, Lukas' normally expressive face closed off, blank and stubborn. "You can't stay here. It's too dangerous."

She turned back to Evrard, pulling at his hauberk. They said it was best to sweat a fever out, but Emelota had seen men overheat in their armour during the crossing of the Anatolian deserts last year, and Evrard showed the same signs—bathed in sweat, clammy skin, racing heartbeat. She must get his armour off at once, even before she took a look at the blood-soaked bandage on his thigh. "You don't need to stay," she told Lukas, trying to push the mail shirt over Evrard's limp head. "We already owe you more than we can ever repay."

He didn't reply. At first Emelota presumed she had missed whatever goodbye he said. But then he heaved a noisy sigh and came over to lift Evrard's shoulders so that she could draw off the mail, and then the quilted jacket beneath.

"I mean it," she told him, looking up into his still-shuttered face. "You needn't feel responsible for me. I'm not..." *Worth it*, she almost said. It wasn't as though she was a trueborn lady. She could endure any hardship, so long as it gave her the chance to repay everything Evrard had done for her. And now that she had her brother back, she no longer felt so desperately reliant on Lukas Bessarion.

But he interrupted her before she could finish the sentence. "I *am* responsible for you," he said gruffly. "I'm a Bessarion. I know my duty. Besides, you were right. They need my gift up here. And I can't seem to use it without you."

* * *

The blessedly cool and silent night was shattered by a gasp and a sudden, convulsive movement. Lukas Bessarion woke and jerked to a sitting position. Emelota tensed, wondering if he'd heard or seen something—maybe enemy soldiers creeping into the camp in the dark?

Instead, with a muffled groan, he bent over his knees and rubbed at his weary face.

She blinked at him, realising she must have dozed off herself. "What happened?"

"Bad dreams," he said, with characteristic brusqueness.

Beside Emelota, Evrard himself stirred and became restless. It was as though a dark spirit had passed through the tent, putting an end to their peace.

The day had been a blur of hunger, thirst, and exhaustion. Emelota had spent it tending Evrard with what few resources she had in the way of tisane and clean bandages; meanwhile, Lukas had gone back into the shield-wall until the fighting ceased at dark. He'd looked like a ghost when he returned, pitching onto his side and falling asleep nearly before his head touched the carpet.

Now, he lifted his head from his hands. "What time is it?"

Emelota was not sufficiently familiar with the night sky to tell the time from the stars, but the waxing moon was already sinking westwards, drenching the tent with a pale light. "About Vigils, I suppose." Once, the pilgrimage would have gathered to observe the early morning office; but on Silpius they would be lucky if anyone was awake to keep guard, still less lead the prayers.

Lukas swore, pressing a hand to his breastbone.

"Is something wrong?"

"I had business in the city. It's too late now." She heard him muttering under his breath, as though he was praying.

Beside her, Evrard also began to mutter. She put a hand on his forehead: hot and feverish. Dipping her washcloth in what remained of her feverfew tisane, she began bathing his face and arms.

Across the tent, visible only as a faint, dark shape outlined against the canvas, Lukas grunted. "If the fever's that bad, he probably needs the leg taken off."

"No!" Emelota said sharply, and regretted it at once, because she felt Evrard jump at the sound.

"He'll die otherwise."

"No," she said more softly. "That's...that's not the intention. He's going to make it."

"If you say so." He spoke only after a long moment, and Emelota wondered whether there was something strange in his voice: as though he was secretly relieved at her certainty, but didn't want to show it. Yet, a miasma of blood and fury still hung about Lukas Bessarion, strong enough to smell. What did it mean?

He didn't speak again, and Emelota was too busy with her own thoughts. In the silence that unspooled between them, Evrard's muttering became more distinct:

"She's dangerous. Get on your knees...Take their weapons, Roger. Take the sling, for God's sake!"

Lukas caught his breath as though he'd cut himself fumbling for his weapons in the dark. "How can I sleep with *this* going on?" he growled, and the tent flap lifted as he pushed through into the night. He didn't go far: beyond the canvas, she heard the faint scrape of a whetstone as he sharpened Evrard's sword.

Emelota didn't try to follow him. For an hour, she sat over her brother laving his face and trying to think through the fog of her exhaustion. Doubt washed through her like waves on the seashore. Why was Lukas helping them, when he hated her brother so much? It might be a sheer matter of survival, but he clearly had other things on his mind. And there was the stench of corruption that hung about him... She remembered his bad dreams, and the cloud that had hung over the tent when they awoke. Crossing herself, she prayed a Paternoster.

Presently, when Evrard became quieter and less restless, she felt her way to the flap and followed Lukas to a white stone where he sat looking out over the few burning lights of slumbering Antioch.

He must have heard her approach, for the night was very still; but he didn't turn or speak to her. Emelota felt as though she was approaching a wild animal, and must do so with slow movements and a gentle voice.

"Do you know what I found beneath his tunic?" she began.

He knew precisely whom she meant. "I have no interest in your brother."

"It was a hair shirt," she said, and let him think on that for a while.

"So he knows he's a sinner," Lukas said at last, with a snort. "Good. I hope it keeps him awake at night."

"That was your wife he was speaking of earlier, wasn't it? The one he said was dangerous?"

She half expected him to tell her that it was none of her business, but after a drawn out silence he said, "Ayla was trying to protect me. She had… we had not always been friends. She wanted to stand by me for once, and it cost her her life."

By the time he finished speaking, his voice had cracked, letting Emelota glimpse some of the boundless sorrow beneath. She offered him her own pain in return. "Evrard never told me. I could see guiltless blood on his hands, and he pretended it was nothing." She shivered. "Did you know Evrard was married himself, once? Her name was Alice, and she died in childbed fever."

"Do you mean to tell me that I ought to forgive him because of that?" Lukas turned on her, almost violently. "Will that bring Ayla back to life?"

She ignored his outburst. "That's why he lied to me. He knows exactly what he has done to you, and he doesn't want to admit it, least of all to me." She paused. "I don't mean to tell you he isn't guilty. I mean that he is, and he knows it. But I don't want him to die with this on his soul."

"It would be no more than he deserves."

How could she look him in the face and tell him she wished his wife's murderer to escape justice, either in this world or the next? And yet there *was* an escape. She believed in the forgiveness of sins, the resurrection of the dead, and the life of the world to come. Not everyone had committed mortal sin, but everyone needed forgiveness, and small or great it was equally undeserved.

Lukas Bessarion said, quite calmly, "I'm going to kill your brother."

Emelota took a long, shaking breath. "Yes, I gathered it would be something like that."

"That's the only reason I'm helping him. So that I can challenge him to single combat for Ayla's sake."

"Will that bring Ayla back to life?"

"Don't speak her name!" he snarled. "Of course it won't. But he took Ayla's life from her; it's only just that his life should be taken from him in return. If these Frankish lords may kill without consequence, what recourse will any of my people have? If I don't teach your brother a lesson, who will?"

Emelota wound her arms around herself. The night was warm, but after the stuffiness of the tent, the breeze at the peak of the mountain seemed more chilling than anything else. Worry plagued her: she was almost certain Evrard was meant to recover, but what if she was wrong? What if she was deceiving herself with false hope?

"Will you do something for me, if I ask it?"

He uttered a bitter laugh. "I've done everything else you asked, haven't I?"

"Ask for a vision about Evrard. I…he's so sick, and…neither of us want him to die like this."

Lukas made a sound of disgust, but then he went still, staring out into the night with eyes that didn't seem to focus on anything in particular. His lips moved soundlessly, and his head tilted back, the eyes rolling up behind the lids. Emelota didn't dare reach out to steady him.

Then he was with her again, breathing hard, pressing a hand to his chest as though to still a racing heart.

"What did you see?" Her mouth felt very dry.

He paused before answering and, just like that, she *knew*.

"Your brother will die. I have seen his dead face in the sunset."

Emelota forgot to breathe. *No.* Not Evrard. What would she do without him? Where would she go? If Alice's death had left her without her only friend, then Evrard's death would leave her without her only family, without any way to survive.

Then she remembered herself and managed to draw in another breath. Everyone died in the end. "How old? Where? From what cause?"

"No older than he is now," Lukas told her. "As for the rest, I cannot tell. But he wasn't within the tent."

She nodded, wordless. If that was all the hope he would give, she would hold onto it with both hands.

Lukas watched her with folded arms. "Why do you remain loyal to that brute?"

"Why do you ask?"

"I'm curious, that's all." His voice thickened with disgust. "I don't understand it. How does a man like that get friends and family and a sister who's willing to die for him? It's the title and revenues, isn't it?"

Emelota sighed, rubbing a hand across her itchy eyes. It had been a long few days, first caring for the sick chaplain and then her sick brother, and whatever sleep she had managed to snatch in the quieter moments was not enough to keep her going. She didn't have the strength to argue with him now: to prove that Evrard's title meant less and less the further they got from home, that his liege lord had fled and his coffers emptied, that his friends had died and his family deserted, and his knights had been forced to take service with anyone who could pay them. Instead she only said: "Evrard still has power, it's true, and he's chosen to use that power to protect me, even when it means he can't pay his knights or feed his horse."

"Of course he does. You're his sister."

"Only half," she said reluctantly, remembering all the women who mocked her for her low birth, all the men who suddenly lost interest or became indecent when they knew. "Our father acknowledged me, but I have no lawful claim on my brother, not even for my support." She sighed. "That's why I'm here, and that's why I hope you both change your minds about killing each other."

There was a long silence. In the darkness, his voice was grim. "If you can really sense my intentions, then you know I will never change my mind."

"Everyone is capable of change. Otherwise there would be no hope for any of us." She stood, holding to the slim hope he'd given her. "If you really wanted to kill him, you could have done it anytime these last two days, just by turning your back."

"That wouldn't be *preux*," he said. "I'm no murderer. I was born a knight."

Surely Lukas Bessarion, of all people, should know that the line between knight and murderer was thinner than most people thought. Emelota only shrugged. She felt bruised—defeated.

Your brother will die, no older than he is now.

She wouldn't believe it. She'd sensed Evrard would live and recover from this illness. But then what? Even if he outlived the week, and even if Lukas Bessarion changed his mind, they were still shut up in a city on the edge of destruction, on a dangerous quest with far to go.

"Emelota." She flinched when he said her name so familiarly. No *mademoiselle* now, as though she had sunk in his estimation. But then he added in a gentle voice: "You shouldn't have told me about your birth, especially not while your brother is sick. You are safe with me, but… Believe me, you don't want to look like easy prey."

People usually treated her with less respect once they knew about her birth, but it had never occurred to Emelota to imagine how much worse it might be without Evrard to protect her.

"I mean it," Lukas added, and she could tell from his voice that he was at least a little worried about her. "These people think it's funny to bait the powerless. They'll do whatever they think they can get away with." He let the air ring a moment before adding, "But you know that already. You've seen the way your brother behaves."

Emelota pressed her lips together. "I'll take your warning. I meant to tell you we have no water left."

"That's nice."

"I…thought that if the battle continues tomorrow, it might be difficult to get more."

A gusty sigh from the darkness. Then, to her astonishment, Lukas got up, unslung his staff, and struck it smartly against the stone upon which he had been sitting. "Flow, water!" he commanded.

Just like my lord Saint Moses in the desert! Emelota caught her breath. "Did it work?"

"Of course not," he said scornfully. "Seems I'll have to work a different kind of miracle. I'll have to get to the cistern without being killed. But, if you don't mind, I'll wait for dawn. If I don't get a little more sleep, my eyes will fall out of my head."

Chapter XIX.

As the grey light of dawn crept towards sunrise, Saint-Gilles rode into Bohemond's camp to find the South Norman count ordering all his men to their positions: a shield-wall spanned the entire length of the gulley, and the towers bristled with spears. Although the Turks were a little slower to commence battle this morning than they had yesterday, Bohemond evidently meant to be prepared.

Three banners waved from the hillcrest dividing the Frankish camp from the battlefield: Flanders, Normandy, and Vermandois. As Saint-Gilles and Adhemar led their reinforcements towards the knoll where the other princes waited, a thin cheer went up from the weary men filing out of the camp. Even fresh from their night's rest they looked pale and exhausted, like corpses walking. Perhaps that was why their cheer rang so hollowly on the air and died away so soon—or perhaps they saw how few and sullen his reinforcements were.

Bohemond, as ever, was indecently full of spirits. "There you are," he sang out as Saint-Gilles reined in his horse and climbed up the knoll. "I began to think you'd gotten lost!"

"My attention has been on the uprisings in the city," Saint-Gilles said, sounding defensive in spite of himself. "It turns out a great number of Turks and Saracens survived the sack, and some of them built barricades. I suspect there may even be ways down the mountain we don't know about—at least, we found some armed men from the garrison. You should be watching the citadel more closely."

"Look on the bright side," Bohemond said, grinning. This close, even he looked tired, but he wasn't allowing it to dampen his mood. "Obviously, if it was possible to get large numbers of men down these secret paths, Kerbogha would have done that already. So long as we hold this road, I don't think we need to worry."

It was a fatuous comment to make—after all, it had been Saint-Gilles who had had to worry about Turks creeping down to the city, and a good thing he had—but before Saint-Gilles could think of a suitably cutting response, Bohemond lowered his voice. "The real problem is our own people. Some of them are wounded, but not all. They slip away, down the mountain, and they don't come back." He nodded towards the men who had followed Saint-Gilles up the mountain. "There must be a scant three hundred there. We should have thousands. They can't all have deserted."

"I scoured the city for this lot of malingerers," Saint-Gilles growled. "And don't forget we have to man the whole length of the wall. Godfrey's crying out for reinforcements on Stauron. If you think you can do any better, you'd be welcome to try."

Bohemond looked towards the city spread out beneath them, and Saint-Gilles instantly regretted his words. There was a gleam of calculation in the Norman count's eyes that Saint-Gilles had learned to distrust. "Perhaps I will," he murmured.

"What exactly are you planning?" Saint-Gilles demanded.

"Nothing I mean to discuss openly." Bohemond sent a warning look towards their small and motley army, where Adhemar was organising the fresh men in a shield-wall across the road. "Do you know that your interpreter's alive, by the way?"

"Lukas Bessarion?" That was a small glimmer of good news.

"He's been up on this godforsaken mountain for a couple of days. Make a point of thanking him for me, if I don't get to it. He saved my life yesterday."

There was something a good deal too innocent in Bohemond's look. Saint-Gilles ground his teeth. What was that supposed to mean? Did Bohemond mean to make him distrust his own interpreter?

His thoughts were interrupted as some of the archers along the gulley surged in their direction, calling his name and Bohemond's. Saint-Gilles realised they must have heard his sharp question a moment ago, and now they were worried. Perhaps they also knew not to trust Count Bohemond too freely.

"One at a time! One at a time!" Bohemond threw a wary glance towards the citadel, but it lay dormant. "What's the matter?"

"Is it true?" someone yelled. "Are you going to steal away and leave us?"

So that's what they were afraid of. Saint-Gilles snorted. "Leave you? Who's been filling your heads with this nonsense? I assure you," he added, conscious of Bohemond standing beside him, "anyone who wants this city will take it over my dead body, for I won't relinquish it while I live."

"The count of Blois left us," someone yelled.

"And the count of Grandmesnil! And Guy of Trousseau!"

"But we are with you still!" Bohemond lifted his voice like a trumpet. He threw out his arm, pointing to each of the princes in turn. "Saint-Gilles, Normandy, Flanders, Vermandois, and the good bishop of le Puy!"

The crowd surged and muttered like the rising sea, the shield-wall fraying as more anxious men pressed around them. Saint-Gilles knew the harsh cold calculations each of them must have been doing in his mind, for the same had occurred to him. For the thousands trapped in Antioch there could be no hope in anything short of total victory. Only small bands of twos and threes had the chance to slip past Kerbogha's watch and escape the city. What was to prevent the great lords from doing just that?

"Open the gates!" someone shouted unexpectedly. "Open the gates and let it be every man for himself! Don't leave us here to face our death!"

"Fools!" Saint-Gilles bellowed in return. "You'll be slaughtered!"

"Friends, friends!" Bohemond didn't have to bellow: he simply raised his hands, and the crowd quieted. "Are we not sworn to you? What good would it do us to escape with our lives, but without our honour? Of course we won't abandon you."

"Swear it." At first it was one voice, and then it became a chant. "Swear! Swear!"

They didn't have time for this nonsense: a pretty set of fools they would look, if Kerbogha chose this moment to attack. But the citadel lay dormant; and Bohemond, as ever, yielded to the crowd's demand.

"Of course!" The South Norman count waved Adhemar over to join them. "My lord, do you have anything on which to swear an oath?"

"We've sworn already," Saint-Gilles protested. "Each of us, on the day we took our oaths to travel to Christ's sepulchre, swore to succour the others on the same journey."

But neither of the others paid any attention to him. Adhemar drew a fine chain over his head, an ornate reliquary in the shape of a crucifix emerging from its hiding-place beneath his mail shirt. "This is a piece of the True Cross," he proclaimed, holding it out to Bohemond.

As a hush fell upon the whole army, the South Norman count reached out and laid his hand on the jewel. "To each man who has shed his life's blood with mine in the past, and to each man who stands willing to shed it with me in the future, I declare myself bound by the laws of fealty! If the day comes that I forsake this trust and save my own life at the expense of yours, let my right hand forget its skill, and let me be delivered to the blades of my enemies." He sent Saint-Gilles a laughing glance as he went on: "Neither will I relinquish this city while I live. In the name of the Father, and of the Son, and of the Holy Ghost, amen!"

In the ringing silence left by Bohemond's words, Adhemar offered the relic to Saint-Gilles. The pressure of all eyes pinned him down. This oath was nothing: he'd already vowed, and to swear again felt tantamount to admitting that he was capable of breaking his oaths. And there was nothing Saint-Gilles prided himself upon so much as on keeping his word.

This oath was nothing, pure mummery. Bohemond was simply giving the people what they wanted, manipulating their passions as a cloak for his own ambitions—vowing never to relinquish the city, indeed!

Saint-Gilles sighed, thinking of Galdemar's words from the day before. Perhaps he wasn't so different from Bohemond, after all. He had become willing to make use of manipulation and mummery himself.

Perhaps that was what you needed in order to get the better of one as subtle as his rival.

All this flashed through his mind in a moment, before he reached out and put his hand on the relic. "On the day that I abandon this pilgrimage and my sacred oath, may God abandon me. Amen!"

In turn, Normandy and Vermandois swore, then Flanders. The moment they had finished, Bohemond thrust his fist into the air. "God's will!" he cried.

"God's will!" Flanders and Normandy dutifully echoed, and this time the cheer was taken up by a few more throats, but it was still a pitifully thin and spiritless sound.

"And God *does* will it!" A thin cry lofted above the host. Saint-Gilles turned to see a priest in ragged vestments, his eyes ringed with darkness above hollow cheeks. Pushing through the crowd, he fell on his knees before the princes. "My lords, I bring you God's message."

Another one. Saint-Gilles glanced at Adhemar. A muscle twitched in the bishop's jaw, but he didn't return Saint-Gilles' look. It had been like this ever since yesterday morning's argument, as though some door had slammed shut between them, leaving Saint-Gilles feeling as bereft as he had when he'd first lost his eye.

"Speak," Adhemar said gently.

"I am called Stephen of Valence," the priest declared, getting to his feet. His voice rang like a trained orator's; this was not the ignorant fanaticism of the boy from the day before. "Last night, I and some of my friends, terrified by rumours of a defeat on the mountain and a Turkish descent from the city, were keeping vigil in the church of the blessed Mary—confessing our sins and chanting hymns. While my friends were sleeping, I was visited by a man fairer than any mortal. He questioned me as to who now possessed Antioch, and whom they worshipped. I told him we were Christians and recited the creed, whereupon he revealed himself in glory to be the Lord Christ himself. Then he told me: *These people have alienated me by their evil deeds. Tell them to turn from their sins and I shall return to them, and as a sign of this within five days I shall send them a great deliverance.*"

At that, Saint-Gilles could no longer contain himself. "Five days," he muttered in a voice pitched low enough only to reach the bishop's ear. "That's just what the other one said."

Adhemar seemed not to hear. "You know you must verify this vision," he said to the priest.

Valence pointed towards Bohemond's tower. "If you do not believe me, then put me to the ordeal! I am ready to scale this tower and throw myself down from it. If I am unhurt, you will know that I speak the truth, but if I suffer any injury, then behead me or burn me. I am unafraid."

"That won't be necessary," Adhemar said quickly. Like most reform-minded clergy, he was uncomfortable with the trial by ordeal. "Here is a piece of the True Cross: swear on that."

Confidently, Valence made the required oath; and then he turned to the men, raising his voice. "Wait for the deliverance of God! You are his chosen people, led through the wilderness by his mighty hand. Humble yourselves before him, and he will give you vengeance upon your enemies! *God's will!*"

This time, the cheers were deafening. In a moment, the entire mood of the army had changed from despair to hope. Bohemond's face split in a grin as he led the chant of their war cry, signalling his captains to shepherd the men back into their place.

This, Saint-Gilles thought, was what Peter Bartholomew offered them: something worth more than oaths and speeches. Hope: to keep them going through the misery of this siege; hope: without which they could not possibly survive. Whether or not the visions were true, or the phantoms of terror and sickness, they *needed* them.

Saint-Gilles pushed a little closer to Adhemar as the other leaders returned to their stations. "What do you think of Bartholomew's vision *now?*"

The bishop looked tired and gaunt. "My friend, I think no differently than I did yesterday."

"What? This Stephen of Valence is an ordained priest—he *swore* to his vision on the True Cross. Don't tell me it's a coincidence that he has promised the same deliverance."

Adhemar shook his head, evidently seeking the right words. "The only thing proven this morning is that Valence *believes* his vision to be true; not that it is indeed true."

"What, you think the visions might be…" Saint-Gilles cleared his throat, nervous of speaking the word aloud, "…diabolical in origin?"

"It would explain both why they confirm each other, and why they point us in the direction of what I suspect to be a fraud."

"This is ridiculous, Adhemar!" Saint-Gilles snapped, out of patience again. "The vision warned all of us to turn from our sins and put our trust in Christ! Does that sound like something the Devil would ask of us?"

"Valence promised us vengeance upon our enemies," Adhemar said heavily. "But we undertook this pilgrimage to liberate Christ's people and patrimony, not to wreak vengeance on his enemies. Don't you remember?"

Of course he remembered, but you didn't win wars by turning the other cheek. Saint-Gilles felt like throwing up his hands. "Maybe you've misunderstood the purpose of this war."

The bishop opened his mouth, but Saint-Gilles couldn't trust himself not to say something he might regret. Instead, he wheeled away to find Bohemond.

"I presume you made a slip of the tongue during your oath," Saint-Gilles growled into the other count's ear. "Or have you forgotten the oath you made on that very relic, to give up Antioch to Alexius when he comes to claim it?"

"Far from it." Bohemond was as unruffled as ever. "Still, men fight harder when you don't threaten to snatch away their prize."

He tried to pull away, but Saint-Gilles tightened his grip. "You also promised to show me the chrysobull Alexius granted you."

"And I will, when I have two spare minutes to rub together."

"Stop snarling, you two!" Flanders broke in on them. "Didn't you hear the drums start? We've a battle to fight."

Saint-Gilles released Bohemond, his teeth grinding. He needed power, real power. The bishop might be paralysed by his own scruples, but Bohemond was not. Meanwhile, morale was cracking, and Kerbogha was outside the city prowling like a lion.

One way or another, he needed to convince the bishop to let Peter Bartholomew dig in the basilica before the Turks overcame them all.

Chapter XX.

God's will! The Frankish battle cry rose above the pound of the Turkish drums, the commotion making Lukas' heart race. The morning's battle must be beginning already. The cistern where he knelt lay within bowshot of the citadel, and although Lukas could see no activity on the battlements, he thought he heard the chime of steel, the tramp of feet on the mountain at his back. In another moment the citadel would be bristling with Turkish archers, and he would be exposed.

With trembling hands, Lukas thrust the stopper into the last of the canteens he'd brought downhill from the camp, slung them across his shoulders, and hastened up the slope towards the Franks. His sudden movement among the scrub and thorn-bushes must have attracted the citadel's attention, for a couple of arrows whined and skipped among the rocks as he climbed. In another moment, he made it to the shield-wall and was safe.

Beyond the steel-bristling line of Franks he paused, fighting light-headedness. He had barely slept since the day before yesterday, and it had been longer since he had eaten. He no longer felt the bite of hunger in his belly, but the dizziness worried him. How was he going to fight when he could barely carry a few bottles of water up a slope?

As he caught his breath, he overheard snatches of conversation from the Franks. They were abuzz with news:

"Within five days, a great deliverance…"

"Vengeance upon the Turks."

"…said Christ was with us…"

There! Lukas thought triumphantly, *someone else is having the visions now and I can go back to my proper calling.* He picked up the strapped jugs again, but staggered as a fresh wave of dizziness washed over him.

He stood atop the tower scenting death and fire, looking down upon an army of dead men and the smoking ruins of a city. Ahead of him, the great red sun was setting in bloody clouds.

Live. The word clawed to get up his throat. But he wasn't a prophet and he didn't want to help these barbarians. Lukas clapped a hand over his mouth to keep the word down. His gut seethed, nauseous.

A voice spoke behind him: an unearthly voice that sputtered and hissed like pure fire, but was also low enough to make the air vibrate in his lungs. *"Speak, or Antioch will be destroyed."*

The next moment he found himself on hands and knees among the rocks. A pair of feet in battered steel gaiters stopped in front of him.

"Lukas Bessarion!" Adhemar knelt before him, delight struggling with worry on his face. "Alive! God be thanked!"

Lukas barely heard the words. Last night in his sleep, Lilith had visited him—again. She had come to him wearing an unearthly beauty, terrifying in its luminous perfection. She had taunted him with his failures, warning that if he refused to serve her, she would see to it that he never recovered the Bessarion Lance at all.

She too, wanted him to become a prophet.

His empty stomach should not be pulling into knots, without food to feed the sickness—yet still, disquiet seethed within him.

"What is it, Lukas? Are you hurt? Ill?"

He looked up into the bishop's worried eyes. *Stop wishing for the moon and tell him, you ostrich,* Ayla would say if she was here. *We always have a choice, and it's usually between death or slavery. How many of us have the choice to be a prophet?*

He could tell the bishop his vision and be relieved of the burning voice, the burden of the word in his belly. But this time, if he spoke, there would be no turning back; it would not be like yesterday, when he lied to the princes about the source of his information. He needed to think about this before he made his choice.

"I'm hungry, that's all, my lord. I haven't eaten in days."

The bishop helped him up. "There's food in the city. If you've been up here, fighting all this time, then I'm sure you can—"

"Bessarion!" another voice cut in. It was Count Raymond, and his weather-beaten, scarred old face actually creased in a genuine smile: the first Lukas could remember seeing from him. "Bessarion, lad, you're a sight for sore eyes! I thought I'd lost you."

It was rather heady to have such a welcome directed at him. "I would have come to report to you, my lord, but I hadn't the opportunity." He sighed. "I fell in with a wounded count. Between the battles I've been trying to keep him alive, but..."

"As long as you're up here making yourself useful, I have no complaints," Count Raymond said. He shot a scowl in Count Bohemond's direction, then lowered his voice. "Besides, if you're up here, you're in the perfect place to do some information-gathering for me. Bohemond is up to something."

The bishop let out a faint, exasperated sigh.

"Don't be naïve, Adhemar," Count Raymond growled. "Of *course* Bohemond is up to something; the only question is what. Listen, Bessarion. Each of us—each of the seven great princes—had a chrysobull from the emperor, encoding our respective promises and duties. I want to know *exactly* what was in Bohemond's, understand?"

The count might have lost an eye, but the one that was left fixed Lukas with a hard, piercing stare. His throat dried. He'd done a few risky jobs for Count Raymond before, but he'd never spied on another count. If he was caught, he would be killed.

But if he succeeded...Count Raymond had begun to trust him; even to respect him. Perhaps after this he might ask for a knighthood. Lukas nodded. "I understand, my lord."

"Good. And be careful, Bessarion. Don't be caught." Count Raymond straightened, turning towards the bishop. "I'd better get down to the city again—who knows what might be happening down there without me.

Coming, Adhemar?"

"In a moment." Bishop Adhemar turned back to Lukas. "This friend of yours—is he dying? Does he need a priest?"

"He's no friend of mine," Lukas muttered. But le Puiset was sick and raving this morning worse than ever, and he'd told Emelota the truth about his vision: he'd seen the count's face, dead in the sunset, still a young man. What did it mean? He'd seen Ayla's dead face in a vision, and it had happened just as he foresaw. And, twice now, he'd seen the whole pilgrimage destroyed, Antioch burning. Was that also immutable fate? If it was, why was he being prompted to warn them?

Was his vision of the count's death a warning? A promise? Or only one of several possible futures? Did heaven's decrees ever relent?

When Saint Abraham had begged Sodom to be spared if as few as ten Watchers could be found within, God had relented. But ten Watchers had not been found, and the city had been destroyed—as Antioch would be destroyed, for lack of Watchers, for lack of *him*.

It was all the same, he thought wearily, coming back from far-flung reaches of thought to find the bishop still waiting for an answer. Unless something changed, le Puiset would die.

"Few need a priest more," Lukas said bitterly.

"Then I'll come myself," the bishop offered.

When Lukas showed the bishop into the tent, Emelota uttered a squeak of surprise and jumped to her feet to make a hurried bow.

"Peace on this place," the bishop replied, but then he blinked at the delirious count. "Is—is that *Evrard of le Puiset?*"

"Yes, my lord. I'm his sister."

"My regard for Lukas Bessarion increases."

Lukas' cheeks warmed, and he could not meet Emelota's eyes. Only a few hours ago he'd made it quite clear that he was only helping them for the sake of his own feud. In another moment, no doubt, she would laugh scornfully and tell the bishop exactly what Lukas Bessarion's help was worth.

Instead, she only gave him an uncertain look, before turning to Adhemar again. "Will you anoint him?"

The bishop smiled warmly at her. "Yes, and *the prayer of faith*—you know."

As Adhemar produced the small bottle of oil he must carry with him constantly these days, Lukas turned his back on them, going to the flap of the tent where he could see uphill towards the wall, the towers, and part of the citadel. Kerbogha must have sent ballistae, for the great crossbow-like machines peered from the citadel ramparts, and engineers were hard at work settling them in place, calibrating them to strike the Frankish battle-lines. In another few minutes the day's work would begin…

Antioch will be destroyed.

Behind him, as Adhemar intoned the last rites, he heard le Puiset's restless movements and the hitch of Emelota's breath as she surrendered to tears. He felt like an intruder here, but if he left the tent again it would be like admitting defeat. Lukas almost felt he should pray that the Frank would recover. But even that would be a selfish prayer, because he meant to kill le Puiset himself. What had Emelota said last night? *You ask and do not have, because you ask amiss.* Something of that sort. She would thank him for not praying. Surely the prayers of a heart like his would only hurt.

He felt so inexpressibly alone. *I wish you were still here. You'd know what to do. You always did.*

It was the twelfth of June, a year since the last happy month of his life. He and Ayla had been friends edging towards something more, before he started seeing her dead in his dreams, before he learned she was spying for the Turks. Perhaps it had been a fool's paradise, each of them keeping secrets from the other, concealing a part of who they were. But, despite their secrets, there'd never been deception. Ayla had never lied to him.

He ran a thumb from the basilica key, up along the faded cord by which it hung, the sling that was all he had to remember her by. No, that wasn't true. The voice in his thoughts might only be a shadow of the true Ayla, but he couldn't fool himself. He already knew what she'd say if she was really here.

Having finished the rite, Adhemar rose to his feet again, and he and

Emelota joined Lukas at the tent door. Beyond the city wall, Kerbogha's drums beat the rhythm of the attack. There was a sound of swords beating against shields, and the shrill of trumpets blowing the alarm. The day's battle had begun.

Beside him, Adhemar spoke nearly soft enough to be drowned out by the din. "I think you are right: there can be no moving him while he's like this. If his fever breaks, come down to me at the palace and I will send a litter for him, if I can spare the men." The bishop put a hand on Lukas' shoulder, and bowed his head to Emelota. "God be with you both. I can do no more."

"You've already done everything," Emelota told him gratefully.

Bishop Adhemar lifted a hand to sketch a benediction, and then hurried up the hill. Lukas started after him with half an idea of asking the bishop to send someone else to watch over the le Puisets, freeing him go down into the city. The key burned around his neck, the Bessarion Lance was still buried in the basilica and, God help him, he *needed* it…but there was more.

Antioch will be destroyed.

The bishop's kindness, Count Raymond's warm welcome… He *had* to say something. He couldn't keep this terrible warning bottled up inside him and watch them die; what kind of return would that be to the men who'd done so much for him?

Emelota caught him by the arm, her smile brittle and flaking. "Are you leaving us?" she whispered as though she'd read his intentions in his face—likely, she had. Even through the mail he wore, her fingers bit into his arm. "Please, Lukas. Don't go into the city."

He hesitated. Her sky-blue eyes were anxious. She'd been nothing but trouble to him, yet he knew how this worked now. If he refused, she'd tell him to have a vision. The vision would come. And it would tell him to stick by them.

Lukas sighed. Not that there wasn't a certain kind of satisfaction in what he'd done. If le Puiset lived, he'd be dancing on hot coals to think he owed his life to the despised Greek. In any case, he could not leave without carrying out Count Raymond's mission.

"Don't fear," he told her. "I couldn't leave you if I tried."

And believe me, he's tried, Ayla put in.

Whose side are you on, anyway? he complained, hastening after the bishop.

"My lord, a moment," he said when he caught up with Adhemar. "It's hopeless up here. You and Count Raymond…" he glanced towards the bishop's attendants, his new squire and handful of knights who'd escorted him up the mountain to the princes' meeting. Lowering his voice, he said, "You should follow the count of Blois before it's too late."

The bishop's eyebrows shot up. "What are you saying, Lukas?'

What *was* he saying? *Antioch will be destroyed.* Perhaps this would satisfy the visions: if he warned the papal legate, if he got the few decent Franks out of the city before judgement fell. Yes, that must be it. "You and Count Raymond don't deserve to die with these people. You should leave over the wall. Tonight."

The bishop shook his head. "Few of us get what we deserve, Lukas, and that's a great mercy. The count and I cannot leave. We have sworn oaths not to abandon the people…but you haven't."

Adhemar gave him a meaningful look, and Lukas' mind stuttered to a halt.

Was the bishop suggesting *he* desert?

Of course he could never do that—not while his father's lance remained in Antioch—but after, perhaps? Once, he would have been insulted by the suggestion that he flee the siege. Today, it struck him only that the bishop cared about him enough to want to save his life.

"My lord!" one of the bishop's attendants shouted, rushing forward to cover the bishop with his shield even as a flight of arrows began falling around them. Lukas jolted back to the present to find that the Turks outside the city had loosed a far-ranging volley of arrows across the wall; their scaling-ladders were already appearing above the ramparts.

He was supposed to be stationed in the postern tower, helping the Franks defend the wall. As Adhemar's men hurried him away, Lukas raced towards the oncoming storm. All questions of the lance and what he would do after he regained it fled his mind. For today, it would be enough to survive.

***

Some hours later, Lukas found himself standing atop the tower with a crossbow, leaning against a rampart. Night had fallen, the sunset little more than a smudge of gold in the west. As the day's alarms faded, he became conscious of his hunger, bone weariness, and the dirt engrained in every pore of his skin.

If this nightmare ever ended, he might actually have the chance to go down the mountain and pay a few coppers for his first proper bath in over a year. A bath with hot water and soap and oil afterwards to rub into his cracked skin and split knuckles.

He might as well wish to pluck a star from the satin evening sky, to hold it in his hand. Lukas took a deep breath, looking around him. The Turks had not withdrawn to their camp: tonight they'd bivouacked just out of bowshot from the wall, and the smell of cooking meat drifted tantalisingly on the air. He swallowed saliva. It had been a terrible day. The tower had been surrounded; two of the knights had been wounded and for a terrible, interminable length of time there had been only Lukas and the third knight to defend the redoubt. Thoughts, hopes, and fears alike had vanished from his mind: there was only the battle, the faces of his enemies, the hissing swing of their blades, and the sting of his wounds. He hadn't even gone to ask Emelota if her brother had survived the day; the moment the Turks had withdrawn he'd been sent up onto this roof to keep watch on them, since they were so near. Now he took the opportunity to probe his own body for cuts and bruises and scrapes. It was a miracle he had suffered no worse.

The visions had kept him safe. Again and again, flashes of premonition showed him coming danger. He dared a prayer of gratitude, feeling guilty even as he made it, feeling the prick of anger at the knowledge that he was only being kept alive in order to be used. *Why* should he do anything to save these ignorant, superstitious, arrogant people? The harder he was pushed to help them, the more he resented the Franks. He wished to save Count Raymond, and Adhemar, and Emelota, but the rest of them deserved nothing.

The choice was stark. If he wanted to save himself and his people—the Watchers, the Syrians, his few friends among the Franks—then he had to save the whole pilgrimage. Otherwise, they would all perish together, the handful of good people right along with le Puiset and the barbarians who had devastated Antioch in a brutal sack.

And what if they *were* saved? Odds were they'd be confirmed in their idea that God was on their side. After that they would lose every vestige of self-restraint, committing any kind of evil without fear.

But at least he and his people would be alive.

All right. He sent his thoughts out defiantly. *I'm ready to submit, if you're ready to show that you care. Send me a raven with food.*

He waited. The day's heat rose off the battlefield in a stench of spilled guts and voided bowels. Dark shapes slunk through the shadows as the Franks staggered back to their camp, but no shape winged from the darkness with bread or meat for him.

So much for the visions. There was one other way to stop this slow, agonising death: he must go back into the city and unearth the lance.

One of the knights called up to him from below: he was to be relieved and sent back to the camp. Lukas shouldered his crossbow and returned to the le Puiset tent, where he found Emelota attempting to rinse some cloths. In the deepening twilight, Lukas could barely see her face: but he thought she seemed calm, as though a burden had rolled from her shoulders.

"What news?" The words clung fuzzily to his tired lips.

"Evrard's fever broke about Nones. He's been sleeping ever since." Emelota gave him a faint smile. "I was right, after all."

"I expect he'll be his old self by dawn," Lukas said, resigned. Otherwise it was good news. He looked again towards the twilight west. Nones was mid-afternoon; it was Compline now, and le Puiset would have had a few good hours of sleep. If they started down the mountain now, he would reach Antioch in time to call Zarides and unearth the lance. Suddenly, he felt awake again. "Let's get off this mountain."

Emelota didn't argue, evidently as eager as himself to leave the accursed place. Back in the tent, she leaned over her brother's quiescent form and smoothed his hair.

"Evrard, Evrard. It's time for you to wake."

The count moved with a groan.

"How do you feel?"

"Like I've been trampled by wild horses." Le Puiset's voice was a whisper, but it had a smile in it.

"Are you in pain?"

"Only my leg." There was no light in the tent—the lamp oil was all used up, and the only light flowed in through the open flap on the west side of the tent where Lukas waited. The count's face was a pale blur as he turned and saw him. "Who's that?"

"It's Lukas Bessarion, Evrard," Emelota said gently. "He has watched over me for two days, while you lay ill."

Lukas steeled himself for an eruption. Instead there was only silence for a long time before le Puiset said, in a curiously empty voice, "I owe you my thanks, Greek."

"Syrian," Lukas corrected him, lest the count think a few words of grudging thanks were going to make any difference to their feud. But the correction was petty, and the pretence of anger was oddly wearisome to him. After three days of gruelling danger, le Puiset was still alive; and Lukas was conscious mainly of a hazy glow of triumph. Turning to Emelota, he said, "Get your brother ready for the journey. I'll see if I can find some beast to carry him."

A few horses and other mounts—mules, donkeys, even a few sheep and oxen—had been picketed downslope from the camp, their numbers gradually dwindling as any chance of further sorties faded and it became too much trouble to cart sufficient water and fodder up the mountain for them. Lukas was surprised when Emelota shook her head.

"Evrard's horse is here. I went and checked this afternoon; someone brought it back within the wall after the sortie."

"What's that?" Le Puiset's whisper sharpened with hope. "My horse is still alive?"

"They're expecting me to fetch it," Emelota said, putting a hand on Lukas' arm. "You stay with Evrard."

She disappeared into the dusk, leaving Lukas standing awkwardly in the entrance to the tent. Inside, a groan as le Puiset pushed himself to a sitting position. "My horse is alive," he said in wonder. "All is not lost."

There were greater things at stake than one man's horse and the status it conferred. He'd learned that the hard way himself. "You'll find it difficult to feed the beast," he heard himself saying, recalling his own attempts to keep a horse alive on the trek across Anatolia. "It's about to be very difficult to find any food in this city."

"No doubt. I don't suppose those ravens of yours deal in horse fodder?"

There was a tremor of humour in le Puiset's voice, and Lukas stiffened. God help him, was he *fraternising* with Ayla's killer now? All this effort to keep the count alive, and he'd allowed himself to forget they were enemies. Perhaps Emelota's misguided compassion had infected him.

He was still parsing the mistake when le Puiset spoke again.

"I'd be dead but for you, Bessarion, and my sister—"

"Don't flatter yourself, Frank." Lukas interrupted in a voice like a rusty blade. "I didn't do this for you *or* your sister, and I don't want your thanks."

"All right, then. Go to hell. I was only trying to be mannerly," le Puiset said.

"And there were no ravens," Lukas added, conscious of some narrow escape, as though he'd stood for a moment at the perilous brink of the cliffs of Silpius. "You've been delirious."

Le Puiset didn't answer at once, but after a moment he gave a soft huff of breath. "Of course not. Who'd waste a miracle like that on an ungrateful peasant like you?"

Chapter XXI.

The shimmering heat of the last few days erupted into a hot storm of wind that lashed at them every step of the way down Silpius. Lukas and Emelota overruled Count Evrard's objections to strap him to his saddle, and Lukas positioned Emelota beside her brother to hold him steady as they began the long, steep descent. It was darker than ever tonight, as great clouds sailed across the face of the nearly full moon, but Lukas was getting accustomed to navigating the path in the dark. The downward journey left his knees and thighs aching and his head once again dizzy with hunger, but they had descended almost to the level of the nearest rooftops when le Puiset jerked upright and mumbled, "What's that?"

Lukas and Emelota came to a halt and looked in the direction le Puiset was pointing. Across the city in the direction of the palace, a yellow glow shone in the streets. As a fresh gust of the desert wind raced across the city, the glow intensified and flames leaped into the sky: not a tame bonfire like the ones several nights ago, but a quickly-spreading inferno. Thin over the gusting wind, they heard alarm bells ringing in the distance.

"Fire!" Lukas' throat was dry.

"That isn't anywhere near your house, Emelota, is it?" le Puiset asked from his vantage point atop a horse as gaunt and weary as himself.

"No." Emelota pointed north. "Mine is that way. We'll be perfectly safe."

"Downwind of the fire, just beyond the basilica," Lukas corrected her, marvelling inwardly that anyone could be so confidently mistaken. "You're right in the path of danger."

Emelota sent him an amused look. "The house is beside a stream, Lukas."

But given a strong enough wind and flying embers, fire could easily leap a stream. Worse, the basilica was to the north—and so was the Bessarion Lance. His pulse was racing again, telling him to run, to get down into the city and find the lance before everything burned. Was this the opportunity he'd been waiting for? With fire in the city, everyone's attention would be taken up with the problem of fighting it. So long as they succeeded in controlling the blaze, he'd never have a better opportunity.

"Come on," he said, hurrying them down the path again.

Two nights ago, the city had been full of roving war bands, barricades and street fighting. By now, the barricades had fallen—apparently Count Raymond had ruthlessly slaughtered some of the insurgents and then offered the others an amnesty, resulting in a quick restoration of peace—but the streets were now filled with buzzing people craning their necks to see the flames, while groups of the city's natives organised themselves in water-gangs.

The occupying Franks, however, had other concerns. Lukas' little party had not gone far when they were stopped by a band of knights who demanded to know why Lukas and le Puiset were not atop Silpius, fighting. Had it not been for Emelota's vocal assurances, they might have been marched directly back up the mountain.

"We expect you to report to your count as soon as these people are safe," one of the knights ordered Lukas. "We need every spare man on the mountain."

"Yes, my lord." Lukas pretended to meekness. The knights spoke with Norman accents: Bohemond had his men combing the crowds in search of defaulters, and a mute, sullen string of Franks shuffled beneath the watchful eyes of the knights as the press-gang continued towards the mountain. He couldn't risk being swept up in their net, not tonight.

Beside Lukas, the le Puiset siblings seemed more dead than alive, pale even in the ruddy lamplight that blazed from open windows and the streetlamps overhead. Evrard swayed atop his horse, eyes half-closed, using all his failing strength to remain in the saddle. Lukas could not imagine he looked much better himself. His heart failed him at the thought of hurrying the Franks the length of the city to their own home, then doubling back to the house at Rhodion, all while trying to evade the press-gangs and circumnavigate the fire. Instead, when they reached the forum outside the palace, he set off purposefully down the street in the direction of Ilkay's house.

"Where are we going?" Emelota asked, running to catch up with him. "Home is that way."

"I'm taking you to some associates of mine," he told her. "They're closer, and not in the path of the fire."

Emelota glanced anxiously at her failing brother. "Whatever you think best."

"I want to know what *you* think. You're the Revealer."

She looked surprised, but pleased. For a moment she stood looking around them. "I—I think you should speak less," she said at length. "Anyone might be listening…"

Lukas wondered what that was supposed to mean. This street, in the opposite direction to the fire, was very quiet, with hardly any passers-by. In the fitful light of street-lamps and the glare of the distant blaze an idler was leaning against a courtyard entrance further down the street, but he could scarcely have overheard them. Clucking to the horse, Lukas hurried the le Puisets towards Ilkay's house. Zarides would be there, and perhaps other Watchers as well. He put a hand once again to the key, cool and heavy against his breastbone. Nearly—

The door to the courtyard stood half open and energetic sounds came from within. Lukas entered to find torchlight streaming from the open doorway and large windows of the main room, casting the bronze Fortuna into sharp relief. Loud voices called out in Frankish—*See what they've got upstairs—*

Lukas shoved his crossbow into Emelota's arms. It wasn't loaded, but no crossbow looked very friendly when viewed from the business end. "Point this at anyone who bothers you," he said. Her mouth dropped open in alarm, but he had no time to say more. Who knew what was going on in there?

"Zarides!" he shouted, unslinging his staff and loosening Evrard's sword in the scabbard. "Are you in there? Call out if you can hear me!"

The sounds of looting ceased. Somewhere inside the house, a cat yowled angrily; one of the Franks swore loudly. The grey tabby he had seen before streaked out of the house, its tail fluffed up in fright. It hissed at Lukas before vanishing into the shadows.

"What are you doing?" le Puiset rasped, waking from his stupor. "Give me that sword." Lukas ignored him.

Presently the Franks spilled out into the courtyard to see who was shouting. Beside Lukas, Emelota stifled a gasp. There were five of them, gigantic blond men whose filthy hair and unkempt beards seemed a calculated intimidation. Lukas gulped as he saw that one of them wore a necklace of human teeth.

"Where is Zarides?" he asked in Frankish.

"Who's Zarides?" one of the Franks asked, using one of the northern dialects he found difficult to understand—Norman or Flemish. He grinned, halfway through chewing a mouthful of bread from the loaf he held under one arm. "Whoever he is, thank him for us next time you see him."

Lukas glanced at the others, realising they must have been looting Zarides' larder: grain sacks, wine jars, freshly killed chickens swung from their hands. One of them nursed fresh scratches, no doubt from the altercation with the cat. Was food already so scarce?

"You have what you came to find," he told them. "Take it and go."

"Coward!" le Puiset hissed from the saddle behind them. "Emelota! Give me that crossbow!" She paid no attention, either, but his words drew the ruffians' attention to her.

"You're being very generous tonight," their leader said, looking at Emelota with an anticipating grin. "Maybe you'll give us the girl, too, to thank us for leaving you in one piece."

Lukas felt ridiculous, facing five big Frankish bullies with a staff and a borrowed sword, supported only by a half-dead count and a girl with an unloaded crossbow.

Ayla's voice rang in his memory. *I know this kind of scum. Just have to scare their leader, and the rest will follow.*

"Come and take her, then," Lukas said mildly. "Just so long as you give her a decent feed when you're done." Using his right hand, he lowered the weighted tip of his staff carefully to the ground behind him, and nodded to Emelota. "Leave us the crossbow."

Without hesitation, Emelota lowered the weapon to the ground.

The Frank shrugged and stepped forwards—into range.

"Poor choice," Lukas told him, and whipped the staff around in that devastating one-handed blow. The Frank saw it coming and raised his arms with a shout of alarm. That probably saved the man's life: there was a dreadful *crunch* as the staff struck his forearms before beating through his guard and rebounding off his skull. He staggered and dropped, not making another sound.

The others yelled in surprise and terror. One of them dropped the bottles he carried, conjuring starbursts of glass shards and frothing red wine across the mosaic of the tree and the snake.

Lukas pointed at this man with the bloodied end of his staff, willing it not to shake, not to give away the depths of his exhaustion. "Pick up your friend and leave."

Cowed, the looters did as they were told. Within moments the courtyard was clear again. Lukas did his best to prop the gate shut, but it had been rammed open and would not close again. The best he could do was to keep the lights burning and hope no one else tried to force a way in.

"What the hell was that?" le Puiset gasped as he returned. "You offered my *sister* to those *villeins*—"

"It was a ruse," he said coldly, but for some reason it unsettled him to know that Emelota had been telling the truth, that, having taken a bastard half-sister under his protection, Count Evrard was willing to risk any kind of harm to protect her.

Le Puiset slumped in his saddle, consumed by wrath and pain. Emelota went up to him and put a hand over his where it grasped the saddlebow. "It's all right, Evrard. I knew exactly what he intended."

"God! You can't—I swore I would protect—who am I—If I had my strength—!"

"I know," she murmured, unclenching his white fingers from their grip. "I know, my little Evrard."

"Don't call me…" He seemed to relax all of a sudden, sliding sideways onto her. With a grunt of alarm Lukas rushed to help, and thus le Puiset reached the ground rather more quickly and heavily than expected. He was pale and sweating, his eyes closed.

"Let's get him inside," Emelota said. The next few moments were a confused nightmare of pushing and pulling and tripping over the mess the Franks had made of Zarides' front room, but eventually they got the count on the carpet just beneath the window, laid haphazardly across scattered cushions and bits of smashed wood from what had once been a low table. The effort left Lukas dizzy and panting, a trickle of heat running down his back from the two-days-old wound on his shoulder. He folded to his knees and elbows, breathing hard.

Saint George help him, what a narrow escape that had been! The Franks had been giants, twice his mass and hardened warriors. Ayla's trick might not have worked. They might have decided to fight. They might have lashed out and killed him before running away. Even now they might take it into their heads to return, to take their revenge. He had to get up, find Zarides, and retrieve the lance. Just as soon as his head stopped swimming.

Footsteps entered the room and he grabbed for his staff, but it was gone; he must have dropped it in the courtyard when the count toppled from his horse. He looked up and found that it was Emelota. She extended his staff to him and said with a frown, "I've looked, but I couldn't find your friend Zarides, nor any food at all."

Lukas pulled himself gingerly upright, accepting the staff. "I'm sorry. I should have made them leave the food." The Franks had even retrieved the loaf their fallen leader had carried.

Emelota shook her head. "I'm just glad they're gone. But when Evrard wakes, he'll need to eat."

"I need to eat," Lukas said gloomily. A new thought occurred to him. "What about you? How long has it been?"

"I…I've dedicated my fast to the deliverance of the city."

He reached out and caught her arm about the wrist. Before she tore away from his grasp, he felt the bones in her arm and the deep hollows between left by shrinking muscle.

"I think you have fasted enough." He didn't add that if the city's dwindling food stores should go to anyone, he would rather they went to Emelota than her brother.

"I wonder if the horses were fed," she said, glancing out into the courtyard. Le Puiset's horse, a grey rouncey, stood with drooping head in the courtyard, looking little better than Lukas felt.

Franks. "You want me to find horse-feed? Anything else you'd like to order while you're about it?" He climbed shakily to his feet. "Bath-oils? Scented candles? Trained monkey? Your wish is my command."

"Oh, I'd love a trained monkey!"

He stared at her, aghast. "Are you serious?"

She shook her head with a puff of laughter. "I didn't mean you to feed his horse. I meant it's the only thing left to eat."

"What, you want me to slaughter his *horse?* For *food?* Are you trying to get me killed?"

"I'm trying to keep my brother alive!"

"You don't know what that animal means to a man like him."

"I think I understand my—"

"He's lost his men, his strength, his mind—I'm warning you, mademoiselle, you should leave him his horse." Hearing his own words, Lukas stopped and bit his lip. It wasn't that he knew, vividly and painfully, exactly what le Puiset must be feeling right now. He simply didn't wish to provoke the count.

Emelota didn't seem to notice. "There's nothing else, and I'm not sending you out into those streets again. It will have to be the horse; we can open a vein and give him the blood."

Drinking blood? What sort of barbarians must these Franks be, to contemplate such a thing? Still, Emelota was right: without some sort of food, le Puiset would only weaken. Lukas beckoned Emelota into the courtyard and had her take the beast's reins. After more than a year in menial service to Count Raymond, he knew exactly how to bleed a horse. Finding the great vein in the neck, he positioned his small eating-dagger against it and tapped it with a sharp blow from the pommel of le Puiset's sword. The horse shivered, but otherwise did not react as the steel went in; it must be exhausted. Lukas took a bowl from Emelota and twisted the blade until the blood gushed out, hot and metallic-sweet. It took only moments to fill the bowl before he removed the knife and the flow of blood slowed to a trickle.

"Here," he said, shoving the bowl into Emelota's hands. The smell was awful, surrounding him with all the sights and scenes of the last year, all the blood, all the bodies. He couldn't imagine drinking it.

She accepted it with thanks. Lukas remained in the courtyard, clamping a hand over his unsettled stomach. The Fortuna statue's scarred eyes watched him dispassionately from her perch atop her bronze rock. Once again he remembered the girl he had seen crying for help in the sack, the onlooker at Ilkay's death. He didn't recall the name Ilkay had given her. He washed the horse's wound—the cut would heal nicely in time, but the beast would be more comfortable without flies congregating to lap up the blood. He was washing his own hands in the trough when he heard voices from the lighted room.

"This is *blood*."

"It's all we have. Drink it, Evrard, please. If you don't regain your strength…"

Lukas sighed. He might have told her she'd have trouble with this. He stalked into the light and looked down at le Puiset. "It's horse blood. You need it."

Le Puiset spat a red spray and dragged himself up on his elbow. *"You bled my horse? You damned Greek!"*

"On *my* order, Evrard."

Le Puiset's head tipped aside as his weakness caught up with him.

"You—you—"

Lukas fell to his knees and took le Puiset's head in a grip like a vice. Emelota put the bowl to his lips and poured the thick, warm liquid down her brother's throat. The count made no resistance, but he sobbed between swallows. At last Emelota must have judged he'd had enough, for she set the bowl aside and wiped le Puiset's bloodied face and neck.

Lukas released Le Puiset's head, which fell back onto the cushions. "My horse," he whispered, and then there were tears rolling down his face and the sound of hard, racking sobs.

"Oh, don't be such a baby," Emelota said, but Lukas found he couldn't stand to listen. *Don't you understand?* he wanted to growl at her. Didn't she know what it did to a man to be systematically stripped of everything that gave him power or purpose, until he no longer had the means to protect even the most helpless of the things that depended upon him? Instead, he reached for the crossbow and wound it, loading it with one of the three bolts he'd stuck in his belt when they'd handed him the weapon atop Silpius. The effort left him sweating again, but he finished and pressed the weapon into Emelota's hands. "I need to find out what's become of my friend Zarides. Take—"

The room swung crazily around him. The next instant, to his amazement, he found himself sitting on the floor with his legs splayed out, shock reverberating through his body. Emelota seized him around the chest with one arm, propping him up in a seated position. He could smell the horse blood from the bowl in her hand.

"I'm all right," he snarled. "Let go of me."

"You're not all right! You fell!"

"I am…" Midsentence, he lost control of his body and his head dropped back on her shoulder. When the dizziness passed a moment later, she had let him down to the floor.

Slipping an arm beneath his head, she put the warm rim of the bowl to his lips.

"No," he protested, but his voice was lost against the hot salty tang of blood. To his disgust, his stomach welcomed it with a growl.

"Now sleep," she told him. A sorcerer might have spoken the words, for they blotted out all present matters from his mind.

***

Emelota was screaming.

A jolt of fear went through him. Lukas was on his knees, staff in hand, before he knew he was awake. There were flying elflocks and the flash of a straight sword before his eyes. A Turk! Reverting to his years of training, Lukas reached for his staff and jabbed it up under the round buckler. The swing of the enemy's sword went wide and he doubled and dropped, winded and retching, offering an easy target. He reached for le Puiset's sword to finish the man—but there was no time; another Turk loomed up behind the first. Abruptly, Lukas' limbs refused to obey his commands. He tried to rise to his feet but pitched drunkenly forwards instead, directly into the path of the Turk's sword.

A crossbow sang behind them and a bolt thwacked into the attacker's eye. All the force went out of the descending sword-stroke. Lukas got le Puiset's sword out at last and dealt with the winded Turk on the floor. After that, silence descended. Lukas sank onto the carpet, breathing hard.

"Well shot, mademoiselle," he said, but when he turned to look behind him, Count Evrard sat with his back against the wall, balancing the spent crossbow on his knees.

Emelota was on the ground beside her brother, white with shock. "I'm so sorry! I meant to keep watch, but I fell asleep."

"Don't apologise to the peasant," le Puiset growled.

Lukas got up and looked out into the courtyard, which stood empty but for the silent Fortuna.

"We're clear," he told the le Puisets, returning to the room. "No more Turks."

Emelota sighed in relief. Lukas reached for the door-lintel to steady himself. Now that the crisis was past, he began to shake as the tension left his body. He felt sick and light-headed, and the nauseating taste of horse blood was still in his mouth. And Evrard of le Puiset was holding a crossbow.

"Give that back to Emelota," he said, stooping to retrieve the bolt from the Turk's eye. "I don't trust you with a weapon."

Le Puiset's mouth thinned, but to Lukas' amazement, he did as he was told. All he said, after a moment, was, "Are you going to pick up my sword and clean it properly?"

If that was all the thanks he would have, he'd prefer le Puiset's threats and taunts. At least those reminded him to stay angry. Lukas wiped the blade carefully on the tunic of one of the fallen Turks and sheathed it before going through the small pouch each man wore at his side. To his satisfaction, he discovered a small packet of dates and almonds. "Here's food," he said, offering the greasy parcel to Emelota. "Eat it. All of it."

"But I…"

"Eat it!" her brother snapped. Emelota obediently put one of the dates in her mouth. Lukas returned to the door, looking out on the night. The courtyard gate stood ajar. The light of the fire still glared in the city, an eerie red light silhouetting the buildings towards the north. The wind had died, but above, the clouds had shredded from the sky, and Lukas judged from the position of the stars that he must have been asleep no more than two or three hours. He felt as though he'd been dragged from his own grave, aching all over and sick to his stomach, with a line of flame marked across his shoulders where his wound had split open. But he also felt a little clearer in the head, and he thought he could go on, if he must.

And he must. Already his chances of finding the Bessarion Lance were dying away with the flames. He closed his eyes, fixing Zarides' face in his mind, seeking a vision. None came.

"Can't it wait until morning?" Emelota sent him a pleading look and he realised with a jolt that she must have divined his intentions. That was unsettling. He shook his head. Of course, it was horribly risky to leave them alone like this, but the basilica key burned against his breastbone.

"My friend is missing," he said. "Am I *meant* to stay?"

Le Puiset looked from Lukas to his sister in evident puzzlement.

Emelota simply bit her lip and shook her head.

"Be careful, Lukas. Something is waiting for you out there."

"I know it is." He finished cleaning the crossbow bolt and laid it, with the others, at Emelota's side. He hesitated another moment, then unbuckled le Puiset's sword and put it beside them. He'd thought he wanted the prestige of carrying a knightly weapon but, if he was honest with himself, he was better accustomed to the staff now, and the sword had only weighed him down. "You take care, too, mademoiselle."

Without a word or glance for the silent le Puiset, he left the house and stepped through the courtyard gates into the flickering darkness of the street beyond. It was quiet, the people driven inside either by weariness or out of fear: the city was full of looters, Turkish resistance, and the princes' press-gangs. Like many of the poorer streets of Antioch, this one was shaded along the footpaths by lattices protruding from the buildings, rather than by the remnants of the old colonnades. The lamps hanging from them must have been snuffed by the wind; the city Watch, whose job it was to keep them burning, had not passed by to rekindle them. All the same, he could see pretty well by the light of the waxing moon, from the yawning black opening of a covered street not far away to the huddled shapes of corpses still rotting in the streets, left where they had fallen after the sack.

He'd never thought he would become so inured to the stench of rotting flesh.

How would he find Zarides? Lukas had no idea where to begin. Tigranants, perhaps, would know; but he didn't know where to find Tigranants either. Still, there were others in this city who knew Tigranants, foremost among them Lusine, the Armenian woman who'd brought a pair of Turks into the basilica during the sack and then agreed to care for the le Puisets' chaplain while Emelota went to fetch her brother. He would find Lusine, then, since he had no better plan.

He had reached this decision when his skin prickled in an unmistakeable warning. Lukas turned, gripping his staff. In the moonlight, the street seemed empty at first. He moved into the centre of the street so that anyone approaching him would need to move through the light. He waited again, but the sense of being watched only became more intolerable. He turned at a sudden movement from the lattice over the house of Ilkay. A great black shadow unfurled immense wings and flapped laboriously into the air. Lukas saw it clearly outlined against the moon as it passed directly overhead, ruffling his hair with the blast of its wings: a black vulture of the sort that had followed his steps from Constantinople to Syria.

Lilith.

Antioch might be full of the dead, but no bird of prey of that size would willingly descend to a city still populated by the living, nor fly through the streets at night.

Be careful, Lukas. Something is waiting for you out there. Was this what Emelota had sensed? Lukas watched as the great bird glided to land upon the lattice a little further down the street towards the palace. He thought he caught a gleam in its eye as it swivelled its head to look at him—but that was ridiculous; there was no light to catch in the mirrors of its irises. He shivered and made the sign of the cross. Then he followed the bird.

Lilith did not lead him directly towards the great forum and the palace, instead angling directly north until he came to the street leading from the palace to the Bridge Gate. Here, the bird quietly swooped down into the street and settled upon a body lying in the shadow of the fitfully-lighted colonnade, setting to work stripping the softened flesh from the bones. Lukas shuddered and turned his back, watching the street.

"Why have you brought me here?" he demanded, but there was no answer from the bird.

There soon came the tramp of marching feet and the glare of torches from the direction of the palace. Recognising a press-gang, Lukas slipped behind one of the columns. The vulture swallowed a strip of flesh and stalked towards him on its clawed feet, watching the procession through little fierce eyes: Lukas saw that its face was striped with black and white, masked and warlike. Following its gaze, he watched as the unwilling recruits marched by—and caught his breath as he saw Zarides among them. The Franks must be so desperate they were now pressing everyone into service, whether Frankish or Syrian.

That explained what had happened to Zarides, but how was he to retrieve the Bessarion Lance now? When the abject procession had shuffled by, Lukas turned on the vulture.

"What's the meaning of this? In God's name, speak!"

The bird was suddenly a ruffle of angry feathers, jumping away from him with a flap of its wings. It fixed him with an outraged stare and then launched itself into the air, struggling to gain height. It had not yet lifted itself above the buildings of the street when a familiar voice spoke behind Lukas.

"I thought you'd never summon me."

He turned with a hammering heart. Lilith stood watching him, her shape smoky and insubstantial in the flickering lamplight. She was half-woman, half-bird, the feathers moulting from arms and talons like melting wax. She smiled with bloody lips and said, "You haven't been sleeping much of late. Are you trying to avoid me that way? It's quite useless, you know. I am paying you *very close attention, Lukas Bessarion.*"

He tried to ignore the way his skin prickled at the back of his neck. "What do you want?"

"Nothing more than I have always wanted from you."

Khalil ibn Hassan's freedom. Lukas ran the tip of his tongue across his lips. "Never."

"You don't understand, do you?" She cocked her head in a quick, birdlike motion too fluid for a human. "*I* filled le Puiset with pestilence. *I* handed Zarides to your enemies. I walked at your side this night as you descended Silpius; I sent the Flemish barbarians to Ilkay's house to meet you. All that has gone wrong for you this past week—did you believe it was just ill luck?"

"You didn't send the ravens."

"No," she said with a laugh. "What can I say? I like to watch people suffer. I didn't send the ravens, but neither have I been prevented from doing as I like with you, Lukas Bessarion. So know this." Her voice became low and caressing. "Until you fulfil your vow and go to Oliveta to release Khalil ibn Hassan to my service, you will *never* retrieve your father's lance. I will be watching every move you make, listening to each word you whisper in your most private sanctuary. There is no bargain you can make, no escape you can find from me."

He felt the heat of her malice on his brow like the sun at noonday, but he was more angry than afraid. So, Zarides had been pressed into service; but that left Tigranants and twenty-four other Watchers at large. Give him a bare dozen and the rest of the night, and he would unearth the lance. He wouldn't surrender so easily, certainly not to Lilith. "You can do nothing," he snarled, turning on his heel and hurrying up the street in the direction of the palace.

She fluttered to his side. "You don't believe me? You will." She swooped at him like a bird, plunging right through him with a chill that dropped him, shaking and crying out, to his knees.

He was still kneeling in the street, breathing hard in the grip of panic, when the Frankish press-gang found him.

Chapter XXII.

"Bohemond!" Saint-Gilles roared when he caught sight of the South Norman, ignoring all civilities of title. *"Bohemond!* What the *devil* do you think you're doing?"

Bathed in the glaring light of flames, the count of Taranto stood at his ease in the broad Colonnaded Street watching as his knights dragged men at sword point into their gangs. Many were Provençals of all stations, from the unarmed poor, snivelling in fear, to counts blustering with indignation. Others—women, children, and the aged—wandered through the streets, driven from their blazing houses.

"Ah, Saint-Gilles!" Bohemond's smile came as easily as ever, but dark circles underlined his eyes. "Congratulate me: I've discovered a solution to that little problem we discussed this morning on Silpius."

The manpower problem. Saint-Gilles *knew* the wily Norman must have been up to something, but the implications of Bohemond's words robbed him momentarily of speech. Even in the heat of flames and wind, his scalp prickled. "This was *your* doing? You set this fire on purpose?"

"How else was I to flush out our defaulters?"

Forget challenging Bohemond to a battle: Saint-Gilles was ready to take him by the throat and throttle him where he stood. *"Our* defaulters?" he said. "You come into *my* part of the city, set fire to *my* holdings, and round up *my* people? Devil take it!" He pointed north with a quivering hand. "If my people can't get this fire under control it'll burn the granary. We'll starve. You *fool!"*

"Kerbogha will kill us quicker than starvation will," Bohemond said.

Though his tone was confident, the smile had vanished from his face.

"Set these people free at once. You have no right—"

"I have every right," Bohemond cut in. "Until Alexius comes, you swore I should have the rule of this city if I was able to encompass its fall. Do you mean to go back on your oath?"

Saint-Gilles was a sinful man, but there was one thing he'd never done. Even when it meant excommunication or worse, he'd never broken his sworn word. Not to his first wife, his beloved Philippa, when he might have abandoned her in pursuit of a more politically advantageous marriage; not to Alexius, when the emperor's underhanded dealings left his men bleeding and penniless after Nicaea; and not to Bohemond, now.

Not unless he was forced into it.

"You did this without my knowledge or consent," he said in a voice thick with rage. "Perhaps you have the rule of this city, but you do not rule my people. Do as I tell you. Free them, unless you wish to make me your enemy."

"If I do that, we will all die tomorrow. I cannot hold Silpius without men." Bohemond's voice rang with utter certainty.

Saint-Gilles looked into the pleading faces of his people, noting how many of them—high and low together—bore the numb and despairing look of men whose courage had broken at last, under unspeakable strain. He swore under his breath. Bohemond was right: these men would not fight unless they were forced to do it, and even starvation was preferable to losing the battle on Silpius. An inner voice whispered that this was his own failure. Had he been more concerned about the safety of the city, rather than his feud with Bohemond, the South Norman count would have had no excuse to come here tonight.

Now that he had, there was nothing Saint-Gilles could do about it. They needed men on the mountain, every last man they could find. The awareness must show on his face, for he saw it reflected in the slight curve at the corner of Bohemond's mouth.

It was unbearable, this necessity to keep his mouth shut, preserving the fiction that both of them were working together to keep the pilgrimage alive.

He turned to meet the terrified eyes of his people, raising a hand for attention.

"I am ashamed of you." He filled the words with all the rage and scorn he felt for Bohemond. "Will you give way entirely to cowardice? For all his might, Kerbogha still has not crushed us. Stand fast, and we may beat him yet. You have my leave to skulk and cower once the fighting is hopeless. But, by God and all his saints, not one moment sooner! God's will!"

There was a little half-hearted cheering, mostly from Bohemond's Normans.

"Not a bad speech." There was no hint of mockery in Bohemond's voice. "My thanks."

His duty to the pilgrimage done, now it was time to speak plainly. Saint-Gilles beckoned Bohemond apart from their attendants.

"Don't for a moment imagine I did that for *your* sake," he growled, pitching his voice to the register that made his own men chime in their armour. "If you think you can get away with this, you're mistaken. I know perfectly well that you did this to strike at me."

"To strike at *you!*" Bohemond raised his eyebrows. "If anything, the only person I've injured tonight is myself, since this city was ceded to me. Besides, a few houses can be rebuilt. It's the safety of this whole pilgrimage that's at stake; or have you forgotten about that?"

"I never forget it for a *moment.*"

"Don't you? That's very strange." Bohemond still wasn't smiling. "As I recall, you spent the whole winter arguing that we should pursue the close siege of this city, even when we all—even Tatikius—warned you the death toll would be intolerable. And it was, but *you* were quite happy, because you had everyone coming to *you* for the emperor's gold. Were you thinking of the pilgrimage then, Saint-Gilles? Or did you consider so many lives a small price to pay for the power of supreme command?"

Saint-Gilles felt the blood rush from his head. Had Bohemond seen through him so easily? "What are you saying?" he whispered.

"No more than I've observed. Here's another thing: you may be very good at making people afraid of you, but there's one thing I've never seen you manage, and that is to make people love you. Why else do you think Tatikius left us last winter? He wished to withdraw to a distant blockade, and you told him it would happen over his dead body."

That had been sword rattling, meant only to show the gold-nosed Greek he had no intention of backing down. Saint-Gilles snorted in disdain. "Tatikius was well aware that wasn't meant seriously."

Bohemond sent him an incredulous look, gilded in the flickering firelight.

A suspicion struck Saint-Gilles as he remembered the miserable February day on which he'd woken to find the Greek camp deserted. The ambush on the road, when he rode in pursuit…Tatikius' cold glare, the suspicion with which he'd been met. Outrage burned through him. "He believed otherwise? How? Why? What did you say to him?"

Now the smile was back on Bohemond's face, but it was the smile of a predator going in for the kill. "And what if I did? Tatikius had instructions from Constantinople to put more faith in me than in anyone else. And no matter what he may have told *you,* he never deviated from those orders."

Bohemond has sworn oaths that even he will find it difficult to break, Tatikius had said all those months ago. Saint-Gilles felt cold sliding down his neck. "You have a special arrangement with him. That's why you won't show me your chrysobull."

Bohemond stepped back, a guarded look shuttering his eyes. "And you have a peculiarly suspicious mind. Which is why you ordered your interpreter to search my tent."

With a mocking bow, the South Norman count returned to his men. Saint-Gilles stood in the shadows, his hands clenching and unclenching, breathing slowly. Devil take it! Someone must have overheard his instructions to Bessarion on the crest of Silpius. He was a fool, a fool…

Without a word, he turned and beckoned to his attendants, who didn't look him in the eye as they followed him back to the palace. Nor did Saint-Gilles acknowledge them. He went directly upstairs to his quarters, locked the door, took up a large vase that stood upon a table there—pottery in a beautiful feldspar green glaze, festooned with a shape like a long, serpentine dragon—and hurled it against the stone floor with all his might.

A shriek sounded from the next room. Footsteps pattered across the floor to the connecting door and it slid open an inch, showing one fearful eye. Elvira. Her nerves had suffered since the child's death, and although he'd sent her to sit out the worst of the siege in comfort at Alexandretta, she had returned at the news of Kerbogha's approach. Consumed by his own affairs, Saint-Gilles had scarcely seen his wife since her return. Her apartments were at the other end of the palace.

He drew in a deep breath and rasped, "What are you doing here?"

"I…" She pushed the door open a little further. A couple of yawning attendants were behind her, but she closed the door between them, leaving them in privacy. Elvira seemed about to say something, but then she saw the shattered pottery on the floor at his feet. Words failed her, and she stared at the mess with her lips parted, pale as death.

"An accident," he said, feeling vaguely guilty. The vase must have been priceless, an import from the farthest East. The lie made him feel even worse, the more so as it didn't seem to set the girl's mind at ease. "What did you want with me, my lady?"

She touched the tip of her tongue to her lips, not looking at him. "I had a dream. It frightened me."

Was he a nursemaid now, to blot the tears of a frightened child? Philippa would have known what to do, but if Philippa were still alive, he would not be married to this helpless girl, would he? He shrugged, at a loss. "Do you need a priest?"

"No, my lord, it isn't…" She swallowed hard. "It was a warning, my lord, about the young prophet they call Peter Bartholomew. I beg you not to put your trust in him. No good will come of it."

Saint-Gilles scowled. Only this morning, a menial stable-hand had waylaid him as he mounted his horse for the journey up Silpius. The youngster's right arm hung useless, perhaps the result of a battle injury, but the left was quite good enough to hold a bridle in the courtyard. Once Saint-Gilles was settled in the saddle, the boy clung to the rein a moment too long.

"You've met with him, my lord. The one called Peter Bartholomew," the boy had said. "You should listen to him. He's a holy man."

"He is, is he? And what makes you say that?"

"He cares for us poor, my lord. He says we're as noble as anyone else in this pilgrimage, that a peasant has the same right to fight for Christ as anyone else." The boy's eyes glowed with fervour. "Do as he tells you. You won't regret it."

The youngster was either naïve or foolhardy, to make such a recommendation to a prince like himself. Saint-Gilles couldn't help liking him. "I'll bear it in mind," he had said, suppressing his amusement. "You haven't worked in my stables long, I think."

"No, my lord. I was a beggar until my lady, your countess, took pity on me. Wrenched an arm in the fighting at Christmas, and haven't been able to use it since. I thought you'd understand, about Peter Bartholomew."

"Quite," he had said dryly. "Will you give me my reins?"

Now, he watched Elvira through narrowed eyes. It seemed that everyone, from his lady to his stable-hands, had an opinion on the young prophet. "What exactly do you fear about Bartholomew?"

She wrung her hands. "I can't say. I don't know."

Saint-Gilles gave a sceptical grunt. "It was just a dream. Don't trouble yourself about such things. You're my lady wife, not a seer. Mind your own affairs." She looked stricken, and he cleared his throat. "You've been doing works of charity, they tell me. I'll speak to my chamberlain in the morning and see to it that you have access to one-tenth of my treasury to bestow in alms as you see fit, in my name."

Her mouth fell open, a flush rising on her cheeks. "Truly?"

It ought to have been his duty, and he'd neglected it sorely this past week. If Elvira would take the whole business off his hands, he'd have more time to devote to greater affairs—like whatever it was Bohemond was up to. "Truly. Now run along." He looked at the shattered clay at his feet, and sighed. "And send in someone to clean up this mess."

Elvira obeyed with incoherent thanks. Saint-Gilles retired to his own chambers and paced the room, gnawing on what he had learned this evening. Bohemond. Bohemond had known all along of his own agreement with Tatikius. Perhaps the Greek general had even told Bohemond the details of the agreement made that night in Marash, with his son's blood upon his hands—Saint-Gilles drew in a sharp breath as the implications struck him. What would happen if Bohemond told the other princes that Saint-Gilles planned to make himself their leader? They'd never understand his reasoning—that safeguarding the alliance with Alexius was the only way to keep the whole pilgrimage alive. Their sense of pride would be stung. Bohemond might turn all of them against Saint-Gilles with a few words.

Tatikius had never really committed to a Provençal alliance: he must have been content to wait, meaning to play the two rivals against each other and profit by it. Instead, it had been Bohemond who played Saint-Gilles and Tatikius against each other, and sent the Greek packing. As a parting gift, Tatikius had even ceded Bohemond the command of fertile Cilicia! No doubt in exchange for his *friendly warning.*

More implications flashed through his mind. Bohemond must have seen his gambit to discard Tatikius as a guaranteed win. In the short term, he was able to refill his empty coffers with the Cilician incomes. In the long term, either Tatikius would return with Alexius, bringing further help, bolstering Bohemond's bid to make himself Grand Domestic of the East… or he would not, leaving Bohemond free to take Antioch for himself.

Somehow in all of this, the bitterest thing was the thought that Tatikius had, in the end, preferred to trust *Bohemond* to himself. Devil take it, the Greeks had been playing a double game. If Alexius *did* return to Antioch, despite all Saint-Gilles' work on behalf of the Greek alliance, likely the emperor would cede the city to Bohemond anyway.

No, here was the bitterest thing: that it was Saint-Gilles' own determination to make himself leader of the pilgrimage, his commitment to a close siege, that had given Bohemond the opportunity to make his move at all.

He ground his teeth in frustration. In all this there was one consolation:

clearly, Bohemond could not resist gloating over his victory. He would have been wiser not to reveal this information, but Saint-Gilles had it now, and it gave him a thread to pull on. A way to expose his rival, if only he could manage it before Bohemond exposed *him.*

Just what *was* Bohemond's relationship with Alexius?

Though Bohemond might keep the details of his oath secret, his actions spoke for themselves. At Constantinople he'd acted as the emperor's enforcer, persuading Saint-Gilles and the other princes to swear and then threatening to fight them if they refused. At Nicaea, he'd acted as the emperor's quartermaster, the Greek merchants setting up their markets to supply the camp under Bohemond's supervision. All the long way through Anatolia, the Greeks and Normans had marched together, camped together, fought together. Now, the Norman boasted that Tatikius acted on Alexius' orders to trust him above anyone else.

Bohemond has sworn oaths that even he will find it difficult to break.

Oh, he had a fair idea of what sort of oath Bohemond had sworn. But without the chrysobull, he had no proof!

Where *was* Lukas Bessarion? Perhaps he should send up Silpius, call the interpreter back. No, on second thought, he would leave Bessarion be. Let Bohemond lift a finger against him, and Saint-Gilles would have the opportunity he dimly craved, and none of the princes would gainsay him…

If only he could ask Adhemar what to do…but all of a sudden he could picture the bishop shaking his head doubtfully. *Does it matter who ends up with Antioch so long as the people are safe?*

Yes. Yes, it did, because Bohemond was arrogant and ambitious and ought not to be allowed to get away with this—with *any* of it. Who knew what he might be planning? Saint-Gilles didn't mean to survive Kerbogha only to be ostracised for the crime of trying to preserve the pilgrimage's most crucial alliance.

When, hours later, Galdemar returned with news that the city's most well-stocked granary had burned in an inferno that smelled, tantalisingly, of bread, Saint-Gilles knew it was time to make use of every tool in his arsenal.

Bohemond had to be stopped, no matter the cost.

Chapter XXIII.

With Lukas Bessarion gone, silence fell once again in the empty, ransacked house. Beside Emelota, Evrard shivered. "I know this house," he told her in a whisper. "This was where Galon died…"

His voice trailed away, but Emelota knew that a part of him had been trapped in this place ever since, watching a disaster he was helpless to prevent. She was glad that Lukas had dragged the Turkish bodies into the courtyard before he went away, but the smell of blood and death was still thick in the room.

"This cursed city," her brother whispered. "It's a trap. Easy to get in. Impossible to get out."

"We can leave this house, at any rate, but not until morning. Try to rest. I'll get up in a moment and do something about the gate."

He slipped uncomplainingly into sleep. Emelota ate the rest of the fruit and nuts Lukas had scavenged from the dead Turks, her stomach welcoming the food eagerly. Afterwards, she sank back against the wall, putting a hand on Evrard's head where he lay exhausted and still against her side. She would find some glass or metalware or something, like the bowl they'd used to bleed the horse, and prop it up against the gate so that if anyone pushed into the courtyard it would make a loud noise and waken them. But she was so tired, and her eyelids were heavy…

Eventually she got up, retrieved the bowl, and went to the door. Light shone into her eyes, momentarily blinding her. After a moment, her vision adjusted: beyond was no courtyard, no mosaic of snake and tree. Instead she stepped out onto the sun-drenched meadow between the city and the river: a different Antioch, a city raw and new, all fluted columns and gilded statues. On the meadow, a group of people in outlandish costumes—soft draperies and laurel wreaths, bronze breastplates and white horsehair crests—had gathered solemnly about a platform of stone atop which burned a great fire. The crowd stood silently in a ring about the altar, carrying baskets festooned with late-summer roses.

Some sort of festival, Emelota guessed, smelling incense and perfume—but where were the crosses and icons? This looked like Antioch, but the fashions were strange, and the chanting voices spoke in a language she did not recognise. Two of the white-clad men moved towards the altar, escorting a slight figure. Emelota caught a vague impression of trailing ribbons, wild black hair and young white limbs as the onlookers tossed handfuls of barley into the air, thick enough to obscure the view.

Emelota stepped forwards, then in a moment of caution glanced behind her. The door stood open behind her like a slash in the air. Through it she could see into the dark, bloodstained room where Evrard lay sleeping.

Beside it, a girl perched on a rock, wearing a diadem and holding a sheaf of grain in her hand. Emelota immediately recognised the bronze statue that had stood in the courtyard—except that this girl was no longer a statue. She appeared now as flesh and blood, her milky eyes showing where she had been blinded, her flowing garments made of fine white linen. Emelota's breath stopped as the girl raised a hand and pointed towards the altar.

"Bear witness," she said in a trembling voice. "See what they did to me."

Emelota turned again, moving forward through the crowd and the showers of grain as the men in white came to a halt beside the fire. It was a girl standing between them—the same girl she had just spoken with. There was something ageless about the living statue, but despite her gangly height, the girl at the altar was little more than a child. Her eyes seemed glassy and unfocused as one of the men bent towards her and whispered in her ear. The other man took a jug of water and poured it over the girl's head, causing her to bend her neck under the shock of cold. The crowd erupted into cheers, a hushed and reverent acclamation.

"They made me drunk on the fumes that come out of the mountain, so that I would not scream or cry." Through the sound of applause, the girl's voice sounded directly into Emelota's ear. "Then they asked my consent, and poured cold water over me to make me bow my head, the way they would an ox or pig. My consent! I never gave it."

A beribboned basket of barley and a bronze vessel on three wrought feet stood on the ground beside the altar. One of the priests bent down and lifted out a large, curved blade—something between a knife and a sword, with a single cutting edge. Emelota tried to turn her head away with a gasp, but the voice of the girl hissed, "Bear witness!" Emelota pressed a hand against her mouth, but she did as she was commanded: she watched as the priests stretched out the girl's neck above the bronze tripod and drew the wicked blade across her throat, spilling her blood like a red curtain into the bowl.

Emelota had witnessed death, violent death, before; but never like this, decked in ribbons and hymned by gentlewomen, as though it was no great horror after all. She surfaced from her dream gasping, opening her eyes to find herself lying beside Evrard in the fading lamplight. The stuffy room smelled of fresh blood and rotting corpses—as did all of Antioch these days. She put her hands over her nose with a whimper, but it made no difference. What did it mean? She was too exhausted to think, drugged with sleep as though she, too, had been breathing the mountain fumes.

At length, she got up and went to open the door again. Beyond, the courtyard was empty and quiet, but the girl still waited, perched on her rock in soft flesh and white linen. *Bear witness,* she had said. For a moment, Emelota didn't know what to say; she didn't even know whether she was awake or dreaming, speaking to a mortal or a spirit.

Whatever this was, it had once been human. Emelota closed the door behind her so as not to wake Evrard and went to put a hand on the girl's shoulder.

"What is your name?"

"Tyche," the girl said, not looking up, "which means Fortune."

"I meant your real name; the one your parents gave you."

Her lips worked soundlessly for a moment. "Aemathe," she said at last, very softly.

"Aemathe," Emelota repeated, taking care with the unfamiliar sounds. Even seated, the girl was taller than herself. She peered up into the tearstained face and said the one, pointless thing she could find to say, which was, "I saw what they did to you. It was cruel—and evil."

Aemathe put a hand over her mouth, drew in a sharp breath. "It was. You think so, too. I have always thought so. I have never been strong enough to say it."

"Why not?"

"I was their slave," Aemathe told her. "Bound into this image, forced to hear and answer their prayers. I had a little power of my own, one of the last of the descendants of the demigods. We had become few, and it was thought more profitable to sacrifice us and make us gods than to let us die mortal deaths and go down to Hades."

Emelota stared. "You mean that all this time…"

"I don't know how many thousands of years I have been the slave of the image. First I served the kings of Antioch, then the senate. When the new religion came, my power dwindled. I slept for many years, until a new master awakened me. But he was only the master of this house, and then he too was sacrificed. I had almost fallen asleep again when you came and I thought…I thought that you might be able to hear me, since the other one could not."

The other one—Lukas Bessarion? "You could tell we had gifts?"

"Gifts? You mean power? Mine dwindled, when the Son came and the old demon that bound me here was cast out. Once I could not just *see* intentions and probabilities; I could affect them too."

Emelota's pulses quickened. "You were a Revealer, like me?"

"Oh, mortal. I was far more than that. I was Fortuna. Men prayed to me for luck, good for themselves and evil for their enemies."

"And you gave it to them? After what they did to you?"

"What choice did I have?" Her voice was bitter. "I was only ever the creature of the lords of Antioch and their unseen guardian. I would have helped them without being enslaved, but they wanted a power that was completely their own."

Emelota felt hot, suffocated. She was beginning to realise this was more than a simple dream. It was one thing to see saints and angels, but Aemathe was neither. Was she endangering her soul, even listening to this story? "Why are you telling me all this?"

"Because there is no one else." The blind eyes were desperate. "Help me escape this bondage. The demon guardian who bound me here is gone. All you need to do is destroy this vessel and I'll be free."

Free—to do what? Emelota made the sign of the Cross. "I charge you in the name of Christ, what are you? Answer me truly."

"I am descended from the demigods, the giants that were in the land in ancient times. Their fathers were demon princes, but their mothers were mortal. Have you not heard of us?"

"I—I think I have," Emelota squeaked, recalling certain half-forgotten tales of Saint Moses encountering giants in the wilderness. Was that the reason for Aemathe's imposing height? Those nephilim had been wicked, but they had also been mortals, as Aemathe had been when she was killed. And mortals, she felt sure, were capable of redemption. "If I free you, what will you do?"

"Anything that lies within my power. Although I fear it will be a small reward, and I do not know if I will be permitted to stay in this world long enough to repay you."

Oh. "You needn't reward me," Emelota assured her. "Only, I cannot free you if it will harm anyone. The city is under siege, and..."

"Would you have me rescue it, then?"

Hope rose up, nearly strong enough to choke upon. Emelota took a deep breath. "Could you?"

"I could try. Perhaps I have one last fortune to make for the city of Antioch. A good one, and not the vengeance I once planned for them." A faint line etched its way between Aemathe's brows. "I am told that Hades was harrowed with the rising of the Son, so that now his enemies go into a place of anguish. I would make peace with him, if I could. Do you think it would be enough, if I returned good for all the evil they did me?"

This was a task for a priest, not an ignorant girl like herself. Emelota bit her lip. "Such peace isn't a thing you can earn, Aemathe, any more than any amount of their worship could make up for what the people of Antioch did to you all those years ago."

"How is it to be come by, then?"

She could hardly ask, say, Evrard's chaplain to make a journey across the city to instruct the statue of a pagan goddess—even if he had recovered from his illness sufficiently to do so. Father Adso would call it blasphemy, and perhaps he would be right. Perhaps she was being very wicked, or only foolhardy. But she thought she sensed something about Aemathe's head, a faint light that owed nothing to the dented bronze diadem the ancient daughter of demigods wore.

So she breathed a prayer and said, "I will tell you what I know."

* * *

"Your hands are wet," Evrard said when she woke him at sunrise. Emelota wiped them guiltily across her skirts. She had done a very presumptuous thing: she had taken it upon herself to perform a baptism. Sometimes, like this morning, she worried she had ceased to follow her gift and begun doing what was right in her own eyes. Still, she *did* think it the right thing to do, and who could do better than that?

"I fetched you water to drink," she told him, and so hid one truth behind another. "There's no other food, except..."

Evrard shuddered. "No more blood, I beg of you."

He sat up—without her help; he looked much better than he had last night—and took the bowl from her. It was already beaded with sweat in the early heat: the day would be shimmering hot. Emelota sat back on her heels, looking out the window. In the courtyard, the bronze statue also glittered with beads of water, although she wasn't entirely sure last night's conversation hadn't been a dream.

"No other disturbances in the night?" Evrard asked, following her gaze towards the window.

Emelota managed a smile. "None of any importance."

His eyes narrowed. "How do you mean? That Syrian madman didn't return, did he?"

"No!" Emelota took a deep breath. "I only wondered…" In truth, she had been wondering how she was to arrange for the melting down of a bronze statue which was larger than herself and the property of someone else. If only she had ever told Evrard about her gift! If only she could ask his opinion, or gain his support in asking someone who *did* know; the papal legate, for instance, or even their own chaplain—if Father Adso was still alive. She sighed and came at the subject more obliquely. "Did you know that Lukas Bessarion has visions?"

Evrard put the bowl down so suddenly that the water slopped over the brim, soaking his lap. "Lukas Bessarion boasts of things he knows nothing about." He shivered and crossed himself. "I suppose he told you the ravens feed him."

"N-o, he didn't say any such thing."

"If there's any truth in it, it's the work of demons," Evrard snarled. "Well? Are we going home?"

Emelota got up. "I'll saddle your horse," she murmured. Outside in the courtyard, she halted to touch the scar-eyed Aemathe on her bronze cheek. "I'm sorry," she whispered. "I have to go, but I'll return, I promise."

* * *

Several hours later, Emelota let herself back into their lodgings to find the place as silent and quiet as when she had left. Evrard lay in the bed she had hastily remade with their last clean blanket, still asleep—a healing sleep, his face flushed a little with the day's warmth but not burning to the touch. Father Adso's shrouded body lay in a corner. Lusine, her Armenian attendant, had tended the chaplain faithfully in Emelota's absence and shrouded his body decently after his death, but Emelota could not help feeling vaguely guilty, as though the chaplain might have lived had she not gone away.

As Emelota put the greasy, fly-speckled parcel she carried into a basket upon the hearth, Lusine left Evrard's side and came to meet her.

"Have you eaten?" Emelota asked the attendant in the hesitant Arabic she had learned out of curiosity and boredom this long winter.

"Only yesterday," Lusine said, although there was a longing look in her eyes as she sniffed the aroma of roasted mutton. "You eat first, *sayyida.* I'll go to see about the father's burial."

Father Adso might already smell a little in the heat, having died yesterday morning, while Emelota had been sponging Evrard with feverfew up on Silpius. He could not remain in the house much longer, but Emelota could not bear to think of his body being stacked in a cul-de-sac somewhere to rot until the siege broke and there was time to bury the bodies. Perhaps Lusine might find a charnel house not yet filled to overflowing. All the same, Emelota hesitated, throwing a glance towards Evrard. "We cannot afford to pay much…"

Lusine touched her shoulder gently. "I am sure I can find something, in charity."

With Lusine gone, the room felt closer and stuffier than ever despite its thick adobe walls. She had not imagined the faint stench of rot, after all. Emelota pushed open the window shutters in hopes of allowing a little air into the room—hot and laden with stink as it was. The shutters creaked, and she heard a gasp behind her. Evrard rolled from the bed with staring eyes, his hands clutching at his waist for weapons that weren't there.

"Evrard," she said softly, "it's all right. It's me. We're safe, remember?"

He focused on her slowly and let out a long, careful breath; then he subsided onto the bed, burying his face in his hands.

"How did you sleep?"

It took him a little too long to answer. "Poorly. Nightmares."

"Well, I'm sorry I woke you. Are you feeling any better? Can I get you anything? A drink?"

"I'll get it." He made it to his feet; then he swayed dizzily and sat down again.

Emelota rushed to the jug of fresh water on the table and poured out a quick glassful. "Is it your leg? Is it paining you?"

"Barely."

"The fever's left you weak. And you should eat. Here—I went out and found some meat."

"I don't have time to be weak," Evrard growled, but he meekly accepted the fresh bread and the collop of roast mutton she offered him. The food seemed to refresh him somewhat. "Where did this come from?"

"Duke Godfrey."

He arrested the meat on its way to his lips. "What? How does the *duke* know about us?"

Famished beyond bearing, Emelota had already put a morsel of bread in her mouth—crisp oily exterior crunchy with salt, a centre still warm from the ovens, it was melting on her tongue—but she swallowed hurriedly and said, "Oh. I told him, that's all."

"Emelota," her brother said with an air of dangerous calm, "did you go to *beg food* from *Duke Godfrey?*"

She'd done something wrong again, but what? "It wasn't *begging.* We've barely eaten for days. Duke Godfrey is one of the only princes not up on Silpius, and people say he's willing to do anyone a kindness."

"That's not the point!" Evrard's voice lifted, but he barely had strength even for that. It took him a moment to go on. "That's not the point," he repeated huskily. "People of my status don't accept charity, Emelota."

Perhaps it was just as well he hadn't heard her accept Lusine's charity, then. "Do people of your status not starve, either? Just eat the food, Evrard. *Please.*"

His mouth twisted with humiliation. "Why should I expect you to understand? You're only the child of a *slave.*"

The meat turned to ash in Emelota's mouth. Suddenly, she wasn't hungry any more, and the small amount of food she'd managed to swallow sat on her stomach like a rock.

"Oh, saints," Evrard said, seeing the look on her face. "Emelota, no. I only meant—"

"I know *exactly* what you meant," she whispered, getting up and putting the food back on the table. She could hear the voices in her head. *Serf-born brat. How do you even know it's our father's, Evrard? People of that sort breed like animals.*

"Emelota," her brother begged again, sounding wretched. "I only meant you can't help seeing things differently—"

"I'm going to wash these sheets," she muttered, bundling up the soiled bedding poor Father Adso had left. "Once you've finished eating, you might like to wash; there's a jug and cloth behind the hanging there, and I laid out clean clothes for you."

Downstairs, she found her way into the house's lower courtyard, where a laundry tub stood near an opening in one of the water pipes that networked the city. A stream of clean, cold water flowed through a pipe projecting from a wall carving and was caught in a basin before trickling away to the next house. A block of hard soap sat on the stone ledge nearby. Emelota wadded the sheets into the tub and then stood staring without seeing them. The truth was, she had no idea how laundry was done. She might be a serf's daughter, but from infancy she'd been pampered like a lap dog. Was it cold or hot water you were supposed to use to wash bloodstains? Her mother would have known. Her mother, like the other bondmaids in her father's house, would have spent her days in backbreaking labour of exactly this sort. But whatever nameless, helpless woman had birthed her had died in the same hour. All her life she'd been told to feel grateful that her father, in a rare moment of piety, had chosen to acknowledge her and see to her upbringing, so that she did not become just another of the slaves who washed and wove, hauled water and serviced the beds in his house. She ought to be grateful. She *was* grateful, even though everyone who knew the secret of her origins hated her—none more than her own half-siblings, who viewed her as an interloper consuming their own rightful inheritance. She was better off than she deserved. She was better off than she could ever imagine. She shouldn't feel this ache.

Emelota sighed, rubbing her temples. Then she wedged the tub beneath the pipe and filled it with cold water, before attacking the stained linen with the soap, rubbing and pounding it until some, at least, of the discolouration was gone. This done, she upended the tub and draped the dripping sheets over the line crossing the courtyard.

Upstairs, she found Evrard still sitting on the edge of the bed where she'd left him, unwashed, his food half-eaten. She had left his armour and weapons in a pile next to the bed, and his half-unsheathed sword lay across his knees. He looked up at her with haunted eyes.

"Did I frighten you?"

"No," he said after a moment, sliding the blade back into its scabbard. "I just…" His voice trailed away.

"You decided not to wash?" she asked, waving the flies away from his meat.

"No, I will. I'll do it now." He didn't move, though, staring at the sword. Emelota's heart wrung. This was not weakness from the fever; it was a strange lassitude of the mind, as though all the tension had bled out of him, leaving him hollow of all purpose and emotion. She went over to him, moving slowly, and eased down on the bed beside him. He tensed a little as she put a hand on his shoulders and reached out with her gift.

He was a perfect blank, and it frightened her.

"Copper for your thoughts," she said lightly, softly.

"It's nothing. I should wash."

"There's a stool you can sit on while you do it, if you're feeling tired."

"I'll be all right," he said gruffly, but he was still staring at his sword as though it was miles away. A dim flicker of intention came from him and Emelota caught her breath.

"You don't need to go back up the mountain right away, Evrard."

"Yes, I do. You brought my horse back, didn't you?"

"You rode him last night, remember?"

"Oh…so I did." A pause. *"You bled my horse."*

Did he expect her to apologise? "I did what I had to, to keep you alive."

"No one lives long without a horse," Evrard said with something of his old spirit. "Don't you understand? When the battle goes ill, mounted men ride to safety and the peasants on foot are left to die…"

"All the more reason you should both take a few days to rest and recover."

"We may not have a few days," he muttered. "Didn't you see what it was like up there? How many days was I sick?"

"You were wounded on Thursday. Today is…" she counted on her fingers. "Today is Sunday! Oh." She hadn't even thought to attend Mass.

"Four days." Evrard shivered. For a moment he was silent. "Saint George, what must they be thinking of me?"

"Evrard, you were wounded…"

"I can't believe I was such a *fool,*" he muttered. "I led them into a trap and then got myself hurt, and now I'm down here hiding in safety while they fight Kerbogha. The other counts already hate me for what happened at Nicaea."

"Nicaea was a year ago—"

"I shamed myself," he insisted.

"Evrard." She put a hand to his cheek and turned his head to look down at her. "Evrard, it's going to be all right. The other counts know you were wounded. They know you need time to regain your strength. They won't think any less of you for that."

He shivered, unable to meet her gaze.

This wasn't like him. Evrard worried what people would think, but ordinarily he could be brought to see reason. He'd just been through desperate fighting and a terrible illness; why was he worried about his reputation? It didn't make sense.

Unless what she read in his face was the truth.

"You're afraid," she said, wonderingly. The next moment she could have bitten off her tongue, for he went very white and looked away from her.

"I had to listen to them die, Emelota. All day while I hid in that gulley to save my own life, I heard them dying, and there wasn't a thing I could do to save them, any more than I could save Galon…" His voice was jerky, almost as though he spoke against his will. "I ought to be stronger than this, but I'm not. Father was right, after all. I'm a miserable weakling."

She squeezed his hand. "Don't say that! You're still *here,* aren't you? You haven't run away in the night, like so many others."

Evrard shuddered, his voice sinking into a whisper. "Only because I haven't the strength to stand. But, God help me, all I want to do is crawl away and hide." He dragged his hands down his face and stared at the moisture of tears shining on his palms. "I was so…*so* afraid, last night, of losing my horse, of dying a common foot-soldier. What's happening to me? I've turned coward."

Emelota closed her eyes, trying to stem her own tears. "Evrard, being weak is not bad, and being strong is not the same as being good."

"It *is* the same as being noble."

"Being noble isn't the most important thing in the world. I should know."

He didn't reply to that. "I was supposed to fight for Christ. I was promised an indulgence for my sins if I went to Jerusalem. Now what? I was supposed to protect my sister, and now she's protecting me. I was supposed to feed my horse, but it's been feeding me."

"Maybe it's time you stopped fighting, and relied on others for a change."

"I can't," he whispered. "I *must* fight. I *must* expiate my sins," and he glanced down at his upturned palms. Emelota saw them once again splashed with red.

"The Turkish girl," she murmured.

"Am I damned?" Evrard whispered. "The indulgence was only for sins committed *before* the pilgrimage. What will I do now? What if I can't fight? No penance can bring back the dead."

Emelota was so often saying the wrong things; she was afraid to say anything now. What if she told him to go and make confession? What if she told him to go to Lukas Bessarion and admit the wrong he'd done? Every answer seemed too glib, too easy. Anyone might confess evil deeds, and go on to commit them again and again.

Evrard wanted to earn forgiveness for something that could never be undone by his own deeds. The Turkish girl was dead, unable to forgive him. Lukas Bessarion had vanished into the night, and Emelota felt sure he never intended to forgive the one he regarded with such implacable hatred.

The only thing Lukas had told her about her brother was that Evrard would die, and soon. How much time did they have left? Emelota opened her mouth and then closed it again, her thoughts a terrible burden within her that could not be lightened because she could not find the words to give them birth.

Instead, she sighed. "Let's get you washed," she told Evrard. "And then you can eat and sleep some more, and I daresay you'll see things differently."

Chapter XXIV.

The night was dark, but an oil lamp burned in Count Bohemond's tent, awaiting his return. The count himself was still in the tower on the wall, holding a council of war with Flanders and Normandy, leaving Lukas with all the time he needed to complete Count Raymond's mission.

In theory, at least.

Lukas closed the barrel lock on the ironbound chest at the foot of the count's bed and sat back, grinding his knuckles into his aching eyes. The casket had been stuffed full of the count's documents, but Lukas had gone through them twice without finding one that bore the purple dye and shimmering gold ink of an imperial chrysobull. He swore softly, under his breath. Count Raymond's mission was only a tiresome job that meant little to his own plans, but his failure—the second in as many nights—boded ill for his future with the count.

After another hard day's fighting atop Silpius, he was beside himself with exhaustion. Lukas got up, checking his surroundings two or three times to be sure he'd left no trace of his presence. It was only on his third survey of the tent that he saw something glinting in a brass bowl that sat upon the table, beside the lamp. Lukas rubbed his eyes again and found himself staring at scraps of burned and blackened parchment. Neatly deposited atop the pile, as though begging for attention, was the gilded imperial seal bearing the image of Alexius enthroned with sceptre and orb.

A chill went through him. It looked almost as though Count Bohemond knew of his coming and had left the burned scraps here to taunt him.

Lukas shivered, remembering Lilith's warning. He'd attracted too much attention, too many listening ears.

Falling to his belly, he wormed beneath the loose canvas he'd unpegged at the back of the tent. It was the same means Ayla had used to search Count Raymond's tent at Heraclea, after he'd stolen the silver scrying-bowl she'd been using to report on the Franks as they crossed Anatolia. Memory swallowed him, overwhelmingly bittersweet. The way she'd looked at him that day. The longing in her eyes. The fierce set of her teeth. The way they'd both sworn enmity against their own hearts. Lukas felt his insides cramp until he didn't know where the bite of hunger ended and the ache of loss began.

He was still standing outside the tent in a daze of memory when mailed footsteps tramped on the rocks nearby and someone shouted, "Oi, you!"

Lukas jolted into panicked consciousness. *Strife!* A strip of glowing light beneath the sagging wall of the tent showed where he'd just crawled through and then neglected to return the pegs. *Fool.* To make it this far, and then be caught!

He looked numbly into the face of a Frankish knight who hoisted a lantern overhead, shedding light in his eyes. "We need men for a mission beyond the wall. Anyone sound in mind and body. You seem well enough. Follow me."

His voice was oddly familiar in a way that filled Lukas with foreboding. Nevertheless, the knight barely broke his stride and didn't even glance at the sagging tent. Anxious not to provoke trouble, Lukas hastened after the Frank.

Was this Lilith's doing? He shivered as he recalled last night's encounter. *I will be watching every move you make, listening to each word you whisper in your most private sanctuary.* Perhaps it was. Lilith was limited in her interactions with the mortal world, yet she had managed to see first Zarides and then himself captured by the press-gangs.

Unless she was lying. In his thoughts, Ayla was deeply unimpressed. *Reckon it'd suit her just fine to be credited with omniscience.*

All the same, he couldn't help the anxiety gnawing at his insides. *She might not be omniscient, but she's watching me. And there's nothing I can do to stop her.*

For once, Ayla had no answer.

The camp was silent, the men exhausted. Since every spare man had been pressed into the fighting, even those of servile or peasant rank, there were few to light fires or cook meals with what little food was available. In the torchlight, Lukas saw many of the Franks nursing wounds or shivering with the haunted eyes of men whose courage had broken. Others lay slumped on the ground asleep, without even the comfort of a blanket to keep off the dew.

Lukas wished he'd had the chance to join them, for his body had become a clumsy puppet that kept moving, speaking, and fighting only by an immense effort of willpower. He had only vague memories of the day's fighting, but it had been brutal and endless, a test of endurance. Kerbogha's Turks were always fresh, always rested, charging from the citadel or scaling the wall in waves as fierce and relentless as the sea pounding upon the cliffs of Lebanon. The counts had taken to rotating the men in shifts: a few hours in the shield wall or the city wall followed by an all-too-brief hour in the camp, and then back to the wall, to sweat and bleed and weep through another punishing few hours. And all the time Kerbogha kept sending fresh men, grinding down the Franks as a jeweller grinds a stone.

They couldn't go on like this forever. The knowledge hung heavy in the air, breathing down everyone's necks, not needing to be spoken. People said it anyway.

We should have marched out of the city when they first came, a greying old soldier in his company had said at one point that afternoon while Lukas had been trying to get some sleep—the one advantage of his daytime naps was that Lilith did not haunt him then. *We should have died in one clean battle and made an end for songs, instead of withering away inch by inch.*

Now, Lukas stumbled among the stones as he followed the Frankish knight through the dark. The Frank chose a man here and there: anyone who still seemed awake and alert. These men fell into the procession and at last followed him to a campfire where the scent of cooking goat made

Lukas' stomach twist in longing.

"Sit and eat," the knight told them.

The meat was unseasoned, and tough from being cooked too hastily, but the bread must have been brought up from the city that day, for it was fresh and soft. Lukas paid little heed to the men around him, and none of them paid heed to him. Instead he ate and drank until, after shockingly little food, his stomach felt full for the first time in days.

Footsteps crunched across the stones towards them and Lukas glanced up to see Count Bohemond and the count of Flanders, with four or five attendants. Bohemond nodded to them with a flash of his white teeth, then crouched down so that the firelight illumined his face. "Men. I know you gave your all today, but I've come to ask a little more from you. We need to block the leak through the citadel. Once we do that, we can laugh at Kerbogha. So, here's the plan: I'm sending the thirty of you out of the city via the postern gate. Wearing the gear of dead Turks, you'll approach the citadel by the rear and gain admission. The watchwords are changed daily, but a prisoner has given up today's; it will be good until dawn. Once inside the citadel, you'll bar the door by which you entered and then fight your way by any means possible to the gate opening into the city, where the rest of us will be waiting to help you. Sir Barisan will be your leader, and Turkish Bohemond here will do the talking. Any questions?"

Behind the Norman count, Turkish Bohemond raised a hand in greeting—a stocky, aristocratic-looking man who had chosen to turn his coat and join the Franks at some point during the siege. Count Bohemond had sponsored the man at his baptism; now they shared a name. Lukas recognised him as the local who had guided them all up Silpius on the night the city fell.

The guide was trustworthy enough; it was the mission itself that would likely cost their lives. The men around the fire looked from the count to each other, their mouths still full with food. No one spoke. Lukas felt their mood become darker; he knew they were thinking the same as him: *so that is what this is, the final meal of condemned men.*

Lukas swallowed a jagged piece of meat and said huskily, "I have a question. What are we getting out of this?"

"Glad you asked," Count Bohemond said smoothly. "Each of you will keep your Turkish gear and whatever spoils you take in the citadel once the mission is done and the gate is open. Beyond that, you shall have a purse of gold and employment in my own household, should you be seeking masters. And my personal commendation to your own masters if you are not."

Lukas glanced around the circle of faces, noting that each of the men sitting here must be fairly low in status—peasants, servants, down-at-heel starved-looking masterless knights.

"Gold isn't much use to us," he said boldly. Perhaps it was foolhardy to speak his wishes aloud where Lilith could hear him; but still. They'd been served watered wine along with the meat and bread, and perhaps that was what gave him the courage; that and the realisation that Count Bohemond, of all people, was likely to understand ambition. "Gold can be spent and everything is expensive these days. If this mission succeeds, I want something more. I want to be a knight."

"Hear, hear," someone called, while another muttered, "No use being a knight without a horse. I'll take the gold."

But Bohemond cocked his head at Lukas with a wolfish grin. "I see it's the young Syrian. Perhaps you're unaware, but knighthood means little apart from a liege lord. To receive the cuff at my hands you should have to leave Saint-Gilles and serve me instead."

Lukas had spent so long waiting for advancement, but now he hesitated, feeling the pull of loyalty. Count Raymond had been good to him, better than he felt he deserved. Still, the offer of a knighthood from Bohemond could be a powerful bargaining tool. Should this mission succeed, the nightmare atop Silpius would end. He could return to the city and tell Count Raymond that Bohemond had offered to knight him. After that, the count would surely see his worth and offer him the same, sooner than lose him to his rival.

"Agreed," he said, and Bohemond grinned.

"Agreed." He straightened from the fire. "Any of you shall have your choice between gold and knighthood. Eat, prepare, and get some sleep. Dream of riches and honour. You're in command, Barisan." He nodded to the knight who had rounded them all up, then trudged away, leaving his Turkish namesake behind.

"I think the Giant has covered the important things," Sir Barisan added, squatting down in Bohemond's place. "There's a stockpile of Turkish gear in that tent over there. Turkish Bohemond here will inspect you, to make sure your disguise is convincing. We leave by Vigils." He looked around the campfire, his gaze fixing on each face in turn. "Godspeed to us."

There was something about this knight's voice that hit Lukas like a jolt of panic each time he spoke. But only when their eyes met did memory supply the answer.

Sir Barisan spoke with the exact same accent, the same dialect as that spoken by le Puiset. Hadn't Emelota mentioned such a name? And, with that memory, others returned. That night at Nicaea, when le Puiset and his men had surrounded Lukas and beaten him, then thrown him into a latrine trench. That day at Malregard when he had had the ill luck to run into le Puiset and his knight. With a jolt of renewed fear, Lukas realised this was one of Count Evrard's own household.

The knight frowned slightly, perhaps recalling the same events. "Wait, I know you. Bessarion, isn't it?"

Unconsciously, Lukas braced himself for flight. He could think of nothing to say, until the knight added, "I've no quarrel with you, Syrian. You've been fighting on this mountain for four days. That's good enough for me."

A surprise…but a pleasant one. Lukas ducked his head, stuffing more food into his mouth. Covertly, he assessed the knight. Sir Barisan, like everyone else, appeared to have fallen on hard times. Although he carried a sword and shield, his ragged hauberk was covered in spots of rust, the telltale mark of a knight who no longer had any squires or servants.

"A knighthood," someone muttered, sending Lukas a dirty look. "Who asks for a knighthood on a mission like this? They'll never knight the likes of us. They're just trying to convince us we have a chance of surviving this."

"Quiet," Sir Barisan ordered. "Eat."

"Oh, stop it! You're in the same boat as the rest of us; don't try to keep up appearances."

"There are thirty of us," someone put in. "The princes would never throw away so many of us unless they thought it was worthwhile."

"The fact that they're willing to throw away so many of us shows just how desperate they are," the first speaker retorted.

A dull silence followed. "Wish I'd made confession," someone said.

"We still can," Sir Barisan brushed crumbs from his hands. Suddenly, he looked abashed. "I confess that I have often felt cowardly and slothful these last days. I have been slow to leave my bed or to diligently perform my duties. Worse, I have felt despair and wished to run away, over the wall. Two nights ago, I was preparing to do so. I was walking along the wall when I found a rope dangling from the ramparts. I tried to convince the other member of my patrol to flee with me, but he refused and begged me to stay. He is the only reason I did not give in to my despair." He bent his head. "May God give me pardon and peace, and absolve me from my sins."

The knight nodded to the man beside him, a ragged-looking Englishman who wove his knuckles together and said, "I confess that I paid a laundress to lie with me the other week." His nose wrinkled. "She smelled of rotten garlic, so I truly regret it. Also I stole a pouch of ten silver coins from a boy in the street, but I was hungry and needed the money. May God absolve me."

One by one, each of the men made their confessions: some sincere, some grudging, some boastful, some defensive. By the time it was Lukas' turn, he had his teeth clamped together in rage.

They watched him, waiting. "Come on," the Englishman said with a guffaw. "Either you're a saint or a greater sinner than the rest of us, and either way we want to know about it."

Lukas took a deep swallow of air. His feelings were like monsters clawing at him from deep within, battling for the chance to burst from his lips. He recalled his dream of the dead men and the burning city, of the bright flaming word that translated these men from death to life.

He didn't know exactly what he was meant to do; he did know the vision had something to do with this moment, that he was supposed to say *something* to them. He struggled a moment in silence. The beasts clawed and fought within him and then at last he spat:

"This is folly! Despair? Lust? Theft? You believe *these* are all you have to confess? You're like the damned Pharisees, straining gnats and swallowing camels. You confess to sloth in slaying the Turks, but you do not confess to the fellow Christians and surrendering Turks you murdered in the sack. You confess to a laundress you paid, but not to the women you raped. You confess to a stolen purse of silver, but not to a stolen city. No, I'll tell you what your true sin is: your true sin is pride. You think you can do no wrong, that you can kill and conquer as you like because God loves you more than other people." Lukas pushed to his feet, brushing crumbs from his hands with a sharp clapping sound. "You're right to despair, Sir Barisan. From where I sit, it looks as though God is preparing to destroy you all. I only wish I and my people were not likely to perish alongside you."

A heavy silence fell on the circle of men around the campfire. They all stared up at him with blank, uncomprehending eyes. Then one of them gave a soft derisive snort and threw a bone at him. "Are you setting up as a preacher, Greek?"

"Quiet." Sir Barisan rose to his feet and faced Lukas with a set jaw. Lukas flinched at the look on his face, wondering if he had made some terrible mistake. Instead Barisan growled, "If this is some kind of clever plan to escape being sent on this mission, boy, it won't work. Once we're outside that wall, they'll be barricading the postern gate behind us. The only way to save your lives—and this goes for all of you—will be through the citadel. I strongly recommend you all do your best, because it's your own lives you're fighting for. Understood?"

The men subsided, but Lukas caught them shooting angry glances his way. Well, what else did he expect? A Message like that was sure to fall on deaf ears. Just as it did at Oliveta.

* * *

A toe in the ribs prodded Lukas awake from where he'd been sleeping on the hard, stony ground. His body was stiff and aching within the uncomfortable shell of poorly fitting Turkish armour and equipment, and his stomach cramped around the unaccustomed food. No doubt he was in for another bout of dysentery. He clambered to his feet with a groan.

By the time they marched out via the newly cleared postern, Lukas had begun to feel a little more himself again. The night was clear, the moon full and bright, though it was sinking in the west so that the shadow of the city wall threw a stark black shadow, providing them with cover. Suicide mission though this was, the counts had laid their plans carefully, and Lukas almost began to imagine he might survive it.

Keeping to the foot of the wall, the company advanced in single file, with Sir Barisan and Turkish Bohemond taking the lead. Lukas was grateful for the cotton tunic he wore, Turkish style, above his mail shirt, for it smothered the jingle of the closely forged rings.

The gulley was a challenge to cross, particularly as there was a Turkish sentry posted on the single narrow path that crossed it, just out of bowshot of the wall. His voice rang out sharply in the night as they approached, but after Turkish Bohemond responded in his own language, Sir Barisan signalled them to move on across the gulley towards the sentry's position. The men hesitated, muttering under their breath: Lukas felt the same nervousness. If it was a trap—if their guide had betrayed them—then the moment they were inside the gulley would be the perfect moment to unleash one of the terrifying Turkish arrow-storms upon them. They would be eels in a barrel.

Still, there was no way to go but forward, and Lukas had knighthood to win. He was the first to follow Sir Barisan down the rocks. Turkish Bohemond was the first up the far side. Lukas heard a murmur of friendly voices that was suddenly cut off by a strange coughing gasp, and the thud of a falling body. He paused scrambling across the rocks, staring upward to slope's crest and the starry sky beyond.

"All clear," Turkish Bohemond murmured in heavily accented Frankish. With a collective sigh of relief, the men stole up the gulley's far side and into the shadow of the citadel. At Sir Barisan's signal they formed up in ranks, following him boldly towards the citadel's outer gate. First they passed a portcullis, then a narrow passage between two walls, and finally a sharp left turn before they were confronted with a small gate, no more than a postern.

Now came the riskiest part of the plan. Lukas tried to breathe deeply to calm his racing heart, but all around him he felt the jingle and rustle as men set their feet, felt for their weapons, crossed themselves.

Turkish Bohemond rapped boldly on the gate.

The sound shattered the night's peace. In the gate, a wooden panel set behind a stout iron grille slid back with a rattle, and a voice barked a challenge. Turkish Bohemond responded. In the brief silence that followed, Lukas had a sudden flash of vision: mottled light and shadow, the leaping flames of campfires and torches, the glint of blades and armour and the colours of brightly-dyed tunics. He put out a hand to grasp Sir Barisan's arm and whispered, praying that the tell-tale sound of the Frankish tongue didn't carry within the gatehouse. "Something's wrong in the camp. We should withdraw."

"Shut up before you give us away," the knight hissed.

The Turk in the gatehouse was still speaking to Turkish Bohemond, his voice calm and unhurried. Lukas wanted to scream a warning, but that would only precipitate the disaster. Were those arrow-slits in the citadel wall overhead? Most likely they were. Somewhere up there, the hinges of a door creaked. Archers were waiting above. Other Turks were coming from the camp. What did it mean? Reinforcements for the garrison, maybe? Another flash of vision left him bent with vertigo. No, it was too many for the garrison. It could only be a night attack. His skin went cold and clammy with the realisation. Kerbogha must be desperate, to commit an attack to the mountain's treacherous terrain in the dark—but Lukas saw at once that the gamble was likely to pay off. Most of the Franks were sleeping like the dead.

Count Bohemond was not the only general seeking to turn this clear sky and bright moon to his advantage.

Ahead, Turkish Bohemond's voice became louder, faster, a note of anger discernible within it. The men shifted nervously. Lukas turned, but the narrow passage behind him was packed with bodies. There was no escape. The best they could hope for was to die noisily, alerting those within the wall to the impending attack. But even then…

The sound of voices at the gate halted. Turkish Bohemond called out in his own language before beating on the postern door. But the hatch slid shut, cutting him off mid-sentence. There was no answer. Then Lukas heard a slight creak from the archway behind them and caught at Sir Barisan again. "Listen to me," he hissed, but his words were swallowed up in another sound.

It came with all the abrupt violence of glass shattering at midnight: the rattle and crash of the portcullis as it descended behind them, trapping them in the passage. Some of the men cried out in fright, before silence fell, broken only by the slap of feet on stone behind the arrow-slits above, and further off towards the camp, the tramp of feet and the jingle of armour.

"They're going to shoot at us," a panicked voice hissed. "Why aren't they shooting?"

"There are Turks coming up from the camp," Lukas said, with the calm of despair. "They mean to issue from the citadel and take the camp. For the sake of surprise, they don't mean to start killing us until the last moment."

"No one speak." Sir Barisan growled. "So long as none of us speak they can't know for sure we're the enemy."

But the men were dissolving into panic. Some of them rushed to the other end of the passage to rattle the portcullis. Someone wailed under his breath, "We are dead men!"

"I did warn you," Lukas said with grim satisfaction. If only his visions would save him now! The preposterous wish crossed his mind that Emelota might be here, that she might tell him what vision to ask for, and he might yet find a way out. Ah, he was helpless! His mother had been a Messenger, and she had never needed a Revealer to act as her crutch. Nor had Kari, the Messenger who'd given him the mission to save Antioch. Useless recriminations, for a dying man.

"Perhaps you ought to have confessed properly," he told them, unable to keep the faint jeering note out of his voice.

"He did tell us," someone said breathlessly. The Englishman. Then a pair of desperate hands clamped on his borrowed tunic. "Please, I killed three women and a man in the sack, just so I could take their purses. None of them were trying to kill me and one wore a crucifix around her neck. I swear to God if he gets me out of this I'll spend twice what I took in masses for their souls!"

More hands plucked at him. Desperate hands, wailing voices, confessions of crimes black as night. Bloodshed, murder, rapine, vengeance. Availing themselves of the indulgence for past sins as an excuse to continue sinning in the present.

Envy. Wrath. Pride. Desperate and shouting, they pressed in on him, promising to change their ways, begging absolution.

Begging for salvation, and Lukas sealed his mouth, refusing to answer.

So they acknowledged their sins? Good. It was not his place to forgive them. It was not his place either to pardon or to comfort them, these cowards who repented only for fear of Hell. He only hoped the Turks would start shooting before they tore him to pieces in their panic.

A brilliant, burning light descended from the heavens.

The clamouring voices fell suddenly quiet. The narrow space was full of lifted faces; the light was white on their bared throats. Lukas craned his own head to peer into the open sky above. With a roar like hissing flames, white-hot light streaked across the sky from the west. It was falling directly towards them; it was about to hit the citadel; Lukas felt the scorching heat on his face. The men screamed in renewed terror; more shouts echoed within the citadel, and from the men encamped both within and without the walls.

In their panic, the Franks rushed towards the portcullis, hacking at it with swords and battle-axes. The barrier broke and they burst from their trap, carrying Lukas along with them as the great fire stormed overhead.

In that nightmarish glare, the whole hillside seemed full of panicked men—his own terrified band, racing for the wall; the Turkish division, fleeing back to their camp.

The meteor's white fire filled Lukas' vision. For a moment he thought he saw a great winged serpent streaking fire as it flew, a being of heavenly, white-hot splendour. As it passed overhead, it turned its head and looked at him—not at the fleeing Franks but at *him*, Lukas Bessarion, where he stood among the stones, disguised as a Turk.

Looked at him and knew him; and Lukas felt the dreadful certainty that it would never forget him, that it would always know where to find him.

He wanted to hide, to burrow beneath the stones. He could not move, but he blinked and instead of a dragon it was a great flaming ball, roaring so loudly he thought his head would burst. It split in three before striking the ground somewhere in the vicinity of the Turkish camp. There was a terrible sound, louder than anything Lukas had heard in his life, and the whole mountain shook. Particles of heated, glowing star and fractured earth rebounded an impossible distance into the sky. Flames leapt up among the thorns, burning yellow and fierce. Silhouetted against them were the small fleeing figures of terrified Turks, their yells of terror thin and clear in the distance.

"Run!" someone yelled, the sound faint and muffled to his aching ears. "Back to the postern! Run!"

Another voice called to him from behind: *Lukas Bessarion.*

He started forwards, but the rocks tripped him and he fell to his hands and knees among the stones. He breathed in and stopped, for the air was scorching in his lungs. Light shone from behind him, sending his own shadow, monstrous and ugly, streaming away before him. The air hissed and shimmered with heat. The tears he shed evaporated at once. Lukas pressed himself into the burning earth, whether to hide or to find cooler air, he did not know.

The voice spoke again, hissing and unbearably bright. *Fifteen days and*

Antioch will be destroyed.

He locked his hands over his head to shield the scorched skin at the back of his neck. But the thing had not finished with him yet.

On your way down this mountain, you will meet a false prophet. Destroy what he carries and you will save these people from a great evil.

The voice released him. Suddenly he could breathe again; the light was gone and the night air was cool on his blistered skin. Lukas scrambled to his feet and fled, not daring to look behind. Afterward, he had a confused memory of scrambling through the gulley and once or twice tumbling headlong among the rocks, followed by a terrifying, interminable time when the men were all battering at the postern gate, begging to be let back in. At length, the gate was unbarricaded and they got in and collapsed—weeping, shaking, swearing, praying—on the stones within.

"What happened? What was that?" Their voices echoed off the wall. Even the guards in the towers ran down to ask for answers. Their sputtering torches blazed into the night, glaring hellishly on wild, weeping faces. Lukas backed away from the light, into the shadows. But the lights followed him and he found himself in the midst of a circle of pale faces and wide eyes.

Sir Barisan confronted him, reverent, almost, as le Puiset had been when the ravens came. "You were right," he breathed. "We confessed our true sins and God spared us."

If he could have backed any further away from them, he would have. "What did you see?" Lukas demanded. "In the sky—*what exactly did you see?*"

The men looked at each other, doubtful. "Fire. A great ball of it. What did *you* see?"

"Nothing. The same," Lukas muttered, leaning on his staff. The truth was a great burden in his mouth, but he bit it back. They were all watching him with those luminous eyes, those parted lips. What would they do if he spoke?

Whatever he'd expected from becoming a prophet, it wasn't this. It wasn't to be *heard.* Now, the thought terrified him.

"I'm going to get some rest," he muttered. They parted to let him through, then silently fell into step behind him. "Why are you following me?"

"It's…this is the way back to the camp," said the Englishman. His voice was hushed. No one else spoke, but they kept *watching* him, as though they expected him to call bears out of the mountain to eat them if they misbehaved. Fidgeting beneath the weight of their silent attention, Lukas stopped at the nearest smouldering campfire and lay down, using his light Turkish buckler to shield his burned face from the light. He wished he was small enough to scuttle beneath the buckler and disappear altogether.

He had gone out of the city in search of a knighthood, and *this* had happened.

He had done as his visions prompted, and *this* had happened.

A star had fallen out of the sky.

A seraph had descended and spoken to him.

A miracle had thrown the Turks into disarray, saving all their lives.

Lukas felt naked and exposed, here atop this mountain beneath the staring eyes of the moon and stars. Something great and holy had chosen him, had given him a task and responded to his grudging obedience with this terrifying, miraculous aid.

He was a Messenger. He'd known that for months, but it went deeper than that: he was, especially, the Messenger to the Franks. Counselling the Franks was the direction in which all his visions tended, and it was the last thing he'd ever wanted to do. He had his *own* people to look after. *These* people had killed Ayla.

What was he going to do?

A seraph had looked upon him. Lukas knew the Watcher lore: an angelic guardian could be powerful protection for a person, a house, a city, or even a people on the road. But there were certain things you must renounce if you wished to avail yourself of such protection. Power, rank, oppression. Pure holiness burned the unjust; that was its nature.

A voice echoed in his mind: the prophecy of his youngest sister Elisa on the night Oliveta fell. *The guardianship of these provinces is taken from you and given to John Bessarion and his heirs, in whom there is no deceit.* But was that true of him? He'd spat the words of warning at the Franks in anger, meaning them to be terrified. He'd been grimly pleased when it looked as though they would all perish, even if it meant he would die among them.

He'd accused *them* of pride, but surely he was filled with just as much arrogance, just as much bloodlust and vengeance.

Lukas didn't dare sleep: he did not want to see more visions, whether they came from Lilith or—elsewhere. When shouts of surprise and joy roused him from a bleary stupor in the grey of dawn, Lukas sat up to find Sir Barisan sitting beside him, watching as though he had been there all night.

"What is it? What's happening?" Lukas croaked. His throat was sore and dry, scorched from breathing the heated air.

"They say the Turks are striking camp." Sir Barisan scratched the scruff on his chin—few of the Franks had had any time to shave in the last week. "They've failed to break in through the citadel, and the falling star last night broke their nerve. So they are running away down the mountain. We are saved. You…"

If one nightmare was over, a new one was beginning. "I did nothing."

"If you say so." Barisan seemed unperturbed—wholly unconvinced. He put out a hand as though he expected Lukas to take it. "My name is Barisan, although if you find it difficult to pronounce, there are some who call me *Balian.*"

"We've met," Lukas said, ignoring the hand. "You tried to gut me on Stauron a couple of weeks ago. And at Nicaea, you threw me in a latrine trench."

Silence. Lukas held his breath, acutely aware of the blood sliding through his veins with every heartbeat. The knight withdrew his hand, his eyes shadowed beneath frowning brows. Here it came—

"At Nicaea, that night," Barisan said slowly. "What we did to you was wrong, but I didn't know what kind of man I was lifting my hand against. Forgive me."

Lukas drew in another breath. "I don't care who you think I am now, but you shouldn't treat anyone that way. Especially not if they are weaker than you."

Barisan bent his head, humble and wordless. Lukas choked on his own bile. Climbing to his feet, he spat on the ground beside the knight and said, "You're not sorry, you're just *scared.*" With that, he limped away to find a latrine pit.

Why was he so formlessly, viciously angry?

Because he listened to you, you walnut. Because you promised yourself last night their repentance would last no longer than their danger, but he came to you to beg your pardon.

He ground his teeth. "One man. *One* man. Out of *thirty.* Am I supposed to relent for the sake of one man?"

If one man is capable of repentance—of really changing, not out of pure fear—then more of the Franks are capable of the same. Any of them, really.

Even...him.

It struck Lukas with sudden, crystalline clarity that he never wanted Evrard of le Puiset to be sorry. If the count was capable of repentance, Lukas would be obliged to forgive him.

This, then, was his choice: to give up his vengeance, or to throw away all their lives—his own and Emelota's and the rest of the pilgrimage together.

Fifteen days, and Antioch will be destroyed.

Chapter XXV.

Kerbogha might have abandoned his camp atop Silpius and retreated to the plain, but he had neither abandoned the siege nor surrendered the citadel. This was a lull, not a victory. To Lukas' relief, not everyone attributed the occurrence to his visions. Certainly Count Bohemond said nothing about a knighthood, and none of the other men who had joined the misconceived sortie received gifts either. They had, after all, accomplished nothing.

Instead, the whole army was put to work fetching and carrying stones to build a makeshift wall along the near brink of the gulley to blockade the citadel. Although the barricade would still need to be manned, it would replace the shield-wall, freeing many knights to retreat to the city—and to whatever fresh assault Kerbogha doubtless intended to make from the plain.

Lukas carried stones all day, moving through a fog of hunger and fatigue. Long before sunset, his whole body ached and his head pounded. Last night's lack of sleep had left him fuzzy and confused. Once the wall was built, Count Bohemond promised, the majority of them would be free to go back down into the city, to rest and sleep. Yet, despite his weariness, Lukas wasn't sure he ever wanted to sleep ever again, now that his dreams had become a battleground where he wrestled with powers far greater and more terrifying than himself.

If he surrendered to the seraph, he would have an ally against Lilith. He would no longer be her helpless plaything. No one simply *fell* into the toils of a demon; it took evil deeds to invite such attention. When had he begun to go so badly astray? When did vengeance become more important to him than his own life?

Mad thoughts danced through his brain. He need not surrender. There were ways to outmanoeuvre Lilith. He might behave erratically, keeping silent so that she could neither predict his movements nor overhear his plans. He might deceive her. He might leverage other, lesser powers against her. She could not kill him, at any rate; not if she wanted him to free Khalil. For days, the key to the basilica had been dragging at his neck, and he was close, so close…

Fifteen days, and Antioch will be destroyed.

His scalp prickled, warning him that he ought not to dream of playing games with Heaven, even if he was mad enough to play games with Hell.

The wall was done by the time the sun descended in a welter of red and purple towards the west. A relief force marched up from the city to hold the mountaintop, and Lukas was finally free to depart. Retrieving some of his Turkish gear from a cache in the rocks near where Emelota had spent a day in hiding, Lukas paused to gaze down on the city. Even at this distance, over the reek of his own unwashed body, he thought he could faintly scent the bodies that rotted in heaps in the street, mixed with the acrid scent of ash from the fire that had ravaged the city two nights before. The wound across his back hurt intolerably, gone putrid after too long without tending. He felt sick and hot, as though he was about to suffocate.

Fifteen days, and Antioch will be destroyed.

Lukas closed his eyes, weary as death. Had he not said enough, *done* enough?

On your way down this mountain, you will meet a false prophet. Destroy what he carries and you will save these people from a great evil.

He opened his eyes with a shiver. The sun dipped beneath a bank of clouds on the horizon and a cool wind blew, rattling his bones. It brought a lashing of rain, fat drops that exploded against his skin but barely damped the dusty ground. Shivering, he staggered to his feet, his belongings in his arms. A company of Franks was just beginning their dead-eyed, exhausted shuffle downhill into the city, and Lukas fell in behind them.

He knew what he was supposed to do: he was supposed to walk down into Antioch and tell the Franks—tell the *princes*—what he had heard in his vision. They must confess their sins and make what restitution they could, or Kerbogha would destroy them all.

It seemed an impossible task. Bishop Adhemar might possibly heed him, but he could already imagine Count Raymond's scornful tongue-lashing. Lukas winced. Or, worse, the count might actually believe him. Might look at him with the same sick awe as those men had last night.

Perhaps it was inevitable, but everything in him shrank from the prospect.

He didn't want to be despised as an upstart, nor revered as a prophet. He only wanted to be the equal to these men, to fit into their world.

Meanwhile, there was the Bessarion Lance to recover. Surely Zarides and the other Watchers would be released from the walls now and they could spend the whole night digging in the basilica. Time enough to think of delivering his message if the night passed without finding what he sought. Yes, it was a good compromise. He would go directly to Ilkay's house.

Not for the first time, he wondered what had become of the le Puisets. What a fool he'd been to rush away and leave them! He might as well have stayed and got some real sleep—if Lilith would have left him alone. Now... he imagined returning to Ilkay's house to find them dead in the wrecked room, killed by Frankish looters or Turkish insurgents. His throat closed suddenly and he nearly tripped over his own feet. Emelota didn't deserve such an end, even if her brother did. As for le Puiset himself, how strangely bereft he felt at the thought of losing the count! Was his life really so empty that only his enemy could give it meaning?

It seemed he had been walking down this mountain in the dark forever. The twilight ebbed until it was hard to tell what was stone and what was shadow on the ground. In his daze he stumbled, jostling against the man walking ahead of him. The Frank turned—Sir Barisan.

"You look half dead," he said, steadying Lukas with a frown. "Do you need to rest a moment?"

Lukas barely heard his words. "Can't rest," he muttered. "I have to get to the city."

"You're with the Provençals, aren't you?"

"For now." Lukas moved on again. It might be easier to walk if he was not so cold, and shivering so hard. At long last, the road levelled out and he found himself wandering through crowded streets beneath the glare of lamplight. Music and light flowed from a public house, filled with people—both Franks and natives—celebrating the reprieve on Silpius. His own feet beat a pattern on the stones beneath his feet: an endless, tuneless rhythm.

Memories came back to him. He had been in the crypt beneath the basilica once before. He thought he knew where Patriarch Anastasius had been buried; knew where his father would have hidden the lance, at the far side of the niche, in the shadows behind the bones. His mind mapped out the basilica, pinpointed the exact location where he would dig first.

If he disturbed the patriarch's bones, he prayed his father's old tutor would understand and forgive him.

A hand touched his elbow, turning him a little to his left. Lukas looked up to find Barisan guiding him across the old forum towards the whitewashed palace, now blazing with lamps. Some kind of procession was coming down the Colonnaded Street from his right; everyone had flocked to see it, and he could hear the boisterous chant of the *Non Nobis*. More celebrations, he thought. He stopped, pulling feebly against Barisan, who had steered him to the palace gates. "No," he protested in a thin scratchy voice. "I can't. I must go to..."

The procession reached them, swallowing up his words. Count Raymond marched at the head of a dozen or so men—his chaplain and some of his great vassals. Beside him was a ragged, wild-looking boy. Lukas recognised him at once: it was the madman who had tried to break into the basilica and slaughter the people hiding within. He marched beside the count with his lips set in a grim triumphant smile: and raised in his hands, which were already decked with garlands of flowers, he carried the Bessarion Lance.

There was no mistaking the weapon. It was as pristine as he remembered it being when his father brought it back from the great battle in which he had won it. Its wood shone with oil and its blade of rippling steel was untouched by rust or corrosion; almost he could have believed that it, like himself, had been transported across the abyss of time in the blink of an eye.

Lukas' head cleared a little, and his heart stood still with something between joy and terror. The lance—his father's lance—*here.* He stepped forward, but then the joyful crowd surged between him and the count, sweeping him and Barisan with them into the palace courtyard itself. Lukas slipped from the knight's grasp and pushed his way up the steps, the count's protective cordon of guards opening to let him through.

He made it to the count's side just in time to see the young Provençal madman turn to the crowd, brandishing the spear in view of the whole crowd.

"Now you understand God's reason in leading you here," the visionary announced in a ringing voice. "Now you see the greatness of his love, the special way he cares for you. These pagan Turks have heaped scorn upon him and upon his chosen ones. Yet his love for you is so great that the saints now resting in peace have begged him to let them return in the flesh and fight by your side, envious of the favour in which he holds you!"

The crowd cheered, but many of the upturned faces were silent, tears of hope running down their cheeks. Lukas wanted to laugh: in the light of his own visions this demagogue's words seemed little but flattery.

On your way down this mountain, you will meet a false prophet. Destroy what he carries and you will save these people from a great evil.

Through an intoxicating wave of exhaustion, Lukas felt an involuntary sound escape him. A false prophet—this madman. But then—

Destroy what he carries.

The Bessarion Lance.

Destroy what he carries.

No. How? No. *No.* He could not. He *would* not. Not his father's lance. Not his *birthright.* There must be some mistake. Heaven could not ask this of him. The lance *belonged* to him, the one thing in this cursed future that did.

A hand fell on his shoulder, startling him. Lukas looked up into the one-eyed count's triumphant face. "Bessarion, you've returned! Don't go anywhere; I want your report."

Count Raymond snapped his fingers to one of his men, who beckoned Lukas to follow him within the palace. As he followed, half in a dream, he heard the madman's voice continue:

"From among all mankind, God has handpicked *you*, pilgrims, like grains of wheat gathered from among oats. You stand out above all who have ever lived, above all who ever will live! Your merit, your grace shines like gold among a heap of silver!"

Long after the false prophet's voice had faded, when Lukas had been shown to an antechamber near the count's cabinet—it should be warmer in this room, but he was still rattling with cold—he could still hear the delirious response of the crowd to their visionary's cries. His thoughts whirled around in his mind, hopelessly tangled. Of course he could not destroy the Bessarion Lance. Filial piety forbade it. He could not dishonour his father so. A *real* seraph would never ask such a thing of him. He took a deep breath. For a moment he had been too tired to think clearly, but now he became calm again. No, there must have been something else he was supposed to destroy, and he had been so distracted he had missed his chance.

Had Lilith not warned him of other prophets in the pilgrimage? This was certainly her doing. Perhaps, if he had not been so reluctant to play the prophet himself, he might have prevented this madman ever gaining power. What did it all mean? How did Count Raymond come to know the secret of the Bessarion Lance's power? A fresh chill assailed him, making him shiver uncontrollably. Now his birthright was in the hands of the Franks! There was too much noise in his head, so Lukas muttered aloud. "I must get it back. That will be easier than digging." Then he remembered that Lilith must be in the room, listening, and he clapped a hand over his mouth. He should take care. She could speak into his thoughts but not read them.

The door slammed open, admitting Count Raymond. At the door, he dismissed his attendants. When they were alone, the count turned eagerly towards Lukas. "You've returned. Did you find it?"

Lukas stared blankly. *"You* found it."

The count's face lit in a grim smile, but he waved dismissively. "Not the Lance; the chrysobull."

Lukas' heart plunged as he recalled the mission on which he'd been sent to Silpius. "My lord, the chrysobull…I found its remnants. Count Bohemond had burned it. All that was left was the seal."

He held his breath, but the eruption never came. Count Raymond only swore once, softly, under his breath.

"I ought to have known he would get rid of it." He glanced back at Lukas with another of his grim smiles, one that boded no good to someone. "You have proven one thing, at least: that Bohemond could not risk the document falling into my hands. You have done well."

Lukas felt cautiously hopeful. "You promised me a reward, my lord. After the sack, you told me I might take something from your treasury."

"Ah, yes, I did. I thought you'd already chosen something."

"Chosen, but not claimed." He gulped. "Grant me the lance you found in the basilica today." And then, because he did not know what he would do if he was denied, he added: *"Please."*

Count Raymond looked incredulous. "I beg your pardon?"

"I know that lance." His voice seemed far away, his wound a line of fire across his shoulders. "Long ago, before it was lost, that spear belonged to my father—to my forefathers, I mean. I'll swear homage and fealty to you if you like. I'll fight for you, even if you mean to rule over my people. Anything you ask, so long as you let me hold the lance of you and carry it into battle." He paused, the look on Count Raymond's face stopping his spate of words. Had he said something he shouldn't? Saints, he was so tired, and he didn't know why he'd felt so cold a moment ago; the room was suffocatingly hot.

The count stepped towards him abruptly, raising a hand. Lukas flinched from the blow he was sure was coming. Instead, Count Raymond laid a rough hand on his forehead, then dropped it with a hard laugh.

"I thought so. You're feverish. That isn't an ancestral weapon, Bessarion. It's the Holy Lance, the same that pierced the side of Our Lord as he hung on the Cross. It's a mighty relic. No one will be wielding that spear in battle."

Lukas stared at him, mouth open. "A *relic?*"

"A relic," the count almost snarled.

But if it would never be used in battle—if it would only be venerated, carried as a standard—then they were all doomed.

"That lance could save us," Lukas whispered. "It's not a relic."

"It *is* a relic," the count repeated. His lips pressed together a moment, pale. "The people need something to pin their hopes on, Bessarion, or we're all certainly doomed. It would be a very great shame if someone injured their faith."

He pulled the door open and called into the hallway for a servant. "My interpreter is delirious," Lukas heard him say, as though from a great distance. "Take him to his chamber."

Chapter XXVI.

Between fear and madness and the pain of the burning summer sun, Khalil had spent days raving. Now, exhausted, he slumped in the day's cooling twilight, staring into the limpid sky and counting the ways in which he had tried to kill himself.

He had gnawed open his wrists.

He had seized a passing viper and made it bite him until his flesh bubbled with venom.

He had called upon lesser demons and taunted them in an attempt to provoke them to rage.

He had gashed the skin at the seam of his waist, where his living flesh turned to stone.

He had screamed blasphemies at the summer thunder.

Yet still he lived. Still trapped upon this mountain, the horror-stricken recipient of a demon's confidence. Conscious that she meant to use him as her tool for a crime greater than any he could have imagined. Helpless to stop it.

Lilith had told him everything.

"Listen, Half-Stone," she had murmured, a note of malicious enjoyment in her voice. "This is the story of how we spat in God's eye, and lived. Thousands of years ago, the flesh creatures weren't only my worshippers; they were like gods themselves then, long-lived, beautiful, wise, and *strong*. And they had been created to be good, for the pleasure of the Enemy. But they were corrupted. They can always be corrupted; can you imagine creating something with that measure of freedom? What a fool!

"In those days, the Fallen were still able to don flesh. We created ourselves bodies and walked among them. We gave them knowledge and power. We showed them how to take every dark thought and twisted passion they had ever had, to forge weapons, to wield them against each other. You've never seen such beautiful slaughters as they committed then! In thanks, they gave us their daughters and we seeded the earth with demigods—the race of djinn. Our plan worked," Lilith added thoughtfully. "With our teachings and our mighty offspring to lead them, the whole race of men became corrupt."

Khalil's scalp prickled. People said that demons could beget children with mortals, only he'd never heard of it happening to someone he knew.

"And what then?"

"Justice," she said with grisly relish. "The whole earth was torn apart in the Deluge, scoured by fire and water. A few short generations—that was all it took to desecrate the Enemy's beloved and reduce them to a pitiful, diseased, and ignorant race crawling on the skin of a scarred and miserable world. Of course," she added thoughtfully, "we might have been more thorough. The Enemy was able to find *one* family worth saving."

It was the words she said afterward that gave him nightmares and set him to clawing his own flesh.

"Next time, I'll be more careful."

Chapter XXVII.

Saint-Gilles closed the door gently but firmly after his interpreter and stood there for a moment with his hand flattened against the carved wooden panels. Bohemond's chrysobull was destroyed: so his guess must be true. He didn't know if he felt more nauseous or angry, but what could he say about it? He had no proof, and any anger he stirred up against Bohemond would rebound onto the emperor as well, threatening both the alliance and the success of the pilgrimage, already teetering on the blade's edge.

Kerbogha may have been frustrated in his attempt to take the mountain, but he had not withdrawn. His next move was easy to predict. He must guess that supplies of food in the city were already desperately low—he might even have been informed, by spies or deserters, how much had been destroyed in the fire. All Kerbogha need do now was blockade the gates and wait. While Yaghi Siyan had been able to bring in supplies from friendly Aleppo via the Iron Gate, the Franks' only hope was the possibility of Greek ships bringing supplies to the port at Saint-Simeon—a port which had now been seized by the Turks, the ships burned to the waterline, so that even that hope was gone.

Saint-Gilles ground his teeth. The withdrawal from Silpius had not saved them: it had only condemned them to a slow, grinding death by starvation, unless Kerbogha allowed them some form of surrender. And it was all Bohemond's fault.

He must pray his message to Alexius was received and answered—and soon. In the meantime, there was the question of Bohemond, who must be chastised for his recklessness and duplicity. Saint-Gilles' people had *needed* that grain, and now what would they eat?

Then there was the matter of the chrysobull. He was now able to guess what Bohemond's secret arrangement with Alexius had been. But how could he forge that knowledge into a weapon?

Brooding on Bohemond's secrets reminded him of his own. Saint-Gilles crossed the antechamber into his own room, checked that the doors were locked, and then reached into his pouch to draw out an old shard of steel. A spear-point. He looked at it for a moment, and a wild desire to laugh came over him, but he felt too terrified to laugh, and his hands were shaking. Next to one of the alabaster-paned windows was a potted lemon-tree. Saint-Gilles dug a hole in the red earth between its roots and buried the shard within. There let it lie until it had been forgotten that he had ever occupied this room…

If Bartholomew hadn't discovered the Holy Lance, it would have been necessary to fake the discovery. Indeed, after they had spent the whole day digging in the basilica, Saint-Gilles had been reaching into his pouch, slipping the shard into his sleeve when Bartholomew had found the real thing.

If it *was* the real thing. Bessarion's protests had the ring of truth—and Adhemar swore he'd seen the true Holy Lance in Constantinople. Saint-Gilles dismissed the thought more by an effort of willpower than genuine faith.

It was necessary that this be the Holy Lance. The people needed a sign of divine favour to keep them from blind panic. But they needed more than this; they needed a relief army, and the Lance could not bring them that.

* * *

"What the devil is going on out there?" In the garden courtyard of the palace, Saint-Gilles put down the bit of coarse bread with which he'd been breaking his fast and scowled towards the sound of a cheering crowd.

292

Opposite him, Galdemar cracked a walnut and said, "Sounds like your demagogue is at it again."

"I can go and find out, my lord," his chamberlain suggested, but Saint-Gilles shook his head. All they had to breakfast on was vinegary wine and bread that seemed to be at least half sawdust. "You go and check on my interpreter," he ordered. "He was running a fever last night. Have an apothecary in to see him if he's no better. Come on Galdemar, let's see what all this is about."

They found Bartholomew perched on an empty hogshead haranguing a crowd gathering in the palace's front courtyard. He was without the Holy Lance this morning—Saint-Gilles had it firmly under lock and key in the palace's hastily re-sanctified chapel—and seemed to be reciting the contents of another vision.

"In addition, the Lord orders you to celebrate the date of the discovery of his lance on the octave of next week, and thereafter on every anniversary of the day. Further, you must pay heed to today's reading of the epistle of my brother, Peter: *Humble yourselves under the mighty hand of God.*"

Galdemar nudged Saint-Gilles with a grin. "Seems that this peasant thinks himself the equal of the great apostle."

"They're both prophets," Saint-Gilles said shortly. "Why shouldn't he?"

He must have spoken too loudly, for he captured Bartholomew's attention. "Behold!" the young prophet trumpeted, turning towards them with an outflung arm. "The count of Saint-Gilles, your chosen leader!"

Every head in the courtyard—even those of his sergeants who should be minding the crowd for signs of trouble—swivelled towards Saint-Gilles, who tensed a fraction. Although he had brushed off the warning, he understood Galdemar's caution: a demagogue like this might be difficult to control, especially if he chose to make trouble.

"Chosen by God himself," Bartholomew said after a pregnant silence. "The blessed Andrew appeared to me last night and proclaimed: *Behold, God has given the lance to the count—in fact has reserved it for him alone, throughout the ages. He has made him leader of the pilgrims because of his great devotion to God, and indeed he shall be the instrument of the Lord's salvation.*"

Bartholomew was a natural orator, his gestures grand and sweeping. The people responded, surging towards Saint-Gilles and crying his name in delirious hope.

He recognised one of the faces: it was the young peasant with the crippled arm. The boy seized his hand and kissed it. "You won't regret this, my lord. With the lance and Bartholomew, we'll be in Jerusalem by Christmas."

Saint-Gilles nodded and moved forward as though in a dream, reaching out his hands so that they could touch him, kiss him. No one had ever chanted his name like this. In his own dominions he was an uncrowned king, feared and respected but never loved, despite his best efforts. He had always known this, and had always accepted it, for there was some justice in the charge that he had come by his title as a usurper.

This, though—this felt a great deal like being loved. The sensation was intoxicating. God had chosen him. The people had come to embrace him. The sins of the past were wiped away. He need never doubt himself again.

"He who holds the Holy Lance will never be defeated in battle!" Bartholomew cried. "Saint-Gilles, the beloved of God! Saint-Gilles, the unconquerable!"

"Remember you are but mortal," Galdemar breathed in his ear. Saint-Gilles turned towards his friend, the spell broken.

"What?"

Galdemar shrugged. "A Greek told me that when their emperors are given triumphs, a slave is made to ride beside them and whisper that in their ears."

"You're not a slave," Saint-Gilles said.

"But you *are* mortal."

"Saint-Gilles! Saint-Gilles!" Behind him the crowd chanted, wanting his attention, but it was caught and held by a movement in the palace doorway behind Galdemar.

In the portico, Adhemar stood watching silently from the shadows, flanked by two other Provençal bishops, Orange and Narbonne. The papal legate's face sagged in heavy pouches and folds, as though he had aged ten years in a single night.

Every feeling of triumph left Saint-Gilles.

Galdemar followed his gaze. "Have you spoken to him?"

"Of course not. He's been busy on the wall." Steeling himself against the bishop's haggard appearance, Saint-Gilles shrugged off the crowd and stalked towards him.

"Adhemar," he said crisply, taking in the bishop's unshaven chin and gaunt frame. "Come and eat with us, and I'll tell you what has been happening here."

The bishop swallowed. "I think I gather what has been happening here, Raymond."

His voice was as gentle as ever, but Saint-Gilles stopped in his tracks when the bishop used his Christian name. For a moment, he was back in Elvira's tent in the twilight of an October evening outside Marash, staring at the broken body of his son. Adhemar hardly ever called him Raymond; only when the worst had happened.

"I suppose Orange has told you all about it," Saint-Gilles said, nodding towards one of the other bishops. "He was with us in the basilica."

"I told you what I thought of this prophet." Adhemar showed no intention of moving on. He planted himself in the doorway and spoke doggedly, as though each word needed to be dragged out against its will. "Nothing I have heard has changed my mind. It is hardly surprising to find an old lance buried beneath a basilica in such an ancient city, and I have already venerated one Holy Lance at Constantinople. Why did you go behind my back? If our friendship was not enough to earn your confidence, then my station as papal legate surely required it."

Saint-Gilles felt sickened, and that set all his hackles up. "Never doubt my friendship, Adhemar. But I *had* to do it. The people needed hope." He let out a huff of frustration. "I didn't want to hurt you..."

"It isn't my feelings you should be worried about," Adhemar's voice lifted, just a little. "Do you even understand what you have unleashed? We have no reason to believe this man is from God, and already he has the people eating out of his hand!"

"Is that what this is? Jealousy?" Saint-Gilles spoke before he could think, and the bishop paled.

"If I am jealous," he said quietly, "it is only for the honour of Our Lord, whose name and favours are being bandied about rather freely out there."

"If they are, it is no more than you and your master Urban have already done, promising all these people indulgence and victory should they leave their homes and venture on this mad quest."

Saint-Gilles was horrified, in the ringing silence left by his words, to find that he meant them.

"Look, Adhemar. I'm sorry. But try to understand my predicament. Here are all these people I have been saddled with—*someone* must keep them alive and give them hope. The city is surrounded, and you want to quibble over a prophet who saw the *truth?* You accepted Stephen of Valence readily enough!"

"If you remember, I had my doubts about him also."

"We had *no* reason to disbelieve him!"

The bishop put a hand to his head. "Raymond, that's not how proof works."

Saint-Gilles wheeled to confront the two bishops. Orange he was sure of; though, as one of the second-highest-ranking clerics in his following, Narbonne was the more strategic piece on this chessboard. "Narbonne, what do you think?"

The other bishop heaved a sigh. "I think the count of Saint-Gilles is right, my lord. Bartholomew has been justified by Stephen of Valence and by his own discovery."

"There," Saint-Gilles turned on Adhemar. "Even your clergymen agree with me."

"You don't—I don't care about the spear," Adhemar said tightly. "I care about *you,* my friend. I care that you seem quite happy to use this doubtful relic for your own ends. I care that the truth evidently doesn't matter to you as much as power does."

"Power?" Saint-Gilles had meant to respond in measured tones, but the word erupted from him like a bolt from a crossbow. "Power? Is that what

you think of me? You think I'm like Bohemond, do you? Do you even understand what that count has done?"

"Raymond…"

"Don't Raymond me!" Saint-Gilles jabbed a finger in the direction of Silpius. "You have *no conception* of what that man is capable of. The way he lied to get rid of Tatikius once the Greek alliance became an embarrassment to him. The way he lied to us about his way into the city so that we would be forced to agree to his terms. The fact that he's told none of us exactly what his oath to Alexius was, then burned the chrysobull that bears record to it. The fact that he burned a swath through this city and destroyed *half our food,* so that we will have good fortune not to die of starvation. Here's an idea: If you're worried about the souls of the princes on this expedition, I suggest you go and pay Bohemond a visit. For if you won't, I surely will."

The bishop looked at him piteously, and suddenly Saint-Gilles could stand it no longer. Turning on his heel, he fled into the peristyle of the courtyard-garden and took a long, jagged breath.

Slower footsteps followed him, and Saint-Gilles looked over his shoulder to see Galdemar.

"Don't you dare say it," Saint-Gilles growled. "I know perfectly well you told me this would happen."

Galdemar held up his hands defensively. "I had no intention of saying anything." He strolled over to the abandoned breakfast-table and threw himself down in his vacated seat, filling his enamelled glass with wine, and pouring it down his throat almost as quickly. Setting the cup on the table again, he watched Saint-Gilles with narrowed eyes.

"So, do you really mean to confront Bohemond?"

Saint-Gilles pressed his lips together a moment, annoyed to have allowed his intentions to slip, even to Adhemar. But he felt terribly in need of action, his body seething with pent-up rage.

"Not Bohemond himself," he admitted. "But I'm told he has a storehouse among the palaces at the foot of Silpius." A small, hard smile tugged at his lips. "Money. Grain. A few guards—not many, for he can't afford them.

Let's go and take back what he owes us, Galdemar."

Chapter XXVIII.

Lukas lay sick, plagued by visions and memories, dreams and hallucinations.

The burning city. *Fourteen days, and Antioch will fall.*

Lilith bending over him, her smile cruel and slashing. *Did I not say I had other prophets in this city?*

The young Provençal madman pounding on the basilica door, his voice a wild chant taken up by the hungry and despairing people, while Lukas tore his hands against stone and packed earth, seeking the Bessarion Lance.

The throbbing pain of the wound on his back. Low voices and the glare of lamplight; a trickle of cold water through his lips, making him shiver.

The burning city again. *Thirteen days, and Antioch will fall.*

Khalil in the mountains, Lilith circling him with a thin smile as the sorcerer groaned in pain. "What you ask is vile—blasphemous. I'll never help you destroy my people."

Lilith circling him, Lukas, the same thin smile on her lips. *Have you realised yet how fruitless it is to struggle against me? Free my servant, and you may have the lance.*

Gentle hands trying to remove the useless key from around his neck, then relenting when he clutched it and fought.

Ayla walking through his dreams, never turning back to look at him as he pursued her through endless narrow streets. He came to the courtyard of her father's house and beat on the gate in desperation until he heard her voice from beyond. *I never asked you to avenge me, Lukas Bessarion.*

The burning city. *Twelve days, and Antioch will fall.*

Get up and warn them.

Lukas awoke. It felt as though a great hand had reached into deep water and plucked him out, casting him alert and confused upon the shores of waking. His fever had gone—only now did he realise that he must have been very sick for days. Light filtered in through the glass panes of his window, making his head pound. His throat was dry and there was a crick in his neck from spending so long on his front, but when he got his elbows beneath him he found that the burning pain across his shoulders was gone.

He reached towards the glass of water sitting by his bedroll, but his hand was too clumsy and knocked it over. The door to his small chamber opened at the sound and he looked up to see one of Count Raymond's servants, a laundress who'd been loosely attached to the count's household since the bad times at the dead of winter.

"You're awake," she said kindly. "Here, let me get that." Sopping up the spreading puddle of water before it could get into his bedroll, she poured out another glassful, slipping an arm around his shoulders and holding the cup to his lips. "How do you feel?"

Dreadful. "Better," he rasped. He tried to sit up, but she pushed him back, and he didn't have the strength to fight her. "Let go! I need to see Count Raymond."

"If you promise to rest, I'll tell him you're awake. He wanted to see you."

She went away, but did not return at once, nor even after half an hour. Restless, Lukas managed to get up, washing his face and hands in a basin and trying to make himself presentable. He was still filthy, but his wounds were bathed and dressed. His chin was now decorated with a patchy beard, the result of nearly two weeks' growth, but Lukas decided against trying to scrape it clean: even if he could summon up the strength to get the razor sharp enough, he was hardly in any shape to be wielding a blade on his own face.

Presently a rap came at the door and the woman entered again carrying a tray upon which was set some coarse bread and a bowl containing some indeterminate stewed meat. "You're to eat this," she told him, although there was a wistful hunger in her eye. "Count Raymond's orders. He'll come when he has the chance. But there's a Saracen who's been coming every day to see you. He's here now and won't be sent away."

Lukas checked his ravening hunger long enough to ask, "A Saracen? What does he want?"

Before the woman could reply, Zarides put his head around the corner, offended. "Did she just call me a Saracen?"

"Thanks, I know this man," Lukas said to the laundress, before addressing Zarides in Greek. "She did. But don't mind her, my friend, she's only an ignorant peasant."

"These Franks are barbarians." Zarides sniffed at Lukas' small cell, but sat cross-legged beneath the small window with its round tracery. "Did you hear the rumours? Some of them are already so hungry, they boast of eating the flesh of the dead. God knows it must be a sore temptation to them, all those corpses littering the streets, amidst this famine."

Lukas felt a ridiculous urge to defend the Franks, as though the relative unlikelihood of their eating the dead could make up for evils committed elsewhere. He only said dryly, "Do you mind? I'm trying to eat. Strife, Zarides, how long has it been since I last saw you? A week?"

"About that long." Zarides tilted his head towards the basilica key, still hanging around Lukas' neck on the cord of Ayla's old sling. "I take it we won't be needing that."

Dimly, he recalled clinging to the key when they tried to take it from him during his illness. Such futility. He untied the knotted cord and slid the key from it, before restoring the sling to its former place on his wrist. "I tried." He couldn't meet Zarides' eyes. "We could have done it, the night of the fire. But by the time I learned you'd been taken by the Franks, I was picked up by a press-gang myself. Now the Franks have the Bessarion Lance, and…"

"Bessarion." Zarides punched his shoulder gently. "You're not about to give up, are you? Not now that the Franks have so kindly dug the lance up for us. Are you a son of John Bessarion or not?"

"How could I ever be anything else? His legacy is all I have left." Lukas drew breath to go on, before remembering that he could say nothing, or

Lilith would hear him. Instead he tilted his head forward, holding Zarides' gaze.

"Do you trust me?"

Zarides hesitated, but only for a moment. "Yes."

"Will you do as I ask without question?"

"Yes." More quickly this time.

"Good." Lukas sat back, looking down at his meal and considering whether he should eat it all now or save some of it. From the corridor came the sound of footsteps rapidly approaching, the thump of the spear Count Raymond used habitually as a walking stick. "A time will come when I have need of you and the other Watchers. I cannot say when. I am being watched."

Zarides watched him with eyes that missed nothing. "I understand."

The door blew open and Count Raymond stumped through it. "Ah, Bessarion! You made it," he said, without a trace of the coldness that had been in his eye last time they had spoken. "They told me it was a sharp battle, especially on top of the last one. You've fought well."

The count had been asking after him during his illness? Lukas could not help feeling like a dog hearing its master's praise. If he had a tail, it would wag. "What day is it? How long was I sick?"

"Thursday. You fell ill on Monday—Saint Basil's eve."

Then the voice in his dreams—the one that inexorably counted down to the destruction of the city—had counted off one day for each that was past. Lukas shivered, wishing the voice had lost track of the days when he had. He would rather lose his wits than be a prophet.

"Eat up," Count Raymond added, pointing at the remainder of his meal. "It isn't much. Kerbogha's blockaded every gate with a battalion and is waiting at his camp across the river to starve us out. But I need you strong again. I tried sending Adhemar to meet with these Watchers of yours, but they swore they'd only speak to you."

Zarides, across from him, had gone very still. Lukas felt the other man watching him as though waiting for some direction. He took the plunge.

"The Watchers answer to me," he said, looking Zarides in the eye. If

Zarides and his people were willing to swear obedience, the least he owed them in return was to declare himself responsible for their actions. "Anything you have to say to them should be said to me."

Zarides bowed his head, but there was a smile on his lips. Lukas lifted his chin, staring almost defiantly at the one-eyed count. *Let us see what you make of this, old man.*

Count Raymond regarded him with a look that was thoughtful and shrewd, but not angry—in the way that a man does not feel anger when he is stung by a gnat. "Do you have ambitions, Bessarion?"

"Show me the man who does not wish to better himself, my lord, and I'll show you a brute who might as well be dead."

"Very good." Count Raymond crouched on the floor to look him in the eye; somehow that was more intimidating than if he had continued to loom over him. "Tell these Watchers of yours that so long as they serve you, and you serve me, we shall do very well together."

There was an unspoken threat in his words, but Lukas felt more relieved than terrified. "Go, Zarides," he told the Watcher, wanting to ask his next question in more privacy. When Zarides had departed, Lukas drew a deep breath and said:

"And the lance, my lord?"

"What of the lance?" Count Raymond's single eye narrowed in displeasure.

"With respect, you do not understand its true value. He who bears it will never be defeated in battle."

"Indeed! Bartholomew told me the same thing—the young man whose visions led him to the lance's hiding-place." Count Raymond waved dismissively. "This thing is too valuable to be given into the possession of a single man. It belongs to Holy Church in trust for all of us. There must be other things you want."

The invitation was too much to resist. "Well, then, make me a knight, that I may have the power with which to protect my people."

"A knight!" The count's eyebrows rose.

"Why not? I was born and trained to it."

"You're too valuable to be wasted on battle." Lukas contemplated the great likelihood that he would lose his life in battle anyway, once Kerbogha took the city, but the count seemed almost incapable of imagining such a thing. "Clerk, interpreter, liaison—you're so much better at that sort of thing than an old battle-axe like me."

"What advancement is there for a clerk?" Lukas said bitterly.

"All sorts! You might go into trade. Or the church, if that suits your taste better. Adhemar would sponsor you if I asked him—or if trade tickles your fancy, I have Genoese friends right here in the city." The count clapped him on the shoulder with a smile, sending a twinge through the torn skin on his back. "Rest well. Eat. You'll be on your feet again in a day or two."

He blew out of the room again, leaving Lukas alone to stare at the wall opposite.

No lance. No knighthood.

He might as well be honest with himself: Count Raymond only saw him as a tool to be used and discarded. If the count treated him well and worried about his health, it was no different to the way he'd treat his horse, or his hound, or any other animal that was of use to him. *You're so much better at that sort of thing.* Lukas was anything to the old count, but not a knight.

Not an equal—not even with the Watchers behind him.

His stomach rumbled, and Lukas picked up the dubious stew. Beneath the sharp aroma of spices was the unmistakeable, sickly odour of rot, but he ate it anyway and felt much better once it was filling his stomach. To his surprise, he slept again and did not wake until the following morning.

Eleven days, and Antioch will fall.

Today he felt much stronger. After washing, Lukas opened his window casement for fresh air. The small window looked out onto a peristyle circling the courtyard garden, on the opposite side of which the count with his great vassals, Raymond Pilet and Galdemar Carpenel and Gaston of Bearn, as well as others whose names Lukas had not learned, were just dispersing from their council.

He leaned there a moment, considering his options. Zarides was right:

the Bessarion Lance was his birthright and he must get it back. Lilith would try to stop him, but there was a limit to what she could do to him. Unlike Count Raymond… He rubbed his throat, recalling the relic thieves the count had hanged out of hand after the sack. If he was caught, he could expect no less.

It was here that he scented opportunity, like a treasure lost in a dark and narrow space. Here, between a count who would think little of killing him and a demon who would do anything short of that…

He had no time to thoroughly consider his plan before footsteps and distinctive murmuring voices sounded outside his door. A gentle knock sounded, and Lukas sighed.

"Come in, Emelota of le Puiset."

The door opened and Lukas turned to find Emelota standing there with a covered dish in her hands. A black veil in the Syrian style covered her face, concealing her features, but she pulled it away to reveal large, awed blue eyes.

"How did you know it was me? Did you see me in a vision?"

He sent her an exasperated look. "I heard your voice."

"Oh." An awkward silence. Lukas looked past her, into the colonnade. She had a retinue this morning: her Armenian maid was with her, as was Sir Barisan. What was the meaning of this very formal visit?

Emelota held out the dish. "This is for you."

It was still hot, a spot of grease melting through the white napkin that covered it. Beneath was a small fowl, perhaps a pigeon, shot as it flew over the hungry city before being roasted brown in spices. His mouth watered, reminding him how hungry he still felt after the morning's bread ration.

"This is too much." He pushed it back at her. "I can't—"

"Please," she interrupted. "It's the least we can do for you. I heard how sick you have been."

"Then at least you'll help me eat it."

"You need it more than I do."

There was a certain amount of pity in her eyes and Lukas felt a compulsion to punish her for it. "I see. A lady doesn't eat with an inferior.

Is that it?"

"No! That's not…" She swallowed her words, turning her head away, and he had the feeling that his words had cut deeper than he had intended. Before he could make an apology, she said: "Where can we eat together, then?"

He took his staff and led her to the garden-courtyard, leaving Barisan and the maid to wait in the vestibule, within sight of them but not hearing. A settle waited in the peristyle, drenched with sunlight, and he eased himself down onto the cushions. Emelota passed him the bowl and he took the dainty legbone of the bird; she seemed to relax a little once he had taken a bite, and used her knife to remove the other drumstick.

"You didn't come only to bring me food," Lukas said when the edge of his hunger was blunted. "You seem well. How is your brother?"

"He's recovering." Emelota sent him a wary look: clearly she had not forgotten his stated intention of killing le Puiset. "I've been feeding him up, so he's recovering very well. In fact, his horse died, so we have been obliged to eat some of it and sell the rest."

So the horse had died, despite their best efforts. What a humiliation for le Puiset! "That puts him at quite a disadvantage," Lukas said dryly. "It was inevitable, though. Feed is nearly as scarce as horses these days."

Emelota nodded, her eyes fixed on the roses flowering in the shade of the silver-leafed Greek poplars in the garden. "Better his horse than his life," she said, as though she had read the jeer he'd hidden beneath his words. "If not for you, he would be dead. He sent me to convey his thanks."

Lukas could hardly breathe for a moment. "His thanks." No longer hungry, he dropped the napkin into the bowl again. "His *thanks.*"

"It was Evrard's idea," she added, quickly answering the question he didn't ask. "He was the one who shot it. I wanted him to eat it but he said no, no, he could not send to thank you without a—a peace-offering."

He wished he had the strength of will to pick up the dish and fling it into the fish-pond, but the whole city was on the brink of starvation and he was not quite strong enough to throw away good food. Instead, he sat frozen in anger. He should never have allowed himself to trust her, even a little. He should have known she would only try to manipulate him into pardoning her brother.

"You deceived me. You tricked me into eating before I knew—"

Her mouth set stubbornly. "It was no deception. Lukas, you need food—"

"Don't speak to me as though you are my friend." He got up, clinging to his staff as dizziness washed over him. "You know very well why I saved your brother's life. Does he think I will relent?"

She tilted her chin up, but did not answer.

"Do you think you can bring me a roast fowl, and I'll forget every wrong he has done me and others?"

"Lukas," she said sharply: "beware."

A dark chill fell on him, like the sun going behind a cloud. Her voice was laden with warning, and he shivered. Then he forced a laugh. "Beware? What is that supposed to mean? Have you seen my fate?"

"I hardly need to. This whole city stands on the brink of destruction, and it will take a miracle to save us now. You know what will happen if this goes on much longer. Please, my friend, don't go to your death full of this pride, this wrath."

"*My* pride? *My* wrath?" Lukas almost choked. "Your brother murdered the woman I love out of *pique.*"

She got to her feet to face him, pale but determined. "Evrard knows precisely what is on his soul. All I ask is that you allow him to confess it before he dies. If he came to you, would you hear him?"

His whole face was burning, perhaps from rage, perhaps from shame. He thought of the falling star, of the fear in Barisan's eyes, of the muttered confession across the campfire.

No. No. *No.*

"So that's what this is about?" he spat. "You think the Turks have put the fear of God into your brother? So what if they have? While he could do it safely he had no compunction cursing and beating and *murdering* those beneath him. There is *no* putting this right. Now you ask me to forgive him, only because he goes in fear of starvation?"

Her eyes were terribly bright. "No, Lukas, but because *you* go in fear of starvation."

That pulled him up. He knew precisely what she was trying to tell him. *Forgive us, as we forgive those who trespass against us.*

"Don't pretend you care about me," he growled.

"And what if I do?"

That was laughable. "Go back to your brother and tell him this: that the only atonement he can make for Ayla's death is death. A life for a life. It is her right. I will accept nothing less."

He turned his back on her and went back to his room, passing Barisan in the vestibule without looking at him. It was a close call; he barely got his door shut before his exertion caught up to him and he sank to his knees on the floor, his head spinning.

His eyes were closed. He saw the falling star, the blazing eyes of the dragon. Felt the shimmering heat beating on the back of his neck.

What if it was true? What if Evrard of le Puiset was capable of admitting the wrong he had done?

Every thought revolted against the idea. Despite the open window, he felt desperate, almost suffocated. Was it the day's heat, or the aftereffects of his illness, or simply his feelings that threatened to choke him? Lukas flattened his hands against the cool stone of the floor as though he could draw strength from the earth.

Damn the Franks—damn them all. Even Emelota. Even Count Raymond. They would never treat him or his people any better than animals; Count Raymond had made that quite clear yesterday. As for Emelota, she wanted him to forgive the unforgiveable. Her precious brother hadn't even come in person. Of course le Puiset felt no remorse at all over what he'd done to Ayla.

He had the means to destroy them. All of them. All he must do was keep his silence and let them walk blindly into their own destruction. Their blood wouldn't be on his hands, after all. Kerbogha would slaughter them for him, and they'd deserve it.

He pressed his lips together, making his plans. *Eleven days, and Antioch will fall.* A luxurious amount of time in which to recover his strength, lay his plans, and warn Zarides.

Then he would take the Bessarion Lance, gather up the Watchers, and flee Antioch, letting God deal with the Franks as he willed.

Chapter XXIX.

Don't pretend you care about me. As Emelota walked home, she presumed Barisan and Lusine were following her, but she could barely hear their footsteps over Lukas' angry words echoing in her ears.

What if I do? Her answer had been instinctive, unthinking. Her cheeks heated, making her glad to recall Lukas' bark of disbelieving laughter. He might have chosen to misunderstand her—as other men had, presuming that her birth made her fair game.

She felt mortified. He had laughed in her face, and now she could scarcely bring herself to acknowledge that deep down, a part of her clung to the idea of Lukas Bessarion like a drowning man to a floating reed.

She had been drowning all her life, fallen into the crack between two worlds that rejected her. Half of her was muck, and the other half was gold. For a short time she had had an honoured place among Evrard and Alice's attendants and the expectation of an undistinguished but comfortable life. But Alice had died and Evrard had ceased to care about his life. She had accompanied her brother on the pilgrimage partly because she too wished to see Jerusalem, to stand before a God who, since he did not scorn to associate himself with prostitutes, would surely not think evil of her. But even if she had not, she would never have been able to remain at home in Le Puiset. There was no one there willing or able to protect her.

Now Evrard faced death, and her only other stay was the gift she'd been given, this world of purposes and intentions that surrounded everyone but herself. Since meeting Lukas Bessarion, she had come to see that, in alliance with him, and for the first time in her life, she had a kind of power.

She could provide the direction; he the certainty. Her sense of purposes and intentions gave him the ability to—not precisely *command*, but to *wield* his visions.

Perhaps she need not be dependent on Evrard. Perhaps she had a purpose of her own—a *value* of her own. The thought almost frightened her, it was so soaring and brilliant.

And then she plummeted to earth again with a thud: must she always be reliant on someone else? If not on Evrard, then upon Lukas Bessarion?

Two stubborn, angry, prideful men. In their feud, she had once more fallen between them.

"You're back," Evrard greeted her when she went up onto the rooftop to find him. The sun was high and the roof would not be a pleasant or cool place until evening, but Evrard had taken to haunting the parapets in silence, gazing towards the encircling city wall and the distant blue mountains beyond. In the last few days his sleep had begun to improve, his fatigue and melancholy gradually fading; but he still suffered from bad dreams and Emelota found that he startled easily and spoke often of France, of home. *I wish I had not been so quick to leave my son in the care of my brother,* he said once, and then *No, perhaps it is for the best, since I shall never see Le Puiset again.*

That made Emelota shiver: she had not informed him of Lukas' vision.

Now he turned his gaunt, bony face towards her and said wearily, "How did he take it?"

"Not well." She had given the leftover meat to the woman Count Raymond was paying to tend his interpreter, telling her to eat it herself if Lukas didn't. "He throws your thanks in your teeth. I told you that you ought to go yourself."

"Why? So that he could throw with greater force and accuracy?" Evrard's jaw bulged stubbornly. "I've been humiliated enough, surely."

"Oh, surely!" Emelota could not help murmuring, but her sarcasm drifted by without notice.

"Can you imagine what would happen if I went to him myself? Bessarion would only take the opportunity to gloat. All these peasants are the same.

Give an inch, and they'll take a mile."

Evrard was always saying such things about peasants, and it struck her now that they had always made her feel ashamed, even when she knew the words were not aimed at her.

He frowned at her. "What is it? What's the matter?"

"Nothing," she said with a sigh. Perhaps Lukas Bessarion was right. Perhaps her brother wasn't ready for forgiveness.

Perhaps he never would be. The old fear returned, sliding cold into her bones. She shivered, watching Evrard closely for some sign. Since Bishop Adhemar had anointed him during the last rites she had seen a glistening mark on his forehead, its smell faintly sweet. It had faded as he recovered strength, until she could no longer sense it at all.

If only she could warn him—but no: he ought to know better than this, and he would never believe her if she came to him now with tales of intuitions and visions—certainly not visions from *that* source. Sighing, she glanced at the sky. "You should come inside before the sun burns you."

"Soon," he promised. Full of misgivings, Emelota went downstairs. What could she do? She could not force Evrard to confess, nor Lukas to hear him. Perhaps Evrard was not meant to be saved—perhaps it was his fate, not merely to die but to burn in Hell for his crime. But if that was his fate, it was one she would battle with every bone in her body. *I pray I may be forgiven for wishing better for him.*

At the door to their own lodgings, Emelota paused, seeing Lusine in the courtyard with two others, a man and a woman about her own age. The three of them held hands, their heads bowed. It was only when Emelota hurried up to them, calling Lusine's name, and all three of them turned to look at her, that she realised they had been praying.

"I beg your pardon," she said awkwardly. "I didn't think…" She stopped, thinking that she had a bad habit of not thinking, especially with people like Lukas Bessarion, or her attendant.

Lusine said, *"Sayyida,* this is my sister Arevik and her husband Toros." She began to make an apology, no doubt for entertaining visitors without leave, but Emelota interrupted.

"Your family is always welcome here. Are you Watchers, perchance?"

The three Armenians exchanged wary looks. "No, *sayyida* We…we don't claim that title. We do what we can in the way of charity and devotion. We don't long for a return of the old empire, nor do we seek to bring it about by force of arms, as Leo Zarides and his followers do."

"Oh." Emelota was quite sure the Watchers at home in France did not care two pins for the Greek emperor. "I thought the Watchers were supposed to be beyond all that sort of thing. I thought they were a lay order doing works of charity, as you mentioned, and devotion."

Lusine and her siblings relaxed a little. "Then perhaps it *is* us you're looking for," Toros said with a grin. "We have worked no miracles, nor are we very rich or holy. But if there is any small way in which we can help you, we are at your service."

Emelota swallowed, hard. She had spent most of the week brooding upon the problem of Aemathe. She had promised the spirit she would return to free her, and she was almost certain it was the right thing to do; moreover, it might mean the saving of Antioch and the sparing of her brother's life, at least so far as the Turks were concerned. All the same, how would she broach the topic with Evrard? *I wish to buy a larger-than-life bronze statue* was, in their penniless state, as unthinkable as *A penitent goddess spoke to me in a dream, asking to be baptised.*

"What do you know of the spirit named Aemathe?" she began tentatively.

"Do you mean the Fortuna?" Lusine gave her another wary look. "Only that she was sacrificed in ancient times to bring the city luck. Do you mean to say she has been seen again?"

Arevik, who had remained silent until now, made the sign of the cross. At that, Emelota's nerve broke entirely. "I—I cannot really say," she said in confusion.

She was saved from further reply by the sound of hoof beats, and looked around in surprise to see Count Bohemond himself dismounting at the gate.

"Is this the lodging of the count of le Puiset? I hear he's been ill," the Norman count said, entering the courtyard with a smile he evidently intended to dazzle her. Emelota felt her face stiffen: her mother's fate and her own experiences had left her with a strong distrust of smooth-spoken powerful men.

"I'll fetch my brother," she said, putting a little emphasis on the last word.

Bohemond followed her as she made for the stairs, seeming too large, too vivid for the dusty courtyard. "On the roof, is he? Mind if I go up?"

Emelota led the way onto the roof, trying to put as much room between herself and the count as possible. "Evrard," she called out before she reached the rooftop, but Bohemond trod close on her heels and both of them saw the look on Evrard's face when he turned to see them. He shivered a little, as though Count Bohemond's presence troubled him. But then the count brushed past Emelota and wrapped her brother in a hug.

"You're looking well, for a man who was close to death last time I saw him," Count Bohemond said. "We'll have you back in armour in no time."

Evrard looked stricken. "I…"

He sent a pleading glance towards Emelota. She had not recovered the presence of mind necessary to understand him, and when Count Bohemond saw the look they exchanged, he waved her away. "I've come for a little private talk with your brother, mademoiselle. Give us this roof a while?"

Emelota ducked her head obediently and scurried down the stairs again, but she stopped once the parapet hid her from view. Something was wrong with Evrard—wrong with his heart as well as his body—and she didn't mean to leave him to whatever mercies Count Bohemond chose to show.

"I know what this trouble is," she heard the count say to her brother, in an off-hand sort of way. "Trust me, I've seen it all before. It's the constant risk and danger—no one can stand it for very long."

"Most men don't let it make cowards of them," Evrard said softly.

Bohemond let out a snort of laughter. "Courage is no more boundless than strength or health, my friend. Bodies break. Hearts break. What do you think I've been doing ever since Kerbogha retreated from Silpius? I've been going around Antioch, to all the men like you."

"Malingerers?"

"Not malingerers. Men that have pushed themselves to the edge of their fortitude and beyond." There was a silence. "I know no braver men."

Emelota put a hand over her mouth to stifle the choking sound she made. Perhaps Count Bohemond could be trusted after all.

"I'm a count. I ought to be stronger than this." Evrard's voice was soft, but in it Emelota could hear the echo of their father's tongue-lashings.

"You will be," Bohemond said cheerfully. "It will all pass in a day or two, and then you'll be back in armour, leading your knights, tougher than ever. I've seen a lot of men succumb to this once. I've rarely seen it happen twice—and if it does, the second time is nowhere near as bad. You'll see."

Perhaps she wasn't needed here, after all. Emelota crept back downstairs to their room and went to work opening windows and tidying away laundry and dirty dishes. Lusine and her siblings were still in the courtyard, and she did not yet have the courage to face them. Emelota had never considered timidity one of her faults, but her whole life she had sheltered behind the virtue of strict decorous conformity. *Please, Sir God, if this is something I am meant to do, you will have to provide a way, for I do not see how I am to do it on my own.*

In the meantime, she had a noble guest to entertain. There was no drink in the house apart from the fresh water that flowed in plentiful streams and pipes throughout the whole city. For food…her eyes went to the small chest where they kept the last hard bits of bread and the remnants of Evrard's horse, now beginning to smell a little despite having been cooked nearly dry. Food was short in Antioch, prices soaring to unbelievable heights. By now, some in the markets had even resorted to selling grass. Emelota sighed. If water was all she could offer, that must do.

By the time the two counts ventured downstairs again, Evrard was looking much better—more alert and more peaceful—than he had in days. Count Bohemond refused the offer of water, but he turned to grip Evrard's hand with a smile.

"Rest well, my friend. This siege isn't over yet, and we'll need all the good men we can get."

A shadow came back into Evrard's eyes. "Do you think there's a chance for us?"

There was a silence. "Not if we go on as we have," Bohemond said gravely. "Saint-Gilles believes Alexius will come for us, but the emperor would be a fool to stick his neck into this trap."

Even Bohemond had lost hope? Emelota's heart wrung. No wonder Lukas had seen her brother's face dead in the sunset.

"If I must die, I would prefer it to be in honourable battle than dishonourable hiding," Evrard said, lifting his chin.

Bohemond gave a wry laugh. "There are other options, surely, than a suicidal charge."

"Have you a battle plan?" Evrard looked hopeful.

"Well…it would be a great risk. If only we had some alternative."

"An alternative to *fighting?*" Evrard looked blank, and Emelota could not resist reaching out to touch his arm. She felt drawn to this idea.

"There is honour in making peace as well as war, count."

"What, go to Kerbogha and ask for terms? Admit our weakness?" Evrard looked scandalised, but Emelota said nothing as she watched the slow realisation settle across his face—that there might be a way out of this trap they found themselves caught in.

If only they could bring themselves to admit defeat.

The idea caught hold, however reluctantly. "We could offer him Antioch in exchange for our lives. We could go to Jerusalem and fulfil our vows." Evrard's throat worked. "What did you tell me just now? There's no honour in pretending to a strength we lack."

Bohemond looked thoughtful—or perhaps calculating would be a better word, Emelota realised in surprise. She'd been too distracted by her brother to pay much attention to Bohemond.

"You're quite right," he said, making a show of surprise. "It could work. We may be starving, but on Silpius we burned Kerbogha's fingers so badly that my spies in his camp report his commanders are beginning to grumble, talking of going home to their crops."

"You think he would be obliged to accept a surrender." Evrard's face lit up with hope.

"Yes, but the problem would be convincing the other counts." Bohemond rubbed his chin. "I would put it to the council myself, but it is your idea and, if it serves, you should have all the credit for it. You might even go with the embassy yourself."

At that Evrard shivered and looked so troubled that Emelota reached out for his hand, wishing it was seemly for her to step in and speak. At last he said: "I cannot go myself. Not after the last embassy. I am not… strong enough for that yet."

She was grateful to Bohemond for bowing his head and saying: "I understand."

"I would be dishonest to take the credit if I am not also willing to assume the risk," Evrard added proudly. "You should propose the idea to the other counts."

"Not on your life! It will sound better coming from you. We counts of the first rank are too often accused of self-interest, and I'd hate for something like that to ruin our chances of making peace." Bohemond clapped Evrard on the shoulder again. "Rest. Get well, and put your idea to the council yourself. As for that other thing I asked…"

Emelota sensed a momentary tension in the air. "My answer will not change," Evrard said. "It is a matter of honour."

"Very well." Bohemond spoke mildly, but as he spoke Emelota felt an unpleasant jolt. Blood seeped from his lips, as it had from Lukas Bessarion's. Fresher, brighter: the sign of a more recent grudge. The hair prickled on the back of her neck, so that she scarcely heard the count telling Evrard that he would try to send food, if he could find any, his stores being depleted…

Evrard saw the count out, and Emelota put a hand over her mouth, suddenly seeing the whole visit in a different light. When Evrard came back, he looked at her strangely.

"What's bitten you?"

Her lips parted. Who did Count Bohemond mean to kill?

More cautiously, she said: "You didn't see what just happened here?"

Evrard's eyes narrowed. "If you're going to spin more fairy tales about reading people's hearts—"

"Not his heart," she burst out. "His eyes. His words. All the things he was careful *not* to say. The way he led you on, step by step. Evrard, this is *his* plan, not yours. He simply doesn't want to be the prince who suggests making a settlement with the enemy."

Evrard seemed indignant at first, but by the time she finished speaking he had gone pale. "You think I'll lose honour by this?"

For a moment she wanted to smack him over the head—not that she could do that, either. Her heart wrung. Count Bohemond had said good and wise things to her brother, things for which she was grateful, since they would lift him out of his melancholy. But it was all in service of some cold purpose. "I'm afraid you'll lose your life if we *don't* make peace with Kerbogha. But he's using you, Evrard, as a tool."

Her brother frowned; she did not miss the way his hand hesitantly moved to touch the sword at his side. "It doesn't matter what anyone says about me," Evrard said at last. "I made a vow to go to Jerusalem. I *must* do penance for my sins. The true dishonour would be failing in that oath. So I will make the suggestion. Don't cry, Emelota. I—I do not think my honour will suffer greatly, and I do not mind being made the count's tool in this."

Her eyes had filled with tears. "Oh, you great simpleton, it isn't your honour I weep for! I am proud of you, that's all. But what did the count mean by *the other thing he asked?* What was a matter of honour to you?"

Evrard's face darkened. "It is not a matter to be discussed with maidens."

Emelota pressed her lips together. "Don't say that, Evrard. There was murder in the count's mind."

He stared at her, startled out of his dignity. "How did you know that?"

"Does it matter? What did you say to him? Does he mean to kill you?"

"Not me, but the Greek. Lukas Bessarion."

"What?" Cold panic seeped through her. "Why?"

Evrard shook his head wearily. "Oh, he gave me some story about Bessarion rifling through his tent. In truth, it must have to do with the feud between himself and Count Raymond. He wished me to carry out the deed, since I have a grudge against the Greek. I refused, of course. I will not have it said that Evrard of le Puiset does not pay his debts. I owed Bessarion my life; now we are quits."

It made a perverse sort of sense that if the princes really were quarrelling, they might sink low enough to feud by proxy through their followers. Still, it was not the prospect of internecine strife that left Emelota numb and terrified. A part of her had come to rely upon Lukas Bessarion, and now he, too, faced death. "We must warn him," she said. "Count Bohemond will not be satisfied with your answer—"

Evrard scowled. "We don't know that for certain."

"*I do*, Evrard. He's in terrible danger."

"Then leave him to it!" Evrard's voice rose. "I won't kill the Greek, but I don't have to save him, either. Not after he's thrown my charity in my face!"

And here they were again, and she was fallen between them. Emelota bit her tongue, as she had tried to do all her life. But, suddenly, it was too much. Silent, she could help neither Lukas nor Aemathe nor Evrard himself.

"If Lukas had behaved in that way then you would be dead, and so would I," she said softly. Lusine and her siblings were still talking in the courtyard; she heard their soft voices from the window. Emelota ran downstairs to find them.

Chapter XXX.

After his confrontation with Emelota of le Puiset, Lukas felt so exhausted that he went back to his cell and fell asleep. In his dreams, Ayla came to him and wound her arms around his neck.

"Avenge me," she whispered in his ear.

"Always," he breathed into the short, waving strands of her hair. Her skin was soft, and slick like feathers.

He woke in a sheen of sweat some hours later, conscious that something had changed. For a moment he almost acknowledged that his dreams, vivid and exhausting, were now troubling him during the day. He shied away from examining this thought too closely, and went to splash water over his face. It occurred to him that one, at least, of his ambitions was within his reach: there must be a bathhouse in the palace somewhere. He closed his eyes, thinking of soaps and oils and hot, cleansing water.

Perhaps he would have the bath now, and then attend to business. Lukas pulled open the door of his cell and stepped into the peristyle bordering the garden-courtyard, only to see Emelota of le Puiset hurrying across the tiles towards him.

"You again," he said roughly. "What do you want now?"

She and her maid—veiled modestly in black behind her—were both breathing hard. Emelota gulped a breath and said, "You're in danger, Lukas Bessarion. Count Bohemond means to kill you. Evrard refused to do it, but I know...I *know...*"

She stopped to draw breath. Lukas blinked at her. "Why?"

"Because he owes you his life," she began. He dragged a hand down his face.

"I meant, *why does Bohemond want me dead?*"

"Oh. Something about you spying on him for Count Raymond."

Lukas remembered the burned chrysobull, the gilt seal lying atop the scorched remnants as though waiting for him to find them. Once again, he felt certain the count had known to expect an intruder: it chilled him a little to think how genial and pleasant Bohemond had been scarcely ten minutes later when Lukas had begged him to be knighted. Perhaps Bohemond had agreed only because he wished to deprive Count Raymond of a trusted servant. At any rate, it was easy to see why the Norman count wished him dead. By now, all Antioch knew the two counts were at loggerheads, but Bohemond could not risk an act of open hostility against a fellow count.

Once again, he was a pawn in a game that would cost him his life, even played in the shadows as it was.

All the more reason he should recover his father's legacy and leave Antioch before this cursed city became his grave. "I understand," he said. "Now I'm curious. Did le Puiset send you?"

Her face, normally so open, shuttered a little. "No."

In her eyes, he read more than she was willing to say, and he felt a little better than he had this morning. "No. It seems his remorse only goes so far. Now if you'll excuse me—"

"If I'd said yes, what difference would it have made?" she cut in wearily. "You would have accused him of trying to earn your favour, and me of acting as his tool. This time I chose to speak on my own account."

Lukas caught his breath, then decided it was no use bandying words with her. "I have business to attend to."

He discarded the thought of a bath with an inward sigh: he was getting used to Emelota, and he didn't fancy the thought of her trailing him into the men's bathhouse, even if he could have relaxed enough to enjoy the experience, with this new threat hanging over him. Instead, he stepped around her and started towards the palace chapel where the lance was being kept. An oblong building to one side of the palace, it was reached by a passage that opened from the peristyle. During the day it was packed with people who had stood in line in the street for hours to adore the supposed Holy Lance. One more would scarcely be noticed in the throng.

"Don't get killed," Emelota said beside him—gently, as though she had swallowed her annoyance.

He stopped, seeing genuine worry in her blue eyes. Why did she care? Saint George, did the girl imagine herself in love with him? Cutting words rose to his lips and stopped there. Emelota was not her brother; she had always meant kindly by him. "Look," he said a little more gently, "I shouldn't have spoken to you as I did, and I'm sorry. But you should no longer concern yourself in my affairs. I have enough—people—interfering in my life as it is. Let them keep me alive. You should go home to your brother."

He turned on his heel and continued down the peristyle towards the chapel but, as usual, Emelota was not to be shaken off so easily. She caught up to him a few long-legged strides and lowered her voice to a whisper.

"There was something I meant to ask you: do you know anything about a spirit named Aemathe?"

The name was oddly familiar, although it took him a moment to recall where he had heard it before: on Ilkay's lips, addressing the blinded statue. "The old Fortuna? What's this about? *You're* having visions now, is that it?"

Emelota looked uncomfortable, as though she was trying to make her tall frame fit inside a space that was too small for it. "Never mind. What's happening here?"

Ahead of them, the pavement ran in a straight line from the peristyle into the shadows of a passage and out again to a small gate set in the palace wall. The passageway was choked with people milling impatiently at the chapel door under the watchful eye of Provençal guards.

"This is where they are keeping my—the Holy Lance," Lukas said. "It was a real question, mademoiselle. Have you seen this Aemathe in a vision?"

Emelota threw a glance behind her, at her maid. Lukas had the impression that, behind the veil, the Armenian was paying very close attention. For a moment, he thought she was going to speak, but then Emelota sighed.

"Likely it was only a dream," she said. "I am only a Revealer, after all."

"True enough." It reassured him, for he did not like to think of Emelota falling into the power of one such as Lilith. It also reminded him that Emelota had been of service to him in the past, and that perhaps it would be well to have her help in the chapel. "Come with me."

Emelota touched the pouch hanging from her waist—a little flat woven bag with tassels of faded silk that must have been bought in Constantinople, a shameless bit of frippery like the reliquary around her neck. It occurred to Lukas that le Puiset must enjoy buying fine things for his sister, and he recalled with sudden, shocking intensity the last day he had seen his own sister Marta, and had tried to buy her an amber ball to cool her hands with.

He would never see her again. The thought made him almost sick, until Emelota's voice pulled him from his memories. "I have no money to make an offering."

"I assure you that God will not be offended," he told her grimly.

As a servant of Count Raymond's, he was permitted to enter the chapel without waiting. Within, the high-roofed church was dark and cool, a narrow space of pillars, round arches and small high windows. At some point its frescoed saints had been painted over, but the whitewash had faded to reveal dim splashes of colour and gilding beneath. Yaghi Siyan must have used it as a granary, for it had the dusty smell of grain, and small kernels of barley rolled underfoot. The chapel had evidently yet to be restored, its furniture and decorations missing: yet two massive golden candlesticks had been placed to either side of the iconostasis, and between them Peter Bartholomew stood, flanked by his guards, the Bessarion Lance in his hand. A great number of people waited in line, the silence broken by their shuffling feet, their whispers and noises of excitement. Lukas felt half suffocated with anger as the filthy, untaught Frankish peasants shuffled past his father's lance, each pausing to pray and to kiss the smooth, oiled wood of the shaft. A box with a slit in its lid stood by the door, coins ringing steadily within as the people filed out; other offerings of flowers and even food lay heaped at Bartholomew's feet.

It's all a sham, Lukas thought as the line approached the lance. Their relic was a hoax, their prophet was a madman, his saints demons. These people would be better off kissing the cross of amber and gold around Emelota's neck, with whatever scrap of bone or thread or dust was housed inside.

For a moment he wondered what would happen if they were confronted with some real holiness—the creature of love and fire that had breathed on him at Silpius. Assuredly it would destroy them.

Perhaps they would deserve it.

The line moved, and he and Emelota stood before Bartholomew. Reaching out to touch the shining wood, Lukas found that he did not need to counterfeit reverence after all. Something shivered through him as his fingers stroked the silk-smooth wood: a sense of recognition, of power. This was his father's legacy, his own birthright, a relic of John Bessarion if not of the Crucifixion, and in that way it was holy to him. He bent to kiss the wood and realised the weapon was quivering. Bartholomew's gnarled hands and ragged nails held a death-like grip on the relic, and when Lukas looked up into the young Provençal's glassy eyes, he almost recoiled. Within them was recognition and white-hot rage.

"I know you," Bartholomew hissed, too quiet for anyone but Emelota to hear. *"Infidel. Oath-breaker."*

The hair prickled on the back of his neck. *Oath-breaker.* He had presumed it was Lilith pulling Bartholomew's strings, but how much had she told him? Lukas glanced at the two knights, the false prophet's guard of honour that flanked him in full armour with swords at their side. If Bartholomew called to them… He might simply snatch the lance and flee, taking Lilith and Bartholomew alike by surprise. He almost did it anyway. But Bartholomew said nothing else, and Lukas swallowed hard, restraining himself. He must take more care than that: he could not have the whole city up in arms and hunting him down, and, besides everything else, he did not want Emelota to be hurt.

"Demon-worshipper," he retorted in the same undertone, taking a backwards step. Emelota heard that too, looking in puzzlement from him to the Provençal seer and thence to the lance. Her eyes grew wide as she reached out hesitantly to touch the weapon, then pulled her hand back as though it had been burned. She turned away from it quickly, without stopping to pray, and went towards the door. The Armenian maid followed; and so, with one more wary glance at Bartholomew, did Lukas.

In the crowded passage outside, despite the jostling and chattering of the people, the atmosphere was less oppressive: a hot wind blew, dry and fierce and cleansing. Lukas took a deep breath and caught Emelota's wrist. "What happened? What did you see?"

She could easily have planted her feet and pulled away from him, but instead her strong fingers wrapped around his in something like desperation. "What *is* that thing, Lukas? That—that weapon, it smelled of blood…"

"They call it the Holy Lance, that pierced Christ's side upon the Cross." He was unwilling to reveal his secrets to this girl. "Did you expect it to smell of roses?"

She shook her head vigorously. "Don't lie to me. You *know* there's nothing holy about that thing. It has been used for great ill and will be again, soon."

He pressed his lips together. "Not if I have my way. What else?"

"You called that man a demon-worshipper. Why did you venerate his relic?"

Lukas felt his cheeks flaming. "You wouldn't understand. *What else did you see?*"

She gasped as his fingers dug into her wrist. "Nothing! I only smelled the blood. I could *taste* the blood. Lukas, I…" Her eyes went unfocused. Her voice hushed. "I think you're supposed to destroy it."

Destroy it. The seraph had told him the same. Lukas allowed her to pull free of his suddenly numb grip. "I can't," he said raggedly. "It's all I have."

He stepped away from her and suddenly outside sights, outside voices poured in; he realised that the Armenian maid had pulled away her veil and put herself beside Emelota, where she was sending him a glare of daggers, as though trying to protect the Frankish girl.

"It's all right, Lusine," Emelota panted. "I—*oh!*"

She had turned her head to look towards the incurious throng of people at the chapel door. Lukas followed her gaze and met the hungry eyes of a tall, grey-haired man in hacked-up armour that hung loosely on a wasted frame.

"Don't look," Emelota gasped, too late to prevent him from looking. "I know that man. I think he's here to kill you."

Her voice faded away beneath a flashing onslaught of visions: Count Bohemond, a glint of gold, an axe folded beneath a ragged cloak. Lukas came back to himself moments later, braced against the passageway. Emelota was still talking, something about how the man had once been a squire in her brother's household before the money ran out and of course Count Bohemond would have—

Lukas gripped her by the arm and steered her into the quiet peristyle that circled the courtyard. "You, go." He gave her a push towards the palace vestibule, whence she and her maid would have no trouble making their way to the forecourt. He had no weapon except his staff, and without his mail shirt, torn and rusted as it was, he felt peculiarly naked.

Emelota resisted. "I'm staying," she declared in a hissing undertone. "He served my brother. He won't attack while I'm with you."

"You can't know that." He glanced at the maid, whose lips were ironed disapprovingly shut. Likely she did not understand Frankish, but he could tell she disapproved of him and would not be overjoyed by the notion of becoming his human shield. "You should leave: it isn't safe for either of you here," he told her in taut Armenian, before turning to Emelota again and saying in Frankish: "Think of your maid and take her home. It's like I said—you aren't the only one interested in my safety, and if anyone is trying to kill me, I'd prefer they try now while I'm expecting it. Go."

He could tell she was unhappy, but this time, at least, she did as he asked. Lukas still did not glance behind as he turned up the peristyle towards his own cell. In the heat of mid-afternoon it was quiet in the courtyard garden, the chatter around the chapel doors distant, the only nearby sound the sleepy warble of doves. For this reason he heard very clearly when his stalker's hurried footsteps sounded upon the pavement behind him. Lukas increased his own speed, stepping as quietly as he could so as not to warn the Frank that he meant to flee. Ahead to the right was a shadowed interior stairwell leading to the upstairs loggia, as good a place as any for an ambush. He was partway there when a blinding flash of vision seared his eyesight: his pursuer going for the weapon at his belt. Lukas dove sideways towards one of the pillars that divided the pavement of the peristyle from the low green hedges, aromatic herbs, and blooming roses of the garden. As he moved, he saw the Frank's arm whip back and circle over with a glint of steely light. A wicked, slender little throwing-axe, all sleek curves, left his fist and flew end-over-end towards Lukas; a fraction of a heartbeat too late, he realised that he had moved too soon and the enemy had corrected to account for his sideways scuttle. He could never arrest his momentum in time—

The thing never reached him. Instead, it broke apart in a cloud of splinters and jagged shards of steel. A particle of the debris struck his cheek, making him flinch. The next instant he slammed against the pillar and slid behind it, breathing hard, dizziness eating at the edges of his vision.

Saint George, he'd miscalculated. He couldn't fight like this; he could barely keep his feet. He was too fresh from the sickbed. And… He glanced around the pillar to find the Frank staring at the debris littering the pavement. *Strife!* The man also carried a sword. Now he was drawing it, although his face looked slack and glassy with fear. Lukas knew better than to expect an easy victory: a frightened man could be deadly. He took a long breath to calm his racing heart. Why, why, *why* hadn't he taken the Bessarion Lance when it was *right there* before him?

Slow, cautious footsteps approached his hiding-place. As the Frank circled the pillar to face him, Lukas retreated into the garden, staff gripped in a low guard. For a moment both of them were still: then the Frank lashed at him with the sword. Lukas parried the blow with his staff and retreated a step, blundering into a rosemary hedge. For an instant he was thrown off balance; he flung out his arms to catch himself, laying himself open to attack.

But the next stroke never came. Instead, a body of Provençal sergeants poured through the vestibule across from him, their shouts filling the air as they spotted Bohemond's assassin. With a muttered curse, the man fled in the direction of the chapel.

Like a puppet with its strings cut, Lukas dropped onto the grass as the Provençals rushed past him. It was over—for now. He sat for a while, sweating and dizzy, until Emelota's scent—a warm, pleasant smell with a fair bit of soap and incense in it—enveloped him again. "I'm sorry, Lukas," she said deferentially, "but he got away. I know it isn't what you wanted; I just thought that after being sick, you might do better if you had some help, so I fetched the guards. I can give you his name, if you like?"

Chapter XXXI.

Saint-Gilles had been waiting for Bohemond to retaliate.

At the time the thing had seemed perfectly straightforward. For once, his vassals had agreed that Bohemond had gone too far in destroying their food supplies: the largest part of the pilgrimage, including most of the poor, relied upon the count of Toulouse for food and protection. Galdemar, Pilet, Bearn, Die, Montpellier, Castillon—all had agreed that some reprisal was necessary. Only…Saint-Gilles heaved a sigh. Only Adhemar had sounded a note of caution.

Saint-Gilles and his council and a strong band of knights had gone to the shabby, down-at-heel villa beneath the shadow of Silpius where Bohemond had made his city headquarters. The South Norman count himself was up on Silpius with the majority of his men, leaving the villa to a handful of wounded knights beneath the command of his chaplain and chamberlain. They had not put up a serious defence, and Saint-Gilles had overseen a calm, bloodless sack. No property except Bohemond's own had been touched: they had taken all the grain and a chest full of gold.

"Tell your master," Saint-Gilles had said to the resigned chamberlain, "that I am recovering only a part of what he owes me, and that if he is dissatisfied with what I have done, he may bring it before the princes."

All the same… he had not expected to fully replace the lost grain, but Bohemond's supplies were pitifully low, filling barely two of the ten carts Saint-Gilles had brought to carry away the spoils. Without a patrimony, Bohemond must never have been rich, Saint-Gilles reflected. And lately he must have spent heavily and gained little: he had not partaken of the sack of the city, nor, during the siege, could he receive revenue from his Cilician holdings.

All this trouble for so little gain—Saint-Gilles had the disconcerting suspicion that he had achieved little beyond making a fool of himself. The feeling was only confirmed a day or two later when Bohemond arrived at the palace carrying, in the palm of one hand, a little sack containing a tiny ration of grain, not enough for a single loaf of bread.

He had proffered it with a sweeping bow and a great many florid words about how sorry he was to have destroyed the granary and how desolated he had been not to have the honour of repaying his debt in person, which he had truly meant to do if business had not kept him on the mountain. Nevertheless, as a gesture of his true repentance and a signal of his goodwill he was contributing all the grain he had left, for he would not like Saint-Gilles to think he had held anything back. Now he begged they would be friends again.

His mien was just grave enough, and the famine in the city beginning to be so severe, that the gift could not *quite* be taken as a calculated insult. All the same, the message was clear: Bohemond had shrugged the insult off with a laugh. He did not mean to retaliate—at least, not openly.

Now, facing the nervous Amalfitan merchants across the table in his cabinet, Saint-Gilles felt almost relieved. He'd spent days waiting for the other foot to drop, and if this was it, there was nothing he couldn't deal with.

"I beg your pardon," he said dryly. "We had an understanding, messieurs. You were to receive an expanded quarter in Antioch, including a second square, a water-cistern, and three churches, to say nothing of certain legal rights including tax exemptions and the right to set up your own court of Amalfitan law. Now Count Bohemond is asking you to transfer your allegiances to him? What more will he offer you than I already have?"

The Italians exchanged dubious glances, but did not immediately reply.

"Has he threatened you?" Saint-Gilles insisted. "I am more than capable of protecting my allies. Ask the Genoese if you doubt me."

"It isn't that." Their spokesman was a capable-looking man whose sleeves were pushed up to reveal black-haired forearms, but his skin was faintly beaded with nervous sweat. "You've heard what happened when Count Bohemond's brother was besieging Amalfi?"

Saint-Gilles nodded. "Count Roger Borsa told me how Bohemond convinced half his knights to abandon the siege and follow him on this pilgrimage."

"Thanks to Bohemond's intervention, Amalfi remains a free city today. Now he guarantees us his support should his brother seek to complete the conquest. We're sorry, my lord. You were most generous. But we *need* Count Bohemond."

"I understand." Saint-Gilles swallowed his ire with difficulty. In their place he would do the same; and, after all, as a neighbour of the rapacious South Normans, Amalfi had fallen on hard times lately. He spared a moment's gratitude that the Genoese, at least, were his own neighbours. And if this was all the revenge Bohemond meant to take for the loss of his grain, it was little more than a token gesture. Perhaps he'd finally done it: convinced Bohemond, the Giant, that he was no one to be trifled with. Saint-Gilles dismissed the merchants with rising spirits.

The presence of so many people had heated the small room, despite its thick adobe walls. Saint-Gilles got up and opened the casement, then the shutters. Vain hope: the air outside was more stifling still than inside—but before he could close the window again, a commotion in the garden below attracted his attention. Saint-Gilles leaned out with a grunt of surprise, tilting his head to focus his single eye on the flurry of activity below—the sergeants running to and fro across the garden, the faded blue of a woman's dress as she knelt beside someone sitting half collapsed by the central pool. Saints—was that…

"Bessarion," he muttered, grasping his spear from where it leaned by the door, and hurrying out into the loggia. "What's bitten him now?"

* * *

Bohemond had attempted to kill his interpreter.

Saint-Gilles listened to Bessarion's tale with confusion and mounting outrage. "And it was one of Bohemond's men, you say? You would swear to this?"

Bessarion ran a tongue across his pale lips. "Not myself, but she will." He turned towards the young noblewoman who had got up and curtseyed demurely when Saint-Gilles approached. Saint-Gilles turned as well, only to find the girl had vanished, together with her veiled maid.

"Mother of God, that woman," Bessarion muttered. *"Now* she chooses to leave. My lord, that was the count of le Puiset's sister, who came to warn me that Bohemond had sent one of her brother's former servants to kill me."

"Le Puiset's sister?" Saint-Gilles raised an eyebrow. "You have mended your quarrel?"

The Syrian's lips pressed together, his eyes baleful. "No, my lord."

"Good." Saint-Gilles breathed in, hard. He'd underestimated Bohemond again. This was unacceptable. "Lukas Bessarion, do you still wish to be a knight?"

Bessarion's eyes widened; his eagerness brought him to his feet, although his grip whitened on his staff, betraying his weakness. "I do, my lord."

"Good." Saint-Gilles took a moment just to breathe, feeling fortunate that neither Galdemar nor Adhemar were here: Galdemar was busy on the wall, and Adhemar, as he might have predicted, had come down with a fever. "Bohemond means to war with me by proxy. Very well. Summon your followers. Go to the count of le Puiset's house and kill him."

Bessarion stiffened. A series of emotions passed over his face: shock, uncertainty—*fear.*

It was not what Saint-Gilles had expected; perhaps it was not what the boy himself had expected. Still, Bessarion's reaction shamed him; it reminded him of what he ought to be feeling himself, ordering the violent death of a man who had never wronged him. He steeled himself, holding fast to the cold black fury that seethed in his heart. "In battle I cannot have cowards at my back, Bessarion. Are you afraid?"

"No." Bessarion lifted his chin with the air of unconscious arrogance he'd always carried with him. "Not of anything that treads the earth."

"Then go. Do not be afraid. You will be well rewarded."

Bessarion nodded tautly and went towards his cell. Saint-Gilles let out another measured breath. He hoped Bessarion would not tarry. He already felt his conscience eating away at him. If Adhemar knew…he realised, suddenly, that Adhemar *would* know. Sooner or later, Saint-Gilles would be unable to keep himself from confessing.

Inward, another deep breath. So, he would confess, and he would be penitent, and he would be forgiven, but only once the deed was done. He need not fear, he comforted himself. The Holy Lance had not been gifted to *Bohemond.*

Chapter XXXII.

No matter what Count Raymond demanded, Lukas couldn't simply murder le Puiset.

It took that thought some time to emerge from the turmoil of his mind. When it did, it brought with it a sharp feeling of relief.

It wasn't that his resolve had softened. Ayla deserved vengeance and Count Evrard deserved death for what he'd done. Still, a Bessarion was no common assassin. Justice, of course, was impossible for such a man as le Puiset, barring a knightly vengeance carried out with full ceremony and challenge.

And for that he would need the Bessarion Lance.

What, are you afraid to fight with ordinary weapons? Ayla's voice echoed in his thoughts. *Why the lance?*

Because I've tried to earn my place without it, and the odds are weighted against people like us; it was you who taught me that.

Once he took the lance, he would need to leave Count Raymond's service; he would need to leave the pilgrimage altogether, for he could not go about Antioch carrying a weapon several thousand of the inhabitants had kissed. In the silence and safety of his own mind Lukas considered the thing quite calmly from every angle, until he was sure his plans were sound. Over the next several days, when he was not taking care to rest himself, he made his preparations. He asked for, and received, access to the count's armoury, where he repaired any deficiencies in his gear: he still had the Turkish armour and weapons he had been given on Silpius, but now he added several other items, most importantly a spear with a point of rippling black Damascus steel. He then went into the city where he purchased beeswax, a piece of rough sharkskin and a saw. A visit to the house of Ilkay satisfied him that the Watchers held themselves in readiness. All the while, he felt sure Lilith was watching him—but he hoped she would not immediately connect his preparations with the lance.

He bathed two or three times. The sensation of cleanliness was exquisite, yet the experience itself left him dissatisfied. Perhaps there was too much on his mind to allow him to really enjoy himself…or perhaps all capacity for rest and healing had been crushed out of him by the events of the past year, and he would never again be able to experience the simple pleasures of eating, bathing, or sleep.

Seven days, and Antioch will fall.

He timed his attempt on the Bessarion Lance for the evening, when the worshippers had been turned out of the chapel, Compline had been said, and the household was preparing for bed. The darkness would help to shroud him from idle watchers, but there would still be enough people about that he would not draw undue attention.

In his cell, Lukas lit an oil lamp and inspected his new spear. He had delayed his work on it until this afternoon, the last possible moment. He'd rubbed the shaft with the rough sharkskin until the existing patina of smoke and rain and oil had been stripped off, leaving the grain clean and bright before rubbing it to a silky gleam with hot wax. He'd used the saw to shorten the spear to an appropriate length, then whittled the end smooth. By the end of the afternoon he'd produced quite a passable facsimile of his father's lance. To be sure, anyone who inspected it closely would see at once that this spear was a decoy—the shape of the head was dissimilar—but Lukas meant to be far away by the time that happened.

Next, he donned his Turkish gear. Included in the gear was a small turban, but Lukas used this to muffle his face, leaving only his eyes visible below the rim of his steel cap. Over that went his threadbare mantle, arranged so that the white cross sewn to one shoulder was clearly visible. The night was hot and stank of carrion; perhaps that was why he was drenched in sweat nearly at once.

Lukas picked up his decoy spear and stepped silently into the peristyle.

Some of the other servants nodded to him as he passed, but no one challenged him. More sweat trickled down his back, and his pulses raced, prompting him to break into a run. Night was Lilith's time of power, and she must have realised by now what he was doing. Still, unless she had actually possessed someone, her power was limited to dreams and suggestions.

He kept going, keeping a sharp watch for one of Lilith's tools—Peter Bartholomew, or Stephen of Valence. The false prophets were popping up like strange fungi in the hot, starving city, all linked by a series of similar visions: the Franks were God's favoured people, destined for victory and greatness.

Not everyone believed in them. Their priests and friars had been telling them for some time now that their pilgrimage was a chance at salvation, blessed by Heaven. Yet here they were, surrounded by enemies and dying by inches of starvation and disease. It would take more than a few visionaries and a relic to soothe their terrors.

Lukas checked that his face was covered as he turned towards the chapel and the small door beyond it which opened onto the street. The latter was locked, but it was one of the bulky, old-fashioned wooden arrangements he had grown up with. He picked it without much difficulty, securing his exit.

He expected the chapel to be more difficult. Instead, when he touched the latch, the door swung inwards with nothing more than a low groan. Beyond, the small narthex—divided by a screen from the church interior—glimmered with faint light.

Was someone in the chapel?

Lukas paused, holding his breath, but there was no sound of movement within. At last, he stepped through the narthex door. Some of the Provençals must have been at work restoring the desecrated chapel, for the plaster had been cleaned from the image of Christ Pantocrator in the apse and now those large serene eyes stared down at him with dispassionate judgement. Below, the nave was cloaked in shadow, but the iconostasis doors stood open, permitting a glimpse of the sanctuary where a lamp burned atop the simple carved table that, for the present, served as an altar. The Bessarion Lance, gleaming and beautiful, rested there in a pair of rough wooden brackets; beneath it, a dark huddled shape lay upon the paving stones. At first Lukas thought it was a fallen cloak, but as he stole nearer he realised it was the unmoving body of a man, his hands stretched out in prayer.

Peter Bartholomew.

Lukas halted with his heart in his throat. Hardly daring to breathe, he waited for the mad prophet to rise.

He did not, and for a moment Lukas wondered if Bartholomew had been struck dead. Nearer, it became clear that his body rose and fell with the rhythm of breath. Bartholomew was asleep—or having visions.

Strife. Lukas' blood ran cold. Lilith's power was greatest at night, when she was able to haunt the dreams of the unjust. Fear spurred him to action. He drew his new Turkish sword from the scabbard and sprang up the stairs towards the iconostasis doors.

In the same moment Bartholomew awoke with a shout that echoed like a thunderclap through the whole echoing chapel. "Help! *Thieves!*"

"Silence," Lukas hissed, digging the point of his sword into Bartholomew's ribs until he hissed with pain.

"Or what?" Bartholomew grimaced, showing broken teeth. "You'll kill me in the Lord's house? *To me, Provençals!*"

Lukas didn't know what to do, and his father's lance was there, *calling* him. For a moment he stood as though paralysed. Then he heard the pound of running feet in the peristyle. Bartholomew's call was about to be answered. He was already out of time. Between himself and the lance, Bartholomew had climbed to his feet and now faced him in a fighter's crouch, weaponless but for his clawed fingers and the feverish light in his eyes.

Lukas swept his sword in a slashing cut for the mad prophet's throat. Before the blow could fall, darkness bloomed between them like a flower. Lilith snarled in his face, raising an arm plated with scaly armour. There came a sharp, high sound that he recognised as the Turkish blade shattered against her. With that, Lilith was gone. For a moment all he could do was stare in shock at the broken hilt, at the shadows surrounding them.

Footsteps poured in at the chapel door and Lukas turned to see half a dozen Provençals—sergeants, a knight, even a meddling servant or two from the cells next to his own.

"Get out of my way," he growled, turning to Bartholomew again, and lunging for the altar, and his father's lance above it. But the Provençal boy threw his wiry arms around Lukas' body.

"Take this man," Bartholomew panted to the count's men. "My saint has shown me his evil intent. He has come to take the Holy Lance. But it is not the relic's will to depart with him."

"Your *saint* is a demon." With each moment, Lukas' last chance to retrieve his father's lance slipped away like sand through his fingers. He tried throwing Bartholomew: but he had not counted on the other man's desperation, nor his own weakness. Instead, he lost balance, staggered and fell. Pain bloomed in firebursts across his vision; the decoy lance rolled, echoing, across the pavement. A weight dropped upon his chest. Bartholomew's rank breath blew hot against his veil.

"Let's see who you really are." Bartholomew snatched the folded cloth and tore it away from the loose stitches that held it to his helmet.

The next instant they were face to face, and for some reason a look of shock passed across Bartholomew's face, as though he had expected anyone but Lukas.

"*You.*"

His confusion allowed Lukas an opening and he took it, slamming the heel of his palm into Bartholomew's jaw and toppling him, stunned. The Provençals had hung back while he and Bartholomew grappled, but now they surged forward, weapons out, calling to him to surrender. Still on his back, Lukas moved with swift economy, pulling the cloth across his face again. In the same moment he slammed a foot against the altar. It slid away; the wooden brackets holding the Bessarion Lance toppled towards him. The lamp smashed between his feet, spattering his legs with hot oil he barely felt through his trousers of thick linen, and then the Bessarion Lance fell into his outstretched hands.

His hands burned with a heady inrush of power as they closed around the enchanted weapon: suddenly he felt as though he could fight his way through a whole army, and take on Evrard of le Puiset at the end of it.

This. This *is why I needed the lance.*

Drunk on that rush of strength, Lukas was on his feet, on guard, before anyone had the chance to react. Peter Bartholomew's eyes were wide and shocked, as though he was still staring at Lukas' uncovered face. Lukas thought of the whispered taunts Bartholomew had made in the chapel some days ago: *Oath-breaker. Infidel.* It was Lilith who had revealed this to her prophet; she must also have warned him not to let Lukas die.

Which meant that he might yet get free of this.

"Surrender," the knight called—Lukas recognised him as one of Count Raymond's household, one of those who commanded the guard in the courtyard. "There's no escape. Put the relic down and we'll petition Count Raymond for mercy."

"No!" Bartholomew snapped. "Kill him! Kill him now!"

So much for *that* hope. But Lukas felt glad: his whole body thrummed with power and finally, *finally* he was ready to step into his father's legacy.

"You die first," he growled, turning upon Bartholomew and drawing back the lance to strike.

Before he could strike, there came the sound of a pair of hands clapping: a soft, gentle sound that filled the chapel with reverberations. Bartholomew's eyes rolled back in their sockets and he sank to the floor—dead or fainting, Lukas did not know. A jingling sound came as Count Raymond's men and servants followed suit, sliding to the pavement. The wick of the fallen lamp flickered and went out; the clapping ceased. Lukas turned, gasping, to stare about him. For a moment the chapel was utterly silent except for sounds of soft breathing, as though the Provençals had simply lain down and gone to sleep.

In the sudden darkness, the shadows seemed thick, *living.* Lukas' skin prickled: he smelled his own sweat.

He did not jump when a familiar voice spoke in a soft, husky murmur. "You have conquered. Are you happy now?"

Lilith. Tightening his grip on his father's lance, he stepped over Bartholomew's body to the door of the iconostasis. "Have I?" he asked, sceptical. "Conquered you?"

"I admit you were clever, to create a situation in which you must take the lance or die. Now I must aid your escape, or I will lose my best chance of freeing my slave in Oliveta."

A little of his tension dissipated. If that was what was happening, his gamble had paid off. Lukas tucked the Bessarion Lance close to his side and strode through the dark nave. Shadows coalesced before him: he saw Lilith at her most monstrous, head of bird, body of woman, eyes of flat obsidian he was too afraid to behold. He tucked his chin and walked through her. It was a mistake: he felt as though he had plunged through something cold and oily and full of nightmares. Battling the urge to surrender to the horrors, he found himself standing motionless at the doors to the narthex, shivering.

"Put it back, Bessarion," she said. "You won't get far, you know. I forgive nothing; I will have my vengeance, and you will suffer tenfold for your defiance."

Her voice was potent: it clawed at his mind with all the formless horrors he had felt in her shadow. For a moment he nearly obeyed. Then he stopped himself and laughed.

"Too much time in the shape of a bird has addled your wits, Lilith."

Passing through the narthex, he stepped into the shadowed passage beyond. On the chapel's threshold he blundered into a body, which roused with a grunt. Lukas found himself looking into the wide, startled eyes of a young Provençal whom he recognised as one of the stable-hands, a boy with a crippled arm. Lukas had the Bessarion Lance and his face was covered: he did not fear discovery now. Grasping the youth by the scruff of his neck, he dragged him to his feet and shoved him in the direction of the peristyle. The boy staggered and fell; Lukas turned contemptuously away. The side door was still open. He yanked it wide and stepped into the Colonnaded Street, making off towards Rhodion and the Watchers.

Lilith appeared by his side, a dark ominous shadow with clicking beak and rustling, knife-sharp feathers. "Do you doubt my power, mortal? Shall I teach you to fear me?"

"Try it," he taunted her, not breaking stride. "How will *you* make me suffer? What will you take from me that I have not already lost? I have lost my patrimony, my family, my beloved. I have suffered wounds, sickness, starvation, and fear. My mind has broken; my body has broken. I know what it is to suffer. At this point, more would be merely tedious."

The streets were quiet and still: Antioch had many sleepless nights to repair. As Lukas passed the palace's main gate, the moonlight showed him a man slumped in the gutter, asleep. He recognised the sword and distinctive torn mantle of the Frank who had tried to kill him some days ago: he had not known the man was still trying to collect whatever price Bohemond had put on his head. He smiled to himself and circled the inert body. Not until the Frank was out of earshot behind them did Lilith speak again.

"I command Bartholomew, and he commands the people. If he accuses you of trying to steal the Holy Lance, not even the great count, your master, will be able to save you. The Franks will tear you to pieces."

"After the past year, I would welcome it as a mercy."

"Or I might abandon you, fool, to the mercy of the firedrake you saw on Silpius."

"And why should I fear Heaven's mercy?"

"Because you don't want it. You want revenge. I can get you that, you know. Against le Puiset; against all of them."

"I hardly need you for that. I got the lance without your help. I will get revenge without your help, too."

"Perhaps you wish to see your wife again."

His step faltered. Only for a moment. "I do." He could not prevent his words coming out soft and yearning.

"Then do as I ask. Promise you will free Khalil, and you shall see her that same day."

"In the grave, you mean." He feared to speak of Hell; he dared not hope for Heaven. "Thanks, but no. There's nothing I want from you, vile fiend. Leave me in peace."

"Peace is more than I can give you, ungrateful mortal," Lilith snarled. "But I will leave you, since you ask it—for just as long as it takes you to beg my return."

With that he was alone: Lukas felt a lightening of the oppressive air despite the day's lingering heat, laden as it was with the corpse-stench that had left him wondering what fresh air smelled like. Taking a deep breath, he looked up at the weapon he carried: his father's lance, finally in his possession. He'd done it: he'd carried off the prize and forced Lilith to leave him in peace. Perhaps he would go to Oliveta after all, and try what an enchanted weapon could do to kill an immortal. His pulse quickened. The world was at his feet. Nothing would stop him now: not le Puiset, not Khalil, not Kerbogha, not the pilgrimage. He could not stay in Antioch, but the mountains beyond Antioch were full of his own people, and he thought they would readily follow a Bessarion—especially once they saw the Bessarion Lance at work.

That left only the problem of what to do with le Puiset. He did not like to leave the count in Antioch, to abandon his vengeance to the Turks. Nor could he simply murder the Frank on his way out of the city: for one thing, Emelota would know and warn her brother the moment she saw his face, and for another, it was hardly *preux.* It wasn't just about making le Puiset pay for Ayla's death: it was about forcing him to acknowledge Lukas as his equal in birth and his better in arms.

But that left only one other choice. He imagined Ayla's reaction, if she were here. *No, you cucumber, that's the worst idea I've ever heard.*

Perhaps it was, but he felt invincible tonight.

He came to the house of Ilkay and found the gate shut, but Zarides had given him a key—a block of carved wood to be slotted into the latch. As the pins clicked into place he felt a jolt like the memory of lightning; his fingers burned, and when he pushed the door open a ray of brilliant light struck him in the face. He put up a hand to shield his eyes: after a moment his vision adjusted and he saw a citrus tree growing at the courtyard's centre, circled by a bright, celestial dragon that turned its head and looked at Lukas with scorching eyes.

Six days, it said with a sputter of flame in the sibilants, *and Antioch will be destroyed.*

Lukas cried out and slammed the door shut. The light winked out. When he opened the door again, his hands trembling, it was dark within the courtyard and Zarides was standing in the open door behind the bronze Fortuna, looking out to see what the disturbance was.

Lukas took a deep breath and stepped into the courtyard.

"I have the Bessarion Lance," he announced. "The time has come."

Chapter XXXIII.

Ordinarily Emelota would have awoken at the customary time, around Vigils, to hear distant chanting from the basilica, but tonight something must have woken her sooner. For a moment, all she heard was the soft breathing of her brother on his bedroll against the wall. Lusine had gone to her sister's house for the night.

Then came a different sound: the soft chime of mail, as though an armed man was inside the room with them. Emelota sat up, narrowing her eyes at the shadows. A little moonlight struggled in at the small windows, but near the door the shadows gathered too thick. Too dark for sight; but not too dark for smell.

Only one man gave off that distinctive scent of blood.

"Lukas Bessarion," she whispered.

His mail chimed. "Keep your silence," he hissed.

"All right." She climbed carefully out of bed and pulled a tunic-dress over her shift. Padding across the room, she found Lukas there in the darkness, his face and hands pale blotches in the shadows. "Why have you come?"

"I think you know why I've come."

"I truly don't," she said in surprise. He smelled of violence, but then, he always had. "I take it you've recovered well from your fever? Have you eaten today?"

"Yes, Count Raymond has given me generous—" Abruptly, he stopped. When he spoke again, his voice had hardened to a growl. "I didn't come to exchange pleasantries. I came for your brother."

Emelota's heart struck her. "Ah."

"I have the house surrounded. Light a lamp and get him armed."

She didn't obey at once, drawing deep breaths through the darkness, listening to the soft promptings of her gift.

"You don't want to do this, Lukas Bessarion," she said, when she was certain of what she needed to say.

"On the contrary, I think I know what I want. Best you do as I say." There was a faint chime of armour as he stepped nearer. Emelota swallowed: her senses were suddenly jangling with alarm. Perhaps there was something different about him tonight, after all; something immeasurably more terrifying, and it didn't matter that she was the taller by half a head: she feared him.

She ran the tip of her tongue across her lips before replying. "Lukas, you should ask for a vision concerning yourself."

"Is that your gift speaking or only your fear for *him?*"

Doubt struck her, but there was only one answer to that. "That's easily proven."

A silence.

"I'm not asking for a vision," he hissed between his teeth. "I'm not a prophet, Emelota of le Puiset. I'm the one who has this house surrounded by men who will break in and drag your brother from his bed if he doesn't come quietly."

She sighed and went to the table, feeling for the flint and steel that lay there. "I'm only trying to spare you, my friend."

"Wait." He took a swift step across the room and his hand closed on her arm. "What do you know?"

What *did* she know? Emelota put out a hand and placed it against his chest, stilling mind and heart and soul. Beneath all his layers of steel and padding, wrath and pride, his heart beat fast and nervous against her fingers.

The certainty washed over her, overwhelming. Sickening, though her fear for her own wellbeing lessened somewhat. She snatched her hand away with a quick intake of breath. "You should ask for a vision."

"Why?"

"Because tonight will not go the way you think. You can't leave this city, Lukas Bessarion." Leave the city—as wildly impossible as the idea seemed, she felt the overwhelming certainty that he meant to do exactly that. "Not while you have a mission to fulfil here."

"Speak more softly. What did you see? Was it the vulture woman? Was it the fiery serpent?"

"Neither," she whispered back, pulling free of him. "I don't see visions: that's *your* gift. All I have is intentions. If you want more, you know how."

He did not answer, but she knew he had no intention of doing as she said. Shaking off his grip, Emelota struck flint and steel together, the sparks catching quickly in the curl of oiled wool she was using as tinder. A moment later she had the lamp lit. In its wavering light she was struck by a new look in his eyes: his bearing was somehow proud, triumphant, and despairing all at once. She had always thought him uncommonly, sometimes uncomfortably handsome, but tonight the word that flashed through her mind to describe him was *nobility,* and she wondered whether it wasn't a good thing after all to be half mud.

He carried the purported Holy Lance in his hand: as in the chapel some days ago, it was almost dizzying to look at, caught in a twisted mass of purposes and intentions. She had never before seen such a nexus of meaning surrounding an inanimate object; no, indeed—she had rarely seen a living being so laden with terrible potential.

"Did you know it's been decided to send an embassy to Kerbogha?" she asked him, tearing her gaze away from the weapon with difficulty. Evrard had put the suggestion to the princes' council only today. He'd come home more at peace than he had seemed for weeks.

Lukas seemed genuinely surprised. "What, the princes are attempting diplomacy? I knew things were desperate, but that hardly seems the Frankish way."

She didn't bother telling him how difficult Evrard had found it to make the suggestion, nor why Count Bohemond had been unwilling to do so himself. "Two days from now, they'll ask for terms. If Kerbogha will grant us safe-conduct through these lands to Jerusalem, the princes will hand the city back to them." She gave him a hopeful smile. "So, you see, if all goes well, you will not need to flee at all."

His face darkened. "It isn't the Turks I'm fleeing. But of course, you've never truly understood that your precious people are a danger to anyone outside their own bloodline." He turned towards her brother, but she caught hold of his lance.

"This weapon…"

"It's why I have to leave," he said, before she could finish the sentence, almost as though he meant to prevent her saying anything aloud. He pulled it from her hand and turned to her brother, but Evrard had already turned over in bed and was blinking at her and Lukas in confusion.

"Bessarion?" he growled. He staggered from his bedroll, fumbling for his sword with sleep-clumsy fingers.

Lukas put a foot on the scabbard. "Get dressed and armed. You're coming with me."

Evrard gulped. "The devil I am." He lunged up and forward, but Lukas levelled his spear directly at her brother's heart. Evrard stilled. For a moment, the two watched each other, pale and wary. Her brother broke the silence first.

"What do you want, Greek?"

Lukas knelt slowly, neither breaking his gaze nor lowering his lance. His purpose thickened, sharpened. Emelota put a hand across her mouth to stifle her alarm, but neither of the men paid her any attention.

Lukas struck her brother across the face.

"I challenge you to battle, Evrard of le Puiset. Put on your armour. Take up your spear."

Evrard flinched beneath the blow, but then he lifted his chin, the colour slowly flooding his face. "You challenge *me?*"

"Are you a saint, that I should not?"

Evrard swallowed hard and looked away—looked directly into Emelota's eyes. She read fear there, and resolution.

"No." She drew in a sharp, almost a painful breath. Once she would have swallowed her fear in silence. Now, she spoke. "Don't do it, Evrard."

He ignored her. "I'll come," he told Lukas. "On one condition."

"No conditions." Lukas stood, turning to the door. "Zarides!"

The door pushed open and the room filled with armed men. Locals, by the looks of them: Syrians and Greeks. All very young, well dressed and well groomed, like a band of avenging angels. None of them paid the least attention to her. Lukas stepped away from Evrard, tossing his sword to one of his followers. "Get him dressed; then bind him."

There was no way around it. Emelota stood for a moment staring blindly at her brother, trying to add up all the different intentions she felt. It all came to this: Lukas would not leave Antioch tonight—none of them would. She wondered, in a detached way, whether that meant danger for Lukas. It certainly meant trouble for her brother, and death for at least one of the others in this room.

Evrard was looking at her. "I'm sorry," he told her softly, pulling on steel gaiters, settling the sleeves of his padded gambeson. "I meant to leave you better provided for, Emelota. If I don't return—"

"Don't," she choked. His shoes were by the door; she picked them up and held them out to him. "You'll be coming back. No one is leaving Antioch tonight."

She spoke without thinking. In the silence that followed her words, she looked up to see Lukas watching her with narrowed eyes. Had that been a mistake?

"You don't insist on coming with us?" he asked.

She hesitated, but she had promised herself she wouldn't stay silent. "I don't need to."

With a sense of foreboding, Emelota watched his purpose harden.

"I don't trust you," he announced. "You will come with us. Bind her," he added, turning to one of his followers.

"No!" Evrard threw himself against the restraining hands, but he was outnumbered and still weak from his illness. "Please. Let her be. I'll fight you. I'll give my parole. I'll do whatever you ask—"

"Yes," Lukas said softly. There was a peculiar triumph in his eyes. "You will, won't you? You'd do anything for your sister. Another reason to bring her with us."

Emelota could barely stand to watch as the gaunt, stubborn lines of Evrard's face melted into blind despair. She could not reach out to him, because one of the young men had her wrists and was knotting them together with a cord. For fear of Lukas, she dared not speak again, dared not tell him that whatever lay ahead, they would get through it together.

As Lukas and his people marched the two of them from their house and set out into the shadowed streets of Antioch, Emelota tended a flickering hope within her heart, as she would tend a candle-flame on a draughty evening.

I'm not just a burden to him, she thought, almost unbelieving. *Evrard cares for me.*

Chapter XXXIV.

As he led his band of Watchers and prisoners into the night, Lukas wondered if he was making a terrible mistake. One hostage was a liability, but two was surely asking for trouble.

Especially when one of them was Emelota. She said he wasn't meant to leave Antioch. She knew he had the purported Holy Lance. He'd had to bring her, lest she raise the alarm to fulfil her own prophecy. Still, he felt her gaze on the back of his neck, and it was making him sweat. Somehow, he wanted her to think well of him—an urge very much at war with his desire to terrify her brother.

No, he shouldn't concern himself with what Emelota thought or wanted. She wasn't the first to underestimate him. She told him he was meant to remain in Antioch—well, he had been *meant* to destroy the Bessarion Lance, and he'd refused. He had been *meant* to free Khalil, and he'd refused that, too.

The only purpose he recognised now was his own: to defy fate, not bow to it. He needed to believe that Ayla's death had not been inevitable. He needed to believe that neither Lilith nor Heaven itself could dispose of him against his will. He needed to believe that he could wrest some victory from the disaster of his life, and if he bowed to Emelota's prediction and stayed within the city, he might as well cut his own throat now.

Zarides pushed ahead of the Watchers, falling into step by Lukas' side as they hurried through the narrow streets. "Surely it would have been better to kill them both."

"No," Lukas said shortly. "They're worth the risk. If we run into trouble, we'll be glad we brought hostages." They came to a crossroads lit by flaring lamps, and Lukas paused. It was a part of the city with which he had never familiarised himself. "Which way to the postern you told me of?"

"Tigranants knows." Zarides beckoned the young Armenian to the front of the column.

Tigranants led them up the narrow street bordering the Parmenius stream towards the Iron Gate, a steady ascent towards the mountains. While they were in the le Puisets' lodgings, the wind had grown stronger and clouds had begun to cover the moon. Not many street lamps burned in this easternmost part of the city, and the Watchers used the few windblown lamps as a guide without venturing into their small, flickering glow. Hidden by shadows, the wind masking the tramp of their feet, they passed through the streets like ghosts.

At length the houses and lamps thinned away as they came to the jagged, rocky valley notched into the mountains, cleaving Silpius from Stauron. The city remained quiet and no one had challenged them. Tigranants paused, explaining that it was time to leave the Iron Gate road and start the climb up Mount Stauron towards the small postern by which he and le Puiset had left the city barely a month before.

Lukas called a halt so that Watchers could light their lanterns. As they clustered around tinder and flint, light flaring fitfully on their faces, he caught Count Evrard watching him in disdain.

"You're *deserting*," he said with a curl of his lip. Lukas didn't even bother to laugh, but le Puiset seemed grimly triumphant. "You'll be dishonoured forever if you do this."

"No, *you're* the one who'll be dishonoured," Lukas responded. "A Greek peasant has no honour to lose, but you—you're a count. The chroniclers will never forget *you* disappearing from the siege at its darkest hour."

As Lukas spoke, a light flickered in the sky and a sound rumbled with it, a low distant mutter that sounded more like words than thunder. Cold perspiration broke out on his forehead. *Strife!* Was Lilith listening? Emelota had already said too much at the house: he had been unable to stop her blurting out his plans to the listening shadows.

Huddled over their flickering lamps, the Watchers looked nervous, even Zarides. Tigranants gulped and whispered, "Did you hear that? A voice on the wind…"

"It's nothing."

"It sounded like a voice." Tigranants whispered. "Demons! They'll rain hail and lightning on our heads…"

"Worry about the hostages, not the wind. I've faced demons before and won." Lukas omitted to mention that this was some time ago. Instead, he pointed to the count. "If he speaks again, gag him."

With that, he signalled Tigranants to take the lead again, striding up the narrow white path with more confidence than he felt. Five minutes on, even he could no longer pretend to bravado. Lightning flickered behind the clouds, and voices muttered incomprehensible words in response.

What if Lilith really attacked them? This was an enemy that could not be fought with the lance. He could no longer defeat her: his prayers, his commands rolled off her like rainwater off steel. He would be shamed in front of his only allies.

That wasn't going to happen. He still had at least one hold over Lilith, and so far it has been enough.

Emelota's eyes itched on his back like a biting insect and whenever he looked back he saw her watching. She shook her head at him pleadingly.

Beside him, Zarides spoke in an undertone to his men, and they began to speak, chanting. Mnemonics, mostly: the sort of lessons a master might teach a very young pupil. Lists of councils, definitions of doctrines, rolls of saints and emperors, medical conditions and their remedies, taxonomies of plants and animals, grammatical declensions.

"What are you doing?" Lukas asked.

"Deflecting attention," Zarides answered.

The wind howled even louder around them as they climbed: the path narrowed, zigzagging its way up a precipice. The lights of Antioch were now visible below their feet. Then a great gust of wind swept past them, scouring the mountain's face. The lamps went out. Lukas put a foot wrong: a stone turned and fell away beneath the thin leather of his sole. A cry of terror escaped him: he flung out his arms, seeking a handhold, trying to regain balance. The next instant, Tigranants caught him and pulled him steady. Lukas fell to his knees, breathing hard, listening to the stones bounce and rattle all the way down the long precipice…

The Watchers' recitations had come to a halt in the confusion and when Lukas looked up again he saw Lilith bending over him. She gave him a slashing smile; then she spread great black wings and leaped into the wind, crying aloud in an unknown tongue. The Watchers, blind to her presence, nevertheless heard her cries and trembled.

Lukas had to clear his throat once or twice before he could speak. "Courage! Here, Zarides, where's the rest of that rope? Have everyone take hold of it. Look to the hostages. Can you lead on in the dark, Tigranants?"

"It isn't much further," the Armenian said, pointing. Above, the city wall was a faint dark line against the boiling clouds of the sky. To the left, lights burned in a tower. "The postern is there, beneath that tower."

The journey that followed was a nightmare. The hot wind buffeted them; occasionally the moon peered from between flying clouds to give them nightmare glimpses of tumbled rock, dizzying drops, and black shadows that reeled and flitted, batlike, in the sky. At length a shoulder of the mountain occluded the light of Tigranants' tower, but still Tigranants climbed, pausing occasionally to feel his way to left and right before choosing to continue. At length the ground became a little more broad and level, but then the path seemed to disappear altogether and they found themselves clambering across great tumbled rocks, torn at by thorn-bushes.

"Are you sure of the way?" Lukas asked at length. The light of the tower had not yet come in view again.

"Yes! Any minute now," Tigranants shouted over the howl of the wind; it was not reassuring when a high distant laugh followed his words. They pushed on a few heartbeats longer. Nobody was reciting aloud now: if they had any breath at all, they were using it to whisper their prayers.

A rotten stench came to his nose. "Stop!" Lukas cried out. "Light a lantern. Quickly."

He'd been living in a city of slowly ripening corpses for weeks: he should be no stranger to bad smells, but this was of a different quality, something very like rotten eggs. When Tigranants got his lantern lit, Lukas snatched it from his hand, raising it to illumine their surroundings. They stood in a narrow gulley somewhat sheltered from the wind by its steeply sloping sides. There was no sign of the wall or of the watch fires, and the lights of Antioch had fallen out of view behind them. Lukas turned, shining the light across the stones until he found what he was looking for: the weathered face of carved stone, marking this place as sacred and dangerous.

Seeing it, Tigranants drew in a sharp breath and crossed himself.

"Don't breathe the fumes," Lukas shouted over the roar of the wind. "The air is dangerous!"

A flicker of lightning darted across the sky; in its light the shadows reeled and Lukas flinched as a succession of dark objects rained down the rock-face towards them. He shouted in the dark and dropped the lantern. Its door broke open, and the ceramic lamp within overturned among the rocks, spilling its oil. Flames flared up, showing Tigranants beside him crumpling beneath the impact of some great heavy object. For a moment, flecks of rock struck Lukas from all directions, raining from above and rebounding from below: the objects he had seen were falling stones, whether dislodged by the wind or by some darker intelligence, he did not know.

"Tigranants!" he yelped, falling to his knee and feeling for the Armenian's pulse. His hands touched hair sticky with blood; his fingers outlined a terrible depression in the other man's skull. The Armenian twitched under his probing fingers and then went still.

Dimly he was aware of the other Watchers gathered around him, pushing and shoving and asking what was the matter.

"Get back," he told them—for all the good it would do, he could still smell the rotten-egg stench and he was breathing in great panicked gulps, his eyes and throat already itching. "Get back, the air is dangerous!" He climbed shaking to his feet and herded them back down the gulley, slipping and barking their shins and cursing until they could no longer smell the sulphur. Some of the Watchers fell to their knees, retching. He wasn't the only one to have breathed too much of the mountain's deadly vapour.

Still there was no sign of light, either from the city or the wall.

"Where are we?" Zarides demanded, wheezing through the effects of the poison. "Tigranants, what the devil did you mean, leading us to such a place?"

"Tigranants is dead. A falling rock struck him." It was just his luck that he spoke into a sudden calm; in the silence after his words, someone cried out:

"Then we're lost on this devilish mountain!"

The words were followed by a terrible laughter, the overwrought sound of a man whose nerve had broken.

"Silence that man!" Lukas wheezed—his eyes were streaming from the fumes—but it was already too late.

"They've got him!"

"Mother of God, he's possessed."

"Kill him!"

"No, beat him until the devil leaves him."

A babel of voices arose; the laughter cut off with a cry as someone struck the sufferer across the face; then came a loud *crack* from above and more stones rained down from above, dislodged by the wind. Lukas did not see if anyone else had been hurt. Screams echoed against the rocks, underlined by a faint and far-off laughter. Panic reigned: another flicker of lightning showed him his Watchers scattering in all directions; and then he turned and saw Lilith descending like a thunderbolt from the sky behind him, and he, too, could bear it no longer. Terror overtook him. He lunged for the darkness, but he was too dizzy to walk straight. He tripped on a rock and fell sprawling.

His outflung hand touched something soft and warm and was caught within a firm grasp. "Lukas," Emelota said out of the dark. "Who is the woman with black wings?"

If he spoke her name, she would hear and pounce on him. But Emelota's voice cleared a little of the panic out of his head. The demon was upon him in any case.

"Lilith," he sobbed.

"Lilith," Emelota said thoughtfully. She sniffled noisily and stood, her voice becoming more decided. "In God's name, Lilith, leave us in peace!"

The wind died, and the moon peered out from between two clouds, illuminating the gulley. Lukas gasped for breath and rolled over on one elbow. Lilith was gone; there was only Emelota standing over him, a pale blur in the darkness.

"She went," the Frankish girl said in a voice of pleased surprise. "Did you see that? I spoke and she had to go. I suppose you were meant to bring me on this journey after all!"

With a pang, Lukas remembered the first time he had commanded Lilith to depart and had been obeyed. That time seemed impossibly far away now, before he swore vengeance and broke an oath and stole a relic, a time bright and far away and half forgotten.

He'd been excited, too.

"Thanks," he said shortly, because she seemed to expect an answer. He got up, retrieved the Bessarion Lance from where it had fallen among the rocks, and caught her wrists by the cord that bound them. "Watchers! Zarides!" he shouted above the wind. "Where are you? Cowards!"

"Bessarion!" Zarides' voice echoed from above the gulley. "This way! I see the tower!"

Five minutes later, somewhat shaken, they had reassembled and counted each other: perhaps five of the Watchers had disappeared entirely, but the rest had not gone far before the panic left them and they flocked back, shaken and shamefaced. Le Puiset, miraculously, was among them.

He really did seem genuinely attached to his baseborn sister.

"The postern is just there, over that rise in the ground," Zarides said, pointing. "I don't know the path beyond it, though. Only Tigranants knew that; he said it was dangerous."

"It will be more dangerous to be caught inside the city." Lukas turned to le Puiset, changing from Greek to Frankish. "Our guide is dead. You know this path, correct?"

"I…" Le Puiset hesitated. "Yes. I can find it again."

He sounded determined—eager, almost. Despite his surprise, Lukas led on without further comment. Zarides turned out to be correct: before the party had gone far, they found a narrow path that lifted them out of the gulley and led them past a craggy outcropping towards the tower they had been trying to reach all along. The square bulk of the tower was dark; its watch fire had gone out, doubtless because of the wind.

As they approached the wall, Lukas saw a glimmer of lamplight in the dark ahead.

The light illuminated a man whose face was shrouded by a hood pulled deep over his head. He appeared to be searching for something on the ground, for he zigzagged to and fro across the path, lantern held low, muttering beneath his breath. When he realised he was no longer alone, he straightened. The light shone on his face, illuminating hollow cheeks, stringy hair, a mouth slack with shock. The next instant, belatedly, he grabbed for the rusty sword at his side.

"Hullo," Lukas said in Frankish, "what's this?"

The man's eyes fixed on the lance. "You're a *thief*," he spat. "It's just as the saint said—I would find the Holy Lance on the road—"

Another of Lilith's tame prophets. Lukas understood now. "Is it just as the saint said? It doesn't look as though you're prepared to face an entire armed company. Perhaps your instructions were to take the lance from a dead man."

The man's mouth hung open a moment. Then he collected himself and said, "I do not fear you and your devils, heretic! My saint will protect me."

"What is this? What is he saying?" Zarides elbowed past Evrard, his face still haggard and shiny from their encounter with Lilith. His sword was in his fist. "We don't have time for this. Even if the tower's empty, there will be a patrol along any minute."

"He's just another of Lilith's madmen. We'll take him prisoner," Lukas ordered in Greek.

Zarides' face darkened. "Sir, with respect, we already have too many prisoners, and this one isn't worth keeping."

This was a fight he couldn't afford to win—not when so much of his future depended upon Zarides' support; not when the Watchers were already frightened and it was, after all, only a lonely Frankish starveling.

"No! Lukas!" Emelota protested suddenly, as though she had divined his intentions.

"Be silent," he told her. Zarides, seeing his decision in his face, lifted his sword.

"No," Lukas told the Watcher. His father's lance was in his hand, a smooth weight charged with some potent energy. He felt the eyes of the others on him, waiting to see whether he had the guts to lead them, whether he had been telling the truth about the Bessarion Lance. He could not afford to give this moment to Zarides.

Before he could think it through any more deeply, he flung the lance with one quick, powerful overarm motion. The Frank had time for nothing more than a whimper before the spear punched its way between his ribs, swift and powerful, as though tossed from the hand of a giant rather than a starved and weakened boy.

Behind him, Emelota made a stifled choking sound. Lukas didn't turn to see the sickened reproach in her eyes. He stepped over the Frank's fallen lantern and pulled the Bessarion Lance with an effort from its place wedged between the ribs of a corpse, reaching into his purse for a rag to clean it with.

Before them, in the flickering light of their lamps, a low, heavy door was set into the wall by the tower.

"Open it," Lukas commanded.

Chapter XXXV.

Zarices unlocked the postern and stood back as they filed through. Le Puiset went first and Lukas followed, holding the dead prophet's lantern high and praying that the light would not blow out in the howling wind. Outside the gate, the path narrowed to a treacherous ribbon as it plunged steeply down the north flank of Stauron.

Lightning flickered in the sky above them; the whole mountainside lit up with the glare, the shadows of thickets and thorn-bushes and pine-trees dancing in wild gaiety. Thunder followed at once, shaking the air like immense enemy drums, so near and so overwhelming that Lukas nearly dropped his lantern. There was something different about the storm now: there were no voices on the wind, no feverish terror stalking them. They were surrounded by clean nature, not malicious but wild and unfathomably powerful.

Lukas should feel more triumphant. At last, everything he wanted had come to him: he had regained his father's lance, put himself at the head of the Watchers, captured his enemy, outwitted Lilith, and won free of dying Antioch. He was the master of his own fate, no longer the plaything either of demons or of angels.

It didn't feel that way. It felt as thought he was running into a black tunnel that led only to a prison.

There were at least two men dead on the mountainside because of him. Well, if he'd sacrificed honour, at least he'd gained power, and power was the only language the Franks truly understood. What was honour without power, anyway? No one expected a peasant to have honour, because no one expected a peasant to have power. Give him power, and honour would surely follow.

The wind was hot and wild at their backs and the lightning drew nearer, thunder shaking the mountains. There was no rain; the heavens strained like a stillbirth. Lukas and his people had just reached safer footing at the precipice's foot when a bolt of lightning slashed across the sky above them. Lukas, who had been peering into the darkness ahead for the way down the lower slopes of the mountain, saw the bolt quite clearly. The whole mountainside was bathed in instantaneous, white-hot light. Thunder accompanied it, a boom like the heavens splitting. A dry tree flashed into stark relief: its limbs and trunk burst open. Then profound blackness rushed in to swallow all sight; but a yellow flame flashed up on the hillside where the tree had been. Lashed by the wind, it licked into the thorny undergrowth.

Within moments, heat and the stench of smoke gusted towards them on the wind. Lukas stood paralysed for a moment, watching the flames build and spread, watching them licking up and along the hill, straight towards them, fast as a horse could run.

Their path led them directly into the fire.

The men behind him gasped and trembled. "We should go back," Zarides said, pale despite the ruddy glare of the flames.

"No." The fire was spreading uphill faster than it was spreading along: by the time they were halfway to the wall they would already be cooked. "This way."

In the growing light, it was now possible to see what looked like another path running along the precipice towards the east. Lukas set out along it half at a run, begging the path not to strand them at the brink of another precipice. Emelota's warning flashed into his mind again—that he wasn't meant to leave the city tonight. For the first time, he wondered if she was about to be proven right, despite every stratagem.

He reached out cautiously for a vision, but none came.

He knew instinctively it wasn't because *she* had made a mistake: it was because he had missed his chance, and now there was wilfully shed blood on his hands. With that, suddenly he *did* feel free. He was a warrior, not a prophet; it seemed that someone had finally figured that out.

All to the good, but the fire had gained on them, and the path was climbing upward again, putting them in greater danger. Desperate, Lukas abandoned the path and scrambled downwards, bruising hands and feet against the tumbled stone, ripping his clothes on thorn-bushes. Suddenly, the rock he put a hand on shifted and, with a yell, he pitched headfirst into a black cleft that opened before him. He shrieked, reaching out blindly with a hand that found and latched onto a rock in the chimney before him; he pivoted in the air and moments later stood on his feet on solid ground, breathing hard but quite safe. It was dark: broken pieces of his lantern crunched underfoot.

"Bessarion!" That was le Puiset's panicked voice above him, followed by others.

"What happened? Where is he, Frank?"

"I'm here," Lukas called up. He stood in one of several tall stone bays etched into the mountain's flank, having fallen barely the height of two men. "Quickly, climb down. There might be shelter."

By now the smoke was thick enough to choke on, the fire a hungry roar in the wind. Lukas took a step further into the bay but came up against rocky walls. He turned and felt in the opposite direction. The smoke blotted out all light. Even when Zarides—having climbed down behind him—got another lantern lit, its light was a tiny flickering halo around the vessel, barely useful to guide the Watchers as they descended the cleft.

Taking the lamp, Lukas went to the bay's opening, where the stony walls opened onto the mountainside. His heart fell as he found their only way out choked with dry, dead thorns. They might tear themselves to shreds trying to escape this chimney, but let the fire get in among the thorns and even this shallow bay would not protect them from being roasted like fowl in an oven.

Despair settled into his bones.

"What next?" Beside him, Zarides' voice was calm, but there was fear in the stink of sweat on his body. The other Watchers crowded after, falling silent as they saw what Lukas saw: the barrier of dry thorns, the illusory nature of their hiding place.

"We're trapped," Zarides said blankly.

Lukas dragged in a breath. The chimney was full of terrified people now weeping, praying, preparing for death. He'd led them here, promising glory and the recovery of a lost patrimony.

"This is my fault," he said, his throat dry and coated in soot.

"You couldn't have known," Zarides said tightly.

"Yes, he could have." Le Puiset's voice cut through the roar of the fire. Lukas turned to face the Frankish count with a feeling of dull inevitability. The taller man loomed over him, but any hostility was swallowed up in terror. Le Puiset's throat worked convulsively. "He's a prophet. He can save us."

The silence was deafening. Lukas was dimly aware of Zarides' shock as the Watcher looked from Lukas to le Puiset and back again.

"*Please*," le Puiset added through trembling lips. "The ravens feed you, Lukas Bessarion. The angels speak to you. Don't let us all die here."

"You're a *Messenger?*" A look of awe crept across Zarides' face.

"I…"

"John Bessarion's heir *and* a Messenger?" Zarides' voice lifted above the commotion, silencing the Watchers and gaining their attention. "Why didn't you tell us?"

"I'm not!" he burst out. "Not any more. Do you think I didn't *ask* for a vision just now? I can't save you. I'm sorry."

"No," le Puiset protested. "You can. You must. You dragged my sister into this danger, and now…"

Emelota had not predicted his death tonight, but his return. Pinned by a dozen or more pairs of despairing eyes, Lukas swallowed. He was trapped: to save his life, he must give up his secret—act the prophet, if it was not already too late to save them.

Desperately he reached for a vision again. Nothing. He risked a glance beyond the narrow bay of rock: his face scorched in the waves of heat that rolled towards them. The flank of Stauron had turned to an inferno.

What he could see of the mountainside above them was alive with racing flames, which crawled more slowly along the slope towards them.

Stalking through the shimmering heat, burning white-hot and haloed by smoke was the dragon he had met on Silpius, the night of the meteor. Its head turned from side to side as though it was seeking something—*someone.*

Lukas recoiled, his heart racing as though he'd tried to run up the mountain. He closed his eyes for a moment, gathering resolve. "Where's the girl?"

A stir within the bay, and Emelota approached him. Someone had cut her bonds, but clumsily in his haste, so that there was blood on her hands. "Take my hands," she said, reaching out.

He did not obey at once: the sight of her blood had unnerved him. "You tried to save that false prophet back there."

"Would you have me apologise?"

He had spoken angrily. He was still angry. "I had no choice but to kill him."

"You always have a choice."

That reminded him of something Ayla had once said. "Yes, and it's usually between slavery and death. Isn't it? We are all only the playthings of powers greater than ourselves." He seized her hands, holding tightly to avoid slipping in the blood coating her skin. "Tell me what I'm meant to do."

She closed her eyes. A faint crease appeared between her eyebrows. "I think…" Her voice trailed away; her eyes opened, startled. "Ask for a vision. Ask for…I think it's supposed to be…*my* future."

He frowned. Emelota had never been able to divine her own purpose, after all. "Are you sure?"

"No," she said raggedly, "of course not. But it's all I have."

All right, he thought, reaching out in invitation.

Indistinct light flashed through his head—but no vision, no distinct images. Before him, Emelota gave a soft sound of surprise, her hands tightening painfully on his. He tried to pull out of her grasp, but she clung to him mercilessly. His senses were drowned by pain and blinding, incomprehensible light. At length Emelota released him and he fell back a step, breathing hard, sick and disoriented as though the vapour-sickness had returned.

Emelota's eyes were unfocused, staring at a point infinitely distant, her lips parted.

"*Oh,*" she said softly.

"It didn't work," he said. "I saw nothing."

She blinked and looked at him, seeming to return only slowly. "You're supposed to go out to it. There's a gap in the thorn, there." She pointed. "The seraph is waiting. It won't leave without you."

"What?" His voice was strained. "How do *you* know about the seraph?"

"There's a *seraph*?" Zarides crossed himself. Le Puiset, like many of the other Watchers, made a soft sound almost like distress. Emelota ignored all of them.

"I saw," she said softly. "I saw…everything. Quickly. There is no time. Go."

She was telling him to go out and meet the seraph—to go out and *die*. Lukas backed away, his whole being rising up in a silent protest. After the things he had done tonight, he knew instinctively he would never survive such an encounter.

But he was about to die anyway; and this way, he might at least save his Watchers. Unslinging the Bessarion Lance from its place across his shoulders, he extended the weapon to Zarides. "Keep this for me," he said. "If I…if I don't return, use it to rally our people."

"No!" Zarides threw his hands up. "You're a Messenger. The angels visit you. How can we send you out to die?"

"It's die out there or die in here," Lukas growled. "Take it."

A stricken silence. "But, the Turks. The *plan…*"

He swallowed hard. "I know. I thought…I was wrong. I don't know any more, who lives or who is destroyed. Ask Emelota of le Puiset. I can't tell you. Goodbye."

Not knowing how else to explain, he pushed the lance into Zarides' hands and turned. Putting up an arm in a futile attempt to shield his face, he used his empty scabbard to thrust aside the thorn-bush Emelota had pointed out, stepping through the gap.

Into the night.

Into the heat.

Into the fire.

The great seraph awaited him where the unburned ground met the black. Lukas felt the skin on his face pull tight with the heat as the creature paced towards him, immense and bright, its flanks rippling with white fire. Lukas, in turn, went forward to meet it, until each breath was agony, an inrush of scalding air that burned his lungs. At last he stopped, burning and shaking and trying to stand upright before the face of his reckoning. He could not put his face against the stones like he had last time.

Serpentine and graceful, the seraph lowered its head until their eyes were on a level, the seraph's burning with a blue-hot flame. Lukas blinked fast, trying to protect his own eyes, trying to meet that fiery gaze.

Its voice hissed and sputtered within his mind.

Why have you run away, mortal? You had a message to deliver.

I'm not who you think I am. I'm no prophet. All I want is to avenge Ayla and protect my people. I didn't choose this.

The thoughts were empty now, lies he told himself for comfort. They shredded away beneath the dragon's blue-hot gaze.

Did you not? You want a better world than the one you awoke into. You want wrongs righted and the weak protected, do you not? This is how it happens. You did indeed choose this.

But I'm a warrior. The Bessarion Lance is my patrimony, Syria my inheritance. My father—

Your father knew that warriors change nothing, Lukas Bessarion. You were meant for something greater. To pierce hearts with something more potent than blades.

"No," Lukas gasped, speaking aloud in a voice raspy with smoke. "No, that's not what I want. I want the Franks to *pay*. I want *justice*."

The dragon gazed down at him. Worse than dispassion was its fiery pity.

I know.

He closed his eyes, feeling the tears dry between his eyelids. *Am I to have no choice in the matter? Nothing between death and slavery?*

A quiet, ruminating moment. *Very well,* said the seraph, *I give you the choice between justice and mercy. Only know that whatever you judge for them will also be meted to you and yours.*

Not so long ago, he would have been glad to die if it meant the Franks were destroyed along with him. But in that moment Lukas could not face the thought of death. Each breath burned him from the inside out, a foretaste of eternal justice, and he found that he did not have the courage to ask for that now.

What a fool he had been: pretending he could chase away his visions as easily as he could a flock of wild ravens, pretending to himself that he could reject this calling when it hunted him in wildfire. He had set out that evening to prove to himself that he could defy fate—that he could defy *Heaven.*

But the mercies of Heaven were infinite, and could be entreated. Wasn't that supposed to be his lesson?

Show me, he said. *Show me this mercy you boast of, if it truly exists.*

Chapter XXXVI.

"The Galileean stripped us of great power," Lilith complained. "We can no longer create bodies for ourselves; in order to walk in the world of flesh we must find a willing vessel to possess, and that is not an easy path. But with *you, Khalil…*" She traced a cold finger under the sorcerer's jaw, forcing him to look into her obsidian eyes. "You will invite me to possess you. Together, we will create more demigods. We will take command of the Franks. We will desecrate everything the Enemy has built since the last Deluge, beginning with his holy places and everyone who calls on his name. We will fill his beloved city with blood until it flows to the horses' bridles. And when we are done, we will make sure there is *no one* left worth saving. No Noahs; no Bessarions. Then the whole cosmos will know who is greater: him, or me."

Khalil swallowed, his voice little more than a faint rasp. "Why me? Why not someone else—one of these prophets you have corrupted?"

"I need a sorcerer to father my children, one who is able to bind and master them. Children are ungrateful creatures, prone to revolt," she added thoughtfully. "Not all my first children always carried out my will. Some turned to the Enemy. No: I have chosen *you,* Half-Stone."

Khalil felt as though he was standing outside his body, watching the great queen of nightmares bending over him, her breath hot with the stink of carrion. Even so, he was unable to keep the terror, the hatred, out of his eyes. Her eyes narrowed, but her voice was full of pleasure.

"You do not like this prospect? You wish to turn and bite me, you insect? I am glad you loathe the idea," she murmured in his ear. "Think on it very carefully in the short time you have left, Half-Stone. Possession is hardly sweet if uncontested."

She had gone then, leaving Khalil in the company of glaring sun, hot wind, and the occasional yelp of a distant jackal—all the privacy a madman might wish for in which to experiment with his own immortality.

He ought to know by now that there was no way in which he could relieve himself of his own cursed existence. All he could do was darken it by self-inflicted pain.

I seek forgiveness from God, he thought wearily, at last, when all his attempts had failed. The Name had not crossed his lips in years beyond measure; barely even his mind, except in terror. Now he turned towards it. Begged it. Threw himself upon its mercy.

I have been consumed by dreams of vengeance, God forgive me, when this devil is my true enemy. No longer will I commit this sin.

I seek refuge in the Lord of mankind, the King of mankind, the God of mankind, from the evil of the sneaking whisperer, who whispers in the hearts of djinn and mankind.

O God, release me from this bondage, and see what deeds I shall do in your name.

Chapter XXXVII.

Perhaps a minute passed since Lukas Bessarion had walked into the storm on Emelota's direction. Then, the storm burst in a torrent of rain that poured from the sky like a spilled ocean. Hailstones rattled and bounced in the chimney above where Emelota, her brother, and the remnant of Lukas' followers hid. The smoke washed from the moon-gilded sky, the flames that surrounded them died with much hissing, and then a trickle started down the chimney overhead, swelling first to a rush, then to a torrent.

The Watchers reacted to this new threat with shouts of alarm. Emelota, standing at the mouth of the cleft staring into the darkness, felt Evrard seize her by the arm. "The way out," he said hoarsely. "Which way?"

"Let me see." Her voice came from a long way off, as though in a dream. She could still scarcely believe the things that had happened to her in the past few minutes. First had come the feeling, so faint that she had nearly missed it—how often had she overlooked it in the past, believing it to be impossible?—that she *did* have a purpose to be discerned, that she was something more than a blank tablet, fit only to receive the impressions of others. After that—the vision. *Her* vision, singular and spectacular and entirely, extravagantly impossible. She closed her eyes, remembering what she had seen: all her choices and purposes, and not merely her own but those of others that affected her, unrolled before her like a map, like a pattern, like a tapestry of twisted threads. Only a fragment of the pattern had come to her: only as much as her mortal mind could comprehend without breaking. But a portion of it she had seen, and now she considered its intricacies in wonder and delight. Certain threads she understood instinctively to be a choice that hung in the balance, likely to go one way or the other at the whim of the chooser; others she knew to be more likely, choices that must be made simply because of the nature of the decision-maker. In either case, one could not leap from one clue to another once taken: a mortal must experience his or her own thread in sequence and it was those choices that determined her way, whether it led to sorrow or bliss.

Emelota dimly sensed that it might be possible to step off the tapestry altogether to a place where all things happened at once and never, when past and present and future existed as a harmonious whole, a tale written in a book. To the tale-teller, only one path was ever intended; the different threads were drawn together into one scarred, beautiful whole, and that was a comforting thing. But to the people of the tale, time occurred in sequence. It was a dialogue between tale-teller and tale-liver, mercies asked for and received, and that was also a comforting thing. From her perspective the future was malleable, changeable, full of hope.

She had been so anxious these past few weeks, but it wasn't necessary, after all. She was no weakling: her gift had tremendous power. She knew exactly what to do next.

She knew exactly where to go, even though the light was gone, the moon blotted out by silvered clouds and the mountain lit only by dying embers.

"This way," she said, pointing to the way Lukas had taken. The thorns parted to let them through. Beyond, the night kept its secrets: she could see nothing of Lukas, whether charred bones or living man.

As she turned left towards the city, one of the Watchers—Zarides—pulled her to a halt, protesting in Greek. Most Antiochenes also spoke Arabic: she said in her broken form of that language, "We must go back to Antioch. I will show the way."

"No. No. It is death to return to Antioch, and the Franks will kill us for the sake of the lance. We will go north, Aleppo maybe." He signalled to the others, having them light their lanterns now that the rain had eased.

"What are they saying, Emelota?—I agree," Evrard added, when she had translated the Watcher's words. A change had come over her brother: he was alert and eager like a man newly come alive. "We can't stay in Antioch. We've been lucky to escape with our lives and each other. These men saved my life once, before. Remind them of that, and tell them that if they will grant us safe-conduct—"

"We're meant to be in Antioch," she protested. "That's where our paths lead."

"What, are *you* a prophet, too, now?" Evrard demanded.

Beneath the bluster there was something uncertain in his voice, but she could not bring herself to try to convince him: not now. Emelota swallowed the objection she had been going to make. "It will be easier if you follow me now."

Evrard was silent a moment. "I can't go back there. Zarides is right. It's death to go back. I can't."

Emelota sighed, but made no objection as the Watchers turned away and began navigating the lower slopes of Stauron in the dark. It was slow, wet, dangerous going for perhaps half an hour until the grey light of dawn began to show in the east and they blundered into a Turkish patrol. It must have been their lanterns that drew attention: without warning, arrows hissed down from the slopes above. One of the Watchers fell, shrieking in pain. Uphill, a drum began to beat. An answer came from further down the mountain, followed a moment later by the sound of horse's hooves thudding towards them.

"Douse the lights," Zarides hissed. "Back!"

This time there was no debate: they turned and fled back the way they had come. The light of dawn provided them with a quicker journey; the rain had stopped, but the mountain was now dissected by torrents of water that in some places had washed away the path. When all sounds of pursuit had been left far behind, Zarides called a halt and the party threw themselves on the sodden ground, breathing hard, their faces pale and exhausted in the early morning light. Emelota was ready to cry from exhaustion and emotional strain: she had never spent such a night in her life, and her feet were bruised and blistered from the hard ground. She was unprepared for Zarides to get up, stalk over to her, and pluck her from the mud so that she stood facing him.

Evrard got up with a shout of warning, but two of the other Watchers tackled him at once and put a knife to his throat.

"Did you know they were waiting for us?" Zarides demanded in Arabic.

"Ye—yes," Emelota panted. "I would have told you, but I didn't think you'd believe me."

Zarides drew back his fist with a sudden, violent motion, as though he meant to strike her in the face. Evrard shouted—warnings, threats. Emelota only laughed.

"It's all right," she told her brother. "He's only bluffing. He doesn't really mean to harm me."

Zarides, not understanding, faltered and then lowered his fist. "What are you? A witch? Perhaps we should have sent *you* out into the flames, and we would still have our Messenger."

"Lukas said I was something called a Revealer," she protested. Why did this man treat Lukas with such reverence, but herself as suspect? Both of them, after all, had the same sort of gift. "If he trusted me, shouldn't you?"

"I don't know: maybe because you sent him to his death?"

"He isn't dead." That much the vision had shown her. "That's why I tried to lead you back to Antioch. If you abandon the city, you abandon him."

There was a silence. Zarides narrowed his eyes, then looked at the lance in his hand.

"Don't listen to the witch," one of the other Watchers said. "We can't go back to Antioch now. What about these Franks? If we take them back, they'll blab on us."

"That's easily mended," said another, drawing his sword. "Kill them both. No one will know. Plenty of others have deserted."

"Emelota, for the love of God, what's going on?" Evrard's voice quivered: he had seen the drawn blade.

She might have been frightened too, if she did not have that tapestry of woven threads in her memory. "It's nothing. I'll tell you later."

Zarides had been weighing up the worth of their lives with a terrifying detachment. "Bessarion wanted both these Franks alive. If he comes back he may not be pleased to find them dead."

"Then don't kill us," Emelota suggested. "Hold us as hostages for your own safety. We will both give our parole not to escape."

The Syrians glowered at her. "Evrard," Emelota added, "they are asking for our word not to escape, should they return to the city. Tell them you will give it."

"What?" He stared at her, incredulous, as though she had bitten him. If it was her command that astonished him, Emelota could not blame him. She had become very bold of late—but she was trying to save their lives.

"It's that or die now," she explained, and he did as she said, with herself as the interpreter.

Later, when they had crept back in at the unguarded postern—with Emelota's guidance and the growing light of day, it was a laughably quick journey—she found herself sent to the rear of the party to walk beside her brother. Evrard's face was set in stark, unhappy lines as they slipped back into Antioch's waking streets, its streets and rubbish-heaps still heaped with corpses. The stink of rotting flesh enfolded them, suffocating after their brief escape: a loathsome medley of rotted meat, swamp water, ordure. In addition to the detritus of the sack there were fresh corpses in the streets now, those of the poor who had been unable to buy or beg food. A small loaf of bread cost a whole gold bezant, a walnut cost a silver penny, and wine was beyond price. People were boiling thistles, fig leaves, or even dried skins to eat, and of late Emelota herself had been obliged to go out and forage on the mountain-slopes for tender green shoots to eat, things she would never have imagined fit for food.

"God's mercy," Evrard said now in something close to despair. "For a moment I really thought we were escaping this nightmare." There was a brief silence. His face was white as he sent her an odd look, half fearful, half hopeful. "Perhaps Kerbogha will grant terms. Does the embassy succeed? Do you—do you know that, too?"

She wanted anything but to tell him the truth—but her face must have betrayed her.

"Tell me!"

"I could," she hedged, "but you won't like it."

His face crumpled. "Blessed Virgin, pray for us. What are we going to do?"

Ah, this was terrible. Emelota bit her lip. "For the present? All we can do is wait."

* * *

That night, Emelota slept like the dead at first. But then, as she had half expected, she began to dream of Aemathe.

In the beginning, it was only a voice, urgently calling her name. Emelota pushed open the door and walked into the Watchers' courtyard to find Aemathe looking for her in a living form that glowed, casting its own faint light.

"You're here," Emelota said, absurdly pleased. Where else would Aemathe be? "When they brought us here, I hoped I would see you again. I am sorry it's taken me so long to think of a way to set you free, but—"

"Hush." Aemathe's gaze was fixed on the courtyard gate, and Emelota became aware that the other girl was trembling. "Something is here. Something older and far more powerful than me."

A lamp burned in the front room, its light streaming into the courtyard through open door and window, and the night was so silent Emelota could almost hear the flame flicker. If Aemathe said something was here, she must be right; but where were Zarides and his men? Surely one of them must be keeping watch?

Even as the thought crossed her mind, a muffled sound came at the gate, followed by a violent blow that made the door shake. Another came, and then another—until, with a loud splintering sound, the gate burst open. Emelota smothered a gasp as she saw what lay beyond.

Three men stood there. Two wore the robes of priests and carried a small post they had used as a battering ram, but the youngest was dressed, albeit well, in the simple clothing of a Provençal peasant. Emelota recognised him at once as the keeper of the supposed Holy Lance: she had seen him in the chapel some days previously.

Emelota felt a shiver as Aemathe reached out to grasp her hand. It was a curiously mortal gesture; but the goddess' hands, not being made of flesh, passed through her without touching. Behind the three men was a shadow, dark and seething even against the blackness of night. It reared up behind them in a vigilant bird-shape.

"It is Lilith," the other girl whispered in a voice so faint that Emelota half thought she had imagined it. Yet, the great bird-shape opened two glowing yellow eyes and fixed them upon Aemathe when she said the name. Emelota's heart stopped, then began beating wildly, recalling the panic upon the mountain the previous night.

She touched her tongue to her lips. "You cannot stop her, can you?"

Aemathe shook her head. "Not bound as I am. That is why I called upon you." Raising her voice, she called: "You are not welcome here, Poison Mother! This house is under my protection!"

"Only the house? Ah, how the mighty have fallen. I remember when the whole city was under your protection." Lilith's mockery sharpened. "Stand aside and do not attempt to hinder me, if you value what freedom you have."

As Lilith spoke, Peter Bartholomew and the two priests strode into the courtyard towards Emelota. Overcoming her doubts, Emelota made herself face up to them. "Why do you break into this house, like thieves in the night?"

They gave no sign of hearing her: their faces were set, and they went through her like a wind, making for the light that burned in the house. In their wake Emelota staggered, looking down at her own ghostly hands. Of course: her body must still be fast asleep in the hidden cellar where Zarides had chosen to imprison her, together with Evrard.

"You are in my realm now, mortal," Lilith observed; but Emelota noticed that she remained hovering in the air beyond the gate. "Don't you know the perils of dreamwalking? Tell me, shall I snatch your soul and send one of my servants to possess your body? Shall I drive your brother the last few steps into madness?"

A day or two previously, that would have frightened her. But she was coming into her power now. Emelota shook her head. "Words are all you have, aren't they? You won't cross the threshold of this courtyard. You fled from me in the mountains." She stepped forward, making the sign of the cross. "In the name of Christ, you may not enter this house."

"I don't need to," the shadow replied disdainfully. "My prophets have already entered it."

Emelota glanced at Aemathe, then dashed for the doorway that led into the lighted front room. Within, Zarides and two of his lieutenants must have been sitting up, laying their plans, but had now slumped over, fast asleep. Bartholomew's two priests must have gone further into the house, but he himself knelt by Zarides, gently drawing the Bessarion Lance from the Watcher's grasp.

So that was their business here.

On the windowsill, Zarides' cat had awoken and was unconcernedly washing its face, but it paused to hiss at Emelota in alarm when she entered. "Really?" she whispered to it. "You don't mind these thieves, but a perfectly friendly dreamwalker is too much for you?"

Bartholomew gave a soft sound of satisfaction as the lance slipped free. Zarides moved in his sleep with a grunt; Bartholomew quickly replaced the lance with an iron-shod staff, the same she had seen Lukas Bessarion using so often. Zarides' grip closed and he went on sleeping. Bartholomew stood, wiping the end of his sleeve across his face to blot out the nervous sweat.

Emelota hesitated, recalling her vision. There were more than a few twisting and parting threads in the tapestry for this weapon. The lance was important, but not in the way anyone thought. She sensed a slumbering spirit within it, bound by many chains and a name of merciless living power. Like Aemathe, another demigoddess…

Divining something of the purpose that stretched out before this captive, Emelota raised a hand to the lance and spoke: "My sister, I bless you to have remembrance of things forgotten."

Some power evidently moved through her in that moment. Barely three paces away, Bartholomew stopped moving: his eyes focused upon her and *saw* her. With a grunt of alarm, he levelled the spear and drove it towards her. Emelota recoiled, all the way through the wall at her back and into the adjoining room. She heard the dull *thud* as the lance struck the wall. Had she been present in body, she would have been spitted like that poor madman on the mountain.

The two priests who had been searching the rest of the house now rushed into the room where Bartholomew stood with the lance's point buried in the plaster. "What is it?" Emelota heard them whisper.

"The witch," Bartholomew panted. "Where is she? Did you see her?"

People were calling her that a great deal lately.

"There are only men in this house. No women. We should go."

"She knows we are here." That was Bartholomew: he sounded…afraid of her. "The saint said she would be here, that she must die."

That was worrying, but no more than she had expected, from her vision. Emelota had heard enough: it was time to act. She drifted cautiously through the wall into the lighted room where the prophets clustered by the door, whispering their arguments: Bartholomew wanted to search the house a second time, the priests wanted to make good their escape. To her relief, neither of them saw her. She threw herself at Zarides' cat, still washing itself on the windowsill. The animal gave a yowl of terror and fled, knocking the lantern from the low makeshift table between Zarides and his lieutenants. Flames flared up. Zarides and his men woke with shouts as they saw, first the broken lamp and fire, then the terrified intruders. Without further argument, Bartholomew and his cohorts fled into the street.

Inside the house, confusion reigned as the Watchers put out the fire and searched for other intruders. Meanwhile, Emelota went out into the courtyard to find Aemathe pacing in impotent watchfulness at the gate. Lilith was gone, and Aemathe was frowning terribly.

"Aemathe! There's another one—a demigoddess, like you—in the lance."

"My kinswoman. I know," she fumed. "They took her away. There was nothing I could do…"

"I'm sorry." Emelota felt as though she ought to apologise; intangible as she was, perhaps she ought to have done something sooner. "If it helps, it won't do them the least bit of good."

"I wasn't thinking of *them,*" Aemathe said.

"No, of course not. But your kinswoman cannot be freed yet. The lance is protected by a living name; it isn't like your statue. Whoever bound you there is long cast out and I need only melt it down."

"I know. Deal with the demon first, then the vessel." But Aemathe still looked furious. "How many more of my kin have been bound in servitude—to rings, to lamps, to weapons and images?"

"I don't know." More lights shone into the courtyard as the house awoke: two or three Watchers, seeing the broken gate, ran into the street. It was hopeless: the prophets must have been long gone by now. In her mortal body, Emelota felt the heavy tread of feet vibrating through the house, tugging her from the depths of sleep. "Listen, Aemathe: I have a task to do in this city. I know how to unbind you, but…it may still take some time. I will need help. A new Watchers' Council."

"What's wrong with this one?"

"They're killers," she said with a sigh. "It was *meant* to be Lukas Bessarion's task, but he has failed the test, and this…this is my purpose now." She had purpose now—the words were a shiver of delight on her lips. "I'm going to free you, Aemathe, and between us we will secure this city. But there will be a cost, I'm afraid."

"Whatever it is, I am ready to pay it," Aemathe promised her. Emelota would have said more, but the dream fled as light and sound burst in upon her sleeping body.

* * *

Zarides was enraged at the loss of the lance; but try as he might, he could find no one to blame. He himself was supposed to be sitting up keeping watch, but sleep had overtaken him. Emelota had been locked in the cellar, or he might have been tempted to accuse her of some sinister design. In the end, he was forced to settle the blame where it was due: upon Bartholomew's demon.

"Very well," he snarled once he had been convinced not to take out his anger on Emelota. "But you live on sufferance, and only until Lukas Bessarion returns. You had best pray he does so shortly."

He would, Emelota thought, but she did not particularly care for Zarides and did not choose to enlighten him. He had been little more than a bully to her. Zarides sent her back to the cellar, where she found Evrard pacing to and fro in a welter of fraternal anxiety.

"Did they hurt you?" he asked. They had been allowed a lamp, and now he raised it to her face, putting a worried hand to her cheek.

"Only my feelings," she told him with a wry smile. "They seem to think I'm a witch."

"That's ridiculous," he exploded. A moment passed in silence, then his voice changed. "What *are* you, Emelota?"

She thought of the vision she had seen the night of the fire on the mountain. "I don't know," she said in a small voice. "A Revealer, Lukas told me. But when I'm with him, strange things happen between us..."

He looked scandalised. "What kind of thing?"

"Nothing evil!"

"There should be nothing good either," he snarled. "That boy was no fit company for my sister, and if by some miracle he *does* come back... I won't have you encouraging him again."

"Encouraging him how? By sending him out into a wildfire?"

Evrard groaned and collapsed, all angular arms and legs. He put his face in his hands. "I can't," he said thickly. "I *can't* watch you run into danger, Emelota. Please, if you know how, get us out of here. *Please.*"

"Out of this cellar?" She frowned. That was no part of her plan.

"Out of this cellar. Out of this house. Out of this cursed city." He sucked in a jagged breath, close to tears. "This room...I hid here for days, after Galon died. Now even these Watchers have turned against me, and—I tell you, I cannot endure it much longer—I'm a *coward*..."

"Count Bohemond didn't think so."

"Well, he's wrong. *Look* at me, Emelota. I have no horse and no men and barely any armour, I can neither feed nor protect my own sister, and I'm…I'm out of my mind with fear. Even if there was a hope of winning a battle, I can't fight…I *can't.* I hoped to get out of this with honour, and now…" His mouth twisted. "Now I'd just be glad to get out of it at all."

Emelota risked putting a hand on his shoulder, and he flinched.

"Don't."

"Maybe honour isn't everything, Evrard."

He said nothing, but she knew what his answer would be: *That's all very well for you to say.* Once she might have felt a sting at such words, but she knew now that, for all his arrogance, he was willing to give his life for her.

That gave her boldness, and she had resolved to speak plainly. "If you want to find your courage, perhaps you should stop worrying about honour and dishonour and what other people think of you. Surely it's enough of a burden for any man to think on his sins."

"That's what frightens me." He lifted a tearstained face from his hands. "I wanted to go to Jerusalem for my sins…but I've done evil even on this pilgrimage and now where do I stand?" His throat worked. "They're both dead now. I can't even confess to them."

She didn't need to ask whom he meant, but what could she say? *Don't worry, you'll have your chance to apologise to Lukas, at least.* She was not sure how he would receive this, so she curled up on one of the mildewed old cushions and tried to forget the emptiness of her stomach in sleep.

Some hours later, the trapdoor opened again. This time the house was full of a terrible hush, almost like that of a funeral; indeed, when Emelota and her brother were hauled up the ladder and into the front room, there was a dead man eating bread and drinking wine in the front room.

Evrard stopped in the doorway with a wordless sound of shock. *"You,"* he breathed.

All the Watchers had gathered around in perfect silence to watch Lukas Bessarion eat. He was worth looking at, too: he almost hurt her eyes, and he smelled of a piercing, ferocious heat. Despite the sunken cheeks and wasted hands of one who had walked too long on the edge of starvation, his skin was smooth, all scars and bruises gone. His silk tunic looked as though it had been taken off the loom that instant, and where his mail armour peeped out from beneath the tunic at wrists and neck, it glittered as brightly as though an army of squires had been scouring it all night.

He swallowed a mouthful of coarse bread and grinned with strong, white teeth. "Saints, this is good. I was perishing for hunger."

Not a spirit, then. Emelota had not thought she would have been so surprised to see him again, but something about his appearance left her speechless with conflicting emotions: relief, fear and suffocating anger.

He nodded towards her, towards her brother. "Have you Franks eaten?"

There—that was what was so different about him. No blood dripped from his lips as he spoke; no strong, overriding purpose drove him. Lukas Bessarion stood at the divergence of two threads and had not yet quite chosen his path. Balanced at a tipping-point, a puff of wind might move him: it was not peace she sensed but instability.

Perhaps Evrard felt it too, for a look of trepidation crossed his face.

"Emelota hasn't eaten," he said. Lukas tossed her a piece of his bread; she caught it and divided it between herself and her brother.

Evrard refused to eat, but she was not so haughty. The bread must have been about half sawdust. It tasted wonderful.

"Why feed us?" Evrard demanded in a low voice. "You meant to kill us, after all. If it's a battle you want, let's go out into the courtyard now and get it over with."

"Not so fast." Lukas sobered. "I call on you from necessity, count. I have a Message for the princes' council, but I dare not go to Count Raymond for fear he will kill me."

Evrard cleared his throat, sending a nervous glance about the room. "A message? What do you mean?"

"Not a message, a *Message*," Emelota told him. That didn't seem to help. She sighed. "A prophecy."

"A *prophecy?*" Evrard glanced from her to Lukas Bessarion.

Lukas misinterpreted his surprise: his face, so open a moment ago, shuttered. "Are we going back to pretending you don't believe me, then?"

"No!" Evrard drew a long breath: there was a tone of inexpressible relief in his voice. "No, I believe you are sent by God to save us. I will take you before the council. I will even return here afterward, to be your hostage. But if Count Raymond really does want you dead…I won't necessarily be able to protect you." He glanced at Emelota. "I want your promise that my sister will be released, no matter what happens."

Lukas watched her brother with a still, waxen face, and once again, Emelota sensed nothing, good or bad. "So it will be. Take me to the council and I will release your sister."

Chapter XXXVIII.

Do not despise the mercy that has been granted you, the seraph had said, a voice of crisp and unbearable heat in his mind. It is not for your sake alone that this is done for you, Lukas Bessarion. Go to Antioch now and deliver your Message.

Despise the mercy granted? That did not occur to him. He did not know how long he had been walking beside the great creature through an arid and burning waste. He only knew, like a dim and mercifully-forgotten memory, that he had walked through fire until there was nothing left of him; and then the seraph spoke again, and Lukas had found himself standing outside the Iron Gate, free of what seemed like an eternity of agony.

No, this was nothing to despise. He was too grateful to be alive, when he ought to have been dead.

Four days, the dragon's voice rang in his mind, *and Antioch will fall.*

He had opened his eyes upon a fresh morning sky. He was unbearably hungry, but his stomach was no longer knotted with the bloody flux and he was free of innumerable aches and pains for the first time in months. His clothes were new and crisp, and the smell of fire—not smoke, but pure scorching *fire*—hung about him.

He had taken one step and fallen to his knees: his legs were as wobbly as a newborn colt's. Before him was the Iron Gate, part wall, part dam, and part gate: the isolated eastern entrance to Antioch, tucked like a secret between Stauron and Silpius. The road was a narrow ledge carved from the precipitous flank of Stauron, skirting a pool of red and turbulent water held back by the wall from flooding the city. Two round arches pierced the wall a little below the level of the road and the water flowed through these with a steady musical sound, tamed to the quiet Parmenius stream that flowed past Emelota's lodgings. Directly ahead, the road led to the gate itself; when Lukas looked up to the high viaduct bridging the walls between Silpius to the left and Stauron to the right, he saw pale faces looking down on him, heard thin clear voices hailing him.

"Let me in," he had called, using the Provençal dialect. It did not even occur to him to question the seraph's instructions. Perhaps, later, he would begin to think again of how he could pick back up the shattered pieces of his ambitions. "I have a Message for the princes."

* * *

Lukas wasn't entirely sure what he expected from the princes' council meeting, but he certainly had never expected this.

At the palace gate, no one rushed forward to seize and accuse him—either of thieving a relic, or of slaughtering a prophet. They only nodded to him in surprise. "Bessarion! Count Raymond's been looking for you," someone said, but that was all. Anyone might have imagined that he was guilty of nothing worse than a few days' absence without leave. In the audience-hall of the palace where the six great princes sat in a ring with their most important vassals packed around them, Count Raymond's single eye fixed on him—and looked briefly relieved.

Nor did le Puiset take the opportunity to denounce him, as he had feared. Instead, Count Evrard led him into the circle of princes and said:

"My lords, this man has a Message for you. Please hear him. I will swear to the truth of his visions."

Lukas' throat went dry as the hum of anxious conversation hushed and he found himself sweating beneath the eyes of perhaps two hundred hungry, fearful Franks. For a moment, he wished he could simply turn and go—but where? There was nothing he could do but deliver the Message.

"Four days, and Antioch will fall," he announced. "I've seen it in a vision.

384

Kerbogha means to burn the city and leave you dead in its ruins."

There was an echoing silence. Count Raymond's scowl reminded Lukas how recently he had been sent on a mission to assassinate the very man who had now introduced him to the council.

If he lived so long, he was going to have quite a bit of explaining to do.

In an amused drawl, Bohemond said, "Thank you for bringing us this insight, le Puiset. Now, weren't you and the Syrian feuding?"

"Please, my lord, listen." Count Evrard tipped his head towards Lukas. "There's more."

"No, there isn't." Count Raymond glared daggers in Lukas' direction, and then addressed the circle of princes. "This is pure nonsense. As I was just telling you, I sent for Alexius weeks ago. If he set out when he received my message, he could be here within the week. All we need to do is hold the city until he comes."

Count Raymond said more, but Lukas didn't hear it: visions assailed him again with bright, unbearable colour. When he struggled back to the present, the princes were loudly debating their next steps, whether the emperor was coming, whether they could bear to watch the people starve until he did. As Lukas drew breath, he found that le Puiset had him by the elbow, watching him in wary concern.

"Pull yourself together, Greek."

"It was a vision," Lukas growled, pulling away from the count's supporting hand. His voice lifted above the debate. "My lords, Emperor Alexius is not coming."

"Of course he isn't." Count Bohemond snorted. "We don't need a prophet to tell us that."

"Don't interrupt," Count Raymond snapped, but Lukas raised his voice to override their debate.

"The count of Blois has left Alexandretta and gone to tell the emperor of Kerbogha's arrival. The Greeks have taken their people, set fire to Anatolia, and retreated to Constantinople. The emperor has deserted you." Hearing his own voice falling like hammer-blows in the stunned silence, Lukas began to feel a sense of grim enjoyment. "Kerbogha *will* destroy Antioch. You fools! The corpses of your victims lie piled in the streets, and you dare to believe that God is on your side? That you are his chosen people, that *you* are better and holier than any other people in the world? Are you so blind that you do not see that Heaven is against you? God has allowed you to be bewitched by demons who assure you of your own illustriousness, and all along he means to destroy you."

This time there was silence—profound silence. Le Puiset was pale to the lips. Beside Count Raymond, Bishop Adhemar had buried his face in his hands: his fingertips were white, making painful dents in the skin.

Mother of God! Perhaps they would believe him. Perhaps he had become the salvation of the Franks. The thought nearly choked him.

"The Greek is raving," Count Raymond burst out contemptuously. "How have we been bewitched?"

"I will vouch for the truth of what he says," le Puiset said. Count Raymond turned dark red, but he did not speak: only he sent Lukas a murderous gaze.

Bishop Adhemar rose and spoken in a shaken, husky voice. "I believe him. If he will swear on the Gospels—"

"What? *Adhemar,*" Count Raymond protested.

"You know that what he says is true! We were sent for the liberation of the east, not its enslavement. Narbonne, will you find a book of the Gospels, to put the Syrian under oath?"

No, Lukas thought desperately. They *mustn't* believe him. They must ignore him and be destroyed, so that once he had tried to warn them and failed, he would be allowed to run away in peace, unhounded by the beast of fire.

But words burned in his stomach, crawled up his throat. "Never mind about an oath. I will give a sign," he gasped, and then clenched his teeth.

The relic you believe to be the Holy Lance will split asunder from haft to tip.

He locked the words behind his lips. No. *No.* Not that. Not his father's lance. Not his only hope to protect his people.

So what if Lilith and her prophets had stolen back the lance in the night? He would recover it, that was all. Seraph or no, burning or no, damnation or no, he couldn't command its destruction like this. It was as Khalil ibn Hassan had said on that night in Oliveta, when he had destroyed a town in order to regain it: he who held the lance held power over men.

His people badly needed power.

The decision was easy to make, in the end. Lukas felt himself flooded, suddenly, with passion and purpose. Anger like his, ambition like his, could not simply be forgotten. He straightened, pointing directly at the lord standing in the place of honour behind Count Raymond's chair. Forced his own words through his lips rather than the ones he had been given. "Lord Galdemar Carpenel. You shall also see my vision and know that it is true."

"The devil I will," the nobleman said with a snort of surprise, but then he cried out, gripping the back of Count Raymond's chair and doubling over as if in pain. Some of the men beside him reached to support him, but others backed away, their eyes flickering from Lukas to the Provençal lord in fear.

The disturbance hardly had time to begin before Lord Galdemar straightened again, breathing hard. "It's true. I've seen it too. Blois told the emperor the situation here was hopeless, that he'd seen Antioch surrounded by our troops." A convulsive swallow. "Alexius has withdrawn. We are alone."

Chapter XXXIX.

"I'm sorry," Galdemar said breathlessly, rushing after Saint-Gilles as he stalked out of the council hall.

"For what?" Saint-Gilles asked, his voice clipped and harsh, not slowing. "If the emperor has abandoned us, it's hardly *your* fault."

"For blurting it out," Galdemar said, not sounding reassured. "I don't know, Saint-Gilles! If I'd had my wits about me… Saints!" He shivered, crossing himself. "You know I'm not the flighty, visionary sort. I never want to go through something like that again."

Saint-Gilles turned to look at Galdemar. Curiosity got the better of him. "What was it like?"

"Something like a very bad sick-headache. Something like dreaming with your eyes open." A shiver. "Let's not talk about it."

"If you say so." Saint-Gilles gnawed a knuckle. *Galdemar,* having visions? *Galdemar,* prophesying? The thing seemed impossible, yet he could not doubt his friend. Glancing up, he saw the rest of the counts following him from the audience hall. Peter Bartholomew, who had been waiting in the vestibule, had arisen and was standing by the door, waiting for them to approach; beyond, no doubt, the courtyard was packed with silent, fearful pilgrims waiting for an announcement.

He'd had a crowd on his doorstep every day for the past two weeks. With Bartholomew's help, Saint-Gilles had felt the real hope of attracting and keeping something like power for the first time since Constantinople. Now Adhemar, Bessarion, and even Galdemar seemed to have conspired to tear that power away from him.

His own closest friends and followers. But what did it mean, that Bessarion had returned, carrying visions and, worse still, sharing them with Galdemar? Devil take it, he'd sent Bessarion to *kill* le Puiset, not to form an alliance with him. Was Bohemond involved? The prophecy surely benefited him: in one fell stroke, Alexius had been removed from the picture.

Alexius had deserted them.

Saint-Gilles felt his dread like a cold hand squeezing his throat.

Never mind Bohemond's schemes; never mind Bessarion's treacherous visions. Alexius had deserted them. No help was coming. No help would ever come again, even if by some miracle they survived Kerbogha, because, after this, the Greek alliance was over.

Numb, Saint-Gilles led the way through the vestibule. Bartholomew fell into step beside him; Bohemond pushed forward to flank him on the left. The sergeants on duty pulled open the great double doors at his signal and the six great princes, together with their vassals, stepped out into the portico to confront the great crowd.

Saint-Gilles lifted a hand for silence. "A decision has been reached," he announced. "We will not ask you to starve in inactivity much longer. Bishop Adhemar will explain."

"Thank you," Adhemar said without looking him in the eye. The detachment in the bishop's manner was one more cut to Saint-Gilles' heart.

"Beginning today and lasting until Vespers on Sunday, I proclaim three days of fasting and repentance," Adhemar announced. "Give alms to the poor. Confess your sins. Let every man, woman, and child cry out to God. Turn from your evil ways, and from the violence that is in your hands. Make amends to those you have wronged. Forgive those who have committed sins against you. Who can tell? Perhaps God will relent from his fierce anger against us, and will save us from Kerbogha."

Saint-Gilles hoped that, to the people gathered below, he looked grimly determined rather than grimly mutinous. In the council, Adhemar had stressed forgiveness and reconciliation: with each other, with the native

Christians, even, devil take it, with such Turks as lived within the city and were willing to accept a Frankish peace. Saint-Gilles knew he had a long list of affairs to set in order—it was like leaving Provence all over again—but he knew Adhemar had been looking at *him* when he mentioned making up quarrels with enemies.

With Bohemond.

Saint-Gilles felt like shouting. How could you forgive someone who wasn't *sorry* for what he'd done? Neither of them were sorry for anything, in fact. Saint-Gilles had done so many terrible things to keep the pilgrimage safe and together. He'd gambled away so many lives, from the indigents who had starved over the winter when his was the loudest voice insisting on a field siege, to his own son.

William.

He knew he ought to feel grief for his son's death, but the truth was, he had ceased feeling anything at all. Even Galdemar had noticed it. *I'm not grieving,* he'd told his friend irritably. *What are any of us, but the stewards of a great legacy? The child served his purpose. I will beget others.*

True enough, Galdemar had replied, *but it's a damned heartless way to think of your own child, Saint-Gilles.*

It was, and he knew it, but he could not allow grief to break him; he had tens of thousands of others to keep safe. His Provençals were his children, even if not born of his body. Divinely appointed to lead them, Saint-Gilles would not shrink from whatever ruthlessness it took to keep them safe.

Adhemar having finished his address, Bohemond raised a hand for the muttering crowd's attention. "Don't worry," he said cheerfully. "We aren't asking you to fast for nothing. Save up your food. If there's any grain in the city, deliver it to the stables for the horses, but everything else is fair game once Vespers rings on Sunday. Slaughter the livestock that can't be ridden and eat everything you can. By Monday night we shall all be feasting like kings, whether here on earth or up in Heaven." As Bohemond paused, Saint-Gilles saw hope dawning in the people's starved eyes.

"We are going out to battle!" Bohemond announced. "And, God willing, I will lead you to victory."

There was a long silence: for a moment. Saint-Gilles wondered whether Bohemond's spell had failed. No one wanted to fight, sick and despairing as they were. But then someone broke the silence with "God's will!" and then the whole courtyard, and the street beyond it, filled with cheers.

In the commotion, Saint-Gilles turned to Bartholomew.

"It seems a new prophet has arisen," he muttered to the visionary. The words left a sour taste in his mouth. Bessarion had been a valuable, if sometimes unreliable, servant. Now, in response to the Syrian's message, the other princes had now voted unanimously to give Bohemond supreme command of the pilgrimage during the battle and for fifteen days after.

Saint-Gilles had been in too much shock to argue, but even he had to admit it was time to throw the dice on one last desperate gamble, before they were all too hungry and weak to lift their weapons. If they were to have any chance at victory at all, Bohemond must lead them.

But he still had to plan as though they were going to win, because that was the only way to keep from going quite mad with despair. So he tightened his grasp on his prophet and said, "You need to step in, Bartholomew. Don't let them forget that it's God who will save them and not Count Bohemond."

Insolently, the boy did not turn to look at him. "Nor Count Raymond."

"I never claimed that," Saint-Gilles said, but he couldn't quite keep the defensive tone out of his voice.

The people were cheering again—Bohemond had been weaving his glamour, telling them all how strong and brave they were. Bartholomew now shoved forward to face the crowd, lifting a hand for silence. Instantly he had it.

"Let everyone, from the great to the small, turn from your sins to God," he proclaimed. "You shall each offer five alms because of the five wounds of the Lord. Or, if these are beyond your means, you shall repeat the Paternoster five times, so that no one may call your devotion into question, despite your poverty. Then you shall open the battle in the name of the Lord according to the princes' commands, and the Lord's hand will be with you! This land does not belong to the pagans, but is the patrimony of

Saint Peter. Your battle cry shall be *God aid us,* and truly God shall aid you. Your fallen comrades shall fight beside you. And you shall hurl down the kingdom of these pagans and grind it underfoot, even as you yourselves are lifted up!"

Bohemond had elicited a trickle, but Bartholomew wrung a torrent of eager acclaim from the crowd. As the people chanted their new battle cry, Adhemar turned to face Saint-Gilles, as though he meant to say something. His face was haggard: he'd been struggling lately with a fever. For a moment his lips worked; but then he changed his mind and turned back to the crowd, putting up a hand for silence. At length he received it.

"Remember the things you are asked to repent of," he told the people. "Remember that you are not come to take vengeance on the Turks, but to liberate your fellow Christians within the city. Be temperate in victory. I charge you, as you fear God and hope to see long life, do not indulge your evil lusts."

"Bring your alms here, to the palace," Saint-Gilles added as the bishop paused. "I will take charge of them and create a common fund for the poor. Anyone who needs assistance should come to me for support. You are dismissed."

As the crowd dispersed, eager to spread the word and bring their alms for collection, Adhemar followed Saint-Gilles into the palace. "I had more to say, Saint-Gilles."

"Did you? I beg your pardon." His mind was only half on Adhemar's words. "I'm going to send criers around the city to make sure everyone knows what they need to. You can add your directions to theirs."

"Saint-Gilles…"

"Can it wait?" He'd caught sight of Lukas Bessarion slinking through the vestibule towards freedom, and now reached out and grabbed the young Greek by his ear. "I have alms to collect and a city to prepare for battle, Adhemar. For heaven's sake, go and eat something and rest; you look like death warmed up. You, Bessarion. I want to see you. Now."

Chapter XL.

First the council meeting; then the announcements in the palace courtyard. Lukas hadn't found a good way to sneak out of either of them. As the council meeting finally broke up, Evrard of le Puiset had caught him. "I have something to say to you."

"You know where to find me," he'd muttered in reply. "Come alone." No doubt le Puiset wanted his sister back. Why had he promised to release the girl? He must have been too focused upon the immediate task. Now it was done and his head was clear again. Emelota was his hostage, probably the only reason le Puiset hadn't betrayed him in the council just now. Now that Lukas had delivered his Message, he needed to see to his own survival. Since Bartholomew knew he had attempted to steal the lance, no doubt Count Raymond knew it too. Lukas shivered. He must get out of this palace, find himself somewhere to hide until he could retrieve the Bessarion Lance and see what happened to the Franks.

He'd known it. All along he'd known *exactly* what would happen if he delivered his Message: there'd be grandiose displays of penitence. Convincing these people that they had sinned was never a problem. The problem was getting it through their thick heads exactly what they ought to be feeling sorry for, and Lukas didn't want to explain to them any more than he had wanted to tell them that they might be spared if they repented. It was Bishop Adhemar who had heard the part of the message he'd repressed: that there was hope for them.

That God was merciful.

Now, just when he thought he had the chance to slip out of the vestibule with the outflow of counts and squires and pages, an arm shot through the crowd and fastened on his ear. "You, Bessarion," Count Raymond barked. "I want to see you."

Terror washed through him, robbing him of speech. He'd been caught. He knew exactly what happened to relic thieves.

The count beckoned to a pair of sergeants who fell in behind him, sealing off any escape that might have been possible. Desperate, Lukas scanned the courtyard for le Puiset, but even his best enemy had vanished into the crowd. He had no choice but to choke down his panic, falling into step with the sergeants as they ushered him towards the stables. How many times had he cheated death already? Count Raymond might never have truly respected him, but he had valued him as a tool. What service could he promise now, to save himself?

"First thing first," Count Raymond led the way, the butt of his own spear pounding the stones with a stiff, angry rhythm. "The night before last, there was a theft."

God help him, there it was.

"The Holy Lance, praise God, was retrieved last night. But there is still the matter of the thief. Shortly before the outrage, you were seen in the vicinity of the chapel." Count Raymond led the way from the forecourt into a smaller courtyard wedged between the stables and a line of secure storerooms. Lukas' mouth went dry. *Breathe. Le Puiset will come looking for you, wanting his sister. So long as it isn't a summary execution—*

Then he saw the beam protruding from the stables. Ordinarily it must be a crane used to raise heavy items from the courtyard through the great doors in the upper level. Today a man leaned out of the doors, fixing a piece of rope to the pulley at the end of the beam. When he was done, a sinister shape hung stark against the grey sky.

A noose.

Lukas pictured himself being shoved from those high open doors. The jerk. The snap. So clear and vivid was the picture that he wondered if he was having a vision of his death.

Count Raymond said something to a sergeant who stood before one of the storerooms. Lukas turned. "Please," he began, but his voice had dried up and his lips moved without sound.

The sergeant fitted his wooden key into the door, reached inside, and pulled out a young man. Lukas' throat dried as he saw a thin young Provençal about his own age and height, nursing a useless right arm. It was the stable-hand he had tripped over on his way out of the chapel with the lance. A witness.

His own fearful gaze was mirrored in the other boy's eyes.

"Bartholomew is the only one who actually saw the thief's face," Count Raymond announced, "but it was dark, and his eyes are weak. We rounded up everyone in the palace who matched the description, and Bartholomew accused this one. Can you corroborate his word?"

Lukas' throat was as dry as a desert and his heartbeat thundered in his ears. Was this a trap? A test? Lilith, evidently, had been at work on her prophet: but what of the count? How was it possible that Count Raymond did not suspect him *at all,* given how often Lukas had laid claim to the supposed Holy Lance?

The count watched him now with narrowed eyes and an unpleasantly shrewd look. God help him, he *did* suspect. Why this play-acting, then? If he wanted Lukas dead for theft, surely he would simply arrest him and hang him, as he proposed to do to this man. Count Raymond was capable of many things, but it was not in his nature to take a crooked path to a straight goal. Which meant that this was a real decision, not a cat-and-mouse game. A warning, certainly; a display of power, meant to intimidate him; but a real way out.

Lukas could escape any blame for the theft of the lance, simply by condemning this man.

A moment ago, staring that noose in the eye, his future had been shattered underfoot. No way to get his father's lance. No way to avenge Ayla. No way to help his people. Now, suddenly, it was all back within his grasp. But at what price?

If he refused to take this way out, he would die. Once again, he felt the drop. The snap.

He didn't look into the eyes of the weeping boy. "Yes," he said. "He brushed past me in the passage just as I was leaving the palace to visit my Watchers in the city. Come to think of it, he might have come from the chapel."

It was the strict truth. As though that made any difference.

"No!" the boy screamed. "It wasn't me! Please!" He threw himself towards Lukas, falling on his knees. "Please! Don't condemn me! Are you not also a villein?"

The sergeants picked him up and carried him towards the stables, leaving Lukas staring at the flagstones where the boy had knelt, not seeing anything.

Are you not also a villein?

No, he was a lord, sacrificing the lives of lesser men for his own ends. Lukas felt a sick sense of self-loathing. Certainly, he did not deserve mercy now.

I take it back, he thought. *I want justice; justice on the Franks, justice for Ayla... Justice on me, if that's what it means.*

A pair of shadowy, sandal-clad feet appeared upon the flagstones and Lukas looked up feeling as though his stomach had turned inside-out. Lilith—Lilith, at midday, wispy and insubstantial but still *there,* visible to his waking eyes.

She smirked at him—she had adopted an almost-human form today. "You didn't seriously think I'd let them execute you, did you? Not before you'd carried out my will to the last *drop.*"

Behind Lukas, the boy's muffled screams cut off. A dead silence followed.

"I'll never do your will," he whispered.

She only smiled and shrugged. "You will, if you want your lance."

"Bessarion," said the one-eyed count behind him. Lukas jumped, his mouth dry in fear as Count Raymond gripped his shoulder, his scarred face set in hard, ugly lines. "Now. You had a mission to carry out, did you not?"

The death of le Puiset. Lukas touched his lips with his tongue. "I was prevented. Should I see to it now?"

"What are you, an imbecile? *Should I see to it now?* Of course you should not. We cannot fight a battle without men. Let the Turks deal with le Puiset! Look, Bessarion, I can overlook delay, or even failure, or whatever cockeyed ambitions you may be harbouring. What I cannot overlook is that you should appear at council with the vassal of *my enemy*, and that you should enlist his aid in destroying this pilgrimage's best hope for aid. You're Greek, for God's sake. Shouldn't you be trying to *preserve* this alliance with Alexius? Or are you utterly without honour?"

It was perhaps the longest speech Count Raymond had ever made to him. Lukas gulped. "No, my lord."

"Answer me this, then: do you think to set yourself up as a prophet?"

It was hard to focus on the count, when behind his shoulder swayed the lifeless body of the man they'd killed between them. Lukas swallowed hard.

"No, my lord. I've never wanted these visions."

Count Raymond's eyes narrowed. "You're lucky Galdemar corroborated you. But I wish to make one thing perfectly clear. If you ever have another vision, you will bring it to *me* first, in private. Do you understand?"

"Yes, sir. Perfectly."

Still Count Raymond did not relax his painful grasp on Lukas' shoulder, nor his hostile glare. "I don't know whether you're a knave or a fool, Bessarion. Perhaps a little of both. Either way, know this." A jerk of the count's head towards the swaying, twitching corpse. "This is what happens to those of my servants who betray me."

Releasing him, the count turned on his heel and stalked away.

Almost weak with dizziness and nausea, Lukas turned, only to find Lilith still watching him with a thin smile.

"I shouldn't worry if I were you. I don't suppose you'll be having more of *those* visions. Not after that." She nodded towards the swaying body.

"You aren't supposed to be here," Lukas muttered, and walked directly through her. Immediately he wished he hadn't, for as he passed through her insubstantial form he felt chill dread creep through his bones.

"My dear little Watcher," Lilith said mockingly, "didn't you know? Once a soul puts itself in my power I will be with it always, wherever it is."

With no way to banish her, Lukas turned towards the palace, afraid to glance behind him for fear that he would see the Poison Mother following at his heels with her blood-red smile. He did not doubt the truth of Lilith's words. A scant year ago he'd been able to send her packing with a few words. And then he'd broken an oath on Oliveta. He'd lied, stolen, murdered, run away from his calling. And with every step he'd handed over another part of himself to Lilith, until now she dogged his steps, night and day.

It didn't matter. He could endure this. He'd brazen her out. She could torment him however she liked, especially now that his Message was delivered and the seraph was done with him—but she would never make him free Khalil. Never, never, never.

Meanwhile, he ought to retrieve his bedroll and other belongings from his old quarters. Within the palace, the peristyle of the garden courtyard was shadowy but full of murmuring voices and echoing feet as the count's servants busied themselves to receive and record the expected influx of alms. Lukas kept his head down, wishing to pass unnoticed. Nevertheless, as he crossed the garden towards the door of his cell a familiar voice, breathless with haste, called his name. He turned to face the newcomer with a sinking heart.

"Lukas Bessarion," said Count Evrard of le Puiset in an unexpectedly humble voice. "Will you give me a moment?"

Chapter XLI.

None of it quite added up, Saint-Gilles thought uncomfortably as he returned to the palace, leaving the relic thief's body swinging in the courtyard and Bessarion looking sick with terror in its shadow. Peter Bartholomew had been very certain in identifying the stable-hand as the thief, but his eyes had skittered around like a liar's under questioning. Nor was Saint-Gilles satisfied with Bessarion's corroboration. Nevertheless, what else could he do? The Holy Lance was all that gave him any influence, any power, and he had very nearly lost it. His vengeance must be swift and harsh, to dissuade any further attempt.

Adhemar was always counselling him to show moderation and temperance in his judgements, but Saint-Gilles had always been of the opinion that a harsh show of force now prevented any amount of rebellion later. With the stable-hand to act as a caution, Bessarion would think long and hard before he repeated this morning's mistake.

Some might call him ruthless. Saint-Gilles simply wished others to share his very high esteem for the rare quality of mercy.

In the vestibule he found the people already queuing to donate their alms for the poor. Many of them, terrified of the Turks and anxious to survive the coming battle, had chosen to be generous. Saint-Gilles heard coins ringing by the score into coffers that had been getting dangerously empty since Tatikius left five months before. After this they'd be overflowing, and not just with coin—with spices, bolts of cloth, vessels of gold and silver. He would no longer need to stint in his charity. His people—if they survived the coming battle—would be safe and well provided-for, for a few months at least. And they'd all know it was him they had to thank for it.

For a while he only watched from the shadows, feeling renewed hope. He had only ever wanted to keep his people alive, and now—even without Alexius—he might actually be able to do it.

"Saint-Gilles?" Adhemar approached, leaning on a crozier. His face sagged in leaden, anxious lines as though he expected to pick another fight, and Saint-Gilles sighed.

When had their friendship become so much work?

"Adhemar," he greeted the bishop briskly. "Didn't I send you home, to get over the last of that fever?"

"Yes, but I wanted to ask you something first." He glanced across the hall, where Count Bohemond lingered with Evrard of le Puiset, gesticulating energetically. "Will you speak to him?"

"To Bohemond? About what?" Saint-Gilles demanded. "Do you want me to tell him I've wronged him? Because I haven't. I think I've treated him very justly."

"The two of you have been at odds since Marash. Isn't it time you made peace?"

Saint-Gilles gritted his teeth. "Make peace? We haven't been at war."

Adhemar looked distressed. "Perhaps not openly, but…"

"This city belongs to Alexius," Saint-Gilles lowered his voice. "Bohemond has even less right to it than the rest of us. Don't you remember him playing the henchman to Alexius all last year? He was the one who strong-armed all of us into making those oaths! He and Alexius had to have had a special relationship. And now he'll start saying the emperor forfeited any right to the city once he turned his back on us in our hour of need. He'll seize it for himself. He'll—"

"My friend, my friend, listen a moment to me."

Saint-Gilles folded his arms, tight-lipped as the bishop searched for words. At last Adhemar sighed.

"I do not think it is about the oath to Alexius, any more."

"Of course it's about the oath to Alexius! What was he supposed to do, run his neck into a trap to save us? It will take more than that to make *me* abandon my sworn word."

"I mean that this is not zeal for honour or piety. This is personal animosity. You might not be openly feuding, my friend, but I've seen how you watch him, how you set your spies on him and rifle his storehouses." Adhemar gulped. "Our Lord said that there is a kind of hatred which, if a man feels it in his heart, is the same as committing murder."

The words fled from Saint-Gilles' lips.

"We have resolved upon one last desperate leap, have we not? There's more at stake than your eternal soul, my friend. The lives of all these many thousands of people and the fate of the eastern church may hinge upon God giving his blessing in the battlefield three days from now."

Saint-Gilles swallowed, hard. "You condemn *me* for wrath and hatred, but you do not confront *him* for his deceit, his lust for power?"

"If I had, would you expect me to gossip about it?"

The bishop had a point there. Saint-Gilles glanced across the room, narrowing his eyes at the sight of his rival. Hadn't he just been telling himself that he must submit to Bohemond, just for a few days, just for the sake of pulling the pilgrimage out of this trap?

All right. But he'd get what he could out of Adhemar, too.

"I'll make my peace with Bohemond, on one condition."

The bishop's relief faded into something akin to despair. "My friend, this isn't—"

"I'll do as you ask for the sake of the people," he interrupted, "if you'll do as I ask for the sake of the people. I want you to recognise Bartholomew and make a donation to the Holy Lance. And it must be carried with the other relics into the battle."

"Raymond!" Adhemar's distress mounted. "I can't do that! I don't believe it's genuine!"

"Maybe not, but the people do." Saint-Gilles let that sink in before adding: "Look at them, my friend. I'm not convinced they'll even consent to go into battle without it."

That was a hit: he watched as the bishop threw an anxious glance at the people flocking obediently to give alms. Bartholomew had stationed himself with the Holy Lance beside the collection-boxes, and with every donation they bowed to kiss the relic.

Adhemar dragged a hand down his face. "All right. The lance can be carried into battle. But I will not offer any donation, and I cannot countenance Bartholomew."

"The bishops of Narbonne and Orange are happy enough to accept the boy. Why can't you?"

A dark look came into Adhemar's eyes. "He's dangerous, Saint-Gilles, and he preaches vengeance. You may think you can control him, but he will burn you in the end."

"Is that a prophecy?" Saint-Gilles could not resist the jibe.

"Call it foresight."

"Well, I don't care what your foresight tells you," he said grimly, "or how you warn me, so long as you don't stand in my way. Understood?"

It wasn't until the words had crossed his lips, and the hurt flooded Adhemar's face, that Saint-Gilles realised he'd spoken as he would to a rebellious vassal.

Not to an ally.

Not to a friend.

"Devil take it," he muttered, but what could he say to undo the sting? What were words, beside actions? "Go and get some rest, Adhemar."

Swivelling on one heel, he marched across the hall towards Bohemond, whose argument with le Puiset had become heated. "If you refuse to give me a straight answer—" Bohemond growled, before straightening as he became aware of Saint-Gilles' approach.

"A word," Saint-Gilles said tersely.

Le Puiset took advantage of the interruption to beat a hurried retreat, and Bohemond gave him a tight, angry smile. "This ought to be interesting."

"In private," Saint-Gilles added.

It *was* interesting: had le Puiset something to hide from his own lord? Saint-Gilles hesitated a moment as the possibility occurred to him that perhaps Bessarion and le Puiset had chosen to form an alliance in order to make fools of both Saint-Gilles and Bohemond. Well, he certainly didn't mean to bring *that* up with his rival. They had more important things to discuss today.

Ushering Bohemond into the council-hall—now empty but for a ring of silent chairs—Saint-Gilles shut the doors behind them and turned on the other man with a savage grin. "I know your secret, Bohemond."

"You don't say!" The other count smiled with offensive cheer. "And which secret would this be, my friend?"

"Your true relationship to the emperor." Saint-Gilles noticed a tell-tale stiffness around Bohemond's lips and felt a moment's triumph. "It's obvious. I should have figured it out months ago. You swore *liege-homage* to Alexius. Your loyalty to him now outweighs any other oath you may have taken to any other lord in the world. *Holy Virgin.*"

"Do you speak to the bishop with that mouth?" Bohemond was still smiling, but only with his teeth, not his eyes. After a moment he added, "It's an interesting story. What gave you that idea?"

"It was something Tatikius said once. He referred to Alexius as your liege, then excused himself for a slip of the tongue." Saint-Gilles permitted himself a grim smile of his own. "It was a slip, but not for the reason I thought at the time. It was supposed to be a secret from the rest of us, wasn't it? You bullied all of us into swearing oaths to the emperor. You arranged in secret to be made the Grand Domestic of the East. You frightened Tatikius into leaving Antioch before the Lake Battle, pretending I meant to have him killed. Why should he have believed you rather than me, unless he had imperial orders to trust you above anyone else? Then, you burned the chrysobull you received from Alexius. To stop me seeing it, to pave the way to your claiming this city in your own name."

Bohemond still wore that faint smile pasted beneath cool, thoughtful eyes. "Did you work all this out for yourself?"

"Did you think I was a fool? You as good as told me, the night of the fire." Saint-Gilles shook his head, incredulous. "You slipped, so take warning. I don't know what you've said to the other princes—how you have cajoled or coerced them into putting you in command of the battle—but know this: when the battle is over, I *will* be insisting that we hand over the city to Alexius, and if you stand in my way, I will make sure everyone on this pilgrimage understands exactly what you owe the emperor in terms of fealty and service."

Bohemond's stiff face cracked—into laughter. "What, do you truly expect me to quake in fear at this—this fairy-tale you've spun yourself out of a few passing remarks? Please. Go ahead. Tell the other princes, and see if they believe you."

"I'll do better than that," Saint-Gilles said evenly. "I'll send to Alexius and ask him myself."

Bohemond shook his head. "And exactly what do you think that will prove?"

"That you're deceitful, unfaithful, unscrupulous, and are constantly scheming for your own advantage?" Saint-Gilles matched Bohemond's urbane expression.

"Is that what you think is happening here?" A grin, somewhere between a girl who has just been complimented and a wolf scenting its next meal. "Saint-Gilles. You flatter me!"

"Go ahead, then. Tell me I'm wrong."

"Hm." Bohemond still looked much too pleased. "Before I do, a question. Even if what you say were true, even if had you been able to find proof, do you seriously think it would have blocked my appointment as battle leader today?"

Saint-Gilles opened his mouth—then closed it again. "I'm not talking about today," he said stiffly. "I'm talking about after."

"If there is an after," Bohemond said with a moment's gravity. There was a cold, weighty moment as they considered the desperate odds that faced them. Then Bohemond stopped in his pacing around the ring of vacant chairs, and leaned on the back of one of them. "You see," he added softly, "I was not obliged to cajole or coerce anyone, Saint-Gilles. For the past four weeks I've had time for one kind of scheming only: finding a way to save all these people from the trap we have blundered into. This is the full extent of my cajolery: that I have saved this pilgrimage on battlefield after battlefield, and therefore they have made me their commander. Where is the trickery in that?"

Saint-Gilles didn't speak—couldn't speak. Had he deceived himself so entirely? There was truth in what Adhemar had said: that he'd become consumed with watching Bohemond, tormenting himself by trying to imagine what the other count could be plotting next. Suspicion had eaten him up even as Bohemond led the fighting atop Silpius, during the four-day battle that had raged from sunrise to sunset each day leaving the men so exhausted they had fallen asleep where they fell. As their commander, Bohemond must have been bone-weary, consumed by worry, bowed by responsibility, and honour-bound not to show it. For more than a week after the capture of Antioch, Bohemond had scarcely had the opportunity to descend Silpius, to set foot in the streets of the city he claimed—let alone to intrigue himself into a position of greater power.

"You see, here's the thing about deceit," Bohemond said slowly. "It will do *something* for you, certainly. It can make you look a little better than you are, or give you a little advantage over your rivals. But there's one thing it can't do."

"Oh?"

"It's no substitute for actually being able to help people." Bohemond straightened, offering a hand. "So what about it, Saint-Gilles? Will you fight with me in Monday's battle? Will you follow where I lead?"

Saint-Gilles felt aware that his rage must be written plainly in his face, but he could do nothing to hide it. Humiliating. Nearly as bad as being read a lesson by Bohemond, of all people.

A true lesson nevertheless. He would never trust Bohemond as far as he could spit, but the South Norman count had a point. Deceit hadn't put him at the head of the pilgrimage at this moment of crisis, and Saint-Gilles' needless suspicion was only going to hurt their chances.

That didn't mean he meant to yield without exacting a price.

"I need a guarantee of good faith," he said, not taking the hand. "We made oaths to Alexius. Before I agree to follow you in battle, I want to know those oaths will be kept. If the citadel surrenders, it should be garrisoned by as many Provençals, North French, and Lorrainers as by South Normans, and you will swear to this in council."

Bohemond considered this for a moment in silence before speaking slowly: "And if I refuse, then what? You'll obstruct my appointment as battle leader? You'll put the whole pilgrimage at risk for the sake of a defunct alliance?"

Saint-Gilles felt the blood rising in his face. "Say, rather, that I fear to go into battle with an oath-breaker."

"A sentiment that does you great credit," Bohemond said dryly. "Very well then. I accept, since the lives of all these people are at stake."

"Then I'll obey your commands, this once." It was Saint-Gilles' turn to offer his hand. Bohemond grasped it, but released it quickly, like a venomous snake that might bite him. After that, Bohemond departed, and Saint-Gilles went back into the vestibule to listen to the coins ringing into the coffers.

The sound did not comfort him as it had before. When did he become so obsessed with power? When did *Bohemond* become the one willing to compromise his own interests to save lives?

Remember what Bartholomew said, he told himself with a deep breath. *God himself chose you to lead this pilgrimage. You have every right to make these demands.*

Chapter XLII.

Will you give me a moment? Once, le Puiset's arrogance would have filled Lukas with anger. Now it was the count's humility that galled him.

"The count is a count," he said stiffly, tightening his grip on his staff. "Surely he will go where he pleases and speak to whom he likes, and we poor beggarly peasants will put up with it as we must."

"I don't wish to impose, but…"

Lukas looked about them. The courtyard garden itself was empty, for it was a place for leisure and no one in the palace had any of that. He lowered his voice. "If it's about your sister—"

"No, it's…it's something else. I must lead a company into the battle on Monday, and there is something I must say to you first."

A premonition struck Lukas with a feeling akin to panic. Perhaps it was dangerous to antagonise Count Evrard now that the escape from Antioch had failed, and le Puiset was free again, restored to his privileges, with only a slight limp to show for his injury. All the same, it would be better to antagonise le Puiset than to let him say the words Lukas feared to hear.

"Still, we will speak of your sister, count. You offered to return as my hostage, but you can hardly lead a battle from the cellar of my house. You are free again, protected by your rank and power. I need a guarantee you will not use it against me."

Le Puiset blinked at him. "My word of honour," he began.

"What honour? You have said it yourself: you think me a villein, and unworthy of honourable treatment. Since I cannot trust you, I must hold your sister hostage for your good behaviour."

"Mother of God," le Puiset began thickly, but then reined himself in, turning his head away. Lukas smiled thinly. After a moment le Puiset turned back to him. "It's true my rank and power protect me, but they also impose burdens too heavy for any man to bear. I cannot show weakness. I must ride into battle whether or not I am willing or able. It doesn't matter," he added, before Lukas could retort. "I did not come to bewail my fate, but to confess my sins."

All words left him.

He knew—he *knew*—this would happen. Lukas's fists tightened on his staff as though it was le Puiset's throat, and he was choking the life out of it. Ever since Barisan, on Silpius, he had known exactly what the seraph intended for the Franks. *Oh, I am God's own fool. Did I not see him being driven slowly to repent?*

I ought to have killed him when I had the chance.

"I was wrong about you," le Puiset went on, his gaze sinking to the flagstones. "I despised you as a coward, but when I could no longer face battle, you kept fighting. I abhorred you as a villein, but while I did you evil, you returned good to me and my sister." A deep breath. "I killed your wife."

"Ayla." Lukas heard himself growl the word from a long way away. He could not move, his feet rooted to the ground. Otherwise he might have turned, stormed away. "Her name was Ayla. *Say it.*"

"I killed Ayla," he said humbly. "I let my pride make me a murderer. But it's worse than you think: I know something of what you have suffered. I know what it means to lose the one you love. The truth is, I persecuted you because I had no other way to blunt my own conscience, except to prove you a villein. Instead, you proved yourself noble in heart, and I proved myself...I don't know. A coward, lacking in honour. Or perhaps true honour lies in the repentance I now offer."

Le Puiset stopped speaking. A sparrow hopped in the peristyle to his left, seeking crumbs beneath the abandoned breakfast-table. Lukas thought, tiredly, that the birds had no right to go about their business on a day like this.

His voice still sounded distant, thick with tears. "Why are you telling me this? Will any amount of repentance bring the dead back to life?"

"No." Count Evrard's lips pressed together; he swallowed. Then he drew his sword.

A moment's wild hope swept through Lukas. He stepped back, raising his staff to guard, before le Puiset dropped to one knee and offered his sword, hilt-first.

"I deserve to die for what I've done, but because I am a count there is no one to pass sentence, no one to swing the sword. Except you."

Lukas stared. The sparrow picked up a tiny morsel the dogs had missed and flew away. The count's sword hilts glistened in the clear, merciless sunlight. Lukas cleared a throat that had gone suddenly dry.

"Did you forget, in your illness, why I risked my own life in saving yours?"

Le Puiset shook his head.

"Then why this?" He gestured at the proffered weapon. "Do you imagine for a moment that I have changed my mind? When I kill you, it will be done properly, on a horse with a lance, like the knight I am."

"No," le Puiset breathed. "Please. I beg of you, kill me now or grant your forgiveness."

"Kill you now? Do you think it will be an easy thing, like drowning a kitten?" Even Count Raymond had withdrawn his permission for le Puiset's death. "I am no one. You are a count. If I kill you in this garden, I'll be dangling from a gallows by evening."

Le Puiset lowered his sword, eyes still shadowed with despair. "Then forgive me."

"Forgive you? Those are my only two choices, to forgive you or die? What kind of penitent asks forgiveness on pain of death?"

"That isn't what..."

Lukas' anger was like the wave after an earthquake, seething and relentless. "Why are you here, anyway? Last time you sent your bastard sister. Did you have no servants to send this time?"

"I can't..."

"If you really want to do justice, do it yourself. Go home and fall on your sword and leave me out of it. But you won't do that, will you?"

Le Puiset's gaunt face was tight, his eyes like the sockets of a skull. "They've put me in command for the battle."

"You say that as though it's an answer."

The count gulped. "I'm supposed to go to battle, and I'm…I'm afraid. I don't want to die with this on my conscience."

Perhaps the count was right to fear death without having performed the works that showed true penitence, but Lukas knew better than anyone the shape of the divine mercy. He trembled at a memory of fire. The problem was that Heaven was both more just and more merciful than himself. Lukas himself was a knot of rage and ambition and selfish bias.

Perhaps this was his way out, then: let God forgive the count, since he could not.

In any case, le Puiset's repentance was hollow. "So this is why you have come," Lukas said. "Only because you are afraid to die, and for this you expect my gratitude? What happens when the threat to your life passes? Will your repentance dissolve like the morning dew?"

"Please," le Puiset begged. "I know my life is forfeit, but do you wish me in Hell?"

"Yes." Lukas bit the word off with his teeth. He knew, as he said it, that he meant it with all his heart. He could not forgive—even though he knew he should, even though he feared not to.

He watched the count's face, the slight recoil, the way his words struck home like a crossbow bolt. *Good.* Turning on his heel, Lukas stalked away.

He went back to his room and bundled up his bedroll. A sort of numb quiet settled on him. He remembered Ayla; how, in Marash, before the judgement seat of Thatoul, she had been given the same choice he did, between revenge and reconciliation. Only then, it had been he who had offended her, and she had chosen reconciliation. Now what? Ayla would not recognise the vengeful monster he had become. Neither, he realised with a bolt of clarity, would his father. He had failed both of them. But what else could he do? He felt nothing, no sorrow for his actions. He might as well be carved from stone.

Well, then: if he could not be a good man, he would simply do what he could. Lukas shouldered his belongings with decision. He'd killed an innocent man today. That had been a waste. The next man he killed would deserve it.

But to do what he had in mind, he must return to his Watchers and to the prisoner they held.

Chapter XLIII.

Lukas Bessarion returned to the house of Aemathe with hands dripping blood, and darkness surrounding him like a cloak. Emelota knew he had made his decision: she knew, too, where the threads of the tapestry led next.

She was not surprised when he summoned her into the front room, where he sat cross-legged with his staff lying across his knees.

"Emelota of le Puiset, shall we make a bargain?"

It was like sitting next to an eruption—all smoke and darkness and noxious fumes—but she made herself kneel before him and folded her hands demurely in her lap. "That depends upon the bargain."

"Your service," he told her, "for your brother's life."

She had foreseen the possibility: now it was true. "You wish to employ my gift."

"Yes, your gift." He leaned forward, putting out a hand that she did not take. "We are stronger together than we are alone, Emelota. You directed my vision, that night on the mountain, and I was able to share it with you. Surely we were *meant* to work together."

"What I saw was more than just a vision." Perhaps she would regret speaking so freely, but she had confided in no one else, and Lukas was the only one who might understand. And oh, how she longed to be understood. "I saw *everything:* not simply one future but infinite possibilities, all the threads of purpose and potential, twisting and dividing. It was..." She shook her head. "It was both our gifts in alliance, the future of all our intentions laid out like a tapestry. In that moment I could have done anything at all."

"Anything?" The darkness that surrounded him thickened. "You might have spared me from the fire, then—and you chose not to?"

"Chose?" Her heart sank. "No. I followed the thread I was *meant* to follow."

"You chose," he repeated. There was a silence, thick and brooding. Zarides' grey cat stepped daintily into the open doorway. When it saw Lukas, it changed its mind about entering: it gave him a wary look and scampered across the courtyard to some hiding-place of its own. Emelota could sympathise.

At last he added, "It isn't only your gift. In the mountains, you chased the Poison Mother away and kept the Watchers from scattering in terror. You…" He swallowed, suddenly looking very young and weary beneath all that seething menace. "You have a pure faith. The Poison Mother cannot withstand that. If you send her away, she must go."

"It isn't as simple as that." Emelota watched him warily. "You know the tale of the washed and cleansed house, how when its ruling demon was cast out, seven more made their homes there, worse than the first."

A muscle flexed at the corner of his jaw. "It was a man, not a house. A man who did not have Emelota of le Puiset by his side."

She almost wanted to laugh. "What do you think I am? I wouldn't know how to deal with a creature like Lilith; still less can I save you from yourself, Lukas Bessarion. The problem with walking down the road to Hell is that sooner or later, you will get where you are going."

He paled a little. "I know where I am going. I only wish to put off the evil day a little longer, until I am able to do at least a little good for my people."

"Such as?"

His eyes slipped away from her to the faded, flaking frescoes on the wall. "Peter Bartholomew must die," he said in a flat voice. "I must recover my father's lance. For either of those things to happen, Li—the Poison Mother must be sent away and warded off for as long as possible."

"I see," Emelota put in gravely. "I am to be your tool, a talisman against evil. Well, it is nothing new. All my life, people have told me I am only a thing to be used. Plaything or mistress or talisman, it is all the same."

Lukas considered that, without rancor. "Fair enough. What would it take to make you feel like a person in this arrangement, and not a thing? I am ready to offer you anything. Except," he added hastily, turning red, "marriage. I had a wife. I'm not interested in another."

"Nor," she said, repressing a laugh, "am I so desperate as you seem to imagine." She watched him for a moment, judging her next words. This day was a knot of divergences, threads radiating out in patterns of light and darkness, and she did not yet know which of them was to prove fated. She wished she was better at predicting how people would respond to the things she said. "Before I answer, there is a charitable deed I must undertake. If you will help me, it may prove beneficial to you."

Lukas raised an eyebrow. "Explain."

So she did.

By the time she finished, they were standing in the courtyard before the statue, Lukas staring up into the scarred bronze eyes. "Aemathe," he muttered. "I have met her once or twice."

"I do not know what will happen when we free her," Emelota added, "but she wants to help us; and I did think, that if the Fortuna of Antioch was liberated, there might be something she could do about the battle, and perhaps, even, about Lilith."

"Don't speak that name aloud," he cautioned her, with a nervous glance to the sky. There was nothing there, at least so far as Emelota could tell. After a moment, Lukas began to pace, staring at the bronze image. "The Fortuna of Antioch...What could I not do with such a creature on my side? I might become powerful. I might become immortal—like him..."

"Like whom?" she asked, unsettled. There was something approaching madness in his glittering eyes, and she thought uncomfortably that this was it, the response she had not foreseen. "Immortality? What do you mean? What are you dreaming of?"

He turned upon her, the darkness flaring about him like a cloak. He seized her hand and she flinched at the sticky, hot feeling of blood against her skin. "I will do as you ask. The statue will be melted down, but I wish to speak to the spirit when she is freed. Will you do this?"

Emelota swallowed, reminding herself not to be intimidated. Now Lukas had made his choice, her next steps had become clear. "As you like. But first I wish to see my brother. And if I am to remain here alone, I ought to have another woman with me. My attendant Lusine…"

"She and the count shall be sent for." Emelota tried to pull away, but his grip tightened. "You did not give me an answer, before. What shall I give you, to secure your help?"

What was the saying? *Wise as serpents, gentle as doves.* "You spoke the truth, before," she began, cautiously. "You and I are stronger together than we are alone. But if one of us is master, the other's gift must be disparaged." A dizzying number of relationships came to mind: lord and vassal, master and servant, man and wife, father and child, abbot and monk…none of them would suit her, for none of them would put her on an equal footing with Lukas. "Give me your friendship," she said at last, "and I will give you mine."

"Your friendship?" His face darkened. "That is not enough for me."

No, Emelota thought sadly. It would never be enough, so long as he wished to command her, for one friend could not rule another.

Lukas beckoned to one of his Watchers. "Take her back to the cellar," he ordered, and Emelota perceived that she was not yet to be trusted.

* * *

"You confessed to him?" Emelota had known there was something different about her brother, just as she had known there was something different about Lukas Bessarion. Now she let out a long sigh, relieved to find that some of the brighter threads in the tapestry were coming into play, as well as the dark. "Evrard, you don't know how that puts my heart at ease!"

He smiled tightly and glanced around—she had been let out of her cellar once again in order to see him in one of the upper rooms, and a Watcher was lounging at the door, armed to the teeth and scowling at Lusine.

"Little good it did me. He told me to go to Hell." Evrard pressed a clenched fist against his mouth. "Saints, Emelota, how can I go into battle like this, unforgiven?"

"You were willing to seek reconciliation. That's the main thing."

"Yes, but was it enough? It was not enough before, when I sent you."

"He isn't God, Evrard."

"I know. I know. But if it wasn't enough for him, how can I know if it was enough for God?" He looked at his hands. "Perhaps it is Heaven's will that Ayla's people execute justice upon me in battle, since Bessarion cannot."

Her heart twisted as she saw his cold purpose take hold, as she remembered the vision Lukas had seen, of Evrard dead in the sunset light, and soon. "Evrard, no. You must not think such things. You must not throw away your life—despair is a sin also." She seized his hands, calling the tapestry once again to mind, trying to see which of the possible threads were marked out by divine purpose. "Promise me you will do nothing rash. I…" *Need you?* "I don't want to lose you," she substituted in a whisper.

From the sorrow in his eyes, she knew he would not promise.

"Then at least promise to remember two things," she added in desperation. "First, that even heretics and infidels are made in God's likeness and are precious in his sight. And second…" *Think, Emelota. Remember the tapestry.* "And second, that the Turks love to outflank their enemies. Watch your back. Don't let them sneak up on you."

Hearing that, Evrard couldn't stifle a snort of laughter. "What, Emelota! Are you setting up as a commander, now?"

"No," she said, reddening. "As a seer."

He blinked at her. "In truth? Holy dame! You are serious." At her nod, he drew back with a sharp intake of breath. "Please don't tell me my fate. I—I will face it better if I am ignorant. I commend you to God, sister." Dropping a kiss on her forehead, he practically fled downstairs, leaving Emelota alone with Lusine and the guard.

She turned to Lusine, changing to Arabic. "I have told him something about what I can do. This time, I think he believed me."

"Then there is hope for him." Lusine smiled at the guard, who scowled more ferociously.

"I hope so," she said, thinking sadly of the grim purpose she had sensed in him. Well, he was out of her hands now, and in the meantime… She pulled Lusine over to the window, lowering her voice to a whisper so that the guard could not hear them. "These people seem to dislike you, Lusine."

"We are acquainted. They do not like my way of doing charity, to strangers as well as to blood kin."

She did not want to be responsible for Lusine's death or injury. "Will you be safe here? Should I send you home?"

The Armenian hesitated, evidently torn. "Not if it means leaving you alone in this house."

"I am willing to risk it." Emelota nodded decisively, her plans becoming clearer as her purpose hardened. "You and your family are the true Watchers in this city, Lusine, and I need true Watchers for what is coming. If I send you home, will you bring Arevik and Toros to me on the day I shall name?"

Chapter XLIV.

Antioch was singing, and it was as though the morning light itself had a voice.

The chanting had begun at dawn. Voices rose in measured cadences, lilting and winging from stone to stone. As the light grew, so did the number of voices as new bands of monks, priests, and even nuns filed onto the wall. Latin Franks, Melkite Greeks, Jacobite Syrians and Armenians: the whole city thrummed in harmony.

Saint-Gilles thought it the most beautiful thing he'd heard in his life. As the singing was taken up by some of the lay bystanders at the Bridge Gate, the words became clear:

"O God, the heathen are come into thine inheritance; thy holy temple have they defiled; they have laid Jerusalem on heaps. The dead bodies of thy servants have they given to be meat unto the fowls of the heaven, the flesh of thy saints unto the beasts of the earth. Their blood have they shed like water round about Jerusalem; and there was none to bury them."

Saint-Gilles tightened his grip on the reins of his horse—a miserable half-starved creature he would scarcely have deemed worth skinning back in Toulouse, but he was not riding out to battle today and all the horses in better condition were needed for the sally.

Rising a little in his stirrups, he scanned the broad road leading towards the palace from the Bridge Gate. Under the lift and fall of the wings of that music, the men of the pilgrimage waited in silent expectancy, their faces turned towards the gate like the congregation towards the altar in a church.

Apart from a modest force atop Silpius, guarding the citadel, the entire fighting-force of the pilgrimage was assembled here. There had been no lack of weaponry in the city after its fall, and every man who could be loosely described as able-bodied had been pressed into service—perhaps even some martially disguised women, God forbid. Still, Saint-Gilles' mouth went dry as he realised how small, how terribly small, their number had become. Perhaps a third of the men who'd fought at Nicaea remained to defend Antioch against the greatest army any of them had ever seen.

If today went badly…Saint-Gilles swallowed hard. From his station atop Silpius, it was possible he would be able to flee should the battle fail. But in that case he must abandon not only his vassals but also the people of his own household to be killed or enslaved in a second sack. He had sworn to die fighting in the East for the love of Christ, and today, if that was all the duty that was left to him, he would not try to escape it. If he was to blame in any way for how he had dealt with them, perhaps, by dying with his people, he might redeem himself.

Next to him under the brooding shadow of the Bridge Gate, Bohemond sat astride his own half-starved horse. Bending forward until his steel cap nearly clanked against that of Count Hugh of Vermandois, his hands made intricate shapes out of last-minute instructions. Saint-Gilles shook his head, thinking of the unnumbered host camped across the river.

Let them get alive to the end of this day, and he would find it in himself to be grateful even to Bohemond.

* * *

"Kerbogha has us outnumbered and surrounded. Therefore, the Bridge Gate is the obvious place for our attack," Bohemond had explained at the council three days ago, stabbing a hastily-sketched map with his dagger.

Another of the princes—Vermandois—frowned at the map. "But Kerbogha's main camp must be two miles north of the Bridge Gate." He tapped his finger on the confluence of the Orontes with another stream, north of the city. "If we wish to put the matter to a *decisive* battle, shouldn't we emerge from one of the northern gates?"

No doubt it was vigil and fasting that had sapped Vermandois' mind, the same as it sapped everyone else's. Saint-Gilles said, "That would be suicide. If we go out the north gates, east of the river where Kerbogha is strongest, we walk straight into his three strongest divisions. He has only one small division west of the river, watching the Bridge Gate. If we attack there, we attack him at his weakest."

Bohemond chimed in. "More to the point, it's at the Bridge Gate that we have what we most desperately need: the chance to deploy outside the city without being cut to pieces, since the river acts as a barrier. If we force our way out, we can come to grips with Kerbogha's dispersed forces before he can come down from his main camp." His teeth flashed, predatory, like a wolf's. "With luck, we can rout the men outside the Bridge gate and they'll rip up their own reinforcements as they flee. We won't even have to fight them."

* * *

"Explain again what you mean to do?" Lukas spoke to Emelota in an undertone.

Not everyone in the city waited to deploy out the Bridge Gate, or crowded on the walls and rooftops to watch. In a metal-worker's courtyard barely two streets away from the house of Ilkay, a large foundry was heating up and beginning to glow; under the artisan's directions, three of the Watchers operated the bellows to heat the furnace where the bronze Fortuna rested, packed with burning charcoal. They were consuming a great deal of precious fuel for the task; Lukas had commandeered the shop and the artisan's assistance without leaving him the choice, but the gift of the melted bronze itself should make a rich payment.

"I'm not entirely sure," Emelota answered him. "But I gather the idea is for Aemathe to make an alliance, of a sort, with Antioch's Watchers. Do you know anything about that?"

"A guardian." Lukas puckered his lips to whistle. It was not uncommon, of course, for cities or monasteries or other institutions to dedicate themselves to a particular patron saint or angel; such guardians, it was hoped, would interest themselves specifically in the welfare of the place, offering prayers and intercessions, or working miracles on their behalf. "I've never heard of the goddess of a city becoming its guardian."

"I've never heard of a goddess offering herself for baptism," Emelota admitted. "But then, I don't know much, I'm afraid."

The furnace glowed hotter, acrid with charcoal smoke and the clean, scouring scent of hot metal. For a long time, it seemed that nothing would happen. Then, just as Lukas was about to demand whether the thing was done, there came a soft, almost melodic sound like a harp-string breaking.

Beside him, Emelota stiffened; a look of joy crossed her face. Lukas blinked, gazing at the furnace: had something emerged from it, or were his eyes only deceived by shimmering heat?

Emelota stepped forward, putting out her hands in welcome. "Aemathe," she breathed. "Poor slave of the image, you are free now."

"I can't see her," Lukas said gruffly, unable to avoid the suspicion that if so, it must be his own fault. "Ask her if she will make a covenant with me and my Watchers, to serve and guard us."

"She can hear you." A pause: Emelota sent Lukas a nervous look. "Of course; but which of us will tell him?"

"Tell me what?" Lukas demanded: and then with a shimmer in the air, she came into view. Aemathe, the Fortuna of Antioch, the tall girl with dark hair who had pleaded with him to save the city. Her eyes, no longer milky with blindness, were a light, reflective brown, cool and unimpressed when they fixed on Lukas.

"Your Watchers slew my last master before my eyes, and you are no less cloaked in violence, Lukas Bessarion," Aemathe said coldly. "I will make no alliances with you."

"What?"

Aemathe turned to Emelota as though he didn't even matter. "I was promised true Watchers," she said.

"I *am* a true Watcher," Lukas snapped, pushing his sleeve back to display his Mark. "I have spoken to the seraph. It was prophesied that the guardianship of these provinces had passed to the line of John Bessarion, to me."

His words fell on deaf ears. Aemathe sniffed the air, cocked her head as though listening to the distant sounds of singing upon the wall of Antioch. "Do you feel that? Lilith is here!" she hissed and, in that same moment, between one heartbeat and the next, Lilith stepped through unfolding shadows into the courtyard.

"What's this?" the Poison Mother asked in a voice like oozing honey. "Are you trying to escape me, Lukas Bessarion?"

* * *

"We are become a reproach to our neighbours, a scorn and derision to them that are round about us. How long, Lord? wilt thou be angry for ever? shall thy jealousy burn like fire?"

Within the shadow of the Bridge Gate, Count Bohemond clasped Vermandois by the right arm and threw his left around the count's shoulders: the farewell of one man sending another to his death. Then, as Vermandois turned his horse, Bohemond lifted an arm to cheer.

"God aid us!"

"God aid us!" the answering call rang out.

The count of Vermandois took his place alone before the Bridge Gate. Behind him in ranks his shock troops tensed for their charge: heavily-armoured archers of North France and England, each with a bow in his left hand and a fist full of arrows ready in his right. Thirty mounted knights took up their positions in the rear.

Saint-Gilles reined his horse backward, pressing against the wall of the houses overlooking the street, leaving as much room as he could for the impending charge. At the gate itself, two Syrians stood ready to unbar the gate. Others coiled heavy ropes around their fists, ready to heave all their weight against the massive double doors.

Above the city, the chant hung serene and untroubled in the gold-shot sky, like an eagle on motionless wings.

"Pour out thy wrath upon the heathen that have not known thee, and upon the kingdoms that have not called upon thy name. For they have devoured Jacob, and laid waste his dwelling place. O remember not against us former iniquities: let thy tender mercies speedily prevent us: for we are brought very low."

A scurry of movement from atop the gate. A runner came down the stairs—one of Saint-Gilles' Provençals. Saint-Gilles leaned down from his horse to hear the message. "The Turks have brought up mounted archers outside. Thousands of them. Should I warn Count Bohemond?"

Saint-Gilles thought for a moment. "No. It will only delay us, and we have no time for that."

"Ready?" Count Bohemond called.

The Frankish archers gave a deep-voiced cheer in response.

"Follow me closely." Vermandois circled his horse to face them, a crossbow cocked at a jaunty angle on his hip. "Be bold or be damned! I will not look behind me to see if you follow. Today, the Turks shall see what manner of men they have thought to crush!"

Another cheer.

"God aid us!" Vermandois shouted.

"God aid us!" Antioch echoed.

"Gate!" Bohemond's voice was lost in the blare of trumpets; and the massive bars groaned from their sockets.

"Clear!" Saint-Gilles signalled to the rope-teams. As they threw themselves against the ropes, the gate fairly crashed open, revealing innumerable ranks of horse-archers waiting beyond, Turks and Armenians, renowned bowmen.

"Shields up!" Levelling his crossbow, Vermandois kicked his horse, howled in defiance, and plunged through the gap. The archers poured across the bridge in a torrent after him. The thrumming song of bowstrings began almost at once, quickly followed by the screams of injured men.

High on Silpius, from the battlements of the enemy-held citadel, a black banner floated in warning. Saint-Gilles scowled at the distant signal.

There had been no way to hide the muster within the Bridge Gate. The citadel had seen, and in response to their signal, Kerbogha had sent mounted archers to stop their charge.

The enemy knew they were coming.

***

"We have thousands of men and one narrow gate by which to exit," Bohemond had told them cheerfully. "The trick will be to get all our troops out the gate and across the bridge in safety, which will require time and co-ordination, likely in the face of immediate enemy attack. Think of sand running through an hourglass. That's what it will be like trying to shift the army out of the gate, except that the grains of sand are a small nation of frightened cats, and the hourglass is on fire." He glanced around the room, at their blank faces, and waved an unconcerned hand. "Terrible imagery. Forget it. Suffice it to say that deployment will be the riskiest stage of the battle. Risky, but not impossible, if someone goes through first to break up the Turkish cordon and buy us the time we need to assemble in battle array on the plain."

He gave them an insinuating grin. "It's likely whoever goes out that gate first will be annihilated within the first quarter-hour, and that the rest of us will be forced to retreat and finish starving."

"We'll hope for better things," Adhemar put in quickly.

"I notice *you* aren't volunteering for the job, count." Saint-Gilles couldn't resist the barb.

"Well, no." Bohemond was unabashed. "I thought you asked me to take charge of this battle-plan, and I hope to be alive to alter it if necessary. Does this post of highest honour appeal to anyone else?"

"I'll do it! For the honour of France." Or for the honour of Hugh of Vermandois, Saint-Gilles thought cynically. Someone like Bohemond could manipulate someone like Vermandois into anything, anything at all, simply by hinting there would be bragging rights after.

"It will be risky," Bohemond went on. "But not impossible. Kerbogha has spread himself dangerously thin, and if we charge quickly enough we can seize the initiative. But there's good sense to it, too."

He leaned forward, his eyes gleaming with suppressed excitement.

"Here is what I would be thinking in Kerbogha's place. I would be thinking: good, here are these Franks trapped inside Antioch, and the citadel provides us with an easy path within her walls. A quick struggle, a thorough slaughter, and this army of madmen will trouble us no more. But the struggle is not quick. I have been inside the city, fighting four days without a pause, yet still these Franks hurl me back and I am no closer to winning. Now I look foolish, and my amirs mutter behind my back. All the same, the Franks are in desperate straits and evidently cannot hold out much longer. I withdraw and begin to choke them to death. I wait seven days. I wait another seven days. From time to time I show my teeth in an assault. I test the way through the citadel. Still the Franks defy me. Still my generals mutter, and some of them begin to depart."

Saint-Gilles nodded, thoughtful. "If you remember, Alexius told us that lately the Turks have passed their time chiefly in fighting each other."

Bohemond grinned and went on. "Therefore, one morning my spies in the citadel warn me that the Franks have mustered and clearly plan to give battle. They are weak, their ranks thinned by disease, desertion, and famine. They have no more horses, asses, or oxen to their name than would serve to mount two hundred knights." He rapped the point of his finger against the table for emphasis. "I have two choices. One is to cut them off before they finish issuing from the gates. The remainder of them withdraw into the city, bar the gate again, and continue to starve, but more slowly, because they have fewer mouths to feed. The amirs I summoned to my banner grow tired of waiting and ride home to reap their crops or to exploit their neighbours' absence. I look yet more foolish and ineffective, and the sultan in Baghdad begins to ask himself if I am really his best commander.

"*Or.*" Bohemond flung himself back in his chair, clapping his hands together and rubbing them. "I allow them to empty the city of every man, so that when all of them are gathered on the plain, I may fall on them and cut them down like ripe wheat."

He grinned triumphantly around the table. The other princes stared at him wordlessly. Saint-Gilles shook his head.

Bohemond seemed to hear what he had just said. "Which may very well happen," he added quickly. "But it will be a last stand for the minstrels to sing about forever, and like Kerbogha himself, I *much* prefer it to this slow death."

* * *

Lusine waited with her sister and brother-in-law in a narrow street running along the city's western wall within sight of the Bridge Gate, wedged among sweating bodies that reeked of nameless and unpleasant foods as the people of Antioch waited to know their fate.

"Any sign of our friend?" Arevik muttered in her ear. Lusine shook her head. Emelota had asked them only to be somewhere near Rhodion, ready to come when summoned. Possibly, she had said, Aemathe would find them of her own accord. After that…she and Toros and Arevik might as well have targets painted on their backs. Zarides and his fanatics would be incensed. Lusine didn't care about herself, but she was fiercely protective of Arevik, and part of her hated herself for dragging her younger sister into this.

From outside the wall came the faint sounds of battle, the shrieks of wounded and dying men. "Tell us what is happening!" someone shrieked at the clergy assembled upon the wall. A monk heard and replied.

"The count of Vermandois is out! His arrows make a cloud like rain upon the ground. The Turks run like water! God be thanked, the Frank has won his ground! The way is open!"

Which, Lusine supposed, meant the next phase of the battle would be going ahead, that the rest of the Frankish army would soon be venturing out to join them. Her fists tightened until her nails were digging into her palms. Like most Christians in Antioch, Lusine had mixed feelings towards these co-religionists from the distant west: but at present they were all that stood between the city and a fresh wave of destruction.

"Now Normandy and Flanders follow them! They circle right, advancing on Vermandois' flank… Duke Godfrey follows them!"

"What about the Turks?" someone yelled. People were just about climbing each others' shoulders to get nearer the wall.

"The Turks attempt a retreat, but we have come to grips with them! The North French are in the thick of it! Ah, now I see the bishop of le Puy at the head of the men of Provence! His standard-bearer is carrying the Holy Lance. They set off across the plain to outflank the enemy, all walking afoot like peasants, God help us!"

A stir came as a young man appeared atop the distant Bridge Gate, thin and rangy like a half-starved dog who is ready to eat anything. Lusine had seen him before in the palace chapel, when Emelota had gone to visit the relic of the Holy Lance. Flanked by two priests, Bartholomew raised his arms for silence and began to speak in Frankish. The Franks in the crowd hushed, listening in rapt silence and then cheering as the boy's voice ebbed and flowed in passionate feeling. Battered by their fervid emotions, Lusine felt sweat prickling on her foreheat and down her back.

"What is he saying?" she asked, tugging at the elbow of a neighbour.

"It's Peter Bartholomew, who unearthed the Holy Lance in the basilica," the reply came, passed through the Arabic-speaking crowd. "He's dedicating the battle to his saints and invoking their aid."

"But they aren't saints," Toros murmured.

"We know." Lusine had passed on to her siblings all the things the lady Emelota had learned, or guessed.

"No. Lusine." Toros pulled her and Arevik around to face him. His eyes were suddenly blazing with a dire warning. "He's dedicated the battle to a *demon*."

It took her a moment to understand, and when she did, it was as though a hand fastened around her throat and squeezed. Arevik had clapped a horrified hand over her mouth.

"We need to find Emelota."

* * *

Within the Bridge Gate, Saint-Gilles gnawed on the forefinger of his glove. A nest of snakes writhed in his stomach, knotting more tightly with each moment. He had been sick again over the past week, and he wondered now whether it was bad food or sheer gnawing worry.

At least the illness gave him a plausible excuse for staying behind in the city—to guard the citadel, he had told the council blandly. Or to seize it, if he had the opportunity. But he had not bothered to spell out that part, and if the others guessed it, they did not complain. The public oath to install a mixed garrison including representatives from across the army seemed to have laid everyone's mind at rest.

So far Bohemond's plan was working smoothly enough: Most of the pilgrim army had filed through the gate. There went Bohemond's young nephew, Tancred. There went Evrard of le Puiset, carrying his own banner at the head of his knights—Saint-Gilles blinked. Where was le Puiset's sword? Surely the hotheaded count was not riding into battle with an empty scabbard?

It was too late to say or do anything: the men moved past him in a flow, so steadily that he felt almost as though he and his horse and the entire city were drifting backward together. As the last sands of the Frankish pilgrimage trickled out by the Bridge Gate, Bohemond flashed Saint-Gilles a white grin and led out the last and largest of their battle-companies, a reserve force of disciplined, battle-hardened South Normans he trusted to hang back, keeping clear of the battle until he might throw them into the balance at the decisive moment, wherever they might be needed.

Almost before the last man and horse cleared the massive double doors, Saint-Gilles kneed his horse forward, signalling the gatekeepers. "Shut the gate!"

He'd had Adhemar and the Syrian Patriarch hand-pick local men for this job, men who could be trusted, men who knew the mechanism of the doors. They flung themselves to their work, hardly even waiting for his signal. With a great creaking and grinding, the gate closed, but Saint-Gilles held his breath until the massive bar was dropped back into the latches of the door. Then he turned to the vassal waiting at his elbow.

"Gouffier, take command." The battle on the plain would have to proceed without him. Nodding to the fifty men he'd risked bringing to the gate—just in case something went wrong with the deployment and he needed to defend the gate before closing it with force—he turned towards Silpius, and his footmen fell into line behind him.

Above, the citadel was black on the skyline.

The time was ripe. Bohemond was outside the city fighting for his life, and he, Saint-Gilles, chosen by God to lead the pilgrimage, was ready to take Antioch.

* * *

"What about horses?"

Duke Godfrey had not spoken much until now, instead quietly tracing his finger across his clean-shaven upper lip as Bohemond explained the plan. Now he leaned forward and added, "I don't know how you all stand for horses, but I doubt my men could find twenty worthy of carrying a knight."

The other princes chimed in, estimating the number of horses they thought they might be able to find—calculated to a nicety, of course, for after a knight's own lifeblood nothing was more important. Godfrey frowned slightly, keeping track of the others' numbers on his fingers. "Two hundred and fifty at the most. That's hardly enough for a proper charge."

Bohemond shrugged with supreme indifference. "Then we will fight on foot."

"Against the mounted Turks?" Flanders grimaced. "They'll go through us like the wind."

"Not if we adopt a close formation," Bohemond pointed out. "Despite the advantage we'll lose in terms of manoeuvrability, heavy armour and long spears in a shield wall will stand against almost anything."

"You will have us *all* fight on foot, then?"

"Saints, no. We'll mount as many men as we can and move them out of the city behind a screen of foot."

"But the horses are not much stronger than the men," Bishop Adhemar interposed. "If we mean to use them, they'll need to be fed."

"So we'll feed them; all the grain in the city, if that's what it takes. Win or lose, we won't need it."

Godfrey put up a tentative hand. "What of those who have lost their horses?"

"Lost your horse?" Saint-Gilles frowned. "What the devil is that supposed to mean? How could you *lose* a horse?"

The duke swallowed nervously. "I had it slaughtered."

"Slaughtered!" Saint-Gilles exploded into the shocked silence. "I've been watching you ride that creature for weeks. Strawberry roan. Splendid animal. You fool."

"I have a splendid household, too. I had to feed them somehow."

"But it was your *horse*," Vermandois burst out. "Who do you think will sell you another now?"

There was a moment's silence. Adhemar shifted and drew breath. *Of course,* Saint-Gilles thought in resignation. It was just like Adhemar to give away the very horse between his knees. One had only to look at his face with its razor-sharp cheekbones, sunken cheeks, and hollow eyes, to see that he had already given away everything else, from the food in his mouth to the hours of his nights.

Saint-Gilles snapped, "I'll give you a horse, Bouillon. My best."

"I was going to say I had one," Adhemar said mildly.

"I'm better able to spare mine, since I'll be watching the citadel. You need yours for the battle," Saint-Gilles didn't look Adhemar in the eye as he spoke. Bartholomew still hung between them, an unsettled question, but they could deal with that later. Right now, the most important thing was to win this battle.

* * *

Lilith smiled at Lukas mockingly, and Lukas threw caution to the wind. "You were supposed to make a covenant with me," he said in desperation, turning to face Aemathe. "Tell her, Emelota. Make her obey."

"Emelota has no more power over me than you do, mortal. Is it likely that I should give up my freedom to you now that I have found it at last?"

"Help me," Lukas begged. "Help me expel *her* from Antioch."

"You are in no position to do that." Aemathe spared him a withering look, before advancing on Lilith. "Hear, Poison Mother. I am Antioch's guardian, and you are *not welcome in my city.*"

What happened as she spoke was almost too quick to follow with mortal eyes. With a blaze of light as Aemathe quickened into motion. She was now clad in plate armour of polished bronze—breastplate and greaves, helm and spear and great round shield, like the Amazons of old. She aimed her deadly spear at Lilith. In the same moment, black wings unfolded from the Poison Mother's shoulders, a beaked mask closing over her face. With one sweep of her great wings, Lilith threw herself backward and up—shooting into the sky—drawing her bow.

Aemathe followed like a lightning-bolt, white and gold. Before Lilith could loose her arrow, Aemathe's spear struck her. A flash of light suffused the city, followed by a rumble of thunder as the two distant adversaries collided. The next instant the spiralling combat soared into the clouds, and a moment later rain began to fall, as though shaken free by the battle of goddesses.

Lukas hitched up his sagging jaw with a snap. Beside him, Emelota smiled up into the clouds, her hands spread to feel the rain. Rage seethed within him; it was only with great effort that he stopped himself from shaking her until her teeth rattled.

"What does this mean? You told me Aemathe would make an alliance with me!"

She turned candid blue eyes upon him. "I told you Aemathe would make an alliance with the *Watchers* of Antioch."

"These *are* the Watchers of Antioch! What did she mean by refusing?"

Emelota followed his gesture, looking from Zarides to the other young men scattered about the courtyard. She gave a little, resigned sigh. "Didn't you know, Lukas Bessarion? To gain holy authority, one must forswear temporal power. You were meant to be a prophet, not a warlord. A servant, not a master. If the angels ally themselves with anyone, it will be such."

Lukas felt his face redden. In the sky there came another flash of light, the thunderous sound of collision. Something bright fell, blazing, through the clouds into the mountains. A dark streak pursued it. The earth shook; a distant cloud of dust arose.

One thing he had gained at least: with Aemathe keeping Lilith occupied, the second part of his plan could go ahead.

"To the palace!" Lukas ordered. "It's time we destroyed Bartholomew and his conspiracy of prophets."

* * *

Saint-Gilles and his men were halfway up Silpius when someone grabbed his rein, pulling him to a halt. The knight must have pelted up the mountain from somewhere in the column behind: gasping for breath, he could not speak, but simply flailed his hand towards the southwest. Turning without a word, Saint-Gilles squinted in the direction indicated.

In that direction lay the southernmost gate of Antioch—Saint George, as they'd dubbed it. In laying their battle plans, Bohemond had disregarded the Turkish division camped outside this gate: since there was no bridge by which they could cross the river, they would theoretically be cut off from the battlefield on the river's west bank.

Except that they'd evidently found a way across.

"Boats," Saint-Gilles groaned.

The Saint George division was now marching up on the battle at the unguarded Frankish rear. Enmeshed in a ferocious struggle north of the Bridge Gate, the pilgrims had no time to watch their backs. Meanwhile, Adhemar's flanking movement across the plain towards the distant hills had run into trouble. Saint-Gilles could see the swiftly moving dots of Turkish horsemen buzzing around the bishop's people, fallen men littering the ground behind them. More of the Turkish cavalry drove between Adhemar and the battle, reaching out towards the men from the Saint George Gate.

Kerbogha had not yet brought his full forces into play, yet the Turks had already begun to encircle the battle. Only let him pour more men onto the battlefield, and the separate Frankish forces might be cut off from each other, slowly strangled by a cordon of the enemy.

Bohemond, waiting with his reserves at the bridge itself, did nothing. Had he even seen the Turkish flanking attack?

"Blow the alarm!" Saint-Gilles ordered. "Signal for danger on the field."

He knew he risked raising a panic, but it was all he could do. The signal rang out thinly in the windy air. Down at the Bridge Gate, a tiny flag waved; faint and far away, he heard the trumpets of Gouffier pass on the warning to the men on the field.

At first, for an agonisingly long minute, he thought his warning had gone unheeded—but then, at last, a column of men detached from the mêlée of the battle and turned south, levelling their spears, locking their shields in place to receive the unexpected enemy behind.

Saint-Gilles lifted a wrist to blot away the sweat on his forehead. He felt feverish, his gut churning, but he couldn't afford to stop to watch: already he could hear the thin sound of swords clashing and voices yelling battle cries atop Silpius. His vassals were already hard-pressed, and he needed to be there with them.

"Onwards," he commanded, putting spurs to his drooping horse.

* * *

At length, Bohemond leaned back and folded his arms, his white teeth flashing in a brilliant smile. "This might just work."

Saint-Gilles thought it looked suspiciously like a grandiose suicide. But that was hardly a helpful opinion to air right now, and besides, he could tell from the faces of the other princes that similar thoughts had occurred to them.

Flanders was most optimistic. "It offers Kerbogha a thorny set of dilemmas. Should he allow us to leave the city, or barricade us within? Should he commit his whole army to the main attack, or should he hold back in caution lest Adhemar strike his flank? I like it."

Duke Godfrey cleared his throat. "We'll need our divisions to stick together in tight, disciplined formations. We can't allow ourselves to become separated and fight a series of small battles, duel after duel. On foot we will be more vulnerable than on horse, and then there are the enemy archers to reckon with. Some of us have had experience fighting in close formation, but most…most haven't trained for this."

His voice trailed away. Saint-Gilles knew what he meant. Most of their battles had been fought and won with small forces, mere shards of the fighting-capacity of the pilgrimage. This one, for the first time, would commit the entire army to the field.

Bohemond nodded. "None of us have had any practice at this battle, it's true. But everyone has been involved in the fighting at some point…and everyone who failed to learn from it is dead." Again, his flashing smile. "Don't be anxious. We may have fewer men, but the men we do have are tempered like steel, worth a force three times their number." He nodded across the room to Evrard of le Puiset, who stood listening among the watching counts. The young count nodded silently, but Saint-Gilles saw his hands interlaced across his sword-hilt, bone-white with pressure.

"Easiest to organise ourselves by realm and fealty," Bohemond added. "We'll pass out word. Everyone should be told to fight with his liege and stand firm."

"I'll send criers throughout the city," Saint-Gilles volunteered.

"Good work." Was it a sense of relief Saint-Gilles read in Bohemond's eye? Gratitude that, instead of clashing heads, they were working together for once, as they had on the long journey through Anatolia?

Whatever it was, it was a peculiarly human expression to see on the face of this lamia-born trickster. Saint-Gilles couldn't help responding to the almost-vulnerability of that look. Feeling a swift smile cross his face, he stood up from the table.

"My lords." There was a cup of the heavy red wine of this country on the table before him, and he lifted it with solemnity. "It has been an honour to fight beside you. Let us die as we have lived, in noble company."

Their cups clinked against his.

In that moment, he almost loved all of them.

* * *

From the foundry, Lukas marched his people through Rhodion to the house of Ilkay, meaning to leave Emelota there with a guard before continuing to the palace for Bartholomew. His plans were diverted when he entered the courtyard to find Emelota's maid there, accompanied by the same man and woman whom he had seen at the basilica on the day of the sack.

Lusine threw herself at Emelota, clasping her arms and speaking in a rush of anxious Arabic. "Speak a civilised language!" Lukas snapped at her in Armenian. "What's the problem?"

Zarides had paled. "She says Bartholomew was on the wall with his cohorts, dedicating the battle to the Poison Mother."

Lukas remembered Oliveta, and the slaughter Khalil had carried out as a sacrifice to gain Lilith's power. Was Bartholomew attempting something similar? "Saint George," he said, aghast. "Where is he now? Where is Bartholomew?"

To his consternation, Emelota answered quite calmly: "He is coming. He is at the door."

She nodded towards the gate, still broken after the prophet's last visit. In the hush that fell upon them, Lukas heard the tramp of feet, the indistinct muttering of a crowd. The hair stood up on his scalp, but there was no time for more discussion; no time to lay an ambush or consider eventualities.

"Swords out," he commanded in Greek, as Bartholomew thrust open the broken gate and entered the courtyard. The Provençal was followed by the two priests—Stephen of Valence and Peter Desiderius—that had become his supporters and fellow prophets. Behind them flowed a rabble of men and even some women—hard-bitten peasants and hedge-knights, many of them limping or mutilated whether from battle or their lords' harsh punishments; all of them carrying clubs, billhooks, or swords. Lukas had little more than a dozen Watchers left; Bartholomew had at least twice as many.

Mouth dry, Lukas backed away from the gate. Evidently, he was not the only one in Antioch with murder on his mind.

He reached out for a vision—nothing. "Emelota," he hissed. "What do we do?"

"*We* do nothing," she said in a murmur.

That was no help at all! As Bartholomew advanced towards him, Lukas levelled his staff. "Do you mean to kill me, Bartholomew? Those *saints* of yours want me alive."

"We're here for the witch, not for you," said the young Provençal. "Hand her over and we'll let you go."

* * *

Once again, the march up Silpius ground to a halt, this time because the snakes in his stomach were writhing again. Saint-Gilles vomited into the bushes before staggering back to his horse, wiping his mouth on the back of his hand.

"What's happening down there?" he asked his men, heaving himself back into the saddle. Their faces were grim, and they didn't answer at once. Saint-Gilles blinked, trying to clear his swimming head, and focused on the battleground with his one remaining eye.

What was happening was carnage.

The ground to the south where the Frankish rear-guard had met the Saint George Gate Turks was strewn with corpses, but the Franks, incredibly, were on the offensive—pressing the Turks back towards the river with a line so thin, Saint-Gilles thought for a moment that the Turks were retreating of their own accord.

Even as he watched, open ground suddenly appeared and widened between the Frankish line and the Turkish body. The Turks turned, fleeing back to the boats and the river. In the steadily-opening gap between the retreating Turks and the ragged rear-guard, a thread of blue rose into the air. A tongue of pale flame flickered in the dry grass.

"By Saint Robert," Saint-Gilles breathed, a weary laugh racking his body. "They've set fire to the battle-ground to cover their retreat." But there were painfully few Franks left north of the fire-line: even from this distance, they could be seen falling to their knees in exhaustion, glad to let the Turks run. Saint-Gilles clicked his tongue. The rear-guard had done their job, but at what cost?

"It was Reinhard of Toul's banner, my lord," his standard-bearer said sombrely. Toul. One of Godfrey's vassals. If they survived the day he would have to ask after the lord of Toul.

Bohemond still held his own squadron in reserve outside the Bridge Gate, but the rest of the army was embroiled in fierce fighting to the north. Thanks to the count of Toul, they had escaped being surrounded—barely. Across the plain to the west, Adhemar's flanking force waited, a dark smudge beneath the blue ridge of the distant mountains, too far for Saint-Gilles to tell whether they were still hounded by the enemy.

Further north again, a great mass of warriors seeped from the Turkish camp, making south towards the battle. The army of Kerbogha at last, dark on the ground, an innumerable host.

"God aid us," Saint-Gilles whispered. So far, Bohemond's plan had worked brilliantly. They'd brought the Turks to close-quarter battle, while Kerbogha had dallied in camp before throwing the balance of his army into the field.

But with the Franks deadlocked on the ground by the Bridge Gate, the initiative was lost, the moment ripe for Kerbogha to seize victory with his vastly greater force.

"God aid us," Saint-Gilles whispered again—less a battle cry than a prayer.

* * *

The witch? Lukas' mind went blank with surprise. Bartholomew could only mean Emelota. Why did Bartholomew want him to hand over *Emelota?*

Probably for the same reason Lukas needed to keep her.

He stepped in front of the Frankish girl. "If you want her, you'll have to go through me." Somewhere behind him, he heard creaking as Zarides wound a crossbow. Thunder rumbled in the mountains: Aemathe and Lilith, still at war. "Your saints are busy, Bartholomew. Leave now, before you regret coming here."

Bartholomew grinned, a terrifying sight. "Why should I fear *you,* Bessarion? I know you are planning to kill me for the sake of the Holy Lance. Yet I hold your life in the palm of my hand. Don't imagine I have forgotten our little meeting in the chapel."

Lukas felt cold. Perhaps it was too much to hope, that Lilith had expunged the memory of his face from her prophet's mind. "If you know so much, why do you not tell the count and have me hanged?"

"Even Judas Iscariot had a part to play in the redemption of mankind, and so do you."

"Oh, so I'm Judas in this pageant? What does that make you? Jesus Christ?"

"His prophet, at least," Bartholomew's grin slanted up at one corner.

"And you call me the blasphemer?" Lukas lifted his voice to reverberate in the courtyard. "Would Christ have accused an innocent man of theft, and allowed him to be hanged, as you did?" It was no more than he'd done himself, his conscience whispered. But at least he'd never pretended to be holier than he was.

"He was a sinner, and deserved it." Apart from the look in his eyes, Bartholomew didn't seem particularly mad; his voice was uncannily reasonable. "We are the chosen people of God, and must remain pure. I—"

"You can eat steel," Zarides said from somewhere behind Lukas. His crossbow sounded like a harp-string as it loosed the bolt.

Bartholomew flinched, but the missile never touched him. Instead, cloaked with blazing light and trailing shadow, Lilith flashed from heaven to earth and landed between them: before it touched her, the bolt burst into shards of wood and steel.

* * *

The climb up Silpius was punishing to a man as sick and weary as himself, and Saint-Gilles was forced to call one last halt as they neared the top. His horse rested a hind hoof and stood with a drooping head as Saint-Gilles curled over his complaining stomach, wishing this day, this year, this gruelling pilgrimage would be over.

"Why isn't he attacking?" Polignac, his standard-bearer, muttered as he stood watching the battlefield. Saint-Gilles gave a stifled grunt. He didn't even have to glance towards the field to know what Polignac meant. Having crossed the river, Kerbogha had come to a halt, refusing to throw his massed forces into the deadlocked fight on the riverbank.

Which meant that Bohemond's gambit had worked. Against all probability, it had worked.

"It's Adhemar," Saint-Gilles straightened dizzily, keeping a tight grip on his horse's saddle. "Kerbogha knows that if he commits to the battle, Adhemar will swoop in and catch him in the rear. So long as his men at the river hold, he has no reason to commit—"

"God in heaven!" Polignac interrupted.

Saint-Gilles saw what Polignac saw. Incredibly, even with Kerbogha's reinforcements waiting half a mile off, the ragged edge of the battle was beginning to dissolve.

First a trickle. Then a torrent. The Turks gave way and the Franks pressed forward, a great dark cloud with light flashing from their blades like lightning. On the heels of the retreating Turks they flooded across the ground towards Kerbogha's great, useless, mounted host. The panic spread like wildfire, leaping the rapidly narrowing space between the fugitives and Kerbogha's reserves, making the Turkish knights mill in confusion even before the running battle crashed into them.

Saint-Gilles knew the exact moment when Kerbogha bowed before his fate. The Franks swept their retreating foes before them, and under the impact of that headlong retreat, the whole great Turkish host shuddered and tore itself to pieces, scattering in every direction. Bodies of men fell like ripe grain beside the river. The Franks pressed on, within a dizzily brief time crossing the pontoon Bridge of Boats to attack Kerbogha's camp. Smoke-plumes unfurled into the sky, perhaps set by the Turks to cover their retreat, perhaps by the Franks wreaking havoc in the camp.

It didn't have to happen this way, Saint-Gilles thought, scarcely able to believe what his eye was telling him. The distant picture was flat but unmistakeable, like a painted capital in a prayer book. Bohemond's plan was designed to give Kerbogha a series of nasty dilemmas, and in every case the Turkish general had done as Bohemond had prompted him.

A miracle. Not even Bohemond could have predicted Kerbogha would stumble so helplessly, so entirely into their trap.

Saint-Gilles sucked in a deep breath. It was like coming back from the dead. All his people were going to *live.*

Jerusalem beckoned.

And nearer, the citadel of Antioch was ripe for the taking.

Chapter XLV.

This time, everyone in the courtyard beheld Lilith.

Lukas flinched. Bartholomew's followers and his own recoiled, letting out cries of surprise or terror. Only Emelota stood her ground, gripping hands with Lusine and her friends.

Lilith seemed battle-worn, with feathers moulting from her injured wings and the tip of her great cruel beak broken. But she had dragged Aemathe with her by the hair, and the fainting demigoddess looked much worse: her spear was gone and her breastplate was full of black arrows. Her blood was the colour of pale honey, and the sight made Lukas almost sick with dread. If Aemathe could not overcome Lilith, even freed—

Bartholomew's face turned grey. *Demon!*" he gasped, pointing at Lilith. "Now we see what gives you your power, Lukas Bessarion!"

"Silence, minion," Lilith hissed. Bartholomew stopped on an indrawn breath. From the distance came the sudden sound of cheering, sounds of rejoicing; the drums of the Turks had fallen silent and now instead came the shrieks of Frankish horns. Releasing Aemathe, Lilith closed her eyes, shuddering. Her wing mended in the blink of an eye. In another, her beak was whole again. "Ah," she whispered. "Now the tide of battle turns! Now I will be glutted with slaughter!"

She rose from her place in the courtyard, shadows unfurling like draperies from her monstrous body. Spiralling upwards, she threw back her head and shrieked, a bloodcurdling sound high on the edge of hearing.

On the battlefield, perhaps, that cry struck fear into the hearts of the enemy. It flooded Lukas with desperation. He turned to Emelota. "Do something. *Now.* Before she gains strength."

"What can either of us do now?" Emelota only looked sorrowful. "Your opportunity is past: my people are set on the path to slaughter, and nothing can stop them making a blood sacrifice that will be mourned for a hundred years."

"Not *them*—Lilith! Cast her out!"

She turned wide blue eyes upon him. "To what purpose? To have her place taken by ten more wicked than herself?"

As Lilith ascended, Bartholomew broke free of her control. "Kill them," he shrieked, pointing at Lukas and Emelota. "Kill them all, the witch and the heretics together!"

"No, you fool!" Lukas backed away, pulling Emelota with him towards the shivering Watchers, the praying Armenians. "We are not your enemies—Lilith is!"

His feet scuffled across the mosaic pavement, the image of the dragon encircling the tree. An arrow hissed by his ear, striking one of the Watchers beside him. They were about to die where Ilkay had died, executed out of hand by a mob of fanatics. There was a measure of justice in that.

The tumble of his helpless thoughts was halted by the sound of laughter. In the blink of an eye, Lilith descended into the courtyard again, seething with shadows and power. "Not so quickly," she announced, advancing upon Peter Bartholomew.

"You are mine now," she murmured to him, almost loving.

With trembling fingers, he lifted a rough-hewn crucifix from where it hung on his chest. "Back, fiend," he cried hoarsely.

Lilith swooped upon him—and vanished.

Bartholomew staggered backward as though something had gone through him like a blade. A moment later he recovered his feet, apparently victorious. His followers shouted, brandishing their weapons in something close to delirium.

"See how God helps us!"

"Kill the heretics!"

"Burn the witch!"

"Wait!" Bartholomew turned, raising his arms. A hush fell over the courtyard.

"Command us," one of the priests begged.

"Kill them all. Keep only their leader alive." Bartholomew turned his head, sending Lukas a smile that chilled his blood to ice. The Provençal's eyes were like shards of obsidian. "That one is mine."

* * *

"What news?" Saint-Gilles emerged onto the rooftop of the tower they had taken over from Bohemond as command headquarters on Silpius. By the time he'd reached the summit, the Turks had retreated into their citadel at the sight of the defeat below, leaving his battered Provençals in command of the facing wall.

Now, Galdemar met him on the rooftop with a jug of wine, a dented silver cup, and a cheer of victory. "Saint-Gilles! Hail, the conqueror!"

The wine sloshed out of the cup as Galdemar all but threw it at him. The spicy aroma of this hot-weather wine was not appealing, but his Provençals were cheering him below, so he took a deep quaff and hoped it might settle his stomach. "The conqueror? You rate yourself too low, Galdemar. Bearn. Pilet." He glanced around at his vassals, weary but ecstatic. "You did all the work."

"But you gave us our orders." Galdemar grinned. "You were right, too. They sent a proper assault across the gulley, determined to break through, but we held them. The fire-pots were a good idea. Are you going to finish that wine?"

Galdemar eyed the cup longingly, so Saint-Gilles handed it back with the best will in the world. "Any sign from the citadel?"

"Not yet."

"Tell me if you see something." He stumped across the stones to the low parapet, shading his eye with his hand. Even at this distance it was clear that Kerbogha had failed to rally his men. By now it was all over: the Turkish foot were scattered dead on the ground all the way from the

Bridge Gate to the camp, the grassfires had burned themselves out against the Alexandretta road leaving black smoking ground behind, tiny far-off bands of cavalry were riding for the north horizon with only a small band of mounted Franks on their trail, and the shattered Turkish camp was a seething mass of distant figures. Saint-Gilles felt a little breathless at the thought of the food, horses, gold, and other plunder that would flow into Antioch tonight.

He almost feared to call it a victory. Surely some other disaster was about to snuff them out altogether. Kerbogha would rally. A new enemy would arise.

"The citadel!" someone shouted. "My lord!"

He wheeled around, squinting up at the black bulk of the fortress. A flash of white—and then it unfurled, a blaze across the wall, the flag of truce.

"Saint George and Saint Demetrius be thanked!" Galdemar's voice at his elbow was dazed and faint. "It's over. It's done. Antioch is ours."

* * *

Lilith had vanished but not gone: she had possessed Bartholomew. Lukas felt her malice beating upon him from within the young Provençal's emaciated body and knew instantly what it meant: this servant had been difficult to manipulate, but now that Lilith had control of Bartholomew, she would rule the whole pilgrimage.

After she had slaughtered Emelota and his remaining Watchers.

"Is there nothing you can do?" Lukas gasped, turning to the Frankish girl.

The Watchers had closed around them, ready to do battle. Emelota still appeared entirely calm. "There is," she said, "but you aren't going to like it."

For a heartbeat he hesitated, bitterness so thick on his tongue that he could almost taste it. According to Lilith, the battle had turned in the Franks' favour. The pealing bells and jubilant shouts that even now echoed in the houses and streets around him bore out her words, but Lukas felt impossibly weary and disillusioned. He'd failed to bind Aemathe. He'd failed to kill Bartholomew. He'd failed to destroy the Franks. Maybe he should simply give in.

The feeling lasted only a moment. He couldn't surrender. Not to Lilith, not to Bartholomew.

"Do it," he said, but Emelota wasn't waiting for his permission.

"Aemathe," she whispered. The demigoddess climbed to her feet, flickering a little as she moved, like a candle-flame in danger of snuffing out. "Aemathe, are you willing to do as I asked?"

"Yes." Aemathe touched her bleeding side. "Need you ask?"

"I would not blame you for choosing otherwise," Emelota said gently. "Call your seraph, Lukas."

"My..." It took a moment for her words to sink in: Aemathe had failed to defeat Lilith in her own strength, so now Emelota turned to the one thing undeniably, immeasurably more powerful.

Words and courage failed him together.

"I cannot," he said jerkily. "If I see it again it will destroy me."

Be at peace: I am here.

The hissing voice sounded in his mind without warning. Lukas flinched as serpentine folds and glittering scales and burning wings unfolded from the mosaic beneath his feet, shimmering with heat. He fell back with a cry, putting up his hands to shield his face. Had the seraph been here all along, in the courtyard, twined about the tree, witness to all he did?

Nearer the gate, Peter Bartholomew had crumpled to the ground. His followers, together with the Watchers, cried out in terror and bolted into the street. Only Lusine and her siblings stood their ground, although their faces had gone pale with terror.

Emelota had called upon Heaven, and Heaven had answered. But at what cost?

"Aemathe." Emelota beckoned the goddess to approach the great burning dragon. Aemathe obeyed, sinking to her knees.

Stand, the seraph commanded. *My sister, you and I look each other in the eye.*

"I sue for peace," Aemathe said, not rising. "If there are consequences for my tardiness, I am willing to face them."

Peace is already granted you. As for consequences: are you willing to become Antioch's guardian? To lay down your weapons; to renounce vengeance; to return good for all the evil they have done you, and to serve these humble Watchers as friend and protector?

"I am." At Aemathe's words, her battered armour and the ichor that stained her clothing dissolved into golden sparks that drifted from her in the wind. The seraph leaned down to kiss her brow; Lukas wondered how she endured it, apparently without pain.

Gleaming like a star, Aemathe rose to her feet.

"Lusine, Toros, Arevik," Emelota said. "Watchers. Here is your guardian."

Lukas could not speak: his throat was closed up with some unexpected emotion. He was the Watcher; he was John Bessarion's heir. By rights he should be standing in Emelota's place, inured to the seraph's fire. Instead he was no more than a spectator, a beggar at the door watching the feast within.

Aemathe exchanged kisses with each of the Watchers in turn. Then, like a bird, she rose into the sky; rose and grew, stretched out shimmering wings, and faded away into the golden clarity of noon.

"We're Watchers now?" the Armenian man—Toros—was saying. "What are we supposed to do?"

Lukas neither paid attention nor replied, for the seraph had turned and now advanced upon him.

"I asked for justice," he protested, backing away. "For the Franks, as well as myself. Now you have made them victors. What manner of justice is this?"

Was it sacrilegious to imagine that the seraph laughed? *You asked at first for mercy, and Heaven saw fit to grant it. Now you must endure it, as you can.*

Lukas flinched at its advance; but when he opened his eyes, it had disappeared.

He was not fool enough to hope it had gone.

Chapter XLVI.

In the space of a single morning they had gone from starving rats to glorious victors. It was too good to be true, Saint-Gilles thought as he handed his banner to the representatives of the citadel's Turkish garrison. Was it a miracle, or was Bohemond in command of black magic? No—if such power was at Bohemond's command, Saint-Gilles would not be up on Silpius, accepting the citadel's surrender.

Having exchanged bows with the emissary, he limped back to the dry-stone wall that now lined the gulley and subsided onto a folding-stool. Most of his men dispensed with the luxury, sitting or lying where they had fallen, laughing and passing to and fro the last of their jealously hoarded wine. All of them looked sick, battered, and emaciated; and Saint-Gilles fought back a wild desire to laugh. By such as *these* this great battle had been won.

Before he could make himself comfortable, there came another movement at the citadel gate and Galdemar spoke sharply, worried. "My lord, they're coming back."

"Coming back—what the *devil?*"

Saint-Gilles levered himself to his feet with the help of the spear he used as a staff. When he saw that the returning emissary carried his own banner, his nausea and fatigue receded.

"What is this?" he demanded as the Turk held out the banner towards them, speaking in one of the native languages. "Where's that interpreter?"

His Turkish interpreter hurried up, exchanging a few words with the emissary before changing to nervous Frankish. "My lord, he says his amir refuses this banner. His amir will take the blood-red banner, not the white."

The blood-red banner—Bohemond's banner.

"Damn him!" Saint-Gilles exploded, before he could stop himself. Then he took a steady breath. It didn't necessarily mean Bohemond meant to double-cross him. "Don't translate that. Tell him we don't have the blood-red banner. He must accept this one, and turn the keys over to me."

He and Bohemond had agreed on a mixed garrison. Probably he should have foreseen this, should have handpicked the garrison and marched them up to Silpius hours before the battle. But they had all been so busy... and he couldn't resist being the man to occupy the garrison first, even if he had to hand it over later.

As the interpreter translated his instructions for the emissary, the Turk's shrewd eyes flickered back and forth between interpreter and count. Saint-Gilles thought sourly that he was the first decently fed mortal he'd set eyes on in longer than he cared to count. At last his answer came through the interpreter:

"The blood-red lord is your leader. Did he not set his standard on this mountain? Did he not bring about this defeat? We have promised him we will not open our gates to anyone else. We have resisted you a month already: surely we will last another hour until Count Bohemond comes."

Saint-Gilles swallowed, hard. Bohemond had been speaking to the citadel behind his back? "You *promised* him...Saints, when?"

He received no answer. The sound of hoofbeats came up the mountain road, and the emissary stepped back with a pleased exclamation as the blood-red banner crested the hill, accompanied by the crunch of marching feet, the tips of spears, and the golden head of Bohemond himself, bared to the wind and bleached by the sun.

Bohemond must have abandoned the battlefield and rushed up the mountain the moment he could see the battle was won. Now, Saint-Gilles' lips pressed together as the Turk handed the banner of Toulouse to Galdemar and advanced to meet the South Norman count. When they met, Bohemond halted his column and descended from his horse: the bloody banner was taken down and offered to the emissary.

Saint-Gilles couldn't speak, could hardly breathe in the hot oppressive air. It felt as though he was the opening to a black and stinking pit.

"Polignac," he said in a low growl. "Have the men fall into a shield-wall across the gulley and road."

"My lord?" his standard-bearer said in a startled voice. Saint-Gilles' vassals turned to stare, and Galdemar opened his mouth to protest.

He wasn't going to consult them on this; his mind was already made up.

"You heard," Saint-Gilles said before Galdemar could speak. "Set them in array against the Normans."

"Saint-Gilles." Galdemar's voice was sharp. "Have you gone mad? What is this?"

"A show of strength." Saint-Gilles marvelled that his voice could sound so level, so reasonable, with all that blackness seething inside him. "Mercy means nothing to a man who doesn't feel conscious of your power."

"We didn't discuss this," Bearn put in.

"We don't have time to discuss it now. Go, Polignac. *Now,*" Saint-Gilles snarled, and his standard-bearer rushed to obey. Saint-Gilles was glad he hadn't permitted the men to disperse into the city, even after the victory on the plain. Now they were easily reassembled into their shield-wall. He saw the moment Bohemond noticed what was happening; his gilded head lifted from the discussion with the Turk, and Saint-Gilles, tight-lipped, held the count's distant stare.

Bohemond clapped his hand on the Turk's shoulder in farewell. Carrying the red banner, the emissary took the road towards the citadel's main gate and the hastily formed shield-wall. He was, like all Turks, a man of supreme courage, and Saint-Gilles lifted a hand, signalling to his men to let the emissary through.

In this battle, the Turks were not the enemy.

Followed by his vassals, Saint-Gilles picked his way across the tumbled rocks towards Bohemond. His rival smiled guilelessly as he strolled forward to meet him.

"This is a somewhat martial welcome, Saint-Gilles."

If Saint-Gilles hadn't been so sick and tired, he might have been tempted to snarl something clever in return. Instead he simply demanded, "Do you mean to go back on your word, count? We were to place a mixed garrison in the citadel."

Bohemond's smile didn't slip. "I mentioned it to the emissary just now, but his amir won't have it. I'm afraid I already promised to take command of the citadel myself in some of our earlier negotiations, and he held me to my word. What can I say? It's out of my hands."

"What does he care? Let him march his men out by one gate as we enter by the other. We won't harass him."

"That's not his plan." Bohemond shrugged. "He and his men have chosen to convert. They'll be joining my men now. So, you see, it's important that they know their safety is in hands they can trust."

And that, of course, was checkmate: if the Turks truly wished to turn coat, of course Saint-Gilles was unable to object. He felt his face redden, but he kept his voice dangerously calm. "You ought to have revealed your standing obligations when you *promised* the council we would *all* garrison the citadel."

Bohemond pulled a long face. "Did I not mention it?"

"No. You did not."

"These things happen," said Bohemond. Saint-Gilles' fists clenched by his side, itching to fly. The Norman count turned, waving towards the scarred battleground. "The main thing is that we survived this, eh?"

The message was clear: *You ought to thank me for pulling your fat out of the fire.* If Bohemond thought to pacify him with such words, he was deceiving himself. Even beyond the small angry sphere inhabited by the two of them, Saint-Gilles heard armour chime softly as Normans and Provençals shifted their weight or tensed for action.

"March your men home, Bohemond." Saint-Gilles put all the menace of which he was capable into the words. "March away now, or there will be fresh blood on this mountain."

"Really? You'd attack me?" Bohemond's lip curled, almost imperceptibly. "How the mighty have fallen. There was a time when you prided yourself on refusing to shed the blood of fellow Christians. You were very superior about it in Constantinople, I remember, and again in Marash."

Saint-Gilles ground his teeth, but Bohemond had not finished speaking. His voice softened as he stepped forward, crowding Saint-Gilles and ensuring his next words were too soft to be heard by the men at his back.

"When did that cease, Saint-Gilles? When you sent your servant to attack the count of le Puiset? When you handed over the pilgrimage and a holy relic to a madman?" A shake of the head. "Sometimes I wonder, if that animal hadn't killed your son, whether you wouldn't have *thrown* the child to the brute."

Saint-Gilles didn't think, just moved. Bohemond recoiled with a shout of pain as the blow landed. A hundred spears and innumerable arrows were suddenly pointed at his heart, but Saint-Gilles grinned as he shook out a right hand that was going to kill him with aching for the next week or so: that is, if Bohemond didn't kill him first. He'd struck the count—humiliated him in front of both their men. The insult was unforgiveable. Blood would be shed before this was settled.

He didn't care. He even felt glad in a cold, remote sort of way. "What, count?" he asked, as Bohemond blinked at him in outrage. He had, at least, wiped the everlasting smirk from the South Norman's face. "Did you think you could bait me forever?"

Bohemond straightened, gently probing the reddening mark across his jaw. When he spoke, his white teeth were bloody and his voice soft as velvet. "What shall it be? Do you mean to fight me, or will you take a second cuff in return?"

"We'll leave the pilgrimage out of it." At long last, all this shadow-boxing was over, and he felt almost cheerful at the prospect of a real fight. "Let this be between you and me and God. The winner takes the citadel."

Bohemond blinked, as though Saint-Gilles had struck him a second time. "Pardon? You are serious? You mean to fight me—*yourself?*"

"Do you think me an imbecile?" Saint-Gilles demanded, contemptuous. "I know what it means to strike a man. I am ready to fight where you please, when you please, with what weapons you please."

Bohemond glanced at his own men, then beckoned Saint-Gilles aside, onto a bare knoll of the hill. Out of earshot of both their followers, he cleared his throat. "You don't want to do this, count. On this pilgrimage—and at your age—"

Saint-Gilles was the older man, prone to sickness, and Bohemond a warrior still in his prime. "You will get nowhere treating me as a child," he snapped. "I meant to fight you and I will; let it be in secret, if you like."

"Devil take it, Saint-Gilles! Just let me return the cuff and call it quits."

Bohemond had what he wanted, control of the citadel, and Saint-Gilles had only this cold lust for vengeance. "I will fight," he snarled.

"You will take the cuff." There was steel hiding beneath the velvet of Bohemond's hushed voice now. "No: hear me. One of my sergeants came to me three days ago with grave news. He was leading one of the clean-up crews, collecting the bodies and putting them into charnel-houses."

Saint-Gilles stared, mystified. The hot summer weeks had left the corpses nearly unrecognisable apart from their gear. Those identifiable as Turks were burned on great pyres, while the rest were stacked in cellars or mountain clefts to rot until the bones were clean. How was this relevant to the citadel?

"There was a cache of bodies in the vicinity of Saint George's church," Bohemond went on, naming a basilica near the Iron Gate in one of the poorer quarters of the city. "We found that the flesh had been cut from the bones of some of them, using knives—the scrape-marks on the bones, you understand."

Bohemond seemed reluctant to continue, instead pressing his lips together until they had gone pale. It took Saint-Gilles a moment to realise what he was being told. "God in heaven," he whispered, some of the rage leaking out of him. "You think…"

"People starved during the siege, until even putrefying human flesh…" Bohemond's voice trailed away. "We asked at the neighbouring houses. It wasn't hard to find the ones that did it. Not a desperate few, before you ask, but an organised band of ruffians. They call themselves Tafurs."

Saint-Gilles frowned. The name was vaguely familiar, as though it had drifted past his hearing in a crowd. Or—no, wait. *That* was how he knew of them.

"When questioned, they said it was all right so long as they ate only Turks." Bohemond looked him in the eye, challenging. "They had permission from the lips of Peter Bartholomew himself. Your prophet is a blasphemous madman, Saint-Gilles, and your relic is a hoax."

"You can't prove anything," Saint-Gilles said hoarsely. The mountain might have fallen on him; he could scarcely think. "Who are your witnesses? A pack of peasants?"

"Peasants, indigent knights, and bones scored by knives." Point made, Bohemond stepped backward and began stripping the stained, battered leather glove from his right hand. "I don't want to humiliate you before the whole pilgrimage, Saint-Gilles, but I will, sooner than fight you."

Saint-Gilles felt physically sick in a way that had nothing to do with his illness. Cannibalism—no, he would not believe it. Bartholomew was a man of God: he would not sanction such a horrible thing. Bohemond was only trying to blackmail him. But what could Saint-Gilles do? With the Greek alliance lost, Bartholomew—and the Holy Lance—was his one remaining claim to power. If he insisted on fighting Bohemond, he might salve his rage and restore his honour, but he would never win the citadel, because he would never overcome the younger count in a duel.

Whereas, if he surrendered to Bohemond, he might yet retain some sort of power.

The South Norman watched him, missing nothing. As resignation set in, Bohemond held up his glove. "Will you allow me?"

Saint-Gilles braced himself. "Not the glove, I beg you."

The smirk crept back to Bohemond's lips, devil take him. His hand flew, delivering a lady-like slap whose very gentleness was an added insult.

"I was raised to treat the aged with deference."

Saint-Gilles gritted his teeth.

"You may have outmanoeuvred me, but don't underestimate Alexius," he said, as Bohemond turned away. "Enjoy Antioch while you have it, count."

As ever, Bohemond could not be cowed. "Thanks. Enjoy your prophet while you have him."

Saint-Gilles led his men down the mountain, hunched atop his weary horse in abject defeat. His stomach was writhing in knots again, but this time it wasn't merely the sickness.

He'd sacrificed his honour—he could feel his men's contempt at his tame acceptance of Bohemond's blow—and for what? For Bartholomew…God help him.

What devil's bargain had he made?

Chapter XLVII.

The seraph disappeared, and Emelota blinked as though awaking from a dream. Turning, she found Lukas Bessarion staring at her—no, *through* her, into an unfathomable distance: he seemed lost and adrift in the storm of his own dark rage.

"What now?" Toros repeated.

Someone gave her a shake: Lusine was looking up into her eyes, a worried line pinched between her eyebrows. *"Sayyida,* your instructions?"

Emelota blinked at her. "I don't know," she admitted, coming back to the present with a shiver. She had been given only one vision, only one fragment of the future to see. "I…I have run out of tapestry-threads."

Lusine nodded, lips pressed together until they went pale. "Zarides will kill us when he returns. We should go."

Seizing Emelota's hand and Arevik's, she brushed past the speechless Lukas Bessarion and into the street. Toros ran to catch them up. Outside, there was no sign of the flown Watchers amid the shouting, dancing people that flooded the street. A drunk tried to seize Lusine for a kiss, but she tripped him up and kept moving. By the time they reached the Colonnaded Street, the first of the victorious army had begun seeping back into Antioch, laden with spoils and eager to distribute bread and meat, wine and fruit, gold and silver, horses and bolts of finely-woven muslin. Emelota felt grateful for the crowd, for it protected them from being seen or followed.

When at last they had crossed the stream into the northernmost quarter of Antioch, Emelota turned aside towards the room she and Evrard had rented. Lusine caught at her. *"Sayyida,* no. Come home with us."

"My brother will be home soon, if he still lives," Emelota said. Even as she said it, her heart beat hard, remembering Lukas' vision of Evrard dead in the sunset. "I will wait for him."

"They know where you live."

"They know where *we* live, too," Arevik pointed out. That seemed to decide them, and Emelota led the way upstairs to the small, dark, stuffy room that she had last seen on the night that Lukas Bessarion came to steal them away. A sturdy bar latched the door: Toros dropped it in place and stood back, assessing the thick stone walls, the narrow windows with their iron tracery.

"We're as safe here as anywhere," he said.

"Forgive the mess." Emelota hurried around the room to tidy things: the beds were unmade, dirty laundry lay heaped in a corner and meat was spoiling in a jar on the hearth, the mess a testament to her normally fastidious brother's perturbation these past few days.

"Be at peace. We can take a little disorder," Arevik assured her, but when Emelota stilled halfway through straightening her brother's bedroll, it was not because of her guests' reassurances.

Something heavy lay beneath the blanket—heavy, and gleaming, and sharp. Emelota uncovered it with shaking hands: her brother's sword.

A horrible flash of understanding struck her: she covered her mouth with her hands and turned towards the door. In the shadowed corner behind it, hiding where a casual observer would not see it, was his tall lance.

"Mother of God," she whispered against her fingers, half sick. She had divined Evrard's purpose correctly, then.

"Sayyida—what is it?" Lusine seized the long iron poker from the hearth and glanced about the room, as though expecting to be attacked.

"It's not—it's my brother," Emelota whispered. "He's gone into the thick of that battle without weapons."

Lusine frowned. "Why would he do that?"

"An act of penitence." Emelota suddenly felt quite certain her brother would not return. She felt no grief, only numb shock. What would she do now? Having dragged Lusine and her family into a rivalry with Antioch's self-styled Watchers, she now had no safety to offer them. As the bastard sister of a dead count, she would scarcely be able to protect herself, let alone anyone else.

"Are you so sure Zarides will try to kill us?" she asked.

By the window, which they had opened a crack to gaze out upon the street, Toros and Arevik glanced at each other. "Others have been ruined, threatened, or made to vanish," Toros said gravely. "Since Zarides does none of the work of a true Watcher, he can only maintain his title by brute force."

So this was the man to whom Lukas Bessarion had pledged himself. Emelota moistened her lips. "This is my fault. I never thought—"

"Don't," Arevik said quickly. "We knew precisely what we were letting ourselves in for."

"But I thought I would be able to protect you. And I can't." Emelota picked up her brother's sword and laid it on the table, seeing a white, drawn face in the reflection of its finely honed blade. "Perhaps we should flee, take sanctuary in a church."

"And then what? Starve there?" Lusine demanded.

"We shall have to starve here, in any case," Emelota pointed out.

"Don't despair," Arevik chirped. "Perhaps your brother will return. Perhaps the false Watchers will not follow us."

"It's too late to hope for that, I'm afraid," Toros said in his level voice. "There is Zarides in the street, and he has his people with him. No, *sayyida!* Stay away from the window!"

"I want to see if Lukas is with him!"

"He isn't." Toros and Emelota reached for the window in the same moment; Toros slammed it shut a moment before Emelota could pull it all the way open.

"Are you sure?" she panted. "Please, just one little—"

Something struck one of the small, thick panes of glass, bursting it from its frame. Shards of glass pattered on the floor; a hissing wind brushed

Emelota's wrist; a crossbow bolt struck the plastered ceiling and stuck there, quivering

Toros swore. "Away from the windows, all of you."

Emelota snatched her brother's sword from the table. "Can you use one of these?"

"Not well." Toros took it anyway, his jaw set with determination.

A knock rattled the door, making Arevik jump. Lusine put her arms around her sister as Zarides' voice called from the narrow steps that reached the door from the outside. "I know you're in there," he called, his voice thick with anger. "Unbar. Let's talk."

Emelota shook her head. "Why? So you can shoot at us again?"

"Let me in and there need be no more shooting." A pause. "Nor, to show my goodwill, will I have my men set fire to this house, and watch it burn over your heads."

Emelota glanced at Arevik and Lusine, half in a panic. This was all her fault. If she had not—

Wait.

If she had not freed Aemathe, the guardian of Antioch.

If she had not set herself in opposition to Lilith, the Poison Mother herself.

If she had not called upon a seraph—and been answered.

She could not help herself: she burst into laughter. So she had lost her brother; she had lost her Messenger. She was still herself: a Revealer, a true Watcher, one who had seen the face of a seraph and lived. In two strides she reached the door, unbarred it, and threw it open. On the doorstep, Zarides flinched behind a raised arm as though he expected some attack.

"Fire!" she said, still half laughing. "Tell me, Leo Zarides, why I should fear fire, when it comes at my call to strike my enemies."

With a sudden movement she reached a hand to the heavens as though ready, then and there, to call down fire upon him. Zarides swore and recoiled, nearly falling into the arms of the Watchers behind him. Why, there were only three of them in all: the rest must still be scattered in their fear. The two behind Zarides wavered, lowering their weapons.

"My lord," one of them protested.

"Stand your ground, you cowards," he snapped at them, pushing upright.

"My lord, do you hear that?"

The tramp of feet; the sound of chanting. A troupe of Franks rounded the corner from the Colonnaded Street and came marching towards the house, surrounded by laughing children and a flock of women and burgesses. Their chant swelled as they approached: they carried a knight on their shoulders, and as they drew nearer Emelota could hear their words.

"Evrard the Merciful! Evrard the Merciful!"

By the time they swept to the foot of the stairs and deposited their burden, Zarides and his men had beat a retreat and melted into the crowd. Emelota clapped a hand to her mouth as she looked down into the weary, smiling face of her brother. Weaponless, blood-stained, but alive.

* * *

"What did you do, Evrard?" she asked, once he was done vomiting up his nerves into a chamber pot.

Her brother wiped his mouth and collapsed onto his bed, slumped against the wall as though too exhausted to hold himself upright. But he was still smiling and, beneath all the sweat and blood, she thought he looked better than he had in months.

"I went into the battle without weapons," he said. "I thought that if I wanted to prove my repentance, I ought to give Ayla Bessarion's kin the opportunity to kill me, if they wished. But they didn't. I lived. I lived. God had mercy on me." A deep, shivering breath. "Now I *know* I am forgiven."

And his hands were clean, she realised. Not because Ayla's death was undone—in that sense there would always be blood on his hands, and perhaps there would yet be justice done for that crime—but because he had at last abandoned all excuses and confessed his guilt.

A lump crawled up her throat: Emelota wanted to cry, or laugh, or perhaps dance. "Yes. Yes, I could have told you that. Oh, Evrard. I thought you were dead. What was the meaning of the cheering—Evrard the Merciful?"

He laughed, rubbing a hand across his weary eyes. "Once the Turks broke and fled, I remembered what you and the bishop had told me, that they are men like us, and beloved of God. I tried to stop my men joining the slaughter. At first they were angry enough to kill me, but then they saw that I had ridden into battle with no weapons. They…" He laughed uneasily. "They decided it was *preux,* and dubbed me *the Merciful* on the spot, and carried me home cheering."

His breath hitched as he laughed and Emelota flew to her knees beside him. "What is it? Are you hurt?"

"Not grievously." His breath hitched again. "Our father would have considered it a sign of weakness, Emelota. To ride into a battle without weapons, to turn aside from the slaughter. In his eyes, I would have been dishonoured today."

"Our father was a fool." Once she would never have had the courage to say so, but today was the beginning of something entirely new for both of them.

"I begin to see that." Evrard's smile faded. "There was more I could have done. *Should* have done. I stayed hands today but saved no lives, Emelota. The Turks I spared were cut down by others. Poor helpless peasants, foot-soldiers, left to die as their leaders fled a-horse. I…"

"You will," she told him, leaning forward to kiss his brow. She no longer had any tapestry-threads to follow, but she could feel his intentions solidifying, bright and bold. "You will."

Chapter XLVIII.

Emelota of le Puiset and her Armenian Watchers had scarcely been gone half a minute when Zarides returned to the courtyard.

"What was the meaning of all that?" he demanded, white to the lips with rage and fear.

Lukas shook himself out of his daze, realising exactly how terrified Zarides had been. Who could blame him? Lilith's victory over Aemathe; her possession of Bartholomew; the seraph's appearance. He himself was sweating all over, trembling. Everything had gone wrong. Aemathe was beyond his control, Emelota escaped, Lilith ascendant, Bartholomew alive, and the Bessarion Lance as far from reach as ever. Power was slipping through his fingers, and how would he get it back?

"Look, Zarides, I know that didn't go according to plan, but—"

"Did it not?" Zarides glared around the courtyard as one or two of the other Watchers ventured within. "Was this not entirely the Frankish woman's plan, to free the slave of the image and make an alliance with it? Whose side are you on, Lukas Bessarion? Are you a traitor, or only a dupe? Are you even a Bessarion?"

His mouth went dry. Zarides had never doubted him yet, but now the man was in a rage, and for some reason Lukas could not forget the vision of Ilkay's death—the blood spreading, sticky, between the tesserae. Would Zarides turn on him, also? "The Frankish woman deceived me. She told me Aemathe would make an alliance with the Watchers. I never dreamed she had other Watchers—"

"They are not Watchers!" Spittle flew from the other man's mouth,

spraying his face. "They are heretics—jezebels—everyone knows Toros and his women have converted to Mahometanism in secret!" He wheeled away, beckoning to the remaining Watchers. "It's time we dealt with these renegades. Come with me, you two."

"No—wait—I'll come," Lukas gasped. "Perhaps we can find a compromise."

"Don't you dare." Zarides sneered. "I thought you were a man, but you are only a weakling. Don't be here when I come back, Bessarion."

He plunged into the street, his men following. Lukas watched them go numbly. Zarides was going to kill Emelota and her friends—and if these Watchers were angry enough to kill Emelota, they were angry enough to kill him, as well. That was all very well for Emelota, who now had Aemathe *and* the seraph running to her beck and call. He, on the other hand…he could not be here when Zarides returned, frustrated of his murderous design.

He waited only long enough to snatch his staff and mantle before heading out into the streets, shoving his way through the press of rejoicing people. The streets were full of music, of people dancing. Whole sheep and goats roasted over bonfires, the first fruits of plunder. There was little wine, but a mood of wild intoxication prevailed anyway. The churches were full of weeping gratitude. A woman rather older than himself seized him, kissed his cheek, and told him in slurred Provençal to cheer up, God loved him—God really *did* love them all. She'd doubted it, but now she was sure. Lukas pushed her aside and moved on, stewing in resentment and disgust.

A black shape fluttered in the corner of his eye and Lukas turned with a jumping heart, but it was only a monk in a dark robe. He had almost thought it would be Lilith, come to gloat. He imagined her voice in his ear. *I can give you the lance, you know.*

He wasn't interested.

Zarides and *the lance. You could yet have followers and power. And for such a small price.*

Never. Sweat beaded his forehead. Time was he'd heard Ayla's voice in his thoughts. Now she was silent, and Lilith had taken her place.

He considered retreating to the palace, but decided against it: he feared Bartholomew as much as he feared Zarides. Instead, he climbed partway up Silpius and then left the road to navigate the steep, treacherous slopes until he found a rocky ledge upon which collapse, gasping for breath. Starvation had left him too weak to run any further. For now, he leaned against the rocks, trying to decide what he must do next.

Below, people flocked out to dance and carouse in every street. Beyond the city walls, his vantage point allowed him to view the battlefield, speckled with corpses and smoking from the fires Kerbogha's men had lighted to conceal his retreat. Tiny, ant-like figures still moved amidst the camp and the battlefield, plundering; black birds of prey circled above the wreckage.

Heaven had abandoned him. Aemathe had rejected him; the seraph had refused to wreak vengeance upon the Franks. That was bad enough, but it added insult to injury to see them granted this mercy.

Black anger seethed within him at the thought. These damned Franks. Killers. Barbarians. Fools, who'd run their heads into a hopeless trap, only to be lifted out of it. What lesson would they take away from this? That God loved them and they could do no wrong?

Barbarians. Fools. Lukas ground his teeth. What kind of justice was this, that the Franks should be *victorious?* It went against all sense. No doubt Bartholomew would ascribe the victory to his presumed relic. It was a miracle, he'd say, and they'd all believe it. Maybe it *was* a miracle, just one of the ordinary, everyday ones that came without a great deal of fanfare and gilding. A gang of desperate men had made a clever battle-plan, and another gang of men had fallen completely into their hands when there was no reason at all to do so.

He pressed into the scant shadow at the foot of the cliffs, angry to realise that here on the mountainside he would quickly be exposed to the full glare of the afternoon sun. He must rest a while, until he regained the strength to move. Where? There was no safety left in the city.

"Why?" he groaned, pulling a fold of his mantle over his head. "Why?" There was no answer but the wind sighing in the dry grasses and naked thorns.

Perhaps he had fallen asleep, then, because for the first time in many days, he dreamed of Ayla—Ayla as he remembered her, neither tantalisingly out of reach nor intoxicatingly close and speckled with oily black feathers. Instead she sat beside him as she had in a hundred conversations, her chin propped on her hands, her short black hair grazing her knuckles as she listened.

He had been speaking for some time.

"What kind of fool am I? I *knew* this would happen. All my visions have been telling me to save the Franks—that was why I tried to run from Antioch in the first place. Mercy was *always* the intention. Mercy for them."

"Mercy for you, too, you walnut," she said, smiling wryly.

"Only that I might become the instrument of mercy for them." He groaned. "People talk as though justice is cruel and mercy is kind. It's a lie. Justice can be kind. Mercy can be cruel."

"And each of them good in its place."

"This is not good. These people are still wicked. Left unchecked, what evil will they do?" When she gave no answer, he narrowed his eyes at the girl by his side. "You aren't my wife. Ayla is dead. What are you? Lilith, or one of her servants?"

"God have mercy! You ostrich! You've been listening to a demon, just because she comes to you wearing my face? I thought you knew me better than that!"

"All right," he muttered. "Maybe you are my wife. Did you…does that mean…" His voice trembled; he blurted out: "What is it like, where you are now? Are you happy? Are you well?"

Her gaze softened; she tucked her hand into his. "All it means is that no matter what Lilith tries, there's a part of you that will always remember me rightly."

But then, she was only a memory. His eyes, unbidden, filled with tears. "That's not what I wanted. I wanted to spend the rest of my life with you—the *real* you—the you that lived and breathed and did wild, terrible things when I least expected them." A pause. "I wanted le Puiset to pay for what he did to you. And I never wanted the Franks to have the power to do the same to anyone else—ever again."

"You once said Watchers were like the good men in Sodom," Ayla said, at last. "How did the story go? Sodom was full of violence and pride; they did not even fear to abuse the angels. Yet God would have spared the city, had it contained but ten just men. Are there not ten just souls in Antioch?"

He thought of Adhemar; of Emelota and her three friends and of Barisan confessing his sins upon the mountain. Doubtless there must be at least a few more. "Aren't you angry?" he asked in a low voice. "Don't you want them to die?"

"What, all these thousands of people? For *my* sake?"

"You aren't the only who's suffered at their hands. Remember what they did to this city when they took it. They deserve to die."

"Most of them have already," she said baldly, and that was true, too. She was silent a moment. "What if it isn't about what they deserve, Lukas? What if it's about what they need?"

He'd tried giving them what they needed. They'd had their mercy today, and what use did they make of it? A slaughter that played right into Lilith's plans, handing her control of the whole pilgrimage. "They can't be saved."

"What about le Puiset?"

"Le Puiset can go to hell." The words burst out of him, angry and cold. A mistake. Ayla smirked.

"And there we have the kernel in the walnut."

"I wish you'd stop comparing me to nuts. It's disrespectful."

"If I disrespected you, you cucumber, I wouldn't bother trying to reason with you. But it's the truth, isn't it? You don't want justice; not really. Justice is measured. Proportionate. It doesn't ask thousands of deaths in return for one. It doesn't demand damnation in return for murder. What *you* want is vengeance."

Her words were a knife, cutting through his pretence. For a moment, Lukas couldn't speak at all, and then he replied the only way he could.

"You're right. I do want vengeance."

It cost him something to say the words. His heart hammered, his hands shook; he felt the dream splinter and sat up, throwing off his stifling mantle, breathing hard in the hot evening air.

Ayla's final words still echoed in his mind:

This is not what I wanted. So don't pretend it has anything to do with me.

For a moment, her words left him feeling curiously unmoored, before his resolve hardened.

All right. He would get this vengeance on his own behalf.

Sleep had left him refreshed, able to think more clearly. The sun sank in the west, painting streaks of blood and gold across the weary horizon. He could not spend the rest of the night wandering this mountain: he must go down to the city and find food, a place to sleep.

There was still one Frank in the city, if he had survived today's battle, who might have mercy on him.

Leaning on his staff, Lukas limped into the city and pushed his way through the streets. The celebrations would last all night, no doubt: bonfires danced on every corner, and the air was full of smoke and the scent of roasting meat. He reached the forum outside the palace to find Bartholomew—or Lilith in his shape—standing atop the palace wall to harangue a crowd of eager listeners. Brandishing the Bessarion Lance, he declared, "Has anyone since the creation of the world witnessed a more marvellous deed than this? Today you have seen a deliverance outshone only by the redemption of world!"

The crowd responded deliriously. Lukas pulled a fold of his mantle over his head to conceal his face. Around him, bodies were wedged into the forum almost too tightly to let him move.

"Consider the secular battles and campaigns in which so many kingdoms have been invaded. Can you think of any army—any exploit—comparable to ours?" Bartholomew boomed. "We have heard that, in ancient times, God was glorified in the Jewish people, but today we must acknowledge that Jesus Christ lives and thrives among us today, here, in Antioch, just as he did among men of old."

Blasphemy, he wanted to shout. But that would get him torn to pieces.

"Again I tell you: such a deed has never been done in this world. No longer can the Jews claim to be the chosen people of God! Let them mention all the miracles which the Lord performed for them in the past; we can show them greater marvels! They fought carnal wars to fill their bellies, for rituals and circumcision. But we fight to cleanse the churches and propagate the faith. To us Christ himself has given hope and strength in proportion to the holiness of our intentions. It is clear that God himself has chosen us from among all mankind for this glorious work! Be assured that any who have died in battle today are blessed martyrs and have been received instantly into heavenly bliss!"

At last he struggled to the palace gate. As the crowd responded to Bartholomew's message with ecstatic cries, the madman turned and saw him. Lukas felt certain then that it was not Bartholomew who looked at him, but Lilith, for a thin, cold smile came over the prophet's face.

"Don't worry," Lilith murmured as Lukas passed the cordon of guards into the courtyard. Her voice carried straight to his ears, making him shiver. "You are safe for now, Lukas Bessarion."

Lukas made no reply, but panic gnawed at his gut as he crossed the courtyard. He'd never felt so alone in his life, nor so desperately helpless. He *knew* this would happen.

How arrogant, to presume themselves any more particularly worthy of blessing than anyone else in the world. How foolish, to imagine the divine presence to be their obsequious servant rather than a consuming fire. Lukas shuddered.

"To whom much is given, much shall be required," a voice said softly as he reached the portico. Lukas looked up in surprise to find Bishop Adhemar standing in the shadows alone, listening to Bartholomew's—Lilith's—sermon. "What do you think of this doctrine, Lukas Bessarion?"

"It's blasphemy," he said shortly. For all his own sins, that still angered him.

Adhemar sighed. "I have read many of the lives and passions of the holy martyrs, and I have not found any martyr who wished to kill his persecutors."

"You're the papal legate. Can't you stop him saying such things?"

Adhemar's mouth twisted. "There's no stopping him tonight. I'll speak to Count Raymond tomorrow. Again." He stumbled a little, and Lukas reached out to steady the bishop. He was still in his battle gear, flecked with blood and padded with layers of quilting and mail. All the same, Lukas' hands closed on wasted flesh and protruding bones.

"You should rest," Lukas said, startled. "Where are your attendants?"

"It's all right." Regaining his balance, he waved Lukas away. "They're outside. Listening to Bartholomew." From the way he said the words, Lukas realised he meant listening—and believing. He turned towards the vestibule. "The princes are meeting…I should be there."

As they moved into the light towards the audience-hall, Lukas' worry grew. The bishop looked ill, his skin pale beneath a sheen of sweat. "My lord, are you ill?"

"Only tired. Perhaps still a little feverish." The bishop moved on a few steps, then came to a halt, distressed. "I told them they were to exercise temperance in victory. Do you know what they did?"

"What did they do?"

"They came to me, very pleased with themselves." The bishop swayed on his feet. "They said that when they reached the Turkish camp, they very temperately refrained from doing any evil to the women there. Rather, they pierced them with swords and spears through the belly."

Lukas could find no answer to that.

"I don't know what to do," Adhemar said bleakly. "I had such dreams, Lukas—such good intentions. But I feel I'm standing on the edge of an abyss shouting to the people on the other side, and the louder I shout, the further away these people become."

"You'll feel different about it in the morning, my lord," Lukas told him. It was a lie. These Franks *were* hopeless, and Adhemar…

Adhemar was the only one of them who was any good at all. Adhemar was the only one who'd ever treated him as a person, not a means to an end. All this time he'd been trying to win Count Raymond's approval, he might have been serving Adhemar.

And now it was impossible. If Adhemar knew what he'd done…*when* Adhemar knew what he'd done, he'd lose that approval altogether. Lukas swallowed hard, surprised to find a jagged lump in his throat.

They were still moving towards the door to the council-chamber when brisk footsteps echoed in the passage leading to the garden, and Count Raymond appeared, taking in the scene in an instant.

"Adhemar," he said in a hollow voice. For an instant, Lukas wondered if there was guilt in the count's eyes. Then the bishop stumbled again, and Lukas had to catch him.

"You're sick," Count Raymond said. "You ought to be in bed. Here, Polignac, fetch my chamberlain; tell him to arrange a litter and bearers to the bishop's house. Hullo, Bessarion. Come back, have you? Guide the bishop home and then come back here. Your old room is waiting for you."

It was like falling asleep again; falling back into old ways, old obedience. Lukas hated that his head dipped in a bow; that he said in a hushed voice, "Yes, my lord," but there was nothing else he could do. The bishop was too weak to protect him, and if Count Raymond was willing to do so, he had no other choice. He needed time to make new plans, to win back Emelota or Zarides or whoever would help him.

This is not what I wanted, Ayla's remembered voice whispered. He pushed the memory away.

Chapter XLIX.

It was an afternoon of hot and brooding sounds: the coo of doves, the aimless buzzing of flies. Saint-Gilles slumped on a carved stool at the head of Adhemar's bed, his elbows on his knees, his fingertips kneading his aching temples.

The bishop's bedchamber was darkened, for he could not endure the pitiless glare of the late July sun, nor the dry southern wind that shook the dusty poplars in the courtyard. With the windows shuttered, the room stank of rotting flesh. The attendants had told Saint-Gilles that it had been a long and unquiet three days, but the bishop was sleeping now.

Saint-Gilles watched, and prayed in weary circles.

Not Adhemar. Please, Sir God, not the bishop.

Saint Robert and Saint Giles, pray for him.

A month had passed since the great battle, and Adhemar's was not the only case of fever in Antioch. Heat, crowded living conditions and the chaos of war had festered in the corpse-clogged city. Most—more than half—were racked by fever for a while, before slowly recovering their strength. Too many fell prey to greater maladies: coughing up bloody spume, rotting from the feet up, or carried off by a sudden recursion of fever that brought stiffness of the neck, discolouration of the skin, convulsions and death.

Saint-Gilles tried not to breathe too deeply in the sickly atmosphere. They were speaking of cutting off the bishop's feet. Even if by some miracle his hunger-weakened body survived, he'd never walk or ride again.

It was cruelly ironic. Adhemar had survived incredible dangers and hardships: cold, dysentery, starvation, fear, battle after battle after battle. His courage had bought them victory on the field; his words peace and wisdom in the council-chamber. Of all the men on the pilgrimage, he was the one Saint-Gilles could least imagine doing without. All the way from Provence, Adhemar had kept them focused on their goal and working together in as much harmony as could be expected.

Now what?

At a tiny motion from the bed, Saint-Gilles lifted his face from his hands. The bishop had turned his head and opened his eyes, lucid but weary in a way that went far beyond the physical.

"They told me you were asking to see me, old friend," Saint-Gilles said.

Adhemar smiled faintly. "I thought you might have left the city."

Saint-Gilles shifted, discomfited by the reminder that even sick, he'd been avoiding his friend. "Some of the counts are considering it. The sickness spreads, and it's cooler in the mountains. But I'm not leaving you."

"I'm grateful." A faint smile. "No one else will tell me what is happening."

"With the pilgrimage, you mean?" Saint-Gilles blew out a breath. "Well, now is no time to be undertaking a march on Jerusalem. It's been decided to wait until November, when the weather's cooler and the men are more rested." *Or dead of fever.* "Vermandois and the count of Hainault have gone to Constantinople to invite Alexius to Antioch. Bohemond was unhappy about it, but I'm glad to say that sense prevailed."

He grimaced, thinking of all the things he'd left unsaid.

"The Patriarch?" Adhemar prompted.

"Has been re-enthroned in the basilica, as you wished." Saint-Gilles couldn't keep the edge out of his voice. The Syrian Patriarch had been completely unhelpful to him, refusing to recognise the authenticity of the Holy Lance and, beyond that, reluctant to take sides in the dispute over the city. Saint-Gilles didn't understand the man's attitude. It was true that if Bohemond succeeded in consolidating his grip on Antioch, the Patriarch couldn't afford to offend him. But didn't the man realise that Bohemond would never trust him anyway? The Patriarch answered to the Greek church authorities at Constantinople, not to the Latin church at Rome. Bohemond would always suspect him of being a tool of the emperor's.

"Bohemond?" Adhemar inquired faintly.

"Still insists he's entitled to the city. *I* say he's usurped it, but no one listens to me. *Oh, send for the Greeks and let them sort it out.*" Saint-Gilles' lips tightened. Humiliatingly, it was not only his fellow princes who refused to support him. His own vassals grumbled at the feud, unconvinced that the Greek alliance could be revived. The only bright spot—if it could be called bright—was that Bohemond had not renewed his accusations against Bartholomew.

He must be feeling secure in his grasp on Antioch.

"Not only has Bohemond held onto the citadel, but a couple of weeks ago, he demanded we all give up our holdings in the city. The walls, the palaces, the fortresses. Godfrey gave up everything like a lamb and went off to Edessa to take service with his brother. And he calls himself a duke!"

"Perhaps he thinks Bohemond has earned the right to the city."

"What, against his oath to the emperor?" Saint-Gilles snorted. "I'm damned if I'll be forsworn so easily. I told Bohemond to go to H—I told him where to go," he added awkwardly as he suddenly recalled to whom he was speaking.

"I'm sure you did," Adhemar said wryly. "I gave up my holdings too, you know."

"You're a bishop," Saint-Gilles muttered, swallowing his anger. "Still, I wish I knew why *everyone* lets him get away with these things. Is it witchcraft, or are people just that stupid?"

"Bohemond wants to be loved," Adhemar whispered. "As conniving and mercenary as he is, as greedy as he is for power, he wants people to like him. But you, Saint-Gilles, as much true compassion as you may feel for your people…you have always been content to be feared."

Saint-Gilles opened his mouth to deny it, but how could he? He was ruthless to his enemies and honest with his vassals, and if he was sometimes rough with his friends, that was only because he cared for them too much to coddle them. Did Adhemar want him to apologise for bludgeoning people out of their own folly?

"I'm not excusing Bohemond," Adhemar went on after a moment. "But you're my friend, Saint-Gilles. Don't let this feud with Bohemond turn you into a monster. Even a man with the purest intentions and deepest devotion in the world can be corrupted by the thirst for power. Don't let that become true of you."

At one time such advice would have filled him with guilt; now he held Bartholomew's words close, like a shield. If Saint-Gilles wanted power, it was only because power was due him. He would not apologise for doing whatever he must to secure it.

"You sound tired," he said. "I should let you rest."

"Saint-Gilles. Think on what I've said." There was an undercurrent of urgency in the bishop's voice.

Saint-Gilles hated that all this had come between them. Hated that all he could say, as he turned stiffly away, was, "Remind me yourself when you get well again."

Chapter L.

"He's asking for *you*." Count Raymond had leaned on the last word as though there was something incredible in the request. "I told Narbonne you'd wait here until he was ready to see you."

Lukas wondered what such a summons might mean. Word was the bishop was terribly ill, that his feet had turned gangrenous. Perhaps there was some final errand the bishop wanted him to run—a message to the Syrian Patriarch, a commission to another bishop, in Edessa or Alexandretta. Another task. Another purpose. Another distraction from the problem he could not solve.

Lukas felt unmoored and helpless, as he had ever since the day of the battle. His father's lance seemed far out of reach. His visions had dried up. He had seen neither Zarides nor the le Puisets since the battle, though this was partly because Lukas had hidden himself on the one occasion that Evrard visited the palace.

As the weeks passed, Adhemar sickened, rallied, sickened again. During the bishop's illness, Lukas had been employed as an interpreter in Count Raymond's meetings with the Patriarch, but he could tell that the count no longer trusted him to liaise independently with the Syrian authorities. Meanwhile, everywhere he went, hostile eyes watched him. Bartholomew—Lilith—and the other prophets delivered their visions, waiting for him to set a foot wrong.

Lukas, like the city itself, lay beneath an enervating spell in the sweltering summer heat. *Don't pretend this has anything to do with me.* Ayla's words sapped away his willpower, held him in check.

Memories assailed him, soft and suffocating like a cloud of moths. A year ago, they were crossing the high Anatolian plateau. Water had been scarce, jealously hoarded. Lukas had been lying awake one night, tormented by thirst. He'd heard a scuffle in the sand and sat up to find a water bottle, still damp, lying on the ground beside his head. It was Ayla's, full. She'd exchanged it for his empty one. He never found out where she got the water, whether she had gone thirsty to share with him. At that stage in the journey, they were barely even speaking.

Now, Lukas sat kicking his feet in the shade of the bishop's loggia until evening, when an attendant came to tell him the bishop would see him. After the scented comfort of the rest of the house, the heat and stench of the sickroom hit him like a slap in the face.

The bishop gave him a faint smile of welcome. "They say you've been waiting since Nones."

"You wanted to see me," Lukas said, as though that explained it. He felt like a fraud. If the bishop knew the things he'd done… "Are you…how do you feel today, my lord?"

Adhemar didn't answer at once. "They tell me I am dying. I think they are right."

He felt it like a knife in the dark. "No," he whispered, and reached for a vision. Surely he should see *something,* since he wanted it for another and not for himself.

But there was nothing. The last time he'd had anything like a vision, he hadn't even seen it himself. It had been given to Emelota, as though he was simply the conduit.

"Believe me, I'd be happy to be proven wrong." Adhemar turned his head on the pillow, and Lukas was struck by how wasted he looked, his skin like paper and his cheekbones sharp above his growing beard. "Please listen: this is important. I will leave a gap, which others will race to fill. Orange. Narbonne. Chocques. There's no lack of great bishops on this expedition, but none of them have the full papal authority, nor the loyalty of the poor. I don't mean to boast. It is the truth."

Lukas nodded silently. None of the other bishops was as beloved as

Adhemar, that was certain.

"When I am gone, the people will turn to another."

"Bartholomew." Dread pooled in his stomach.

"We both know he's dangerous. I'm not sure you understand *how* dangerous."

Lukas might have laughed if the situation had been less dire—a demoniac in command of the pilgrimage. "I have a fair idea, my lord."

"I'm not sure you do." Adhemar coughed feebly. "It isn't merely his own madness; it's his influence over the pilgrimage that concerns me. Bartholomew believes the purpose of this campaign is vengeance. It was always meant to be liberation—of the eastern church, of the holy places. A war for liberation lays down its arms once peace is achieved, but a war of vengeance has no goal beyond bloodshed. Pure destruction."

Lukas ran a finger around the collar of his tunic, trying to breathe. Within the sickroom, the scent of rotting flesh was horrible. A dove warbled out in the courtyard, soft and soporific.

"It happened before," Adhemar's voice was far away. "How do you convince men like these to abandon their homes and lives, to travel across the world on a quest as desperate as this one? When the pilgrimage first began to be preached, we told them that Christ was their liege lord, that they must fight for him as they would their own secular lords. But to fight for a secular lord is a matter of honour, feud, and vengeance. In their untaught eyes, the Turks had done Christ less dishonour by occupying his lands and oppressing his people, than the Jews had done in condemning him to death. Bands of them gathered in the Rhineland, hunting the Jews to a merciless slaughter, hounding them to convert and gutting them to seek for gold. What, didn't you know that? It was only two years ago. Senseless cruelty! The Jews are peaceable folk, oppressors of no one, and Holy Church forbids conversion by force."

His own mother was of Jewish blood. Lukas ran a tongue over his lips before daring to reply. "Did...did anyone I know..."

The bishop shook his head. "Most of the malefactors were in an early expedition, which was attacked and destroyed before we ever came east.

Still...I wish I could say they all perished, but some of the culprits are here, with us, on the pilgrimage. And make no mistake, Lukas: the demon of vengeance has followed us every step of the way."

Lukas could hardly breathe. Beads of sweat rolled down his chest. Honour, feud, and vengeance? He'd despised the Franks for their ignorance and violence, but now he could not help wondering if he was truly any better.

This is not what I wanted, Ayla's voice echoed in his mind.

"I fear," the bishop said faintly, "that when I go, Bartholomew will forge these silly sheep into a weapon of terrible destruction. I fear that whatever good they accomplish will crumble beneath the burden of pride. I fear a great many things."

"At least your soul is safe," Lukas said bitterly. It was more than he could say of his own. In that moment he regretted what he had done; he would have taken it all back, if he could. But it was too late for him.

"What good is it, to escape the wrack of this world with one's own soul?" Adhemar whispered. "A good man should leave a good legacy. This was mine—the answer to a thousand prayers, the enterprise of a lifetime. And see how it has been corrupted, despite all that I could do…or perhaps it was corrupted from the beginning."

There was no answer he could make to that. Lukas stared at his loosely clasped hands, the veins swollen in the heat. He hated all the Franks, except this one. He could give no comfort.

Yet he found himself blinking back the tears.

"The divine judgement doesn't always look like fire from a clear sky," Adhemar said with a sigh. "Sometimes it looks like natural physical consequences—say, an epidemic in the aftermath of a senseless slaughter. Perhaps it is fitting that I go with it, unready as I am. But promise me something, Lukas Bessarion."

Lukas had been avoiding the bishop's eyes some time, but now he glanced up with a premonition. Of course he had not been summoned here merely to commiserate with the bishop's grief.

"You're a prophet," Adhemar said. Neither worshipfully, nor mockingly—not in any of the ways anyone else had said similar words. Simply, as though he had said *you're an interpreter* or *you're a Greek.* "A true one. It was you, not Bartholomew, who saved us in the battle a month ago. It's you, not Bartholomew, who should lead this pilgrimage when I am gone. Expose Bartholomew. Counsel these people. Warn them away from vengeance, or I shudder to think what crimes they may yet commit."

Lukas had turned to stone. Counsel the Franks? *Help* the Franks?

Adhemar saw the look on his face. "I know it is a great deal to ask."

He jumped to his feet, blurting out the first words that came to mind. "Who told you to ask this of me?"

"Ah. So you have considered it."

He raked his hands across his face, forcing his voice to be calm. "You don't understand what you're asking of me, my lord."

"Perhaps I do," Adhemar said, very gently. "I knew Ayla too." It startled him that the bishop remembered her name. For a moment he was incapable of speech.

This revenge is not what I wanted.

Again, he felt half suffocated. Counsel the Franks—how? His visions were gone. The seraph had rejected him. Even if he wanted to, he could not turn back now.

He realised, dizzily, that he was considering it. If he capitulated, he would no longer be at Lilith's mercy. Somehow there might be a way to retrieve the lance—but no; his instructions had been quite clear. He was meant to destroy the lance.

His only other option was to do as Lilith asked, and free Khalil.

"I won't force you to promise." Adhemar had been watching him hopefully. "Do this willingly or not at all, Lukas Bessarion. But at least, tell me you'll think on what I said."

Lukas moistened his lips. "That I can promise you, my lord."

Chapter LI.

Adhemar of Monteil, bishop of le Puy, papal legate, went to his rest on a cloudy day at the kalends of August. Three days later, his withered remains were buried in the excavation where the Holy Lance had been found.

The great basilica of Saint Peter must have been crowded with bishops, princes and counts as the burial service was sung. There was no room for Lukas within the church. Adhemar, who had always found time for Lukas during his lifetime, was unable to make a place for him at his death.

Beyond the church, the great courtyard and even the streets were packed with a silent, watching crowd. When Lukas bothered to look around him, he found more than one face drenched with tears, pale with grief. During the bishop's illness, and in the few days since his death, Lukas had heard many stories. It seemed that everyone knew someone who had received help, comfort, or counsel from the bishop. The knife in his heart twisted. They called him their Moses, their leader through the wilderness towards the Promised Land.

Lukas wondered whether it would have consoled Adhemar to learn that his people loved him so much and grieved so sincerely at his death…or whether he had already known; whether it left him yet more racked by guilt and failure in his final days.

And Adhemar had asked *him* to take his place. Not as papal legate, of course. To be a prophet was to be set apart from every mortal hierarchy. As Emelota had said, to gain holy authority, one must forswear temporal power. But what other choice did he have? He had tried to take a middle course between Heaven and Hell, and he had failed. Now Adhemar begged him to choose: to give up the claims of birth and training, to accept his fate as a prophet.

The longer he thought it over, the clearer it became that he could not pretend he had gone too far to draw back. Despite the things he'd done, despite the blood he'd shed…if there was a way back for le Puiset, then there was certainly a way back for him. He could taste the sourness in his mouth. He didn't have to do anything or earn anything; he had only to lay down his dreams.

I could do it, he thought wearily. *Give me the Bessarion Lance—give me this one small thing—and I will do it.*

The funeral must have ended: there was a stir at the basilica door as sergeants pushed the crowd back, making room for the princes and the Patriarch. Before they could emerge, however, a wild figure stepped out in front of them, arms spread as he faced the courtyard.

"A message!" Bartholomew cried. Since Lilith had taken possession of him, the young peasant had deteriorated: his clothing was unwashed and ragged, his hair and beard untrimmed. He looked—and smelled, Lukas thought—like a starving animal; but in his right hand, he carried the Bessarion Lance.

Instantly, the crowd hushed to hear what the prophet might say. Behind Bartholomew, the princes were forced to come to a halt in the basilica door—doubtless it was part of the prophet's appeal that he, a peasant, was able to take precedence of these princes, and none of them dared to object.

Bartholomew spoke—or rather, Lilith within him spoke.

"The Lord orders you, Raymond and Bohemond, the custodians of Antioch, to make peace with one another. If you are in agreement, nothing will destroy you. You must take counsel for the wise governance of this city, and choose one from among yourselves to rule. Do not delay this task, for you have sworn to complete your pilgrimage to Jerusalem."

The crowd cheered their approval of his words with every pause.

"Let every man declare his wealth and give everything he can to the poor. Do not trust the Turks, even if they say they wish to keep the Christian commandments! Seize them and force them to give up the names of all their people. When this is done, you must ask the Lord's advice on your journey to Jerusalem, and he will counsel you well, through the mouth of his saints. But if you refuse to follow these commandments, although Jerusalem lies ten days distant, you will not reach it in ten years."

More shouts. Bartholomew held up his hand again, wanting silence.

"Behold, the blessed Andrew visited me in the night, and with him came the good Bishop Adhemar! The bishop came to me in great sorrow and suffering by reason of his lack of faith, his head and face severely burned. He told me that he deeply regretted his sin in disbelieving the Holy Lance, for at the moment of his death he was drawn down to Hell and whipped most severely."

No. Lukas felt as though he was listening from a great distance away. His mouth filled with bile as he observed the looks on the faces of the people surrounding him, their murmurs of horror and excitement as Bartholomew described how a garment Adhemar had once given to a beggar protected him in the flames of Hell.

How dare he? How *dare* Bartholomew and Lilith desecrate Adhemar's memory in this way? Perhaps Lukas was not fit to sand the bishop's armour or sharpen his sword, but it was more than he could do to stand by and hear a holy man's memory so abused.

"Finally, because of three pennies he presented as an offering to the Holy Lance before his death, the good Bishop Adhemar was released from the sufferings of Hell. Now," Bartholomew finished in triumph, "he repents in great sorrow and honours the Holy Lance of God, the instrument of Our Lord's passion."

For so many weeks, Lukas had bit his tongue, standing by in silence while Lilith used Bartholomew as her mouthpiece for falsehood. But now she had certainly put a foot wrong.

He *had* them.

Bartholomew drew breath, ready to utter more blasphemies.

Not this time.

"You lie!" Lukas bellowed.

Everyone stared at him, even the princes. For an instant, the silence was nearly suffocating. The crowd drew away from him, a silent rejection. He took advantage of the space to push towards the front of the gathering: he was trembling, but he would not stop himself now.

The die was cast. He would try fulfilling Adhemar's final wish; the bishop's memory deserved that much.

"You lie!" He turned towards Count Raymond. "Bishop Adhemar never donated money to the lance, as you know perfectly well!"

Lilith-Bartholomew seemed untroubled. "If anyone doubts what the bishop told me, let his grave be opened! You will see the marks of the fire on his head!"

Perhaps agreeing would be an easy way to disprove Bartholomew. On the other hand, perhaps Lilith had already taken liberties with Adhemar's corpse as a way to back up this story. That kind of thing was no proof at all.

Instead, Lukas turned to Count Raymond, pleading. "My lord! You know perfectly well that Adhemar never accepted the veracity of this relic."

Count Raymond's lips thinned stubbornly. Count Bohemond smirked and said something behind his hand to the count of Flanders. Lukas caught something about *seems terribly convenient, you must admit* before Bartholomew lifted his voice again.

"If Adhemar denied the holy relic it was on account of *your* tempting and prompting. Blasphemer! Heretic! Liar!"

The crowd muttered. Such accusations could get a man killed. Repressing his terror, Lukas turned to face his rival. "Beware," he murmured. "You need me alive, remember?

"Do I?" It was strange to see one of Lilith's slashing smiles on Bartholomew's face. "Perhaps you are the one who should beware. I am perilously close to dispensing with you."

That struck real fear into his heart; but it also made him bolder. The crowd around him had turned ugly, shouting at him to recant, but Lukas was done keeping his mouth shut.

"My lord, you know I'm no liar," he declared, still addressing Count Raymond. *"I told you of the emperor's withdrawal. I counselled you to repent of your sins before the battle.* Count Galdemar will tell you whether I am a true prophet or not."

Count Raymond shook his head. "Enough, Bessarion."

"Please, my lord! He would have hated this," Lukas pled. "Don't let them misuse his memory like this."

The count's jaw set. "Adhemar was a mortal like any of us. Would you have him incapable of confessing his faults, even after his death?"

Lukas drew breath to answer, to point out the undeniable falsehood of the offering, but Count Raymond repeated in a voice that brooked no defiance: *"Enough!"*

The crowd behind him was seething, hostile. A pair of meaty hands latched onto his shoulders; a voice spoke with chilling levity. "Want us to deal with him, my lord?"

"Kill the heretic!" someone else yelled, less jovial. More hands latched onto his clothes, yanking him about.

"No, you simpletons, don't tear him to pieces!" Count Raymond strode forward, beckoning to his knights. "I wish to make full inquiry. Hand him over."

"One moment." Lilith-Bartholomew rapped the lance against the pavement, stilling the crowd. Count Raymond hesitated, as did his knights. "We'll make our inquiry here and now. Should I fear to confront this heretic? As I am a true prophet, no."

At a gesture from the prophet, his captors released Lukas with a shove that sent him staggering towards Bartholomew. Regaining his balance, he cast a glance behind him and caught a glimpse of blue in the crowd. It was Emelota of le Puiset, watching them with a frown etched between her brows. He tore his gaze away.

In front of him, Lilith-Bartholomew emanated pure unconcealed malice.

"This man claims to be a prophet," they proclaimed. "Let us put the matter to judgement. I will show you the power that is in me, and let this man show the power that is in him; and you will decide which is the true prophet."

Lukas' throat went suddenly dry. Bartholomew had Lilith. And he had… nothing.

He glanced at the people laughing and cheering at Bartholomew's words, and tried to find Emelota, but all the faces blurred into one.

He was alone. He would die, torn limb from limb, and the last thing he saw would be his father's stolen lance. He almost wished he had accepted Lilith's help when she was willing to offer it.

Lilith-Bartholomew was also scanning the crowd. "Not all of you are true men," they announced. "Not all of you are holy…You!" Their roving finger fixed upon a man. "A pox is upon you, you sinner!"

Before the astonished onlooker could protest, hands reached out and tore away his clothes, revealing a pale torso speckled with a red rash. Someone in the crowd shrieked; others backed away. The man fell on his knees, weeping and begging alternately Bartholomew and God to absolve him of his sins. Lukas felt a sudden desire to laugh. He'd seen that rash before: everyone who came down with the pestilence had it, even the bishop.

"That is nothing," he said with scorn. "Anyone can play that game."

He paced the fringe of the watching crowd, staring into eyes as wary as his own until he found a man who looked as Adhemar had the night of the battle—pale, feverish, sweating. Around his neck were the telltale signs of the rash. Lukas pointed his staff, careful not to touch the man, and everyone else backed away. "This man has the same pox," he called. "In a crowd this large, anyone might have the pestilence!"

Lilith-Bartholomew raised the lance, pointing to a woman. "You, hold up your bottle. Tell the people what you have inside it."

"Water, sir," she said with a bob of her head.

Bartholomew waved his hand over the skin bottle, then took it from the woman's hand. "It is wine," he announced, throwing it to one of the sergeants bordering the crowd. "Taste and see, brother."

The sergeant took a mouthful, and his eyebrows climbed. "It *is* wine," he gasped. "Just like they grow at home in Gascony."

Some in the crowd gasped or cheered; others fixed their gaze—hostile or assessing—on Lukas.

If he was about to get himself killed by a vengeful mob, he might as well do it properly. Lukas strode to the sergeant and held out his hand for the skin. "And in God's name, I say it is water," he said.

In the instant that passed before he moved again, he wondered whether Lilith could have really turned water into wine. Whether she was toying with him in this contest or really trying to win.

Whether there was still some power in his words.

He tipped the skin over and a clear stream ran out of it, sparkling in the sun. Lukas caught some of it in his hand and raised it to his lips.

"It's water," he repeated huskily, tossing the skin back to the woman who had brought it.

This time, when Lukas turned to face them, Lilith-Bartholomew looked almost murderous.

"Try this!" Lilith snarled, catching the end of Lukas' staff. Lukas tried to yank it out of Bartholomew's hands, but their eyes had unfocused, their teeth were bared, and their grip was like steel. Then, suddenly the staff changed in his hands to supple folds of muscle and flesh and cool, slippery scales.

Lilith released their hold even as Lukas gave an involuntary cry of surprise and let go. The staff fell to his feet, no longer a staff but a snake writhing and spitting in fear. A viper, spotted like a leopard. Its diamond-shaped head rose, a stiff S-bend in its neck as it prepared to strike.

The crowd recoiled, crying out in fear and wonder. Lilith-Bartholomew backed away, eyes hot with victory.

Lukas stood as though changed to stone. His mouth had gone perfectly dry. "Stop it," he whispered. "You're a staff. You're *my* staff."

It seemed to think about that. After a few moments it lost its watchful rigidity, melting to suppleness.

Lukas inched away and instantly it reared up again, hissing, neck flattening.

"Go on, Bessarion!" Lilith-Bartholomew jeered. "Turn *that* back to what it was!"

Behind Bartholomew, the princes watched in silence. One of them—Duke Godfrey—made as if to step forward, but Count Raymond put out a hand to stop him.

Lukas looked at the snake again, not daring to move, because if he moved he was dead.

And if he didn't move—if he didn't *do* something—then he was a fraud, and he was also dead. Bitterness welled up in his mouth. He was no fraud. Visions had haunted him. Ravens had fed him. Seraphs had spoken to him.

Please, he thought. *Please. I've done what you asked.*

In answer, there came a flash of eggshell-blue as a soft hand reached out. Emelota of le Puiset caught the snake by its tail and offered Lukas his staff.

"He's no fraud, my lords," she announced in a clear voice, sending Lukas a slight frown. "But he is terribly stubborn."

Lukas couldn't speak, couldn't move. The smooth, cool wood of his staff seemed slightly mottled, its colours still resembling those of the viper. He almost wanted to cast it from him.

He almost wanted to chastise Emelota for pushing in where she wasn't wanted. It had been *his* opportunity to prove himself a prophet, to overawe the crowd. Instead, his prayer was answered—by the Frankish girl who had taken his place.

"Witch!" Lilith-Bartholomew hissed, losing their temper for the first time. "You're in league with him!"

"Be silent, demon," Emelota said.

Silent, swift, unsummoned, Aemathe appeared beside the Frankish girl in a blaze of light. The crowd still hung back, muttering. Even if they could not see Aemathe, they must be able to sense her presence, sweet and pungent like the smell of lightning.

Unburdening Lukas of her weighty regard, Lilith fixed Bartholomew's gaze on the city's guardian. "Do you think to challenge me? You, a miserable suckling with a few weak drops of divine blood, whom I have already defeated once in battle?"

"In battle, you have the power," Aemathe acknowledged. "But in this city, I have the authority."

Lilith seemed suddenly wary. "Bartholomew is my lawful prey. You cannot take him from me."

"Nor can I permit you to deceive people in *my* city." Aemathe stepped forward, raising a hand. "Sleep now, and for a time forget the judgement that awaits you."

Bartholomew reeled a step backward.

Everyone's eyes were on Emelota and the prophet; no one paid any heed to Lukas and, for an instant, as Lilith's control of the prophet was broken, the Bessarion Lance hung loose in a slack hand.

His visions might have left him, but he could still have the Bessarion Lance. Lukas swooped forward, caught the weapon, felt the surge of power and recognition that flooded him when his fingers tightened upon the shaft.

"Come now, come to me," he panted. The lance came willingly enough, sliding from Bartholomew's slack fingers to his own.

With it came something else.

A great cloud of dust whipped up in the centre of the courtyard—condensed, congealed, and became the form of a gigantic woman wearing a rich tunic of impossible green. She kneeled before him, reaching out brown arms covered in bracelets of rich gold. Aemathe had been invisible to the crowd, of insubstantial form; but this woman had created a body for herself of earth. Everyone could see her.

Lukas dropped the spear with a sob of terror. The crowd shrieked and backed away.

"Child of the Bessarions!" Her voice shook the earth. "Have you come to break my chains?"

Lukas could not answer, only stare. She towered over him like a mother over her child, but held out her hands like a supplicant. He was still gaping when Bartholomew recovered sufficiently to snatch up the Bessarion Lance and shove Lukas aside, brandishing the weapon in the woman's face.

"Depart to whence you came, unholy spirit!"

Lukas had barely begun to recover from the first marvel: now came the second. The great, liquid eyes went dead, the face slack, before the giantess crumbled like a castle of sand. A moment later, there was only a heap of dust where she had knelt. Bartholomew gaped at it, looking as horrified as Lukas himself felt.

"Bartholomew," Lukas gasped, pushing to his feet. He understood nothing, but this he could insist upon. "Give me the lance."

Bartholomew turned on him, looking like a child newly awoken from bad dreams. "Stand back!" he gasped, lowering the lance to Lukas' breastbone.

Lukas raised his hands, palm-outward. "Lilith has you in her grip, Bartholomew. We can free you. Just—give me the lance."

"You lie!" Bartholomew feinted with the weapon; Lukas staggered back a step. "What have you done to me? Heretic! Witch! Devil-worshipper!"

"Witch!" The cry was taken up by a hundred terrified voices. Lukas flinched as a stone flew past him. The princes at the church door watched with gaping mouths, but the crowd surged close, faces distorted with fear and rage. Some already seized stones and clods from the street to fling at him.

Aemathe put herself between Lukas and the crowd, so that their missiles flew wide. Beside him, Emelota caught Lukas' hand. "Barisan!" she called.

"Seize them!" Bartholomew shrieked.

"That's all right, sir," a large, rumbling voice said from behind him. "I'll take charge of them."

Lukas turned with a start to see Barisan leading five other men, all wearing the badge of le Puiset. Before anyone could react, the armed men surrounded them and swept them away.

* * *

It was just as well that the le Puiset lodgings were barely a quarter of a mile

488

away. Within five minutes, Barisan had them up the stairs and inside the dim upper room from which Lukas had abducted the count and his sister on the night of the adventure on Stauron. Bedrolls now bordered all four walls, save for a small partition where Emelota and her maid doubtless slept. Elsewhere, the room was adorned with rugs and tapestries; a large chest at the end of the bedstead stacked high with new, shining weapons. The le Puiset fortunes had evidently risen after the battle, since the count was able to afford men and supplies again.

The room was empty of people, however: Count Evrard himself must be away from home. As they ushered him inside, Lukas shrugged free of his escort and turned to face them, staff ready in one hand.

"What is this? Le Puiset's revenge?"

"Mademoiselle..." Barisan rumbled, turning towards Emelota protectively. The look he shot Lukas was injured, uncomprehending. "Should I..."

Emelota shook her head at him, but her eyes were fixed on Lukas. "Not everything is about vengeance, Lukas Bessarion."

"Then what *is* this about?"

"Consider it the payment of a debt. You were in trouble; I did what I could to help."

Glancing around the empty room, Lukas let out a jagged laugh. "Le Puiset doesn't even know about this, does he? Would he be pleased to see you offering sanctuary to me?"

"Evrard is guarding the wall." She tilted her head, watching him gravely. "A question, if I may?"

"If it's about the giantess, I have no idea."

"Oh, dear, no! I know all about the slave of the lance. I meant—"

"The slave of *what?*"

She pulled herself up. "Oh! It is one of Aemathe's kin, that is all. Only as Aemathe was enslaved in a bronze image, this one is enslaved in a lance. Where else do you imagine it gets its power? You called the spear to you, and the slave obeyed; then Bartholomew seized it back and ordered it away."

Lukas was speechless. *Have you come to break my chains?* The slave of the Lance expected him to free her. To free Aemathe, they had destroyed her vessel, the statue.

The seraph had commanded him to destroy the Bessarion Lance, and now he knew why.

He closed his lips stubbornly. It was still his birthright. Giantess, or demigoddess, or djinn, or weapon—he and his people still needed its protection.

"I meant to ask why you did it," Emelota said in a gentler voice. "It was *preux* to face Bartholomew and his disciples like that."

She was all wide eyes and eager, expectant looks—as though she saw something in him besides the killer and liar who'd been rejected by every pure spirit, from the seraph to Aemathe to Ayla's own memory.

"Why do you care?" he countered. He could not admit the answer to her question, that he had accepted Adhemar's challenge because he thought it might win him the lance. He felt so raw, so furious. Perhaps with her for intervening in the square; or perhaps with Heaven itself, for sending her as his answer.

"Why should I not care for my friends?" She faltered. "We are, are we not? You did so much for me, during the siege."

"Do not make the mistake of believing me to be your friend." Why must he be saddled with this naïve girl? She was a hundred times worse than his sister Marta had been, because Marta at least had always had the sense to know when she was not wanted. Emelota lacked any shyness at all. "A friend is no use to me. You have said it yourself: if you trust in me, I will destroy you."

A certain light went out of her eyes. "I thought you might have done at least some of it out of…oh, I don't know. Stay here tonight. I can protect you. You can leave in the morning if you like, before Evrard comes home."

"Is that what you think I need? Protection?"

"In all fairness, they *were* trying to stone you." She paused, and he thought he might have exasperated her at last. "What would you have of me, then?"

"Not your charity, and certainly not your forgiveness." He hadn't meant to go on, but the thought came to him unbidden. "I've only ever wanted to be respected."

"Respected," she repeated, and now her eyes had kindled to blue fire. "What do you know of respect? You saved my brother's life. You protected me. When you might have remained safely in the city, instead you chose to care for both of us until we could leave the mountain. When you only wanted to flee the city, you walked into the fire to save us. I have never entirely trusted you, Lukas Bessarion, but there was certainly a time when I respected you."

He was not so weary that he did not hear the finality in her voice. "A time that is past, I think."

"I don't know where you went or what you learned there, the night of the fire," she added softly, "but it ought to have changed you and it didn't. It frightens me that the fire made no difference to you. It frightens me that you refused my brother when he begged your forgiveness. It frightens me that even now I can still see you cloaked in fumes and breathing out murder. How can I respect someone like that?"

He didn't know why that hurt him as much as it did.

"If I can't be respected," he said, "I am happy to be feared."

With that he turned and went back out into the street, too dazed to do anything else. It was probably a mercy that the first people he met were a band of Provençal sergeants who closed ranks around him with the friendly observation that the count of Saint-Gilles wanted to see him.

Chapter LII.

Saint-Gilles was in the room he used as a cabinet, alone but for a bottle of strong red Cyprus wine, when his chamberlain knocked to say that Lukas Bessarion had been found.

He waved his assent. Bessarion ventured into the room and Saint-Gilles leaned back in his chair, folding his arms wearily on the massive table. He had no explanation for the vision in the basilica's forecourt, and today of all days he was loath to unravel such portents.

"Bartholomew accuses you of witchcraft," he said without preamble. "Well?"

Bessarion didn't speak at first. With fresh food flowing more freely into the city, the Greek's slight frame was beginning to fill out again, but there was something fey and dangerous in his narrow face and angry eyes.

His throat worked and at length he said, "I cannot explain the vision."

"A vision," Saint-Gilles said flatly. "Seen by how many others?"

"I cannot explain it." Bessarion's anger burned like a banked fire. "But that is beside the point, surely. The point is that Ad—the lord bishop would never have made an offering to the lance, because he never accepted it. Bartholomew is lying for his own benefit."

Adhemar was dead and buried. The last thing he wanted to do right now was to adjudicate a debate over his memory—or his ghost.

Saint-Gilles sighed and took another sip of his wine. If Adhemar truly was appearing to Peter Bartholomew, then surely that was a good thing. His heart ached to know that Adhemar saw in death, if not in life, the sense of what he had done. That he might reach back from beyond the grave to say *I'm sorry, you were right.*

That Saint-Gilles was not now left alone to lead this great pilgrimage.

He *wanted* to believe Bartholomew, but there was one problem: Lukas Bessarion was correct. As far as Saint-Gilles knew, the bishop had died refusing to acknowledge the Holy Lance. But he couldn't start disbelieving Bartholomew—not now. With an inward shudder he thought of the evidence Bohemond had collected, the clean-scraped bones and the impenitent Tafurs; the accusations that Bartholomew had sanctioned a terrible crime.

No. He could not begin to doubt—not now.

"Perhaps the lord bishop saw the error of his ways, but was embarrassed to say so in public."

"But you knew him, my lord!"

The note of desperation in Bessarion's voice hinted at a depth of feeling that surprised Saint-Gilles—as though the boy cared for the bishop more deeply than his nearest friend did. Saint-Gilles set the glass on the table top with an irritated *clack* and went on the offensive:

"You say this lance is not the Holy Lance."

"I told you it belongs to my family."

"How can you know that for sure? It must have been buried in the basilica for generations, by an earthquake that happened hundreds of years ago."

The Syrian pressed his mouth shut. Saint-Gilles shrugged. "No answer?"

"You can't trust Bartholomew." Bessarion tried another line of approach. "He's preaching vengeance, not liberation. Didn't you hear him say to round up the Turks? For what? Slaughter? I'm not saying he doesn't have visions. I'm saying he's become a mouthpiece not for saints, but for demons."

Saint-Gilles pursed his lips, took a sip of wine. Hope flickered in Bessarion's eyes.

Saint-Gilles thought of the other thing Bartholomew had advised: that he should hand over Antioch to Bohemond, and lead the pilgrimage to Jerusalem.

Bohemond had smirked at that. Was Bartholomew in Bohemond's pay, or only playing into his hands?

Slowly, Saint-Gilles lowered his cup. "Are you offering to replace him?"

Bessarion's eyes widened.

He sat forward. "Like it or not, Bartholomew—and the Holy Lance—have become desperately important to the success of this campaign. I need a prophet. Are you able to act in that capacity? Because I didn't notice *you* turning any staves into snakes."

Bessarion's throat worked. "I'm not like Bartholomew. I can't tell these people what they want to hear, or do flashy marvels to impress them."

Saint-Gilles snorted. "I didn't think so." Another drink, pouring the rest of the wine down his throat. Perhaps it was a waste.

Perhaps he needed the fortification in order to say what he knew he had to say. Bessarion's prophecy before the battle had been correct, after all. Galdemar wasn't the only one who'd verified his message: a group of Frankish pilgrims newly on their way from the west had refused to turn back when the emperor did. They had arrived in Antioch mere days ago, confirming that Alexius had fled back to Constantinople, burning Anatolia in his wake.

The boy's record was impeccable. And against Bartholomew he had Bohemond's accusations of cannibalism; Adhemar's firm resistance during his lifetime; and those three damned silver pennies after.

His fist clenched on the empty glass. Say the worst *was* true. Say Bartholomew *was* the mouthpiece of demons. Could Saint-Gilles afford to do without him? Now that the Greek alliance was in ruins, now that Bohemond had seized Antioch and the emperor had abandoned them, how could he command this pilgrimage if he didn't have *power?*

The die was cast. Even if he was making a devil's bargain. He pinned the boy with a forbidding glare.

"Very well, Bessarion. Hear this, because I will only say it once: I will not have anyone question the lance, or Bartholomew. Not you. Not anyone."

A look of disgust came into the boy's eyes. "And Bishop Adhemar? You'll stand by while his name is bandied in support of things he would have opposed in life, and you expect me to keep silent? Which of us was his true friend?"

That shouldn't have cut as deep as it did. "You are entitled to voice your opinions, so long as you do not do so within the walls of Antioch," Saint-Gilles said stiffly.

"You aren't the lord of Antioch."

Saint-Gilles managed a laugh at that. He picked up a small pouch of gold that had rested on his desk since a visit from a Genoese embassy this morning, weighed it thoughtfully in his hand, and decided to be generous.

"You came from these parts, didn't you? You must have some people somewhere. Go and find them." He tossed the pouch to the youth.

Bessarion sidestepped, letting it fall to the ground. A muscle jerked in his jaw.

"Go on, boy: take it. You've served me faithfully, and you'll need it on your journey."

"I'm not taking a journey."

"I advise it."

"What if I choose not to take that advice? Will you send someone after me with a throwing-axe? What would the bishop say to that?"

"Don't be a fool." Saint-Gilles struck the tabletop with a fist, making the glass jump. "It's for Adhemar's sake I'm giving you this chance at all. Bartholomew knows you're his rival. He has the whole pilgrimage in the palm of his hand. Do you really want to be ripped to pieces in the street one morning, as they nearly did today? Take the money. Leave."

Bessarion met his gaze mutinously, as though he meant to force Saint-Gilles into changing his mind by sheer force of will. Saint-Gilles felt a prickle of unwilling respect for the boy: he didn't know many men who would meet such a gaze so unflinchingly.

But then the Greek shrugged, bent down, and picked up the purse. "I will use it," he said bitterly, "to comfort the orphans Bartholomew will make."

Chapter LIII.

Lukas closed the cabinet door behind him and stood in the loggia of the palace, weary and boneless. The count's purse weighed in his hand like a burden. When was the last time he'd held so much money? Could it really be less than two years?

Another world, another life, now immeasurably distant.

He looked up at the sky, noting that it was afternoon and the sun was slipping towards the horizon. That woke him a little. He didn't want to be under the count's roof tonight. Moving like an automaton, he went downstairs, begged some food in the kitchen and then strapped his bedroll shut around his belongings. Donning the Turkish armour he'd won on Silpius the night of the meteor, he slung the swag across his shoulders and took his staff in hand.

There was no one to say goodbye to, no one who might notice his absence or worry for his safety. He paused for a moment on an image of Emelota, then pushed it aside. She no longer thought well of him, she'd said it herself.

He ventured through the palace gates and stood in the Colonnaded Street, uncertain where he would go. At least he had armour, and money enough for the purchase of a horse and a sword.

The day was warm, overcast, almost suffocating. When a passer-by glanced at him in curiosity, he turned away to conceal his face. He could not linger here forever…

All this trouble, and in the end it had come to this: he was leaving Antioch friendless and alone, with no Bessarion Lance and no protector.

Worst of all, in that moment, was the knowledge that he could do nothing for Adhemar. His heart wrung. First Ayla, then the bishop—he could well believe that it delighted Lilith to desecrate the memories of the dead in support of things they would have been adamantly opposed to in life.

No matter what Lilith tries, there's a part of you that will always remember me rightly. Ayla's words should have been comforting, but a small voice in the back of his mind that was neither she nor Lilith was telling him what to do next, and he could well imagine what she would say to the idea.

He had listened to Adhemar and done as the bishop asked. He'd asked for only one thing in return: the Bessarion Lance, his birthright. His request had been denied.

That left only one option—but it was the last thing in the world he'd ever wanted to do.

Lukas was still deliberating when a hand fastened on his shoulder. He turned with a growl, bringing his staff up on guard. But his assailant was too close, and his wrist smacked into a calloused palm, halting his strike.

"Bessarion," Zarides said, low and urgent. "What are they saying in the streets? You summoned another spirit? What does it mean?"

Lukas stared at the older man. A cicada was chattering in a garden nearby, pitched loud and uncomfortably high. Lukas felt strung tight, his teeth on edge. "What if I did? It doesn't matter to you. I'm only a weakling, remember?"

He turned away, but Zarides moved to get in front of him. "Listen, Bessarion, I spoke in haste. We need you. You're a Messenger. You're a Bessarion. You have the bloodline, the gifts. Toros and his women have the Franks' protection and the loyalty of the people. We can't fight that." A pause. "Please."

The thoughts in his mind churned, slowly, inexorably. The cicada was high-pitched, an alarm-bell. "Don't forget they have Aemathe," he told them. "We can't fight her, either." He turned down the Colonnaded Street.

Zarides ran after him. "So what are you going to do? Leave Antioch altogether?"

"Naturally."

"Take us with you." Zarides pulled him to a stop. "We have horses. Armour. Money. You have…"

"A djinn," Lukas said softly. "This one, under my control."

A deep breath from Zarides. A smile. "I knew it."

But only if he had the Bessarion Lance. He took a deep breath, making his decision.

"Good. Buy whatever else you need to go on campaign. I must leave Antioch tonight on…a matter of private business. I'm going…" His mind worked busily. He might strike south to Jerusalem at once if he was alone, but if he would be bringing an armed troop with him, the risk was too great. He would be striking into enemy-held territory with just enough followers to be a threat, and few enough to invite attack. It made better sense to wait and travel with the Franks.

But which Frank? Count Raymond led the Provençals; le Puiset was with the Normans. That left the Lotharingians. The longer he thought of it, the better he liked the idea. Duke Godfrey had listened to him on Silpius; during the siege, rumour had it he had killed his own horse to feed his household. Count Raymond spoke of the duke with friendly scorn, believing him to be a soft fool, but Lukas had had his fill of hard men.

"I'm going to join Duke Godfrey in Ravenden." Ravenden was the name of the town that the duke's brother, who had taken Edessa, had given him in the Syrian highlands. "He'll be glad of the extra men, I'm sure. We can be spears for hire until we've amassed enough plunder and new followers to strike out on our own. What do you say?"

Zarides' face was full of excitement, but he stepped backwards and fell to one knee in an attitude of genuflection. "Forgive me for doubting you. From now on, Lukas Bessarion, you are our Presbyter."

Our Presbyter. The word was intoxicating. His father, too, had been a Presbyter. Lukas reached down, clasping arms with the Watcher. "Say no more of it, but meet me at Ravenden."

Zarides departed. Lukas drew a deep breath, hoping he wasn't about to make a terrible mistake. First, he would search the marketplaces for a good horse.

Then—it was time to claim his birthright, once and for all.

* * *

It was all so easy.

As night fell he walked in at the palace gates, half expecting to be challenged, but the guards didn't give him a second glance. Count Raymond, having sent him away, had evidently not imagined he would be back. Lukas went directly to the chapel, where a light was burning and Bartholomew kneeled, keeping vigil before the altar.

Hearing him enter, the prophet jumped to his feet, his face ugly with rage. "You," he hissed, but Lukas waved an imperious hand.

"I don't want you. I want the Poison Mother. Wake, Lilith. I have come to bargain."

Bartholomew's eyes widened in a flash of panic—then crinkled into cold laughter as Lilith slid smoothly back into control.

"Tell me your wishes," she crooned to him. "I'll make them all come true."

"Thanks, but I only want my father's lance."

"You know the terms."

Lukas took a deep breath. Perhaps it would always have come to this, in the end. "Swear to me you will leave me in peaceful possession of the lance, and I swear to you I will release Khalil ibn Hassan from his long imprisonment."

Her smile was triumphant, unbearable. "So I do solemnly swear." With a mocking bow, she stood aside, motioning him to the Bessarion Lance.

He reached out towards the smooth, oiled haft. Before his fingers touched it, he stopped with the sweat beading on his forehead. That woman in green—huge, terrifying, alien—surely—

Lilith rolled Bartholomew's eyes. "You have to summon her, simpleton."

Swallowing, he reached out and took his father's spear.

It fit into his hand, smooth and deadly, the most beautiful thing ever made for war, with its blade of rippling steel, its well-oiled haft, its iron-shod foot. Ageless, unaffected by the passing of the centuries, its strength and vitality flowed into him with a rush of power. Now that he knew the source of that power, he found himself trembling as he lifted it down and turned to face Lilith-Bartholomew.

For a moment the blade of the spear wavered in Lukas' hand. His agreement with Lilith had not covered Bartholomew. Perhaps he ought to destroy the mad prophet before he led the Franks to some terrible deed of blood.

Lilith must have read the temptation in his eyes, because Bartholomew made a motion like the aiming and releasing of a bow. Lukas cried out as a shaft of pain pierced his body. As he staggered, Lilith-Bartholomew's hand fastened on his jaw, forcing him to meet their eyes.

"It would be very foolish of you to make further trouble for me, mortal."

"What—what did you do to me?"

"Nothing you need to worry about if you obey me. Now go. Do as you have promised."

They released him and swept through the iconostasis doors, producing an item from the shadows: the decoy lance with which Lukas had replaced the Bessarion Lance the first time he had taken the weapon. Lukas did not stay to watch them settle it into the hooks by which it was displayed above the altar. Determined not to rue his bargain, he fought the lingering pain in his chest and went out again, through the side door and into the night.

** * **

By now the city's gates were locked, but even this gave Lukas no trouble: he had a pass to leave the city, sealed by Count Raymond that afternoon lest he be harassed on his way out. Within minutes, he had ridden out by the north gate, taking the road leading into the Syrian highlands towards Ravenden and his rendezvous with Zarides.

A bowshot from the gate he paused, noticing a light that flickered uphill to the right, at the top of a dark, squat shape.

The tower of Malregard.

So much had happened in the few short weeks since he had last passed through the shadow of the tower. Since the battle, the Franks had secured the tower again, staffing it with a small garrison to watch the northern hills. With so much of the Syrian hinterlands still in the hands of the Turks, the Franks would undoubtedly be keeping a watch on the road for any unexpected travellers. Making sure his pass was within easy reach, Lukas kneed his horse to a walk again.

It was with a dull sense of inevitability that, a moment later, he heard hoofbeats echoing from the direction of the tower, and looked up to see bobbing torches streaming forth to meet him. They moved fast, cutting ahead of him and swarming onto the road to block his path.

At their head sat Evrard of le Puiset, holding a crossbow. Lukas' heart turned to ice, remembering what happened last time he and Count Evrard met on the road outside a city at night. He had never believed that le Puiset had really changed. With the battle over and the danger past, why should the count fear for his soul?

Why should tonight end any differently than it had the last time?

One thing, at least, was different: tonight, he had the lance. Tonight, he had no reason to fear.

"Who goes there?" le Puiset challenged.

Lukas didn't answer, instead urging his horse to a walk. When the shadows thinned enough for le Puiset to recognise him, the count's face darkened in wary surprise. Lowering his crossbow and making a gesture to his followers to remain behind, he trotted towards Lukas.

"Keep your distance," Lukas growled, lowering the lance as the Frank approached. Le Puiset reined in.

"Easy, Bessarion," he said in a voice too low to carry to the onlookers behind. "Just state your business and be on your..."

His voice faded; Lukas saw the moment at which le Puiset realised what he was seeing. *Strife.*

"Where are you going with the Holy Lance?" le Puiset asked in a dangerously conversational tone. "What is this, the second time you've taken it?"

For an awful moment, Lukas felt paralysed. For so long le Puiset had tried to catch him in wrongdoing, determined to condemn him as a malefactor—and now he'd played right into his enemy's hands.

No fear, he told himself. No shame. It was time to take his vengeance. Lukas straightened in the saddle, the blood humming in his veins.

"I came to challenge you."

Le Puiset's eyebrows climbed. "To battle?"

"You said you were sorry for what you did to Ayla. Did you mean it? Fight me now, like a knight and an equal, and prove that you did."

The torch shed flickering shadows across the look of utter shock on le Puiset's face. "I'm not going to fight you," he said at last, softly.

"Because you think I'm a peasant?"

"Because I have no quarrel with you." His face, once so gaunt and skeletal, had filled out again with good food and rest. "Go your way in peace."

No—no, it mustn't end like this.

"What are you? A coward?"

Barely two months ago, le Puiset would have risen to the bait. Tonight, he shrugged. "Fighting you would be a poor penance for the evil I've already done. I won't repeat my sins."

Lukas ground his teeth. How long had he waited for this moment? And now that it had finally come, le Puiset meant to refuse him—meant to take the high ground? For a moment he could barely speak.

"Are you going to sit there while I spit you?"

"If you meant to do that, you'd have done it already." After a moment, le Puiset lifted the crossbow from where it rested against his thigh.

Bessarion Lance or no, there was nothing Lukas could have done to defend himself. As le Puiset lifted the crossbow, he sat paralysed by memory.

Torches. Drunken laughter. Jeering voices.

She has a sling!

A sound like an egg cracking. The light fading from Ayla's eyes.

The trigger clicked. Lukas jolted with a tiny sound of distress, but the bolt never touched him: he dragged himself back to the present to find that Le Puiset had discharged the bow into the road. The count's horse shifted nervously, stung by a ricocheting pebble.

"I'm not fighting you," le Puiset said with finality. "Go where you like, Bessarion, and take the Holy Lance, since it has chosen to accompany you. I won't stop you. Come on," he called to his men, raising his voice. "This is only Saint-Gilles' interpreter." Laying the rein across his horse's mane, he headed back up the path towards Malregard.

The path was dark again, and Lukas was left shaking in his saddle, half terrified, half furious. With each passing moment, his fury increased until there was no more terror left. At Nicaea he had been too mean to fight such a one as Count Evrard, and now at Antioch, Count Evrard was too great a man to concern himself with such a battle. Either way the outcome was the same, but the sense of inferiority was worse somehow. At Nicaea he had comforted himself that he was the better man. Now all he felt was his meanness.

Chapter LIV.

There was a moment when Lukas tried to run from his fate.

It happened on the high plateau, when he reached the crossroads where the Antioch-Aleppo road was bisected north to south by the road leading south to Oliveta. He'd been travelling most of the night, stopping only briefly for a few hours' sleep before dawn. Now the morning glared hot and angry upon his surroundings: red earth, stunted olive-bushes, tufted grass scorched white by the summer, and far off, a distant cluster of adobe dwellings. It all struck him with a painful sense of familiarity: August in the Syrian highlands, the sky a bright bowl of pitiless blue, just as it had been all those centuries ago when he first travelled this road with his family.

Memories flooded back to him: the burning of Oliveta, the slaughter of its inhabitants, the chant by which Khalil had summoned Lilith and bound himself to her. Suddenly, Lukas wanted to retch. What had he done, entering into his own bargain with Lilith? Agreeing to loose Khalil once more upon the world? Was he mad?

Lilith couldn't *make* him do it, could she? Hadn't Aemathe trapped her in Antioch within the confines of Bartholomew's body? He should be turning right towards Oliveta, but instead he turned left up the road leading to the monastery of Saint Simeon and beyond towards Ravendel.

That pain burned through his chest, the same he had felt the previous night as he hesitated over killing Bartholomew. At the same moment, Lilith appeared in the air before him, her feet hovering several feet from the ground.

"Please," she told him, lowering her bow. "Try again. I love it when my pets try to disobey me."

"I don't belong to you," Lukas gasped.

"There you are mistaken," she said with a smile as hard as diamonds. "You handed yourself over to me when you made this bargain."

Bartholomew is my lawful prey, she had told Aemathe. Lukas shivered. Now he, too, was Lilith's property and subject to her commands. How often had he told himself he had no choices? Now, perhaps for the first time, it was true.

He reached Oliveta late that afternoon, sweating in hot armour beneath the pitiless sun. In the sky were some far-off signs of life, like an eagle drifting lazily to the east, but in the Dead City itself, Lukas saw not so much as the quick liquid flicker of a lizard or snake.

Dead trees punctuated the landscape. Deep-graved labyrinth patterns wrinkled the brows of old friezes: lions snarled from the cornices of villas. The crumbling walls and arches on either hand seemed somewhat like dead trees themselves: stripped of all perishable trappings, they stood revealed in their fundamental structures, a skeleton city.

At the centre of the village forum was a well with a crushed and mangled parapet. There was no tripod or bucket over it, but Lukas used a length of cord from his pack to lower his canteen to the dark, shimmering surface below. When the container was full he drank, then refilled it. His horse lipped sadly at the wet spots that fell on the stones before vanishing. Lukas sighed, wishing he could promise the beast a drink on the way north, when they reached neighbouring Bara.

But he didn't know if it was a promise he could keep. He was about to free Khalil, the enemy he most feared. What would happen after? He didn't know.

Instead he pulled off the saddle and its blanket and left his mount in a patch of shade behind a west-facing wall. Fastening the dripping canteen to his belt, he approached the basilica courtyard.

Khalil sat exactly where he had nearly a year ago, cross-legged at the centre of the tessellated pavement. Wrapped in the rags of a black robe, his head was bowed in silent misery over his linked hands—so still that Lukas paused in the arch of the corridor, wondering if the sorcerer was asleep…or dead.

When Khalil didn't move, Lukas slung the Bessarion Lance across his shoulders and stepped warily into the courtyard. At his footfall, Khalil jerked upright. He looked dreadful, the skin of his face reddened and blistered by the sun, his hair and beard untrimmed and wild.

"No," he rasped hoarsely. "Not you!"

"I haven't come to kill you," Lukas snarled, yanking his canteen from his belt. Now that he was actually here, he wanted this over and done with. "I came to keep my word."

"I release you!" Khalil's voice was like the scrape of steel and stone. "I forgive your oath! Go and leave me!"

Lukas stilled, blank with surprise. On his previous visit, Khalil had begged to be free. "You're raving," he said at last. "You can't really mean to—"

"For God's sake, stop telling me what I mean and hear me." Khalil ran a tongue over his cracked, bleeding lips: his eyes flickered nervously around the courtyard, as though fearful of being overheard. "You don't know what she means to do. The Poison Mother…She means to desecrate Jerusalem. Fill it with blood. And that's only the beginning."

"How will she…" The words died away on his lips as he realised how. Lilith had control of Bartholomew, and in that way she had control of the entire Frankish pilgrimage. Hardened warriors, accustomed to death.

It wasn't just the heat of the sun making him feel dizzy. She could do it, he realised. She'd already profited from the bloodshed in Antioch. What could she do at Jerusalem?

"Jerusalem is holy to us also, you know," Khalil whispered. "It's worse than that, though. She means to corrupt all humanity. Breed a race of wicked djinn, as she did in the days of Noah. Please. I don't want to—"

"You talk too much, Half-Stone." Lilith appeared beside them with silent abruptness. "Do you think I won't hear you, just because the sun is high and I must conserve my strength?"

Khalil's lips closed, and he turned his face away from his mistress. Lukas clasped a hand over his jumping heart. Although the day was hot, he shivered like a man with the ague. Khalil's ravings were only madness, he told himself. How could Lilith breed more demigods? If she had the power to take on flesh, she would have done so already.

"Do it, mortal," Lilith ordered him. "Pour it down his throat if you must."

She looked eager, feverish. Lukas' mouth was suddenly dry. "Why *do* you want this man freed? What is he saying, about corrupting—"

That lightning-bolt of pain flashed through him again, leaving him crumpled on the pavement, sobbing with pain.

"Don't be so squeamish," she told him contemptuously, and he was too beaten to object.

With a heaving breath he got to his feet, uncorked the canteen and offered it to Khalil. The sorcerer must have smelled the water, for his face screwed up and he let out a sob.

Then his resolve shattered and he grabbed for the container, pouring the water down his throat with small, desperate sounds, as though he had become more animal than man. Lukas watched, fascinated, as Khalil lowered the vessel at last, his shoulders heaving as he gasped for breath.

He moved a leg. It slipped out from between his robes, a smooth ankle encased in new, supple leather. Khalil stared down at the limb, touching it in wonder.

"Enough," Lilith said in a bored voice. "Kill the Greek, Half-Stone. *Now.*"

With the final word, her voice became a snarl. Khalil responded as though he'd been pricked with a blade, coming off the ground with a grunt of pain. He collided with Lukas, snatching for his throat, and Lukas went down on the cracked pavement with a huff of pain as the wind was knocked out of him.

Somewhere far away, dimly heard through the rushing in his ears, Lilith was laughing.

Lukas couldn't move, couldn't speak. The Bessarion Lance was trapped beneath his shoulders, unreachable. He ought to have seen this coming. Lilith had only protected him so long because she needed him to free

Khalil, and now that was done, he was to be disposed of.

As Khalil's right hand fastened around his throat, his left found the dagger Lukas wore at his belt and tore it from the sheath. The point found the tender skin below his jaw, cold and ticklish. For the second time in the space of a day, Lukas steeled himself for death.

Khalil did not strike.

"Do it, Half-Stone!" Lilith hissed. Khalil glanced up at her.

"You do not command me," he said in a low, taut voice. "Not yet. Not ever."

"What did you just say to me?"

It was now or never, while Khalil was distracted by the infuriated Lilith. Lukas bucked and the sorcerer's body, sustained only by magic, toppled like a bundle of sticks and bones. Rolling away, Lukas climbed to his feet, unslinging the Bessarion Lance from his shoulders.

"Pay attention when I speak to you, mortal!"

Khalil pushed himself to his knees, breathing hard, but he had no attention for Lilith. Instead, his eyes widened as he recognised the weapon Lukas held on guard, the lance for which he had slaughtered Oliveta.

"You have it," he choked. "My lance!"

Lukas moved forward, jabbing with the blade.

"Give me one reason not to kill you," he snarled.

Khalil shook his head. "Not even *she* can kill me, boy. Not while I'm bound to the Poison Mother." Another pause. "There are bigger things to worry about than our vengeance, Bessarion. Tell me: are you with the Franks, or against them?"

"I'm against them." Lukas spat. "What does it matter to you?"

"Good," the sorcerer said briskly. "If you will oppose the Franks, if you will prevent them from destroying my people, I will let you live. I'll even allow you the lance. Just so long as you leave me to deal with *her*." He nodded towards Lilith. "Perhaps the Poison Mother will allow me to escape while she toys with you."

"I'll drink your blood first!" Lilith's voice had risen to a vicious scream.

Lukas could think of nothing to say: he was utterly speechless. Knife in hand, Khalil turned to scan the courtyard. He seemed to find what he sought in a dead tree, blackened with soot, that peered over the courtyard wall. He snapped off a branch and took the knife to it—*scrape, scrape*—removing the scorched shell to reveal the silvery old fibres beneath. He looked up at Lukas, giving a smile that spread drops of blood down his chin as his dried lips cracked.

"I suggest you do something similar," he told Lukas. "It's your only hope of escaping her."

With that, he circled towards the courtyard arch. Lukas found his hands shaking on the haft of the lance. Perhaps he ought to stop the sorcerer—the murderer of Oliveta—from escaping. Instead he called, "Wait! What did you mean—the corruption of humanity?"

Khalil paid him no more attention than he had paid Lilith: Lukas could still hear the *scrape, scrape* of his knife.

"Wait," he began again, but Lilith was beside him, her face disfigured with fury.

"Where is he?" she screeched. "Where did he go?" She glared around her as though struck blind. "Speak, mortal!"

"I..." Lukas shook himself, started after the retreating sorcerer.

"Answer me!" Lilith screamed. Her bow twanged: that invisible dart pierced him through. Lukas fell to his hands and knees with a groan, darkness floating before her eyes.

From beyond the courtyard came the sound of hoofbeats.

"Devil take it!" he gasped, forcing himself to his feet, staggering to the courtyard entrance. He was too late. Khalil was on Lukas' horse, already dwindling into the distance. At a sound behind him, Lukas turned, steeling himself for another of Lilith's arrows—but the courtyard was empty, the harpy gone, the only sound the sighing of the wind.

Lukas sagged against the stone archway, sobbing for breath. *Escape.* Khalil had a way to escape Lilith? Khalil meant to stop her destroying Jerusalem—and more?

It ought to have been a comforting thought, but it was not. The grim truth was that Khalil might be able to escape, but he could not.

He'd fallen deeper into Lilith's power than even the sorcerer had.

Lukas stood there a little longer, alone and aching. At length, moving painfully, he took the north road towards Ravendel, where Zarides was waiting for him with horses and Watchers. The hot breath of the southern wind beat against his neck as he moved through the dead city; once he looked back, half fearing, half hoping to see the fiery seraph.

It wasn't there—not unless the heat-shimmer of the summer air meant something.

Turning, Lukas continued on his journey. A black vulture wheeled in the sky above him, watching, waiting.

S.D.G.

Lukas Bessarion will return in **A Covenant of Salt**

Watch out for the next Watchers of Outremer book
The House of Mourning

Historical Note

One of my goals in the *Watchers of Outremer* series is to draw on the best academic research to bring the medieval crusader states to memorably fictionalised life. Therefore, I have tried to remain as faithful to the history as possible, simply embroidering my tale in the margins. When I look back on the events that occurred in Antioch in the summer of 1098, however, there seems relatively little embroidery needed. The history itself is a grand drama, and the second siege of Antioch in June of that year may be the most well-documented event in medieval history.

A number of the people in this story are fictional: Lukas Bessarion, Emelota of le Puiset, Leo Zarides and the Watchers, Lusine and her siblings, Ayla and her family, Khalil ibn Hassan and Lilith. For the historical characters—Saint-Gilles, Bohemond, Adhemar, le Puiset, Barisan, Bartholomew, and others—I have copied and extrapolated from the history, and sometimes invented personalities and histories out of whole cloth.

The events themselves unfolded more or less as I have depicted them, though I have done quite a bit of embellishment. For instance, I have only a few hints in William of Tyre's history, written decades after the siege, to evidence fighting or unrest in the city of Antioch itself during the battle on Silpius from 10-13 June. Similarly, the fire kindled by Bohemond on the night of 12 June is not recorded as having destroyed a granary, though it is true that the portion of the city most affected was the part occupied by the Provençals.

Peter Bartholomew is an enigma by any measure. As a charismatic figure attracting religious enthusiasm, Bartholomew performed a role that was fairly well known to medieval society around the turn of the first millennium. Older scholars thought him a clever charlatan. His visions and speeches certainly served a specific agenda, to the point that John Hill and Lauritia Hill have suggested they were fabricated by Saint-Gilles' chaplain and chronicler, Raymond of Aguilers. However, these days most modern scholars agree that Bartholomew likely believed in his own visions. If he acted as the mouthpiece for any particular temporal interest, it was that of the *vulgus,* the poor commoners who formed the backbone of the crusade. Although Bartholomew would soundly discredit himself before the crusade was over, for several heady months he acted as a focal point around which elements of the poor were able to coalesce to make their voices heard and their wishes known to the powerful. Himself impoverished, Bartholomew always advocated that a large share of plunder should go to the poor, and the religious observances he commanded were always of a type that even the destitute could participate in.

Crusading could be brutally difficult for the poor, some of whom turned to desperate measures to survive. It is a matter of historical fact that at the siege of Marrat an-Numan in early 1099, the crusade was rocked by scandal when some of the poor resorted to cannibalising the bodies of dead Turks. Historical rumour attributes this as a regular practice of the "Tafurs", a poorly-documented extremist group among the larger body of the poor, whom Lewis Sumberg has conjectured may have been impoverished Flemish knights. The fictionalised *Chanson D'Antioche,* written around 1180, depicts the Tafurs resorting to cannibalism during the siege of Antioch in the winter of 1097-1098—on this occasion sanctioned by Peter the Hermit, another popular demagogue on the crusade. It was this rumour that I repurposed for this story, taking the dramatic liberty of linking the Tafurs with Peter Bartholomew during the summer of 1098.

The dispute between Raymond of Saint-Gilles, Count of Toulouse and Bohemond of Taranto over the rulership of Antioch, may not have begun as early or developed to the point that I depicted it in this story. The Hills, for instance, argue that Saint-Gilles and Bohemond acted in successful cooperation throughout both sieges, and that their rivalry over Antioch did not heat up until after the Great Battle. According to them, the rift only formed when news arrived that, upon hearing of the crusaders' predicament, Alexius had packed up his army and rushed home to Constantinople, burning Anatolia behind him. On the other hand, Jonathan Shepard convincingly argues that Bohemond tipped his hand on 25 May, when he proposed that the rulership of Antioch should be ceded to the man who should bring off its capture. Such a request was utterly at odds with his oath to Alexius, especially if that oath (as Shepard argues in a very fine bit of historical deduction) was actually one of liege homage, which ought to have superseded any other loyalties owed by the slippery South Norman.

I have adopted Shepard's account of events, imagining the dispute to heat up around late May and escalating from there through a largely fictionalised progression. There are conflicting accounts of the surrender of the citadel. The Provençal chronicler Raymond of Aguilers says that the citadel was in fact surrendered to a joint garrison, which Bohemond forcibly ejected shortly after the battle under the pretext that he had promised the Turkish commander, ibn Marwan, that he would hold it himself. This account is a little difficult to believe, since on Aguilers' own showing ibn Marwan *had* surrendered to the joint garrison. The anonymous author of the *Gesta Francorum,* however, says that ibn Marwan had been about to surrender to Saint-Gilles, only to change his mind and surrender to Bohemond instead. I have taken the liberty of picking and choosing from both accounts as best fit the purposes of the story.

Count Evrard of le Puiset, his sister Humberga, and his brother-in-law Galon of Beaumont are all real people with whom I have taken significant creative liberties. Having left his infant son in the care of his younger brother, Hugh of le Puiset, Evrard joined the crusade in the following of Stephen of Blois together with a large number of family members. Various sorts of attrition—including the death of Galon during an abortive embassy into Antioch on 20 May and the desertion of Guy Trousseau of Montlhery on the night of 10 June—would have left Evrard more isolated.

At some point, probably after his feudal lord Blois deserted the crusade on 2 June, le Puiset entered the service of Bohemond and is mentioned as wounded in Bohemond's tower during the intense fighting atop Silpius from 10–13 June. He is next mentioned leading a division of the Frankish army during the Great Battle. There is no firm evidence that the humble knight Barisan, the progenitor of the powerful Ibelin family, was in fact one of le Puiset's knights, but historians consider it likely—it has even been suggested that he may have been le Puiset's illegitimate half-brother.

Adhemar Monteil, bishop of le Puy and papal legate, has long struck me as being one of the few genuinely sympathetic figures of the First Crusade. While historians argue over whether he was the diplomatic glue holding the crusade together, or simply a revered mediocrity who would have been unable to deal with the crusaders' subsequent wrangling had he lived, certain facts remain clear. Adhemar, unlike many of the secular knights on the pilgrimage, understood the mission of the crusade to be liberation rather than vengeance. Tasked with repairing strained relations between the western church based in Rome, and the eastern churches based in Constantinople, Antioch, and Jerusalem, Adhemar interacted with local ecclesiastics in a spirit of remarkable humility. His policy of confirming local ecclesiastics in their positions of authority was abandoned abruptly after his death. From then on, the Franks would install bishops of their own rite to rule over the local populations. Adhemar's attitude towards the various Islamic peoples of the east is less well attested, and it's more than possible he may have shared the prejudices of his fellow Franks. I've chosen to hope that his focus on liberation, rather than the knightly motivation of vengeance, enabled him to adopt a more gracious attitude towards them.

Throughout the gruelling winter of 1097-1098, Adhemar took a keen interest in the welfare of the poor, but he never joined them in their faith in Peter Bartholomew and the Holy Lance. Agreeing to allow Raymond of Aguilers to carry the relic into battle with his troops was a significant concession to popular enthusiasm. Bartholomew claimed that Adhemar had even made a small donation to the Lance: this may very well have been the truth, but certainly didn't warrant the prophet's subsequent claims that Adhemar had visited him in a vision to repent of his scepticism.

As always, I would like to return a word of thanks to the wonderful beta readers who gave of their time and insight to make this book what it is: Christina Baehr, David Noor, Lucy Holdsworth, M.L. Farb, Stella Dorthwany, and Leila Ammar. Thanks are due also to my cover designer, Jenny Zemanek and to my editor, Shelby Judge. I couldn't have done this without any of you.

Suzannah Rowntree
December 2021

Further Reading

This is the second book I have written set in the 1090s, and there were a number of books I revisited in their entirety: Thomas Asbridge's *The First Crusade: A New History*, a very accessible work for the lay reader; Jonathan Riley-Smith's *The First Crusade and the Idea of Crusading*, which fleshed out the conflicting motivations of liberation and vengeance on the First Crusade; John France's *Victory in the East: A Military History of the First Crusade*, which meticulously details the fighting of June 1098 and the terrain on which it took place; and Malcolm Barber's *The Crusader States*, which fills in the aftermath to the campaign. Meanwhile, Jonathan Shepard's article *When Greek Meets Greek: Alexius Comnenus and Bohemond in 1097-1098* is a stunning work of historical deduction and laid the foundations for my understanding of the personalities and relationships at play: not just Bohemond and the emperor, but also Saint-Gilles and Tatikius.

I also added a few new studies to my library. Tom Holland's *Millennium* is a wonderful popular history of the turn of the first millennium, vital in understanding the social and religious context in which the First Crusade took place, especially regarding the rise of the feudal system and popular religious enthusiasm. John Hill and Lauritia Hill's *Raymond IV Count of Toulouse*, while somewhat partisan, gave me new insights into Saint-Gilles' character and history. It is unfortunate that the most comprehensive available history of Antioch is E.S. Bouchier's 1921 study *A Short History of Antioch, 300 B.C.—A.D. 1268*, since it interpolates its fascinating historical details (like street lights, running water, and the human sacrifice of one Aemathe to act as the city's Fortuna) with truly startling amounts of racism and anti-Semitism.

Among the articles I consulted for this book are included: Randall Rogers' *Peter Bartholomew and the Role of "The Poor" in the First Crusade*, Lewis A Sumberg's *The "Tafurs" and the First Crusade,* and James A Brundage's *Adhemar of Puy: The Bishop and His Critics.*

I continue to return to several foundational books for help understanding the crusader states in general: *Medicine in the Crusades* by Piers Mitchell; *The Atlas of the Crusades* edited by Jonathan Riley-Smith; *The Crusades and the Christian World of the East: Rough Tolerance* by Christopher MacEvitt; *Western Warfare in the Age of the Crusades* by John France; and Carl Stephenson's *Medieval Feudalism.* As always, van der Toorn, Becking, and van der Horst's *Dictionary of Deities and Demons in the Bible* provided helpful inspiration for writing Lilith, the seraph, and other fantastical elements. I'll also mention *The Body Keeps the Score: Mind, Brain and Body in the Transformation of Trauma* by Bessel van der Kolk, which I hope has assisted me in depicting the aftermath of trauma.

I continue to refer to the medieval chroniclers themselves, who produced what remains some of the most readable and vivid crusader literature available. Christopher Tyerman's Penguin Classics compilation of *Chronicles of the First Crusade* was my constant companion, including selections from the *Gesta Francorum* and the chronicles of Fulcher of Chartres and Raymond of Aguilers, with some excerpts from Muslim and Jewish sources. William of Tyre's *History of Deeds Done Beyond the Sea* was also helpful as it provides a synthesis of earlier accounts, and Malcolm Barber's compilation of *Letters from the East* includes many missives from the crusaders themselves.

About the Author

Suzannah Rowntree lives in a big house in rural Australia with her awesome parents and siblings, reading academic histories of the Crusades and writing historical fantasy fiction that blends folklore and myth with historical fact.

You can connect with me on:

🌐 https://suzannahrowntree.site

Subscribe to my newsletter:

✉ https://www.subscribepage.com/srauthor

Also by Suzannah Rowntree